SPECIAL MESSAGE TO READERS

Lisa Genova graduated valedictorian from Bates College with a degree in Biopsychology and has a Ph.D. in Neuroscience from Harvard University. With more than half a million copies of her critically acclaimed *New York Times* bestselling novels in print, she has captured a special place in contemporary fiction, writing stories that are equally inspired by neuroscience and the human spirit. She lives with her family on Cape Cod, Massachusetts.

Visit her online at: www.lisagenova.com
Follow her on Twitter: @LisaGenova

LOVE ANTHONY

Olivia Donatelli's dream of a normal life was shattered when her son, Anthony, was diagnosed with autism at age three. He didn't speak. He hated to be touched. He almost never made eye contact. And just as Olivia was starting to realise that happiness and autism could coexist, Anthony was gone. Now she's alone on Nantucket, desperate to find meaning in her son's short life, when a chance encounter with another woman brings Anthony alive again in a most unexpected way. In a piercing story about motherhood, autism and love, Lisa Genova offers us two unforgettable women who discover the small but exuberant voice that helps them both find the answers they need.

LISA GENOVA

◆

LOVE
ANTHONY

Complete and Unabridged

CHARNWOOD
Leicester

First published in Great Britain in 2012 by
Simon & Schuster UK Ltd.
London

First Charnwood Edition
published 2014
by arrangement with
Simon & Schuster UK Ltd.
London

A catalogue record for this book is available
from the British Library.

ISBN 978–1–4448–2128–4

Published by
F. A. Thorpe (Publishing)
Anstey, Leicestershire

Set by Words & Graphics Ltd.
Anstey, Leicestershire
Printed and bound in Great Britain by
T. J. International Ltd., Padstow, Cornwall

This book is printed on acid-free paper

For Tracey

In memory of Larry

Prologue

It's Columbus Day weekend, and they lucked out with gorgeous weather, an Indian-summer day in October. She sits in her beach chair with the seat upright and digs her heels into the hot sand. The ocean in front of her sparkles white and silver in the sunlight. There are no fishing boats or yachts in the distance, no kite surfers or swimmers near the shore, nothing but a pure ocean view today. She inhales and exhales.

Soak it up.

Her three daughters are busy building a sand castle. They're too close to the water. It'll be flooded and destroyed within an hour, but they wouldn't heed their mother's warning.

Her oldest daughter, almost eight, is the architect and foreman. *More sand here. A feather there. Go get some shells for the windows. Dig this hole deeper.* The younger two are her loyal construction workers.

'More water!'

The youngest, barely four, loves this job. She skips off with her pail, charges knee-deep into the ocean, fills her bucket, and returns, struggling with the weight of it, sloshing at least half of the water out as she walks a drunken line back to her sisters, smiling, delighted with her contribution to the project.

She loves to watch her daughters like this, absorbed in playing, unaware of her. She admires

1

their young bodies, all in little-girl bikinis, skin still deeply tanned from a summer spent outside, skipping, squatting, bending, sitting, utterly unselfconscious.

The weather and the holiday combined have invited a lot of tourists to the island. Compared to the last many weeks since Labor Day, the beach today feels crowded with walkers and a few sunbathers. Just yesterday she walked on this same stretch of sand for an hour and saw only one other person. But that was a Friday morning, and it was foggy and cold.

Her attention becomes drawn to a woman sitting in a similar beach chair at the water's edge and her boy, who is playing by himself next to her. The boy is a skinny little thing, shirtless in blue bathing trunks, probably a year younger than her youngest daughter. He's creating a line of white rocks on the sand.

Each time the water rushes in, momentarily drowning his line of rocks in white foam, he jumps up and down and squeals. He then runs into the water as if he's chasing it, and runs back, a huge smile stretched across his face.

She continues to watch him, for some reason mesmerized, as he methodically adds more and more rocks to his line.

'Gracie, go see if that little boy wants to help you build the castle.'

Outgoing and used to taking orders, Gracie bounces over to the little boy. She watches her daughter, hands on her hips, talking to him, but they're too far away for her to hear what her daughter's saying. The boy doesn't seem to

2

acknowledge her. His mother looks over her shoulder for a moment.

Gracie runs back to their beach blanket alone.

'He doesn't want to.'

'Okay.'

Soon, the ocean begins to invade the castle, and the girls grow bored of building it anyway, and they start grumbling about being hungry. It's lunchtime, and she didn't bring any food. Time to go.

She closes her eyes and draws in one last warm, clean, salty breath, then exhales and gets up. She gathers a handful of stray shovels and castle molds and carries them to the water to rinse them off. She lets the water roll over her feet. It's numbingly cold. As she rinses her daughter's beach toys, she scans the sand for seashells or sea glass, something beautiful to bring home.

She doesn't see anything worth collecting, but she does spot a single, brilliant white rock peeking out of the sand. She picks it up. It's oval, tumbled perfectly smooth. She walks over to the little boy, bends down, and carefully places her rock at one end of his line.

He glances at her so quickly, it would've been easy to miss them altogether — stunning brown eyes, twinkling in the sun at her, delighted with her contribution to his project. He jumps and squeals and flaps his hands, a happy dance.

She smiles at the boy's mother, who mirrors a smile in return, but it's guarded and weary, one that doesn't invite anything further. She's sure she doesn't know this woman or her little boy and has no particular reason to think she'll ever see them again, but as she turns to leave, she waves and says with total conviction, 'See you later.'

1

Beth is alone in her house, listening to the storm, wondering what to do next. To be fair, she's not really alone. Jimmy is upstairs sleeping. But she feels alone. It's ten in the morning, and the girls are at school, and Jimmy will sleep until at least noon. She's curled up on the couch, sipping hot cocoa from her favorite blue mug, watching the fire in the fireplace, and listening.

Rain and sand spray against the windows like an enemy attacking. Wind chimes gong repetitive, raving-mad music, riding gusts from some distant neighbor's yard. The wind howls like a desperately mournful animal. A desperately mournful wild animal. Winter storms on Nantucket are wild. Wild and violent. They used to scare her, but that was years ago when she was new to this place.

The radiator hisses. Jimmy snores.

She has already done the laundry, the girls won't be home for several hours, and it's too early yet to start dinner. She's grateful she did the grocery shopping yesterday. The whole house needs to be vacuumed, but she'll wait until after Jimmy is up. He didn't get home from work until after 2:00 a.m.

She wishes she had the book for next month's book club. She keeps forgetting to stop by the library to check it out. This month's book was *The Curious Incident of the Dog in the*

5

Night-Time by Mark Haddon. It was a quick read, a murder mystery narrated by an autistic teenage boy. She liked it and was especially fascinated by the main character's strange inner world, but she hopes the next one will be a bit lighter. They typically choose more serious literature for book club, but she could use a pleasant escape into a hot summer romance right about now. They all could.

A loud bang against the back of the house startles her. Grover, their black Lab, lifts his head from where he's been sleeping on the braided rug.

'It's okay, Grove. It's just Daddy's chair.'

Knowing a big storm was on its way, she told Jimmy to take his chair in last night before he left for work. It's his 'cigar-smoking' chair. One of the summer residents left it on the side of the road in September with a sign taped to it that read FREE, and Jimmy couldn't resist it. The thing is trash. It's a cedar Adirondack chair. In most places on Earth, that chair could weather a lifetime, but on Nantucket, the salty, humid air eventually degrades everything but the densest man-made composite materials. Everything needs to be extraordinarily tough to survive here. And probably more than a little dense.

Jimmy's moldy, corroded chair belongs at the dump or at least in the garage, as Beth wisely suggested last night. But instead, the wind has just lifted it off the ground and heaved it against the house. She thinks about getting up and hauling the chair into the garage herself, but then she thinks better of it. Maybe the storm will

6

smash it to pieces. Of course, even if this happens, Jimmy will just find some other chair to sit in while he smokes his smelly cigars.

She sits and tries to enjoy her cocoa, the storm, and the fire, but the impulse to get up and do something nags at her.

She can't think of anything useful to do. She walks over to the fireplace mantel and picks up the wedding picture of Jimmy and her. Mr. and Mrs. James Ellis. Fourteen years ago. Her hair was longer and blonder then. And her skin was flawless. No pores, no spots, no wrinkles. She touches her thirty-eight-year-old cheek and sighs. Jimmy looks gorgeous. He still does, mostly.

She studies his smile in the photo. He has a slight overbite, and his eyeteeth jut forward a touch. When she met him, she thought his imperfect teeth added to his charm, lending just enough to his rugged good looks without making him look like a hillbilly. He has a self-assured, mischievous, full-out grin for a smile, the kind that makes people — women — put forth considerable effort to be the reason for it.

But his teeth have started to bug her. The way he picks at them with his tongue after he eats. The way he chews his food with his mouth open. The way his eyeteeth stick out. She sometimes finds herself staring at them while he talks, wishing he'd shut his mouth. They're pearly white in this wedding photograph, but now they're more caramel than cream-colored, abused by years of daily coffee and those smelly cigars.

His once beautiful teeth. Her once beautiful skin. His annoying habits. She has them, too. She knows her nagging drives him crazy. This is what happens when people get older, when they're married for fourteen years. She smiles at Jimmy's smile in the picture, then replaces it on the mantel a little to the left of where it was before. She takes a step back. She purses her lips and eyes the length of the mantel.

Their fireplace mantel is a six-foot-long, single piece of driftwood hung over the hearth. They found it washed up on the shore one night on Surfside Beach during that first summer. Jimmy picked it up and said, *We're hanging this over the fireplace in our house someday.* Then he kissed her, and she believed him. They'd only known each other for a few weeks.

Three pictures are on the mantel, all in matching weathered, white frames — one of Grover when he was six weeks old on the left, Beth and Jimmy in the middle, and a beach portrait of Sophie, Jessica, and Gracie in white shirts and floral, pink peasant skirts on the right. It was taken just after Gracie's second birthday, eight years ago.

'Where does the time go?' she says aloud to Grover.

A huge, peach starfish that Sophie found out by Sankaty Lighthouse flanks the Beth-and-Jimmy picture on the left, and a perfect nautilus shell, also huge and without a single chip or crack, flanks the Beth-and-Jimmy picture on the right. Beth found the nautilus shell out on Great Point the year she married Jimmy, and she

8

protected it vigilantly through three moves. She's picked up hundreds of nautilus shells since and has yet to find another one without a flaw. This is always the arrangement on the mantel. Nothing else is allowed there.

She adjusts her wedding picture again, slightly to the right, and steps back. There. That's better. Perfectly centered. Everything as it should be.

Now what? She's on her feet, feeling energized.

'Come on, Grover. Let's go get the mail.'

Outside, she immediately regrets the idea. The wind whips through her heartiest 'windproof' winter coat as if it were a sieve. Chills tumble down her spine, and the cold feels like it's worming its way deep into her bones. The rain is coming at her sideways, slapping her in the face, making it difficult to keep her eyes open enough to see where they're going. Poor Grover, who was warm and happy and asleep a few moments ago, whimpers.

'Sorry, Grove. We'll be home in a minute.'

The mailboxes are about a half mile away. Beth's neighborhood is inhabited by a smattering of year-rounders and summer residents, but mostly summer people live on her route to the mail. So this time of year, the houses are empty and dark. There are no lights on in the windows, no smoke billowing from the chimneys, no cars parked in the driveways. Everything is lifeless. And gray. The sky, the earth, the weathered cedar shingles on every empty, dark house, the ocean, which she can't see now but can smell. It's all gray. She never gets used to this. The tedious grayness of winter on Nantucket is enough to unravel the most unshakable sanity. Even the proudest natives, the people who love this island the most, question themselves in March.

Why the hell do we live on this godforsaken spit of gray sand?

Spring, summer, and fall are different. Spring brings the yellow daffodils, summer brings the Mykonos-blue sky, fall brings the rusty-red cranberry bogs. And they all bring the tourists. Sure, the tourists come with their downsides. But they come. Life! After Christmas Stroll in December, they all leave. They return to mainland America and beyond, to places that have such things as McDonald's and Staples and BJ's and businesses that are open past January. And color. They have color.

* * *

Cold, wet, and miserable, she arrives at the row of gray mailboxes lining the side of the road, opens the door to her box, pulls out three pieces of mail, and quickly shoves them inside her coat to protect them from the rain.

'C'mon, Grover. Home!'

They turn around and begin retracing their route. With the rain and wind pushing behind her now, she's able to look up to see where she's going instead of mostly down at her feet. Ahead of them in the distance, someone is walking toward them. She wonders who it could be.

As they get closer, she figures out that the

person is a woman. Most of Beth's friends live mid-island. Jill lives in Cisco, which isn't too far from here, but in the other direction, toward the ocean, and this woman is too short to be Jill. She's wearing a hat, a scarf wrapped around her nose and mouth, a parka, and boots. It would be hard to recognize anyone in that getup in this weather, but surely, Beth must know who it is. There are only so many people who would be out walking in this neighborhood in this weather on a Thursday in March. There are no weekenders or day-trippers out for a stroll on Nantucket today.

They're a few yards apart now, but Beth still can't identify her. She can only see that the woman's hair is long and black. Beth prepares to say *Hello*, and she's already smiling when the woman is directly in front of her, but the woman is fixated on the ground, refusing eye contact. So Beth doesn't say *Hello*, and she feels sheepish for smiling. Grover wanders over for a sniff, but the woman skirts by too quickly and is then behind them before Beth or Grover can learn anything more about her.

Still curious after a few steps, Beth looks back over her shoulder and sees the woman at the row of mailboxes, toward the far end.

'Probably a New Yorker,' she mutters as she turns around and presses on toward home.

Safe inside, Grover shakes himself, sending water everywhere. She'd normally scold him for doing this, but it doesn't matter. Just opening the door splashed a bucket's worth of water into the mudroom. She removes her hat and coat, and

11

the mail falls to the ground. She kicks off her boots. She's soaked through.

She peels off her wet socks and jeans, tosses them into the laundry room, and slips into a pair of fleece pajama bottoms and a pair of slippers. Feeling warmer and drier and immediately happier, she returns to the front door to collect the mail from the floor, then walks back to the couch. Grover has returned to the braided rug.

The first piece of mail is the heating bill, which will probably be more than their monthly mortgage payment. She decides to open it later. The next is a Victoria's Secret catalog. She ordered one push-up bra three Christmases ago, and they still keep sending her catalogs. She'll toss it into the fire. The last piece of mail is an envelope hand-addressed to her. She opens it. It's a card with a birthday cake pictured on the front.

May all your wishes come true.

Huh, that's strange, she thinks. Her birthday isn't until October.

Inside, the words *Happy Birthday* have been crossed out with a single, confident ballpoint blue line. Below it, someone has written:

I'm sleeping with Jimmy.
PS. He loves me.

It takes her a few seconds to reread it, to make sure she's comprehending the words. She's aware of her heart pounding as she picks up the

12

envelope again. *Who sent this?* There's no return address, but the postmark is stamped from Nantucket. She doesn't recognize the handwriting. The penmanship is neat and loopy, a woman's. Another woman's.

Holding the envelope in one hand and the card in the other, she looks up at the fireplace mantel, at her perfectly centered wedding picture, and swallows. Her mouth has gone dry.

She gets up and walks to the fireplace. She slides the iron screen aside. She tosses the Victoria's Secret catalog onto the fire and watches the edges curl and blacken as it burns and turns to gray ash. Gone. Her hands are shaking. She clenches the envelope and card. If she burns them now, she can pretend she never saw them. This never existed.

A swirl of unexpected emotion courses through her. She feels fear and fury, panic and humiliation. She feels nauseous, like she's going to be sick. But what she doesn't feel is surprised.

She closes the gate. With the card and envelope squeezed in her fist, she marches up the stairs, emphasizing each loud step as she heads toward Jimmy's snoring.

2

Olivia strips down to her underwear and changes into sweatpants, socks, and her oldest, favorite Boston College sweatshirt. Drier but still freezing, she hurries downstairs to the living room and presses the button on the remote to the fireplace. She stands in front of the instant blaze and waits and waits, but it doesn't throw off any noticeable heat. She touches the glass with the palm of her hand. It's barely warm. It was David's idea to convert the fireplace to gas. Better for the tenants. More convenient and less messy.

Although they've owned the cottage for eleven years, she and David have never actually lived here. They bought it as an investment just before the housing market boomed and prices skyrocketed. David, a business major who reluctantly stepped into his family's real estate business after college, is always keeping his eye on properties with potential. He's all about location, location, location. He looks for a fixer-upper in the right neighborhood, buys it, hires contractors to renovate the kitchen and baths and to paint the interior and the exterior, then he sells it. The goal is always to flip it fast, a SOLD sign on the front lawn and a tidy profit sitting fat and pretty in his pocket.

But Nantucket was different for David. With almost 50 percent of the island designated as conservation and 'forever wild,' leaving only half of the almost fifty square miles buildable, David wasn't interested in flipping this house. He assured Olivia that the property value would never dip below what they paid for it. The house is nothing special, a modest three-bedroom cottage with little remarkable about any of the rooms or layout. But situated less than a mile from Fat Ladies Beach, it's a highly desirable vacation property, and David correctly guessed that they would always more than cover their annual mortgage payments with summer rentals.

It's a smart investment for our future, he'd said, back when they could so blissfully imagine a future.

They stayed in the house for a week or two each year in the shoulder seasons, usually in October, but stopped coming altogether after Anthony turned three. Pretty much everything stopped after Anthony turned three.

A violent gust of wind screams in the distance, sounding to Olivia like a small child crying out in pain. The windows rattle, and a cold breeze dances along the skin of her bare neck. She shivers. Nantucket in winter. This is going to take some getting used to.

She rubs the palms of her hands together, trying to create some friction to warm them. Dissatisfied, she wonders where she might find a blanket. She's only been here nine days, and she's still learning where everything is, still feeling like a guest in someone else's home. A stranger at the inn. She searches the linen closet, finds a gray, woolen blanket she vaguely

15

remembers buying, wraps it around her shoulders, and snuggles into the living-room chair with the mail.

The bills are still sent to their house in Hingham, a small, suburban town on Boston's South Shore, so she hasn't yet received anything but home-repair-service advertisements, local election postcards, and coupon flyers, but today she knows she has some real mail.

Before even opening the first, she knows it's a book from her old boss, Louise, a senior editor at Taylor Krepps. The envelope has a yellow forwarding-address sticker on it. Louise doesn't know that Olivia has moved to Nantucket. She doesn't know about Anthony either.

She doesn't know anything.

Olivia hasn't worked as a junior editor to Louise in self-help books at Taylor Krepps Publishing for five years now, but Louise still sends her advance reader copies. Maybe it's Louise's way of keeping the door open, of trying to entice Olivia back to work. Olivia suspects Louise has simply never gotten around to taking her off the mailing list. Olivia's never hinted to Louise that she'd ever come back; it's been a couple of years since she's sent a note thanking her or commenting on a book, and even longer since she's read any of them. But they keep coming.

She doesn't have the heart or stomach to read anybody's self-help anymore. She's no longer interested in anyone's advice or wisdom. What do they know? What does it matter? It's all bunk.

She used to believe in the power of self-help

books to educate, inform, and inspire. She believed that the really good ones could transform lives. When Anthony turned three and they were told with certainty what they were dealing with, she believed she'd find somebody somewhere who could help them, an expert who could transform their lives.

She scoured every self-help book, then every medical journal, every memoir, every blog, every online parent support network. She read Jenny McCarthy and the Bible. She read and hoped and prayed and believed in anything claiming help, rescue, reversal, salvation. Somebody somewhere must know something. Somebody must have the key that would unlock her son.

She opens the envelope and holds the book in her hands, rubbing the smooth cover with her fingers. She still loves the feel of a new book. This one is called *The Three Day Miracle Diet* by Peter Fallon, MD.

Hmph. Miracle, my ass.

She used to attend conferences and seminars. *Please, expert Dr. So-and-So, show us the answer. I believe in you.* She used to go to church every Sunday. *Please, God, give us a miracle. I believe in you.*

Sorry, Dr. Fallon. There are no miracles, she thinks, and tosses the book to the floor.

She holds up the cardboard envelope from David next, staring at it for a long moment before carefully tearing the tab and upending it.

Three white, round, perfectly smooth rocks fall into her lap. She smiles. Anthony's rocks. And three of them. She shakes the envelope.

There aren't any more. He would've liked that there are only three and not one or two or four. He loved things that came in threes. The Little Pigs, One-Two-Three-Go, Small-Medium-Big. Of course, he never said the words to her, *Mom, I like the 'Three Little Pigs' story*. But she knew.

She rolls the three small rocks in the palm of her hand, enjoying the cool, smooth feel of them. When she's done with the mail, she'll add them to the glass bowl on the coffee table already containing at least fifty more of Anthony's white, round rocks. A shrine in a bowl.

Anthony wouldn't have liked his rocks in Olivia's bowl on the coffee table, however. He preferred them lined up like perfectly straight rock parades on the floor, all over the house. Heaven forbid Olivia should ever clean up and put his rocks back in his box in his bedroom. But sometimes, she couldn't help herself. Sometimes she simply wanted to walk through the house and not kick through a rock parade. Sometimes she simply wanted to walk through a normal house. It was always a huge mistake. They didn't live in a normal house. And change, however small, was never Anthony's friend.

She peeks into the envelope and sees a folded piece of stationery.

Found these three under the couch.
Love, David

She smiles, thanking him for taking the time to send her three rocks, for knowing she'd want them. And the *Love, David*. She knows these

18

words aren't throwaway or insincere. She still loves him, too.

The rest of Anthony's rocks are in his box, now in her bedroom. It was one of the few things she insisted on bringing with her on her final trip over, and it was no small feat getting it here. She lugged it, sweating and questioning her sanity, from the backseat of David's car to the ferry in Hyannis, from the ferry to the taxi in Town, from the taxi to her bedroom here. More than once she thought about dumping the rocks overboard on the way over, freeing herself from the physical and emotional burden of carrying all the damn rocks. But they're Anthony's damn rocks. Beautiful damn rocks collected from the beach and obsessively lined up in rows by her beautiful boy, now artfully displayed in the glass bowl on the coffee table.

So the damn rocks came with her. She left behind her cookbooks, her collection of books she helped edit at Taylor Krepps, all of her novels. She didn't take any of the furniture, the appliances, or any dishware. She left Anthony's clothes still folded in his drawers, his bed unmade, his Barney DVDs in the TV console cabinet, all of the educational toys he never played with, his toothbrush in the holder in the bathroom, his coat on the hook by the front door.

She brought her clothes, her jewelry, her camera, and her computer. And she brought her journals. Someday, she'll have the courage to read them.

She also left all of her photographs — her

college album, their wedding and honeymoon albums, the collection of arty shots she used to take of sunsets and trees and seashells, the best of which adorn the walls of their house, Anthony's baby album. She left it all with David. She feels as if that life didn't happen to her. It happened to some other woman.

She kept only one picture. She looks up at the eight-by-ten photograph framed, matted, and hung on the wall over the fireplace, that one picture that took many hours over many days of patient waiting to get. She remembers how she sat cross-legged in front of the refrigerator, camera over her face, finger on the button, ready to click, waiting. Waiting. Anthony passed by her many times, skipping on his toes, squealing and flapping his hands. Each time she held her breath. She didn't move. He didn't look at her.

One day he sat down only a couple of feet in front of her and spun the back wheel of a toy truck with his index finger for at least an hour. She didn't get up and demonstrate how to play with the truck appropriately. *See, Anthony, the truck goes vroom, vroom.* She didn't redirect him. She didn't move. He didn't look at her.

With each attempt, her knees, arms, and ass would eventually ache and scream for her to shift position. Her mind would try to talk her out of it, too, mocking her for wasting another morning sitting on the floor like an idiot. She ignored herself and sat, silent, unthreatening, invisible.

Then finally, it happened. He looked directly into the lens. He was probably thirsty, looking to the refrigerator, wanting juice. It was probably a

20

complete accident, but she clicked the button before his eyes darted away. She looked at the LCD display, and there they were. His eyes! Wide-open windows into a shiny, clear day. Not disconnected or wandering eyes. Deep, dark, melted-chocolate-brown eyes belonging to her little boy, looking at his mother. Seeing her.

She sits on the living-room chair with the mail in her lap and loses herself in his eyes, wiping tears from hers, grateful for the chance to look into them and see real meaning, even if she doesn't understand what that meaning is, even if it was only one moment in almost nine long years, and even if she only ever saw them like this through her Nikon lens and then on two-dimensional paper. She's grateful to have it.

She wipes her eyes again with the edge of the blanket and turns her attention to the last piece of mail, a manila envelope from the law offices of Kaufman and Renkowitz. Olivia slides out the stack of papers and reads the top of the first page.

Separation Agreement for David and Olivia Donatelli

She closes her eyes and listens to the wind and rain banging at the windows, pounding on the roof, raging all around her. She tucks the blanket over her feet and holds on tight to the three rocks still inside her hand. Like everything, this storm can only last so long.

3

Facing away from her side of the bed with their puffy down comforter pulled up to his chin, Jimmy is still sound asleep.

'Jimmy,' Beth says loudly, just shy of shouting, startling even herself.

He lurches upright. 'Huh? What?'

Jimmy doesn't wake up well, never has. His thinking is all jumbled at first, staggering around and bumping into the walls of his skull as if he'd just thrown back six beers. He wouldn't be able to recite the alphabet or the full names of his three girls within the first few seconds of waking. He might not even know he has three girls right now. She hesitates, giving him a minute to let the fog clear from between his ears. Or maybe she hesitates because she's giving herself one more minute of not going where they're about to go.

'What is it?' he asks, rubbing his eyes and nose.

'What's this?' She throws the card and envelope at him, aiming for his head. But they're like a poorly constructed paper airplane, fluttering weakly onto his lap instead of smacking him in the face. He picks up the card.

'It's not my birthday,' he says, still rubbing his eyes.

'Open it.' She shakes with anticipation as he does.

'I don't get it.'

'Don't act dumb. Who sent this?'

'Hold on, let me get my glasses.'

So now he's dumb and blind. What next? Deaf? As much as a part of her doesn't want to hear his answer, another part of her can't resist it, compelling her toward what feels inevitable.

Jimmy reaches for his glasses on the night table, puts them on, and reads the card again. He opens and closes and opens it, studying it as if it were a crossword puzzle or one of Sophie's algebra problems, like it's some kind of test.

It is a test, Jimmy. It's a test of your integrity. This is a test of your character.

She watches his face as he keeps his eyes focused on this most mysterious riddle, refusing to look up at her. He's stalling.

'It's not the tax code, Jimmy. Who sent this?'

'I have no idea.'

He's looking at her now. They pause here, eyes locked, unblinking, unmoving, nobody saying a word. A showdown.

Jimmy ends it by getting out of bed and tossing the card and envelope into the wastebasket. He then walks past her and down the hall. She hears the bathroom door shut. Apparently, he's said all he has to say about the card. Incensed, adrenaline now surging through her veins, she retrieves the card and envelope from the wastebasket and storms down the hall to the closed bathroom door.

Manners stop her with her hand on the doorknob. She and Jimmy aren't one of those couples who share bathroom intimacy. She doesn't floss while he sits on the toilet, he

23

doesn't chat with her while she's in the shower, she doesn't change tampons while he shaves. She wouldn't normally go in. They don't have that kind of marriage.

But what kind of marriage do they have? She shoves the bathroom door open and stares at him as he stands over the toilet.

'Jesus, Beth, can you give me a minute?'

'I'd like a real answer.'

'Hold on a second.'

'Tell me who sent this.'

'Wait.'

He flushes. He turns and faces her. She's standing in the doorway, arms folded across her chest, blocking the way out. He's wearing nothing but plaid boxers and glasses, his hair mussed, his hands hanging heavy by his sides, looking vulnerable, defenseless. Caught.

'You don't know her.'

The joints of her legs suddenly loosen, and she leans into the doorframe, steadying herself. She feels like she's standing on train tracks, tied to the rails, staring at the oncoming train, so close she can feel the hot wind on her face from its relentless forward motion.

'Who is she?' she asks with slightly less demand and a lot more fear clinging to each word.

'Her name is Angela.'

There it is. He admits it. This is really happening. He's cheating on her with a woman named Angela. She fights through crashing waves of dizziness and thickening nausea, trying to picture Angela, but she can't come up with a face. She's not a real woman if she doesn't have a face. Maybe this isn't really happening.

'Angela who?'

'Melo.'

Angela Melo. It's the dead of winter on a fourteen-mile-long-by-three-mile-wide island. Everyone knows everyone. But he's right. Angela Melo. She doesn't know her. Petra will.

'Do you call her Angie?'

He sighs and fidgets his feet, his face struggling, as if only now has she asked him something too personal. 'Yes.'

She focuses on the blankness of the white tile wall behind him, unable to inhale. Jimmy's been having sex with a woman named Angela Melo. Angie. He's been naked with her, kissing her mouth, her breasts, her everything. She wonders if he uses a condom, but she's too embarrassed and disgusted by the thought to ask him.

She walks back to their bedroom and sits on her side of the bed, not sure of what to do or say or feel next. She wishes she could go back in time and undo this. Crawl back into bed, wake up, and start the day over. And not get the mail. Jimmy has followed her and is standing over her, waiting.

'How long?' she asks.

'A while.'

'How long is a while?'

He hesitates. 'Since July.'

She doesn't know what she was expecting him to say. She hadn't developed any specific suspicions or scenarios in her imagination. A few stolen nights. Maybe a month or two. Since July?

25

She ticks off the months in her head. Too many stolen nights for her to count or imagine. Hot tears start streaming down her face.

Damn it, Beth, don't cry. Don't fall apart.

She doesn't want to feel like a victim. Like a cliché. But she can't help it. She gives in and sobs on her side of the bed against her own will while Jimmy continues to stand a few feet away from her.

'Do you love her?' she asks, choking out each word, shaken and airy.

'No.'

She studies her hands in her lap, her engagement and wedding rings on her finger, rings that came with vows that didn't protect her from this, afraid to look at him, to see if he's telling the truth or lying. He's been lying to her for months now, so maybe he's lying about this. Would she know the truth if she saw his eyes? What does she really know about him now? Ten minutes ago she would've said, *Everything.*

She closes her eyes and retreats into crying. Something has to happen now. She can't simply walk downstairs, finish her cocoa, and vacuum the house.

'I think you should go,' she says. 'I think you should move out.'

He's still. Beth quiets her crying and holds her breath, holding on for his reply.

'Okay.'

Then he's in motion. He's at the closet, pulling clothes from hangers, he's at his dresser, emptying drawers. He's stuffing his gym bag.

She wants to let out a scream, but her voice is

too devastated for sound. *Okay?* He's not even putting up a fight. He's not apologizing or begging for forgiveness. *Okay?* He's not asking her to work on this with him, to let him stay.

He wants to go.

She wants to hit him, shake him, hurt him. She wants to throw something hard and heavy at him. She considers her iron bedside lamp. She wants to hate him. But to her shame and confusion, she also wants to hug him, soothe him, stop him. She wants to tell him that everything will be okay. She wants to go to him and kiss him the way they used to kiss. Those deep, long kisses that melted her.

Now he's kissing some woman named Angie and melting her.

He's banging around in the bathroom now, probably gathering his things from the medicine cabinet. She looks over to the indent where he was just sleeping. Was he with Angie last night before coming home to sleep and snore here?

She can't sit on this bed, their bed, for one second longer. She gets up and begins stripping it. Still crying, she tugs the comforter, the blanket, and each sheet off the mattress and whips them into a heaping, defeated pile on the floor. As she's peeling the pillowcases off the pillows, she notices Jimmy's socks lying on the floor, lazy and careless, waiting for her to pick them up and put them in the hamper. She's always picking up his stinky socks. His stinky socks, his dirty underwear, his coat, his shoes, his crumbs all over the floor from the pastrami sandwiches and chips he eats without using a plate, the gobs of dried toothpaste spit he leaves in the sink, the sand he always tracks throughout the house. She's picking up his stinky socks and wiping up his crumbs and sand and spit and doing his laundry while he's out having an affair.

Jimmy appears at the foot of the bed, carrying his gym bag and their big red suitcase, the one they bought at Kmart in Hyannis for their road trip to Disney World back in October. Back in October, when he was cheating on her with Angie Melo.

'I'll call you,' he says, sounding reluctant.

'Uh-huh,' she says, holding all of their bedding and his dirty socks in her arms, trying not to look at him.

He stands there, struggling to say something more, possibly hoping for her to say something more, for her to stop him. She can't be sure. She sneaks a quick glance at him. His face is pained, tears pooled in his eyes. She looks away. He doesn't say anything. She doesn't either. He turns and walks down the stairs. She doesn't move an inch until she hears the sound of the front door closing behind him.

In the laundry room, she carefully measures out the detergent. The engine of Jimmy's truck turns. She pours the liquid fabric softener into the dispenser. He backs out of the driveway. She turns the dial to SHEETS and presses START. His truck shifts into first gear and rumbles down their street. She watches the hot water pour onto their bedding. Steam fills the barrel of the washing machine. Everything begins to spin.

He's gone.

She walks into the kitchen, stands at the sink, stares out the window, and does nothing. She doesn't know what to do. With determined effort, she directs her thoughts over to her routine, hoping the comfort and safety of her daily schedule might counter the wild panic rising mightily within her.

She still needs to vacuum the house. And she can get dinner started in the Crock-Pot soon. She's making chicken-noodle soup. And she'll bake brownies for dessert. The girls get out of school at two. Sophie has drama club, Jessica has basketball, and Gracie has a playdate.

She won't tell them, of course. Not today. They won't notice. Jimmy's hardly ever home for dinner or bedtime.

She stands at the sink, motionless. The wind screams. The radiator hisses.

Jimmy is gone.

She takes a deep breath and releases it through her mouth. Okay, time to vacuum. But first, before she does anything, she's calling Petra.

4

It's predawn and still dark out. Not pitch-black the way it is on Nantucket nights that are moonless and starless, when she can't see her hand in front of her nose. The world around her is colored like a photographic blueprint, an anticipation-of-morning shade of blue-gray. But it's also foggy, which is typical at this early hour, especially near the shore, and the lack of visibility makes it seem darker than it really is. Even with the headlights of her Jeep on and the windshield wipers flapping as fast as they can, Olivia is having a hard time seeing where she's going. She drives slowly, carefully. She's in no hurry.

The Wauwinet Gatehouse is empty. She parks the Jeep, gets out, and releases air from all four tires to 12 psi. She climbs back in and continues, the road changing now from pavement to sand. The sand turns soft, and her Jeep dips, bounces, and sways as she inches along. The fog is even thicker here. She can see nothing to either side and only a few feet in front of her.

Maybe a little over four miles into this drive — she can't be sure, not having seen any landmarks along the way — the path is blocked by fencing. Vehicles are restricted from further progress down the beach, an effort to protect the endangered piping plovers who might unwittingly nest in the tire tracks. She parks her Jeep at the fence and gets out.

She hikes through deep, smooth, wind-caressed sand along the ocean that she can hear and smell but not see, the fog still obscuring everything. It can't be far now. She pulls a flashlight from her coat pocket and aims it in front of her, but the beam of light scatters, diffusing among the water molecules suspended in the air, proving useless. She presses on. She knows where she's going.

When the soft give of the sand changes to firm ground, wet from an earlier high tide, she exhales with relief. Each step is finally easy to take. Despite the cold, she's sweating, and her leg muscles burn. She licks her lips, enjoying the taste of sea salt. Still unable to see the water, she knows it's directly in front of her now and is disappointed that she can't see the lighthouse, which must be only a few feet from her path, hidden behind the wall of fog.

Great Point Light has been destroyed twice, once by fire and once by storm, rebuilt both times. A seventy-foot, cylindrical tower of white stone, it stands resilient and majestic on this fragile pile of sand, where the Atlantic Ocean meets Nantucket Sound, its existence continually threatened by erosion and gale-force winds. Surviving.

Aside from the gulls and maybe a few piping plovers, she expects to be alone here. From May to September, she imagines this seven-mile stretch of beach is probably crawling with four-wheel-drive vehicles, hikers, families led on natural-history tours, people on vacation. But on

March seventeenth, no one is here. She's alone, thirty miles of water separating her from Cape Cod to the north and about thirty-five hundred miles of ocean between where she stands and Spain to the east. It's the closest place to nowhere that she can think of. And nowhere is exactly where she wants to be today.

In the past, not that long ago, being this far away from anyone or anything else would not have been appealing to her. More than that, it would've scared her. A woman alone on a secluded beach, miles from anyone who might hear her if she needed help — like most girls, she'd been taught to avoid this kind of situation. But now, she's not only unafraid, she prefers it. She's not worried for a second about being raped or murdered out here alone on Great Point. Walking through safe, suburban Hingham, surrounded by ordinary people doing everyday things — that was what had been killing her.

The chips-and-snacks aisle in the grocery store. A Little League baseball game in progress. St. Christopher's Church. Escalators at the mall. Her old friends blessed with typical children, one innocently bragging about her daughter in the school play, another unassumingly complaining that third-grade math isn't challenging enough for her son. She avoids them all.

All of those places and people and things are charged, filled with memories of Anthony or the Anthony she prayed for or the Anthony that might have been. And they all have the potential to turn her inside out in an instant, to make her cry, hide, scream, curse God, stop breathing, go

32

insane. Any and sometimes all of the above.

She would drive many blocks out of her way to the bank or the gas station so she wouldn't have to lay eyes on her church. She stopped answering the phone. Last summer at the grocery store, she noticed a boy she guessed was about Anthony's age walking alongside his mother. Olivia was fine until the chips-and-snacks aisle, when the boy asked, *Mom, can we get these?* He was holding up a can of salt-and-vinegar Pringles, Anthony's favorite. Without warning, all of the oxygen vanished from the store. She was paralyzed, gulping for air, drowning in panic. As soon as she could move, she ran from the store, abandoning her cart full of food, and cried in her car for almost an hour before she could collect herself enough to drive home. She hasn't stepped foot in the chips-and-snacks aisle since. It isn't safe there.

The world is littered with traps like salt-and-vinegar Pringles that swallow her whole, which would be fine with her except that they eventually spit her back out and say, *Carry on, now.* Everyone wants her to carry on now. Carry on. Move on. She doesn't want to. She wants to be here, alone on Great Point, far away from all the traps. Standing still, moving nowhere.

She squats down and writes *Happy Birthday Anthony* with her index finger in the wet sand. He would've been ten today.

She remembers the day he was born. His birth was uncomplicated but long. She'd wanted a natural childbirth, but after twenty hours of painful and unproductive labor, she surrendered

33

and asked for an epidural. Two hours, a hint of Pitocin, and six pushes later, Anthony was born. Pinkish purple, the color of petunias, calm and wide-eyed. She loved him instantly. He was beautiful and full of promise, her baby boy who would someday play Little League baseball, star in the school play, and be good at math. She didn't know then that she should've had much simpler dreams for her beautiful son, that she should've looked upon her newborn baby boy and thought, *I hope you learn to talk and use the bathroom by the time you're seven.*

His first couple of birthdays were normal — cakes she chose and bought at the bakery, candles that Olivia blew out, presents that she and David opened and acted overly delighted and animated about. But he was only one and two years old, so this was to be expected. After two, birthdays began deviating further and further away from normal.

Anthony stopped getting invited to other kids' birthday parties when he was four, and when he turned five, she and David followed in turn, hosting private celebrations, family only. It was easier this way. Anthony didn't participate in the party games or pay attention to the birthday clown anyway. It still broke her heart.

And while the maturing interests of other little boys his age were reflected in the party themes with each passing year — from Elmo to Bob the Builder to Spider-Man to *Star Wars* — Anthony had and was perfectly pleased with a Barney birthday year after year. Sure, she could've gone with another character. But there was no point in pretending that he loved superheroes or robots or ninjas. He loved Barney, and there wouldn't be any other little boys at his parties to tease him for loving a purple dinosaur.

So each year, Olivia and David lit the candles on his Barney cake and sang 'Happy Birthday.' Then she'd say, *Come on, Anthony! Make a wish and blow out your candles!* And then he wouldn't, so she'd blow them out for him. She always made a wish, the same one every year.

Please don't get older. You have to talk before you get any older. You have to say 'Mom' and 'Dad' and 'I'm six years old' and 'I want to go to the playground today' and 'I love you, Mom' before we put another damn Barney cake on the kitchen table. Please stop getting older. We're running out of time.

She never stopped wishing.

They went through the motions every year, but his birthday was not a fun day for her or David. Instead of celebrating like other parents whom she imagined and so passionately envied and sometimes hated, instead of marveling over the past year and how much her child had changed and grown, she and David felt only unspoken dread and desperation on Anthony's birthday. March seventeenth was the one day each year when they were forced to stare the severity of Anthony's autism straight in the eye, to be fully cognizant of how much progress he hadn't made. When she shopped for his present and considered toys for age five-plus or ages five and up, she would be forced to admit to herself that these toys would hold no interest for him,

35

that he couldn't possibly play with any of them. There it was, printed on too many Fisher-Price boxes — Anthony was impossibly behind for his age.

So she would buy him an educational toy recommended by Carlin, his applied-behavioral-analysis therapist, or a new Barney video, or one year she wrapped a can of salt-and-vinegar Pringles. Pringles always made him happy. But the gift he loved the most each year was the card.

When he was four, she bought him the first of countless musical greeting cards. This one was a Hoops & Yoyo. She showed him first. He watched, pretending not to look. She opened the card. A song played and the characters sang. She shut the card. The music and the singing stopped.

To this day, she remembers his face, wondrous and joyful with the unexpected discovery of a new fascination, like when he found light switches. He opened the card. Music. He shut it. No music. Open. Music. Shut. No music. These cards were heaven to Anthony. The same song every time it's opened, the same music; everything the card did was predictable and entirely under his control.

He'd spend the rest of the day smiling and squealing and flapping his hands as he opened, shut, opened, shut, opened, shut. That's all he wanted every year. Unlimited time alone with his card. So this is what she and David gave to him.

She wonders how David is doing, if he's awake yet, realizing the date, thinking about Anthony. She hopes he finds comfort today. Her heart

36

aches thinking this, wishing she could be this to him. But she can't. Comfort doesn't exist within her, and she can't offer what she doesn't have. He doesn't have it either. They know this.

Olivia sits on the beach, waiting for sunrise, listening to a gull squawking above her, sounding like laughter. The tide is coming in. With each pulse of waves, she watches as a little more of *Happy Birthday Anthony* washes away, until it's pulled into the sea entirely. Wiped clean, as if it never existed. If she still believed in God, she would ask Him to send her birthday note written in sand to her son in heaven. But she doesn't ask for this. These are only words scratched in sand with her finger, swallowed by the ocean.

In front of her feet, she writes *I love you* and waits. The water comes, steady and sure, pooling and bubbling into each letter. The words wash away, reaching no one.

The fog has started to lift, and the day begins to lighten. The metallic-gray ocean tumbles out in front of her. The lighthouse materializes to her left. The next wave crashes, dissolving into a bed of fizzing foam, and deposits a single white, round rock at her feet. Her heart stalls, then quickens. She squats down, picks up the beautiful, smooth stone, and rolls it inside her hand.

Anthony.

I miss you, my sweet boy.

The sun rises, glowing pink on the horizon over the ocean, the color of petunias, beautiful and full of promise.

5

Beth and Petra are sitting in Jill's living room, waiting for Courtney and Georgia. It's book club night, but Courtney teaches yoga on Thursday evenings, and her class doesn't get over until six thirty, so they know she'll be running a bit late. And Georgia is always late. Jill knows this, but she's still irritated. She's holding them in the living room until everyone arrives because she wants the entire group to see the dining room at the same time. She's imagining a grand entrance.

Beth is growing antsy, too. Petra's planning on outing her tonight, and Beth is feeling less and less certain about this decision each time Jill sighs. It's not that she doesn't want her girlfriends to know that Jimmy's having an affair and has moved out. She doesn't want the whole island to know. And they will — Len, the school principal; Patty, the checkout woman at Stop & Shop; Lisa, Beth's hairdresser; Jessica's basketball coach.

But Petra's right. Beth needs to stand tall in her truth, draw strength from the collective love of her friends, and something else. Another platitude from Petra's pep talk earlier today sounded good at the time. Beth can't remember it now. Petra reads a lot of inspirational books. She also reads tarot cards and sees a shaman once a month instead of a regular therapist. A lot of people on the island think Petra's a little cuckoo. While Beth agrees that Petra can lean a bit eccentric, she also believes Petra possesses an inner wisdom that most people never know, a spiritual center that Beth admires and is drawn to and is certain that she herself lacks.

Plus, honesty, friendship, and New Age mumbo jumbo aside, it's nothing short of a miracle that Jimmy's affair isn't public knowledge already anyway. Beth knows. Petra knows. Jimmy and Angela know that Beth knows, so they're probably less careful now. Someone from the restaurant must know. And that someone will sooner or later tell someone who will tell Jill or Courtney or Jessica's basketball coach.

And the girls now know that he's moved out. Sophie was the first to notice that Dad wasn't inhabiting any of his usual spots — the bed, the couch, his cigar chair. *Where's Dad?* turned out to be a harder question to answer than *What's sex?* or *Have you ever smoked pot?* Beth teetered her way through her answer, purposefully keeping the explanation short and vague (and honest — she doesn't know exactly where he is either), a vain attempt to protect them from having the kind of father who would cheat on their mother. So the girls know that he's not living at home, but they don't know the ugly reason. Yet. Sadly, their father is, in fact, cheating on their mother, and it's only a matter of time before everyone on Nantucket, including his three beautiful daughters, knows it.

Beth picks up the copy of *Nantucket Life* from Jill's coffee table and thumbs through it, hoping for distraction while Jill frets about how late it's getting. Beth agrees. It's taking too long to get started. She feels like she's in the waiting room at her dentist's office, knowing that she needs to get her teeth cleaned and that they'll look and feel great when she's done, but the waiting around gives her anxiety and her memory too much time to play together. She'll begin to fixate on the anticipated sound of the metal instruments scraping against her teeth, the throbbing soreness in her gums, the shame she feels when the hygienist scolds her for not flossing enough, the taste of latex and blood in her mouth. If she has to wait more than ten minutes for the hygienist to call out her name, it takes every ounce of self-control she possesses not to leave for another six months.

Her hygienist and dentist are going to know that Jimmy is cheating on her.

Beth tries to forget about Jimmy and her dentist and what she and Petra talked about earlier and focus on Jill. She's telling them a story about Mickey's latest transplant project. Jill's husband, Mickey, runs his own construction company. The most incredible jobs he contracts aren't new construction or elaborate additions, but the moving of existing homes a few critical feet. The historic cottages and mansions positioned on the cliffs in 'Sconset are all in imminent danger of tumbling over with the eroding edge, as if each home were sitting on a piece of pie, and every year Mother Nature carves out another bite with her fork. Mickey's crew can miraculously move an entire house back, one hundred feet, four hundred feet, but eventually the owner will run out of frontage. The front door will be at the road. There'll be nothing left but crust, and Mother Nature will still be hungry.

Mickey's now transplanting a seven-bedroom monstrosity on Baxter Road, but this one's different. The owners recently bought the house directly across the street. Mickey's crew razed it, and now they're moving the cliff house to the other side of Baxter, to an entirely new piece of pie. Only on Nantucket.

'Crazy, huh? Mickey says if he lives long enough, he'll move that house again,' says Jill.

'This is why I live mid-island,' says Petra, who lives mid-island because that's where she grew up and because she can't afford to live closer to the ocean.

It's a good story, but Beth is now busy testing out the believability of different exit strategies in her head and can barely keep her butt on the couch. *I forgot my book. Gracie's not feeling well. I'm not feeling well.*

Petra, who is sitting next to Beth and somehow senses her approaching flight, reaches over and discreetly slides Beth's hand between their laps. She squeezes it, firmly but not too hard, offering both comfort and an anchor. *I love you, and you're not going anywhere.*

They hear a perfunctory knock at the door, and then Courtney and Georgia enter at the same time, a study in contrasts. Courtney's round, makeup-less face is flushed pink, her hair is loosely gathered into a ponytail high on her

41

head, her hairline is wet with sweat. She's wearing a lavender tank top under an unzipped thrift-shop winter coat, black cotton yoga pants, and flip-flops. She has her book in hand. Bright and smiling, she takes a seat on the couch on the other side of Beth, her energy floating into the room along with her, landing softly, like an airy, white dandelion puff blown in on a gentle breeze. She smells of patchouli.

Georgia, on the other hand, is hurried and harried, wearing smoky evening eye shadow, lipstick, and bold, dangling gold earrings, clomping in on her black business heels, struggling against the weight of the stuffed leather laptop bag on her shoulder, cursing the latest bridezilla who kept her on the phone for forty-five minutes agonizing over aisle runner choices, peeling off hat and gloves and scarf and coat as she apologizes for being late. If Courtney is a wispy seed sailing in on a warm breeze, Georgia is a tree limb snapped by a hurricane wind, crashing to the earth. It's hard to imagine from the sight of them that Courtney and Georgia are best friends, but they are.

Relieved and now called to action, Jill excuses herself and runs into her kitchen. Before Georgia can sit down, Jill returns, claps her hands twice like a schoolteacher demanding her class's attention, and ushers the group into her dining room. Georgia is the first to gasp, then they all do. Jill beams, delighting in all the oohs and aahs, gratified to have elicited the exact reaction she'd imagined.

The book this month takes place in post-World War II Japan, and clearly Jill was inspired by this setting. An origami animal sits on the center of each plate — a purple crane, a white swan, an orange tiger, a green turtle, a gray elephant. A gob of green wasabi and a neat pile of fleshy, pink ginger are placed to the right of each paper animal, and each plate is flanked by a pair of chopsticks and a tiny bowl filled with soy sauce. White tea lights are scattered around the room, and two bottles of sake are on the table. California, salmon, and tuna rolls are displayed on an oval platter at the center of it all.

'Wow, Jill. Tell me you didn't roll these yourself,' says Courtney.

'Of course she did,' says Georgia.

'I did,' admits Jill.

'And did you make these, too?' asks Courtney, holding up a purple paper crane.

'It wasn't hard. They have simple directions on the Internet,' says Jill.

'It wasn't hard for you. You're amazing,' says Courtney. 'You must've been preparing all day.'

'It didn't take that long,' says Jill, taking great pleasure in all the fuss.

'You could do this for a living,' says Beth.

Jill's been a stay-at-home mom for sixteen years, and she certainly doesn't need to work as long as Mickey keeps moving houses, but it's not a bad idea. She could hire herself out to the wealthy summer residents, hosting lavish book club parties. They'd love her.

'Okay, now everyone choose a seat. Each place

43

card has the name of one of the characters, so you'll — '

'We're not talking about the book tonight,' says Petra.

Beth's stomach tightens. She wishes she could at least down a glass of sake before they dive into this.

'What?' Jill smiles nervously. 'Of course we are.'

'No, we're not,' says Petra.

Petra is five years younger than the youngest of them, but she's without question the alpha male of the group. The oldest of seven children, daughter of Polish immigrants, and owner of Dish, one of Nantucket's most beloved restaurants, Petra is tough and bossy and will say with a shameless, crooked smile that she comes by it naturally. But she's also fair-minded, and there's not a nasty bone in her tall body. If anyone can derail Jill's book club extravaganza without tears or a friendship-ending argument, it's Petra.

'And we need something stronger than sake. You have any vodka?' asks Petra.

'But that's not Japanese,' says Jill, still trying to resist the suggestion of deviating in any way from the book's theme.

'Jimmy's cheating on Beth with the hostess at Salt, and he moved out,' says Petra.

Again, Georgia is the first to gasp. Jill turns to Beth and absorbs the fear and apology in Beth's eyes. Without another word about Japan, she walks into her kitchen and returns to the table with a bottle of Triple Eight vodka in one hand

44

and a bottle of Ocean Spray cranberry juice in the other.

'Will this do?' she asks as she sits down.

'Perfect,' says Petra, and she begins pouring vodka into wineglasses, leaving little room for juice. 'Show them the card.'

Beth pulls the card and envelope out from her book and obediently passes them to Georgia.

'Oh, Beth,' says Georgia after reading the card and passing it along to Courtney. 'This is from the hostess at Salt? Who is she?'

'Angela Melo,' says Beth.

'I don't know her,' says Jill, skeptical of there being anyone on Nantucket whom she doesn't know.

'She's only been here a couple of years. She's from Brazil. Came over with her sister as summer help,' says Petra. 'They applied for jobs at Dish, but I couldn't use them.'

'I don't know her either,' says Courtney. 'How long has this been going on?'

'Since July,' says Beth.

'Oh my God, Beth,' says Jill.

'I know,' says Beth.

She takes a big gulp of vodka from her wineglass. It's warm, it doesn't have enough cranberry juice, and it scorches the back of her throat. The sake would've been better. Talking about the book would've been better. She tips down another big gulp.

'I told you not to let him work at Salt,' says Georgia. 'That place is too sexy. The music, those martinis. Even I want to have sex with someone after I've spent an hour in that place.'

Jimmy used to scallop from October to March and bartend a few shifts here and there over the summers when scalloping is prohibited. But he never actually needed to bartend. Nantucket scallopers used to make great money. He bartended mostly to stay busy, not because he had to. Jimmy made a proud and reliable living over the years, and Beth enjoyed having him around for summer vacations with the kids.

But the scallops started disappearing from the harbor a few years ago. Then, in a frighteningly short amount of time, they were essentially gone, and Jimmy was essentially out of a job. He blames the McMansion owners with their lush, green carpet lawns laced with fertilizers that leach into the harbor, poisoning the aquatic infrastructure, killing the scallops and God knows what else.

He continued to bartend part-time in the summer, but he had no work in the winter, and for a while they had a hard time paying their bills. Jimmy moped around the house, frustrated and in denial, still hoping for the scallops to make an unlikely comeback. Then, a little over two years ago, Salt asked him to work there full-time, year-round. Year-round work of any kind is a rare and precious gem on Nantucket, and they desperately needed the money, so Jimmy the scalloper became a bartender at Salt.

'How long have you known?' asks Georgia.

'About a month,' says Beth.

The longest month of her life. She's seen Jimmy three times since he'd moved out, all unannounced visits. He came by once in the morning, after the girls were already in school but before she'd had a chance to shower, to retrieve a pair of work shoes. The other two times, he came over in the evening. He milled around in the kitchen, talked to the girls, never sat down, asked if he had any phone messages. He never has any phone messages.

Each time he showed up, her heart lifted, hoping, almost assuming that he was there to tell her that he was sorry, that he'd been crazy, that he didn't want to live without her and the girls, that he wanted to come home. But he never said any of this, so her heart felt stupid and betrayed all over again. She faked indifference toward him, acting nonchalant as she peeled potatoes at the sink while he chatted with Jessica, pretending to be absorbed in a book while he bumped around the house searching for his shoes (not a chance in hell that she was going to fetch them for him, and she knew exactly where they were).

Whenever she's home now, she finds herself glancing out the windows, listening for noise in the driveway, straining her vision and her hearing, holding her breath, even checking herself out in the mirrors, making sure she looks okay, just in case. She hates not knowing when he's going to show up next. Even more, she hates that he assumes he can simply walk through the front door whenever he wants, day or night. What if she's busy? What if it's not a good time? What if she starts having an affair, too? He can't just waltz in anymore. He moved out. She hates him for moving out. But what undoes her the most, when she allows an unguarded and honest

47

moment to settle over her while she's peeling potatoes or looking out the window, is the thought that at some point he might never walk through the front door again.

'Do you know her?' asks Jill.

'No,' says Beth.

'You haven't been to Salt yet to check her out?' asks Georgia.

'God no!' says Beth.

'I'd be dying to know who she is. You don't want to be in line with her at the bank and not know it. We should all go together and give her the evil eye. Petra, you and your witch doctor should put some kind of curse on her,' says Georgia.

They all laugh, including Beth, despite her self-conscious misery. She imagines a cloth voodoo doll dressed in a miniature, black Salt T-shirt with sewing pins stuck in its eyes. She can feel the vodka now, warm in her stomach, buzzing in her head. Normally, she'd say she'd had enough. She doesn't want to feel wrecked in the morning. But she hasn't been sleeping well, and she feels wrecked most mornings anyway, so what the hell. And Petra's driving her home. She refills her wineglass with vodka.

'I don't know if I could. Maybe.'

'Have you guys gone to counseling?' asks Courtney.

'No.'

'Maybe you should go,' says Georgia. 'Phil and I used Dr. Campbell. He was good. Well, not that good, I guess, he didn't fix us. But we were beyond fixing.'

48

Phil was Georgia's second husband, the one she loved the most. She's been married four times. Her friends will say that she's 'in between husbands' now, but Georgia insists she's 'divorced.' End of story. She keeps a Post-it note under a refrigerator magnet at eye level: DO NOT GET MARRIED EVER AGAIN. But they all know that she will. She can't help it. She's a hopeless romantic.

As the wedding coordinator for the Blue Oyster, twice a week for at least twelve weeks a year she's surrounded by brides looking like Disney princesses in Vera Wang, grooms looking like James Bond in Armani, 'Ave Maria' playing on the harp (sung or played at all four of her own ceremonies), weddings that are stunningly perfect down to the most microscopic detail. Every week each summer, she gushes about the most beautiful wedding cake she's ever seen, the most elegant bridal bouquet ever carried down the aisle, the most moving toast she's ever heard, as sincere, wide-eyed, and excited as she was for her very first bride and groom. Those weddings never get old hat to her. For Georgia, each wedding has its own real magic, a belief in true love and destiny and God that permeates her soul. Then she transfers all of that over-the-top fairy-tale romance onto whatever unsuspecting guy she's dating. Next thing they know, the Post-it note is gone from her fridge, and she's got another new last name.

'I don't know if he'd even want to,' says Beth.
'Do *you* want to go to counseling?' asks Petra.
'I don't know.'

'Do you want a divorce?' asks Courtney.

'I don't know.'

Beth doesn't know what she wants. She wants this to be a regular book club night. She wants to drink sake and talk about Japan. She doesn't want it to be the Thursday night that everything officially and publicly changed. Her marriage, her picture-perfect life as wife and mother of three on Nantucket, is gone now. Her marriage is broken.

I'm broken, she thinks.

Tears spring from her eyes and roll down her face. Georgia scooches her chair over toward Beth and puts her arm around her.

'I can't believe this is happening,' says Beth, embarrassed to be crying in front of everyone, to have a cheating husband in front of everyone.

'You're going to be okay,' says Georgia, rubbing circles with her hand on Beth's back.

'I'd divorce the bastard,' says Jill.

'Jill!' scolds Petra.

'Well, he is, and I would,' says Jill, looking to Georgia for support.

'You know I'd get rid of him. Already been there and done that. But I was probably too quick to end things, especially with Phil. It's something I should work on, *if* I were getting married ever again, which I'm not.' Georgia lifts her wineglass in a gesture of cheers and drinks the rest of her vodka in a toast to her own proclamation.

'You have to figure out what you want,' says Petra. 'You and Jimmy can recover from this if you both want to. Or this is the way out. But you should decide what *you* want. Don't let him or anyone else decide for you.'

Petra's right. She's always right. But Beth's head is swimming in vodka, and the only thing she can think of that she wants right now is for Georgia to keep rubbing her back.

'And we love you, no matter what you decide,' says Petra.

Georgia squeezes Beth's shoulders, and everyone nods, everyone except for Courtney, who looks lost in thought, her eyebrows knotted. Beth feels drunk and embarrassed, broken and uncertain, but suddenly, surprisingly grateful.

'I love you, too,' says Beth, smiling through tears, because even if Jimmy doesn't love her anymore, she feels lucky to have a handful of girlfriends who will love her no matter what.

6

Mourning doves whistle back and forth in plaintive conversation while sunlight eases its way into Olivia's bedroom through the unshaded windows, bathing her in a soft and gentle glow. This is generally how she begins each day now, in synchrony with the birds and the sun. And if it's a cloudy or stormy morning and the doves aren't feeling chatty, she sleeps and sleeps, probably until at least noon. Maybe much later. She doesn't know. She's lost all track of real time. The power went out for a day last month, the first of too many times to count now, and she never bothered to reset any of the clocks. She also stopped wearing a watch. This hasn't been a problem as she has nowhere that she needs to be. She's existing outside of time.

She looks over at the other side of the bed, the comforter and the pillow unbothered, and remembers all over again that David isn't here. He's in Hingham. She's on Nantucket. Separated. She still sleeps curled on her side with one arm hugging the edge of the mattress, leaving room for him. She shimmies over to the middle of the bed and lies flat on her back, arms and legs spread wide, taking up as much space as possible. It feels strange.

She stretches and yawns, in no hurry to leave her bed, enjoying the extravagance of emerging slowly from a full night's sleep. It seems like only yesterday that she woke too early every morning to David's alarm clock or to Anthony's eeya-eeya-eeya, shocked into consciousness, still exhausted. More than exhausted. Eroded. A little more of her missing each day. Those mornings were just yesterday, and yet they were a million years ago. Time's a funny thing, bending, warping, stretching, and compressing, all depending on perspective.

It's April, but she only knows this because the letter she received from her lawyer the other day was dated April fourteenth. Without that letter, she would've guessed that it was still March, still winter given how cold it's been and how nothing has changed.

The springs she spent in the Boston area were unrecognizable compared to the lush, warm, green springs in Athens, Georgia, where she grew up. Spring in Boston is just another word for winter, the second half. Right about when the magnolia trees are blooming in Athens, it snows in Hingham. And not just a dusting. Snowfall in March in Hingham is school-canceling, street-plowing, where-are-we-going-to-put-it-all snow. Olivia made no secret of her hatred for March snow, but she had to admit, the white at least brightened up the barren, grim, preblossom landscape.

It doesn't snow on Nantucket the way it does near Boston. Surrounded by ocean, the air is usually too wet to support the structure of a delicate flake, and it rains instead. A couple of times here, she noticed the ground was slushy, but she never saw any actual snowfall this year

53

and hasn't had to shovel once. She's not sure she even owns a real snow shovel here. The only shovel she can think of is in the backseat of her Jeep, kept there to dig herself out of sand, not snow, if (when) the Jeep gets stuck.

But even though it doesn't snow here like it does on the mainland, it still doesn't feel like spring. Even on sunny days, the cold is unrelenting. And somehow everything seems tinged gray, the way the world looks through sunglasses. It's been the same cold and gray winter day for months. Time feels literally frozen here.

According to the letter from her attorney, her divorce proceedings are frozen as well. The agreement is uncontested and no-fault, their divorce being one of the few things she and David haven't fought over in a long time. She's read through the entire document three times now. She likes to linger on the words *no-fault*, typed in black and white right there on the official, legal page, as if the state of Massachusetts is acknowledging them personally, exonerating them both of any blame. The failure of their marriage wasn't really his fault or hers.

Within a few breaths of the word *autism*, Anthony's pediatric neurologist actually asked them, *How's your marriage?* Olivia remembers bristling, thinking, *What business is that of yours?* And, *We're talking about Anthony here, not me and David.* But the neurologist knew their future. He'd seen it too many times before, the comorbidity of autism and divorce.

She doesn't remember if she answered him.

54

She doesn't remember most of whatever followed the word *autism* in that office on that day, but she's thought about his question and her answer many times since. If she managed to voice a polite reply on that day, a day she thought for sure would be the absolute worst day of her life — only to be irrefutably unseated for all time a few short and long years later — she probably said something like *Fine*. And their marriage might've remained fine had they not been pressed and pulled and gutted in ways that two married people could never have imagined when they dressed up and said *I do*.

No, they most certainly weren't fine after that day. But how could anyone be? That would be like throwing a glass vase against a brick wall and expecting it not to smash into a thousand broken pieces, acting surprised and upset that it no longer holds water. The vase will always shatter. That's what happens when glass hits brick. It's not the vase's fault.

When they were still dating after college, when they entered the 'real world' and things got serious, Olivia questioned whether David was husband material. She made a mental list of necessary qualities and began checking off boxes: Handsome. Smart. Funny. Good provider. Handy around the house. Loves children. All checks. They married when she was twenty-four.

She never imagined the additional boxes she should've had on that list: Can function on little sleep for years. Willing to have his heart and will broken every day. Doesn't mind dumping all the money he earns down a bottomless drain.

Like the state of Massachusetts says — it's not his fault.

They agree on all the terms. She gets the cottage on Nantucket. He gets the house in Hingham. There's no money. They already spent all of their savings on Anthony.

Applied-behavioral-analysis therapy, speech therapy, Floortime, sensory integration, metal chelation, gluten-free diets, casein-free diets, B^{12} shots. Pediatricians, neurologists, gastroenterologists, occupational therapists, physical therapists, energy healers. From the mainstream to the alternative to the practically voodoo, Olivia doesn't remember much of any of it being covered by their health insurance. David worked more and more hours. They refinanced the houses. They emptied their IRA nest eggs. Because how could they retire with money in the bank and a son with autism, knowing that there was a therapy out there that might've helped him but they didn't try because it was too expensive?

They were about to sell the cottage.

Olivia remembers those late-night conversations in bed with the lights off, she on her side, David on his, hope and hopelessness living and breathing between them and every other word. She'd read or heard about some new treatment. *It's not FDA-approved for autism, and I agree, it sounds a bit cockamamy, but expert Dr. So-and-So said at this year's conference it works on a subset of kids. It costs a fortune. What do you think?* She remembers the sound of his exhale and then the silence, knowing he was nodding in the dark.

They tried it. They had to.

So there's no money left, and half of nothing is nothing. There's no alimony. And no child support, of course. That's basically it. Clean and simple. They can set each other free.

But David hasn't signed the agreement. Olivia knows he will. He just needs more time. And since time isn't going anywhere, she doesn't mind waiting.

She gets up and walks into the kitchen. She opens the cupboard and sighs. She forgot to buy more coffee.

If David were here, he'd say something like *No problem, let's go to The Bean*. Before they had Anthony, they'd make a morning of it. They'd settle into a table, hopefully the one in the corner by the front window, he'd read the *Globe*, and she'd read a book for work, he'd have two large coffees, both black, and she'd have a large latte and a blueberry scone. Every now and then he'd read part of a news story to her, and she'd share either some particularly insightful, gorgeously worded nugget of wisdom or some hideously atrocious paragraph of trash. She loved those easy, unstructured mornings, back when they were newly married.

She wishes he were here. As she stews on this a bit more, she realizes that what she's really longing for is a latte, a scone, and a leisurely morning at The Bean. She doesn't need David here for that. Seized by a sense of purpose and a desire she hasn't experienced in a long time to be out in the world, she throws on a pair of jeans and a sweater, zips her coat, grabs her hat, purse, and keys, slides her feet into her boots by the front door, and, before she can talk herself out of going, leaves the house.

★ ★ ★

Downtown is mobbed, crawling with cars and people. The few times Olivia has driven through Town since she arrived on the island this winter, it's been deserted, even on a weekend. The storefront windows have been darkened, sporting naked mannequins and signs reading SEE YOU NEXT SEASON. Most of the restaurants have been closed in the middle of the day. Parking spaces have been everywhere, just as anyone would expect in winter, when too few people are on the island to support most businesses.

But today everything has come alive as if it were the middle of August, not the middle of April. *What's going on here?* She can't imagine.

She turns right onto India Street, beginning to loop the block for a third time, and vows to abandon the mission if she can't find anything this go-around. She's about to give up, planning a consolation trip to Stop & Shop for a bag of coffee or maybe the Downyflake outside Town, but then she spots an opening in front of the Atheneum in between a Hummer and a Land Cruiser.

The Atheneum is Nantucket's library, an imposing white building, the front entrance flanked on either side by colossal Ionic columns. It looks like an architectural anachronism, more like an ancient Greek temple than a modern library, as if it belongs on the Acropolis and not in the heart of the otherwise quaint, New England-style, historically restored town of Nantucket. Since she's right there, and she's now imagining how nice it would be to read a book while she drinks her latte at The Bean, just like old times minus David, she decides to run inside and find something to read.

As the bumper-to-bumper traffic outside might've predicted, the library is swarming with people. There are strollers everywhere, mothers and fathers reprimanding and calling to their kids, kids yelling and running away from their parents. A baby in one of the strollers is wailing, inconsolable. The whole place is buzzing with activity and voices that echo and skip off the high ceilings. The energy feels all wrong, disrespectful, like when kids talk and goof around in church, and Olivia second-guesses her decision to come inside.

She gets as far as the front desk and pauses, wondering if she wants a book badly enough to wade through the clogged chaos before her, deciding, in the end, that she'd rather get the hell out of there. She's about to turn around and leave when she catches sight of a familiar book cover sitting alone on a TO BE SHELVED metal cart. *The Curious Incident of the Dog in the Night-Time*.

She read that book years ago, just after Anthony was diagnosed, part of her mission to read everything ever written about autism. She remembers thinking at the time how different the main character's autism was from her Anthony's. Exact opposite ends of the spectrum, like red and violet in a rainbow. In the most obvious ways, they were entirely different, yet she found subtle and surprising similarities that comforted her, restored her hope. Violet isn't blue because it also contains red.

'I'll take this, please,' she says, deciding that she might be ready to read it again.

After filling out the paperwork for a library card, she hustles out the door and down the front steps of the library with her loaned book in hand, relieved to be out of there. She walks around the corner to The Bean, expecting to stroll right in, but her progress is stopped well outside the entrance by a snaking line of customers. It's freezing cold, and the line is long, yet everyone around her appears to be in exceptionally good cheer. Olivia hasn't left her neighborhood much, but when she does venture out — to the grocery store, to the bank — there are never any crowds. She hasn't waited in a single line since she's moved to Nantucket. She's become used to the quiet bubble of her life here, the convenience of getting in and getting out with whatever she needs with minimal human contact.

She glances down at her bare wrist, looking for the time, wondering how long this is going to take. It's got to be well after noon. Why are all these people here? She pulls the collar of her coat up over her chin, shoves her hands into her pockets, closes her eyes, and breathes.

At long last, the line inches forward, and she

steps inside. The café is exactly as she remembers — the worn wooden floor, the teardrop crystal chandelier, the antique copper and pewter teapots on the shelves, the glass canisters filled with biscotti. But her air of enjoyment in the familiar surroundings deflates when she notices every seat in the house is occupied.

'Can I help you?' asks the girl behind the counter.

'I'd like a large latte and a blueberry scone, please.'

'We're all out of scones.'

'Oh, okay, just the latte then.'

'Milk or soy?'

'Milk.'

'Regular, two percent, or nonfat?'

'Uh, regular. What's going on today?'

'Sorry?'

'Why are there so many people here?'

'The daffodils.'

Olivia thinks. 'Is that a band?'

The girl looks Olivia up and down, sizing her up, the way young people look at older people who don't have a clue. 'The flower? You don't know? Why are you here?'

'I live here.'

'Huh,' says the girl, not believing this at all.

'So all these people are here to see some daffodils?'

'Yah, there's like three million in bloom all over the island.'

Three *million*. Really? She hadn't noticed any. And is someone actually counting these? Olivia suspects that this girl must be exaggerating, the way young people do. 'So, what, people drive around and look at flowers?'

The girl hands Olivia her latte, and Olivia pays for it.

'There's like a whole festival, the parade, the tailgating — '

'Tailgating?'

'Over in 'Sconset.'

'Is there a football game?'

The girl laughs.

'Excuse me, are you done? There's a long line here,' says the guy behind Olivia.

'Sorry.'

Olivia steps out of the way and looks around the room one last, hopeless time. No seats. She nudges her way against the incoming line back outside and returns to her car. As she bounces over the cobblestones of Main Street and then turns onto the smooth pavement, she notices, for the first time, all the daffodils — planted in gardens and window boxes, lining fences and front yards, 'wild' crops of them dotting the sides of the road. They're everywhere. How did she not notice any before?

Daffodils and tailgating. Curious, she decides to take a quick detour over to 'Sconset. She and David used to tailgate with their friends before every home football game at Boston College. Everyone wore BC sweatshirts and jackets and hats. Someone always brought a grill and a couple of kegs — charred cheeseburgers and Milwaukee's Best in plastic cups. David and his friends would talk in passionate detail about the

62

players, and someone would invariably compare the quarterback to Flutie, and they'd argue over who was better. They'd all be rowdy and drunk by midmorning, well before kickoff.

As she approaches Main Street in 'Sconset, there they are, the tailgaters, parked one after another along the strip of grass between Milestone Road and the bicycle path. She's in a thick parade of traffic now, but she slows down even more than she needs to for a better look. A car parked on the grass ahead of her begins to pull out as she's approaching it, and she decides to take the spot.

She grabs her mirrored sunglasses, gets out of her Jeep, and begins walking. Main Street is blocked off to car traffic, so she walks down the center of the road. The tailgating cars are now mostly antiques or fancy convertibles and must've had special permission to be here. Most of the license plates are from New York or Connecticut. These people aren't year-rounders.

All of the cars are decorated with daffodils — huge bouquets tied to mirrors and roof racks and hoods. The people are decorated in daffodils, too. Hats, leis, corsages, boutonnieres. Most everyone is dressed for the occasion, casual but festive in some combination of yellow clothing with daffodil accessories, but some of the women are wearing elegant spring dresses and heels, and a few of the men are wearing seersucker suits and ties, as if they were out for tea in the English countryside. It feels like a Mardi Gras parade thrown by the Kennedys.

There are no kegs. There are wineglasses,

champagne glasses, and martini glasses. There are Bloody Marys with green olives and sticks of celery. There are lawn chairs and card tables adorned with tablecloths and, of course, centerpiece vases bursting with daffodils. The tables are also piled with food, and not hamburgers and hot dogs, but beautiful food, food that could be served at a wedding. Baskets of bread, boards of cheese, fried clams, sushi, salads, and chowder.

It's all very civilized. Although everyone appears to be drinking in public, and she's sure that plenty of these people are feeling tipsy, none of them is drunk enough to be a public nuisance. No one's calling the campus police here. No one is reliving a Hail Mary pass or doing keg stands or puking. No one has taken off his shirt and finger-painted GO EAGLES or YOU SUCK on his chest.

These people aren't here to cheer on their beloved home team or celebrate a winning season. These people have packed up their suitcases and traveled hundreds of miles by plane or car and ferry, they've prepared picnic baskets full of crackers and cheese and lobster and wine, gotten dressed up in their wacky yellow outfits, and driven over to 'Sconset to sit by the side of the road on a freezing-cold day in April to celebrate a flower. These people are crazy.

Olivia avoids eye contact and walks at a brisk pace down the middle of the road, as if she's on her way somewhere specific, looking for someone she knows, and doesn't have time to stop and visit. The air smells like wet earth and buttery-sweet flowers, ocean and garlic. Her stomach growls. She wishes she had that blueberry scone. Or a bite of that woman's lobster roll.

Satisfied that she's seen all there is to see at this bizarre roadside holiday, she turns around, returns to her car, and heads to the other side of the island, enjoying the cheery sprays of yellow that decorate the landscape all around her as she drives. Back in her driveway, she spots six daffodils in her own front yard, three gold and three white, fully open and bobbing in the wind as if they were nodding and happy to see her. She wonders who planted them. She smiles, feeling not only hungry now, but also strangely inspired.

She heats up a bowl of clam chowder in the microwave and shakes a heap of oyster crackers on top. She grabs a spoon, her latte, a blanket from the couch, and her library book and sits on the rocking chair on her front porch. Cold coffee, three-day-old chowder, and six of the three million daffodils all to herself. Her own private tailgating party to celebrate Daffodil Day, or whatever they call it. Perfect. Or at least, not bad.

She eats a spoonful of chowder and studies her flowers shivering in the wind, impossibly bright and fragile and brave against the cold grayness of April on Nantucket. It must be hard to be a daffodil here. They probably wish they could stay in the ground another month. But they have no say in the matter. Some biological alarm clock inside them tripped the germination switch, telling each bulb to sprout and go forth, whether it's sunny and seventy in Georgia or still feeling like winter in April on Nantucket. They come, year after year.

She takes another spoonful and thinks about all the people partying in 'Sconset months before the weather has welcomed them to celebrate the daffodils. What's the big deal? She finishes her chowder and drinks her latte. She continues to sit on her porch, facing the flowers and the sun, feeling the warmth on her face through the frigid air. She closes her eyes, soaking in this small pleasure.

Maybe it's the promise of summer. After a long and bleak winter that often extends straight through spring, maybe the daffodil is a sign that summer will come again. The earth will spin and turn around the sun, and the clocks will tick even if Olivia doesn't reset hers, and time will move along. Winter will end. This, too, shall pass. There's the promise of a new beginning. The daffodils will bloom by the million, and life will return to the island.

And whether Olivia wants it to or not, life will return to her as well. She sits on her porch, tailgating before her daffodils, and notices that the sun has moved across the sky past her bedroom windows. It must be nearing midafternoon. Time passing.

Time heals, they say.

She reads the back cover of her library book. She's definitely ready to read about autism again. She feels ready to face what happened, to

66

remember it all, to try to understand Anthony's life and why he's no longer here, to begin healing. But if she's feeling brave enough to face autism again, it shouldn't be through fiction. She carries her library book back into the house and returns to the porch a minute later with something else.

Rested and full and feeling like today, Daffodil Day, might just be as good a time as any, she opens one of her journals to the first page and reads.

March 19, 2001

We had Anthony's one-year doctor appointment today. He's 29 inches and 21 pounds, the 50th percentile for height and weight. He had a bunch of shots — my poor baby boy. I cried right along with him! I can't stand to watch him in any kind of pain. I was so proud to show off that he's already walking. Dr. Harvey says we can switch him over to whole milk now. It's going to be SO nice to not have to deal with buying formula anymore.

I can't believe he's already one! He's growing up so fast. He's always on the move now. He only lets me hold him to give him his bottle, otherwise he wants to get down and explore. He's not my snuggly little baby anymore. He's officially a toddler!

This must be what happens. He's already beginning the long process of growing up, pulling away, becoming an independent little person. It's what he's supposed to do, but I wish it didn't have to happen so soon.

This is why mothers have more babies. We forget about the pain and discomfort and wild inconvenience of pregnancy and childbirth so we can feel that heavenly feeling of holding a warm baby snuggled and content against our chests again. It's like nothing else in this world. Maybe David and I should start trying. We want a big family, and I'm not getting any younger.

I told Dr. Harvey that Anthony's not talking yet and asked if we should be concerned. He said that not all babies talk at a year and that we should start to hear some words by around fifteen months. So not long now. But Maria's kids all talked before one. I remember Bella saying 'mama' and 'dada' and 'moon' and signing 'more' and 'all done' before her first birthday.

Dr. Harvey said girls usually talk a little sooner than boys. He said not to worry. But it's there. The worry. I can't help it. It's like telling me not to have brown eyes. I have brown eyes. I'm worried. Why isn't Anthony talking yet?

David's not worried at all. He says I worry too much about everything. I know he's right. I do worry a lot, but this feels different from my normal, everyday neuroses about switch-plate protectors and sterilizing his pacifiers and the possibility that his formula could be contaminated with bugs.

I wonder if his hearing is okay. Anthony

doesn't seem to hear me. When I call his name, he doesn't look at me. In fact, he really almost never looks at me. The other day, I clapped my hands as loud as I could, and he didn't even turn his head. He just kept sitting on the floor looking out the slider glass doors at the leaves blowing around on the deck. It was as if I didn't exist.

Is he deaf? He's not. I know he's not, which is probably why I didn't mention it to Dr. Harvey. I see him bounce to music when we have it on. He loves reggae. And the other day, I dropped a pan in the kitchen, and I saw him startle, and then he cried. So he's definitely not deaf. So why does a part of me keep hoping that he is? What a crazy thing to think. God, what's going on with Anthony? Please tell me everything's okay with him.

What am I worried about? Dr. Harvey says he's fine. David thinks he's fine. I'm sure he's fine.

I'm such a liar.

7

Beth has been staring vaguely into her bedroom closet for twenty minutes, about nineteen and a half minutes longer than she typically spends in this position. Her closet is a modest, rectangular pocket in the wall, enclosed by two doors that slide past each other. A single rod runs the length of it, and a single shelf sits above the rod. Nothing fancy. Beth's side is on the left, and Jimmy's is on the right. Or rather, it was.

She slides the doors to reveal the other side — the bare rod, the empty shelf, those nasty dust bunnies on the floor she needs to vacuum. She complained about their lack of closet space to Jimmy for years. She practically drooled over the walk-in that Mickey built for Jill (there's even an ottoman in the middle of it for sitting — for sitting!). Now Beth has what she wished for, twice as much space, but she can't bring herself to spread her hangers out onto his side of the bar or to walk her shoes over to his side of the floor. She can't.

She slides the doors again and returns to the problem at hand. What to wear. Like everything else in the house, Beth's side of the closet is tidy and organized. All of the hangers are the same — white, plastic, and facing the same direction. Hanging from left to right are tank tops, then short-sleeve shirts, long-sleeve shirts, dresses, and skirts. A short stack of sweatshirts and sweaters are folded on the shelf above the rod, and two rows of shoes are lined up along the floor. One pair of each — sneakers, snow boots, leather boots, clogs, low heels, sandals, flip-flops. With the exception of the sneakers, which used to be white but are now many-years-old gray, all of her footwear is black.

Most everything in her closet is black. Not edgy black. Not New York City, metropolitan-chic black. Not even Gothic black. Everything is blah black. Safe and boring, nothing-interesting-to-see-here black. Invisible black. What isn't black is gray or white.

She thumbs through her shirts, cotton and boxy crewnecks and turtlenecks. The sweaters are shapeless and long. They all cover her butt. She holds an androgynous, black T-shirt up to her neck that might look okay with jeans. But her jeans aren't dressy enough for Salt. Her jeans are baggy, practical, and comfortable, good for driving the kids in the minivan or cleaning the house or sitting on the couch or gardening, but not good for going out to Salt. Not good at all.

She pulls out her only two dresses and lays them side by side on the bed. They're both black, but neither can be described as a 'little black dress.' The first is the dress she wears to wakes and funerals — high neck, long sleeves, no waist, hem at her ankles. She originally bought it for Jimmy's dad's funeral because it looked respectful and nondescript, and she liked that it didn't call attention to her in any way, but as she's inspecting it now, she's embarrassed by it. It looks like a costume for a school play, and the

71

play is about a seventeenth-century Quaker spinster.

She turns her attention to the other dress, hoping it might be her savior. It's a scoop neck, short sleeve, Empire waist, with a flowing skirt hitting just below the knee. It's not bad. It could work. It's actually kind of cute. She holds it up and studies herself in the full-length mirror on the back of the bedroom door, trying to figure out if she looks cute, but suddenly she remembers the last time she wore it, and any possibility of pulling off cute flies right out the window. She checks the tag. Mimi Maternity. She was nine months pregnant with Gracie the last time she wore this dress. She can't wear a maternity dress to Salt, even if it is the sexiest thing she owns, and no one will see the tag.

She chews her nails as she scrutinizes her only two dresses, hating them. She returns them to their spot on the rod on her side of the closet and searches through her black clothes. Her old, dowdy, stupid black clothes. She can't do this. She can't go. She can't.

She grabs the phone from her bedside table and dials.

'I can't go,' she says to Petra.

'Why not?'

'I have nothing to wear.'

'What are you, sixteen? Wear a black top and a skirt.'

'I need to go shopping first. Let's go next weekend.'

She needs time for a trip to the Hyannis mall, an involved and expensive excursion requiring

72

ferry tickets and bus schedules. Even if she could afford to shop downtown, which she most certainly cannot — hell, even if they were giving the clothes away for free — she wouldn't be caught dead wearing ninety-nine percent of it. She'll never understand why women who can afford anything and everything would *choose* to wear pineapple-print dresses, Pepto-Bismol-pink tops sporting sequins and embroidered dogs, skirts patterned with starfish and whales.

'Next weekend is Figawi, we'll never get in. Come on, you've been putting this off all month. Put on some jewelry and some makeup, you'll look great.'

She's right. Next weekend is Memorial Day weekend and Figawi, an internationally celebrated sailboat race from Hyannis across the sound to Nantucket harbor. It's also the grand, official kickoff to Nantucket's summer season. There are clambakes, fancy fund-raisers, award ceremonies, and parties all over the island. And all the restaurants will be jammed.

'I don't know.'

'You want to check this woman out or not?'

'I think so, but — '

'Then let's go check her out.'

'What does she look like?'

In the infinite pause that follows, Beth presses her fingers to her lips and holds her breath. Her heart pulses in her temples. She's wanted to ask Petra this question so many times since book club last month, but her fear of every conceivable answer has always shoved it down, silencing her. If Angela is beautiful, then Beth

73

must be ugly. And *ugly* is being kind. *Hideous* is the word Beth has been trying on for size, feeling as if it might fit her perfectly, better than any black thing hanging in her closet. And if Angela's not beautiful, then she must be sweet or funny or attractive in some other compelling way that Beth is not, else Jimmy wouldn't have to stray to find it. So if Angela is beautiful, Beth is ugly, and if Angela is ugly, then Beth is a bitch, either way redefined by whatever Jimmy sees in this other woman.

'That's what we're going to find out tonight.'

'Yeah, but you've seen her. What do you think?'

'I think she doesn't hold a candle to you.'

Beth smiles, but then her eyes return to her closet. 'How about after Figawi?'

'How about tonight?'

'Petra, I don't have to go at all.'

'True.'

'But I can't stand not knowing who she is.'

'Well then.'

Beth chews her thumbnail. 'Can I borrow your turquoise necklace?'

'You got it. I'll be over a little before seven. You okay?'

'Yeah.'

'It's not even noon. You should get out of the house. Step away from the closet.'

'I will. Once I figure out what I'm wearing.'

'Black top, skirt, turquoise necklace. You'll look great. See you tonight.'

Black top and a skirt. She pulls out her white peasant skirt and considers it. She walks into the hallway and stops in front of their most recent family photo hung on the wall, the one taken last summer on Miacomet Beach. She wore this skirt. She, Sophie, and Gracie wore white skirts and black tops; Jimmy and Jessica, who won't wear anything but pants, wore white shorts and black tops. It's a beautiful photograph. They're all sitting in the sand, beach grass, wispy white clouds, and soft-blue sky behind them. Jimmy has his hand on her knee, touching her skirt, this skirt now in her hands, touching her so easily, so naturally.

She remembers those days early on, when they were dating and first married, when he touched her, even in passing, and she felt it. Really felt it. That magnetic, electric heat of his hand on her. That invisible, magical, chemical connection. Where did that go?

He was cheating on her when this picture was taken. Beth pinches her eyes shut and swallows, trying to keep it together. What does Jimmy feel when he touches Angela? Does he feel an invisible, magical, chemical connection? What doesn't he feel when he touches Beth? When he used to touch her. She opens her eyes and steps back, taking in the whole wall — seven years of family portraits and a black-and-white photo of her and Jimmy from their wedding day. She looks at everyone's smiles, her happy family. Her life. She clenches her teeth and blinks back tears. Her life is a fraud.

She straightens two of the frames that were tipped just slightly to the right of level, returns to her bedroom, and crawls back into bed. The bed feels good. The bed feels safe.

And she knows how to dress for bed. She's wearing her old, pink flannel pajamas, covered in nubs, the most colorful things she owns. She should go to Salt in her pajamas. Then she'd really make an impression. Not the kind of impression she wants to make though.

But what kind of impression does she want to make? She wishes she didn't have to make one at all, that she could go in disguise, sporting a wig and dark glasses, so she could see and not be seen. But she also fantasizes about going and being noticed by everyone. She'd strut into Salt, looking confident and sexy (tastefully sexy, not trashy sexy), and shy of that, at least better than Angela, a difficult goal to set since she has no idea what Angela looks like. She's terrified of giving this woman any reason to feel any more superior to Beth than she probably already feels. Unfortunately, realistically, there's an awful good chance of this. Beth's not feeling confident or sexy. And she never struts. She looks into her pathetic closet, rolls over, closes her eyes, and tucks the blankets up to her chin.

Behind her closed lids, she envisions Jimmy shaking a martini, then stopping midpour, struck by the sight of her as she *struts* into the restaurant with her friends. She imagines him pulling her aside, telling her that he feels like an idiot for leaving her. She imagines him begging her to take him back right there at the bar, right in front of Angela.

She directs the entire Salt scene, smiling as it plays out in her head. She's even cast a fictitious

Angela, devastated and defeated, with sleek black hair, thick eyebrows, severe makeup, and a spandex dress (trashy sexy). The only person she can't see in this little fantasy is herself.

Damn it, what am I going to wear?

It occurs to her that she's on the other end of this ridiculous question at least once a week with Sophie, her thirteen-going-on-eighteen-year-old. The other two girls will be dressed and ready and waiting at the front door, and Sophie will still be in her room, half-dressed, crazed and crying, clothes tossed everywhere. *I can't go to school! I have nothing to wear!*

Worried more about the girls' being late for school than Sophie's fashion crisis, Beth typically offers something quick and admittedly too glib.

You look beautiful. Just be yourself and it won't matter what you wear. C'mon, let's go!

Now Beth gets why Sophie rolls her eyes and cries harder. She owes her daughter an apology and a trip to the Hyannis mall.

She tries for a moment to take her own advice. *Be yourself.* But who is she? She's Jimmy's wife, and she's a mother. And if she gets divorced, if she's no longer Mrs. James Ellis, and she's only a mother, then is there less of her? She fears this and feels it already, physically, as if a surgeon has taken a scalpel to her abdomen and removed a whole and necessary part of her. Without Jimmy, she doesn't recognize herself. How can that be? Who has she become?

She rolls over and looks into her closet. It's organized. That's her. But otherwise, she's not in there. She sits up and looks at herself in the mirror on the back of the bedroom door, her blonde, chin-length hair a matted mess, her blue eyes deeply set and dull, her pajamas pink and nubby. *That's not who I am.*

She gets out of bed and returns to face the pictures on the wall in the hallway. The most recent portraits offer her nothing more than wife and mother. She'd always approved of how she looks in these pictures, her hair not too frizzy from the humidity, her makeup subtle, her nails polished, her clothes pressed. But as she studies herself now, her smile appears forced, unnatural, her posture stiff, like she's a cardboard cutout of herself. Like she's posing. She moves back in time and visits the oldest family photo and the portrait from her wedding. Here she sees more of the woman she thinks of as herself. Her smile contains an unself-conscious abandon, her eyes are bright and happy. Where did that woman go?

For some reason, she looks up at the ceiling, and there it is, as if the answer were delivered to her from above. The attic!

She stands on her tiptoes, pulls the dangling white string, unfolds the wooden stairs, and climbs up. A wall of dense, stagnant heat greets her in a hurry at the top. Nearing the end of May, the days have been sunny, but it's remained cool, only in the sixties, yet the trapped heat up here feels like summer against her skin.

She pauses before fully committing to going in. The roof is pitched and low, and the wooden ceiling is riddled with protruding nails, making it both impossible and dangerous to stand up straight. And the floor is unfinished, with only a few planks of wood running the length through the center, like a bridge crossing a sea of pink insulation.

Beth doesn't like coming up here for fear of either forgetting about the low ceiling and impaling her head with a nail or accidentally stepping off the planks and falling through the fluffy fiberglass floor into the living room. Because of this, she normally visits the attic only twice a year — the day after Thanksgiving to take the Christmas decorations down and New Year's Day to put the Christmas decorations back. Up and in, out and down, she's never dallied in here.

Jimmy's got a bunch of his stuff strewn all over the far end — fishing rods leaning against the angled ceiling, two of them fallen over, tangled nets, tackle boxes, one of them open, a collection of golf clubs crisscrossed and loose on the floor like a pile of pick-up sticks, the empty golf bag, a single golf shoe, a surfboard, a clamming rake and bucket.

'Jimmy.'

With her hands on her hips, she scolds him in her head and has to resist the urge to tidy it up. That's not why she's here.

Separate from his mess are three standing fans and two window-box air conditioners. Six plastic storage tubs, all labeled in her printing with a black Sharpie on masking tape, sit in a neat row, two each: CHRISTMAS, HALLOWEEN, WINTER.

The winter boxes are both empty. She and the girls have still been wearing their winter coats in the morning and at night, and they've also been getting good use out of their winter boots, the

79

ground finally fully thawed, the height of mud season. Each year, about a week or two from now and under Beth's directive, Jimmy carries all of the winter gear up to the attic and comes back down with the fans and air conditioners. She sighs, recognizing that this will be her job from now on.

One last tub, apart from the others, way at the back, is labeled BETH. The lid is coated with dust. She hasn't opened this bin in at least a decade. Feeling both excited and scared of what she might discover inside, she sits cross-legged next to it and opens the lid.

First, she pulls out a red Frisbee signed by everyone on her ultimate Frisbee team, turning it over in her hands as she studies each note and signature. Johnny C! Her four-year, unrequited crush from Reed College. She hasn't thought about him in years. He was such a sweet guy. He was premed. She wonders where he is now. He's probably a successful doctor somewhere, not cheating on his wife.

She finds a stack of ticket stubs held together by an elastic band. Rolling Stones, *Stomp*, *Rent*, Cirque du Soleil, the Metropolitan Museum of Art, an airline ticket from Portland to New York, another to New Mexico, even movie stubs, each labeled with the names of the friends or boyfriend who went with her. She can't remember the last concert she's been to (it might've been the Stones), and her last plane trip was from New York to Nantucket, one way. She misses vacations to new places, Broadway shows, and museums (and the trips with each daughter's third-grade class to the whaling museum don't count).

She shuffles through her college ID cards, photos from parties and summer vacations. She laughs at her huge hair and aqua-blue eyeliner. The nineties!

Then she finds a stack of birthday cards, and she hesitates, gathering emotional courage. Eight birthday cards from her mother. She reads through them all, starting with sweet sixteen, treasuring each handwritten word, each *Love you, Mom*, wiping her eyes with her pajama sleeve every time the words get too blurry to read through her tears.

Her mother had a lumpectomy the summer before Beth moved to Nantucket. Her doctor said they got it all. She had radiation and chemotherapy after the surgery. Everything was standard procedure. Everything looked good.

Her hair was gone when Beth moved to New York in September. It was her first job out of college, an editorial assistant for *Self* magazine. Her mother insisted she go and start her life and assured her that she would be fine.

But she wasn't fine. They didn't get it all. In November, she went back into surgery, this time to remove the whole breast and some lymph tissue. Beth's heart tightens. If only they'd done this in the first place. Again, the doctors said they got everything. She and Beth celebrated over Thanksgiving weekend, relieved and grateful.

But they shouldn't have celebrated anything because some microscopic flecks of cancer had

81

already broken free of her breast before the doctors removed it, and they floated off into her mother's body, looking for a new residence. They found her liver first. And then her lungs. She died in January.

Beth holds the last birthday card, the last *Love you, Mom.* It was her twenty-third birthday, and she never imagined her mother wouldn't be here to see her turn twenty-four, thirty, thirty-eight.

She's often wondered if she'd be married to Jimmy if her mother hadn't died. She found getting out of bed and going to work nearly impossible after her mother's funeral. She remembers feeling utterly unable to do her job, even though it only consisted of fairly mindless office duties such as answering the phones, checking faxes, and scheduling meetings. She remembers trying to hide a torrent of tears at so many unprofessional moments. She needed some time off. She clawed her way through each week until June, then she quit and left New York City. She quit and went to Nantucket.

She had inherited a little money from her mother, enough for her to rent a cottage with three friends for the summer and attend graduate school in the fall. She'd been accepted into Boston University's MFA program in creative writing. Other than that, there was no plan. She didn't plan on meeting Jimmy and falling in love with him. And she certainly didn't plan on marrying him and starting a family instead of going back to school.

But this is exactly what she did. On Labor Day, when her friends got on a plane and flew back to the real world, Beth stayed. A year later, she and Jimmy got married, and a year after that, Sophie was born.

She's often wondered what her mother would've thought of Jimmy. She probably wouldn't have liked him. She certainly wouldn't be a fan of his right now. Her mother never had a high opinion of men. She and her father divorced when Beth was three, and they never saw him again after Beth turned four. She doesn't remember her mother ever dating. She was entirely devoted to making a living and raising her daughter, her only child.

Beth digs through the tub, now looking for a specific picture. She knows it's in here. She finds it at the bottom of everything, the only picture she has of her father. He's wearing a men's white undershirt and black-rimmed glasses. His light brown hair is receding. He's smiling. His arms look strong. He's holding Beth in his lap. Her blonde hair is in pigtails, and she's wearing a pink party dress. It's her second birthday. She's also smiling. They look happy together. She has no memory of this man or of herself as this little girl, but she believes that it's them. The writing on the back of the picture, her mother's writing, reads *Denny & Beth, 10-2-73*. She breathes a dense sigh and discards the photograph back to the bottom of the bin.

She presses the stack of birthday cards from her mother against her chest. She misses her, especially now. She smiles and dabs her wet eyes with her sleeve, lost in a bittersweet thought about her own daughters. Her mother may not have cared for Jimmy, but she would've loved her grandchildren.

Beth returns the cards to the tub and pulls out a paperback book. *Writing Down the Bones* by Natalie Goldberg. The book that made her believe she could be a writer someday. Why is this book in here and not on her bookshelf in the living room or on her bedside table?

When she first moved here, she wrote event pieces for *Yesterday's Island*, nothing earth-shattering, but she was writing and getting paid for it. After she had Jessica, she landed a better job as a staff writer for the *Inquirer and Mirror*, but after she had Gracie, she found working and raising three young girls too much to juggle, and she quit the paper. But still, for a while, she kept her pen active.

She finds her essays, poems, and short stories. She finds her notebooks — ordinary, spiral notebooks, floppy and worn, every inch jammed with blue ink — writing exercises, ideas for short stories, vignettes, her imagination, her thoughts and emotions, her tender, naked insides laid out on the eight-and-a-half-by-eleven, college-ruled pages. She flips through them and becomes absorbed in reading one in particular, a short story about a peculiar boy who lives strictly within the confines of a bizarre yet beautiful imaginary world. She remembers when she wrote that story. It was about six or seven years ago after a morning on the beach with the girls, inspired by a little boy she saw there playing with rocks by the shore. She used to find inspiration in her everyday life here, and she used to write about it. When did she stop writing? When did her life become uninspiring?

One of the notebooks she finds is brand-new, untouched. She holds this notebook in her hands, makes a promise to herself, and sets it aside.

Next she comes to the clothes — the faux-leopard-print coat that was her mother's; leather pants (rock-star black); her Goldie Hawn, pink-and-orange, geometric mod dress. She used to *love* that dress. She wore it everywhere — parties, dance clubs, weddings, first dates. Her first real date with Jimmy.

She carefully strips out of her nubby pajamas and slides the dress on over her head without hitting the ceiling. Miraculously, it fits! She doesn't need the mirror in her bedroom to see if it looks cute. She knows.

She finds piles of cheap jewelry — huge silver-hoop earrings, chunky and colorful plastic bangle bracelets, lots of rhinestones, a bunch of tangled necklaces, all very Madonna circa *Desperately Seeking Susan*. She slides a moonstone ring onto the middle finger of her right hand and admires it, wondering why she ever packed it away.

She wonders why she packed any of this away. Some of it has to do with moving from New York to Nantucket and wanting to fit in here. Year-rounders on Nantucket wear oversized L.L.Bean fleece jackets and hip waders, not Goldie Hawn dresses and mood rings. And some of it has to do with the swelling and weight gain that comes with being pregnant three times.

Those skintight, leather rock-star pants haven't been humanly possible in years. But leather pants aside, these things, the notebooks and clothes and photos and cards, are pieces of herself, her history, her sense of adventure and style, her dreams for her future.

This is me, she thinks, staring into the bin.

She and Jimmy used to throw impromptu parties with nothing in the house but a bag of potato chips, a six-pack of beer, and a cheap bottle of wine. Everyone would bring something, and they always had plenty. They always had fun. She and Jimmy haven't thrown a party in a long time. The parties somehow changed, no longer arising spontaneously from the quick and playful thought, *Hey, why don't we invite some friends over tonight?* Instead they required planning and cooking and cleaning the house. Everything had to be *just so*. They became work, and she doesn't remember the fun, only the fights between Jimmy and her ignited over some stressful aspect of getting ready, her anger and resentment sticking to her ribs long after the last guest went home.

She used to wear blues and greens and orange. She used to have moxie. She used to skinny-dip at Fat Ladies Beach and dance to the music she liked. Now she always wears a loose and large cover-up over her bathing suit at the beach, and she only listens to whatever the girls want to hear, usually Britney Spears or some Bambi-eyed teenage girl from the Disney Channel.

She used to write.

She can't believe she stuffed so much of

herself into a box, banished to the attic for so many years. At least she didn't donate herself to Goodwill or, worse, throw herself out. She continues to dig through the box, skipping down memory lane with each item until she picks up the locket, the first gift Jimmy ever gave to her. She opens the smooth, tarnished silver heart and holds it in the palm of her hand. She and Jimmy kissing. She and Jimmy in love. She studies this picture of herself and Jimmy, and it's as if she were seeing two other people, as if they were old friends she was so fond of once, friends she's long lost touch with and who have moved far away. Her heart sinks. She wore that locket every day for years and loved it. Then, at some point, she doesn't remember exactly when, the silver heart began to tarnish, and what once looked new and romantic and sophisticated to her suddenly felt old and boring and childish. She grew tired of wearing it and packed it away.

Careful not to stand up straight or step too far to the side, Beth drags her bin to the top of the stairs, then carries it down and into her bedroom. Balancing the bin on her hip, she slides the closet door open and plops the bin on the floor of Jimmy's side. She gathers *Writing Down the Bones*, her old notebooks, including the one that's blank, and sets them on her night table. She nods. Then she clasps the locket around her neck, rubs the silver heart between her fingers, and turns to check herself out in the mirror on the door.

There I am.

Ready for Salt.

8

It's the hour before sunset on Fat Ladies Beach, and Olivia is walking with her camera in hand. She's been walking this beach every evening and has come to appreciate why photographers call this time of day the magic hour. Lighting this patch of earth for the last minutes of the day from across the horizon rather than from directly overhead, the sun coats everything in a soft, diffuse glow. Colors look more saturated, golden, romantic. Magical.

Olivia had been walking without her camera, uninspired, all spring. Everything everywhere was gray. But then the pervasive gray seemed to lift and vanish for good this weekend, as if it finally became warm enough for Nantucket to unzip and peel off its gray winter coat, revealing the remarkable beauty of this place, especially at this hour. The astonishing blues of the sky melting into the ocean, the crisp, apple-green blades of beach grass, the glittering sand, and soon the showstopping sunset, an intensifying blood-orange sun sinking out of view, trading places with a sky increasingly drenched in hot pink and lavender, unbelievably more magnificent than it was just seconds before. It all begs to be photographed.

Olivia loves the feel of her Nikon in her hands. She admits that the teeny, deck-of-cards-size pocket cameras would be more convenient to carry, and technically they can do most of what she wants from a camera, but they feel like cheap toys. She prefers her bulky Nikon, the responsive click of the button beneath her index finger, the dialing action of the manual focus, its overall heft.

It reminds her of how she used to love the feel of one of her new books hot off the press, the culmination of years of writing by the author and months of editing by her, its smooth and shiny new cover, maybe with embossed lettering, and the satisfying weight of it in her hands. She still loves the feel of a new book. While she appreciates the convenience of those thin, slick e-readers, they don't give her the three-dimensional sensory experience that comes with a real book.

She walks along the water's edge, stopping now and then to snap a wide shot of the horizon, a macro of a seashell, a sandpiper, the silhouette of a woman walking her dog in the distance. Unlike the previous months when she could walk here for as long as she wanted in complete and almost guaranteed solitude, other people are always on the beach now. The island is coming to life, and as Olivia walks, she realizes how out of step she is with the world around her. The pervasive gray surrounding *her* hasn't lifted; it's still winter in her heart. She feels that she's witnessing her life more than she's actually living it, this woman who lives on Nantucket, drinks coffee, reads her journals, goes for walks, and takes pictures, as if she were watching a movie, a boring movie about a boring woman where nothing much happens, a movie she'd like to shut off or change to a different channel, but for some reason, she's glued to the screen. If she keeps watching, something will happen.

In one respect, something does have to happen soon. She needs to find a job here. Even with her meager existence, there are the expenses of daily living. David agreed to pay for her first six months, which means she only has a little longer left on his dole. Either she'll need to make a living here, or she'll have to sell the house and move, probably back to Georgia to be near her mother and sister, Maria, and her family. Or maybe she'll sell the house and run away to somewhere even more remote, some island in the South Pacific where she can disappear.

She's thought about it, about really disappearing. Several suicides on Nantucket have been reported in the paper since she moved here. Counselors and psychologists weighed in as to why suicides are more common on Nantucket than elsewhere, pointing fingers at depression and seasonal affective disorder layered onto the extreme abyss of winter on this isolated speck of land. She's imagined her own name in print, the star subject of a similar newspaper article. She gets it. An almost unbearable emptiness unfolds before her every morning. And then come the questions.

Why?

Why was Anthony here?

What was the purpose of his short life?

No answer.

Why am I here?

Why?

No answer. There are never any answers, not in her prayers or dreams, not so far in her journals or in the faith she used to have in God and the church, not in the magic of a sunset on Fat Ladies Beach. A part of her has accepted that these questions will never find their answers, that there is no point to this life, but another part of her continues the search, asking these questions over and over, with the deepest sincerity, repeating this inquisitive loop many times a day, perseverating.

Like someone with autism.

The silence that follows the last *Why?* of the day always hangs in the air, echoing for a long moment before floating off into infinite nothingness, leaving her so utterly and painfully alone that she often wishes she could dissolve right there and disappear with her question into that nothingness. But something deep inside her insists on holding on, enduring. Witnessing and waiting. And soon, finding a job. But a job doing what? What can she do here?

Why am I here?

Why?

She squats down low, looks through her viewfinder, adjusts her focus, and clicks a photo of the shore, the white foam, the wet, metallic sand, the layers of liquid blue. She looks up and sees the slick, black head of a seal in the surf. She zooms in and clicks. Still zoomed in, she can clearly see the seal's round, black eyes, and it appears to be looking directly at her. She lowers her camera, and they hold each other's gaze for a

91

long moment before the seal dips below the water's surface, disappearing, leaving her alone.

Behind her, a bunch of voices tumble onto the beach. She turns and looks. Two boys are running toward the ocean, toward her, laughing. Their mother, weighed down by a large beach bag on one shoulder and a toddler on her hip, unable to give chase, yells after them, warning them not to go in the water. The father walks beside her at first, then begins to run. They're all barefoot and wearing matching light blue shirts and khaki pants.

The father catches the older two boys, scoops them up in his arms, one in each, just before their toes hit the surf. The boys scream with laughter. The father spins them all dizzy and falls to the ground, and the three play-wrestle in the sand.

'Are you Rebecca?'

'Sorry?' asks Olivia, not because she didn't hear the mother's question, but because she can't quite process it, so unaccustomed to any human voice directed at her on this beach, to anyone penetrating the gray layer that is wrapped so tightly around her skin.

'Are you the photographer?' the mother asks, nodding down to Olivia's Nikon.

'Me? No.'

'Sorry. I thought you were her.' The mother looks back over her shoulder at the parking lot and sighs, hoisting her toddler, who is aiming to get down, higher on her hip. 'I don't know how long I can keep all three clean and dry. Max! No!'

Max is the middle boy, Olivia's guessing around five, and he's now chasing a seagull down the beach. He's fast, ignoring his mother. The father goes after him.

The oldest boy, around eight, wanders over to his mother, no longer interested in the cold water without a brother to race. He stands by her side and holds her free hand.

All three of these boys are familiar and foreign to Olivia, two sides of the same sword, each equally capable of carving her in two. They are the size and shape of Anthony — his feet when he was two, his legs when he was five, his eight-year-old hands.

Max, the boy running down the beach not heeding his parents' calls to stop, is just like Anthony. And yet, he's nothing like Anthony. This boy leaps up and takes off with a glint in his eye and the devil in his smile. He's playing, and he's involving his parents in the game. *Chase me!* And he'll delight in being caught.

When Anthony ran on the beach, he ran to feel the impact of the solid ground compressing his joints, to feel the cool wind on his skin, to feel the hot, granular sand between his toes, to get to the water he loved more than anything else. He ran and didn't listen to her or David's calls to stop, but it was never a game that included them in his world.

The photographer arrives, the father returns with the middle boy, carrying him tucked under his arm like a football, and the mother gathers them all together, encouraging the boys to smile.

'Look at me,' says the photographer, and

unexpected chills tremble through Olivia's center.

Look at me.

How many hundreds of thousands of times did she hear those three words, spoken by her, by David, by doctors, by a series of applied-behavioral-analysis and speech therapists.

Anthony, look at me, while she held a Pringle to her nose.

Anthony, look at me, while she held her breath.

Anthony, look at me, while he did not.

The toddler is throwing his head back and stiffening his limbs, crying, his face puffed and red, his eyes squeezed shut. The mother hands him over to the father. She pulls a toy still inside its packaging from her beach bag and hands it to the photographer. It's a truck. A bribe. She's smart.

'Look at the truck.'

It works. The toddler's attention is drawn to the truck, which the photographer has strategically placed on the top of her head. The toddler stops crying and points. The toddler points and says, 'Mine.'

Until that moment, Olivia wondered if he were on the spectrum. She'd already decided that the other two were neurotypical, but she wasn't sure about the toddler on his mother's hip. After Anthony's diagnosis, every boy she saw — pre-schoolers and teenagers, sons of women she knew and sons of strangers, boys sitting in front of her in church and boys playing on the playground — she observed for signs of autism.

Even now she can't look at a boy and simply see a boy. She has to see or not see autism, too. Like looking at the letters of a word and reading the word, she has to do both. They are inextricably linked.

And where she feels an unspoken bond, a compassionate kinship, with mothers of children on the spectrum, she often feels all sorts of unflattering emotions toward the parents of typical boys and girls. Jealousy, irritation, hatred, rage, grief. Their normal, blessed, easy, unappreciated lives flaunted right there in front of her.

Look at them, she'd usually think, jealousy, irritation, hatred, rage, and grief consuming her, poisoning her.

But today, quite unexpectedly, she feels none of this. Instead she feels relieved and hopeful that this mother will get at least one decent picture with her whole family smiling and looking at the camera. The toddler continues to point at the truck while sitting on his mother's hip, his older brothers are yelling, '*Cheeeeeese*,' and the father has his arm around his wife, his other hand on the shoulder of the oldest boy while the photographer clicks away, still saying, 'Look at me.'

Olivia pulls her Nikon up to her eye and looks at this family through the viewfinder. It's almost sunset now. The light on their faces is warm and flattering. Click. Click. Click. She looks down at her LCD, at the last image she captured. She sees the saturation, the brightness and contrast, the composition, and approves. It's a good picture. Then something shifts, maybe some of the gray surrounding her lifts, and she forgets the technical aspects of the photograph. She looks at the image on her LCD, and she sees joy, intimacy, family, love. Magic captured.

I could do this.

9

Beth and Petra meet up with Jill, who is waiting for them, always early, in front of Salt. Courtney's not coming because she's teaching two yoga classes tonight, and Georgia can't come because she's overseeing a wedding down the street at the Blue Oyster. But with Petra and Jill by her side, Beth has more than enough girl power in her corner, and she's feeling confident and ready in her Goldie Hawn dress. But as Petra walks up the steps, leading the way, Beth realizes that her heart is beating way too fast, urging her body to spring into some kind of large physical action to match her racing pulse. *Run!* She focuses on the back of Petra's neck, on the clasp of her turquoise necklace, the one Beth asked to borrow but didn't wear, as she forces each forward step, walking behind her friend, slowly, deliberately, against her heart's instinct, into the lion's den.

'Hi, welcome to Salt.'

Before Beth can notice anything else, there she is, smiling at Petra. Salt's Saturday-night hostess. Angela.

She's younger than Beth, possibly in her late twenties. Her hair is long, curly, and dark brown. She's wearing a plain, boring black top, but on her it's tight and has a plunging V neckline. That and a small gold cross at the end of a long gold chain draw Beth's eyes, and probably everyone else's, to her big, exciting boobs. Of course. Twentysomething and big boobs.

Beth rounds her shoulders and folds her arms over her own chest, already neatly covered by the thick polyester blend of her Goldie Hawn dress. Even pushed up and in to the best of her Victoria's Secret bra's ability, even before pregnancy stretched them and breast-feeding sucked the bounce out of them, her boobs never looked like *that*. Angela's eyes, big and black and unnervingly beautiful, are still smiling as they move to include Jill, but then they stumble when they see Beth.

She already knows who I am.

Angela clears her throat and pulls her fake, professional welcome smile back on. 'Table for three?'

'No, thanks,' says Petra. 'We're going to sit at the bar.'

We are? Beth wants to correct Petra, to say that they'd prefer a table, please, one facing the street and not the bar actually, but a sour-tasting panic has risen at the back of Beth's throat, and she can only manage to swallow. Like a lamb being led to slaughter, she follows Petra and Jill to the bar and takes the empty seat between them. And there's Jimmy.

He at first greets them with a neutral cheerfulness, the way he might acknowledge any three women who sit down at his bar, clearly without really seeing them. But then it registers. His smile softens on Beth, becoming genuine, but only for the slightest moment before it's replaced by a tensed grin, holding surprise and

98

uncertainty between his teeth, and then finally his jaw clenches tight to keep him from saying what he's probably thinking. *Oh, shit.*

'Ladies.'

'Jimmy,' says Petra.

'Beth,' says Jimmy.

'Hi,' says Beth.

'So what are you ladies up to tonight?'

'This,' says Petra. 'We're here to spy on you.'

Jimmy laughs and shakes the martini he's making with noticeably extra vigor. Beth wipes her hands on the lap of her dress. She didn't know her hands could sweat.

'Not exactly subtle, are you, Petra?' he asks.

'Never,' says Petra.

Direct and fearless, Petra would never tap a nail gently a hundred times with a rubber mallet when she could whack it once with a sledgehammer and get the job done. While Beth admires this quality in Petra, Beth has never been comfortable with the trait herself. She's too afraid of missing the nail head altogether, of creating a huge and ugly hole in the wall next to her intention.

'What can I get for you?' he asks.

'What do you recommend?' asks Petra.

'What are you in the mood for, beer, wine?'

'Something stronger. Something you make,' says Petra.

He pours off some of the drink he's just mixed into a small glass and places it down in front of Petra, who takes a sip.

'That's good. Espresso martini?'

He nods.

'I'll have that,' says Petra.

'Me, too,' says Jill.

'Try some?' asks Petra, offering what's left in her glass to Beth.

'No, no, I — ' says Beth.

'Can't have caffeine after four,' says Jimmy, knowing her answer. 'She'll be up all night.'

Beth shifts in her seat.

'How about something sweeter?' he says, already pulling bottles.

It's strange to see him mixing all these fancy drinks. Jimmy's a beer-in-the-bottle kind of guy. And not the new kinds of beers infused with nutmeg or pumpkin or blueberries. He likes 'real' beer. Budweiser and Coors. He reluctantly admits to liking Cisco's Whale's Tale, but only because the brewery is down the road from their house.

And this isn't Jimmy's kind of bar. He likes a guys' place, not necessarily a sports pub, although the Red Sox, Patriots, Bruins, or Celtics had better be playing on the flatscreen. He likes a bar that's dark and dirty, a glass jar of hard-boiled eggs and bowls of peanuts on the counter, wooden floors warped from years of soaking in spilled beer, Def Leppard playing on the jukebox. The menu might have mozzarella sticks and buffalo wings but certainly not anything with foie gras or truffle oil. There's a pool table and a dartboard and a bouncer because at least one sloppy drunk is going to throw a punch at somebody before closing.

Salt is the opposite of Jimmy's kind of bar. The coppery-orange globe pendants glow against the

100

tin ceiling, giving off a romantic light. The mixed crowd here — some locals, most not — is more women than men, and everyone is dressed well, refined looking, out for a civilized evening. Beth reads the list of cocktails on the drinks menu and gasps at the prices. At $20 a pop, everyone here is out for a civilized and *expensive* evening. She looks down the length of the bar, at the men and women seated next to them, trying to get a sense for who comes here. She notices nothing worth mentioning until she sees the large Nantucket basket purse perched on the bar, owned by the blonde woman next to the bald man in the seersucker suit jacket. Too expensive for anyone actually from Nantucket to own; Beth has seen Nantucket baskets much smaller than that sell for over $1,000.

The bar itself is a honed, rugged stone slab embedded with amber-colored pieces of sea glass. Beth slides her hand over the cool surface. It's beautiful, a piece of art. The music is techno and loud. No one will be singing 'Pour Some Sugar on Me' here.

'Here you go,' says Jimmy, presenting Beth with a martini glass brimming with pink liquid. 'The best drink on the menu.'

Beth takes a sip. It's sweet and spicy with a strong but not unpleasant kick, the kind of drink she could easily get drunk on.

'It's good. What is it?' asks Beth.

'Vodka, rum, chili, lime, and ginger. It's called a Hot Passion martini.'

Hot Passion? What is he doing? Beth feels

embarrassed, indignant, and then strangely flattered.

'What's with the beard?' asks Petra.

'Just trying it out,' says Jimmy, scratching the hollows of his newly hairy cheeks with his fingers. 'You like it?'

'No,' says Petra.

He's been growing the beard for about a month now, and Beth thinks it looks good on him, rugged, masculine. It makes up for his weak chin. And she knows him, that he's not just trying it out. Jimmy stops shaving whenever he's going through a hard time — when his dad died, when scalloping dried up and they couldn't pay the bills, when Jessica had surgery on her ears in Boston. And now. Beth smiles to herself, pleased to realize that at least their separation ranks up there with the death of his father, that she still matters to him. And he stops shaving not simply because he's too distracted and overwhelmed with the stress in his life to bother, but mainly because his beard makes him feel protected, hidden. Jimmy wearing a beard is like Beth wearing one of her big, black, shapeless sweaters that covers her butt.

But she's not wearing one of those sweaters tonight. She's wearing her Goldie Hawn dress, and Jimmy's wearing a beard. Interesting. It hadn't occurred to her that he might be having a hard time without her. Maybe this isn't what he wants. Maybe he's suffering, too.

Angela wiggles her way behind the bar and says something to Jimmy that Beth can't hear. Angela laughs, and he smiles, flashing those

102

crooked, charming teeth. It's quick and then guarded, but there it was. She made him smile.

Keep suffering. Keep hiding. I hope you end up looking like Grizzly Adams.

Jill leans into Beth. 'I think he's trying out enough new things at the moment.'

Jimmy turns his attention to the couple next to Jill and begins opening a bottle of wine for them. Beth sips her martini, aware that Angela is a few feet behind her, that her estranged husband is inches in front of her, that she is sitting between them. This is too weird. She downs her drink. She hates the thought of Angela looking at her right now, checking her out, without her knowing. She feels self-conscious, exposed. Beth rubs her arms as if she's cold and checks her phone. No messages from the girls.

Unable to watch Angela, which is what she thought was the entire point of this outing, she sits and watches Jimmy instead. She can't remember when she last looked at him for this long. Before he moved out, they slept facing away from each other, a habit that began because of his snoring and his cigar breath. Because of his schedule, they rarely ate meals together, and when they did, it was usually in the living room with their plates on their laps while they faced the TV. And she withheld regard for his very existence whenever they were in a fight, which for the past few years was often.

Now she has a front-row seat with nothing to do but watch him. She's never seen him bartend before. He's in constant motion back there, in command, at ease. His hands, uncorking wine bottles, pouring martinis to the rim, muddling limes, are confident, efficient, graceful. He knows where every bottle and bar tool is. He knows from memory how every drink is made. He's good at this, and he enjoys it.

She didn't know any of this. She feels surprise and a twinge of hurt to discover that there's anything about Jimmy that she didn't know. He's not exactly a complex guy. Work, sleep, TV, kids, cigars. Not that bartending is brain surgery or race-car driving, but still, he's got skill and talent. The bar is the hub of this place. Everything revolves around it, and Jimmy is keeping the cogs moving, keeping the customers happy.

This is vastly different from scalloping, which was solitary and outdoors, a job she thought suited him well. But here he is, in a crowded restaurant, confined to a small indoor space, chatting up strangers, mixing 'girlie' drinks, and appearing to love it. He looks so at home.

But he's not dressed the way he dresses around the house. At home, he wears jeans or shorts that used to be jeans — frayed and uneven where he cut them with scissors at the bottom — T-shirts, a Red Sox hat, and work boots. Here, he's wearing a button-down shirt with vertical blue and white stripes. It's even ironed. He's wearing it untucked with the sleeves rolled up to his elbows and unbuttoned one button more than most men would wear it, revealing the top of his chest. He has a handsome, muscular chest. The beard, his smile, his forearms, his chest — he looks relaxed and, she could kill herself for thinking this, sexy. Fueled at least in part by the Hot Passion, she's at once helplessly attracted to him and completely pissed at him.

How is it that he can be present and engaged and so competent here, whereas at home he drags himself around, too exhausted to do anything but lie on the couch? How is it that he can pull himself together, look handsome and cleaned up for work, but at home he only wears T-shirts stained with barbecue sauce on the front and sweat under the arms? How can he save this alive and fun part of himself for work and not share it with her and his girls?

'So, Jimmy, is it always this busy?' asks Petra.

'This? This is nothing. Wait another hour, it'll be three people deep behind you.'

'Huh,' says Petra.

Her restaurant, Dish, does well, but not three-people-deep-behind-the-bar-without-a-seat well, not this time of year anyway.

'How was your drink?' he asks Beth.

'Okay.'

'You want another?'

'No, thanks,' says Beth, thinking that she's had quite enough of his Hot Passion.

'You didn't like it?'

'I did, I just want to try something different now.'

'How about a glass of wine? You'd like the — '

'I can decide what I want without your help.'

'Okay.'

'I'll have an espresso martini.'

'You sure?' asks Jimmy.

'Really sure.'

He shrugs his shoulders, acquiescing. He grabs two bottles and inverts them over a stainless-steel martini shaker. 'How are the girls?'

'Good.'

'How was Jessica's game?'

'It was long. They lost.'

'And Soph?'

'She's upset about a math test, thinks she failed it, but I'm sure she did fine.'

'How's Gracie?'

'Good.' *She misses you. They all do.*

'Good.'

'Don't you want to know how Beth is?' asks Petra.

'Of course. How are you, Beth?'

'Good.'

'You look good.'

'Thanks.'

'I like your necklace.'

She places her hand over her locket. Her face flushes hot. She almost forgot she was wearing it. Before she can respond, Angela is behind the bar again, this time showing Jimmy something on her phone, capturing his interest. She laughs and touches his forearm. Angela's hand on Jimmy's arm. Beth could stomach the laughing and the smiling and the flirting and the boobs, but something about that small touch, the intimacy of it, undoes her.

'You okay?' Jill asks Beth in her ear. 'You look a little pale.'

Beth nods as she clenches her teeth and swallows. She can't speak. If she talks right now, she'll cry. Whatever goal she had for tonight, the goal now is to get out of here without crying in front of Jimmy and Angela.

'You probably just need to eat.'

Beth nods again, rubbing her silver locket between her fingers, disgusted with the foolish girl who put it on a few hours ago.

Jimmy serves Beth her espresso martini and then all three women their dinners. Petra ordered the grouper; Jill, on a sushi kick ever since that April book club, got the spicy tuna roll; and Beth got a burger with fries. Truffle-oil fries.

'How is everything?' asks Jimmy after a few minutes.

'Good,' says Petra. 'The food is really good, Jimmy. Who's your head chef?'

While Petra and Jimmy discuss the restaurant business, and Jill is texting her boys, Beth stays focused on eating and drinking. After finishing her second martini, she notices that she doesn't feel like crying anymore. She mostly feels numb now, as if a thick layer of fuzzy static is wrapped around her like a cocoon, impenetrable, more effective than a beard or a black sweater.

She's on her third drink, another espresso martini, when she hears someone yelling her name from behind her. She turns around. It's Georgia, waving and weaving her way through the crowd, knocking into bodies and glasses and splashing drinks as she pushes toward the bar, leaving a sea of hostile faces in her wake.

'I'm so glad you're still here!' she says, out of breath. 'How's it going? Where's the Salt mistress?'

Beth, Petra, and Jill look at each other and then at Jimmy, who definitely heard that. Petra laughs.

'You mean *hostess*?' Petra asks.

Georgia laughs. 'Whoops, yes! And I haven't had anything to drink yet. Where is she?'

'You didn't see her on the way in?' asks Petra.

'No, where?'

'Behind you. By the door.'

'Where?'

'The dark, curly hair.'

Georgia stands on her toes and squints her whole face.

'The one in the black shirt,' says Petra.

Georgia shakes her head, still searching.

'The one with the boobs.'

'Ah, got her!' says Georgia. 'Bimbo. I never pegged Jimmy for a boob guy.'

Beth presses her hand over her own insulted boobs. It's true that Beth's are unremarkable, and Jimmy is more of a leg guy. Beth has great legs, long and toned. She's always walking, at the beaches, at Bartlett's Farm, all over New York City before she moved here.

It occurs to her that she's never heard of a man referred to as an eyes guy or a brains guy or a personality guy. She downs the rest of her martini. Guys suck. Maybe this is a blessing. Maybe she's better off without Jimmy. No man in the house. Her home will stay clean and organized, and it will smell pretty. And no more fighting. It's been peaceful since he left. Somewhere in her brain, Marilyn McCoo is singing 'One Less Bell to Answer,' a song her

108

mother used to like when Beth was a young girl and that Beth hasn't heard or consciously thought of since.

'Not that there's anything wrong with yours,' says Georgia.

'Just wait until she has babies,' says Jill. 'Hers will be hanging like the rest of ours.'

The fuzzy numbness of Beth's martini armor must have a chink in it because that comment punched right through and knocked the wind out of her. What if Angela gets pregnant? Beth thinks about how easily she conceived. Each and every time they pulled the goalie, it was one shot — score! She feels dizzy. The edges of her vision turn dim and blurry. She's got to get out of here.

'Hello, Georgia,' says Jimmy.

'I'm not happy with you,' says Georgia.

'I know.'

'But I'll forgive you if Beth does.'

'That's fair,' he says, looking to Beth for input like he's looking for an opening in a window, even the slightest crack.

'Beth, you're looking pale again,' says Jill.

Jill is sitting right next to Beth, but her voice sounds as if it's coming from way off in the distance somewhere.

'Beth, you okay?' asks Petra.

'I don't feel well,' says Beth with more air than sound.

'I'll take her home,' says Petra.

'I'll stay and have a drink with Georgia,' says Jill.

Petra pays her and Beth's part of the bill, and Georgia hugs Beth as she gets up.

109

'She's a bimbo,' says Georgia.

'Thanks.'

'And you're a queen.'

Beth smiles.

'And I love your dress.'

'Thanks.'

Jill gets up and hugs Beth.

'You did great. I'll call you tomorrow.'

Beth nods. She looks up at Jimmy before she turns to leave.

'Good night, Beth,' says Jimmy.

'G'night, Jimmy.'

Petra takes her by the hand, and they worm their way through the crowd, leaving Salt. Leaving Jimmy. Leaving him there with Angela. Leaving him feels so wrong. Somewhere beneath the static fuzz and above the Marilyn McCoo song still playing in her head, a voice is screaming, *Don't leave him! Don't leave!* But it's late, and she's had enough to eat and more than enough to drink, and she's had enough of seeing Angela's boobs and Jimmy's smile, so there's nothing left to do but leave.

'Have a good night,' says Angela's voice from somewhere behind her.

It sounds as if Angela's smiling, maybe even gloating, but Beth doesn't know. She's already out the door, and she doesn't look back.

★ ★ ★

Petra pulls into Beth's driveway. The house is dark. The girls forgot to flick on the porch light. At least they went to bed.

110

'You okay?' asks Petra.

'Yeah.'

'You're too quiet.'

'I'm fine.'

'You don't have to hold it together in front of me.'

'I'm not holding anything. I'm fine,' Beth says, having some difficulty enunciating *holding anything*. 'I'm a little drunk, but I'm fine. I'm drunk and fine.'

'You guys really need to talk soon and figure out what you're doing.'

'I know.'

'Drink some water and go to bed.'

'I will.'

'Love you.'

'Love you, too.'

Beth follows the beams of Petra's headlights to the front door. It must be a cloudy night because Beth can't see the moon or any stars in the sky. Outside of Petra's headlights, the whole world is pure darkness. The air is cool and smells of salt and fish and forsythia. Spring peepers shriek in a loud and noxious chorus all around her, sounding not unlike the techno music from Salt still ringing in her ears. She hears Petra pull away as she opens the front door and turns on the hall light.

She walks upstairs and opens the door to each of the girls' rooms, checking on them, asleep in their beds. Sweet, beautiful girls. She shuts off Sophie's computer and tosses her dirty clothes into her hamper; she hangs Jessica's wet towel on a hook in the bathroom; and she pulls the covers up over Gracie. She walks downstairs and into the kitchen and pours herself a tall glass of water.

Back upstairs, she pauses in the hallway and stares at the pictures on the wall. She looks at Jimmy touching her skirt, and she relives Angela touching his arm, and an anger colored with humiliation rises up inside her, swelling. In another picture, she's wearing the locket he gave her, the one she's wearing now that he noticed on her tonight.

She can't take it. She can't take one more walk down this hallway, looking at his smiling teeth, his hand on her, the locket around her neck, the lie of their perfect marriage, his deception mocking her every time she walks from the living room to her bedroom, from her bedroom to the bathroom. She's had enough of this. Enough.

She starts with her wedding picture. She loosens the latch, removes the back plate and the cardboard filler, yanks out the photo, and returns the empty frame to the wall. She does this methodically, breathing hard, with each picture until she has them all in a nice, neat stack.

Sitting on the floor in the hallway, she flips through them. She gets to the most recent one, the one from last summer, and studies it. Some reasonable part of her not affected by the vodka and rum and humiliated anger urges her to put the pictures in a drawer, that she'll regret what she's about to do. But she's too furious and drunk and hopped up on caffeine to hear reason, and she's tired of feeling like a passive doormat.

The first tear is slow, hesitant, and then

deliberate, straight through Jimmy's smiling face. Then the rips come fast, one after another, after another. There's no stopping now. She tears and tears until the shreds are too small to rip any further, and now she's sobbing, hating him for making her do this. She hears one of the girls sneeze. She stops crying and listens, afraid of waking them. She can still hear the techno music from Salt buzzing in her ears, the spring peepers shrieking outside, and she can feel-hear her heart thumping in her chest and pulsing in her fingers, but the girls are quiet. She wipes her eyes and exhales.

She collects the heaps of torn paper, shreds of what was her happy family, and throws them into the wastebasket in her bedroom. She then returns to the hallway and looks at the wall, to witness what she's done. There. Eight framed, matted pieces of cardboard. He's gone. There's no undoing it now. Like his infidelity. This is what is real.

She adjusts two of the frames so that they're level, flicks off the hall light, and returns to her bedroom. She strips out of her Goldie Hawn dress and slides into her pink, flannel pajamas. She crawls into bed, forgetting the locket still around her neck, facing the side where Jimmy used to sleep with her, her feet restless and her eyes wide-open.

Awake all night.

10

Everything changed in June, and Olivia, naïve to this time of year on this tiny island, never saw it coming. It started with Memorial Day weekend, when the cocooned and quiet simplicity of her daily life became bombarded on all sides by the rapid and sure-footed influx of invaders. The summer people. It took her a couple of weeks not to feel like she needed to hide inside her home, not to feel threatened or violated by their presence, to regain her composure and reestablish a routine. But after a couple of weeks, she finally exhaled, thinking, *There, this isn't so bad.*

And then came July. June did so little to prepare her for July. June is a gently sloping hill in the Berkshires, and July is Mount Everest. The roads are now crammed with mopeds and Jeeps and monstrous SUVs, engine exhausts and radios spewing their pollution into the sweet summer air. The previously desolate, private-feeling beaches are now cluttered with families and their chairs and umbrellas and boogie boards and their picnic garbage and constant conversation, and every rental house is full, every bedroom and driveway, the occupants celebrating their week's vacation with outdoor parties and cook-outs night after night.

These are the real summer people, and they came by the tens of thousands, quintupling the island's population. They came by air, and they came by sea, and they came with their kids and their dogs and their nannies and their assistants and their personal chefs and their houseguests. And everyone (except the dogs) brought a cell phone. Olivia imagines the geological shelf that Nantucket sits on, fragile and precarious, and worries that it might actually crumble under the weight of all the tourists and their stuff, causing the island to sink to the bottom of the ocean. A modern Atlantis.

Even the sky is crowded. Commuter planes and private jets from Boston and New York roar overhead every few minutes. All day long.

If she adjusted in June, she's merely coping in July. She feels a kinship with the other locals, easily identified and distinct from the summer people, like picking out wild horses from circus zebras, even though she knows that the feeling is onesided. Although she's earned some level of respect for having lived here through part of the winter and an entire spring, she hasn't lived 'on island' a full year yet. She's not a real member of the herd. She hasn't put in enough time. But even after a full year — in truth, even after fifty years — she'll always be viewed as a wash-ashore, a transplant, never a true local, and absolutely never a native (a person has to be born here to own that title).

She's made some adjustments already that have become her summer laws for living:

Never go to the beach between the hours of ten and three. That's when they all go.

Avoid Town at all costs. If you must go, do not drive downtown at lunchtime or anytime after

6:00 p.m. There will be no parking anywhere.

Never go to Stop & Shop anytime Friday through Sunday.

Allow an extra thirty minutes for everything.

She's written these rules out on a piece of paper and taped it to the wall by her front door, a cute but serious reminder in case she should grow forgetful or cocky. Which is why she's cursing herself right now, as she stands at the edge of the pasta aisle in front of Newman's Own marinara sauce near the end of a discouragingly long checkout line in Stop & Shop on a Saturday afternoon.

She needed more coffee and eggs and thought it would be nice to have a salad for dinner without thinking about the calendar or her summer laws. She didn't realize what day it was until she pulled into the crowded parking lot and knew immediately. She hesitated, thinking she should forget about the salad and go home, but then the woman in the Land Rover behind her honked, urging Olivia to move along, and so she did, thinking, *How bad can it be?*

That was over an hour ago. She counts the items in her basket. Fourteen. If she reshelves the loaf of bread and the toilet paper (she can get by on what she has until Monday), then she can move over to the express line, but that line is even longer and appears to carry more hostility in its ranks.

'This is taking forever,' mutters the woman in line behind Olivia. 'I'm definitely going to be late.'

Olivia's grateful that she's at least not in a

hurry. She has no beach-portrait session tonight. The family she had scheduled for this evening canceled this morning.

Becoming a professional beach-portrait photographer ended up being far easier than she imagined it would be. First, she did some research by calling around to the other portrait photographers on the island, inquiring about their rates. Then she did the math and figured out that if she could do four sessions a week from June to Labor Day, she'd make enough money to live the whole year. More than enough.

But then she had the problem of how to get any customers, never mind four a week, to hire her, an unknown with no professional training or experience, just a good eye and a natural facility with a camera. To address this rather big problem, she did two small things. First, she printed flyers and posted them all over town — the Visitors Center, Young's Bicycle Shop, The Bean, the library, the Chamber of Commerce, the Hy-Line and Steamship Authority docks, even here at Stop & Shop. And second, she made sure to set her price at $200 cheaper than the 'cheapest' going rate.

The calls and e-mails started coming in, and she's booked more sessions than she thought possible, four to six times a week, often twice in the same evening. She's already scheduled one family for Labor Day weekend. The prints are all ordered online through a separate company, so all she has to do is shoot with her digital camera, edit with Photoshop on her computer, and upload the images to the ordering website.

Payment is online, by credit card. There are no paper invoices to send, no waiting to receive checks in the mail. She has no overhead other than Internet service. It's clean and simple.

The women in front of her have calmly been chatting the whole time, seemingly unfazed by the long lines and the increasingly impatient mood surrounding them. One, the natural-looking blonde, is wearing a black cotton tank with no logo, no embellishments, a plain white cotton skirt, and flip-flops, and the other is wearing yoga clothes. No flashy jewelry, no designer labels, their fingernails aren't manicured, and their purses look like they cost less than $50. Locals.

'Is it weird that I don't want to hire Roger?'

'No, of course not.'

'He's done all the others and has always done a great job. I don't know, I feel like I'm being disloyal, but it'd just be too weird showing up without Jimmy.'

'I get it.'

'He'd be like, 'Where's Jimmy?' And then I'd have to admit that he's not coming, and that would be weird.'

'So don't hire Roger. He won't even know.'

'Everybody knows everything here.'

'True. So then he probably already knows about you and Jimmy.'

'I guess, maybe.'

'And you know, he wouldn't even care. These things happen. I think he just got divorced, didn't he?'

'I don't think so.'

'He did. His wife left the island, moved to Texas.'

'Oh, yeah, that's right. So who would you hire?'

'I don't know, you should ask Jill. They used someone last summer.'

'They used Roger.'

'Oh.'

'I know I shouldn't spend the money, but I need the pictures. They're going to be a visual reminder that my life is fine without him, that I still have my beautiful girls, and I don't need him to be happy.'

'Visualization is good.'

'This is my first step in really moving on.'

'You manifest what you envision.'

'Yeah. And I need to do it soon. Those empty frames in my hallway look depressing.'

'Why don't you have Gracie draw some cute pictures, put those in the frames for now?'

'I asked, she wouldn't. None of them would. They're all mad at me for ripping up our family photos. I don't blame them. Such a stupid thing to do.'

'Jimmy cheating on you was a stupid thing to do. You get a free pass.'

'Shhh.'

'What?'

'We're in Stop & Shop, someone will hear you.'

'Oh, for God's sakes. Kevin Bacon knows Jimmy cheated on you.'

'You're right, I know.'

Olivia touches her purse, knowing she has a

beach-portrait flyer inside. She should tap this blonde woman on the shoulder and offer her the flyer, but as she imagines doing this, it feels too aggressive. And she doesn't want to interrupt or admit to listening to their personal conversation. She decides to keep to herself and hopes that the blonde woman will notice her flyer pinned to the bulletin board on the way out.

Their line is finally out from the pasta aisle, and Olivia can now see every checkout line in the store. To her left, she notices a woman and her son. He's about six or seven, and he's sitting in the toddler seat of the grocery cart. His long, tan legs dangle down, almost reaching the floor. He's spinning a pinwheel, which he has pressed up against his nose. Autism.

He's so completely pulled inside a spinning world of blurred metallic color that he doesn't seem at all affected by the long line, the crowds of irritated people around him, the harsh lights, or Michael Bublé singing Tony Bennett over the speakers. Then something changes. Maybe he realizes he's hungry, or he's bored, or he hates Michael Bublé, or the tag on the back of his shirt is itching him at last more than he can stand. Who knows why? He throws the pinwheel to the ground, and he starts screaming, thumbs in his ears, his eyes squeezed shut.

His mother retrieves the pinwheel and spins it, holding it up to his face, trying to lure him back into its magic spell, but he won't open his eyes. She tries to soothe him with her voice, straining to remain calm, reassuring him that they'll be home soon, but his thumb-stopped ears are unavailable to logic or lies. She doesn't attempt to touch him. Olivia knows this would probably make everything worse. A lot worse.

Then it appears as though she's doing nothing. She's ignoring him.

Olivia sees the looks and hears the murmured judgments being passed around like mints among people in line.

He's too old to be acting like that.

My children would never be allowed to behave that way.

Spoiled.

What kind of mother?

They don't get it. Olivia does. Shy of picking him up and carrying him out of here, that mother is doing what any mother of a child with autism and a cart full of groceries would do. She's breathing, holding on white-knuckle tight to her cart and her courage, and praying to God.

God, please help him calm down.

God, please, before I lose it, too, get us out of here.

God, please.

'I don't blame him,' says the woman in the yoga clothes. 'If this line doesn't start to move a little faster, I'm going to start screaming, too.'

'Not very Yogi of you,' says her blonde friend, the one who needs the pictures.

'True. But it sure would release all the negative energy I've been absorbing in this place. Stop & Shop is totally clogging up my fourth chakra.'

The blonde laughs. Olivia smiles. The blonde stares at the boy and his mother while they wait

121

in line. The expression on the blonde's face as she watches them doesn't seem to carry a trace of judgment, but rather an intense interest, even wonder. Olivia would love to know what she's thinking but says nothing.

At long last, Olivia reaches the checkout. She greets the cashier with a friendly hello, bags her own groceries, carries her canvas tote to her Jeep, and drives home.

Thirty minutes later, she is there.

★　★　★

At home Olivia boils two eggs. She slices the tomatoes, cucumbers, and a red pepper. She shreds the lettuce and tosses it all into a large bowl. She adds olives, Vidalia onions, Parmesan cheese, croutons, and, when they're done, the eggs. She drizzles on a touch of olive oil and red-wine vinegar, a pinch of salt and pepper. A glass of cold sauvignon blanc, a slice from the ciabatta loaf, and she's done.

She carries her dinner, a citronella candle, and one of her journals out onto her backyard deck. She sits with her well-earned feast, opens her journal, and begins to read where she last left off.

July 5, 2003

My life right now is all about communication, or rather, the lack of it. I spend all my waking hours demanding communication from Anthony. Anthony, say JUICE. JUICE.

JUUUUICE. Say the word. Tell me what you want. Say *I WANT JUICE.* Say *SWING.* Say *I WANT TO GO OUTSIDE AND SWING ON THE SWING.* Please. Look at me, Anthony, and tell me what you want. Tell me what you're feeling. Tell me why you're screaming. I can usually tell if it's happy-excited screaming or frustrated-panicked screaming, but right now, I'm too tired, and I can't figure it out. Why are you screaming? How can I help you if you won't tell me what you want?

And then there's me and David. We don't know how to communicate either. We don't look at each other anymore. I can't stand to look into his eyes and see his despair, his exhaustion, sometimes the blame, and too often the wish that he'd stayed at the office another hour. Maybe I'd be in bed by then, and he wouldn't have to deal with me and what's in my eyes.

We don't talk to each other anymore. Not really. We say plenty about what has to be done. Did you buy Anthony's JUICE? I'm going to the grocery store, do we need JUICE? Will you push Anthony on the SWING? He's screaming because he wants to go outside and swing on the SWING. Will you take out the trash, go to the store, do the laundry, pay the bills? The bills, the bills, the bills.

We say all these words, but we don't talk about anything. It's all meaningless. Blah, blah, blah.

I don't tell David what I'm thinking, that we're the parents of a permanently disabled child and our marriage is crippled. I think this every day, but I never say the words. I don't tell David.

We don't have sex anymore, and I don't want sex anymore, but I miss the part of me that used to feel connected to David, that felt horny and wanted sex. We don't talk about this.

And who would want sex after the days I have? I'm exhausted from worry and the physical job of taking care of Anthony. I have bruises from his pinches and kicks, and bite marks all over me. I look abused. I feel abused, but I don't tell David.

I don't really feel abused by Anthony, I feel abused by this life. What happened to my life? My life is all about autism. If I'm not living it, I'm reading about it or talking about it, and I'm just so damn sick of it, I could puke. I'm scared that this is all it's ever going to be. Anthony has autism, and he won't say JUICE or SWING or why he is screaming, and David and I aren't speaking, roommates in the same prison cell.

Or at best we're colleagues, self-trained therapists working on the same patient, a beautiful boy named Anthony, trying to fix him. Only we're failing. We're not fixing him. His autism isn't going anywhere, and it's this huge pink elephant in our living room, and we're not talking about what's real, that we're going to be living with autism for the rest of our lives, and we need to accept this. As much as I want to scream and cry and break everything in this world, as much as I want to resist and fight and beg, we need to accept Anthony with autism.

Why can't we talk about this? Why don't we tell each other how we feel, what we want, what we're afraid of, that we still love each other? Do we? Do we even still love each other?

What great role models we are for Anthony, huh? Hey, Anthony, TALK. See how Mommy and Daddy DON'T do it. We have Anthony in therapy for thirty-five hours a week to learn to communicate. I wonder how many hours a week David and I would need . . .

She and David never went to couples counseling. Maybe they should have. But between all the occupational and behavioral and speech therapists for Anthony, the parent support groups, and then the grief counseling, none of it effective, they weren't exactly jumping at the idea of inviting yet another counselor, and another expense, into their already therapy-saturated lives.

Olivia closes her journal and thinks with her eyes shut. She's been going through her entries a little each day, reading her past, trying to come to terms with it all, looking for peace. She opens her eyes. Not today.

She sighs and returns to the kitchen for

another glass of wine. As she opens the refrigerator door, she hears a shrill ding. She pauses, trying to decipher what it was. She's always hearing things in this house, eerie, unexplained noises that used to spook her when she first moved here, but now she's grown more curious than afraid.

The fog that often settles over the island usually insulates sound, muffling it. The silence of a thick fog on Nantucket can be palpable. But sometimes, and she has no idea why, the fog amplifies, warps, and scatters sound, sending it miles away from its source. She swears she's heard fishermen talking on their boats from her bedroom. And she sometimes hears a creepy, melodic moaning that she likes to think is the sound of seals barking offshore.

A fog is rolling in tonight, so the ding might've been a neighbor's wind chime, a kid's bicycle bell from around the block, an ice cream truck at the beach. But the ding sounded louder, more immediate. More *here*. She pulls the wine bottle from the refrigerator, and there it is again. Is it the doorbell?

She sets the bottle of wine down on the counter, wipes her wet hand on her shorts, walks to the front door, and opens it.

'Hi, Liv.'

She gasps. She didn't actually expect to find anyone there. And she certainly didn't expect it to be him.

'David.'

11

It's nine fifteen, and Beth has already dropped the girls off at the community center. Gracie and Jessica love it there, but Sophie hates it. She showed signs of outgrowing the games and crafts and activities toward the end of last summer when she was twelve, complaining that camp was 'boring.' Well, if last year was boring, this year is pure agony. But it's where all the other kids who are still too young for summer jobs go for camp, and Beth would rather she be in agony at the community center than skulking around the house all day, bored and in agony at home.

When Beth pulled into the community center parking lot, she said to all three, 'Have fun!' Jessica and Gracie smiled and waved, but Sophie replied, 'Don't worry, I *won't*!' — and slammed the car door. Ah, thirteen.

Camp runs until two. Jimmy has the night off and offered to pick them up, spend the afternoon with them, and then take them to dinner at the Brotherhood. He said he'd have them home by eight.

Beth has the next almost eleven hours stretched out in front of her to do whatever she pleases. A completely free day. A week ago, she would've used that time to clean, a big project such as washing all the windows, or bleaching the mold and mildew off the deck furniture, or weeding. But she's been rereading *Writing*

Down the Bones and going through her notebooks, her old poems, her short stories, her many unfinished vignettes, enjoying them all. And she's started dreaming again.

So she's letting the mold and mildew and the pollen spots and pesky weeds be. Instead, she's gone to the library for a quiet place to write, free of distraction. Today, she feels ready to dust off that creative part of her that she boxed up years ago and see if it still works. She's finally giving herself the space and the time to explore that expressive voice inside her that became unconsciously stifled, lost first to the demands of young motherhood, then seduced into ennui by her daily routine.

She walks up to the second floor and sits in an armless Shaker-style wooden chair at a substantial wooden table, much larger than the one in her own dining room, facing a window that is also oversized, at least eight feet tall. The window is open, and a fresh-smelling morning breeze fills the air in the room. Nine other matching chairs surround the table, all unoccupied.

She pulls out her blank spiral notebook, the one she bought years ago, and opens it to the first blank page. It's been a long time since she's written anything other than checks to pay the bills. She feels excited, nervous. She pulls out her favorite pen and stares at the page, trying to think of how to begin. Beginnings have always been difficult for her. She taps her teeth with her pen, a habit she developed as a teenager whenever she was stuck on a homework problem, and she can hear her mother's voice in her head saying, *Stop that, Elizabeth*, and so she does.

She looks up at the clock on the wall. It's nine twenty-five. Like the window and the table, the clock is larger than most. It's oak with Roman numerals on an ivory face. The wood has elaborate scrolls carved into it that look like curled ocean waves. The clock appears old and probably is, and it probably has a story and historical significance, but Beth doesn't know what. It's quiet in the library today, so quiet that she can hear the clock ticking.

Tick. Tick. Tick.

Why is the library so empty today? She looks out the window. Blue sky, no clouds, a gentle and steady breeze. It's a perfect beach day. That's what she could do with her free day. She could go to the beach! She slides her chair out, but before she caps her pen, she recognizes the real motivation behind this impetuous idea. Fear. Fear of this blank page in front of her. Plus, it's a stupid impetuous idea, going to the beach in the middle of the day in July, fighting the summer people for a square of sand. That's where everyone is. She knows better than to put herself through that madness.

She slides her chair back in, tucking her legs under the table, and tries to get comfortable. Okay. Begin. But begin what? Does she want to expand on one of her unfinished short stories? She should've brought those with her. Should it take place on Nantucket? Maybe New York? The questions keep coming, echoing in her head, paralyzing her hand.

She looks up at the clock. Nine forty-five.

Tick. Tick. Tick.

Maybe she should do one of the exercises in *Writing Down the Bones*, get the pen moving, the ink flowing, grease the rusty wheels a bit. She remembers now that this is how she used to begin.

She unzips her purse, a big, bulky, worn, black nylon bag. Someone gave it to her. Was it Georgia? It's so long ago now, she can't remember. It was a baby-shower gift. Her purse is really a diaper bag. Jill thinks it's really a disgrace.

Beth admits that it's not the prettiest thing, and, yes, the girls have now been potty-trained for some time, but she likes the wide shoulder strap, that it's water resistant and wipes clean of pretty much anything, that it has tons of useful pockets. The pocket for the baby bottle is now where she keeps her water bottle. The wipes pocket now contains her wallet. The zipped compartment she used for pacifiers is now where she keeps her cell phone. The middle compartment is where she dumps everything else.

Everything else, it seems, but *Writing Down the Bones*. It's not in there. She forgot to bring it. Damn. Maybe she should go home and get it. She looks down at her notebook.

Blank.

She has to go get it. But if she leaves, she knows she won't come back. If she leaves, she'll be wearing yellow latex gloves and carrying a bucket of bleach in twenty minutes. She plants her feet flat and heavy on the floor as if they were two anchors and breathes. She's staying.

She thinks she wants to expand on the short story she wrote about a boy who found comfort and meaning inside an imagined world where colors had emotions, water could sing, and the boy could become invisible. But then she remembers the boy she once saw on the beach, the curious intensity and joy he showed, even for a child, as he created a line of white rocks, and the briefest moment they shared that felt like an exquisite secret between them. She feels compelled and captivated by both boys. Maybe she can combine them. But how?

She taps her teeth and thinks of the saying *Write what you know.* What does she know? She looks down at her blank page.

She looks up at the clock and sighs. Ten twenty-five. Maybe she should go to The Bean, get a coffee and a snack. Maybe that's what she needs, some caffeine, some food, and a change of scenery. Maybe the atmosphere here is all wrong. She looks around her — the many bookcases painted creamy white, packed with hardcovers; the Persian rugs; the oil paintings of famous writers like Ralph Waldo Emerson, Henry David Thoreau, and Herman Melville on the walls; that damn clock. It's all too serious, too scholarly, too intimidating. Too much pressure.

She has enough reasons to leave, excuses absurd to valid, and yet she stays. She wants to write. She looks around her, at the books on the shelves. Hundreds of books, each one written by somebody. She chooses to feel inspired instead of intimidated. Why not somebody like her?

Her eyes settle upon a book positioned face out on the bookcase closest to the window, second shelf from the top. *The Siege*. The cover is gray and white and has a black-and-white photograph of a young girl on it. The girl maybe looks a bit like Sophie when she was a toddler, but that slight resemblance isn't what's catching her attention. None of it — not the title, the cover, not even the picture of the girl — feels remarkable or particularly interesting to her, yet she feels drawn to it, oddly pulled by it.

She forces herself to look away, browsing the other bookcases from her seat. She finds no other books facing out on any of the shelves. Not one. She returns to *The Siege*, feeling again as if she can't look away, not because it's a distraction like the clock or her purse, not to avoid looking at her blank page, but because she feels strangely *compelled* to look at it.

It's the same feeling she had when she met Jimmy. It was a late night at the Chicken Box, Nantucket's legendary dive bar. She couldn't stop looking at him. It wasn't because he was attractive, although he was. Plenty of attractive single guys were all over Nantucket that summer, everywhere she looked. And it wasn't because she was drunk on beer and Jell-O shots, although she was. That night, there was only Jimmy. The whole bar was static, and Jimmy was a clear channel. She felt almost spellbound by him, as if he were a magnet pulling her to him.

Now this book on the shelf feels the same way.

She stares at it, mesmerized by its nonmesmerizing, simple cover, and wonders what it's about. With considerable willpower, she shakes off its spell and returns to her blank page.

Blank. Blank. Blankety-blank.

Tick. Tick. Tick.

She looks up at the book, now feeling as if the girl on the cover were staring at her.

Oh, for God's sakes.

She walks over to the bookcase and brings the book back to her seat. *The Siege* by Clara Claiborne Park. She reads the front and back covers. It's a true story, written by a mother about her autistic daughter. Beth enjoyed *The Curious Incident of the Dog in the Night-Time*, but autism isn't a subject she would normally read about on her own. But she's obviously not going to begin writing the great American novel today. And she's *not* going back and cleaning the house. She caps her pen, opens the book, and begins to read.

* * *

Hours later, someone taps her on the shoulder, startling her. She looks up. It's Mary Crawford, the librarian.

'Sorry, Beth, I didn't mean to startle you, but we're closing in five minutes.'

Beth looks up at the clock. It says four fifty-five. She looks out the window. The light coming in is softer, more diffuse, suggesting longer shadows and evening. She looks at her watch. Four fifty-five. How did that happen?

133

She looks down at her notebook.

Blank.

'I'm sorry, I got completely caught up in this book.'

'Would you like to borrow it?'

'Yes, please.'

Beth didn't write anything, and she didn't clean anything, but at least she found a good book to read.

★　★　★

Back at home, she still has plenty of time left in her free day before the girls come home. She could clean something or eat something. She chooses the second. She's famished. She hasn't had a thing to eat today since breakfast.

She fixes herself a ham-and-cheese sandwich and, in celebration of her free day, decides to make herself a real drink. She pours vodka, lime juice, cranberry juice, and a splash of ginger beer into Gracie's lunch thermos because she doesn't have a martini shaker. She adds ice, shakes, then pours some into a wineglass. She takes a sip and smiles. It's good. See? She doesn't need Jimmy. She can make her own passion.

The air in the house is hot and stale. No one was home today to turn on the air conditioners or open the windows. Beth takes her meal and drink and her library book out onto the deck, and she sits in one of the mildewed chairs.

The moldiest chair of them all, Jimmy's cigar-smoking chair, is pushed off to the side, facing the corner of the deck, as if it'd been sent there for misbehaving. Beth asked Jimmy to get it out of here, once and for all, weeks ago. It was bad enough before, but she's certainly not going to keep his cigar chair here while he shacks up with another woman. She angles her own chair so that his disappears from view. She eats her dinner and reads.

She's still absorbed in reading and on her third Passion à la Beth cocktail, which she feels she's now perfected (less lime, more vodka), when she hears the front door open and shut.

'Hello?' she yells.

Sophie and Jessica appear on the deck.

'Where's Gracie?' asks Beth.

'In the kitchen, working on a project for camp,' says Jessica.

'Oh, what project?' asks Beth.

'I dunno,' says Jessica.

'What did you have for dinner?'

'Hot dog,' says Jessica.

'Hamburger,' says Sophie.

It frustrates Beth that they live on an island and none of her children will eat fish. She loves seafood but can't cook it in the house without the girls pinching their noses and complaining about the smell.

'Where's your dad?'

'He left,' says Sophie.

'Oh,' says Beth, strangely disappointed that he didn't come in. Must be the vodka talking.

'How was camp today?'

'Lame,' says Sophie.

'Can you please change your attitude and not

wreck it for your sisters? You loved it when you were their age.'

'Fine. It was *delightful*!' says Sophie, delivering the word *delightful* in a high-pitched squeal, her face stretched and dimpled in a too-sugary-to-be-real, Shirley Temple smile.

'Okay, okay. How was dinner?'

Sophie says nothing and looks to Jessica.

'It was *delightful*!' says Jessica in the same tone and manner as her older sister.

'It totally sucked,' says Sophie.

'Hey! Language,' says Beth.

'*She* was there,' says Sophie.

'Oh,' says Beth.

'I don't like her,' says Sophie.

'Me either,' says Jessica.

Beth tries to summon some kind of maternal wisdom or politically correct advice or at least something positive for her girls, but the Passion à la Beths are working against her, and so she goes with something honest. 'I don't like her either.'

'Yeah, but you don't have to spend time with her like we do. I wish we didn't have to see her,' says Sophie.

'I wish Dad would come home,' says Jessica.

Beth's heart breaks.

'He's not going to, is he?' asks Sophie.

'No, I don't think so,' says Beth.

Tears pool in Jessica's eyes, fury in Sophie's.

'I'm sorry, sweeties. I'm so sorry. This does totally suck.'

'I miss him, Mom,' says Jessica.

'I miss him, too,' says Beth.

'I thought you hated him,' says Sophie. 'I

thought that's why you ripped up the pictures.'

'That wasn't why, and sometimes I do hate him. I miss and hate him at the same time. It's complicated.'

'Do you hate him more or miss him more?' asks Jessica with big, wet, hopeful eyes. Beth wipes Jessica's face with her hand and kisses her cheek.

'Miss,' says Beth, having compassion for her sensitive middle child.

'Well, I hate him,' says Sophie.

'Soph,' says Beth in the tone that typically begins one of her lectures.

'Why do you get to hate him and I don't?'

It's a good question, but Beth doesn't say anything. She doesn't say because even if he's no longer her husband, he'll always be Sophie's father. She doesn't say because it's not good to hate anyone. But is it okay for Sophie to hate her father if that's how she feels? It can't be healthy to stuff those honest feelings down. Beth should probably make appointments with the school's guidance counselor for all three girls to talk about all this stuff.

'Because I'm the mother,' she says finally, waving that irritatingly vague, all-powerful parental wand over the whole discussion, ending it. 'It's getting late. Go get ready for bed.'

Sophie rolls her eyes and walks back into the house. Her younger sister follows. Before Beth goes into the house to see how Gracie's doing and to direct the process of going to bed, she reads just a few more pages.

Shortly after the girls go to sleep, Beth brings her book with her to bed, more tired than she has any reason to be after such a luxuriously free day. She hopes to finish the next chapter, maybe even the whole book, but her eyes close before she turns a single page.

As she falls into a deep sleep, unprocessed thoughts about the autistic girl in the book she's reading search out similar elements learned some months ago about the main character in *The Curious Incident of the Dog in the Night-Time*. Detached from people. Bewildered by emotions. Enthralled by repetition. An uncelebrated intelligence. A primal need for order. A row of blocks. A series of numbers. A sensitivity to sound and touch. Persistent. Silent. Honest. Brave. Misunderstood.

These elements combine while she sleeps, blending into something new, something that can no longer be distinguished as belonging to either the girl in *The Siege* or the boy in *The Curious Incident*. It is a prethought, a shadow of an idea forming.

The shadow travels through her mind, gathering energy, weaving through the short story she once wrote about a peculiar boy's imaginary world, merging with the image of a spinning pinwheel and the sound of a scream, absorbing the memory of a small boy and the joy in his eyes as he lined up rocks on the beach. And now, having collected the elements and the power they needed, through a neurological

138

alchemy not yet described in any book, these many-images and sounds within the shadow in her mind assemble, first into a chorus, and then, finally, into a single voice. The shadow is no longer a shadow. It has become inspiration.

That night, a brown-haired, brown-eyed boy inhabits her dreams, a boy who sees and hears and feels the world in a unique and almost unimaginable way. She doesn't know him, yet her mind does. She sees him clearly. He is vivid and real. She understands him. She's still dreaming about this boy when she is awakened in the morning by her alarm clock.

At nine, she drops the girls off at the community center and tells them to have a great day, and Sophie slams the car door. Beth then drives directly to the library.

She goes upstairs and looks up at the clock. It's nine fifteen. Sitting in the same seat she sat in yesterday, she opens her notebook, uncaps her pen, takes a deep breath, and begins to write in the voice of the boy in her dream.

12

I am lying on the deck in the backyard, looking up at the sky. Looking up at the sky is one of my favorite things to do, especially on a no-cloud day. On a no-cloud day, I stare at the blue sky, and I love it. I stare at the blue sky for so long, and I love it so much, that I leave my skin and scatter out into it, the way rain puddles return to the sky on a hot day.

I leave the boy lying on the deck, and I become the blue sky. I am blue sky, and I am high above the earth and the boy lying on the deck, and I am floating and free. I am blue sky, and I am air, gliding on waves of wind, swirling and blowing, weightless and warm under the sun, above the earth and the boy on the deck.

I am blue sky, and I am air. I am everywhere.

I am blue sky and air blowing into lungs. I am breath. I am air moving in and out of squirrels and birds and my mother and father and the green leaves on the trees. I am air turning into energy inside bodies, becoming pieces of what is living inside. I am hearts and bones and thoughts, unspoken words inside the head of the boy lying on the deck, my father's muscles, my mother's sorrow. I am blue sky and air and breath and energy, a part of every living thing around me.

I look up into the no-cloud sky, and I am everywhere, connected to all living things. I look down at the boy lying on the deck. He is happy.

13

David follows Olivia into the kitchen, hanging back and looking around as he walks, probably inspecting the condition of the floors and the window casings, assessing the current value of the place. He can't help it. She pours him a glass of wine and hands it to him.

'The cottage looks good.'

'Thanks. You hungry? I made a salad,' she says.

'No, I had a lobster roll on the way over. Wine is good. Here, I brought you this.' He hands her a small, white paper bag.

'Aunt Leah's,' she says, smiling, shaking the bag, knowing even before she opens it and sees the hunk of chocolate fudge.

'You look good,' he says.

'You, too.'

He does. He's wearing a plaid, cotton, button-down shirt, unbuttoned and untucked over a gray T-shirt, jeans, and black, Italian leather shoes. His hair, black but graying at his temples and in his sideburns, is much longer than he used to wear it. Thick and straight when it's short, this new length, uncombed and tousled, reveals its natural waves and cowlicks. She likes it.

Everything else is the same David. His olive skin, his darkrimmed glasses, his pronounced Adam's apple, his brown eyes, like hers but

141

blacker. Like Anthony's. Then she notices his hands, his bare hands. No ring.

'I'm sorry I didn't call first, but I felt like I really needed to see you, and I thought you might tell me not to come.'

'Let's go sit in the living room.'

He follows her, and they sit down next to each other on the couch, a polite distance apart. David looks up at the wall above the fireplace, at the photograph of Anthony. Love and joy and grief wash over David's face, all at once and in equal parts, as if each emotion is fighting to possess him. He blows out a long, audible breath, trying to shake it off. He drinks some of his wine.

'I'm moving.'

'Where?' asks Olivia, immediately fearing that he's going to say *here*.

'Chicago.'

She's still catching up to the surprise of this unannounced visit, to David's being here, sitting with her on the couch in the living room. And now this. Born and raised on Boston's South Shore, educated at Boston College, and running a real estate business with his parents and brother ever since, David has ties to the Boston area that are knotted good and tight. If she was surprised at the front door, she's shocked now.

'Why Chicago?'

'Not sure. Sully's there, and he's always saying I could come work for him. Mostly because it's not Hingham. I need to get out of there. Everything reminds me of losing Anthony.'

He looks up at the picture over the fireplace,

as if he's including Anthony in the conversation, and then back to Olivia.

'And you, Liv. Everything reminds me of losing Anthony and you.'

The room becomes still. Olivia doesn't drink her wine or eat her fudge. She stares into David's eyes and waits, remaining still, hoping not to scare away what he's finally ready to say.

'I gotta go somewhere new, where I don't see you and Anthony in every room. If I even walk by his bedroom, I'm done for the day. It's awful. And it's not just the house, it's everyone. My parents and Doug, they all talk to me in that sad, careful voice and look at me with worried eyes, and it's what I would probably do if I were them, but I can't take it anymore. I can't be that sad guy all the time, you know?'

She nods. She knows.

'I can't be that guy every single day. I want to be David Donatelli.' His voice evaporates when he says his own name. He wipes his eyes. 'I can barely remember who I used to be. I thought it would get easier, but it's not. It's not even close to getting easier.'

'I know, David. I know.'

'I even had to change laundry detergent because I smelled like you guys. Isn't that crazy?'

She shakes her head. It's not crazy at all. She did the same thing.

'So, Chicago,' he says, as if it were the obvious answer, *four* in solution to *two plus two*.

'Moving helped me. It'll help you.'

143

Nantucket has saved her from seeing anyone she used to know, from bumping up against everyone's good-intentioned but devastating well wishes and pitying stares, from smelling Anthony's pillow and holding his shoes in her hands, from living inside the pretty-colored walls of what was supposed to be their happy home. She's amazed that she and David have experienced so many of the same feelings. She's even more amazed that he's sitting here now, able to articulate these feelings so well, communicating.

If only.

'Plus, I'm a single guy in a four-bedroom house in the suburbs. It's time to move on to something that makes more sense, right?'

'Are you selling the house?'

It's a bad market to sell right now, and she's guessing that David will hold on to it, rent it, and wait for the market to improve.

'I already listed it with Doug. I can leave your things with him for now if you want.'

'Yeah, okay.'

'What about you? Do you think you'll move?'

'Where would I go?'

'I thought maybe back to Georgia, near your mom and sister.'

She used to think that she'd eventually return home, back into her mother's arms and her childhood bedroom, especially during those first cold weeks in March. But now, she knows she won't. She'll return to Georgia to visit, but she'll never move back there. She'd end up running into the same thing David is now running from

— the well-intentioned pity, the relentless reminders of grief and loss.

'No, I like it here,' she says.

'How are you doing? Moneywise. I know we said six months, but if you need more — '

'I'm okay. I've been taking pictures again. I do beach portraits. I make enough for now.'

'You sure?'

'Yeah, it's plenty.'

He looks up at Anthony again. 'I bet you're good at it.'

She smiles. 'No one's demanded a refund yet.'

He looks around the room, again with his Realtor eyes, but maybe also to avoid looking at Olivia next to him and Anthony on the wall. 'I thought you would've done more with the place.'

'Hey.'

'No, it's nice. I mean, it doesn't look like you yet.'

In Hingham, she painted every room as soon as they moved in. Golden yellow, bird's-egg blue, sea-foam green. Warm and cozy walls embracing every room. Here, all the walls remain unpainted, white. And the furnishings, artwork, and knick-knacks are sparse and neutral, the same items they hastily filled the place with right after they bought it, in time for the first tenants.

'I like this,' he says, referring to the glass bowl on the coffee table, filled to heaping capacity with white, round rocks. She finds them everywhere.

'Thanks.'

'I like it here. I always thought we'd end up here. Together. Someday.'

'Me, too.'

'We had all kinds of great dreams, before . . . '

Before. The word hangs in the air alone, refusing further company.

He leans over the table and picks up one of the rocks from the top of the pile. He holds it in his fist and closes his eyes, as if he's making a wish. He then opens his eyes and his hand and returns the rock to the bowl.

'It's getting late,' he says, checking his watch. 'I've got to go if I'm going to catch the last ferry.'

'You can stay, if you want.'

He tips his head and studies her, not quite understanding the invitation.

'The guest-room bed is already made. It's no problem.'

He looks relieved. And disappointed. 'You sure?'

'Yeah, we can go to The Bean in the morning before you go, like old times.'

He smiles. 'I'd like that. And more wine if you have it.'

★   ★   ★

It's late. Olivia's been in bed for a couple of hours now, and she's still awake. She hears the guest-bedroom door open and David walking in the living room. Then she hears the creak of the back door opening. She hears the screen door thwap shut. She waits and listens. She waits and hears nothing. She gets up, walks through the living room, opens the back screen door, and steps outside. David is lying on his back on a

146

blanket on the grass, staring up at the sky.

'David?'

'Hey.'

'What are you doing?'

'I couldn't sleep.'

She walks over to him and lies down on the blanket next to him. It's a small blanket, and she finds it difficult to lie next to him without touching him. She pins her elbows to her sides.

'The stars here are awesome,' he says.

'Yeah. I love the sky here.'

'I've never seen them like this. And that moon. It's incredible.'

The moon is just shy of fully round, bright yellow-white and glowing, the man-in-the-moon face on its surface clearly visible, the sky immediately around it lit daytime blue. The rest of the sky is ink black, dotted all over with brilliant white stars. She finds the Big Dipper first, then the Little Dipper, and Venus. That's all she knows. She should really learn more about the constellations.

They continue to stare at the sky. Her eyes adjust, and more stars appear. And then, unbelievably, more. Stars behind stars, dusty hazes of light, layered galaxies of energy existing, burning, shining, unfathomable distances away from them. She pictures David and herself in her mind's eye as if viewed from above — two tiny, breathing bodies lying on a blanket on the grass on a tiny island thirty miles out to sea. Two tiny bodies who once dreamed of a life together, who had a beautiful boy together, now lying side by side

147

on a blanket on the grass, observing infinity.

'See that?' He points, drawing the letter W with his finger on the sky. 'That's Cassiopeia.'

'Amazing.'

A clear night sky on Nantucket truly does amaze. If it's even noticeable enough to draw attention upward, the sky at night doesn't amaze in Hingham. It won't amaze in Chicago either. She thinks about David living there, surrounded by skyscrapers and city lights, walking along the edge of Lake Michigan and looking up at the sky on a clear night and seeing only darkness when Olivia can see all of this.

It's a cool night with no mosquitoes thanks to a steady wind. Olivia shivers, needing more than her sleeveless, cotton nightgown. David moves closer to her so that their shoulders, hips, and legs touch. He laces his ringless fingers through hers; her hand accepts his. The touch of his body, the heat from his hand, familiar and comforting, warms her.

'I miss you,' he says, still staring up at the sky.

'I miss you, too.'

'I signed the papers.'

As she has witnessed before, it takes David longer to arrive at acceptance, but he eventually gets there. And here he is.

She squeezes his hand.

'I needed to see you, to be sure you're okay before I go,' he says.

'I am.'

'You are.'

'You will be, too.'

They hold hands and watch the night sky. The moon, the stars, the heavens, the universe. It's a sky that could almost make her believe in God again, that the incomprehensible is actually divine order, that everything is as it should be.

If only.

14

Startled awake, Beth sits straight up in bed, holding her breath, eyes wide, listening. *What was that?* She looks at her alarm clock: 3:23 a.m. There it is again. Her nerves jump. She sits straighter, eyes wider.

Someone is walking around downstairs, someone heavy-footed, someone big, not one of the girls. She hasn't locked anything, not the house or the car, since she moved here. No one she knows does. Only summer people lock their houses and cars on Nantucket. Anyone could walk right in. There it is again. Someone is here. A thief? A rapist?

Jimmy?

She leaves her bedroom, her heart pounding, wishing she weren't the only adult in the house, that she could send someone else to investigate the sound. She stops at the top of the stairs and listens. She doesn't hear anything. Maybe she imagined it. She's been having such vivid dreams lately. Maybe she dreamed the sound. As she turns to go back to bed, she hears the floorboards creak. Not imagined. Not a dream.

Before braving the stairs, she notices Jessica's tennis bag in the hallway. She unzips the bag, pulls out her daughter's tennis racket, and holds it in front of her as if it were a sword. She's not sure what good a tennis racket will do her if she finds an actual thief or a rapist in the house (she's never had a strong serve), but it feels at least mildly reassuring to hold on to something.

Aiming her racket-sword in front of her, she tiptoes down the stairs, through the dark living room, and into the kitchen. At the count of three, she flips on the light, and there he is, smiling, looking caught. And really drunk.

'Jimmy, what the hell are you doing?'

He blinks and squints and cups his hand over his eyes like a visor, trying to adjust his vision to the bright kitchen lights after fumbling around in total darkness. His face is sweaty, his Red Sox hat is on backward and crooked, and he reeks of cigars and booze.

'I came to give you this.' He holds out a white, greeting-card-size envelope.

'Oh, no. You can go tell your girlfriend that my birthday is in October, and I don't want any more cards from her, ever.'

'It's from me, and she's not my girlfriend.'

Beth's heart stops. If he says, *She's my fiancée*, she'll beat him to death with this tennis racket. She swears to God she will.

'We broke up. I moved out.'

Blood returns to her head. She loosens her grip. 'Well, I'm sorry it didn't work out for the two of you, but you can't just come back here.'

'I'm not. I just wanted to give you this.' He thrusts the card toward her.

Apprehensive of touching whatever is in that envelope, she cautiously holds out her racket-sword, and Jimmy drops the card onto the head. Extending the racket well out in front of her as if she were carrying a dead mouse or something gross and potentially poisonous, she walks the card across the kitchen and flips it onto the table.

'There, I have it. You can leave now.' She points her racket-sword at the door.

'Can we talk first?'

'No, you're in no condition to talk about anything.'

'I'm fine.'

'You don't smell fine.'

'Please.'

'It's the middle of the night.'

'I need to talk to you.'

'You've had *months* to talk to me. You only want to talk now because your girlfriend kicked you out.'

'She's not my girlfriend, and she didn't kick me out. I left. I ended it.'

'You have to leave,' Beth says as forcefully as she can without raising her voice. She doesn't want to wake up the girls.

'Will you open the card before I go?'

'No.' She turns to walk out of the kitchen. If he won't leave, she will. It's the middle of the night. She's going back to bed.

'Beth.' He grabs her free hand, stopping her. 'Look at me.'

She does.

'I miss you.'

'Good.'

'I really do.'

'You only miss me now because you're alone.'

'I've missed you the whole time.'

'You have to go.'

Still holding her hand, he pulls her into him and kisses her.

He tastes like sweat and beer and cigars. She should be repulsed and offended. She should kick him out on his sorry, drunk ass. She should whack him over the head with her racket-sword. But for some illogical reason, she drops her weapon and melts into his kiss.

Now he's pulling her nightshirt off, and she's letting him. He's still kissing her, scratching her face with his beard, and she's kissing him back, and somewhere in her head, an outraged part of her is screaming, *WHAT ARE YOU DOING?!* But another part of her is quite calmly replying, *Shhh. We'll talk about it later. Now be quiet and unzip his pants.*

The next thing she knows, they're on the kitchen floor. She's naked, and his pants are down below his knees, his shoes and shirt still on. In the fifteen years that they've known each other, they've never done it on the kitchen floor. In fact, Beth's never been naked anywhere in the house but in her bedroom and bathroom.

The whole shebang is urgent and hungry and straight to the point and, despite the pain of the hardwood floor against the bones of her spine and its being over in about a minute, surprisingly good. Completely foolish and probably regrettable, but surprisingly, undeniably good.

Her ears prickle. Did she just hear one of the girls upstairs? Oh my God, she and Jimmy made too much noise, and now one of the girls is probably on her way downstairs to see what's going on. Beth pushes Jimmy off her and

153

scrambles back into her underwear and night-shirt.

'Quick, I think the girls heard us,' she whispers. 'Pull your pants up.'

He listens and doesn't move. 'I don't hear anything.'

He's right. Everything's quiet.

'You have to go.'

'Okay, but can we talk?' His pants are still around his knees.

'Not now. Another time. When it's daytime, and you're not drunk, and you have your pants on.'

He smiles at her, that crazy smile that still undoes her. 'Okay.'

'Now go.'

'Okay, okay. Where's my hat?'

'There.' She points to the counter where she threw it.

He fixes it onto his head, forward and straight this time. 'I missed you.'

'Go.'

'Okay.' He walks to the front door. 'I'll see you later, right?'

She nods, and he leaves. She hopes he's sober enough to drive wherever he's staying. She wonders where he's staying. She wonders what he wants to talk about. She wonders what on earth just happened here.

The part of her that will have to face Petra and the rest of her friends, even Georgia, feels ashamed and stupid about what just happened. The part of her that has felt constantly threatened, like it had been thrown unasked into an unfair competition with that tramp Angela, feels victorious about what just happened. But the rest of her doesn't know what the hell to make yet of what just happened.

She walks over to the kitchen table, picks up the card, and opens it.

Beth, I'm sorry. I love you. Please take me back.
Yours, Jimmy

15

It's ten thirty in the morning, and Beth is in the library. She's writing. What she's writing began as a short story, inspired by a dream, but it's fast growing into something else, something more substantial, either a collection of related stories or a novella or maybe even a novel. She doesn't know yet.

She's writing about a boy with autism, but his story is different from those of *The Siege* or *The Curious Incident of the Dog in the Night-Time* or any of the other books that she's now read about autism. The story she's writing is about a boy with autism who doesn't speak, and yet she's telling it from his point of view, giving a voice to this voiceless child.

This morning, she is writing in her notebook instead of on Sophie's laptop. She can write significantly faster than she can type, but even with a pen, she's struggling to move her hand as fast as the words appear in her imagination, gripping her pen so hard her fingers cramp. She pauses to shake out her hand and look over what she's written about how her character believes his mind works.

I'm always hearing about how my brain doesn't work right. They say my brain is broken. My mother cries about my broken brain, and she and my father fight about my broken brain, and people come to my house every day to try to fix my broken brain. But it doesn't feel broken to me. I think they're wrong about my brain.

It doesn't feel like my knee when I fall outside in the driveway and break the skin, and the broken skin bleeds and hurts and sometimes turns pink and white or blue and purple. When I fall and break my skin, it hurts and I cry, and my mother sticks a Barney Band-Aid on my broken skin. Sometimes the Barney Band-Aid loses its sticky in the tub and comes off, and the skin is still pink and broken, and I'll get another Barney Band-Aid. But after a few tubs, the Barney Band-Aid will come off, and the broken skin will be fixed.

My brain doesn't hurt, and my brain doesn't bleed. My brain doesn't need a Barney Band-Aid.

And it's not broken like the white coffee mug I knocked off the table yesterday that split apart into three pieces when it hit the floor and that my father said he could glue back together but my mother said to *forget it, it's ruined*, and she threw the three pieces that used to be one white coffee mug into the trash. Broken things are ruined and go into the trash.

My brain didn't fall on the floor, it didn't split into three pieces, and it doesn't belong in the trash.

And it's not broken like the ant I stepped on and cracked and flattened so it couldn't move anymore, making it dead. Dead things are broken forever. That ant is broken, but my brain isn't. My brain can still think about the ant and remember the sound of its body cracking under my shoe, so that is my brain still working.

My brain isn't dead like the ant.

I wish I could tell them that my brain isn't broken so they could stop crying and fighting and people could stop coming to my house to fix me. They make me tired.

My brain is made up of different rooms. Each room is for doing a different thing. For example, I have an Eyes Room for seeing things and an Ears Room for hearing things. I have a Hands Room, a Memory Room (it's like my father's office, full of drawers and folders and boxes with papers), a New Things Room, a Numbers Room (my favorite), and a Horror Room (I wish this room would be broken, but it works just fine).

The rooms don't touch each other. There are long, looping hallways in between each room. If I'm thinking about something that happened yesterday (like when I knocked over the white coffee mug), I'm in my Memory Room. But if I want to watch a Barney video on the TV, I have to leave the Memory Room and go into Eyes and sometimes Ears.

Sometimes when I'm in the hallways traveling to a different room, I get lost and confused and caught In Between and feel like I'm nowhere. This is when my brain feels like maybe it's a little bit broken, but I know I just have to find my way into one of the rooms and shut the door.

But if too much is happening at once, I can get into trouble. If I'm counting the square tiles on the kitchen floor (180), I'm in my Numbers Room, but if my mother starts talking to me, I have to go into my Ears Room to hear her. But I

158

want to stay in Numbers because I'm counting, and I like to count, but my mother keeps talking, and her sound is getting louder, and I feel pressure to leave Numbers and go inside my Ears Room. So I go into the hallway, but then she grabs my hand, and this surprises me and forces me into Hands, which isn't where I wanted to go, and she's talking to me but I can't hear what she's saying because I'm in my Hands Room and not in Ears.

If she lets go of my hand, I can go into Ears. She's saying, *Look at me*. But if I look at her, I have to leave Ears and go into Eyes, and then I won't be able to hear what she's saying. So I don't know what to do, and I'm wandering the halls, and I can't make a decision on where to go, and I'm In Between, and that's when I get into trouble.

If I hang around in the hallways too long and don't get safe inside a room, I can get sucked into the Horror Room, and it's not easy to get out of there. Sometimes I'm locked inside that scary room for a long time, and the only way out is to scream as loud as I can because sometimes my really loud scream can pop open the door and push me straight into Ears.

The sound of my own voice screaming is the only thing that can get rid of everything else.

My voice makes screams and sounds but not words. But this isn't a broken room inside my brain. I talk to myself with words inside my brain just fine. I think I might have broken lips or a

159

broken tongue or a broken throat. I wish I could tell my mother and father that my voice is broken but my brain is working, but I can't tell them because my voice is broken. I wish they'd figure it out on their own.

16

Yesterday was not a good day. I had a huge, ugly meltdown. That's happening more and more. My therapist thinks I should go on an antidepressant. I think this is some kind of perverse joke. I've been searching and begging and praying for a medication that will fix everything, and this is the answer to my fucking prayers? Anthony has autism, so give ME an anti-depressant — problem solved!

How about a medication for HIM?! How about that? And one that actually works, please. How about a prescription for him that will make him talk and stack blocks and stop flipping the light switches and moan-shrieking and grinding his teeth? And how about one that doesn't turn him into either a doped-up zombie or a raging psy-chotic on crack? How about that? How about one that doesn't make him puke all over his sheets and the rugs and me? How about that?

But, no, let's medicate ME. There. Every-thing's all better now.

Anthony has at least one meltdown a day, and now I'm having at least one melt-down a day, and we can't manage his, so

161

let's manage mine. Let's fix me, and then everyone can cope with Anthony's autism.

My therapist wrote me a prescription for Celexa last month. I threw it out. I see her logic, and I hate it. I'm trying not to hate her. If I'm depressed, so be it. Feels like a pretty normal reaction to my life right now. If she had my life, she'd be depressed, too. Anyone would. She can keep her nice and tidy solution to all my problems. I'll stick to wine, thank you.

So yesterday's meltdown. I went to the grocery store alone, and David stayed home with Anthony, and I was in a good mood. I love going to the grocery store alone. Then I got home, and first thing I saw when I opened the front door was Anthony standing in the middle of the living room. He shot me a sideways glance and then started jumping up and down, elbows tucked at his ribs, flapping his hands, screeching. This is Anthony excited to see me. And the first thing I thought was *Hi, Anthony. I'm happy to see you, too.*

And then I thought, Maybe I should try it. If he won't mimic us, maybe I should try copying him. I dropped the bags of groceries and forced a loud screech, and I jumped and flapped.

So there we were — David on the couch watching the football pregame and Anthony and I shrieking and jumping and flapping. It felt so unnatural and weird, like I was

162

making fun of him. It felt wrong. This is not how people express joy or excitement or love. And I thought, This is what retarded looks like. And I felt so ashamed for thinking that word. I hate that word.

Why can't he just smile and say, Hey, Mom, glad you're home? Because he can't. Because he has autism. I HATE autism. He shrieks and flaps and looks retarded instead, and this is Anthony showing joy, and I can't join in and feel joy along with him.

And then I thought, This is it. This is all I'm ever going to get. No hugs and kisses. No 'Hi, Mom!' No 'I love you, Mom.' No Mother's Day cards made by him. He jumps and flaps and screeches, and that's how he shows joy. That's how he shows love. And that's it.

On some days, I can be grateful for this. I can. But yesterday, I couldn't take it. I was purely pissed. Rationally, I know it's the best he can do, and I love him for it. I wasn't pissed at him. I was pissed at God.

I left Anthony and the bags of groceries, and I called Father Foley on the phone and unloaded on him. What kind of horrible God would give a boy autism? What kind of God would afflict a small child with this kind of suffering? Why? Why can't Anthony talk to us? Why can't he look at me and smile and say 'Mom!' and come running into my arms like other little boys? Why does he have to live like this? What did he do to deserve this kind of life? What did I do to deserve this? Why?

Father Foley then said a bunch of completely useless words, something about the permissive will of God and manifestations of evil and original sin. I don't really know. It all turned to meaningless static. I didn't say anything. I was still holding the word WHY in my mouth, waiting for a real answer.

Then he said, Keep praying, Olivia. God will hear you if you pray to Him.

And here's where I had my meltdown. I said something like I don't want Him to HEAR me. I want Him to DO something. I want some fucking ANSWERS. I'm so sick of praying. Fuck praying. I'm done praying. I'm done with God.

And I threw the phone across the room and shrieked and wailed like I was being murdered, like this is killing me. And you know, I think it is.

This is killing me.

David missed the first half of the football game trying to calm me down. I drank a bottle of wine while he watched the second half, and I went to bed without dinner.

Today I woke up with the worst headache of my life. I swallowed four Motrin with a tall glass of water, and the worst headache of my life was gone by lunch.

We have pills for headaches. We have antidepressants for sadness. We have God for believers.

We have nothing for autism.

Olivia had forgotten about that meltdown entirely, stuffed it in a box, locked it up, and buried it in the basement of her mind, but after reading her journal entry earlier this morning, she remembers it now as if it were yesterday. Those powerful and ugly emotions that took hold of her that day six years ago, awakened by the memory, stir inside her again, but they feel softer and misplaced now, like a shadow belonging to someone else.

It's now late morning, and she is walking among the throngs of tourists in Town, an attempt at distracting her from herself. She doesn't have an exact destination in mind, maybe The Bean or the library or Aunt Leah's for more fudge, or maybe she'll simply walk. Walking is the plan.

When walking is the plan, she typically goes to Fat Ladies Beach or Bartlett's Farm, places where she can move freely and lose herself in nature. So it's strange that she's chosen to come here, confined to the narrow brick sidewalks, her natural pace impeded by the crawl of tourists in front of her, bombarded on all sides by shoppers and one-sided cell-phone chatter.

She feels her own phone vibrate inside her purse and stops walking to search for it. She grabs it on the fourth ring.

'Hello?' She waits. 'Hello?'

She looks at the area code and doesn't recognize it, but that's not unusual. People come to Nantucket from all over the world. She's already shot beach portraits for families who are from as far away as California and Germany. She begins to worry that she's forgotten a portrait session scheduled for this morning, and the family is anxiously waiting for her on some beach. But the worry isn't real. She knows she has today off.

She looks up and notices that she's standing in front of St. Mary's Church. It's a pretty church with a white clapboard exterior, large, polished-teak front doors, and a two-story tower with no bell. A simple statue of Our Lady, sculpted of white marble, stands on its front lawn, welcoming parishioners with wide, outstretched arms.

But Olivia is not a parishioner. Mary isn't welcoming *her* inside. Olivia vowed the day she had that meltdown that she'd never go to church again. If God was going to turn His back on her, she would do the same to Him. Two could play that game.

But even though she stopped attending Sunday mass and receiving the sacraments, even though she blamed and hated God, she still prayed. She didn't make a show of it, and she stopped making the sign of the cross, but she still whispered her prayers for Anthony. She prayed in the shower, while she brushed her teeth, while stopped at red lights, while she stood in line at Costco to buy diapers for a six-year-old, before dinner, before bed. She kept praying because even though she'd turned her back on Him, her boycott of God was more posture than real conviction. She still believed.

Until last year, when she stopped believing in Him altogether.

166

She continues walking down Federal Street. People are everywhere, taking up every conceivable outdoor space. They're eating and drinking at outdoor tables, pedaling bicycles, walking their dogs, sipping iced coffees as they sit on benches, window-shopping as they walk and talk on their phones. A continuous stream of people in their cars inches along every road, breaking the line only to allow clumps of pedestrians to cross at the crosswalks.

She pauses for a moment, debating whether she should return to her Jeep and go somewhere with fewer people or keep walking here. As she considers a hike on Bartlett's Farm, someone bumps into her, knocking her sideways.

'Watch it, lady,' says a tall, lanky man over his shoulder as he continues past her, not even breaking his stride.

YOU walked into ME, she thinks.

She plants her feet in the middle of the brick sidewalk, partly as an act of defiance and partly because she doesn't know where to go, holding her ground as dozens of people weave around her in both directions, as if she were a rock surrounded by wild river rapids. She feels oddly stuck in this spot and, at the same time, a building anxiety over remaining there.

She should've gone to the beach.

Then she registers where she is. She's standing in front of St. Mary's Church. Again.

She knows she vowed she'd never return to the Church, but she also vowed to love and honor David until death parted them. And now she's getting divorced. So she's already a vow-breaker.

And maybe she does still believe in God. Ever since David left for Chicago, she finds herself talking to Him again. She came to this island to disconnect from everyone and everything, to be alone, and her self-imposed isolation has been a needed salve for her battered soul. But knowing that David was still in Hingham was a lifeline she held on to with both hands. She could go back. Maybe not back to David or their marriage, although, if she's being honest, there was that possibility, too, but back to their house, her home, her life. Now David's in Chicago, and there's nothing to go back to. There's nothing connecting her to her old life, to before. Before is gone.

Some other family will be living in their house, where Anthony was supposed to grow up, to become the best Anthony he could be, whatever that might've been, where David and she were supposed to grow old together. Maybe someone else will have that life there. Someone luckier than her. Someone blessed.

When David was still in Hingham, she could consider her life on Nantucket to be a trial run, a visit, a sabbatical, a temporary state of isolation. It was practice, pretend, a rehearsal. Now it's real. This is her life. She is alone on Nantucket, and there is no undoing it.

She has become an empty space, and despite her grief and resistance, God has wandered back in. She finds herself talking to Him while cooking in the kitchen, as she's doing the laundry, while walking on the beach. She recognizes that she's not simply talking to herself. She's talking to God. And so, there it is. If she's talking to God, she must believe He exists.

She's asking the same familiar questions, waiting in silence for answers. And in those silences, her loneliness feels too sharp, like it might slice her in half. It's not loneliness for David or even Anthony. She's not lonely for her old home or friends. She's lonely for answers. Answers are the company she seeks.

And whether or not she still believes in God, she has always believed in signs. Someone or something is calling her into this church. She hastens by the marble Mary, climbs up the steps, and, with more than a little reluctance, pushes open one of the shiny teak doors and walks inside.

This church is smaller than St. Christopher's in Hingham, probably seating about three hundred at a Sunday high-noon mass. It's dimly lit, and after her eyes adjust, she notices that everything looks brand-new — the red carpet, the polished pews, the gorgeous pipe organ, the woven Nantucket collection baskets. And it's air-conditioned. The money on this island trickles everywhere.

No one is here. The daily mass would've been said earlier in the morning, and confessions are heard on Saturday afternoons. Before walking to the front of the church, she kneels at a table of prayer candles. The candles here aren't real. They're plastic, battery-operated lights in the shape of candles. The town of Nantucket has burned down so many times that everyone on

169

this island is, if not openly fearful, at least a little superstitious about fire, even, it seems, the Catholic priests.

She flips one over, clicks the button to ON, and replaces it on the table. It glows orange, but it's not nearly as satisfying as a real flame. She 'lights' another candle for Anthony as she always used to, and then one more. One for David. She closes her eyes and tries to pray, but she can't find any words. She hasn't prayed to God in church in a long time. She presses the palms of her hands together and tries again. No words.

Maybe she should go with someone else's words, a ready-made prayer like a Hail Mary or the Our Father. She begins whispering a Hail Mary but stops after *the Lord is with thee*. The words feel memorized and meaningless, like she's reciting a nursery rhyme. These are not the words that drew her inside here. Leaving her three 'lit' candles, she wanders to the front of the church, behind the altar, and finds a closed door. She stands there for more than a minute before she finds enough courage to knock.

'Yes? Come in.'

Olivia opens the door to a small sitting room. A priest is sitting in the center of a brown sofa directly under a brass crucifix hung on the wall. He's holding a closed book in his hands. A reading lamp to his left is turned on. An untouched cookie on a white plate centered on an ivory doily sits on a small wooden table to his right.

'I'm sorry to disturb you,' she says.

'I'm not at all disturbed. Please come, sit.'

170

There are two chairs, one modest and covered in a floral slipcover and the other a Queen Anne upholstered in a bright peacock blue. She chooses the Queen Anne and sits with her hands clasped in her lap. She stares at the floor for a moment. It's tiled in black and white hexagons. Anthony would've loved this floor.

'I'm Olivia Donatelli. I haven't been to this church before.'

'Welcome to St. Mary's. I'm Father Doyle.'

Father Doyle has a full head of silver hair and a bright pink face, flushed from within rather than from a sunburn. He's wearing a short-sleeve, black T-shirt, black pants, black sneakers, and no collar.

'I'm not exactly sure why I'm here.'

Father Doyle waits.

'I left the Church five years ago, but I've been praying.'

'You haven't left the Church if you're communing with God.'

'Well, I wouldn't call it communing. There's no conversation. I'm asking questions and not getting any answers. It's just me talking to myself, I think.'

'What are your questions?'

She squeezes her hands together and takes a deep breath. 'My son had autism. He was nonverbal and couldn't make eye contact and didn't like to be touched. And then he died from a subdural hematoma following a seizure when he was eight. So what I want to know is why? Why did God do this to my son? Why was he here and then gone so soon? Why did I have

171

him? What was the purpose of his life?'

'These are hard questions.'

She nods.

'But they're good questions. They're important questions. I'm glad you haven't given up on asking them.'

'What do you think?'

'I don't know a lot about autism, but I know that every human being is made as an expression of God's love.'

She's received this kind of pat, Catholic-textbook response before from the priests in Hingham, and it was always the end of the conversation. A vague reference to God's universal love isn't helpful. If anything, it used to intensify the violent storm that was already raging inside her. She would normally be up and heading for the door after 'expression of God's love.' But for some reason, maybe because she doesn't feel affronted by Father Doyle's soothing voice, maybe because today she possesses more patience than rage, maybe because she likes the blue chair she's sitting in, she stays in her seat.

'Every night of his life, I always tucked him into bed and said, 'Good night, Anthony. I love you.' And I don't know if he ever understood what that meant. I mean, it's not that he didn't understand us. He understood a lot, but love, I don't know. He was good at concrete things, black-and-white rules and routines. He liked order. But social things, people, shared emotions, he didn't seem to notice or care much about these. So I don't know.'

She knows that he loved his rocks and Barney

172

and swings, but loving things is different from loving another person. Reciprocal love is different. He wouldn't let her hug or kiss him. They couldn't stare into each other's eyes. He couldn't tell her what he felt. He couldn't say the words *Good night, Mom. I love you, too.*

'But you loved him anyway.'

'Of course. I loved him desperately.'

She grinds her teeth together and swallows, trying to hold back her tears, but it's no use. There's no stopping them. Father Doyle passes her a box of tissues.

'I don't know if he felt loved.'

'Children who are deaf and can never hear or say the words *I love you* feel love. Children who are born with no limbs or who lose their arms and can't hug still feel love. Love is felt beyond words and touch. Love is energy. Love is God.'

'I know. And I know other parents have children born with disabilities or who have cancer or a tragic accident, and I know I'm not special or deserve anything better, but I still don't understand. I feel like those other parents at least get to say that they love their child and it's mutual, it matters. And there's comfort in that.

'At least those other mothers get to hug their children and cradle them in their arms and say, 'It's okay. I'm here. I love you.' And those kids can see their mother's love in her eyes and feel it. I never had that with Anthony. If Anthony was suffering, he'd scream and cry and we couldn't know what was wrong or how to fix it. We wouldn't know if he had a stomachache or a

173

toothache or if he wanted to go on the swings or if I'd accidentally moved one of his rocks out of place. I felt like I could never reach him close enough to comfort him.'

'And what about you? You needed love and comfort, too,' Father Doyle says.

She nods and wipes the tears from her face. 'And now Anthony is gone, and his father and I are getting divorced, and there's nothing left. There's nothing.'

'There is you, and there is God.'

'So where *is* He then? Where has He *been* for the past ten years?'

'I know it can be difficult to keep faith. These kinds of hardships can either strengthen our faith or destroy it. Even Jesus on the cross said, 'My God, my God, why have you abandoned me?' As difficult as it can be for us human beings to comprehend, He is always present.'

'I feel completely alone.'

'You're not alone. God is with you.'

'I don't hear any answers to my questions.'

'You won't hear Him with your ears. You have to listen with your heart, with your spirit. His answers are there, within you.'

'I don't know,' she says, shaking her head.

'Keep asking your questions. Keep communing with God and try listening with your spirit.'

She nods, but she's skeptical and unsure of what exactly she's agreeing to. She thanks Father Doyle for his time and tells him that she has to leave. He puts his hand on her shoulder and tells her to come and see him anytime.

She walks past the altar, past her three lit

candles, and back outside. The bright sunlit day assaults her vision, forcing her to squint her eyes shut and wait. And in those few seconds with her eyes closed, she pictures Anthony — his uncut brown hair, his deep brown eyes, the joy in his smile. She smiles, loving him.

Then, before she descends the church steps, she thinks. If she can see Anthony without her eyes, maybe she can hear God without her ears.

God, why was Anthony here? Why did he have autism?

She opens her eyes and tries to listen with her spirit as she walks onto the crowded sidewalk below her.

17

Beth showers and dresses and makes pancakes for breakfast. She packs three lunches, washes the table and the dishes, and waters the plants. She drops the girls off at the community center, drives downtown, and finds a parking space on India Street without a problem, grateful as she always is that tourists sleep late. Everything about this morning is typical until she enters the library. And then everything is different.

Someone is sitting in her seat.

The offender is an older woman, at least seventy, with short, brilliant white hair and thick glasses attached to a beaded chain looped around her neck. Pencil in hand, she's working on what appears to be a Sudoku puzzle. Balls of yarn, knitting needles, and a paperback peek out from the top of a quilted bag on the floor next to her. Good God, this woman could be parked here all day. Here in Beth's seat.

Of course, Beth understands that the chair doesn't belong to her. It's not 'her seat.' But she's sat in this chair every morning since she began coming here to write at the beginning of the summer. She likes sitting with her back against the stacks of books, facing the window, able to see the clock. She likes the left corner of the table, with plenty of room to her right to spread out her notebooks and papers and laptop. And if she's being honest, she believes in the magical powers of that seat. In that particular seat she's been writing page after page without second-guessing her prose, without ridiculing her dialogue, without becoming seized with fear, without stopping. As long as she sits in that wooden chair at that wooden table facing east, the boy's story keeps coming, and she keeps writing it down.

And now some elderly woman with bad vision is using up its magical powers for solving Sudoku puzzles.

She considers her options. She could sit in the chair next to the woman, slide it too close, blow her nose, clear her throat, chew gum, and tap her pen on her teeth until the woman is annoyed into finding a new location. She could ask the woman in a polite and nonthreatening voice if she would kindly move to another chair. She could go home and clean. Or she could be a mature adult and find another place to sit.

She picks a chair on the other side of the table, a respectful distance but close enough that she could gather her things in a heartbeat and regain her rightful spot should the woman decide to leave. She opens Sophie's laptop, which Sophie is now begrudgingly sharing with her mother, and stares at the screen. She's facing west, and her chair wobbles. She taps her teeth with her fingernail and sighs, resigned to the obvious truth. There's nothing magical about this seat.

After a while, she twists around and looks up at the clock. She's now been here for an hour and has done nothing but read what she's already written. And as she feared, the woman is now knitting. Maybe Beth should go home. She stares at the cursor, willing it to produce something as if it were a planchette on a Ouija board. No words appear, but a reflection of a woman emerges within the screen. She spins around in her ordinary chair. Courtney is standing behind her, smiling.

'Hey, have a seat,' says Beth, relieved to have a distraction. 'What are you doing here?'

'Had to come into Town for something. Thought I'd stop by and see how you're doing. How's it coming?' Courtney points to the blank, white nothing on Beth's computer screen.

'Good, good, I think. We'll see when it's done.'

'Do you have a title yet?'

'Not yet.'

'We should all read it for book club when you're done. Wouldn't that be fun?'

Beth smiles and nods, loving the idea if her book actually turns out to be 'good,' imagining her unbearable humiliation if it sucks.

'This is for you.' Courtney hands Beth a book. *Mending Your Marriage* by Johanna Hamill. As Beth flips through the pages, she notices passages underlined in pen, handwriting in the margins. Courtney's handwriting. She looks over at her friend, confused, wondering.

'It's my copy. I thought it was pretty good, better than most of the crap out there on how to save your marriage.'

'But, so, you read this? Why?'

'Steve cheated on me.'

'He *did*?'

The old woman looks up from her knitting.

'When?' asks Beth, lowering her voice.

'Four years ago.'

'What? My God, I thought you were going to say 'last week.''

Beth stares without focus down at the cover of the book and shakes her head, unable to decide whether she's more stunned by Steve's infidelity or that Courtney has kept it a secret for four years.

'Who?'

'Some rich-bitch divorcée. He was working with Mickey's crew over in Madaket, remodeling her bedroom and master bath. He said she came on to him, which I believe. You know how some of those wealthy summer biddies act like they're entitled to everything. He said they only did it once.'

'So you're okay? You've forgiven him?'

'Well, not at first. I wanted to kill him. That lasted awhile. Then I stopped wanting him dead, but I couldn't forgive him. I read all these books, and that one might help you, but none of them helped me. I couldn't forgive him. I couldn't trust him. The power balance was all wrong. He had all of it, and I had none.'

Beth nods, following her, empathizing.

'So I cheated on him.'

'You *did*?'

The old woman looks up from her knitting again, this time really meaning it, down her nose, disapproving. Good. Maybe either the subject or the volume of their conversation will drive her out of here. Courtney nods and smiles.

'With who?'

'Some twentysomething, young thing. His name was Henry. I picked him up at 21 Federal. It was just a one-nighter.' Courtney grins, knowing she's blowing Beth's mind. 'The next day, I told Steve. And I said, 'Now we're even. No more.' And we promised that was the end of it, and we moved on.'

'That's crazy.'

'I know. It was, but it was the only way I could stay with him, and I wanted to stay with him. I love Steve and our life here. I didn't want to lose him. So I'm just saying, if you want to take Jimmy back, read the book, and if that doesn't do it for you, I say, go have your own Henry.'

'But Jimmy cheated on me for a whole year, I don't think — '

'You only have to do it once. Once makes it even.'

'Is *that* in the book?'

'I'm just saying. Marriage isn't only about whether you love each other. You have to have mutual power, mutual trust. Do you trust Jimmy?'

'No. But sleeping with someone else is going to help?'

'It worked for me.'

Beth shakes her head, struggling with the math of this adultery equation, to imagine that cheating on Jimmy would accomplish anything but giving them both reputations for being unfaithful scoundrels who should never be trusted. 'I keep thinking, 'Once a cheater, always a cheater.' Who said that, Oprah? Dr. Phil?'

180

'I don't know. Not the case with me and Steve.'

'So you guys were just a onetime thing.'

'Yeah.'

'And you're happy.'

'Yeah, we really are.'

'And you trust each other.'

'Enough. You're always at the mercy of the people you're in a relationship with, right? Anything can happen. But I trust him enough.'

'What if he cheats again?' asks Beth.

'I'd kill him.'

'No, really.'

'I don't know, maybe another Henry.'

'I don't know, Courtney. I don't think I could.'

'Do you want it to work out for you and Jimmy?'

Beth used to think that Jimmy and she were soul mates. They had so much in common when they first met. They're both only children, raised by single parents. His father died of lung cancer the year after her mother's death. Independent and somewhat fearless, they both held a fierce determination to follow their dreams, to do something they loved for a living. For Beth, that was writing. For Jimmy, it was scalloping.

Jimmy grew up in Maine. His father was a lobsterman who saved every penny so Jimmy might go to college, hoping for his son to discover a more reliable, less backbreaking way to earn a living. Jimmy attended the University of Maine and after graduating got the desk job of his father's dreams at a small software company. But Jimmy hated his desk and his cubicle, and he hated being trapped indoors, and he admired his father's life as a fisherman.

He went to Nantucket the following summer, after he'd been at his 'soulless' job for a year. It was supposed to be a long weekend, a vacation with friends. Like Beth, he fell in love with the place. He decided to stay, but instead of lobstering, which he knew, he learned how to scallop, which was where the big money was at the time.

They loved the same music, the same food, Nantucket. They loved each other. And now, here they are. Jimmy gave up scalloping, and until recently she forgot about writing, and Jimmy's been sleeping with another woman, and she doesn't know what they both love anymore.

She looks over at the old woman. Beth's still young. She could start over, and not necessarily with another man. She could regroup, redefine her life as a single mother. She could finish this book, maybe move off-island, get a job at a newspaper or a magazine, maybe somewhere with mountains or a city, maybe back to Portland. Somewhere with no sand or fog or tourists. Somewhere with no Angela Melo.

The possibilities, even contemplating the words *I could*, feel exhilarating. She could do anything she wants. But what does she want? She's happy that Jimmy wants her back, but she doesn't entirely trust her own motivation for feeling good about this. He picked her. She wins. She beat Angela. So maybe she feels more victorious than happy.

And who's to say that he won't change his

mind in a week, in a month, next year, that he won't someday show up in Angela's kitchen at three in the morning with a card in his hands and his pants around his knees? No, she has no desire to be strung to that yo-yo.

Maybe there are no soul mates. Maybe husbands are simply men women eventually put up with so someone is there to haul air conditioners in and out of the attic, to love their children, to keep them company. But Beth can haul the air conditioners herself, her friends provide her with plenty of company, and he can still love their kids even if she doesn't love him. But there's the thing. She might still love him.

'I don't know.'

'Look, Jimmy's got all the power now. It's not just about whether you can love each other again or trust each other again, it's about evening out the power.'

As Beth thinks about these ingredients of marriage, about love and trust and power, her mind wanders over to truth and takes an east-facing seat. A marriage should have truth.

'I had sex with Jimmy the other night.'

'I know, Petra told me. That's why I brought you the book.'

For a second, Beth feels indignant at Petra for betraying her confidence, but she shrugs it off. 'That didn't even out anything, did it?'

'Right idea, wrong guy.'

'He wants to talk.'

'That's impressive for Jimmy.'

'I know.'

'You could try counseling.'

Beth wonders if Jimmy would agree to go.

'If you do, go to Dr. Campbell.'

'The guy with the falcon?'

'I know, but the only other option is Nancy Gardener.'

Nancy Gardener is a twice-divorced marriage counselor whose sister is Gracie's fourth-grade teacher.

'I don't know,' says Beth.

'He's good. Jill and Mickey go to him.'

'They do?'

Courtney nods, eyebrows raised knowingly.

'Why? What's going on with them?'

Courtney shrugs. 'Everyone has stuff, Beth.'

Courtney looks over at the clock on the wall and gets up. 'I've got to run. Read the book, go see Dr. Campbell, go find your own Henry. Or be done with him. That's a fine choice, too.'

Courtney leaves, and Beth is alone again in her wobbly chair staring at her blank computer screen. She looks over at the old woman whose knitting is fast taking the shape of a mitten. Magic seat.

She sighs and shuts off Sophie's laptop. She packs her notebooks and pens into her bag, holding on to Courtney's book for an extra second, considering it, before she tosses it into her bag, too. As she's leaving the library, feeling defeated, she thinks about love and trust and power. And truth. As she walks down the front steps, she thinks about what is true in her life, and four simple, honest thoughts jump up and raise their hands.

1. She's not going to read *Mending Your Marriage*.
2. She's not going to go have her own Henry and call things even.
3. She'll make an appointment with Dr. Campbell if Jimmy is willing to go, and she hopes he is.
4. That old woman had better not be in her seat tomorrow, or she's going to lose it.

18

Beth didn't write anything yesterday, and the words she didn't write have been gathering and growing louder inside her, building to a crescendo, feeling full and urgent, like floodwaters pressing against a failing dam. She woke up this morning at dawn with this boy's words already in motion, rushing at her, through her, insistent, dogging her everyday, routine thoughts until each and every one of them surrendered. She can now think of nothing else.

She arrives at the library only seconds after it opens, hurries upstairs, and is relieved to see no one there. No one sitting in her seat. She sits down, opens her notebook, uncaps her pen, and writes.

I wake up, and it is daytime. I get out of bed and say Good Morning to the tree outside the window, to my box of rocks, and to the calendar on the wall. Yesterday was Sunday, and today is Monday. Danyel comes after lunch on Tuesdays.

I stand on every step with both feet until I do all twelve, and I'm downstairs. I walk into the kitchen and sit down on my seat at the kitchen table. My Barney cup is filled with purple juice, and my fork and white napkin are on the table, but there are only two French Toast sticks with maple syrup on my blue plate, and there are always three.

I can't eat two French Toast sticks because breakfast is three French Toast sticks. I can't eat two because three is finished, and two is stopping in the middle, and stopping in the middle hurts too much. I can't eat two French Toast sticks because then I won't ever be done with breakfast. And if I don't finish breakfast, then I can't brush my teeth in the bathroom and play with water in the sink. And then I can't get dressed in dry clothes on the bottom step. And then I can't go outside and swing. And I can't have lunch if I haven't finished breakfast. And Danyel won't come because she comes after lunch.

If I don't have two plus one equals three French Toast sticks for breakfast, I'm going to be stuck at this table forever.

I NEED ANOTHER FRENCH TOAST STICK!

I run over to the freezer and open it. The French Toast sticks box is gone. There is always a yellow box of French Toast sticks in the freezer. And now there isn't. Something terrible has happened. I'm getting tingly shivers in my hands, and I'm racing around in my head trying to think about how to make the French Toast sticks box come back into the freezer, but I'm breathing too fast, and my hands are too tingly, and I can't think.

My mother is now standing between me and the freezer, showing me an empty French Toast box. Empty is zero, and zero French Toast sticks is a disaster. I flap my tingly hands and moan.

My mother walks me back over to the table and says something in a loud and pretend happy voice, but I can't hear what she said because I'm looking at my blue plate. One of the two French Toast sticks has been cut in half, so now there are two Medium-size sticks and one Big stick, which is even worse than before because two is in the middle and one is the beginning, and none of this can be eaten because this is not breakfast. Breakfast is three of the SAME French Toast sticks. I cannot eat this.

The French Toast box has zero, and my blue plate has one Big stick and two Medium sticks, and nothing has three. Everything is zero or the beginning or the middle, and I can't eat breakfast because it can't be finished if it doesn't have three. I can't get dressed and go outside and swing because getting dressed and going outside and swinging happens AFTER breakfast and I can't have breakfast until I have three French Toast sticks.

I know how to solve this. If my mother would cut the one Big stick in half and get rid of one of the halves, then I'd have three Medium-size sticks. And then I could eat breakfast. Or she could cut one of the Medium-size sticks in half and get rid of one of its halves, and then there would be a Big, a Medium, and a Small stick. This is not as good as three SAME-sized sticks, but it's a three that I can handle. I could eat a Big, a Medium, and a Small French Toast stick breakfast because that is three, and three is finished and safe. Then I could eat breakfast and brush my teeth and play with water in the sink and get dressed and swing outside and see Danyel.

But I can't tell my mother my solutions because my voice is broken. And I can't cut the Big or Medium French Toast stick myself because I can't feel my hands anymore. I can't go into my Hands Room because I'm stuck in Ears. I'm stuck in Ears listening to the sound of someone screaming.

While I listen to the screaming, I lose my body. I have the distant and dreamy feeling of leaving the kitchen, moving through air. I don't want to move through air. I want three French Toast sticks. But I don't have a voice, and I don't have a body. I have the distant and dreamy feeling of struggling, hot and angry, then sweaty and cool. But mostly, I'm in my Ears, listening to the sound of screaming.

Now I'm back in my body. I'm in the bathroom, watching water run in the sink, when I realize that the someone screaming is me. I scream louder, and I lose my body again. I keep screaming so I can become the scream, and then I am the sound of how I feel and not a boy in a body who is in the bathroom without having eaten three French Toast sticks for breakfast first.

19

Beth checks her watch. They still have five minutes before they need to leave the house. Gracie and Jessica are ready, wearing identical gauzy, white shirts and faded blue jeans, waiting at the kitchen table, but Sophie is still upstairs fussing with herself.

'Sophie!' Beth yells. 'Two minutes!'

She steps into the bathroom for one last quick check in the mirror. With her fingers she smoothes down a section of hair threatening to frizz and wipes a bit of shine from her forehead. She fake-smiles. Nothing stuck in her teeth. Even though she knows she should stay out of the sun with her fair skin and tendency to freckle and burn and, more recently, wrinkle, she's been lying out on the deck for an hour each day for the past week, trying to achieve a healthy glow. Her cheeks are pink, and her eyes look bright. Mission accomplished.

She found a beach-portrait photographer with cheap rates on a flyer at Stop & Shop and the perfect beach-portrait shirt online at Old Navy last month. She ordered four, one for each of them, and she laundered and ironed the matching shirts weeks ago. Last night, they all painted their toenails the same shade of peacock blue. They're all wearing tiny pearl earrings and matching silver bracelets. They're perfectly coordinated from head to toe. Beth smiles, congratulating herself on being so organized, for thinking of everything.

'*Mom!*'

The urgent shrill in one of her daughters' voices sends Beth running into the kitchen. She looks Jessica up and down. No blood. No tears. She looks fine. But then Beth turns her attention to Gracie. The entire front of her beautiful gauzy, white shirt is drenched in red fruit punch. Gracie, teary-eyed and shocked, is holding a tall and mostly empty glass in her hand. Not fine. Not fine at all.

'My God, Gracie! What did you do?'

'Jessica did it! She pushed me while I was drinking!'

'I didn't push her.'

'You did!'

'It was an accident,' says Jessica.

'Why were you even drinking anything?' asks Beth. 'I told you we were leaving in two minutes.'

'I was thirsty.'

'Come here.'

Beth doesn't wait for Gracie to move. She yanks the shirt over her daughter's head and leaves Gracie in the kitchen, naked from the waist up and crying. Beth runs into the laundry room, pours a capful of detergent onto the shirt, and scrubs it under running water. The stain lightens from deep red to pink, but it's still there. And now the whole shirt is soaking wet. Gracie can't wear this. Beth checks her watch. They need to leave the house *right now*.

Think. Think. Think.

Beth scrubs the shirt again. Still pink. Still

wet. There's no time. She has to accept it. They can't wear the beautiful matching gauzy, white shirts. That dream is gone.

She has to come up with a plan B. Okay, they won't all be in the same style white shirt, but they can still all be in white.

'Gracie!' Beth calls. 'Go to your room and put on a white shirt!'

'Which one?'

'Any! Go!'

Beth takes a deep breath and blows the air out slowly through her mouth, trying not to freak out. She walks back into the kitchen and eyes Jessica, who is standing awkwardly still, as if she were afraid to blink.

'Why did you push your sister?'

'I didn't mean to.'

'Fine. Just stay there, and don't touch anything. And don't drink anything.'

Gracie returns to the kitchen wearing a white T-shirt with the words GIRLS RULE, BOYS DROOL written in puffy, purple lettering on the front.

'No, no, no,' says Beth, crazed impatience curling into her voice. 'Not that one. No words. It can't have words on it. Go get a plain white shirt!'

'I don't have a plain white shirt!' says Gracie, still crying.

'You must.'

'I don't.'

'Then go get one of Jessica's!'

'It'll be way too big!'

Beth scans through a mental catalog of the

girls' wardrobes. Gracie's right. All the white shirts are graphic T-shirts. Beth looks at her watch. They're late. She's never late. She likes to be early. Her face feels hot. Her soft, sun-kissed glow is now blazing red with stress.

Plan C.

'Okay, listen. Everyone has a solid-color tank top. I don't care what color, no words, go find one and put it on. Go! Go! Go!'

Gracie and Jessica skedaddle up the stairs, and Beth races right behind them.

'Sophie!' Beth yells through the gauzy, white fabric of her beautiful white shirt as she disrobes in her own bedroom. 'Change into a tank top!'

'What? Why?' yells Sophie.

'Just do what I say!'

All of Beth's tank tops are black, so she re-dresses in a flash. She waits for her girls at the top of the stairs, in the hallway of sad and lonely picture frames, each second smacking the center of her forehead as it ticks by. Sophie, surprisingly, is the first to join her. She's wearing a red tank top, no words, and she looks great, except for her face.

'Excuse me, are you wearing makeup?' asks Beth.

'Only a little.'

'Where did you get it?'

'Alena. *Her* mother lets her wear it.'

'Well, *your* mother doesn't.'

'So not fair.'

'Life's not fair. Come here.'

Beth looks at Sophie's made-up eyes, which are a striking blue and only a couple of inches below Beth's. She won't be able to keep her oldest daughter from wearing makeup for too much longer, but she can at least keep it off for this picture.

She resists the urge to lick her hand and wipe Sophie's face with her own spit and instead grabs her by the hand and pulls her into the bathroom. She pumps some hand soap into a facecloth, wets it in the sink, and scrubs Sophie's eyes and cheeks clean.

'Ow, my zit!'

'Sorry. You can keep the lip gloss on, but that's it.'

The other two are now in the hallway. Gracie is in a pink tank top, and Jessica is in blue. No words. No stains.

'Okay! Let's *go!*'

They run down the stairs, Beth claps and calls for Grover to follow them, and they all race into the car. Beth eyeballs her girls in the backseat through the rearview mirror as she slides the key into the ignition. Gracie's eyes are puffy from crying. Sophie's face is splotchy from being rubbed too hard with the facecloth, and she does have one honker of a zit on her cheek. Jessica's jaw is clenched, and her arms are folded. She looks angry, but Beth can't imagine why. They're all wearing different colored tops, and Beth's face still feels red-hot.

They're all supposed to be wearing white. They're all supposed to be calm and happy. They're supposed to be on time. And Jimmy. It's their family portrait. Their family is supposed to include Jimmy.

Maybe she should call and cancel. She thinks about the beautiful gauzy, white shirts and her hallway of sad and lonely frames. She looks back at her three girls again and then at the empty passenger seat. This is her family. She takes a deep breath, blows it out through her mouth, shifts the car into reverse, and drives her late, mismatched, puffy, splotchy, zitty, angry, Jimmy-less family to Cisco Beach.

20

Olivia checks her watch. Her client is late. This, she has already found in her brief experience, is typical. If it isn't the entire family, then it's a stray cousin who didn't get the directions, or it's an indispensable sister who is coming straight from the ferry, or it's a father who is actually here, but he's still in the car wrapping up a call from work. He'll be done in a minute. Or thirty.

This is why she started toting a beach chair to these portrait sessions. She doesn't mind waiting on a beautiful beach if she has somewhere to sit. Today was overcast, threatening rain all day, and Olivia doubts that the beach was crowded at any point. It's mostly emptied out now. There are more seagulls here than people.

Olivia likes the seagulls on Nantucket, which resemble the seagulls on Nantasket Beach — the beach she always went to when she lived in Hingham — only in that they're both white-and-gray shorebirds. Those gulls from Nantasket are insatiable, thieving rats with wings that prey upon anything labeled Nabisco or Frito-Lay. They stalk the edges of beach blankets, waiting for an unguarded moment to peck open a sealed bag of potato chips or fly off with an entire tuna sandwich.

The seagulls here pay little attention to people and their processed food. She watches one nab a crab from the shallow water, then settle into a warm dimple of sand, where it rips off the legs and devours the meaty body. She watches another fly overhead to the parking lot, where it drops a clam on the pavement, cracking open the shell. Why settle for cheese puffs when an abundance of fresh seafood is on the menu? These gulls are handsome and respectable birds.

Olivia follows the flight of another seagull across the cloudy horizon and wonders if it's possible ever to grow indifferent to this view. The water closest to the S-shaped shoreline is a metallic blue dance of rippling waves, but as her gaze travels out to sea, everything goes still and flat and almost white. A laser-sharp line of crisp, dark blue separates the ocean from the blushing pink sky at the horizon. Gorgeous.

The gull disappears in the distance. Olivia checks her watch. At thirty minutes late, she makes a point of calling the clients to verify that they are in fact coming and haven't forgotten or changed their minds. As she digs through her camera bag for her schedule sheet and phone, she sees them walking toward her, the mother and leashed dog leading the charge, three girls in different-colored tanks and jeans lagging behind.

'Olivia? Hi, I'm Beth Ellis. Sorry we're late.'

'Hi, Beth. No problem.'

'We had a wardrobe issue. I know everyone normally matches. Do you think this will look okay?'

Beth's right. Every family always wears matching outfits, like uniforms on the same team. All faded-blue shirts and khakis or all white shirts and Nantucket reds. The matching theme looks nice, but it's hardly necessary. She wonders who came up with this very autistic rule about family portraits.

'You look great.'

Beth rolls her eyes. 'We looked great a half hour ago. I'm hoping for not too embarrassing.'

'No, the colors are fun.'

'Again, so sorry. Before we get started, my oldest would like to know if you can Photoshop out her pimple.'

'Mom!' says the oldest.

All three girls are now gathered behind Beth. Olivia glances down at her schedule sheet. Sophie, Jessica, and Gracie.

'Consider it gone, Sophie. No one will ever see it,' says Olivia.

Sophie smiles just enough to be polite. That pimple looks painful.

'Can you get rid of this line right here while you're at it?' asks Beth, pointing to a deep vertical crease between her eyebrows. 'And anything that looks over thirty-five around my eyes?'

Digital plastic surgery. Olivia can erase all evidence of dark circles, crow's-feet, and age spots with a few precise clicks of her computer mouse. Whatever else her photographs have going for them — magic hour, the correct f-stop, composition, meaningful expressions captured at just the right moment, everyone smiling with their eyes open — her ability to subtly edit years off a woman's face is probably her most marketable skill.

198

'You won't look a day over thirty. Let's start over by the water.'

Olivia has developed an Eat Your Veggies First philosophy when it comes to beach portraits. She always takes the most difficult shot first. Ninety-nine percent of the time, this is the photo of everyone in front of the ocean, the one necessary photograph her client came here for, the one her client will be pissed about if it isn't perfect. All the other pictures, individuals and pairs and combinations of various people and pets and backgrounds, are bonus. Those are the Dessert shots.

Today, the Veggie shot will be easy. Three well-behaved-if-a-little-grumpy girls, a mellow dog, and a mother. No crying babies, no sugar-crazed toddlers hell-bent on running into the ocean, no preschoolers who refuse to smile, no preschoolers who refuse to do anything but smile, freezing their faces into the most unnatural-looking *Cheese*, and no husband.

Although couples don't openly fight right there on the beach in front of her, and Olivia never witnesses the actual argument, she's seen it too many times now. Irritation, blame, contempt, the negative energy between husband and wife over whatever skirmish they had earlier still simmering, bleeding through their eyes and smiles, as obvious as the zit on Sophie's cheek. And there's not a tool in Photoshop that can edit that out.

It's also a small group, much easier to catch eight eyeballs open than twenty. Groups of ten and more are truly difficult. Someone is always misbehaving, not looking at the camera, out of place, blinking. Four is a piece of cake. She'll snap about six hundred shots with the expectation of producing about two hundred quality pictures for Beth to choose from.

They line up in a straight row in front of the incoming tide.

'Smile. Look at me,' says Olivia.

They all do, except for the middle girl.

'Sorry, in the blue, what's your name?' asks Olivia, looking up over her camera.

'Jessica.'

'Jessica, give me a big smile.'

'She won't,' says Beth. 'She has braces. She won't show her teeth.'

'Uh, okay,' says Olivia. 'How about just less angry?'

'Jess, look happy,' says Beth.

'But I'm not,' says Jessica.

'Then fake it, please,' says Beth through a clenched smile, in a threatening singsong voice.

'Fine.'

Jessica pulls her pursed lips into the shape of slight amusement. Close enough. Olivia clicks away. She checks her LCD display and scrolls through the images. Veggies done. Now on to Dessert.

She shoots the girls in all possible combinations together without their mother, with and without the dog, sitting and standing. She shoots Beth with each daughter, then each girl alone, then the dog alone.

'Now how about just you?' asks Olivia.

'Me? By myself?' asks Beth.

'Yeah.'

'No, I don't need one of just me.'

Olivia has also learned this — a client can't purchase a shot that doesn't exist. Get every shot.

'Let's shoot it anyway. You don't have to decide if you want it now.'

She might want a headshot for her job, whatever it is that she does. She's a young, single mother. She might want it for Facebook or Match.com.

'Okay,' Beth says.

'Great. Look at me. Chin up, shoulders down.'

Click. Click. Click.

After Olivia finishes with Beth, they all move over to the dunes and smile at the camera in a similar round of poses. Even though the Veggie shot comes first, Olivia has often found that the second round of pictures is better. Everyone is more relaxed in the new location, and true personalities and relationships begin to emerge here. She can now see that Sophie and Jessica are close, that Sophie is edgy and bossy, and Jessica idolizes her. Gracie is goofy, and despite being around nine or ten, she is still Beth's baby girl. In the solo shots of Beth up against the dunes, Olivia sees a resolve peeking through a well-worn uncertainty, an openness in her posture, an authentic happiness alive in her smile.

After an hour and 652 images in the camera, Olivia declares that they're finished.

'Girls, go walk Grover for a few minutes while I talk to the photographer. Here's a baggie.'

Beth follows Olivia over to Olivia's camera bag and beach chair.

'So when will the photos be ready?'

'I'm running about six to eight weeks.'

'Wow, that long?'

'They might be sooner, but, yeah, probably at least six weeks.'

To her own pleased amazement, Olivia's had steady business all summer. She's done an average of five portraits each week, which means she's actually earning a living. But the editing piece of this beach-portrait-photography gig is more labor-intensive than she anticipated, and she's now considerably backed up. Editing the large family portraits is particularly time-consuming. She had one family of thirty-two who were gathered on Nantucket for the grandparents' fiftieth wedding anniversary. Editing that session was a beast. And erasing any signs of aging on all these women takes time.

'And that's when we'll get the proof book?'

'Yes, I'll e-mail you the link.'

'Link?'

'Yes, it's all online.'

'Oh, so we don't look through an actual book?'

'No, I do it all online.'

'Oh,' says Beth, sounding disappointed.

'It's great. You'll like it. You can choose the size, black-and-white or color. It's easy to navigate, but if you have any questions, feel free to get in touch.'

Olivia places her camera in her bag and zips it shut. She folds her beach chair. It's time to go.

She will happily hold Beth's hand via phone or e-mail through any step of the purchasing, but this is the end of the face-to-face part of this relationship.

'Okay. Thanks. Sorry about Jessica's sour puss.'

'She was fine. She'll look great.'

'I think she was upset that her father wasn't here. We separated this winter, and it's been hard on them.'

'I'm sorry.' Olivia stands with her heavy camera bag over one shoulder and her beach chair tucked under the other.

'It's been hard for me, too. Do you see this a lot? Families without the father?'

Struck by something familiar in Beth's question, Olivia pauses in her haste to leave. She studies the expression on Beth's face, and it registers. The need to feel normal. The desire to be accepted.

'All the time,' Olivia lies.

Beth smiles, grateful.

Olivia senses something else familiar in Beth but can't quite put her finger on it. And then, there it is, like looking in a mirror. Loneliness. Olivia decides to wait with Beth until her daughters return with their dog.

The sky has completely clouded over now, and the sun is just about to set. The air is noticeably chillier than it was only five minutes ago. Beth grabs a sweatshirt from her bag. As she's pulling it over her head, Olivia notices a marriage self-help book sitting faceup at the top of Beth's bag.

'That's my book,' says Olivia aloud instead of to herself as she'd intended.

'What?'

'I mean, I helped edit that book. I used to work at a publishing house.'

'Oh. I haven't read it yet. It belongs to a friend.'

Both women stand in awkward silence. Beth turns and looks down the length of the beach. Her girls are three dots in the distance. She turns back and rakes her toes through the sand. 'So you used to work in publishing?'

'Five years ago. Feels like even longer.'

'I know this is a little forward, but I'm writing a book. It's a series of related stories, or maybe it's a novel, I'm not really sure yet, but I'd love for someone professional to take a look at it.'

'Oh, I edited self-help, not fiction — '

'That's okay. I'd really appreciate your feedback, if you have the time.'

Outside of her job, Olivia's never offered to read anyone's anything. She's never wanted to be the one to tell someone not to quit her day job, to crush someone's dream. She looks down at Beth's bare feet, at her blue-painted toenails, at her copy of *Mending Your Marriage*, at the wedding and engagement rings she still wears on her finger, at the hopeful expression hung on her lonely face. She sighs. She has time.

'Sure. I'd be happy to take a look at it when you're done. Just let me know.'

'Thank you so much!' says Beth, her face lit up.

Olivia smiles. She adjusts the beach chair

204

under her right armpit. It felt light when she first picked it up, but now it's feeling heavy and unwieldy. And the strap to her camera bag is digging into the bare skin on her shoulder. She didn't bring a sweatshirt, and she's cold in her sleeveless sundress. She looks over Beth's shoulder.

'Here come your girls.'

Beth turns and sees her daughters and her dog walking toward her. 'Oh, okay. Thanks again. I knew there was a reason I picked you to do our pictures.'

Olivia extends her somewhat free hand to shake Beth's, but Beth maneuvers around this formal gesture, the camera bag, and the beach chair and gives Olivia a sincere hug. Chills run down Olivia's arms, but not because she's cold. It's been a long time since anyone has hugged her.

'You're welcome.'

The girls file in next to Beth. Sophie is holding a huge seagull feather in one hand and the dog's leash in the other, and Jessica is holding a bag of poop.

'Mom! Look what I found for you!' yells Gracie, smiling, excited.

She holds out the palm of her hand, displaying the amber-colored exoskeleton of a baby horseshoe crab.

'Cool, sweetie,' says Beth.

'And this is for you,' says Gracie, extending her other palm toward Olivia.

Olivia offers her somewhat free hand to Gracie, and Gracie rolls a white, almost

205

translucent, wet, oval pebble into Olivia's palm. Chills run down her arms again.

'It's a pearl,' says Gracie.

'Thank you,' says Olivia, her voice catching at the back of her throat. 'I love it.'

'Okay, we're off. Thanks again,' says Beth, and they all begin walking toward the parking lot.

'We'll talk in six weeks?' Beth asks at her car door.

'Six weeks,' says Olivia, even though it could easily be eight.

Beth waves, disappears into her car, and drives away.

Olivia tosses her camera bag and chair into the backseat of her Jeep and gets in. The warm air inside feels like a thick blanket wrapped around her bare skin. As she backs up, it begins to rain. She turns on her lights and wipers, relieved that the weather held for her portrait session. She pulls out of the parking lot, grateful for Gracie's gift still in her hand, smiling as she drives down Hummock Pond Road in the pouring rain.

When she gets home, she adds Gracie's rock to her growing collection in the glass bowl on the coffee table. She then connects her camera to her computer and retrieves one of her journals from the kitchen table. As the images from today's shoot are downloading onto her computer, she sits in her living-room chair and thinks about Beth and her three daughters, about her loneliness and her book. Olivia wonders what it's about.

Then she opens her journal and reads.

21

I spent today back in eighth grade. It started at the playground. We got there late morning, and Anthony ran straight to the swings, as usual. His body is way too big for the toddler bucket seats, but he refuses to even try the big-boy swings, so I hoisted him into one of the buckets and pushed my five-year-old next to another mother pushing her two-year-old. She smiled nervously at me and said nothing.

It was finally warm out today, and the playground was crowded. There were lots of kids Anthony's age playing with each other. Two boys and a girl were chasing each other up and down the slides, laughing, having a blast. A line of four kids were playing Follow the Leader, moving across the field of grass next to the playground, all arms up, then down, all jumping, then crawling, then clapping. Another group of kids were playing under the jungle gym.

A couple of girls were selling wood-chip ice cream. The customer kids waited their turn at the 'ice cream stand,' placed their orders, paid with wood-chip money, and 'ate' their delicious treats. They went back for

207

seconds and thirds. It would've been adorable to watch if it didn't make me want to sob.

Anthony is light-years away from any of this. Interactive play. Imaginative play.

Friends.

All these things that other kids do spontaneously and naturally would have to be broken down into discrete behavioral pieces, and Carlin would have to work on each one with Anthony for hours and weeks and months before he might learn to pretend that a wood chip is vanilla ice cream. But it wouldn't be for the pure, innocent joy of it. He'd do it to get the Pringles he wants or to get Carlin to stop bothering him about it, to be finally left alone already. Because that's what he wants. To be alone. That's what gives him joy.

All Anthony wants to do at the playground is swing. But I see these other kids playing, and my heart wants more, and I get bored just standing there, pushing him over and over. I stopped his swing a bunch of times and asked him if he'd like to try the slide, if he'd like to play with the other kids, if he'd like to go over to the sandbox. He loves sand. But nothing rivals the swing, and he wouldn't budge. So we stayed there, swinging. I felt self-conscious and defeated.

Why can't I just be happy that he's happy alone on the swing? Why do I have to insist that happiness is doing what I want him to do? Because the world is full of people,

Anthony, not swings, and I want you to be happy in the world and not just happy in a swing. Is that too much to want? Is it selfish to want this?

Because the other kids at the playground can play independently and don't stay on the swings all morning, the other moms were free to sit together at one of the picnic tables. I pushed Anthony on the swing and listened at a distance to these moms chatting and laughing, having a grand old time. I felt like I was in eighth grade all over again — the awkward outsider, not part of the 'in' crowd.

They say 1 in 110 kids have autism now, but I don't know any other mothers in town with an autistic kid. Where are they? I've been out of work entirely now for six months, and I miss adult company. Conversation. Morning meetings.

Friends.

Carlin and Rhia are over every day, but they're Anthony's therapists. They don't count. And David acts like I'm asking him to re-shingle the roof every time I ask him the simplest question. I know I'm probably being sensitive because I've got my period, but I felt how lonely I am while I watched this group of moms. A group I won't ever be a part of. Like the popular girls in eighth grade with their perfect Farrah Fawcett hair and their fancy Jordache jeans. I hated them and wished I could be one of them in the same breath.

We'd been at the swing for over an hour when the moms called their kids over to the picnic table for lunch. The kids came. The moms opened pretty, insulated lunch bags and passed out sandwiches, yogurts, orange slices, string cheese, Goldfish crackers, and juice boxes.

A fun picnic. Not for us.

It was time to go. I gave Anthony a 1, 2, 3 warning, which sometimes helps, but not today. He gave a quick screech and flapped his hands when I stopped the swing, but when I didn't immediately return to pushing and instead began lifting him out, he lost it. His body went stiff and his screeching escalated to an I'm-being-murdered decibel. I had to use all my strength to pry him out of the bucket, to carry him, forty-five pounds of dead weight screaming in agony over being separated from a swing that he'd just spent the last hour and a half on, to not look back at the moms at the picnic table who I'm sure were looking at me the whole time, judging me, thinking, Thank God I'm not HER. Just like eighth grade.

I got Anthony in the car and turned on Barney as fast as humanly possible, and he calmed down. God bless Barney. Then, I stupidly decided to stop at CVS on the way home. I just got my period this morning, and I only had a couple of tampons left. For any of those other mothers at the playground, it wouldn't be a stupid idea to go to CVS when you have your period and only two tampons left. They'd breeze in, zip out, no problem. They might not even remember the quick errand by the end of the day. But for me, this was a colossally stupid idea. And I'll never forget it.

We always go straight home after the playground, and I always take Center Street to Pigeon Lane, but CVS is the other way. I hoped Anthony wouldn't notice. I hoped it wouldn't matter. It would only take a few minutes. *Stupid girl.*

As soon as I went left instead of right out of the parking lot, Anthony started screeching. When I kept going, he started kicking. I should've turned around then and there, but I kept going. He started screaming, whipping his head and flapping his hands, fighting against the buckle of his car seat as if he were being repeatedly stabbed with a knife.

Fueled by sheer and again stupid determination to run a simple and necessary errand, I got all the way to CVS, but there was no way I could go in. There's no way I could physically carry him given the state he was in; I would never leave him alone in the car, and there was absolutely no way to reach him with a rational explanation.

Mommy needs tampons, sweetie. Please stop freaking out. We'll be home in five minutes.

So I drove home.

By dinner, I was out of tampons. But I wasn't going to risk another meltdown in the car, so I had to wait for David so I could go to CVS alone. I made a homemade pad out of wadded toilet paper to hold me over until he got home. But David was forty-five minutes late (with no phone call), and the wad of TP was no match for my period, and I bled through onto my favorite skirt.

Eighth grade all over again. At least my accident happened at home and not at the playground in front of the 'in' moms.

It occurred to me while I was driving to CVS for the second time today that I've spent my whole life since eighth grade terrified of being the outsider, doing almost anything to fit in, always desperate to belong. Anthony doesn't worry about any of this. He doesn't mind being by himself. He enjoys it. He doesn't care what people think. He's not going to get caught up in wanting expensive designer clothes or the latest $100 sneakers. He's not going to drink or smoke pot to look cool. He's not going to do anything because everyone else is doing it.

He doesn't care what other people wear or think or do. He likes what he likes. He does what he wants to do. Until I say it's time to go and rip him out of his swing.

I thought about those kids playing Follow the Leader today. Anthony will never be a follower. He won't be the leader though either. This thought would normally shred my heart and make me weepy, but as I drove to CVS, I felt unexpectedly at peace.

He's simply not playing that game.

22

I am swinging on the swing at the playground. I love swinging. Swinging puts me in my body.

I usually know I have hands, but if anything interesting is going on, if I'm counting or thinking or watching TV, my body disappears from me. I don't have a voice, so people sometimes treat me like I also don't have a body, like I don't exist in the world. And because most of the time I'm not aware of my body, I think they might be right. Maybe I don't really exist in the world.

Swinging makes me exist in the world.

My thinking often gets stuck repeating. If I find a thought I like, I think it again so I can keep enjoying it. These kinds of thoughts are like Pringles. Pringles are so yummy, I never want to eat just one. I want to eat another and another and another. If I find a yummy thought, I want to think it again and again and again. But if I think it too much, then I don't just want to think it. I NEED to think it because I'm afraid if I don't always keep it with me, I might lose it forever. So my thinking gets stuck a lot on the same idea again and again and again. And when this happens, nothing else exists.

The other day I got stuck on Three Blind Mice. I said these three words inside my head, loving them for a whole morning. Nothing else existed. Not even me. I became those three words. Three Blind Mice.

But I don't get stuck on Three Blind Mice right now because I'm swinging. When I swing, I am no longer my repeating thoughts. When I swing, I am a repeating body. I am moving through air, forward and down and up, backward and down and up, forward and down and up, backward and down and up. I am Anthony's body, repeating this perfect rhythm. I swing, and I am here!

I am forward and down and up, backward and down and up, feeling the cool air tickle my face. My face is smiling. My face is real.

Then my mother stops the swing and says something about going over to the sandbox. I flap my hands and make a noise to let her know that I don't like her idea. I don't want to get off the swing. I flap and make a noise because my voice won't say the word NO.

My mother understands me and starts the swing moving again.

I love sand. I love to scoop up as much as my hands can hold, raise my hands high, and let the sand spill down. I love the feel of the sand moving through my fingers, how it drizzles and sparkles in the air like music as it falls. It's almost as good as water.

But sand in a playground sandbox is not like sand at the beach. Sand in a playground sandbox is always too close to other kids. When I play with sand in a playground sandbox, another mother will tell me I can't play with the sand. She'll say, *Please stop doing that, the sand is blowing into people's eyes*. And my mother will take me out of the sandbox because I won't stop doing that, and I also don't know how to *share the sand*.

My mother stops me again and wants me to go over to the slide. I make a noise and flap my hands, and she starts the swing moving again. Forward and down and up, backward and down and up.

I don't like the slide. Sometimes kids will walk up the slide on their feet instead of sliding down the slide on their bottoms, and that is breaking the rules. If I'm at the top of the slide and another kid starts climbing up the slide, then I don't know what to do. I can't slide down because the kid is in the way, but I can't climb back DOWN the steps because the slide steps are for climbing UP. That is the rule. So on the slide, I might have no solution to my problem, and I don't want that.

And out on the playground, a kid might hit me or push me or ask me a question. The mothers always ask me a question, invading me with their eyes and an UP sound at the end of their voices. *What is your name?* But my voice doesn't work, so I can't even tell them that I don't want to answer their questions.

On the swing, I feel protected from all of this. No one can touch me, no one wants me to say my name, and no one is telling me not to play with sand. I only want to swing.

My mother stops the swing again, but this time she doesn't say anything about the playground. She starts taking me out. I make a loud noise and flap my hands, letting her know that this is not okay with me. She keeps taking me out.

NO! More swinging! I'm not done. I want to stay in the swing! I want to stay in my body! NO! I want to exist in the world! I need to keep my body repeating or I might lose my body forever. I might be gone forever!

I scream really loud, trying to show my mother that I need to keep swinging or I might die, but for some reason, she doesn't understand what I'm showing her. I go stiff, trying to keep my body in the swing, but she's too strong and she doesn't understand, and she grabs my body away. I squeeze my eyes shut so I won't see my body leaving the swing. I scream even louder so everything about my stolen body and the swing disappears, and only the sound of my screaming exists.

The next thing I know, I'm not outside anymore. I'm in the car, watching Barney. I'm watching Barney and his friends, and they're doing what I know they should be doing. I stop screaming. I'm not dead because I'm watching Barney. I'm okay.

But then I'm not okay. The car is going the WRONG WAY. The way the car is going is not the way home. The way home is by three white houses, then one brick house, then a street, then one yellow house and two white houses, then a red light/green light. Then church, the trees, one brown house, one white house, one gray house with peeling paint, then Pigeon Lane, the street that HOME is on.

But we did not go this way. This way is a sign with a picture of a girl on it, then a brown house, a white house, a blue house, then a street, a building, a parking lot, a red light. This is not the way HOME. We ALWAYS go HOME after the playground, and this way does not match the map in my head that shows the way home.

I don't know where we're going, but we're not going home. I am not going home to have three chicken nuggets with ketchup on my blue plate with juice in my Barney cup for lunch at the kitchen table. I'm not going to see Danyel after lunch because Danyel comes to my home, and I will not be home. I will be somewhere else.

Maybe we are lost, and maybe I will never see my

home again. The rule is we ALWAYS go HOME after the playground, and this is breaking the rule. If this rule can break, then anything can break. Maybe the world is breaking.

I am screaming. I want to go HOME. I want to get out of this car that is going the wrong way, but I am trapped in this seat. I am screaming, filling with hot, scary liquid. The hot, scary liquid keeps filling me, until I'm too full and burning on the inside. I shake my hands to spill some of the hot, scary liquid out through my fingers, but the hot, scary liquid keeps filling me, too huge and hot and fast for my fingers to empty.

I close my eyes so I don't have to see the wrong houses and buildings and streets. I'm screaming as loud as I can so I can become the sound of my scream and not a boy trapped in a car seat who is no longer swinging but going very fast in the wrong direction.

When I open my eyes, I realize I'm no longer screaming. I'm lying under my Barney blanket in my bed. I see the tree outside the window, my box of rocks, the calendar on the wall. I know this is good because this means I am home, and this also means that the world didn't break, but I don't feel good yet. I feel sweaty and tired, and I still feel too much hot, scary liquid bubbling and sloshing around inside that needs to leak out to make room for feeling good.

I lie in bed and wonder how we got home. There must be a different way. I wonder why we went a different way.

Today is Monday. It is sunny and warm. I am wearing brown pants and a red shirt. Maybe on sunny, warm Mondays when I wear brown pants and a red shirt, after my mother says I'm done swinging at the playground, we go a different way home. Maybe on sunny, warm Mondays when I wear brown pants and a red shirt and we leave the playground to go home, we go by the sign with a picture of a girl on it, then a brown house, then a white house, a blue house, a street, a building, a parking lot, and a red light. Maybe this is a new rule.

I'm hungry now. I go downstairs with both feet on all twelve steps and into the kitchen. My three chicken nuggets with ketchup on my blue plate, my Barney cup with juice, my fork, and white napkin are all on the table for lunch, just like they always are. My mother isn't sitting at the table, but I feel her nearby. I flap my hands and jump and let out one of my happy sounds, getting rid of the last drops of the hot, scary liquid inside me.

I sit down and eat my lunch. I feel good. But then I have a thought I don't like. I didn't know there were a NUMBER of ways home from the playground. Now there are TWO ways to come home from the playground. I don't like that number two. Two is in the middle of things. Two is unfinished. Two is in between, and I don't like in between. I wish there were THREE ways to come home from the playground.

The first way, which is the old way, goes by three white houses, then one brick house, then a street, then one yellow house and two white houses, then a red light/green light. Then church, the trees, one brown house, one white house, one gray house with the peeling paint, then Pigeon Lane. The second way, the new way we go on warm, sunny Mondays when I wear brown pants and a red shirt, is by the sign with a picture of a girl on it, then a brown house, then a white house, a blue house, a street, a building, a parking lot, and a red light, and some other stuff I didn't see before Pigeon Lane because I had my eyes shut.

There has to be one more way. There have to be THREE ways on the map from the playground to home. But what if there are only two ways, and that is it? What if we are stuck with two?

I feel the hot, scary liquid rushing at me again, but I see it coming this time. I shut the door on it before it can even touch my toes, before it has the chance to flood me.

Three Blind Mice. Three Blind Mice. Three Blind Mice.

Three Blind Mice. Three Blind Mice. Three Blind Mice.

Three Blind Mice. Three Blind Mice. Three Blind Mice.

23

After finishing another chapter, Beth left the library early and is now sitting on a couch in Dr. Campbell's office, which is really the living room in Dr. Campbell's house, wishing she'd waited in the car. She's on time, and Jimmy's late, and she feels unbearably self-conscious sitting alone on a marriage counselor's couch with nothing to say.

And the couch isn't helping anything. When she sat down, she sank deep and back into the cushion, her knees forced apart and up, her feet lifted off the ground. She tried to reposition herself without looking as if anything was wrong, but the more she wiggled, the deeper she sank. Dr. Campbell's couch is quicksand.

Dr. Campbell is sitting opposite her in a sturdy leather chair, sipping his coffee, studying her, saying nothing. Maybe this is some kind of psychological test. He told her to 'have a seat' and waved her over here. Maybe he's judging what type of person she is based on how she reacts to being swallowed by a couch cushion. Does continuing to sit like this mean she's an easygoing, well-adjusted woman, or does it mean she's a doormat who will silently endure anything? Should she politely ask for a different seat?

She decides to keep quiet. She waggles her feet in the air as if to the beat of a playful melody and browses the room, trying to act normal.

Dr. Campbell has long, wavy, gray hair, glasses, and a beard. He'd look like Santa, but he's rail thin. He's wearing a gold wedding band. That's good. A marriage counselor should be married. It's always bugged her that the girls' pediatrician has no children. Textbooks and degrees from expensive universities are great, but for her money, there's no better school than real life.

He's drinking coffee from a large, white Starbucks mug. This interests her. She's never seen a Starbucks. She left New York City just before the first one there opened. She only knows they exist because she's been stopped many times over the years by tourists asking her, *Can you tell me where the Starbucks is?* She'll never forget the look on the man's face when, that first time, she replied, *What's Starbucks?* As if he were talking to a woman who'd just been released from an insane asylum. Now she simply says, *There aren't any here*, and she points their astonished faces to The Bean.

She wonders where Dr. Campbell got the mug. He must travel off-island. She wonders where he goes — Boston, New York, exotic parts of the world where they have Starbucks coffee.

Despite there being no bookshelves in the room, books and magazines are everywhere, piled in teetering towers as tall as Beth up against the walls, on either side of Dr. Campbell's chair, on random spots in the middle of the floor. It's a library constructed by Dr. Seuss. Several towers look as if they're one magazine or book shy of collapsing, like a book

221

version of the game Jenga just before someone loses.

The white walls are bare but for one picture, an elaborate family tree drawn in calligraphy on tea-colored paper meant to look old. As she traces the branches, she realizes that it is Dr. Campbell's family tree and that, if the tree is true, he's a direct descendant of Edward Starbuck, one of the original 1659 settlers of Nantucket. She's impressed and surprised that she didn't know this about him.

Island lineage carries a lot of status here. Jimmy's lived here for twenty-one years, and she's been here for fifteen, but they'll both always be considered 'wash-ashores.' Outsiders. Peasant people. Their children were born here, so Sophie, Jessica, and Gracie are natives, but only first generation. Insiders, but direct descendants of peasant outsiders. Dr. Campbell is a native whose ancestors go all the way back. On Nantucket, Dr. Campbell is royalty. It's an understated royalty, without the paparazzi or a castle or pomp and circumstance or even any real wealth, but it's recognized. It's there.

She wonders if the Starbucks coffee store has anything to do with the Starbuck families of Nantucket. Probably not, else the island would surely have one. She doesn't ask.

By far the most interesting thing in the room is the falcon in the enormous cage next to the fireplace behind Dr. Campbell. The bird is about the size of a small hawk with dark gray wings, a white belly flecked with gray, and gray feathers that wrap around its creepy black eyes like the mask of a villain. One of its wings looks as if it might be mangled, broken. The falcon is perched on a piece of driftwood, almost motionless, staring at Beth. It looks menacing, like it wants to peck her eyes out.

'That's Oscar. Don't worry, he's domesticated. He won't bother us,' says Dr. Campbell.

Beth nods, bothered.

The doorbell rings. Thank God. Dr. Campbell gets up and lets Jimmy in.

'This is for the bird,' says Jimmy, handing Dr. Campbell a black trash bag.

Dr. Campbell peeks into the bag and smiles. 'Wonderful. Have a seat. I'll be back in a minute.'

Nantucket locals love to barter. Beth and Jimmy used to pay for car repairs with scallops. Jill's husband, Mickey, does construction work in exchange for dental work. Dr. Campbell accepts roadkill as a copay.

Jimmy sits on the opposite end of the couch, an empty cushion between him and Beth. He sinks just like Beth did, but he doesn't look nearly as uncomfortable as she feels. His feet still reach the ground.

'You're late,' she whispers.

'I had a hard time finding something.'

'What was in the bag?'

'Squirrel.'

'Ack. Gross. Why didn't you just get some pet food at the grocery store?'

'Because the whole point is to save twenty bucks. Kinda defeats the purpose if I go *buy* him food.'

'Where did you find the squirrel?'

'Milestone Road.'

'Did you wash your hands?'

Before Jimmy can answer, Dr. Campbell returns with what she can only assume from the smell is dead squirrel, opens the birdcage for a moment, latches it shut (she's careful to notice), then settles back into his leather chair. He slaps his thighs and smiles.

Is anyone going to wash his hands?

'Let's begin,' says Dr. Campbell. 'Why are we here?'

No one answers. Beth and Jimmy sit, comfortable in their respective, familiar silences, uncomfortable in their respective, sunken seats. Beth looks over at Jimmy, who is staring into his germy, roadkill-covered hands. She looks over Dr. Campbell's shoulder at Oscar, who has a bit of squirrel slime hanging from his yellow beak, his black, predatory eyes still sizing her up.

'Jimmy,' says Dr. Campbell. 'Let's start with you.'

'Well, ah, we're separated. We've been married fourteen years, and we're separated, and we're trying to get back together.'

Jimmy clasps his hands and waits. That's it. That's his summary.

Get him, Oscar. Gouge his eyes out.

'We're separated because he *cheated* on me, and I don't know if I want to get back together.'

'Okay,' says Dr. Campbell, not at all visibly outraged or moved to her side, as Beth would've hoped. 'Jimmy, why did you cheat on Beth?'

Jimmy fidgets and sinks a little deeper into his

cushion. A black cat with white paws struts into the room, brushes against Beth's dangling feet as it walks by, and curls up in a sunny spot on the floor by one of the windows, just outside the shadow of one of the book towers. Jimmy is allergic to cats.

'I dunno.'

'Beth, why do you think he cheated on you?'

Salt is too sexy, Angela is too sexy, I'm not sexy enough, he isn't attracted to me anymore, he doesn't love me anymore, he's a jerk, he's a liar, he's a cheater, he's a man. 'I'd really like to hear Jimmy's answer.'

Beth and Dr. Campbell look at Jimmy and wait. Another cat, this one gray, runs into the room and chases the black cat off its sunny spot on the floor. They both disappear behind the couch. Oscar chirps and flaps its one good wing against the cage. Jimmy rubs his nose and clears his throat.

'Look, I know I was wrong. I'm the bad guy here, and I'm really sorry. I was hoping we could put it behind us and start over. Wouldn't rehashing all this stuff just hurt Beth all over again?'

'Rehashing would mean that we've already hashed it. We haven't talked about this at all,' says Beth.

'Beth, have you forgiven Jimmy?'

'No.'

'Are you ready to put his infidelity behind you and start over?'

'No.'

'If you're going to get back together, it's

important for both of you to understand why this happened and to make some sort of peace with it. If you stay unconscious to why this happened and get back together, it'll likely happen again. So you're going to have to risk talking about some things that are uncomfortable and a little painful for both of you, yes?'

The phone rings somewhere in Dr. Campbell's house. Dr. Campbell sips his coffee as if he doesn't hear it. The three of them sit in silence. The phone stops ringing. The three of them sit in silence.

'She was always unhappy with me. I can't remember the last time I came home and she was happy to see me.'

'You get home at two a.m.! I'm asleep, Jimmy. I'm sorry I don't wake up and throw on a smile and something pretty and greet you at the door with slippers and a cigar.'

'Even before the bartending job, you hated having me around.'

'You weren't working. I hated you not working. You were miserable, moping around the house, making messes for me to clean up all day, like the house was your hotel, and I was housekeeping.'

'Everything in that house has to be exactly how she likes it. Everything has to be perfect. I'm not perfect, Beth. No guy is.'

'Not looking for perfect, Jimmy. Something in between miserable cheating bastard and perfect would be great.'

He says nothing. She folds her arms over her chest and waggles her foot, satisfied to have delivered the last word there.

'Okay, Jimmy. Let's get back to the question,' says Dr. Campbell, redirecting the two the way a parent might talk to a pair of preschoolers. 'You felt unwanted and unhappy. Did you talk to Beth about how you were feeling?'

'No, but it was obvious.'

'Maybe, maybe not. By not telling her, you didn't give her the chance to help you or change anything. You have to communicate what you need, open yourself, give Beth the opportunity to understand what's really going on with you. Unfortunately, we humans can't read minds.'

Jimmy nods.

'Beth, were you unhappy with Jimmy?'

'Before I found out he was cheating?'

'Yes.'

'Well, yeah, anyone would've been. After he stopped scalloping, he was out of work. He wasn't fun to be around.'

'You weren't exactly supportive,' says Jimmy.

'What does that mean? How wasn't I supportive?'

'Everyone we saw, she had to talk about me being a bum.'

'I never said that. I only mentioned it to people so they'd know to call you if anyone had any work.'

'And how about you? I didn't see you out looking for a job to help us.'

'I checked all the papers. None of them had any positions open. And I did work. Remember I did caretaking for those summerhouses?'

'That was like a couple hundred dollars a

227

month, that wasn't a real job.'

'What am I supposed to do here, Jimmy? I quit my *life* fifteen years ago to marry you and have these kids and live on this godforsaken island. I was supposed to go to school and become a writer.'

'I never stopped you from writing.'

When Gracie was a baby and Jessica and Sophie were preschoolers, Beth could barely manage to take a shower, never mind write anything creative. This was probably when all of her essays and short stories and writing notebooks went into the attic. She didn't have the time or space. But the girls got older and more independent. They went to school, and Beth had plenty of time for showers. She had plenty of time and space to write again, but she didn't. Something stopped her, but it wasn't Jimmy.

'Well, I'm writing now,' she says, like it's a threat.

'Do you think it's my life's dream to be a bartender?'

'You love it.'

'I didn't at first. And I'd still rather be on a boat.'

'And I'd rather have a husband who wasn't screwing the hostess.'

Her voice is now hollow and shaken with anger. She blinks back tears. She hates that she always cries when she's angry, as if her emotional wiring is crossed. Her heart is pounding to support her anger, her red-hot face feels her anger, and her mind understands the reasons for

228

her anger, but her eyes take in all this information and conclude, *She's sad. Make tears.* It's infuriating.

'I'm sorry,' says Jimmy.

'You should be.'

'Is the affair over now?' asks Dr. Campbell.

'Yes. She wanted me to get a divorce and marry her, but that was never going to happen. The whole thing was a huge mistake. It's over, I promise, and it'll never happen again. Beth, I don't want to lose you.'

'Beth, do you believe him?'

Beth thinks. She doesn't know what to think. She'd like to think that he leaves Salt alone now, that he goes straight to his friend Harry's apartment, sleeps alone in Harry's extra bedroom until noon, spends the afternoon feeling bad about what he's done, then goes to work again.

But *she's* at Salt. Beth thinks about the two of them there. She imagines a smile, a laugh, a touch, *her* hand on his arm, a kiss. Those pictures in Beth's head are easier to envision, more vivid and real than imagining Jimmy alone in some apartment she's never seen. She pictures Angela's necklace dangling between her big boobs and breathes in a powerful whiff of dead squirrel and something else. Cat pee? She feels physically sick.

'I don't know what to believe. They spend every night together.'

'We don't 'spend' the night together. We work at the same place.'

'Fine. She works where he bartends. I don't

229

know if I can trust him again.'

'I promise, it's over.'

'Yeah, well, clearly you don't always keep your promises.'

Dr. Campbell lowers his Starbucks mug and cocks his head. Everyone waits.

'Did you hear that?'

Beth shakes her head. Jimmy says nothing.

'Listen,' Dr. Campbell says.

Beth hears Jimmy sniffling and a car drive by outside.

'Excuse me, I'll be back in a second,' says Dr. Campbell, and he rushes out of the room.

Beth and Jimmy sit in silence, staring straight ahead, expecting Dr. Campbell to return within a few seconds. When this doesn't happen, Jimmy starts to fidget. He clears his throat, much louder than he would if Dr. Campbell were still in the room. Beth picks at her cuticles. Jimmy checks his phone. She checks hers.

She didn't hear any noise. Maybe this is some kind of test, some kind of time-out for misbehaving couples. Maybe the 'listen' was meant for them.

Well, it's not working. They don't know how to talk to each other. They don't know how to listen. This is why they're here. In addition to feeling ridiculously wedged in Dr. Campbell's couch, stalked by a falcon, angry at Jimmy for betraying her, embarrassed that she cries when she's angry, and sick at the thought of Jimmy and Angela still seeing each other, she now feels abandoned and manipulated. This therapist doesn't know what he's doing.

Dr. Campbell doesn't come back, and the silence between Jimmy and her expands. Dr. Campbell is gone, and the silence develops, forming itself into an actual presence in the room as real and as predatory as the falcon. It has its own evil eyes, pursuing them, uncaged in Dr. Campbell's absence, licking its chops, waiting for the right moment to attack. The silence between Jimmy and her would like nothing more than to devour them, as it's been aiming to do for years.

Finally, after what seems like their entire session but was probably only a few minutes, Dr. Campbell returns to the room, sits in his leather chair, and sighs.

'My apologies. The dogs got out. Now, let's go over where we're at. Jimmy, you need to feel wanted and that you make Beth happy. Beth, you need to be able to trust that if Jimmy is feeling unhappy, he'll come and talk to you about it and that he'll never be unfaithful again. Yes? Does this sound fair?'

'I don't think it's fair to say that Jimmy's the only one who feels unwanted. He cheated on me. That's not exactly wanting me. I didn't go out and 'want' another man.'

'Yes. True. Okay, let's add that in. You both want to feel wanted, happy, secure, and loved, yes? Fair to say?'

'Yes,' says Beth.

'Yes,' says Jimmy.

'Then this is what we're going to work on,' says Dr. Campbell, slapping his thighs.

'But shouldn't those things come naturally if

231

you're right for each other?' asks Beth.

'Some of it does, and some of it requires communication and effort.'

Jimmy sneezes. Beth says, *Bless you*, in her head and offers Dr. Campbell a tight-lipped, timid smile.

'Okay,' says Dr. Campbell, checking his watch. 'Here's your homework. I want you each to get out four pieces of paper, one for *wanted*, one for *happy*, one for *secure*, and one for *loved*, and I want you to write down specific actions and words that you need to see and hear in order to feel each of these things. Come up with as many as you can. Don't hold anything back.'

'Uh, like, what do you mean?' asks Jimmy.

'Well, these four feelings are necessary to both of you, but they probably mean different things when actualized. For example, feeling loved to you might mean a hug and kiss from Beth every time you come home from work. It might mean cigars and slippers. It might mean sex. For Beth, it might mean the same things, probably not the cigar and slippers, but it also might mean something else. Love for Beth might show up as doing the laundry or taking her out to dinner.'

Beth nods.

'Love, happiness, security, feeling wanted — these are the basics, yes? And because they're so basic, people often assume that they should happen automatically. But what floats your boat might not float hers. We're all different. Unless you *communicate* the specific and quirky ways that make you feel loved and happy, your partner can miss the mark. And then we feel unloved and unhappy. Yes?'

Jimmy nods.

'Okay, that's it for today. Good work,' says Dr. Campbell.

Jimmy pops up like a boy who just heard the recess bell. He pays Dr. Campbell in cash for the session, minus the twenty dollars for the fresh roadkill, while Beth rocks herself up and out of her hole. Beth thanks Dr. Campbell and smiles with her hands in her pockets, and she and Jimmy walk out to the driveway.

'What did you think?' she asks once she's sure they're out of earshot.

'I think that guy is really odd.'

Beth laughs.

'He probably needs therapy more than we do,' Jimmy says, smiling.

'Really though?' she asks, needing something more from him than a laugh.

'Therapy's not really my thing.'

She nods.

'But it's worth it if it works, right?' he asks.

She nods.

'All right. I gotta go do my homework,' he says, smiling. 'See ya.'

'See ya,' she echoes.

She gets into her car and laughs, more a nervous release than over anything funny. That whole experience was odd. The living room, that couch, the roadkill copay, the falcon's black eyes, the cats, the 'noisy' dogs.

She thinks about her homework assignment as she drives back to the library, already itching to begin the next chapter. Wanted, happy, secure, loved. What does she need to feel wanted? What does she need to feel loved? What will Jimmy's four pages look like? What does the boy in her book need to feel these things?

Her mind wanders through their therapy session, replaying it as she drives.

Trust. Anger. Silence. Communication. The falcon. That couch. The smell. The cats and dogs.

Her thoughts then shift to the brown-eyed boy in the book she's writing, wandering through the chapters she's already written.

No spoken words. The blue sky. Repetition. His mother.

Wanted. Happiness. Security. Love.

Dr. Campbell might be odd, but he's also brilliant.

24

I am lining up some of my rocks in the living room. This line is made up of rocks that I've collected in the past week. It is a line of new rocks. The line stretches from the coffee table to the wall. It will be a line of 128 rocks when I am done. I'm picturing the line of 128 rocks in my head before I get to the wall, and I'm already excited.

This is why I stopped lining up plastic animals and dinosaurs. I never had enough. I could line them up by type or size or color or in order of what animal could get eaten by another or by who can run the fastest, but the line never stretched all the way from the coffee table to the wall. I always needed more animals and dinosaurs.

I had to wait for my mother or father to buy more plastic animals and dinosaurs from the store, but they never bought enough, and sometimes they wouldn't buy any at all. Even if I went to the store with them, and I begged them for more, they didn't always get me the animals and dinosaurs that I needed:

No. You have enough elephants. Not today. You don't need any more dinosaurs.

But they were wrong. I didn't have enough elephants and I did need more dinosaurs. And their *Nos* and *Not todays* would make me feel like exploding, to leave those animals and dinosaurs I needed at the store when I had lines of animals and dinosaurs at home that didn't even reach the wall.

So I decided to stop needing those animals and

dinosaurs. The rocks are much better. My mother takes me to the beach almost every day, and I can always find more of the rocks I need there. My mother can even forget to bring my green bucket and that's okay because I can fit twenty-one Big rocks in one pants pocket and forty-eight Small rocks in the other. And if it's cold, and I'm wearing a coat, I can fit twenty-seven Big rocks in one coat pocket and fifty-four Small rocks in the other.

My mother never says *No* or *Not today* at the beach. The rocks at the beach are free. I can collect and bring home as many rocks as I need.

There are rules for collecting rocks. They have to be mostly white and mostly smooth and mostly round. I am the judge of what is *mostly*.

Sometimes I collect a candy-corn-shaped rock, which really isn't round. It's really a triangle. But if it's very smooth and very white, I will collect it. If a rock is really good at being round, but it's a little too yellow or has a few bumps or cracks, I will collect it. My mother would call these *exceptions to the rule*, but I just call them part of the rule, and that makes it okay.

At home, I like to count them, organize them, and arrange them into lines that stretch across my bedroom floor, the living-room floor, the kitchen, or, if it's warm outside and not too cold or snowing or raining, the deck. The kitchen floor is difficult because of the tiles. I have to think and plan ahead to make sure the entire line will space out so no rocks fall into the grooves in between the tiles. Every rock has to be on a tile, and I can't break the line with a big space to jump over a groove, because then I've really made two lines and not one. And I don't like that number two.

The kitchen is also a difficult place to make my rock

lines because my mother is usually walking around in there, but I don't notice her until it's too late. She sometimes walks through my line of rocks and kicks some of them out of place, or she tells me to *Clean this up and get these rocks out of the way*, and in either case the line gets ruined. And if my rock line gets ruined, I get ruined. So I like to line up my rocks somewhere where they and I won't be disturbed or kicked or cleaned up or ruined.

Once I get to know my rocks, they can be lined up in all kinds of ways. They can go by size, from smaller than a pea (these are also usually my roundest and whitest) to the size of my hand (always oval). They can go by smoothness, from no cracks or bumps to cracked and bumpy. They can go by roundness, from perfect sphere through every egg and glob and candy corn to perfect oval.

They can line up by whiteness. People call my rocks *Anthony's white rocks*, but this isn't fair to call them Anthony's white rocks because it's not the whole truth. A few of my rocks are only white, but most of my rocks are mostly white, which means that there are other colors, like yellow and gray and pink, living inside. If you take the time to get close to them and really see them, you will understand that most of my rocks have more inside them than only white.

I was so excited the day I learned the names for the different mostly whites. On Sunday, August 22, my mother and father were getting ready to paint the wood around the windows and doors, and my mother spread out a bunch of paper tickets across the kitchen table. Each ticket had six rectangles on them, all different mostly whites! Just like my rocks! I was so thrilled to see all those mostly whites!

My mother saw my excitement about the colored rectangles on the tickets, so she pointed to each one and told me their names. Super White. Decorator's White (white with gray). White Dove (white with yellow). Atrium White (white with orange). Antique White (white with yellow and orange).

More yellows: Linen White. Navajo White. Cameo White. Ivory White. Seashell. Grays: Bone White. China White. Oxford White. Paper White. Cloud White. Dune White. Blues: Fanfare. Blue Veil. Pinks: White Opulence. Alabaster. White Zinfandel.

I spent the rest of August 22 in my Memory Room, and I memorized the names of all the mostly whites. This made me so happy because now I have names for the colors of my rocks. So I can line up all the Alabaster rocks. Or I can line up all the yellow-white rocks by name. White Dove comes first. Seashell comes last.

Today the sky is cloudy. I have made a line of Super White, Cloud White, and Dune White rocks to match the color of the clouds in the sky. The line begins with the smallest pebble rocks at the coffee table and ends with the biggest rocks at the wall. There are 128 rocks in the line. There are 11 Super White rocks, 78 Cloud White rocks, and 39 Dune White rocks; 36 are Small, 80 are Medium, and 12 are Big.

Eleven are Super White and Small, 0 are Super White and Medium, and 0 are Super White and Big. Twenty are Cloud White and Small, 50 are Cloud White and Medium, 8 are Cloud White and Big. Five are Dune White and Small, 30 are Dune White and Medium, and 4 are Dune White and Big.

I lie down with my head on the cold wooden floor at the corner of the coffee table and look down my line of rocks. It's so beautiful. My fingers fill with happy.

My mother sometimes looks at my rock lines and has something to say about them:

That one looks like the bones of a dinosaur tail.

That one looks like my pearl necklace.

That one could be a row of clouds in the sky.

I don't know why she says these things about my rock lines. They are rock lines. Sometimes I organize them according to a certain rule. Sometimes I make a line that is all oval or all White Dove (the color painted around our windows and doors) or all Medium. But they are always rock lines. And they are always beautiful.

My mother also says my rocks are very old and came from volcanoes. She says the energy from the ocean water is what made them so smooth. But I think she's making up a funny story because volcanoes make something called lava, which is orange, hot liquid that turns into rock that is black and not white. And I've taken some of the bumpy rocks into the sink and turned the water on them for a long time, and they're not any smoother. So I don't think volcanoes or water made these rocks. I think my mostly white rocks were just born this way.

I move from the corner of the coffee table to the middle of the line. I get down with my eyes on the ground again and look across my line of rocks. It's perfect. I smile and let my eyes go blurry, so the rocks go on forever.

But in the edges of forever, something is happening. Another rock line is forming. I rub my eyes because I think they might be tricking me, making another line of rocks inside my head and not really on the living-room floor. Then I notice a hand. The hand is adding more rocks. I know that hand. That's my mother's hand!

My mother's hand is adding more rocks in a straight line next to my line. Her line contains rocks that are Ivory White, Cameo White, and Linen White and are all Small and mostly round. Her hand stops. The line stops growing. My mother's hand is done. There are 21 rocks in this yellow-white, small, mostly round line.

As I am admiring this new line of rocks, I see my mother's nose and mouth and chin on the floor behind the rocks. I quick look and see my mother's eyes. I put them together and see my mother's face. My mother's face is on the ground just like mine.

Your line of rocks is beautiful, Mom! Does it make you calm and happy, too? Do you love lining up rocks, too?

I wish my voice weren't broken, so I could ask her. But then I look more closely at her mouth, and I see my mother's face is smiling, and I don't need a voice to know her answer.

25

It's the beginning of October, a new page on the calendar and the first real chilly day of fall, but the change in season, the shift from summer life to something markedly different, felt as if it happened a month ago. The summer families with school-age children evacuated the island in a mass exodus immediately after Labor Day. On that Monday holiday, the island was mobbed and bustling as usual, but by Tuesday afternoon, it was eerily empty and quiet, as if the island itself could be heard exhaling. Olivia can now relax again, go to Stop & Shop any day of the week, turn left without waiting several minutes, and walk on the beaches alone; but strangely, just as the influx of summer people had required a large and conscious adjustment, so did their abrupt absence.

A full month after Labor Day, Olivia still finds herself trapped in a funk. She enjoys solitude, prefers it even, but for some reason, when everyone left Nantucket in September, she felt abandoned, like she literally missed the boat. She has no more beach portraits scheduled. The pages of her calendar for October, November, and December are unmarked. She has plenty of photo editing still to do, work that should keep her busy for at least the next month, but she wakes up each morning feeling as if she has nothing to do. No routine. No purpose.

She thinks about Anthony all the time, experiencing vivid sensory flashes of him in unanticipated moments. She closes her eyes, and she sees the curl of his hair against his neck, his small hands and fingers that looked exactly like hers, his knobby shoulders, the peaceful stillness of his face asleep. She listens to the crickets in the evening, and she hears the sound of his bare feet running across the floor, the melody of his laugh, his *eeya-eeya-eeya*. She inhales the crisp fall air, and she smells his skin the way it smelled after a day in the sun or after a sudsy bath.

She's still trying to understand the why of it all, praying, still trying to listen for answers from God with her spirit, still completely unsure of how to do this. She feels like she's trying to smell with her eyes or hear with her nose, or even more impossible, like she's trying to cajole some part of her anatomy or being she's not even sure exists into becoming an antenna, a satellite dish capable of receiving wisdom from heaven. It feels unproductive and more than a little crazy.

Today is a good day though, a distraction from unanswered prayers and aimless solitude. Today she is the assistant photographer to Roger Kelly at a wedding at the Blue Oyster. Roger is *the* sought-after wedding photographer on island. His assistant had some kind of family emergency off-island that left Roger scrambling. Olivia shot the Morgan family beach portrait in July, and Mrs. Morgan is the bride's maid of honor's mother's best friend, and through this last-minute, word-of-mouth reference, Olivia got the job. It's a long day and doesn't pay much, barely

242

more than a portrait session, but she won't have to edit anything, and she's grateful to have something to do.

Roger has asked her to capture the more documentary-style, photojournalism shots that are trendy these days, while he makes sure to get the posed, more formal and traditional pictures. He's in charge of the Veggies, she's in charge of Dessert. She scrolls through some of the images already in her camera, pausing and nodding at her favorites. The father of the bride kissing his daughter's cheek. The bride laughing. The groom whispering in his bride's ear. The preschool-age flower girl lifting up the tulle of her dress to see her patent leather Mary Janes.

The ceremony took place on the Blue Oyster's modest, man-made beach overlooking the harbor, and the reception is now in full swing on the hotel's terrace. It's evening now, and the sky is lit with a bright moon and twinkling stars. A blazing fire in the stone fire pit and outdoor heaters positioned like lampposts among the tables keep the nippy night air from penetrating the edges of the elaborate white tent. Olivia shoots the moon over the harbor, the tea lights and glass bowls filled with cranberries on the white linen tablecloths, the bride's white-rose bouquet next to a glass of champagne.

The action is now taking place on the dance floor, but Olivia's attention is drawn to a boy sitting alone at his table for six. He looks to be seven or eight, he has long, surfer-shaggy, blond hair, and he's dressed in a white shirt, khakis, and boat shoes. He's adorable. His index fingers are plugged into his ears, his elbows jut out sideways, and he's rocking back and forth in his seat. Click, click, click. Olivia looks at the LCD display of her camera. His gaze is far-off, unfocused.

The band finishes playing 'Love Shack,' and the boy's mother returns to his table to check on him. She kisses the top of his head. Click. Click. Click. She returns to the dance floor. He continues rocking with his fingers in his ears.

The band is loud. People have to yell to talk. The singer's voice amplified over the microphone, the thumping bass, a hundred people yelling to be heard, the dancing, the lights, the smell of the fire — it's all too much. This little boy is fighting against an onslaught of stimuli, doing his best to block it all out, rocking to create his own stimulus to zone in on, a soothing back-and-forth rhythm, a cradle.

The father comes to the table and sits down next to his boy. Click. Click. Click. The father finishes his drink and stays for another song. The mother returns to the table, sweaty and happy. She says something to her boy. He rocks and doesn't look at her. She pulls the father by his hand. He smiles. Click. Click. They return to the dance floor.

Olivia feels her stomach tighten and realizes that she's been holding her breath. She exhales. She's been here. She's lived this. That sweet little boy is only going to be able to cope for so long. What is celebration to everyone else is misery to him. None of this is fun for him, and Olivia wishes that his parents had left him home with a babysitter or that they'd call it a night and leave early. But she also understands their desire to include him, to dress him up like any other boy invited to the wedding and bring him along, to risk one more song, to enjoy themselves, to be a whole family here together.

She and David eventually stopped going to weddings and birthdays and holiday parties with Anthony because it was easier and safer to leave him home than to risk what might happen in public. Autism and noisy parties do not mix well, and if this boy's parents stay too long, it's not going to end well. At some point, rocking in his seat with his fingers in his ears won't be enough, and his nervous system is going to freak out, unable to tolerate one more second of this madness. He'll either melt down or bolt. Fight or flight.

Olivia assumes his parents well know the dice they're rolling, and while she's holding her breath again, worried about their boy, she's also rooting for them, hoping they manage to get through at least one more dance as husband and wife before the fuse on this invisible time bomb detonates, before their entire world transforms from a lovely evening at a wedding reception to a harrowing escape mission. But for now, they dance, seemingly oblivious to the hissing fuse. Olivia checks her watch, knowing it's getting late.

The band changes the mood with a slow song. The boy's father gathers his wife into him, and she snuggles her head into the nook of his neck. The two sway back and forth, pivoting in a small circle, and although they're surrounded by a crowded dance floor, they appear totally focused on each other, on the singular rhythm they've created together, as if no one else exists but them. Click. Click. Click.

Olivia lowers her camera and observes the couple without the mask of her lens between them. A wave of emotion swells in her throat, and she swallows several times to push it back down.

David.

Why couldn't they do that? Why couldn't they hold on to each other and block out the world? Why couldn't they surrender to what they couldn't control? Why weren't they brave enough to celebrate a life that included autism? She wanted to, and she thinks she eventually got there, but it took her too long. Just as she was ready to dance, the music stopped playing.

She glances back over at the boy's table. He's gone. Panic floods her every cell, paralyzing her for a second, but then a powerful and well-trained instinct kicks in.

Where are the exits? She eyes the door to the hotel that leads to the parking lot. He wants to go home, and the car is how to get there. The car is familiar and safe. Or maybe they're staying at the hotel. Either way, he'd have to worm through the crowds of people going in and out to use the restrooms, milling around in the loud lobby, by the concierge and the front desk.

She looks the other way, away from the people and the tent and all the noise, down the lawn, to the windy path that leads to stairs, to the beach, to the harbor. To the water. If Anthony were here and bolted, that's where he'd go.

Olivia forgets everything and runs. Her heels sink and stick with each step into the soft earth beneath the Blue Oyster lawn, slowing her down. She kicks them off and races barefoot down the cold stone stairs, praying to God that he'll be there when she rounds the corner and sees the beach.

26

Beth is peeking out the kitchen window, watching Jimmy and the girls drive away, feeling left behind. It's late Saturday afternoon, and Jimmy popped by about an hour ago, said he had the night off, and offered to take the girls for a hike at Bartlett's Farm and then dinner. She hesitated to allow it at first, not because she had other burning plans for her and the girls, but because she wasn't included.

When in past months an unannounced Jimmy visit would've unnerved or angered her, today she quite enjoyed his company. He wiped his feet on the doormat before coming in the house, he changed the burned-out bulb in the overhead living-room light, he told her he'd line up the chimney sweep, and he asked the girls all kinds of questions about school. And he asked Beth lots of questions about autism and the book she's writing. He was considerate, useful, and sincerely engaged in conversation.

Before they left, he made a proud point of telling Beth that he'd finished Dr. Campbell's homework and looked more than a little crushed when she admitted she hadn't started hers yet. She needs to do the assignment. She knows she's been avoiding it. She's also been avoiding asking herself why she's avoiding it.

She finds a sheet of printer paper and sits down at the kitchen table. She draws a cross, dividing the paper into four squares, and writes one word at the top of each quadrant: *Wanted. Happy. Safe. Loved.* Her eyes go unfocused as she stares at the page. She taps her teeth with her pen and daydreams for several minutes. She snaps out of it and returns to the task. *Wanted. Happy. Safe. Loved.* Blank. Blank. Blank. Blank.

She sighs, folds the paper, and stuffs it into her pocket. She'll do it some other time. Later.

She's grateful this kind of writer's block is limited to her personal life and not to her novel, still untitled. She still goes to the library almost every day, excited every morning to be there. The story has been coming easily, and she's proud of what she's written so far, fully believing when she rereads her chapters that she's somehow able to capture the voice of this fictional boy with autism.

A pen still in her hand and scenes from her novel now running through her mind trigger an almost compulsive urge to write. She checks her watch. She looks out the kitchen window at the spot in the driveway where Jimmy's truck was parked a few minutes ago. With a sudden burst of intention, she gets up, grabs her keys and her bag, and leaves the house. Instead of doing her marriage-counseling homework or cleaning the bedrooms or crashing on the couch in front of HGTV for the rest of the evening while she waits for the girls to return, she's going to the library to write.

She bounds up the steps to the second floor, but then her heart sinks. Four people are sitting at her typically empty table. Eddy Antico from the Chamber of Commerce is sitting in her seat, and Pamela Vincent is reading aloud at the podium on the stage. Beth steps over to Mary Crawford at the reference desk.

'What's going on?' Beth whispers.

'It's the twenty-five-hour reading of *Moby-Dick*.'

'Really? What hour are they on?'

Mary looks up at the clock and counts to herself. 'Six hours, forty minutes. You want to read? We can fit you in pretty much anytime between four and six a.m.'

I'm sure you can!

Mary shows Beth the roster. Rose Driscoll, head of the garden club and at least seventy years old, is scheduled to read at 3:00 a.m. Mary Crawford is signed up at six.

'No, no thanks,' Beth says, trying not to laugh, unable to imagine why any sane person would actually plan to be at the library to read or listen to *Moby-Dick* at four in the morning, or at any time for that matter. Excitement on Nantucket during the off-season is a highly subjective experience.

Beth looks around the room, searching in resigned vain for a way to stay and write, wishing she didn't have to leave. She could try writing downstairs or at The Bean, or she could write at the kitchen table in her quiet house, but she's become more superstitious than a baseball player on a hitting streak about where she writes. She has to be in the library, sitting at the long table in the seat closest to the stage, facing the window. She knows her complete faith in this set of rigid conditions borders on diagnosable, and it can't really be true, but she believes in it. It is true. This is where she feels the inspiration. This is where Anthony's story comes to her. This is where the magic happens.

Reluctantly, she walks outside and zips her coat. She hesitates at her car door. She came all the way downtown and doesn't want to turn around and go home without accomplishing anything. What else could she do here? Maybe Georgia is at the Blue Oyster. Maybe she'd be up for a break and a drink at the hotel bar. A perfect plan.

She makes a brisk walk out of the four quick blocks, excited about seeing Georgia and a deep martini, but as she arrives at the edge of the Blue Oyster property, she spots a wedding ceremony in progress down on their fake little beach, and she stops walking, deflated. A wedding means Georgia is busy and won't be free for a drink. Now what? She's come all the way downtown and walked all the way over to the Blue Oyster.

She sees Georgia standing well behind the two neat rows of white folding chairs and decides to sneak over to her and at least say a discreet hello.

'Hey,' whispers Beth, now standing next to her friend.

'Hey!' whispers Georgia.

Georgia's face is flush with admiration and weepy joy. She dabs her eyes with a tissue. 'They wrote their own vows. I love it when they do that.'

Beth looks over at the bride and groom and strains to hear them. She can hear the groom's voice, but because he's facing the other way, she can't make out what he's saying. The bride's face is young and glowing. Beth wonders if her own face looked anything like that when she married Jimmy. She believes it did. She glowed on her wedding day. But sometime down the married road, she can't pinpoint exactly when, the glow disappeared. Jimmy's right. She hasn't been happy to see him in a long time. In bed, on the couch, at the kitchen table, walking through the front door — no glow. Can she get it back or is her Jimmy glow gone for good? Did she feel a little of that glow rekindled today?

She looks over at Georgia, who can't possibly decipher what the groom is saying, and she looks like she's glowing with his every word. But it doesn't take much for Georgia. She glows over Cotton commercials.

'I should go,' says Beth.

'Why? Stay. I'll be done soon, and then we can go get a drink.'

'Okay.' Beth smiles, pleased that her friend has read her mind.

The bride and groom kiss, and everyone claps.

'Come with me. I have to herd them over to the terrace.'

Georgia ushers the guests over to the tented terrace, where they are met with passed hors d'oeuvres, champagne, and live music. The bride and groom are still at the beach, posing for the photographer. Beth and Georgia stand at the back of the terrace, behind the dance floor and the tables, near the door to the hotel.

'We just need to wait for the bride and groom.

Make sure they get settled over here before I can leave.'

'Okay.'

'Such a lovely ceremony, wasn't it?'

'Yeah. Seems like a million years ago that that was me and Jimmy.' A million years and yesterday.

'What's going on with you guys?'

'I don't know. We're seeing Dr. Campbell. I don't know though. What do you think I should do?' asks Beth, already sure of Georgia's answer.

'If you can forgive him, I'd take him back.'

'What? You've never taken any of them back!'

'I know, but I wish I did. I wish I knew how to love through all the messy stuff. I've never had that love-conquers-all kind of love. Wish I did, but I don't think it's in me. I can't love someone no matter what.'

Georgia has always wanted the fairy tale, the happily ever after. But so far, her princes haven't possessed the kind of character and stamina it takes to reach a proper storybook ending. Prince Charming doesn't go and sleep with the village tramp, he doesn't make a habit out of drinking twelve beers before noon, and he doesn't stop doting on his beloved. But even after four failed princes, Georgia still deep down believes marriage can be a Disney movie. If only she could find the right prince.

What does Beth believe in? Does she believe in Jimmy, that he'll never cheat on her again? Does she believe that she'll get her own happily-ever-after ending? Will Jimmy be there with her? Does she believe in love?

'I don't know if I can either.'

'But I never had any kids to consider, so it was easier for me to end things and not look back.'

'I can't stay with him just for the girls, right?'

'No, you shouldn't. But I think it would make me hang around longer to work on things.'

'So you'd take Jimmy back?' questions Beth, not believing this for one second.

Georgia tilts her head as if she were giving this real consideration but quickly gives up the charade and laughs at herself. 'No, I couldn't do it. I'd be done. But I'm not saying I'm right.'

Beth could argue that restoring her marriage is the right thing to do. Forgive Jimmy, take him back, and everything can go back to normal. Forgiveness is good. Normal would be bliss. The girls would get their father back. They deserve to live with their father. It feels like the kind of selfless decision a good mother would make for her children. It would be big of her.

For the sake of the children, take him back!

But the argument against taking him back is ranting with just as much volume and confidence, heated words scratching against some thin inner membrane of her wounded heart, barely containing her spite and self-loathing.

Are you kidding me? If you don't divorce his ass, you're a pathetic, spineless martyr with no self-esteem!

She imagines Pamela Vincent whispering to Debbie McMahon in the Atheneum while Eddy Antico reads the seventh hour of *Moby-Dick*. *Did you hear Beth and Jimmy Ellis got back*

254

together after he cheated on her for a year? What a fool!

She imagines Jill and Courtney gossiping over goblets of iced chardonnay. *Those poor girls, to have to grow up without their father. Beth didn't even give him a chance. We're all human. We all make mistakes.*

She worries that everyone she knows will judge her either way. She shakes her head and closes her eyes, trying to ignore all arguments about what she *should* do, what everyone else thinks, even her kids, to clear it all away and focus inward, to discover what is real and true for her in her own once-glowing heart. It's a simple question really.

Does she love Jimmy enough to take him back?

She opens her eyes. The bride and groom have made their grand entrance at the reception and are now dancing their first dance as husband and wife. The groom's face is tight and concentrated, and their movement together across the floor is hardly fluid, the obvious product of not quite enough dance lessons, but the effort, despite its being awkward, is sweet. Beth and Jimmy didn't even try to learn actual steps for their wedding. They just sort of waddled back and forth like teenagers at a school dance.

The bride is relaxed and beaming. Her clumsy groom probably took dance lessons with her, probably one night a week, and he probably loathed every second of it, but he did it. He did it because he loves her. He's willing to dance like a fool in front of a hundred people for his darling's happiness. Fast-forward ten years, and she'll be lucky if he's willing to replace the toilet paper or use a plate.

'I love a man who can dance,' says Georgia.

'He's not exactly Gene Kelly.'

'He's trying. I love it.'

The first dance is then followed by the other traditional dances — the bride with her father (he can't dance either), the groom with his mother, and then the groom with his grand-mother, which generates even more adoration from Georgia. If he hadn't just got hitched, she'd be all over him. The dance floor is now open to everyone. The five-piece brass band is festive and loud. Unable to hear each other without yelling, Beth and Georgia have stopped chatting. Georgia checks her watch. She snatches a glass from a tray of champagne flutes.

'Here, stay and have some champagne! I have to take care of one quick thing, and then we can go!'

'Okay!'

Beth leans against the wall, sips her champagne, and people-watches, self-conscious now that she's alone, keenly aware that she's wearing jeans and attending a wedding reception she wasn't invited to. She avoids eye contact with every stranger who walks past her on the way to the restrooms, hoping no one talks to her or asks her how she knows the bride and groom or, God forbid, asks her to dance.

She becomes interested in watching a young boy sitting alone at one of the front tables. He's blocking his ears and rocking in his seat. Autism.

She knows enough about autism now, from both the books she's read and the book she's writing, to recognize it anywhere. And like an obscure vocabulary word she'd never heard of, once learned, she sees it everywhere.

But her writing has done more than simply allow her to recognize it. When she notices a child with autism now, like this cute little boy sitting at the table, she feels a compassionate connection, a softness in her heart, like they're friends who share an intimate secret. Before she began writing her book, she would've looked at this boy and thought, *He seems odd. Something's wrong with that boy.* And then she would've intentionally looked away. Now she smiles as she watches him and thinks, *I know, it's way too loud in here. I want to get out of here, too.*

The boy's parents keep checking on him, but he's not paying them any attention. Good boy. He's smart. If he acknowledges their presence, if he listens to what they're saying, if he cracks open the door to receiving input from outside himself, it might swing wide-open, and then the trumpet and the trombone and the singing and a thousand other aggressive sounds would stampede into him along with the voices of his parents. And that would be disastrous.

He's rocking faster now. His eyes, although still mostly unfocused, have started glancing around. His defense mechanisms aren't doing the job. He's starting to come undone. She can feel it.

Just as she guessed he would, he hops off his

chair and bolts. He runs right out from under the tent and onto the lawn, into the night. Beth scans the dance floor and finds his parents in each other's arms, slow-dancing, oblivious.

Without thinking, Beth loses her champagne flute and runs after him. He's fast, scrambling down the stone path, back toward the beach where the wedding ceremony had been. She loses sight of him as she slows down on the stone steps, careful not to fall, but reassures herself as she keeps going that he'll be at the beach when she gets there and not gone. If he's not on the beach, he could be anywhere.

She reaches the sand, and there he is. He's up to his knees in the water. He dips his hands beneath the surface and then raises them overhead, creating a splash. He smiles and squeals, flapping his wet hands, spraying water from his fingertips. He throws his hands back into the glassy, calm water, creating an even bigger splash. He squeals and laughs. He repeats the process.

Beth stands with her hands on her hips, catching her breath, relieved the chase is over and the boy is safe, asking herself what the plan is now. She wishes she'd alerted his parents before she took off, but by now they've probably noticed he's missing. She'll simply stay with him until they come.

The boy is walking parallel to the shore and doesn't seem to want to go any farther out, any deeper than his knees. Good. Beth has no desire to plunge into the freezing ocean to save a drowning boy. He's unbothered by Beth, who is

258

now standing quite close to him, still delighting in his splashing hands, when Beth hears someone coming down the path. She turns around, expecting to see the boy's parents, but instead it's a woman. Beth knows her, but maybe because she was expecting someone else, she can't at first place who it is. Then she notices the serious camera in the woman's hand, and it registers. It's Olivia, her photographer.

Olivia runs straight to the water, her face pale with dread. But the boy is squealing and laughing. He's totally fine. Olivia stops at the water's edge and breathes hard with her hands on her hips, smiling as tears stream down her cheeks.

'Olivia.'

Olivia startles, placing her hand on her heart. 'My God, Beth, I didn't see you,' she says, wiping her eyes and face. 'Do you know his parents?'

'I know who they are, but I don't know them.'

'Same. Will you go find them while I wait here with him?' asks Olivia.

Beth agrees, but just as she turns around, his parents appear at the edge of the stone steps.

His mother, already barefoot, runs straight into the cold water, soaking the bottom of her black dress. 'Owen! You gotta stop taking off! We don't want to lose you!' She picks Owen up by his armpits and spins him, dragging his feet across the surface of the water, drawing circles around them. His face is pure joy.

Happiness.

Olivia aims her camera. Click. Click. Click.

'Thanks for looking after him,' says his father to Olivia and Beth. 'I thought for sure he'd be in the parking lot.'

'No problem,' says Beth.

The boy's father, Beth, and Olivia stand next to each other for the next many minutes in silent relief, watching the boy and his mother splash and spin and laugh together in the bright moonlight. Glowing.

Loved.

Click. Click. Click.

'There you are!'

Beth looks over her shoulder and sees Georgia waving and teetering in her heels on the last step of the stone stairs. Georgia slips out of her shoes and walks over to this small, unlikely gathering, visibly unable to piece together why they're all here. 'Is everyone okay?'

'Yup,' says the father, removing his shoes and rolling up his pants. 'We're all good now.'

Safe.

'Great,' says Georgia.

Probably dizzy, the mother has stopped spinning her boy and now hangs behind him as he splashes. The father joins them and holds his wife's hand.

Wanted.

Click. Click. Click.

Happiness. Loved. Safe. Wanted. Beth can identify these qualities, these necessary ingredients for a relationship that works, so readily among this family in front of her. She sees each one in this little boy with autism as easily as she sees the bright moon in the night sky, yet she still can't form a specific image of what these elements look like in her.

'I thought you ditched me,' says Georgia.

'Never. You ready to go?' asks Beth.

'Yeah, let's.'

Before Beth ascends the stone path, she looks back toward the harbor to say good-bye to Olivia, but she's squatting at the edge of the water, photographing the boy and his parents, and Beth doesn't want to interrupt her. Beth smiles, imagining how beautiful those pictures will be. She can't wait to see her own portraits. They should be ready soon. She meant to ask about them.

As they walk up the steps, Beth wonders what motivated Olivia to chase after the little boy. It was probably the concern any adult would have who notices a young child who takes off alone toward open water. But as she walks with Georgia across the lawn of the Blue Oyster, she remembers Olivia's panic-stricken eyes and the tears on her blanched face and wonders if it was something more.

She'll have to ask her when she sees her again.

27

Beth's been champing at the bit all morning, dying to get to the library, but she had too many household chores that couldn't be ignored, and now she's at Jessica's soccer game. Jimmy is there, too. Alone. They're both watching Jessica run up and down the field, standing separately but next to each other on the sideline in awkward silence.

'So how's your book coming?' asks Jimmy finally, still staring at the field.

'Good. It's coming along,' says Beth, similarly not averting her eyes from the game, but not because she's worried about missing a play.

'That's great. It's really great that you're writing again. I'm proud of you.'

'Thanks,' she says, unexpectedly flattered.

She turns to look at him. He's watching her now and not the game, smiling.

'I'd love to read it.'

Her face flushes hot, and she diverts her eyes down to her black shoes. She's been pouring her heart and soul into her writing, weaving everything she feels and knows and believes into this story. Jimmy's sudden and unsolicited interest in her book, in her, makes her happy. But the thought of Jimmy reading her heart and soul, of revealing herself so intimately and completely to him now, pokes at something inside her not yet ready to be touched. Trust.

She lifts her eyes to meet his and flashes a timid smile before forcing herself to focus on the girls on the field.

When the game ends, Jessica goes off with Jimmy, and Beth drives straight to the library. She walks up to the second floor and peeks through the doorway. Eddy Antico and Pamela Vincent are gone. No one is reading *Moby-Dick*, and no one is in her seat. She smiles and gets settled.

She dreamed about her book last night and woke with the next chapter fully formed, vividly detailed, waiting for her, like a gift. She was thrilled but then increasingly anxious every second that it lived only as knowledge likely to vaporize at any moment in her head and not as letters written down in ink, safe on a page. She opens her notebook, uncaps her pen, and writes as fast as she can to release the words before they vanish.

My one name is Anthony. When I was a smaller boy, I used to think I had two names: Anthony and YOU.

My mother and father would say things like:
Anthony, come here.
Do YOU want to go outside?
Do YOU want some juice?
Anthony, here's your juice.
Can YOU say TRUCK?
Anthony, say TRUCK.
Anthony, put your shoes on.
Go ahead, YOU do it.
YOU can do it.
Anthony, do it.
So it's easy to see the cause of my earlier

confusion. These nickname words — YOU, I, ME, WE, HE, SHE — they can still confuse me, but I'm mostly okay with them now even though I don't like them. Nickname words depend on the situation, and I've never liked things that depend on the situation.

This is why I like numbers. 6 + 3 = 9. Always. 6 + 3 Pringles or 6 + 3 doughnuts or 6 + 3 rocks in a line or 6 + 3 silver minivans in the parking lot. The answer is 9. Always.

But YOU can mean Anthony or my mother or my father or Danyel or a total stranger in the parking lot.

How are YOU?

YOU is my mother if my father is talking and my mother is there, but YOU is Danyel if my mother is talking and Danyel is there, but if both Danyel AND my father are there, then YOU could be my father or Danyel or BOTH of them. So the owner of YOU depends on who is talking and who is there to be spoken to. Like I said, YOU depends on the situation. YOU follows a Depends Rule, and this is not the kind of rule I like. I like Always Rules, rules that always stay the rule no matter where you are or who is talking.

Always Rules are perfect because they always follow something called cause and effect, and this makes me calm and happy. I used to think light switches were an Always Rule. If I flipped the switch up, the light turned on. If I flipped the switch down, the light turned off. Over and over and over. Always.

Until light switches turned into a Depends Rule. Last winter a big storm came, and the *power went out*, and I flipped all the light switches in the whole house up and down and up and down and nothing happened. The lights stayed off.

So light switches turn out not to be an Always Rule, the kind I like, but a Depends Rule. Flipping the switch up will turn the light on as long as the power hasn't been stolen by a big storm. Light switches depend on the weather. I stopped loving light switches after that big storm last winter.

Eyes are also a Depends Rule. Eyes can be happy or angry or interested or sad, they can be awake or asleep, bright or tired, they can stare or move away. Sometimes eyes cry. Eyes are always something different depending on the situation. Some days when my mother and I go to the grocery store, her eyes are bright, but other times at the grocery store, her eyes are tired. And sometimes at church, her eyes are happy, but other times at church, her eyes cry. So even the same situation can't tell me what eyes are going to do. This is why I don't like eyes.

Things that are Depends Rules like YOU and light switches and eyes are bad because they can't be trusted. I can't know for sure what is going to happen next with YOU and light switches and eyes, which means that ANY-THING can happen next, and anything is too much. I end up wandering the halls in my brain, not knowing what room to go in, scared and confused. I usually end up hiding in the corner of the Horror Room if I'm dealing with a Depends Rule.

So I avoid Depends Rules like eyes and light switches. But there was no avoiding the nicknames like YOU. Nicknames like YOU are everywhere, so I had to learn to accept YOU.

But mostly, I only like Always Rules. I like cause and effect. Something makes something else happen, and I know what's going to happen before it happens because it always happens. This makes me feel good.

When something is a Depends Rule, anything can happen, and this makes me scared. It makes me scream and cry.

I have a thing called AUTISM. My mother and father don't understand the cause of my autism, and this makes them scared. It makes them scream and cry. They must like cause and effect and Always Rules like I do.

Being a boy doesn't mean having autism because most boys don't have autism and some girls do. Getting shots doesn't mean having autism because lots of boys and girls get shots and they don't have autism. So having autism must follow a Depends Rule. Autism is not like math. Autism is like YOU and depends on the situation. So I avoid thinking about autism because I don't like Depends Rules.

All this thinking about YOU and light switches and eyes and autism has me wandering the halls. I'm going into my Counting Room now.

I'm counting the tiles on the kitchen floor. 180. There are always 180 tiles on the kitchen floor. Always.

Always makes me feel good.

Always makes me feel safe.

Always.

28

Olivia sits in her living-room chair with one of her journals in her lap and stares out the window at the trees in her yard. She doesn't like the trees here, the scrub pines and the scrub oaks. They're too skinny and too short. They appear brittle and emaciated to her, as if they're undernourished or sick. But that's just the way they are. The trees back in her old yard in Hingham are real trees — huge, several-hundred-year-old oaks with trunks thick enough to hide behind and branches that spread across the sky. This time of year, the leaves would be red and gold and breathtaking. She sighs as she looks out the window at the rusty brown leaves on the tiny scrub oaks in her yard, daydreaming of fall in Hingham.

October 1, 2006

I think I want to stop Anthony's ABA therapy. I know it's helped with a lot of things. His attention span is better. They've used it to teach him how to stay in his seat, do puzzles, stack blocks, get dressed, brush his teeth.

I have to admit, it does work. Anthony performs a desired behavior, or in the begin-ning, a close approximation to what we want him to do, and he gets a positive reinforcement. Reward for good behavior. Pick up a puzzle piece, get a Pringle. Stick your head in the middle hole of your shirt. Pringle. Put your feet inside your shoes. Pringle.

I remember not liking the idea of ABA at first. Scientists use this same kind of behavioral conditioning to get pigeons to peck a button for food pellets. Anthony's a boy in a house, not a pigeon in a cage. But it works. ABA has given Anthony so many skills I worried he'd never master.

But lately, instead of adding skills, Carlin's been focused on eliminating undesired behaviors. The ABA language for this is 'extinguishing.' I'm not at all comfortable with that word. I picture a candle burning, glowing orange in the center of Anthony, and Carlin is huffing and puffing like the big bad wolf, trying to blow it out. Trying to extinguish him.

They've been working on trying to get rid of Anthony's most prominent autistic behaviors, the stimming ones that most get in the way of his functioning or appearing normal. Hand flapping is the biggest offender. HANDS DOWN. Carlin says this every time he flaps. She places his hands by his sides to prompt him, and if he keeps his hands still at his sides, even for an obvious second, Pringle.

The stated rationale for 'extinguishing' the hand flapping — it's a crutch. Anthony is hand flapping instead of talking to communicate what he wants and feels. If we eliminate flapping as an option, he'll have to find some other way, hopefully spoken words, to communicate.

The unspoken motivation for trying to get rid of the hand flapping is that it just looks weird. It tips everyone off. He looks like a regular, if aloof and quiet, kid until the flapping starts. Then I notice the looks. Something's wrong with that kid. Parents are careful to keep themselves and their children at a safe distance once they see the hand flapping. It might be contagious.

When Carlin first spoke to me about the agenda for extinguishing Anthony's hand flapping, something in me resisted, but I didn't have the words yet to explain it. Plus, she's the therapist. She's the expert. She knows what she's doing. So I went along with it and made a joke instead.

'He's Italian. Of course he talks with his hands!'

Carlin smiled and then proceeded to outline the precise plan for silencing Anthony's hands.

But here's the thing. I don't think his hand flapping is a crutch. I don't think, Oh, if only Anthony weren't flapping his hands, then he'd talk to us! He can't talk, and thank God he flaps his hands. Anthony communicates through his undulating bundle of ticking screeches and flapping. This is how he tells us what he wants and how he feels.

Granted, it's a limited form of communication, but this is what he has. And I've become pretty fluent in this bizarre language. I know when his hands mean This is TOO good or This is the best thing I've ever seen or I don't like what's happening or It's too noisy in here or I want MORE swinging or I want to go home right NOW. Like with any language, the quality and emphasis of the flapping plus the context communicate the specific meaning.

HANDS DOWN. Are we silencing an already muted whisper? Shouldn't we be doing the opposite? Hands, tell us more!

Another behavior on the 'extinguish' list is his obsession with Barney. Anthony still insists on watching Barney, and only Barney, over and over and over. If I try to redirect him before he's done watching, or if I shut off the TV because we need to leave the house or it's time for his ABA therapy, he loses his mind. 'Perseverating' and 'addiction' and 'obsession' are the words his therapists and teachers and doctors use, and so I've been using them, too. And again, like the theory that removing Anthony's hands might force him to use his voice, the hope is that by eliminating Anthony's preoccupation with Barney, this will make room for other, more age-appropriate interests.

At first, I was on board. Barney drives me crazy. I wish Anthony would move on, even to a new obsession. I like his rock obsession much more. At least this lets us spend time at the beach, and even I enjoy combing for beach rocks, so it's an activity we sort of do together. I don't understand the joy he gets from lining them up, but I don't mind the rocks. But the purple, singing dinosaur, he can go.

I thought about our contribution to his Barney obsession. We buy the DVDs, record the show on the DVR, and at least once a day I actually encourage him to zone out in front of the TV, in need of thirty minutes of peace. And today's technology really does feed this symptom of autism. When I was a kid, there were no DVD players, no On Demand, no DVRs. I'm sure I would've been obsessed with The Sound of Music or The Wizard of Oz if I could've watched them every day instead of only once a year. So it's easy to enable this kind of addiction today. And I've been his dealer, happily handing him his drug of choice each and every day.

Carlin said we could go cold turkey if we wanted. We could simply throw out all the Barney DVDs, stop recording it, delete all the existing episodes, get rid of his blanket and all the Barney toys. That'll end it. Or she could work with him using ABA to wean him off it. That seemed more humane to me. The methadone-clinic approach to Barney rehab.

But yesterday, when he was in hysterics in front of the blackened TV screen, Carlin refusing him access to the remote control, I had a different thought. We've been calling this thing with Barney a 'perseveration,' an 'obsession,' an 'addiction.' What if instead

271

we called it 'love'?

When I watch Anthony watching Barney, he's completely enamored. Delight dances all over his beautiful face every time the little, purple, stuffed animal turns into the giant, live Barney. He squeals, Eeeya-eeeya-eeeya, and flaps his hands.

This is too good!

He recently discovered the REWIND button on the remote, and he's learned how to replay the same thirty seconds over and over and over. He laughs a deep belly laugh every time and flaps his hands.

I love this so much!

Anthony LOVES Barney. How can we take away something he loves? Don't we want to encourage love? Why would we extinguish love?

I wish he loved something other than Barney. I really, really do. But why should we get to pick what he loves? I love books and the beach and cooking. David loves football and hockey. What if someone decided that I spent too much time at the beach and reading and cooking and insisted that I give up these things I love? What if someone 'redirected' me and insisted that I love hockey instead? Instead of reading and going to the beach and cooking, I had to watch hockey and learn the rules and play it. I hate hockey. I'd be miserable. I wouldn't be me.

I know getting rid of the flapping and Barney would probably help Anthony in some ways. He'd appear more normal. It'd be easier for him to be mainstreamed in school, to engage with other kids his age (there's not a neurotypical six-year-old kid on this planet who loves Barney).

But here's the thing. Anthony isn't normal. There. I wrote it down, and the world didn't end. I didn't die, and neither did he. He's not normal. He has autism, and his autism makes him flap his hands instead of saying *That noise you're not even aware of is making me crazy* or *I love Barney so much!*

So I don't want to extinguish Anthony's hand flapping or his love of Barney, but I'm afraid to tell David this. He's going to disagree. He's going to say it's giving up on Anthony. Not long ago, I would've said the same thing. But now I don't see it that way. The way I see it, we can look at Anthony's hand flapping and see an abnormal behavior that needs to be eliminated, or we can see our son bravely communicating what he wants and feels the only way he knows how to. We can look at Anthony rewinding Barney over and over and call it an obsession that needs to be treated, or we can call it love.

David's going to say, *If we don't get rid of these autistic behaviors, then he'll never be normal. He'll always be different.*

And my answer to this is going to be Yes. He will always be different.

And the world won't end, and I won't die. And Anthony will be in the living room, loving Barney.

29

It's now November, and the island continues to thin out, shedding the fat, each passing week seeing fewer weekenders and day-trippers. Olivia can go for long walks on the beach or along the roads of her own neighborhood without seeing anyone. Downtown is still open for business, but only because the merchants are all hanging in there for Christmas Stroll, one final bonanza chance to squeeze big dollars out of the tourists before winter officially sets in. After December, she knows most retailers will shut their doors for at least three months. Until the Chamber of Commerce invents some kind of organized excuse for people to come in the winter — the Nantucket Ice Sculpture Festival in January, the Nantucket Winter Olympics in February, the Nantucket Coffee Festival in March — no one will be back until spring. Nantucket is a quaint and seasonal island playground, not a winter destination, and certainly not a place any reasonable person would live year-round.

Olivia's professional life is about to close for the season as well. She has one portrait session left to edit and then no more work. Her days are becoming lean and slow, unpressured and simple, and she now welcomes the change.

It's late afternoon, and she is walking to her mailbox because she forgot to go this morning before breakfast and after reading from one of her journals as is her routine. Reading and rereading her journals these past many months has given her the gentle time and space to go back to what happened with compassionate eyes and a loving heart, to discover what she didn't know then, what she couldn't have known because it was all too raw, too immediate. She was too inside the emotions and the journey then to see them, never mind understand them. Now she does.

She sees her denial and then the scary anger that replaced the denial. She sees her despair and David's, too, and the boundless chasm that grew between them. But more than anything, the thing that she sees now with the most clarity that stays inside her for hours and days after she closes her journal, is Anthony. Not the denial of Anthony's autism or the anger about his autism or the despair over his autism. Not even Anthony and his autism. Just simply Anthony.

She sighs, wishing she knew then what she understands now.

She strolls alone in the middle of the road over long shadows, mindful of the sounds of seagulls overhead, wind chimes in the distance, the rhythm of her footsteps scratching sand against the pavement. The air is wet and salty and cold. Walking feels good. It enlivens her brain, convincing scared and buried thoughts that it's safe to come out of hiding, inviting incomplete thoughts to show their jagged edges, welcoming the wandering and the weak. When she walks, her thoughts line up in her mind like white rocks where they can be clearly seen and cared for.

Today, as she walks, she's thinking about her sister and mother.

Maria wants her to come home to Georgia for Thanksgiving. It would be good to see her. Olivia misses her older sister. But the work of packing, leaving the island by ferry or plane, enduring at least one connecting flight, sleeping on the couch in Maria's living room, all feels impossibly overwhelming.

And despite her substantial and growing guilt over not having seen Maria's kids in ages, Olivia's still not ready to spend time with them, her beautiful niece and nephew, Anthony's cousins, older now, thriving, so capable. Alive. And it's not just the kids. It's Maria's entire life. Maria has always, effortlessly had it better, easier. She had the better grades, the cuter boyfriends. She attended a more prestigious college, landed a higher-paying job. She's taller. And now look at her, happily married with two healthy children. Olivia knows this comparison isn't fair or productive, but if she goes to Maria's house for Thanksgiving, it's also inevitable.

And she's definitely not ready to deal with her mother, who, according to Maria, is still going to church every day, clad head to toe in black, where, in addition to still praying for Anthony, she now prays for Olivia's divorced soul. She's also probably saying a few rosaries to clear her own name, to be sure God knows she's in no way responsible for Olivia's shameful and sinful act against the Church. Olivia doesn't have the strength to go home and be judged by her religion and her mother.

Maria says Olivia can't stay in hiding forever. This is without question why Olivia came here in March, but without intending to, and just as the rest of the island prepares to go into hibernation, she feels the possibility of emerging, of beginning a new life. Maybe Nantucket isn't simply a temporary asylum for her, a shelter from her grief and the life she didn't get to live. Maybe this is her home.

Her remote residence is also the perfect excuse, her refuge from dreadful air travel, unbecoming jealousy, and eternal damnation. No, she's not going to Georgia for Thanksgiving. She's staying home on Nantucket, grateful to be here.

She arrives at her mailbox, opens the door, and pulls out a small stack of mail. As she turns around, she sees a woman and her black dog walking along the side of the road. Olivia pauses with her mail in hand, realizing the woman and her dog are walking directly toward her. It's Beth Ellis.

'Hey!' says Beth, smiling. 'You live *here?*'

'Yeah, I'm on Morton.'

'You're kidding. I'm on Somerset. We're neighbors. How could we not know this?'

Olivia shrugs. Beth's dog sniffs Olivia's shoes and jeans for a few seconds before turning its feisty attention to her crotch. Beth pulls on its leash.

'Grover, no! . . . How long have you lived here?'

'Since March.'

'Really? Tough month to move here.'

'Yeah.'

'Are you married?' asks Beth, not finding an answer on Olivia's gloved hand.

'Divorced.'

Olivia watches Beth digest this bit of information as she opens her own mailbox and retrieves a thick stack of catalogs and envelopes.

'Do you have kids?' Beth asks.

'A son.'

'Oh, how old?'

'Ten.' *He would be ten.*

'Same age as my Gracie! Is he in fourth grade with Mrs. Gillis?'

'No, he doesn't live here.'

'Oh.'

That ended the inquisition, but Olivia can sense the additional questions tumbling in Beth's mind. *What can that mean? Does he live with his father? What kind of mother doesn't live with her child? Where is he?* Before she can verbalize any of them, Olivia changes the subject, hoping Beth will follow.

'Funny, I was just about to e-mail you. Your pictures are ready. Sorry it took so long.'

'Oh, good! I was getting worried. I can't wait to see them. I want to use one of them for our Christmas card.'

'I'll e-mail you the link as soon as I get home. They're great. You're going to love them.'

The two women begin walking.

'I think my book is almost done,' says Beth after an apprehensive silence.

'That's great. Congratulations.'

'But I'm not sure. This might be a stupid

question, but how do you know when it's done?'

Endings are difficult. Wrapping everything up in a tight, elegant bow. Leaving the reader with a satisfying *The End*. Saying good-bye.

'It has to have all the essential elements, a beginning, middle, and end. You just feel it. It's intuitive, I think. When you're done, you know.'

'I don't know what I know. I've read it so many times now, my eyes skip over the words. I can't see it anymore.'

'Maybe take some time away, then go back to it with fresh eyes.'

Beth nods as she walks.

'I'd still like your feedback if you're still willing.'

'When you're ready, I'd be happy to read it.'

'Thanks so much,' says Beth, smiling. 'I'll put it in your mailbox when I know it's perfect.'

'Don't aim for perfect. Aim for complete.'

Perfection is an unattainable illusion.

'Okay,' says Beth, uncertainty in her voice, as if she doesn't quite understand the difference. 'I will.'

They pause, facing each other at a fork in the road. Beth is staying straight, and Olivia is turning right. Beth waves, smiling, then walks away.

Olivia gets back to thinking as she walks home. She thinks about Beth and her novel. She wonders what it's about. She forgot to ask. She thinks about endings and intuition. She thinks about her marriage, how she and David both knew it was over, how they both saw their ending spelled out long before they arrived at the final page. She's thinking about the last time she saw him, lying under the stars and holding hands, when she reaches her front door and thumbs through the mail in her hand.

Tucked between the electric bill and a newsletter from the library is a letter from David.

30

Beth is sitting in her seat in the library, holding the printed pages of her novel in her hands, reading. She thinks it might be done, but then again, whenever she approaches this thought, an itch flares up inside her chest, nagging her from within like a burning-hot rash. Something's not quite right. Even if she doesn't aim for perfect, only complete, she can't declare her book finished.

Today she's reading what she's written, enjoying the story, but she's yet to identify what might be missing. She's on Chapter 10 now, the one about the Three Little Pigs.

I love when my mother reads the Three Little Pigs book to me. I love Three Little Pigs, but it's not the story about a wolf and pigs that I love. I'm not 'obsessed' with pigs, and I'm not afraid of that big bad wolf. It's the music of my mother's voice, singing in threes. There are perfect threes all over that story:

Lit-tle pig. Lit-tle pig.

One-two-three. One-two-three.

Let. Me. In.

One. Two. Three.

Even the title makes me smile. Three words AND the number three.

My mother reads Three Little Pigs, and I feel the big drumbeats inside those words thump-thump-thumping. I jump to the sound of the book's drum, thumping in perfect threes:

Knock. Knock. Knock.

One. Two. Three.

Jump. Jump. Jump.

My mother reads Three Little Pigs, and she sings a waltz. I spin and dance to her beautiful song.

Not by the
Hair on my
Chinny-chin-chin.

Then I'll huff.
And I'll puff.
And I'll blow
Your house in.

My mother finishes the story and closes the book. I jump and squeal and flap my hands, begging her to sing it again. She says she's tired of the Three Little Pigs book. She says I'm getting too old for this story. She wants to read something else.

She pulls two books that are not Three Little Pigs from the bookcase and shows me their shiny covers. But I don't want to hear those books that are not about the sounds of three.

My mother sighs and puts those books I don't want away. She opens Three Little Pigs and reads again:

Lit-tle pig. Lit-tle pig. Let. Me. In.

One-two-three. One-two-three. One. Two. Three.

My mother reads my favorite story, and my world sings.

31

'So why aren't you writing today?' asks Petra.

Beth and Petra are sitting at a corner booth at Dish, splitting a heaping plate of sinfully rich and fattening lobster mac-n-cheese. It's early afternoon on a Wednesday in November, and the restaurant is dead. The two people who came in for lunch left an hour ago. This is how it goes midweek in the restaurant business on Nantucket in November. Petra will limp along until Christmas Stroll, then close down until April 1.

'I think it might be done,' says Beth.

Petra's eyes widen, excited.

'Really? You finished your book?'

'I don't know, I'm not sure. I'm taking some time away from it so I can see it clearly and then decide if it's really done.'

Petra mutters a laugh through a mouthful of lobster and macaroni.

'What?' asks Beth.

Petra swallows.

'What you just said. Are you talking about your book or your marriage?'

Interesting. Beth wonders if the two are in any way related.

'I have this homework assignment from our marriage counselor that I haven't touched that I should've done like two months ago. I made Jimmy cancel our next appointment because I didn't do it yet. I don't know what my problem is.'

'Maybe you're afraid of what you'll discover.'

'Maybe.'

'Probably.'

Petra looks straight into Beth's eyes, straight into Beth in a way that most people never do. Her gaze is focused, unrushed, unafraid to stay there, and kind.

'I think I'm scared he'd cheat on me again.'

'He might.'

'If I take him back, I'd wake up every morning and think, 'He could cheat on me today.''

'He could, but that was true before he actually did, you know. Every day is a commitment and a choice, for both of you.'

'I know, but he chose to cheat. I'd worry after every little fight that he'd be off with someone again. Every time I see him, I think, 'You slept with another woman.' And I picture them together. It's disgusting, and I can't help it. I feel obsessed about it. I wish I could erase it.'

'Do you still love him?'

'Yeah, but I hate him, too.'

It's true. Beth loves him, and she hates him. She misses him and never wants to see him again. She's disgusted by the thought of him, yet she can't stop thinking about that night on the kitchen floor.

Petra sighs.

'I just wish I knew what to do,' says Beth.

'Do what you're doing with your book. Take some time away from thinking about it, guilt-free. Then go back to it with a clear mind and fresh eyes when you're ready.'

Beth nods. She discovers a big hunk of lobster hidden in the creamy cheese and stabs it with her fork.

'But what do you think?' asks Beth.

'About what?'

'Jimmy. Do you think I should take him back?'

'Only you can answer that.'

'But what would you do?'

Petra scrapes a crusty, caramelized section of macaroni and cheese from the side of the dish and eats it. She drinks her water and wipes her mouth with her napkin. Beth waits. Petra smiles with her lips closed.

'Petra? Really, I want your advice.'

Petra raises her eyebrows and says nothing.

'That's what I'd do,' she finally says. 'Stop all the chatter. Stop looking outside yourself for the answers. Get quiet and still and ask yourself those homework questions you're so afraid of. Whatever you find in that space, that's the truth. That's your answer. That's what I'd do.'

Beth sighs, disappointed but not surprised. She should've known that Petra wouldn't do her homework for her.

'You're too wise to be single.'

Petra laughs.

'That's exactly why I'm single! No, I'd love to share my life with someone, have a family. I will. I just haven't invited it yet. I've been so focused on Dish and all these people who need their jobs and taking care of my mom and dad. But someday. Someday, I'd like to have what you have.'

'Had.'

'And have. I'd be lucky to have what you have.'

Beth smiles, grateful for the reminder. She has three beautiful, healthy girls, a lovely home, great friends, and a possibly finished first novel. She has so much. She checks her watch.

'Oh my God, I have to go! I have to pick up the girls.'

Beth wraps her bright purple scarf around her neck, grabs her bag, and hugs Petra good-bye. 'Thanks for an amazing lunch.'

'Anytime,' says Petra, hugging her back. 'So good to see you.'

'You, too.' Beth rushes for the door, not wanting to be late.

'You'll figure it out,' says Petra, but Beth is already outside and doesn't hear her.

* * *

It's Tuesday evening, the week of Thanksgiving. Beth and the girls have just finished eating macaroni and cheese for dinner, but Beth doesn't feel at all satisfied. Petra's lobster mac-n-cheese has probably ruined the Kraft version for her forever. She browses the refrigerator for something else, maybe something sweet, but nothing appeals to her.

All three girls are in the living room. Sophie has the remote control and is in charge, scrolling through the On Demand movie options while Jessica and Gracie yell out different titles. They have no school tomorrow and nothing going on tonight — no basketball practice, no play rehearsal, no homework. Beth is grateful to have a relaxed night with no schedule and no one to drop off or pick up, and, if they can ever make a decision, a movie to watch with her daughters.

She starts a fire in the fireplace and pops a bag of popcorn in the microwave. The girls are still watching trailers, undecided. Beth grabs a blanket and tries to get settled on the couch next to Grover, but she's feeling inexplicably restless. She stands up and looks out the kitchen window. It looks cold and dark and entirely uninviting, yet, for some reason, she needs to get outside. She grabs her coat, hat, scarf, gloves, and a flashlight.

'I'm going for a walk. I won't be long. Don't start the movie without me.'

'Okay!' says Gracie.

Hypnotized by the TV, Sophie and Jessica don't even acknowledge that their mother has said anything. Gracie can tell them where she is if they ever wonder.

It's a dark night with no moon, but the stars are amazing, and it's not as cold as she expected. She points her flashlight in front of her and walks, not conscious at first of a destination, but after a couple of minutes she has one. Fat Ladies Beach. It's a bit farther than she'd planned, but she'll walk fast.

She's walking on the dirt road, focused on the uneven ground within the beam of light in front of her, the visible puffs of her breath, the tempo of her breathing coordinated with her pace. She can't see anything to either side of her, but she

287

knows her surroundings well, the flat, grassy, uncultivated, and mostly treeless landscape that looks like African savanna. It feels good to walk, to move. She spends most of her days, her entire life really, sitting — at the kitchen table, in her car, in her seat at the library. Sedentary. Stuck.

Her exposed nose and cheeks are freezing cold, and her eyes are watering from the wind on her face, but otherwise, she's bundled well. She feels her heart beating hard, the muscles in her legs burning. She's both hot and cold, holding two opposing energies at once, sparking something within her that feels unfamiliar but exciting.

She reaches the beach, which feels far enough without walking along it, but before turning straight around, she stops for a minute to simply take it all in. She turns off her flashlight and listens to the waves, which sound to her like the earth itself breathing. She tips her chin up and stares at the starry sky, at its vast, complicated, unfathomable enormity but also at its simple, accessible beauty, its existence explained by the logical laws of physics and, at the same time, ultimately, utterly unexplainable.

She's the only person here. She's completely alone, yet she feels strangely and beautifully connected to everything. Two opposing energies, held within her, sparking something.

It's time to go home, to blankets and popcorn and a movie with her daughters. She's off the beach and back on the dirt road when her flashlight catches two glowing white lights, like two fallen stars hovering just above the earth, and she stops fast in her tracks. It's a deer, an adolescent, positioned directly in her path only a few feet in front of her. They both stand still, face-to-face, breathing and bearing witness to each other for at least a full minute. Beth observes its black nose, its perky ears, its long, erect neck and wonders what the deer sees of her. And then, without warning, it takes off into the dark and wild Nantucket savanna.

Back at home, the girls had grown equally annoyed and worried by Beth's absence. They're ready now. They've been waiting. But first, Beth makes root-beer floats for them and a mudslide for herself. Then they all settle into the couches under blankets and watch *Marley & Me*, a movie they already own and have all seen at least three times.

It's late when the movie ends, and Beth goes to bed shortly after she tucks her girls in. It normally takes her a while to fall asleep, at least a half hour of tossing, the day replaying, tomorrow already tugging at her sleeve, but tonight, the walk and fresh air must've tuckered her out because she falls straight to sleep.

An hour later though, her eyes pop open. She's fully awake, her heart pounding, demanding something of her. She gets out of bed. She finds a sheet of paper and a pen. She draws a cross, creating four squares, and writes. She can barely write fast enough. Words she didn't know she had within her pour out.

When she finishes, she looks over the four squares. She reads the entire sheet three times. There it is, her homework assignment completed. Her answer. She reads it one more time and knows what she needs to do.

WHAT I NEED TO FEEL WANTED
Choose to spend time with me (instead of sleeping late, smoking cigars outside alone, staying out past closing, sleeping with other women)

Be happy to see me

Compliment me every now and then, something more specific than 'you look nice'

Never cheat on me again

WHAT I NEED TO FEEL HAPPY
My girls

My friends

My writing

For you to see and appreciate the love and care I give to our family/household

A neat house

Spending time off this island, in a big city or near mountains

Believing I deserve to be

WHAT I NEED TO FEEL SAFE
Knowing my girls are okay

Not going into debt ever again and always being able to pay the bills

You never seeing Angela again

Believing you would never cheat on me again

WHAT I NEED TO FEEL LOVED
Hugs and kisses

Hearing you say the words 'I love you'

32

Olivia stands over the kitchen counter where two dozen glass jars filled with hot, homemade cranberry jelly are cooling in pans of water. She's been in busy motion for two weeks, ostensibly preparing for winter. She stored the deck furniture and the grill in the shed. She raked the yard and turned off the water to the outdoor shower. She ordered a dozen books and a case of her favorite merlot. And she's been cooking.

She's made old favorites — pasta fagioli, clam chowder, butternut squash risotto, and black bean soup — and she's tried new recipes, Pad Thai and lobster macaroni and cheese, insane quantities of food for a woman who lives alone and never has company. She's been cooking every day, creating gallons of savory dinners that are barely tasted before being aliquoted into plastic containers and stacked neatly in the freezer. Once the freezer was full, she turned her attention to cranberries — cranberry-walnut bread, orange-cranberry muffins, and now cranberry jelly.

She tells herself that all this cooking is good planning. If it's a harsh winter, if it's a season of nor'easters, if she gets snowed in (she still only owns that one, small sand shovel), she won't need to leave the house for food. But this is just what she tells herself. In truth, the cooking has been necessary for other reasons.

She started cooking right after she read the letter from David. The first recipe she turned to was the pasta fagioli, the one she knows by heart, the soup her mother used to make on Saturdays. Her eyes burned as she chopped the onions, and she welcomed the stinging tears. She cried while she chopped the garlic and the celery and the tomatoes. She sobbed while she stirred in the broth and the beans, then she stopped when the soup was done. She did the same thing while making the black bean soup, the tomato bisque, and the meatballs, but when she got to the onions for the butternut squash risotto, she ran them under cold water, wiped her eyes with her shirtsleeve, and finished the recipe without weeping.

She's done crying, emptied out, but she keeps cooking. It seems the only thing to do to keep herself sane. Fill a pot, fill the void. She keeps her hands moving, stirring, chopping, pouring. Her hands move through the steps for making cranberry jelly, and she can think about David and his letter without becoming leveled by it. She's read through it, dissected it, and cried over it so many times now, she knows it as well as her mother's recipe for pasta fagioli.

Dear Liv,
I wanted to write you rather than call. It seems somehow more proper, and I wanted you to hear this news from me before anyone else. I'm getting married. Her name is Julie. She's a math teacher. I met her here in Chicago. I know it's fast, but it feels right. I feel ready.

I wish I could've gotten back to this place with you, Liv. I'm sorry that I didn't. I know I didn't give my best self to you and Anthony. I guess I got a bit lost in all that we went through. I forgot how to be happy. I think we both forgot.

I hope this news doesn't hurt you, but I know it probably will. That isn't my intention. It never has been. I wish every day that you're okay, that you find happiness again, too. Call me if you want.

Love,
David

Now that the initial shock of the letter has worn off and onions no longer trigger hours of soul-scrubbing tears, other, less explosive feelings have been taking their due turns. Where she'd felt content to be alone the minute before she opened David's letter, she now feels abandoned in her solitude. She checks to see if the jelly lids have sealed, and she feels scared of being alone forever.

A math teacher named Julie. She sounds young. And pretty. And for some reason, blonde. Olivia removes the jars one at a time from their water bath and wipes each one dry against her apron with her jealous hands.

They'll probably have children. She pictures David holding a baby swaddled in his arms, a house full of kids who belong to him and not her, a big family. These pictures in her mind, vivid and achingly beautiful, punch the air right out of her, as they always do, and she wishes she could somehow stop imagining them. She holds on to the edge of the kitchen counter and waits to either breathe or cry. Today, she breathes.

She reads the letter in her mind again, and it's the sound of David's voice she hears. His voice is light and happy. He's happy, and he's found a woman named Julie he can share his happiness with.

He's right. She forgot about happiness. At first, it wasn't a priority. Anthony had autism, and every ounce of energy went into saving him. Her happiness was irrelevant. Then it didn't seem appropriate. How could she be happy when they were living a tragedy? And then, just when she was starting to realize that happiness and autism could coexist in the same room, in the same sentence, in her heart, Anthony died, and happiness was no longer a concept she could fathom.

He died, and for a long time after that worst of all mornings, she replayed his death in her mind, unleashing the massive sorrow that still clings to those images, consuming her in a tsunami of devastated grief every day. She thought she would do this forever, that she should do this forever. Her grief was her daily duty, her misery a humble tribute to her son.

But reading her journals has helped her to remember more than that morning. There was more to Anthony's life than his death. And there was more to Anthony than his autism. So much more. She can think about Anthony now and not be consumed by autism or grief.

But not being consumed with grief is a far cry

from being happy. She stacks the jars of jelly on a shelf in the pantry but keeps one on the counter. She pictures David now, and he's smiling. The image changes from David to Anthony. They have the same mouth, the same dimpled cheeks. Anthony smiling. It's an easy picture to sustain, an accessible memory, real. For all his frustration and aggression and inability to communicate, Anthony was mostly happy. It was his nature. Given time, it's David's nature, too.

She cuts a large slice of bread, slathers the jelly on it, and pours a glass of merlot. She gets comfortable in the chair in the living room in front of a glowing fire and takes a bite of the bread. Her homemade jelly is sweet and tangy, scrumptious.

She listens to David reading his letter in her head while she looks at Anthony's picture on the wall and decides she's done cooking. After two weeks of chopping and dicing and sautéing and sobbing, she's finally done with it all. She's done and left with a freezer stocked full of comfort food and a vague yet real feeling of hope.

If David can find happiness and begin again, maybe she can, too. Happiness. Shared happiness. Maybe it's human nature. And all she has to do is invite it in.

As she eats her bread and jelly and considers this new outlook, she gazes up at her photograph of Anthony on the wall. She drinks her wine and admires her collection of white rocks in the glass bowl on the coffee table in front of her — Anthony's rocks, plus the rocks she's collected here on Nantucket and the one Beth's daughter gave to her. She leans over, chooses a rock from the top of the pile, and holds it in her hand. It feels unexpectedly warm in her palm, as if someone had already been holding it.

Oh, my beautiful Anthony, why were you here?

The penetrating, hollow ache that usually follows this question doesn't come. Instead, a calm energy fills her heart with the assurance of a truth already known, more an intangible feeling, though, than a fact that can be verbalized. She sits still and listens but not with her ears.

She feels her attention being nudged elsewhere. She considers the new books on the table next to the fireplace. She gets up and squats in front of them, contemplating the spines, mysteries and memoirs and novels she's excited to get lost in. She lays her hand on the book at the top of the pile. *Not these.*

She walks into the kitchen, finds a red pen, and returns to her living-room chair carrying a thick stack of paper bound with red-and-white bakery string.

Untitled by Elizabeth Ellis.

She looks up at her photograph of Anthony on the wall and smiles at him with her eyes. She places the white rock back in the glass bowl, wraps a blanket around her lap, unties the bakery string, and begins to read.

33

'Man, it's nasty out there,' says Jimmy, parking his boots at the door before taking a seat on the couch across from Beth.

He blows into his hands, pink and wet from the cold rain, then rubs them together. The wind howls, sounding determined, as if the big bad wolf were roaming the neighborhood, bent on blowing every house down. One of the shutters rattles, and Beth feels a breeze whisper across her face, a current of uninvited air sailing into the living room through the many cracks around the old, warped windows. She cups her hands around her mug of cocoa, absorbing its comforting heat.

It occurs to her that this is exactly how everything started. A winter storm, a mug of cocoa, a fire in the fireplace, Grover asleep on the rug. Everything feels familiar, as if she's done this before, yet she has the sensation of standing tiptoe at the edge of a precipice, leaning out, about to free-fall into the unknown.

'You look good,' says Jimmy.

She allows a self-conscious smile and picks a fleck of white lint off the front of her red shirt. 'Thanks. You do, too.'

The beard is gone, but he left the sideburns long, which she likes, and his face looks smooth and young. He smells nice, like citrus, an aftershave or cologne she doesn't recognize. He holds a piece of notebook paper folded into the size of a playing card in his hand.

'I'm glad we're finally doing this,' he says, smiling, exuding excited anticipation, like a child about to unwrap a Christmas present, sure that it's the very thing he asked for.

Beth's paper, folded once, lies on the couch cushion next to her.

'How do you want to do this?' asks Jimmy.

'I don't know.'

'You want to go first?'

'How about we just swap and read?'

'Okay.'

Beth passes her homework to him, and he hands her his wadded piece of paper. Oily and worn on the folds, it's probably been in his pocket for two months. She unwraps it and reads.

WANTED
  Wait up for me every now and then and sleep
    late with me
  Come to the bar for dinner some nights
  Initiate sex

HAPPY
  Be happy to see me
  Stop being mad at me all the time
  Don't talk to me like I'm one of the kids

SECURE
  Be proud of me

LOVED
  Tell me you love me

His list is short and reasonable, straightforward and simple. It's almost too simple, yet she believes him. His list is sincere, and she feels unexpectedly ashamed. This is all he needs from her, and she's been unwilling to give it to him, even before he began cheating on her.

Her list is similarly uncomplicated. She's not asking for diamonds and luxury vacations. She doesn't need roses and chocolates on her pillow. She's not asking for the moon. It should be easy. Love, happiness, security, feeling wanted, the most basic elements, like air, water, earth, and fire — missing for both of them. No wonder they're both sitting here with sorry pieces of paper in their laps, husband and wife, strangers.

When and why did they start withholding these basic needs? For her, was it in response to the changes in him after he stopped scalloping, before he started working at Salt? Was it a subconscious reaction to his affair? Did she unknowingly sense his infidelity and withdraw? Or did she maybe set aside too much of her creative and passionate self years ago, storing it in a box in the attic, not leaving her with enough love and happiness to share with Jimmy? Did she deprive him first, and he reacted in kind? It's a chicken-and-egg question, probably unanswerable.

She rereads his list, afraid to look up at him. On paper, it all looks so achievable, with the obvious exception of going to the bar for dinner. Not with Angela there. Not a chance. But it also confirms what she's suspected for too long. She looks over his piece of notebook paper and sees words that should've been spoken aloud, chatted about on this couch, whispered in bed, needs that could've been conveyed through a look, a note, a tap on the shoulder — all in uncharged, day-to-day moments. But none of that ever happened. They don't know how to communicate.

And even if they did, even if they worked on it and learned the tools, there is one item on her list, one nonnegotiable need as essential as the drafty air she breathes and that Jimmy can't give her.

She looks up, and Jimmy is done reading, waiting and grinning at her, and a heavy, hollow pit plants itself in the middle of her stomach.

'This is great, Beth. I can do this, all of it. And I want to. I want to get back together and give you these things. I've missed you so much.'

He's still smiling, ready to celebrate, high atop the opposite end of her seesaw.

'We can't.'

'What? I can, Beth, really. This won't be hard.'

'Then why couldn't we do it in the first place?'

'I don't know, but we will now, we — '

'I can't, Jimmy.'

His smile collapses, and the pit in her stomach expands. He stares at her and blinks.

'What are you saying?'

She swallows and tries to take a deep breath, but the pit in her stomach now feels like it's taking up all the space inside her where air goes. She looks at Jimmy, at that face she still adores, afraid of saying what she's about to say. But it's the truth, and she knows it. She leans forward and falls.

'I want a divorce.'

'No. Beth, please. We can do this.'

'I can't.'

'You can. What part of that can't you do?' he asks, pointing to the piece of paper she holds.

'It's not your list, Jimmy. It's mine. I can't get past the cheating. I need to believe that you'd never do it again, and I can't. The kind of man I thought you were, the kind of husband I need, would never cheat on his wife.'

'It was a mistake.'

'Thinking it's Wednesday when it's only Monday is a mistake. Sleeping with her once, in the heat of the moment, I could even call that a mistake. But — '

'I'm sorry. It was stupid and wrong, and I swear, I promise it'll never, ever happen again.'

'I can't believe you. I don't trust you anymore.'

'Let's start over, and you'll trust me again because I won't give you any reason not to. Let me earn it back.'

She shakes her head. Trust shouldn't be something he needs to earn. It should be a given. And he shouldn't need instructions on a piece of homework paper to remind him, DONT CHEAT ON YOUR WIFE.

'I have something for you.' He pulls a small, white cardboard box out from the front pocket of his jeans.

'What's that?' asks Beth, not wanting whatever it is.

'It's a gift.'

'Jimmy — '

'Here, open it,' he says, handing it to her.

Beth stares at him for an uncomfortably long moment. She lifts the lid and the square piece of tissue paper, revealing a necklace. A single, large, round moonstone hanging on a silver chain. She holds the gem in her hand, a shimmering, smooth, almost translucent bluish-white stone. It's beautiful.

'Jimmy — '

'When I saw you wearing the other necklace at the bar, I started thinking about when I gave it to you. It was the year we got married. That locket reminds me of our beginning and the commitment we made to each other. It reminds me of how much we loved each other. I know I ruined that. I'm so desperately sorry for what I've done, Beth. I want to start over with you, and I thought you should have a new necklace, something to symbolize a new beginning and a new commitment.'

She clenches her teeth, swallowing down the urge to cry. Not now.

'Jimmy, it's beautiful.'

'I noticed the ring you've been wearing and thought they'd look good together.'

'And it's a beautiful thought. But I can't accept it.'

She dangles the necklace back into the box, lays the tissue paper over it, closes the lid, and places the box on the coffee table. She looks up at Jimmy. All color and expression have drained out of his face. She suspects she looks the same way.

'Please,' he says.

'I'm sorry.'

'What about the girls? Don't they deserve their parents to be together?'

'Were you thinking about what they deserve when you were sleeping with that woman?'

'No.' He looks down at his socks. 'I wasn't thinking about anything I should've been. But I wish I had. Come on, Beth. We have to at least try to make it work.'

'I have been trying this whole time, but I don't trust you anymore, and if I don't trust you first, then none of this other stuff can happen,' she says, waving Jimmy's homework in the air.

'See, I think the opposite. I think if you have all the other stuff, then the trust will come. I can give you what you need, Beth. I love you. Let me earn it back. You can trust me.'

She remembers attending a reception at one of the art galleries downtown with Jimmy when they were dating. They were there for the wine and to see some of Courtney's husband's oil paintings. Beth fell in love with one of his more abstract representations of a woman standing on the shore. The unexpected colors and strange lines captivated her interest and awe. She remembers the look of puzzled disgust screwed onto Jimmy's face as he studied the same canvas. She wanted to buy it, and Jimmy said, *Looks like something some kid did in kindergarten class.* She remembers feeling disheartened, that they could look at the exact same thing and experience something so completely opposite. And here they are again.

'I'm sorry, Jimmy.'

'I can't believe you won't even try.'

'I did.'

'How?'

She says nothing.

'I think we should go back to Dr. Campbell.'

'I'm done, Jimmy.'

He reads her piece of paper again, shaking his head.

'You still love me, Beth. I know you do.'

'This changed who you are to me.'

She sees her words piercing him, his face pinching in pain, and she can't stand to be the cause of it. She looks away, over to the fireplace mantel, the piece of driftwood he knew would be theirs. The starfish and the nautilus shell are still there, but the old pictures are gone, replaced by a single framed photo of Beth and the girls in mismatched tank tops, arms around each other, laughing.

'I still love you, but it's not enough.'

'It is. It has to be. I love you. If you still love me, that's everything. Please, Beth. Please forgive me. I know we can do this.'

She looks down at her hands in her lap, at her diamond ring and wedding band she still wears.

I promise to be true to you.

A belief shattered into pieces too jagged and sharp, leaving her now holding what feels more like a weapon than a vow. She looks up at Jimmy, at the vulnerable desperation and love in his eyes, and unexpectedly, instinctively maybe, her guard drops and she mirrors his emotions with her own, with the reciprocal love and desperation she still has for him. An uncertainty niggles at

304

her throat. She coughs and drinks a gulp of cocoa.

'I'm sorry. I can't.'

She watches his eyes change, retreating into a familiar fortress.

'So this is it?'

The brutal enormity of what is about to happen hits her full on. This feels nothing like that morning last March when she found out about Angela and told him to leave, not truly wanting him to go, lost in crazed disbelief that he actually did. Today is different. This is their ending. She's losing Jimmy, and a deep and aching sadness fills her heart, but like witnessing death after a prolonged and ugly illness, there is also relief and peace.

'This is it.'

He rakes his fingers through his hair and shakes his head.

'This is wrong, Beth. We should be together. We love each other. We deserve a second chance,' he says, his words struggling against the oncoming force of unstoppable tears.

He gets up and rushes out of the room. She hears him putting on his boots, zipping up his coat. The front door opens and closes. She listens to his truck start and pull away. Her heart is pounding. She did it. It's over.

She walks into the kitchen, pulls a bottle of Triple Eight vodka from the cabinet, fills her mug of lukewarm cocoa to the rim, and returns to the couch. She listens to the storm, the fire, the radiator, the silence. She takes a sip of cocoa and notices that her hands are shaking. She stares at the white cardboard box left on the coffee table, afraid to pick it up.

The doorbell rings, and she startles, splashing cocoa onto her lap. She wipes her jeans with her hand and eyes his homework page, left on the couch. Maybe he came back for it. Or maybe he has more to say. She takes an apprehensive breath and heads for the mudroom.

She opens the front door, and she startles again, this time spilling cocoa down the front of her red shirt. It's not Jimmy. It takes her emotionally exhausted brain a few seconds to adjust her expectation and identify who is standing in front of her.

It's Olivia, soaking wet, holding a white cardboard box in her hands, looking as if she's just seen a ghost.

34

'Olivia, you're soaked through,' Beth says. 'Come in.'

'Sorry to stop by unannounced,' Olivia says, hoping to sound casual. She doesn't pull it off. Her voice sounds wired, tight, too high.

'That's okay, come in.'

Olivia steps inside. She's in a mudroom — gray-tiled floor, a braided green-and-blue rug, girls' shoes and boots arranged in a tidy row under a long wooden bench, coats hung on hooks on the wall. The house is warm. It smells like cookies.

Beth hesitates before shutting the front door, looking out at the empty road. She appears distracted, shaken even. Maybe now isn't a good time.

There is no other time.

'I have your book,' says Olivia, clutching the box she holds tight to her chest, protecting what's inside like it's a precious gift, a sacred offering, a beloved baby.

'Oh, great!' Beth's face lights up. 'Let me take your coat. Come into the living room, and we can sit by the fire.'

Beth hangs Olivia's drenched coat on an empty hook. Olivia removes her shoes and follows Beth into the living room.

'Sorry about the mess.'

Olivia looks around the room, her senses heightened, raw and wide-open, trying to take in every possible detail. White walls, cream-colored Roman shades on the windows, a faded blue area rug on the hardwood floor, a modest TV set inside a white wall unit, all cabinets closed, firewood piled high in an iron trolley, a candle and a small, white gift box on the coffee table, two brown couches facing each other opposite a traditional brick fireplace, a single framed photograph taken by Olivia of Beth and her daughters sitting at the center of the mantel, leaning against the wall, flanked by a large shell on one side and a starfish on the other. A blue plastic laundry basket full of unfolded clothes sits on the floor next to one of the couches, but otherwise, the room is immaculate.

Olivia sits on the couch opposite Beth.

'There's one of your photos,' Beth says, smiling and pointing to the mantel. 'We have eight more framed in the hallway upstairs. We love them. I'll show you before you go.'

'Sure. Glad you like them,' says Olivia, trying to sound breezy, not knowing how much longer she can maintain normal, polite chitchat.

'Can I get you something to drink?'

'Uh, okay. Whatever you're having,' she says, noting the blue mug in Beth's hands, assuming it's coffee.

But caffeine is the last thing she needs right now. When she started reading Beth's manuscript last night, she began underlining and marking up words and phrases that reminded her of Anthony in red pen. She smiled as she read those first few pages, admiring Beth's depiction of a boy with autism, so similar to

308

Anthony. She marveled at the coincidence, that Beth's book was about a subject so close to Olivia's heart. She applauded Beth's choice to tell the story from the boy's point of view, in his voice.

By the third chapter, the words she read and the voice she heard began to feel uncanny, surreal, impossible. Her hands trembled, and her heart pounded. Goose bumps spread across her skin and stayed there. She switched to a highlighter, highlighting whole passages she felt could only be about Anthony and no one else. By the time she reached Chapter 4, she was highlighting every word of every sentence on every page.

She devoured the words, finishing the book just after midnight, breathless, stunned, her heart racing, tears streaming down her face. She sat still for a long while, staring at the last page, crying and smiling, believing and disbelieving.

Finally, she turned over the last page, gathered the rest of the manuscript, and held the pages in her lap, feeling the weight of it, believing. *These words written by Beth are Anthony's words. The voice of this boy is the voice of my voiceless son. The boy in this book is Anthony.*

She went back to the beginning and read it straight through twice more. She's been up all night, and yet she's never been more awake, every cell in her being on high alert, wide-eyed, plump full of adrenaline, ripe to the point of bursting.

'This is hot cocoa,' Beth says, then hesitates. 'And, don't judge me, a little vodka.'

'Okay.'

'Yeah?' Beth smiles and darts into the kitchen.

Olivia removes Beth's manuscript from the box and holds the pages on her lap, trying to contain what she feels for just a bit longer, imagining that she might actually explode into a million bloody pieces of flesh and bone if she doesn't soon say what she came here to say. She listens to the sounds of a microwave cooking and Beth opening and closing cabinets in her kitchen. Any minute now. Her head buzzes, and her stomach is dizzy, like what an actor must feel before going onstage on opening night, or maybe like what a death row prisoner must feel on the day of execution, but like neither of these really. She hears the microwave beep. Beth returns with another blue mug and an eager smile.

'I can't believe you're here with my book. I'm so nervous.'

She places the mug on the coffee table in front of Olivia, then sits, attentive and leaning forward, like a good student.

'Your book.' Olivia's voice catches. Her heart is slamming against her chest like a fist pounding on a locked door, demanding to be let out. 'Your book,' she tries again. 'How did you write this?'

'What do you mean?'

'This story. This is my son's story.'

'Oh?' Beth raises her eyebrows and tilts her head, not understanding but not yet alarmed.

'My son's name is Anthony, and he had autism.'

'Oh my God.' Beth lowers her mug, floored. 'That's unbelievable.'

'Yeah.'

'That's an amazing coincidence. I had no idea.'

'No. Not a coincidence. You didn't just write a story about an autistic boy named Anthony. You wrote about *my* Anthony.'

Beth knots her eyebrows and says nothing.

'The details. You knew everything. Barney, his rocks, the Three Little Pigs. He died when he was eight, almost two years ago.'

'Oh my God, Olivia, I'm so sorry.'

'Do you hear the sound of his voice?'

'Sorry?'

'Does he speak to you in words?' Olivia clears her throat and blinks back tears. What she wouldn't give to hear the sound of Anthony talking.

'I'm not sure I understand what you're asking me.'

'I don't know how else to say this. Your book isn't fiction. This is my son's voice,' Olivia says, lifting the pages.

Beth tentatively explores Olivia's face, like she's waiting for her to explain the punch line to a joke she doesn't quite get.

Olivia stares at her, waiting for her response. Olivia tunes in to the refrigerator humming in the kitchen, the wood popping and hissing in the fireplace. She's aware of her own eyelashes each time she blinks and water from her wet hair dripping down her neck and back.

'Look, I'm really so sorry about your son, but I didn't — '

'How did you write this?'

'I don't know what you mean.'

'How do you know about autism? Do you know anyone else who has it?'

'No. But I've read about it — '

'You couldn't know this from just reading what's out there.'

'And I've observed kids who have it. Even before I ever read anything, I think I've always been tuned in to the kids who have it.'

'This is my son,' Olivia says, raising the pages up off her lap.

'I'm sorry, Olivia. I didn't realize you had an autistic son named Anthony. I had no idea I'd be asking you to read something that's so personal. It's amazing that he reminds you so much of your own boy.'

'This is my son's voice. I know I sound like I'm some desperate, grief-stricken mother who wants to believe someone is in contact with my dead son. But I'm not crazy. This is my Anthony,' Olivia says, flipping the pages.

Beth's eyes widen as she notices all the red and pink ink on the sheets of paper.

'I'm sorry. I don't know what to say,' says Beth.

'I know. I know I've freaked you out. Believe me, I'm freaked out, too. But there's no other way to explain this.'

'It's a coincidence.'

'It's not. This is my son,' says Olivia, rubbing the top page with the palm of her hand. Her hand is shaking.

'Look, I'm sorry, I really am. But I didn't hear any voices. The book was inspired by a short story I'd written years ago about a boy I'd once seen creating a line of rocks at the beach. And then recently I read some books on autism that somehow seemed to fit the boy in my short story and the boy on the beach, and I combined them all into this character. Honestly.'

A boy creating a line of rocks at the beach. Olivia used to take Anthony here, to Nantucket, to Fat Ladies and Miacomet Beaches, when he was little. The boy Beth remembers is Anthony. Olivia's sure of it. An electric chill runs through her.

'I don't know how or why, but my son gave you his story. It didn't come from you. It came *through* you.'

Beth stares at Olivia in disbelief and says nothing. Olivia holds on tight to the pages on her lap. She can't leave this living-room couch without somehow convincing Beth. She exhales and regroups.

'Let me start over. I love your book. I do. It's beautiful and compelling and so real.'

A smile breaks through Beth's guard, a small ray of light peeking through a pinhole in a concrete wall.

'But you didn't quite finish it. Where you ended the story, that's not the ending.'

Beth's smile vanishes, but she's listening.

'We need to know what Anthony thinks about his time here, about his life and his autism. What does he believe was his life's purpose? This is the big, unanswered question in your novel. What did his life mean to him?'

Olivia's voice leaves her. She feels as if she

needs the answer to this question more than she needs the air in this room. She's been asking this question, praying for an answer, for so long, and sitting in front of her is an ordinary but now completely spooked woman, a neighbor she barely knows, who somehow, for some reason, has access to the answer. Access to Anthony.

'Even if you think I'm completely nuts, please listen to me here. Go back to your story and write a little bit more. Trust me. You haven't gotten the right ending yet.'

Beth still looks a little freaked, but she's listening. She nods.

'I'll think about it.'

Olivia searches Beth's eyes. This is as far as she can push.

'Thank you. I can't thank you enough. And trust me, you'll see. You'll know you have the real ending once you write it.'

Beth chews the nail of her index finger and stares at her book on Olivia's lap. 'You really believe what I wrote came from your son?'

'I know it did.'

Olivia's eyes are brown. This book is Anthony. It's not similar to him or based on him. It doesn't remind her of him. It *is* him.

As Olivia stands up to leave, she notices Beth aiming with her eyes to pry the pages of her manuscript from Olivia's hands. Oh my God, she can't leave Anthony's words here. She can't.

'Can I please take this copy with me?'

Beth hesitates. She looks bewildered and exhausted.

'Okay.'

314

'Thank you. I can't thank you enough for writing this. You've let me know my son in ways I was never able to know him.'

Olivia slides the manuscript back into the box, and Beth walks her to the front door. Olivia looks Beth in the eye, making sure Beth really sees her, then embraces her in a hug.

'Thank you.'

Beth nods and whispers, 'You're welcome.'

Olivia retrieves her still-soaked shoes and coat, says a reluctant good-bye, and leaves. As soon as she steps outside, the wind whips her hood off her head. She runs across the lawn to her Jeep but pauses before opening the door. She tips her head back, giving her face to the enormous gray sky, to the wind and the rain, and prays.

Anthony, I know it's you. Please, tell her more. Give me just a little bit more.

She stands in the road, exposed to the wind, vulnerable to the rain, to heaven, to God. She can't imagine why Anthony would choose to communicate through Beth and not her. But he did. She believes. She more than believes. She knows. This is Anthony, and the unwritten ending to Beth's novel is the answer to Olivia's prayers.

35

It's early Sunday morning, and Beth is sitting on Petra's living-room couch, waiting for her to return from the kitchen with herbal tea. She pulls a speck of black fuzz off the couch cushion and flicks it to the floor. Petra's couch is white and many years old, but it still looks brand-new without a single stain, only one of many signs in the room of a woman who lives without a husband or children.

Opposite the couch sits Petra's meditation chair, a low, espresso-colored rattan seat with a high back and a white cushion (again, no stains). A beautiful, handwoven pink-and-gray blanket is curled around the seat, revealing the shape of where Petra was sitting only moments before. A lavender candle burns on the low, round coffee table next to a copy of *Cook's* magazine and a deck of tarot cards. The room is sparsely decorated — a black-and-white photograph of Petra with her siblings and parents, a painting of a sunrise over the ocean, a wooden carving of a sperm whale, a jade plant in a large, blue ceramic pot on the floor, its branches decorated with tiny goldball Christmas ornaments, a glass bowl filled with colored sea glass. There is no TV.

Petra walks into the room, still in pajamas, barefoot, toenails painted bright pink, and hands Beth a steaming-hot mug. She sits cross-legged on her chair, wraps the blanket around her, sips

316

her tea, and leans forward, directing herself toward Beth.

'So this is incredibly cool,' Petra says.

'This is crazy, not cool.'

'Well, it's kind of mind-bending cool, but I think it's cool.'

'Petra, this is unbelievable, impossible.'

'It's a lot to process,' Petra says.

'It's pure coincidence.'

'Or not.'

'It has to be.'

'Why does it have to be?'

'So you believe in this kind of stuff?'

'What stuff is that?' asks Petra, knowing full well what Beth is referring to.

'You know, channeling dead people. Talking to ghosts.'

Petra laughs and tucks her hair behind her ear.

'I believe in divine beings and spirituality.'

'But what does that mean?'

'I believe that we're more than flesh and bone, that we are all spirits living here on Earth for a spiritual purpose.'

Beth sighs and sips her tea. Her own experience with religion, with concepts and beliefs about spirituality and life after death, is extremely limited. Her mother wasn't a church-goer. Beth's not even sure what denomination her mother might have belonged to. For a while when Beth was a teenager, she and her mother went to different churches on the weekends, sometimes even to other towns, with the purpose of at least exposing Beth to organized religion.

She remembers little about any of them. There

were strange choral songs that she didn't know the words to and statues of Jesus nailed to the cross that gave her nightmares. That's about all. They usually went for jelly doughnuts after. She remembers the doughnuts. Then one weekend the church field trips stopped, and her mother left it up to Beth to choose. She was about sixteen. She chose to sleep in on Sundays.

When her mother died, Beth wished she hadn't made that choice. She assumed her mother was in heaven, but she had no religion to help her believe in heaven as a real place. She could only imagine heaven as a part of the sky filled with puffy, white clouds and chubby, naked babies with wings. And it was hard to include her mother in that image. It still is.

'Okay, what about what Olivia believes?' asks Beth. 'Do you believe that's even possible?'

'Yeah, I do. I sometimes experience the presence of spiritual energy when I meditate.'

'So do you hear actual voices?'

'No, but some people do, and some people see images, visual flashes. For me, it's not like hearing or seeing, it's more a sudden knowing, but the knowledge doesn't come from me.'

'That's what we call *thinking*, Petra.'

'It's not. It's different, it's information I wouldn't normally think, or it's communicated to me in a style that's not mine. It doesn't come from me, it comes to me or through me. It's hard to explain.'

'Okay, but even if I believed in this, why would this boy's spirit choose me? I mean, why not communicate directly with his mother?'

318

'I don't know. Maybe his mother wasn't open to receiving him. Too much grief blocking the channel.'

Beth looks around Petra's living room — the tarot cards, the rose quartz crystal in the shape of a heart hanging from a string, sparkling in one of the windows, the meditation chair. If the spirit of a boy named Anthony was looking to channel his story through a woman on Nantucket, why not use Petra? Why not choose someone who believes in this stuff?

'Yeah, but why me? Before writing this book, I had no connection to him or autism.'

'We're all connected, even if we don't know how. Maybe his communicating through you gives you something that you need in this lifetime.'

'Me? Like what?'

'I don't know. Maybe the chance at a new life, a creative life. Maybe it's a lesson, something in the story you've written that you need to learn.'

Writing this book has given Beth access to a part of herself that she'd forgotten about, the creative dreamer she stored away in the attic so many years ago. But a lesson for her? Her book is about autism. It's not about her. She shakes her head.

'Did you ever feel like you were tapping into something or someone else while you were writing?' asks Petra.

'Not exactly.'

Hearing the obvious uncertainty in her own voice surprises Beth. She never heard any voices.

She didn't. But at times when she'd write, hours would go by, a whole morning and afternoon, and it'd feel like only a few minutes. And sometimes she'd read back what she wrote and think, *How did I come up with this? How did I know how to write this?* And there were the dreams. Those full and vivid dreams about Anthony.

'But, Petra, *I* wrote this book.'

'I know you did, but maybe his spirit provided you with inspiration, guidance toward an intended path, some necessary truth.'

Beth chews on her thumbnail and concentrates hard on what Petra just said. 'Okay, but if I was going to be a conduit for someone's spiritual message, why would it be for this boy and not my own mother or my grandmother or my grandfather? Why this boy?'

'I don't know. Again, maybe there's a reason you're connected. Maybe there's something in what he's saying for you to learn. Or maybe Olivia's just a mother who really loves and misses her son, and there's something unresolved with him.'

Beth sips her tea and thinks for a minute.

'She wants to know what purpose his life served.'

'There it is. And your book reminds her so much of him, she sees the story you've written as her chance to understand why he was here and heal. What about that?'

Beth nods.

'I can live with that.'

'Okay, then what do you think about her

feedback? Do you think you have the right ending?'

There it is again, just like when Olivia was in Beth's living room, that electric, sick, sinking feeling.

'I don't know. I'm not sure of anything right now.'

'I would go back to the library and try to write a little more. See if Anthony has anything more to say. It can't hurt.'

'There's something else,' Beth admits.

Petra raises her eyebrows and waits.

'Every time she said, 'You don't have the right ending yet,' I swear I felt a zap and my stomach dropped to my knees. I'd *just* ended things with Jimmy.'

'Interesting.' Petra taps her mug with her index finger. 'Are you having second thoughts?'

'I don't know, but every time she said, 'You're not done,' it was like a lightning bolt. She was talking about me and Jimmy, not the book.'

'So maybe you and Jimmy aren't done.'

'Petra, she was talking about the book. She doesn't know anything about me and Jimmy.'

'Yeah, she was talking about the book, but what you heard was Jimmy.'

Beth sighs. She thought her book was done. She thought she and Jimmy were done. Now this woman she barely knows walks into her house and suddenly she's questioning everything.

'You can believe the spiritual stuff or not,' says Petra. 'Call it a wild coincidence if you want. I believe in it, and I believe in you. Go write. You don't have the right ending yet.'

There it is again. Lightning bolt. Woozy stomach. Jimmy.

'I don't know, I'll think about it.' Beth checks her watch. 'I need to get going.'

'Come here.'

Both women stand and hug close, heart up against heart.

'Thanks for the talk,' says Beth.

'Anytime.'

Beth pulls on her coat, grabs her bag, and waves as she walks out the front door, still uncertain of everything, including the smooth, round moonstone necklace in her pocket.

36

Olivia is sitting at her kitchen table, reading. She had planned to sit and read from one of her journals, but she opened the mail first, and she unintentionally got sucked into reading an advance reader copy sent to her from Louise, a book called *Believing in Bliss: Twelve Steps to Finding Happiness from Within*. She finishes the first short chapter, closes the book, and studies the cover, surprised by her interest in it. She sets the book aside for now.

She sips her coffee, thinking about Beth. Still no word from her. Every day, Olivia prays that Beth decides to write just a little bit more. Olivia can think of little else, consumed and desperate with the desire to read more of Anthony's words, to hear his voice, to have the answer she needs.

Why were you here, Anthony?

She sips her coffee and sighs. Her journal will have to do for today. She opens it and finds one of her favorite entries.

December 7, 2008

Today we had David's father and brother over to watch the Patriots game. Artie is really going deaf, but he refuses to admit it and get a hearing aid, so the TV volume was on screaming loud all day long. And they all yell a lot when they watch the game, especially when it's against the Jets (and it doesn't matter if they're winning or losing, they yell either way). So with all that noise, I knew Anthony would be avoiding the living room today.

I spent the first part of the afternoon in the kitchen. I made an antipasto, chicken Parm, and lasagna for supper. Anthony doesn't like being in the kitchen when I'm cooking. I think it's all the noise I make banging pots and pans and dishes, and maybe all my unexpected moving around, and maybe even the smells. I don't know for sure why, but when I'm cooking in there, he tends to steer clear.

So with the men hollering at the loud TV in the living room and me busy cooking in the kitchen, I worried Anthony would be out of sorts in the house. It was a nice day, so after lunch I sent him outside.

I'm so glad we got that new, fancy Fort Knox lock for the gate so he can be outside alone on the deck or in the yard, and we don't have to worry about his bolting God knows where. I don't ever want to have to search the neighborhood for him again. It's the worst feeling, not knowing where he is, if he's hurt or scared, if we'll be able to find him before something awful happens. And I hated ringing some of the neighbors' doorbells, watching their human faces change to stone as I explained what was happening. He's a sweet, nonverbal boy on the autism spectrum, not an escaped sex offender.

So I knew he was outside and that he couldn't leave the yard, but I didn't know what he was doing out there, and I didn't check on him for a long time when I probably should've. I would normally poke my head out every few minutes, but today I felt greedy — I just wanted a few more minutes of peace and quiet. A few more. A few more.

And it was interesting but of course not surprising to notice that David didn't get up off the couch once to see how Anthony was doing. He assumes I'll do it. I chopped and stirred and boiled and resisted the urge to check on Anthony in the yard, and I didn't tell David to do it or fight with him because he didn't think to do it himself.

I finished cooking the chicken Parm, had the lasagna baking in the oven, and even made the antipasto, all without interruption. No screaming from outside. That was good, but sometimes quiet that lasts too long is just as bloodcurdling as one of his screams, and I started to fear what he might be doing out there. He could be naked and playing with his own poop. This spring, he decapitated all the newly bloomed tulips. You never know. But most likely he's just swinging on his swing or playing with the sand in his sandbox or lining up his rocks.

I finally went outside, and he was lying on his back on the deck in a square patch of sun. His arms were by his sides, palms up, his feet splayed, his eyes open. He was just lying there, staring at the sky.

The square of sun was big enough for two, so I decided to lie down next to him. It was a crisp fall day, cold in the shade but warm enough to be comfortable without a coat in the sun. In fact, the deck boards were hot, and the heat felt like heaven on my sore back.

The sky was a perfect blue, not a cloud anywhere. I looked over at Anthony looking up at the sky and wondered, How long has he been lying like this? Has he been doing this the whole time? What is he looking at? There are no clouds, no birds, no planes. What could be capturing his attention for so long? What's going on in that head of his?

I started to feel antsy, like I should get up and do something. I thought, I can't just lie here. I should be accomplishing something. I still had a sink full of dirty dishes. I should pretend to care about the Patriots and join the men in the living room for a while. I should throw in a load of laundry.

And I felt guilty for ignoring Anthony for so long. I thought I should get him up, redirect him, get him engaged in doing something he should be working on. I thought (with dread) about his upcoming IEP meeting. He's so behind. He has so much to work on, so much to learn.

But luckily, for some reason, I stopped myself. I decided to continue to lie there and do what Anthony was doing, seemingly nothing, for as long as he wanted to do it. So we lay there on the deck, side by side, only a couple of inches separating his entire body from mine, and watched the unchanging blue sky.

My mind wandered all over the place at first. I imagined all those dirty dishes sitting in the sink, not even soaking in water, begging me to come wash them. I worried about his IEP meeting and thought about everything that I need to do to prepare for it. But I stayed. And I eventually let it all go. I did nothing, and I experienced simply being — the blue sky, the warm sun, the cool air, the hot decking, and Anthony next to me.

At some point, I looked over at him, and he had the biggest smile stretched across his face. God, his smile makes me so happy. And so there we were, the two of us lying on the deck together, smiling at the sky.

And then the sun moved on, and our square turned to shade. Anthony sat up and shot me a sideways glance and a pleased grin that I swear said, Wasn't that AWESOME, Mom? Didn't you have the best time looking up at the sky with me?

And then he screeched and flapped his hands and ran into the house.

Yes, it was, Anthony. It was one of the best times I've ever had.

37

Beth is sitting in her seat at the table in the library with Sophie's laptop opened to the last page of her book. She's rereading the ending. She likes it. It works, but she begrudgingly admits that it doesn't knock her socks off.

But how else would she end it? She taps her teeth with the chewed nail of her index finger and reads it again. She leans back and stares vaguely at the stage and the oil paintings of Thoreau, Emerson, and Melville on the wall behind it.

You don't have the right ending.

Why should she listen to Olivia? Endings are so subjective. She reads the last chapter again. It's a perfectly reasonable way to end this story.

What purpose did Anthony's life serve?

It is a powerful question, and if Beth is being honest, she can see how she skirted around answering it, how readers might be left wondering after turning the final page. But what's wrong with leaving them wondering? Isn't that a good thing? Leave the reader with something to think about. Resonance.

Beth sighs and pushes the laptop aside. She pulls out a brand-new notebook from her bag and opens it to the first blank page. She taps her teeth with her pen and stares out the window. No one else is here today except for Mary

Crawford, who is sitting behind the circulation desk.

The library is hot and quiet and still. The clock ticks. She looks down at her notebook.

Blank.

She doesn't need to write any more. The ending she chose is good enough. Even if she does write another ending, it might not provide Olivia with the answer she wants. Beth can't guarantee that. She caps her pen and closes the notebook, but she doesn't leave. She stares out the window, debating with herself, listening to the ticking clock.

You don't have the right ending yet.

The ending you wrote is fine.

What was the purpose of Anthony's life?

Maybe there's a lesson in the story for you.

Jimmy.

Tick. Tick. Tick.

She stretches her arms up over her head and arches her back. She plants her feet on the floor, sits in her seat a little straighter, opens her notebook, and uncaps her pen. She stares down at the blank page.

Blank.

She hasn't bumped up against this kind of resistance since she first started writing here all those months ago. But here it is again, feeling bigger than ever, a fifty-foot brick wall standing between her and the possibility of a new ending. Maybe there *is* nothing left to write.

What was the purpose of Anthony's life?

Tick. Tick. Tick.

'Hey, Anthony. Do you have anything more to

say here?' she whispers.

She holds her breath and listens.

Tick. Tick. Tick.

No voice from another dimension. She exhales, feeling relieved. But then something does come to her, a question asked in her own voice.

What's the purpose of my life?

And then a thought barrels through her mind, big and full of confidence, not composed of sound or an image in her mind's eye, but knowing, ethereal, yet as real and sure as the chair she's sitting in — the answer to her question.

They are one and the same.

She closes her eyes and breathes. She breathes to the rhythm of the ticking clock, and soon both seem to slow down and stretch out. She pictures the fifty-foot brick wall of resistance towering over her in her mind's eye, but instead of trying to scale it or knock it down, she imagines walking along it. She smiles as she assesses the wall from this new perspective. That impossibly tall wall is only a few feet wide. She strolls around it, and standing there before her in front of a pure blue sky, looking straight into her eyes and smiling, is Anthony. She mirrors his smile and nods.

She opens her eyes and picks up her pen, feeling suddenly and powerfully inspired as her hand flies across the page.

38

Olivia awakens still tired to yet another dark gray morning, not thinking yet, not realizing what day it is. She lingers in a steaming-hot shower, gets dressed, and then sits at the kitchen table with a book and a cup of coffee, like any other morning. Not until she drains the last sip does today's date slap her across the face.

January tenth. And any semblance of a normal day evaporates in that realization.

Like today, January tenth two years ago started as a typical morning. It was a Sunday. Anthony got up first, and Olivia followed him downstairs. He parked himself on the couch in front of Barney while she got coffee and breakfast started, and David took a shower.

She toasted three French Toast sticks and served them with maple syrup on Anthony's blue plate. She arranged his plate, his grape juice, a napkin, and a fork on the kitchen table at Anthony's seat and went back upstairs to take a shower while David was still home. By the time she dressed and came back downstairs, Anthony had eaten his breakfast and David had downed his coffee. David said good-bye and left for an open house at least a couple of hours before he really needed to go, part of his daily practice of avoiding her.

Anthony was now upstairs in the master bathroom, playing with water in the sink. It was their typical weekend routine. After breakfast, Anthony played with water in the sink while Olivia cleaned up the dishes, drank a cup of coffee, and read some of the *Globe*. She'd long ago stopped chaperoning him in the bathroom while he played. He knew not to use the tub without her there. Tubby time was at night, and he understood that rule. He liked rules.

And he was finally potty-trained. He typically peed before breakfast, and he normally didn't need to go again until after lunch. So while he played in the bathroom in the mornings, she didn't worry about his using the toilet or poop and all the unsavory adventures that often came with poop.

This was what they did every weekend. She drank her coffee and read the paper, and Anthony played in the sink. He loved to run the cold water over his hands. He loved to fill a large plastic cup and dump the water down the drain over and over and over. He also loved to close the stopper and fill the sink. Then he'd scoop some water into his cup and pour it back in, water into water.

He also loved shampoo. She bought lots of travel-size bottles of shampoo for him and made sure to keep her expensive bottles hidden and out of reach. He'd take off his shirt first. He liked to empty the entire bottle into the sink and make bubbles. He also liked to rub the shampoo on his arms and body. He liked the feel of his skin wet and slippery with liquid soap.

When she was done with her cup of coffee, she'd go upstairs to his room, grab his clothes, go into the bathroom, hand Anthony a dry towel, and tell him that it was time to get dressed. Then they'd go to the bottom step, and she'd help him get into his clothes.

On January tenth, two years ago, she drank her morning cup of coffee and read the paper while Anthony played with water in the bathroom and David hid from her at work. Maybe if she'd drunk her coffee faster. Maybe if David had stayed home longer. Maybe if she hadn't been absorbed in reading the paper.

The taste of this morning's coffee still lingers in her mouth, a taste she loves, but it's suddenly too bitter, foul, nauseating. She rushes to the bathroom and retches over the sink. She brushes her teeth, rinses her mouth with mouthwash, then sits on the cold bathroom floor.

She drank that cup of coffee two years ago in complete peace and quiet. She was reading the Arts section when something about the silence radiating from upstairs crawled under her skin and screamed. She put the paper down and listened. She heard nothing out of the ordinary, just the sound of water running in the pipes.

He's fine, she thought, then the second she finished thinking it, she heard a thud.

THUD. Too big, too heavy, too loud to be a travel bottle of shampoo or a plastic cup full of water. She doesn't remember anything between the kitchen chair and the bathroom. She remembers THUD, then instantly there was Anthony, lying on the tile floor, seizing.

She now peels herself up off the bathroom floor. She gets bundled in her winter coat, hat, and boots and heads outside for a walk, trying to evade the memory of what happened next. Maybe if she keeps moving, maybe if she's not sitting in one easily found, stationary spot, maybe the memories from the rest of that morning won't invade her.

It works at first. She focuses on walking, on bracing herself against the painful cold, leaning into the biting wind. But soon she is literally numb to the weather, and everything she walks past is gray — the houses, the streets, the trees, the sky. Walking becomes one long, familiar, gray, numb blur, not enough to keep her mind and body distracted. And the memories begin marching through her.

Anthony lying on the bathroom floor. Anthony's eyes rolled back in his head. His toes curled. Every muscle in his small, shirtless, pajama-bottomed body squeezing him, shaking him, distorting him.

She'd seen him like that once before when he was four. Just before it happened, he had an odd, blank look on his face. He was staring off at nothing, more so than usual, and he looked sort of washed-out. Then he dropped to the floor, unconscious, his whole body gripped tight and shuddering. It lasted about a minute, a completely terrifying, hour-long minute. Then it released him, and he came to about a minute later, drained but okay.

She and David were both there when it happened. David called 911, and she rode in the ambulance with Anthony while David followed in his car to Children's Hospital. Anthony had an EEG and some other tests she doesn't remember. The neurologist said Anthony had a seizure. He said that seizures are common with autism, that about a third of kids with autism also have epilepsy. He said that seizures are usually controlled well by medication and that Anthony might never have another one.

She watched him like a nervous hawk for a long time after that, but Anthony didn't have another episode. She relaxed and convinced herself that the seizing was gone for good, that it was a onetime fluke. Finally, they were lucky.

The experience of that first seizure when Anthony was four did nothing to prepare her for the sight of this one. This seizure was different. It kept going. One rolled into the next, each one gripping him tighter, shaking him harder. As if someone were adding kindling to a fire, the blaze kept growing bigger, hotter, brighter.

She tucked a towel under his head, unaware that he'd already banged it against the porcelain tile floor with way too much force, and watched in helpless horror. Then it released him. The seizing stopped, and he just lay there. His eyes were still rolled back. His feet were splayed. His lips weren't pink enough. His lips were purple. Purple turning blue.

Anthony!

As she wrapped her arms around him, she felt his limp wrists and his neck with her fingers. She couldn't feel anything. She put her ear on his slippery, wet chest. She thinks that's when she started screaming.

She called 911. She doesn't remember what

she told them. She doesn't remember what they said to do.

She pinched his nose and began breathing into him.

Breathe!

She pressed on his small, naked chest with her hands the way she'd first been taught as a teenager on a lifeless doll named Annie.

Anthony, breathe!

Then there were two men. The firefighters. They took over. A bag on Anthony's mouth, a large man repeatedly pushing the heels of his large hands down on Anthony's chest. She remembers thinking, *Stop! You're hurting him!*

Then two more people. Anthony on a board. Anthony down the stairs. Anthony on a stretcher. Another man, bigger than David, straddled over Anthony, sitting on his knees, pumping Anthony's chest over and over with his hands. Violent. Unrelenting. A bag squeezed over Anthony's mouth. All while they were moving. Two men carrying Anthony and the big man on the stretcher out the front door to the ambulance in the driveway.

The images are surreal and all too vivid. Even as she's remembering each moment now, reliving that morning and crying as she walks, it still feels unbelievable, as if it couldn't have happened. She walks faster.

She sat in the front of the ambulance, facing backward, trying to see Anthony, to see what they were doing to him, trying to will him to breathe, to open his eyes.

Anthony, look at me.

She doesn't remember calling David, but she must've. Or someone did. He was there, standing next to her in the ER hallway when a short, balding, bird-nosed man, replaced in her mind's eye with the image of her grandfather who was similarly small and bald, approached them.

I'm sorry is all she remembers before the sound of her own voice screaming. The sound of her own voice screaming is the last thing she remembers with any clarity for the rest of January tenth.

She's on her third loop through her neighborhood, circling the same gray, empty houses and gray, barren fields, with no intention of altering her route or going home. She pauses only once each time around, in front of Beth Ellis's house.

The black truck and blue minivan are both in the driveway, and the lights are on. Beth's home. Olivia stands in the street in front of the house, desperate to ring the doorbell. She hasn't seen or heard from Beth since that morning in her living room. But each time she passes by, she talks herself out of it. She's in no condition to talk sensibly to anyone.

Not today.

She walks the loop three more times and stops. She's freezing and exhausted. She checks her watch.

My God, it's only noon.

Twelve more hours of January tenth. She can't walk anymore. She has to go home.

On her way, she takes a quick detour over to

her mailbox. She pulls out a couple of bills, a catalog, and a manila envelope with only her first name on it and no postage. She shoves the other mail back into the box, and with a scared and hopeful heart she opens the envelope.

In her hands, she holds a thin stack of printer paper, stapled together at the top left corner. The top piece of paper is blank, but a pink Post-it note is stuck to the middle of the page.

Olivia —

For you and for me.

Thank you,

Beth

She pulls the sticky note off the page, revealing a single word.

Epilogue.

39

Today is a Sunday-brunch book club at Jill's house. It was Beth's turn, but Jill insisted on hosting. Beth is early, the first to arrive. Jill walks her into the dining room.

'What do you think?' asks Jill, beaming, anticipating Beth's reaction.

Beth surveys the room. Blue dinner plates on blue-and-white gingham place mats. A white bookmark lying on the center of each plate. A single, large, smooth, white rock placed on top of each folded blue linen napkin. A large glass-vase centerpiece packed with purple tulips sitting in the middle of a round metal tray covered with small, white stones. Skinny champagne flutes. A glass pitcher of orange juice and a pot of coffee. The food on the side table — a bowl of mixed berries, bagels and cream cheese, some kind of egg casserole, bacon, and French Toast sticks.

'It's spectacular,' says Beth. 'You're amazing. Thank you for doing this.'

Jill waves off the compliment and excuses herself to tend to something still cooking in the kitchen. Beth chooses a seat and picks up the homemade bookmark on her plate.

Reading Group Guide followed by ten questions created by Jill, printed in an elegant calligraphy font. Beth smiles.

They were here in Jill's dining room for book club this time last year. This time last year, they talked about Jimmy's affair and her separation instead of the book. She remembers that night as if it were yesterday and a million years ago. She remembers feeling terrified, humiliated, sick with worry, and drunk on vodka. She thought that night was the beginning of the end of everything.

What a difference a year makes.

The front door opens.

'Hello?' someone calls.

'Come in!' hollers Jill from the kitchen.

A few seconds later, Courtney and Georgia come into the dining room. They pause for the slightest moment, taking in the spread and Beth. They look ready to burst, like children absorbing the sight of presents beneath the tree on Christmas morning.

'Beth!' says Georgia. 'I just finished it last night! This morning actually, you kept me up till two a.m. It was *so* good!'

'I finished it weeks ago. Read it in three sittings. I've been *dying* to talk about it,' says Courtney.

'Really?' asks Beth, grinning, her face flushed.

Jill made them all promise not to speak a word about the book until this morning, to save any discussion for book club, when they could all talk about it together. Even though Beth found this request to be more than a little controlling, even for Jill, Beth agreed. They all did. But she found sticking to her promise almost unbearable, as if she were stewing neck deep in a puddle of her own anxiety, every day for the past month battling the almost irresistible urge to ask each of her friends, *Have you read it yet? What did you think?* Every time she talked to Petra, she wanted to pepper her with at least a dozen questions, especially about the ending. But she held her tongue. It's been an agonizingly long thirty days.

Petra walks in next, carrying a thick stack of white paper under her arm. Instead of paperbacks or library books or e-readers, they've all come to book club today with 186 pages of printer paper. Beth's manuscript.

Petra plunks her stack of pages down on the table and smiles.

'It's *beautiful*.'

'Who knew you had this in you? How did you come up with this? Do you know a boy with autism?' asks Georgia.

'No,' says Beth. 'Not really.'

'I just heard a question,' says Jill, coming in from the kitchen with a bottle of champagne in each hand. 'No questions until we're all here.'

'Well, it's inspired, it really is. To get inside his head the way you did. I really understood him. I loved him,' says Georgia.

Beth looks around the room. Jill, Petra, Courtney, and Georgia. It's usually just the five of them, but today, there's an extra place setting and one seat still empty.

As if on cue, the doorbell rings. Jill smiles at Beth and heads toward the front door.

'You look great,' says Georgia.

'Thanks.'

A book club held in her honor, discussing the book she wrote, her first novel, called for a new outfit. She made a special shopping trip to the Hyannis mall. Sophie came with her. Beth's wearing a red-and-orange, floral wrap dress, a new pair of cream-colored, open-toed wedges, a pair of dangly earrings that Sophie picked out, and even a little makeup.

'And I love your necklace,' says Courtney. 'Is it new?'

Beth places her hand just above her heart and rubs the shimmering bluish-white moonstone between her thumb and forefinger.

'It is,' says Beth, smiling.

Jill returns to the dining room followed by Olivia. She's holding 186 pages in her hands. Beth gets up and walks over to her — her photographer, her neighbor, her editor, her friend — and hugs her.

'Thanks for coming.'

With a hand on Olivia's shoulder, Jill guides her to the chair next to Beth's and introduces her to everyone.

'Ready? Let's raise our glasses,' Jill says, waiting for everyone to lift her flute. 'To Beth and her beautiful book!'

'Cheers!'

They all clink glasses and drink champagne.

'That's my only big problem with your book,' says Courtney.

Beth swallows and waits, her stomach clenched.

'It doesn't have a title.'

'I know,' says Beth, relieved. 'I can't decide.'

'She was awful at naming her kids, too, remember?' says Jill.

She's right. Poor Gracie was still Baby Girl Ellis when they left the hospital. She was almost a week old before she had a name.

'How did you pick the name Anthony?' asks Georgia.

Beth glances over at Petra and then Olivia and smiles, like she's sharing a secret.

'I don't know. I just liked the name.'

She doesn't know why she never considered any other names for her main character. And she doesn't know anyone named Anthony.

'I'm still crying over that ending,' says Georgia.

'I cried, too,' says Jill. 'It gave me goose bumps.'

Beth looks over at Petra with raised eyebrows, waiting, holding her breath.

'It's the perfect ending,' says Petra.

Beth exhales, and she swears she can feel her heart smile.

'Thank you so much. I love the ending, too,' she says, locking eyes with Olivia. 'It's my favorite part of the whole book.'

When Beth began writing this story, she remembers thinking how alien this character was to her, this boy with autism who didn't speak, who didn't like to be touched, who didn't make eye contact, who loved Barney and the number three and lining up rocks. But as she kept writing, as his autism became more familiar to her, she began to see more and more the ways in which they are similar — she chews her fingernails as a form of self-soothing, she feels calm when her house is clean and all the picture frames are level and centered, she can't stand the thought of someone else sitting in her seat at the library, she feels agitated when there's too much noise around her, and sometimes, she just needs to be alone.

But their real similarities have nothing to do with autism. As she continued to write, she began to realize that this story was more about Anthony the boy than Anthony the boy with autism. Autism became almost irrelevant, and eventually she was simply writing about Anthony, a boy worthy of happiness and safety, of feeling wanted and loved. Just like her. The more she wrote about Anthony, the more she realized that she was actually writing about herself.

She loves the whole book, but the last chapter, the one she almost didn't write, is without question her favorite. And the most essential. It was the lesson her heart needed, the advice her true self wanted to hear.

Now, her book is done. She rubs the smooth, cool moonstone on her necklace between her forefinger and thumb and presses it against her heart.

Thank you, Anthony.

'I think we should talk about the ending after we talk about the beginning,' says Jill. 'I've made a discussion guide for us on the bookmarks. Food is there. There's plenty more champagne, and coffee and orange juice, but please don't use the Moët for mimosas. Use the Korbel. Okay, let's eat and discuss the book!'

40

It's early in the day, and the sun feels soothing on Olivia's back as she walks along the water's edge on Fat Ladies Beach. It's a clear morning, no fog, and only a gentle wind. The sky is a pure, soft blue, and the air smells clean. Yesterday, when the sky was crowded with heavy, gray clouds, and the wind was fierce, kite surfers in black wet suits were all over this beach, riding parallel to the shore, playing on the choppy waves. Today, the thrill-seeking kite surfers have stayed home, replaced by the dog walkers. Olivia has already nodded hello and good-morning to at least a dozen people and their pets. So much activity on Fat Ladies Beach is unusual for April. But this weekend, it's to be expected. This weekend is Daffodil Festival weekend.

She feels done walking, but she won't leave until she finds one more. With her jeans rolled up to her calves and her shoes hanging from her peace fingers, she strolls barefoot on the smooth, packed sand, wet and cold from a recent high tide, a trail of her own sunken footprints following her. She walks with her head down, her eyes focused on the golden grains of sand in front of her. The beach is washed clean. It's mostly fine sand, only a few broken clamshells scattered here and there. She persists.

As she knew she would, she finds one, only partially exposed above the sand, white and glistening in the sunlight. She picks it up, then squats by the lip of the ocean, waiting for it to come and lick her rock clean. She beholds it in the palm of her hand. White and round and smooth. Anthony would love it. She smiles. She's ready to go now.

Back in her neighborhood, she walks in the middle of the road, taking notice of all the daffodils, bright, unexpected explosions of jubilant color, like three million yellow phoenixes rising above the ashen gray. Life returns. It's been unseasonably warm this year, and the daffodils bloomed two weeks early. They're everywhere. They're beautiful.

There are cars in many of the driveways now, windows open in many of the houses. As she walks, she hears a lawn mower nearby and someone hammering in the distance. She smells mulch and paint. Spring is here.

She stops in front of Beth's house. The driveway is empty. They're probably already out in 'Sconset. She said they'd be tailgating today. Two Adirondack chairs sit side by side on the front lawn, bright and slick white, freshly painted. Olivia smiles. She checks her watch. She won't have time to say goodbye to Beth before leaving, but she'll see her again soon.

Before turning to go home, she walks to check her mailbox one last time. She opens the door. No mail. Good.

She makes her way back to her cottage, a home that she and David bought for their future. It was a lovely and romantic plan, but it wasn't meant to be. For someone else maybe. She

346

stands in the street before her house, its gray cedar shingles and white trim, the farmer's porch, the stone walkway. The FOR SALE sign staked in the front lawn by the edge of the road shines brightly, reflecting the sunlight. She sighs. For someone else.

She's already packed. She shipped most everything yesterday, and the rest is in the Jeep. Her load is actually lighter today than it was just over a year ago. There's no need to go back inside.

Before getting into her Jeep, she sits on the grass in the sun, already much higher in the sky than it was on the beach, and admires her daffodils. She planted a dozen more this year, so now there are eighteen. Eighteen happy yellow and white flowers, dancing in the gentle breeze, celebrating Daffodil Day.

The promise of a new beginning.

And they celebrate the day today above a bed of white stones, spread evenly over the earth around them. A rock garden and eighteen daffodils. The perfect home for Anthony's rocks.

She thinks about tossing the rock she found this morning, still in her hand, onto the pile but changes her mind. Instead, she chooses two more from the ground and holds all three in her hand. There. Three rocks. That's all she needs.

She picks a single daffodil, inhales its buttery-sweet fragrance, and tucks it into her hair over her right ear. Then she gets into her Jeep, takes one last look at her cottage, her daffodils, and Anthony's rocks, and drives away.

The high-speed ferry to Hyannis isn't crowded, and she has her pick of window seats. People aren't leaving Nantucket today. They're here to see the daffodils. Olivia has seen enough. The ferry engine rumbles, and they begin to move.

She leaves her bag at her seat and walks up the stairs and outside to the back of the ferry. As the ferry approaches Brant Point Lighthouse, she pulls a penny from her pocket and tosses it into the ocean, a tradition symbolizing a promise to return to the island. She'll be back. She'll be back to visit Beth and Jimmy.

She's standing at the railing, facing backward, as more and more ocean separates her from this tiny island. She watches the boats in the harbor, the two church steeples, the buildings in Town, and the gray houses dotting the shoreline shrink smaller and smaller. And soon, Nantucket is gone.

The ferry picks up speed. Olivia returns to her seat inside, facing forward. She's going back to work, back to Taylor Krepps, but as a fiction editor this time. She's ready and excited. Her first book will be the one she brought to Louise herself, the debut novel by Elizabeth Ellis. She can't wait for its publication, to see it in the bookstores, to hold it in her hands, to feel the cover and the weight of it.

She opens her bag and pulls out a thick stack of paper. Beth's manuscript. She holds it in her lap. This is why she came to Nantucket. For this. Her answer. Her peace.

As the ferry takes her back to the mainland, she flips to the last few pages and smiles as she rereads her favorite part, savoring each word, listening with her spirit to the beautiful sound of Anthony's voice.

41

EPILOGUE

Dear Mom,

You already possess the answers to your questions. You already hold them in your heart. But your mind still resists. I understand that sometimes we need reassurance, to hear the words. A two-way conversation.

I wasn't here to do the things you dreamed and even feared I'd do before I was born. I wasn't here to play Little League, go to the prom, go to college, go to war, become a doctor or a lawyer or a mathematician (I would've been great at that one). I wasn't here to grow to be an old man, to be married, to have children and grandchildren. All that has been done or will be done.

And I wasn't here to help others understand immunology, gastroenterology, genetics, or neuroscience. I wasn't here to solve the riddle of autism. Those answers are for another time.

I came here to simply be, and autism was the vehicle of my being. Although my short life was difficult at times, I found great joy in being Anthony. Autism made it difficult to connect with you and Dad and other people through things like eye contact and conversation and your activities. But I wasn't interested in connecting in those ways, so I felt no deprivation in this. I connected in other ways, through the song of your voices, the energy of your emotions, the comfort in being near you, and sometimes, in moments I treasured, through sharing the experience of something I loved — the blue sky, my rocks, the Three Pigs story.

And you, Mom. I loved you. You've asked if I felt and understood that you loved me. Of course I did. And you know this. I loved your love because it kept me safe and happy and wanted, and it existed beyond words and hugs and eyes.

This brings me to the other reason I was here. I was here for you, Mom. I was here to teach you about love.

Most people love with a guarded heart, only if certain things happen or don't happen, only to a point. If the person we love hurts us, betrays us, abandons us, disappoints us, if the person becomes hard to love, we often stop loving. We protect our delicate hearts. We close off, retreat, withhold, disconnect, and withdraw. We might even hate.

Most people love conditionally. Most people are never asked to love with a whole and open heart. They only love partway. They get by.

Autism was my gift to you. My autism didn't let me hug and kiss you, it didn't allow me to look into your eyes, it didn't let me say aloud the words you so desperately wanted to hear with your ears. But you loved me anyway.

You're thinking, *Of course I did. Anyone would have*. This isn't true. Loving me with a full and accepting heart, loving all of me, required you to grow. Despite your heartache and disappointment, your fears and frustration and sorrow, despite all I couldn't show you in return, you loved me.

You loved me unconditionally.

351

You haven't experienced this kind of love with Dad or your parents or your sister or anyone else before. But now, you know what unconditional love is. I know my death has hurt you, and you've needed time alone to heal. You're ready now. You'll still miss me. I miss you, too. But you're ready.

Take what you've learned and love someone again. Find someone to love and love without condition.

This is why we're all here.

Love,
Anthony

Author's Note

As of the writing of this story, the neuroanatomical, neurochemical, and neurophysiological underpinnings of autism are poorly understood. While I look forward to the day, hopefully in the near future, when scientists have identified the causes, elucidating the neuroscience of autism wasn't the goal or within the scope of this novel.

About a third of children with autism also have epilepsy. For most of these children, seizures can be well managed with medication. However, managing the proper dosing and effectiveness of any medication with children who are nonverbal is particularly challenging.

Boy with autism or *autistic boy?* The specific use of language can powerfully influence how we perceive and treat people. I have read and understand the arguments for both choices here.

Boy with autism — the focus is on the person. The boy is a person first, not defined by and only by autism. On the other hand, *boy with autism* can be perceived to treat autism like a disease, like describing a person with Alzheimer's or a person with cancer. It can be perceived as something negative, a malady to cure.

Autistic boy — the argument for this language asserts that autism is a trait to be accepted. It is part of the person, like being brown-eyed or blond.

Seeing the merits of both sides, I consciously used both ways of referring to autism in this book, as they are used in today's culture, aware of this ongoing discussion, respectful of both opinions.

When I began writing this novel in 2010, the incidence of autism in the United States was 1 in 110 children. A report released by the CDC in March 2012 states that the rate has risen to 1 in 88.

This is a fictional story about a boy on the autism spectrum. Over and over, I read and heard this statement from parents and professionals:

'If you've met one child with autism, you've met one child with autism.'

Anthony, the fictional boy in this novel, is one child with autism. While he cannot possibly represent all autistic people, I hope that through the story of Anthony and his mother readers will gain an insight and sensitivity that can be extended to every person with autism.

After talking with parents, physicians, and therapists and reading as much as I could about autism for the past two years, here's what I've come to believe:

The spectrum is long and wide, and we're all on it. Once you believe this, it becomes easy to see how we're all connected.

Acknowledgments

First, I need to thank all the amazing parents who so generously shared their experiences with me. I can't thank you enough for opening your personal lives to me, for teaching me what you know about autism, and for trusting me with this knowledge. I know that what you gave to me is extraordinary. Thank you Tracey Green, Kelly Gryglewicz, Kate Jacobson, Jackie Maust, Susanna O'Brien, Holly Shapiro, Ginger Shephard, and Jim Smith.

Thank you Dr. Barry Kosofsky, one of my first teachers, for your insights as a pediatric neurologist and for describing the current scientific and medical understanding of autism. It was great to learn from you again.

Thank you Corinne Murphy Genova, MEd, BCBA, for your insights as an applied behavioral analysis specialist.

Thank you Jennifer Buckley and Reine Sloan for your generosity, for helping me better understand what happens before, during, and after seizures. Thank you Dr. Jessica Wieselquist for explaining the clinical perspective.

Thank you to Jessica Lucas for sharing her expertise as an emergency medical technician.

Thank you to everyone who helped me come to know and love the quirky and beautiful island of Nantucket: John Burdock, Sarah Crawford, Michael Galvin, Dr. John Genova, Wendy

Hudson, Tina and Richard Loftin, Jacqueline and Vincent Pizzi, Nancy and Peter Rodts, Susan Scheide, Dr. Louise Schneider.

Thanks also to Anne Carey, Sue Linnell, and Christopher Seufert for accompanying me on various trips to the island.

Thank you to Father Jim Hawker for providing information about the Catholic Church.

Thank you Mary Ann Robbat for sharing your insights about channeling.

Thank you Addie Morfoot Kauffman for helping me to imagine the details of Beth's professional life in New York City prior to moving to Nantucket.

Thank you Jill Abraham for role-playing a pivotal scene with me at Starbucks (Jill was Petra, I was Beth).

Thanks to my baristas and good friends at Starbucks for guarding 'my seat' and for providing me with all the chai tea lattes I could drink: Lauren Fowler, Desiree Gour, Brandon Lopes, Erin McKenna, and Mary Trainor.

Thanks to Ann Hood for the glorious writing retreat at Spannocchia.

Thanks to the Peaked Hill Trust for the truly amazing artist residency in the Margo-Gelb dune shack in Provincetown.

Thanks to Danyel Matteson for providing me with the opportunity to spend some uninterrupted time writing in a stunning room at the Chatham Bars Inn.

For the time and space to write this book, I thank my parents, Mary and Tom Genova; my in-laws, Marilyn and Gary Seufert; Sue Linnell; and especially my husband, Christopher Seufert.

For reading each chapter, for sharing this journey with me, and for the many needed pep talks along the way, I thank Vicky Bijur, Anne Carey, Laurel Daly, Kim Howland, Mary MacGregor, and Christopher Seufert.

Thank you to my incredible team at Simon & Schuster for believing in this story — Kathy Sagan, Jean Anne Rose, Ayelet Gruenspecht, Anthony Ziccardi, Jennifer Bergstrom, and Louise Burke.

Thank you to Vicky Bijur and Kathy Sagan for reading and rereading, for your invaluable insights. This book is infinitely better because of your input.

Thank you to Chris, Alena, Ethan, and Stella for your love and patience.

Finally, I thank Tracey Green. Thank you, Trace, for trusting me to write this story. I wrote this book for you, with all my love.

We do hope that you have enjoyed reading
this large print book.

Did you know that all of our titles
are available for purchase?

We publish a wide range of high quality
large print books including:
Romances, Mysteries, Classics
General Fiction
Non Fiction and Westerns

Special interest titles available in
large print are:
The Little Oxford Dictionary
Music Book
Song Book
Hymn Book
Service Book

Also available from us courtesy of Oxford
University Press:
Young Readers' Dictionary
(large print edition)
Young Readers' Thesaurus
(large print edition)

For further information or a free
brochure, please contact us at:
Ulverscroft Large Print Books Ltd.,
The Green, Bradgate Road, Anstey,
Leicester, LE7 7FU, England.
Tel: (00 44) **0116 236 4325**
Fax: (00 44) **0116 234 0205**

SKETCHER

Roland Watson-Grant

Nine-year-old 'Skid' Beaumont's family is stuck in the mud. Following his father's decision to relocate and build a new home, based on a drunken vision that New Orleans would rapidly expand eastwards into the wetlands as a result of the 1970s oil boom, Skid and his brothers grow up in a swampy area of Louisiana. But the constructions stop short, the dream fizzles out, and the Beaumonts find themselves sinking in a soggy corner of 1980s America. As things on the home front get more complicated, Skid learns of his mother's alleged magic powers and vaguely remembers some eerie stories surrounding his older brother Frico . . . Atmospheric, uplifting and deeply moving, *Sketcher* is a novel about the beauty of life no matter how broken it is.

FLORA

Gail Godwin

Ten-year-old Helen and her summer guardian, Flora, are isolated together in Helen's decaying family house while her father is doing secret war work in Oak Ridge during the final months of the Second World War. At three, Helen lost her mother — and now the beloved grandmother who raised her has just died. A fiercely imaginative child, Helen is desperate to keep her house intact with all its ghosts and stories. Flora, her late mother's twenty-two-year-old first cousin who cries at the drop of a hat, is ardently determined to do her best for Helen. Their relationship and its fallout, played against a backdrop of a lost America, will haunt Helen for the rest of her life.

THE TRUTHS
WE HOLD

ALSO BY KAMALA D. HARRIS

*Smart on Crime: A Career Prosecutor's
Plan to Make Us Safer* (2009)

THE TRUTHS
WE HOLD

An American Journey

KAMALA HARRIS

THE BODLEY HEAD
LONDON

1 3 5 7 9 10 8 6 4 2

The Bodley Head, an imprint of Vintage,
20 Vauxhall Bridge Road,
London SW1V 2SA

The Bodley Head is part of the Penguin Random House group of companies
whose addresses can be found at global.penguinrandomhouse.com.

Copyright © Kamala D. Harris 2019

First published in the United States of America by Penguin Press in 2019
First published in the United Kingdom by The Bodley Head in 2019

www.penguin.co.uk/vintage

A CIP catalogue record for this book is available from the British Library

Hardback ISBN 9781847925794
Trade paperback ISBN 9781847925800

Designed by Meighan Cavanaugh

Second insert, page 2, top and bottom, and page 3, bottom: Justin Sullivan via
Getty Images; page 3, top: Bethany Mollenkof/Los Angeles Times via
Getty Images; page 10, top: Aaron P. Bernstein/Getty Images; page 13,
bottom: Alex Wong/Getty Images; page 16, bottom: Zoe Ghertner.
All other images courtesy of the author.

Printed and bound in Great Britain by Clays Ltd, Elcograf S.p.A.

Penguin Random House is committed to a sustainable future
for our business, our readers and our planet. This book is made
from Forest Stewardship Council® certified paper.

To my darling husband:
Thank you for always being patient, loving,
supportive, and calm. And most of all,
for your sense of "the funny."

CONTENTS

PREFACE

Most mornings, my husband, Doug, wakes up before me and reads the news in bed. If I hear him making noises—a sigh, a groan, a gasp—I know what kind of day it's going to be.

November 8, 2016, had started well—the last day of my campaign for the U.S. Senate. I spent the day meeting as many more voters as I could, and of course cast a vote myself at a neighborhood school up the street from our house. We were feeling pretty good. We had rented a huge place for my Election Night party, with a balloon drop waiting to go. But first I was going out for dinner with family and close friends—a tradition dating back to my first campaign. People had flown in from all across the country, even overseas, to be with us—my aunts and cousins, my in-laws, my sister's in-laws, and more, all gathered for what we hoped would be a very special night.

I was staring out the car window, reflecting on how far we'd come, when I heard one of Doug's signature groans.

"You gotta look at this," he said, handing me his phone. Early results for the presidential election were coming in. Something was happening—something bad. By the time we arrived at the restaurant, the gap between the two candidates had shrunk considerably, and I was inwardly groaning as well. *The New York Times'* probability meter was suggesting it was going to be a long, dark night.

We settled in for a meal in a small room off the main restaurant. Emotions and adrenaline were running high, but not for the reasons we had anticipated. On the one hand, while polls hadn't yet closed in California, we were optimistic that I was going to win. Yet even as we prepared for that hard-earned celebration, all eyes were on our screens as state after state came back with numbers that told a troubling story.

At a certain point, my nine-year-old godson, Alexander, came up to me with big tears welling in his eyes. I assumed one of the other kids in our group had been teasing him about something.

"Come here, little man. What's wrong?"

Alexander looked up and locked eyes with mine. His voice was trembling. "Auntie Kamala, that man can't win. He's not going to win, is he?" Alexander's worry broke my heart. I didn't want anyone making a child feel that way. Eight years earlier, many of us had cried tears of joy when Barack Obama was elected president. And now, to see Alexander's fear . . .

His father, Reggie, and I took him outside to try to console him.

"Alexander, you know how sometimes superheroes are facing a big challenge because a villain is coming for them? What do they do when that happens?"

"They fight back," he whimpered.

"That's right. And they fight back with emotion, because all the best superheroes have big emotions just like you. But they always fight back, right? So that's what we're going to do."

Shortly after, the Associated Press called my race. We were still at the restaurant.

"I can't thank you all enough for being with me every step of the way all the time, all the time," I told my incredibly loving and supportive family and friends. "It means so much to me." I was overwhelmed with gratitude, both for the people in that room and the people I had lost along the way, especially my mother. I tried to savor the moment, and I did, if briefly. But, like everyone else, I soon turned my eyes back to the television.

After dinner, we headed to our Election Night venue, where more than a thousand people had gathered for the party. I was no longer a candidate for office. I was a U.S. senator-elect—the first black woman from my state, and the second in the nation's history, to earn that job. I had been elected to represent more than thirty-nine million people—roughly one out of every eight Americans from all backgrounds and walks of life. It was—and is—a humbling and extraordinary honor.

My team clapped and cheered as I joined them in the greenroom behind the stage. It all still felt more than a little surreal. None of us had fully processed what was happening. They formed a circle around me as I thanked them for everything they'd done. We were a family, too, and we had been through an incredible journey together. Some of the folks in the room had been with me since my first campaign for district attorney. But now, almost two years after the start of our campaign, we had a new mountain to take.

I had written a speech based on the assumption that Hillary Clinton would become our first woman president. As I went onstage to greet my supporters, I left that draft behind. I looked out at the room. It was packed with people, from the floor to the balcony. Many were in a state of shock as they watched the national returns.

I told the crowd we had a task in front of us. I said the stakes were high. We had to be committed to bringing our country together, to doing what was required to protect our fundamental values and ideals. I thought of Alexander and all the children when I posed a question:

"Do we retreat or do we fight? I say we fight. And I intend to fight!"

I went home that night with my extended family, many of whom were staying with us. We all went into our respective rooms, changed into sweats, and then joined one another in the living room. Some of us were sitting on couches. Others on the floor. We all planted ourselves in front of the television.

No one really knew what to say or do. Each of us was trying to cope in our own way. I sat down on the couch with Doug and ate an entire family-size bag of classic Doritos. Didn't share a single chip.

But I did know this: one campaign was over, but another was about to begin. A campaign that called on us all to enlist. This time, a battle for the soul of our nation.

In the years since, we've seen an administration align itself with white supremacists at home and cozy up to dictators abroad; rip babies from their mothers' arms in grotesque violation of their human rights; give corporations and the wealthy huge tax cuts while ignoring the middle class; derail our fight against climate change; sabotage health care and imperil a woman's right to control her own body; all while lashing out at seemingly everything and everyone, including the very idea of a free and independent press.

We are better than this. Americans know we're better than this. But we're going to have to prove it. We're going to have to fight for it.

On July 4, 1992, one of my heroes and inspirations, Thurgood Marshall, gave a speech that deeply resonates today. "We cannot play ostrich," he said. "Democracy just cannot flourish amid fear. Liberty cannot bloom amid hate. Justice cannot take root amid rage. America must get to work. . . . We must dissent from the indifference. We must dissent from the apathy. We must dissent from the fear, the hatred, and the mistrust."

This book grows out of that call to action, and out of my belief that our fight must begin and end with speaking truth.

I believe there is no more important and consequential antidote for these times than a reciprocal relationship of trust. You give and you receive trust. And one of the most important ingredients in a relationship of trust is that we speak truth. It matters what we say. What we mean. The value we place on our words—and what they are worth to others.

We cannot solve our most intractable problems unless we are honest about what they are, unless we are willing to have difficult conversations and accept what facts make plain.

We need to speak truth: that racism, sexism, homophobia, transphobia, and anti-Semitism are real in this country, and we need to confront those forces. We need to speak truth: that, with the exception of Native Americans, we all descend from people who weren't born on our shores—whether our ancestors came to America willingly, with hopes of a prosperous future, or forcibly, on a slave ship, or desperately, to escape a harrowing past.

We cannot build an economy that gives dignity and decency to American workers unless we first speak truth; that we are asking people to do more with less money and to live longer with less security. Wages haven't risen in forty years, even as the costs of health care, tuition, and housing have soared. The middle class is living paycheck to paycheck.

We must speak truth about our mass incarceration crisis—that we put more people in prison than any country on earth, for no good reason. We must speak truth about police brutality, about racial bias, about the killing of unarmed black men. We must speak truth about pharmaceutical companies that pushed addictive opioids on unsuspecting communities, and payday lenders and for-profit colleges that have leeched on to vulnerable Americans and overloaded them with debt. We must speak truth about greedy, predatory corporations that have turned deregulation, financial speculation, and climate denialism into creed. And I intend to do just that.

This book is not meant to be a policy platform, much less a fifty-point plan. Instead, it is a collection of ideas and viewpoints and stories, from my life and from the lives of the many people I've met along the way.

Just two more things to mention before we get started:

First, my name is pronounced "comma-la," like the punctuation mark. It means "lotus flower," which is a symbol of significance in Indian culture. A lotus grows underwater, its flower rising above the surface while its roots are planted firmly in the river bottom.

And second, I want you to know how personal this is for me. This is the story of my family. It is the story of my childhood. It is the story of the life I have built since then. You'll meet my family and my friends, my colleagues and my team. I hope you will cherish them as I do and, through my telling, see that nothing I have ever accomplished could have been done on my own.

—Kamala, 2018

One

FOR THE PEOPLE

I still remember the first time I walked into the Alameda County Superior Courthouse, in Oakland, California, as an employee. It was 1988, during the last summer of law school, and I, along with nine others, had been offered a summer internship in the district attorney's office. I had a sense that I wanted to be a prosecutor, that I wanted to be on the front lines of criminal justice reform, that I wanted to protect the vulnerable. But having never seen the job up close, I hadn't made up my mind.

The sun shone brightly on the courthouse. The building stood apart on Lake Merritt, taller and more regal than other buildings nearby. From certain angles, it looked like an architectural marvel from a foreign capital, with its granite base and concrete tower rising to meet a golden rooftop. Though from other angles, it bore an uncanny resemblance to an art deco wedding cake.

The Alameda County District Attorney's Office is itself something of a legend. Earl Warren led the office before becoming attorney general of California and later one of the most influential chief justices of the United States Supreme Court. He was on my mind that morning as I walked past the stunning mosaics in the lobby that depict the early history of California. Warren's words—proclaiming segregation "inherently unequal"—had taken a long fifteen years to make it to Berkeley, California. I was grateful they had come in time for me; my elementary school class was only the second class in my city to be desegregated through busing.

I was the first to arrive at the orientation session. Within a few minutes, the rest of my fellow clerks showed up. There was only one woman among them, Amy Resner. As soon as the session was over, I went up to her and asked her for her phone number. In that male-dominated environment, it was refreshing to have at least one female colleague. She remains one of my closest friends today, and I'm godmother to her children.

As summer interns, we understandably had very little power or influence. Our job was primarily to learn and observe, while assisting where we could. It was a chance to get a taste of how the criminal justice system worked from the inside, what it looked like when justice was served—and when it wasn't. We were placed with attorneys who were trying all kinds of cases, from DUIs to homicides, and had the chance to be in the room—and part of the process—of putting together a case.

I'll never forget the time my supervisor was working on a case involving a drug bust. The police had arrested a number of individuals in the raid, including an innocent bystander: a woman who had been at the wrong place at the wrong time and had been swept up in the dragnet. I hadn't seen her. I didn't know who she was or what she looked like. I didn't have any connection to her, except for the report I was reviewing. But there was something about her that caught my attention.

It was late on a Friday afternoon, and most people had gone home for the weekend. In all likelihood, a judge wouldn't see her until Monday. That meant she'd have to spend the weekend in jail.

Does she work weekends? Is she going to have to explain to her employer where she was? Is she going to get fired?

Even more important, I knew she had young children at home. *Do they know she's in jail? They must think she did something wrong. Who's taking care of them right now? Is there even someone who can? Child Protective Services might get called. My God, she could lose her kids.*

Everything was on the line for this woman: her family, her livelihood, her standing in her community, her dignity, her liberty. And yet she'd done nothing wrong.

I rushed to the clerk of the court and asked to have the case called that very day. I begged. I pleaded. If the judge could just return to the bench for five minutes, we could get her released. All I could think about was her family and her frightened children. Finally, as the minutes in the day wound down, the judge returned. I watched and listened as he reviewed her case, waiting for him to give the order. Then, with the pound of a gavel, just like that, she was free. She'd get to go home to her children in time for dinner. I never did get the chance to meet her, but I'll never forget her.

It was a defining moment in my life. It was the crystallization of how, even on the margins of the criminal justice system, the stakes were extraordinarily high and intensely human. It was a realization that, even with the limited authority of an intern, people who cared could do justice. It was revelatory, a moment that proved how much it mattered to have compassionate people working as prosecutors. Years before I would be elected to run a major prosecutor's office, this was one of the victories that mattered the most. I knew she was going home.

And I knew the kind of work I wanted to do, and who I wanted to serve.

The courthouse wasn't far from where I grew up. I was born in Oakland, California, in 1964 and spent the formative years of my childhood living on the boundary between Oakland and Berkeley.

My father, Donald Harris, was born in Jamaica in 1938. He was a brilliant student who immigrated to the United States after being admitted to the University of California at Berkeley. He went there to study economics and would go on to teach economics at Stanford, where he remains a professor emeritus.

My mother's life began thousands of miles to the east, in southern India. Shyamala Gopalan was the oldest of four children—three girls and a boy. Like my father, she was a gifted student, and when she showed a passion for science, her parents encouraged and supported her.

She graduated from the University of Delhi at nineteen. And she didn't stop there. She applied to a graduate program at Berkeley, a university she'd never seen, in a country she'd never visited. It's hard for me to imagine how difficult it must have been for her parents to let her go. Commercial jet travel was only just starting to spread globally. It wouldn't be a simple matter to stay in touch. Yet, when my mother asked permission to move to California, my grandparents didn't stand in the way. She was a teenager when she left home for

Berkeley in 1958 to pursue a doctorate in nutrition and endocrinology, on her way to becoming a breast cancer researcher.

My mother was expected to return to India after she completed her degree. Her parents had an arranged marriage. It was assumed my mother would follow a similar path. But fate had other plans. She and my father met and fell in love at Berkeley while participating in the civil rights movement. Her marriage—and her decision to stay in the United States—were the ultimate acts of self-determination and love.

My parents had two daughters together. My mother received her PhD at age twenty-five, the same year I was born. My beloved sister, Maya, came two years later. Family lore has it that, in both pregnancies, my mother kept working right up to the moment of delivery—one time, her water broke while she was at the lab, and the other while she was making apple strudel. (In both cases, knowing my mom, she would have insisted on finishing up before she went to the hospital.)

Those early days were happy and carefree. I loved the outdoors, and I remember that when I was a little girl, my father wanted me to run free. He would turn to my mother and say, "Just let her run, Shyamala." And then he'd turn to me and say, "Run, Kamala. As fast as you can. Run!" I would take off, the wind in my face, with the feeling that I could do anything. (It's no wonder I also have many memories of my mother putting Band-Aids on my scraped knees.)

Music filled our home. My mother loved to sing along to gospel—from Aretha Franklin's early work to the Edwin Hawkins Singers. She had won an award in India for her singing, and I loved hearing that voice. My father cared about music just as much as my mother. He had an extensive jazz collection, so many albums that they filled

5

all the shelving against one of the walls. Every night, I would fall asleep to the sounds of Thelonious Monk, John Coltrane, or Miles Davis.

But the harmony between my parents didn't last. In time, things got harder. They stopped being kind to each other. I knew they loved each other very much, but it seemed they'd become like oil and water. By the time I was five years old, the bond between them had given way under the weight of incompatibility. They separated shortly after my dad took a job at the University of Wisconsin, and divorced a few years later. They didn't fight about money. The only thing they fought about was who got the books.

I've often thought that had they been a little older, more emotionally mature, maybe the marriage could have survived. But they were so young. My father was my mother's first boyfriend.

It was hard on both of them. I think, for my mother, the divorce represented a kind of failure she had never considered. Her marriage was as much an act of rebellion as an act of love. Explaining it to her parents had been hard enough. Explaining the divorce, I imagine, was even harder. I doubt they ever said to her, "I told you so," but I think those words echoed in her mind regardless.

Maya was still a toddler at the time of their separation, a little too young to understand what was going on, to feel the hardness of it all. I have often felt a pang of guilt because of something Maya never got to experience: I knew our parents when they were happy together. Maya never really did.

My father remained a part of our lives. We would see him on weekends and spend summers with him in Palo Alto. But it was really my mother who took charge of our upbringing. She was the one most responsible for shaping us into the women we would become.

And she was extraordinary. My mother was barely five foot one, but I felt like she was six foot two. She was smart and tough and fierce and protective. She was generous, loyal, and funny. She had only two goals in life: to raise her two daughters and to end breast cancer. She pushed us hard and with high expectations as she nurtured us. And all the while, she made Maya and me feel special, like we could do anything we wanted to if we put in the work.

My mother had been raised in a household where political activism and civic leadership came naturally. Her mother, my grandmother, Rajam Gopalan, had never attended high school, but she was a skilled community organizer. She would take in women who were being abused by their husbands, and then she'd call the husbands and tell them they'd better shape up or she would take care of them. She used to gather village women together, educating them about contraception. My grandfather P. V. Gopalan had been part of the movement to win India's independence. Eventually, as a senior diplomat in the Indian government, he and my grandmother had spent time living in Zambia after it gained independence, helping to settle refugees. He used to joke that my grandmother's activism would get him in trouble one day. But he knew that was never going to stop her. From them, my mother learned that it was service to others that gave life purpose and meaning. And from my mother, Maya and I learned the same.

My mother inherited my grandmother's strength and courage. People who knew them knew not to mess with either. And from both of my grandparents, my mother developed a keen political consciousness. She was conscious of history, conscious of struggle, conscious of inequities. She was born with a sense of justice imprinted on her soul.

My parents often brought me in a stroller with them to civil rights marches. I have young memories of a sea of legs moving about, of the energy and shouts and chants. Social justice was a central part of family discussions. My mother would laugh telling a story she loved about the time when I was fussing as a toddler. "What do you want?" she asked, trying to soothe me. "Fweedom!" I yelled back.

My mother surrounded herself with close friends who were really more like sisters. My godmother, a fellow Berkeley student whom I knew as "Aunt Mary," was one of them. They met through the civil rights movement that was taking shape in the early 1960s and was being debated and defended from the streets of Oakland to the soap-boxes in Berkeley's Sproul Plaza. As black students spoke out against injustice, a group of passionate, keenly intelligent, politically engaged young men and women found one another—my mother and Aunt Mary among them.

They went to peaceful protests where they were attacked by police with hoses. They marched against the Vietnam War and for civil rights and voting rights. They went together to see Martin Luther King Jr. speak at Berkeley, and my mother had a chance to meet him. She told me that at one anti-war protest, the marchers were confronted by the Hell's Angels. She told me that at another, she and her friends were forced to run for safety, with me in a stroller, after violence broke out against the protesters.

But my parents and their friends were more than just protesters. They were big thinkers, pushing big ideas, organizing their community. Aunt Mary, her brother (my "Uncle Freddy"), my mother and father, and about a dozen other students organized a study group to read the black writers that the university was ignoring. They met on Sundays at Aunt Mary and Uncle Freddy's Harmon Street home, where they devoured Ralph Ellison, discussed Carter G. Woodson, debated W. E. B. Du Bois. They talked about apartheid, about African decolonization, about liberation movements in the developing world, and about the history of racism in America. But it wasn't just talking. There was an urgency to their fight. They received prominent guests, too, including civil rights and intellectual leaders from LeRoi Jones to Fannie Lou Hamer.

After Berkeley, Aunt Mary took a job teaching at San Francisco State University, where she continued to celebrate and elevate the black experience. SFSU had a student-run Experimental College, and in 1966, another of my mother's dear friends, whom I knew as Uncle Aubrey, taught the college's first-ever class in black studies. The campus was a proving ground for redefining the meaning and substance of higher education.

These were my mother's people. In a country where she had no family, they were her family—and she was theirs. From almost the moment she arrived from India, she chose and was welcomed to and enveloped in the black community. It was the foundation of her new American life.

Along with Aunt Mary, Aunt Lenore was my mother's closest confidante. I also cherish the memory of one of my mother's mentors, Howard, a brilliant endocrinologist who had taken her under his wing. When I was a girl, he gave me a pearl necklace that he'd brought back from a trip to Japan. (Pearls have been one of my favorite forms of jewelry ever since!)

I was also very close to my mother's brother, Balu, and her two sisters, Sarala and Chinni (whom I called Chitti, which means "younger mother"). They lived many thousands of miles away, and we rarely saw one another. Still, through many long-distance calls, our periodic trips to India, and letters and cards written back and forth, our sense of family—of closeness and comfort and trust—was able to penetrate the distance. It's how I first really learned that you can have very close relationships with people, even if it's not on a daily basis. We were always there for one another, regardless of what form that would take.

My mother, grandparents, aunts, and uncle instilled us with pride in our South Asian roots. Our classical Indian names harked back to our heritage, and we were raised with a strong awareness of and appreciation for Indian culture. All of my mother's words of affection or frustration came out in her mother tongue—which seems fitting to me, since the purity of those emotions is what I associate with my mother most of all.

My mother understood very well that she was raising two black daughters. She knew that her adopted homeland would see Maya and me as black girls, and she was determined to make sure we would grow into confident, proud black women.

About a year after my parents separated, we moved into the top floor of a duplex on Bancroft Way, in a part of Berkeley known as the flatlands. It was a close-knit neighborhood of working families who were focused on doing a good job, paying the bills, and being there for one another. It was a community that was invested in its children, a place where people believed in the most basic tenet of the American Dream: that if you work hard and do right by the world, your kids will be better off than you were. We weren't rich in financial terms, but the values we internalized provided a different kind of wealth.

My mom would get Maya and me ready every morning before heading to work at her research lab. Usually she'd mix up a cup of Carnation Instant Breakfast. We could choose chocolate, strawberry, or vanilla. On special occasions, we got Pop-Tarts. From her perspective, breakfast was not the time to fuss around.

She would kiss me goodbye and I would walk to the corner and get on the bus to Thousand Oaks Elementary School. I only learned later that we were part of a national experiment in desegregation, with working-class black children from the flatlands being bused in one direction and wealthier white children from the Berkeley hills bused in the other. At the time, all I knew was that the big yellow bus was the way I got to school.

Looking at the photo of my first-grade class reminds me of how wonderful it was to grow up in such a diverse environment. Because the students came from all over the area, we were a varied bunch; some grew up in public housing and others were the children of professors. I remember celebrating varied cultural holidays at school and learning to count to ten in several languages. I remember parents, including my mom, volunteering in the classroom to lead science and art projects with the kids. Mrs. Frances Wilson, my first-grade teacher, was deeply committed to her students. In fact, when I graduated from the University of California Hastings College of the Law, there was Mrs. Wilson sitting in the audience, cheering me on.

When Maya and I finished school, our mother would often still be at work, so we would head two houses down to the Sheltons', whom my mother knew through Uncle Aubrey, and with whom we shared a long-standing relationship of love, care, and connection.

Regina Shelton, originally from Louisiana, was Aubrey's aunt; she and her husband, Arthur, an Arkansas transplant, owned and ran a nursery school—first located in the basement of their own home, and later underneath our apartment. The Sheltons were devoted to getting the children in our neighborhood off to the best possible start in life. Their day care center was small but welcoming, with posters of leaders such as Frederick Douglass, Sojourner Truth, and Harriet Tubman on the wall. The first George Washington Maya and I learned about when we were young was George Washington Carver. We still laugh about the first time Maya heard a classroom teacher talk about President George Washington and she thought to herself proudly, "I know him! He's the one who worked with peanuts!"

The Sheltons also ran an after-school program in their home, and that's where Maya and I would spend our afternoons. We simply called it going to "the house." There were always children running around at the house; lots of laughter and joyful play. Maya and I grew incredibly close to Mrs. Shelton's daughter and foster children; we'd pretend that we were all going to marry the Jackson Five—Maya with Michael and me with Tito. (Love you, Tito!)

Mrs. Shelton would quickly become a second mother to Maya and me. Elegant and warm in equal measure, she brought traditional southern style to her grace and hospitality—not to mention to her pound cake and flaky biscuits, which I adored. She was also deeply thoughtful in both senses of the term—exceptionally smart and uncommonly generous.

I'll never forget the time I made lemon bars to share. I had spent one afternoon making a lemon bar recipe that I'd found in one of my mother's cookbooks. They had turned out beautifully, and I was excited to show them off. I put them on a plate, covered them with Saran wrap, and walked over to Mrs. Shelton's house, where she was sitting at the kitchen table, sipping tea and laughing with her sister, Aunt Bea, and my mother. I proudly showed off my creation to them, and Mrs. Shelton took a big bite. It turned out I had used salt instead of sugar, but, not having tasted them myself, I didn't know.

"Mmmm, honey," Mrs. Shelton responded in her graceful southern accent, her lips slightly puckered from the taste. "That's delicious . . . maybe a little too much salt . . . but really delicious." I didn't walk away thinking I was a failure. I walked away thinking I had done a great job, and just made one small mistake. It was little moments like those that helped me build a natural sense of confidence. I believed I was capable of anything.

Mrs. Shelton taught me so much. She was always reaching out to mothers who needed counseling or support or even just a hug, because that's what you do. She took in more foster children than I can remember and adopted a girl named Sandy who would become my best friend. She always saw the potential in people. I loved that about her, too. She invested in neighborhood kids who had fallen through the cracks, and she did it with the expectation that these struggling boys and girls could be great. And yet she never talked about it or dwelled on it. To her, these deeds were not extraordinary; they were simply an extension of her values.

When I would come home from the Sheltons', I'd usually find my mother reading or working on her notes or preparing to make us dinner. Breakfast aside, she loved to cook, and I loved to sit with her in the kitchen and watch and smell and eat. She had a giant Chinese-style cleaver that she chopped with, and a cupboard full of spices. I loved that okra could be soul food or Indian food, depending on what spices you chose; she would add dried shrimp and sausage to make it like gumbo, or fry it up with turmeric and mustard seeds.

My mother cooked like a scientist. She was always experimenting—an oyster beef stir-fry one night, potato latkes on another. Even my lunch became a lab for her creations: On the bus, my friends, with their bologna sandwiches and PB&Js, would ask excitedly, "Kamala, what you got?" I'd open the brown paper bag, which my mother always decorated with a smiley face or a doodle: "Cream cheese and olives on dark rye!" I'll admit, not every experiment was successful—at least not for my grade school palate. But no matter what, it was different, and that made it special, just like my mother.

While she cooked, she would often put Aretha Franklin on the record player and I would dance and sing in the living room as though it were my stage. We listened to her version of "To Be Young, Gifted and Black" all the time, an anthem of black pride first performed by Nina Simone.

Most of our conversations took place in the kitchen. Cooking and eating were among the things our family most often did together. When Maya and I were kids, our mother sometimes used to serve us what she called "smorgasbord." She'd use a cookie cutter to make shapes in pieces of bread, then lay them out on a tray with mustard, mayonnaise, pickles, and fancy toothpicks. In between the bread slices, we'd put whatever was left in the refrigerator from the previous nights of cooking. It took me years to clue in to the fact that "smorgasbord" was really just "leftovers." My mother had a way of making even the ordinary seem exciting.

There was a lot of laughter, too. My mother was very fond of a puppet show called "Punch and Judy," where Judy would chase Punch around with a rolling pin. She would laugh so hard when she pretended to chase us around the kitchen with hers.

But it wasn't all laughs, of course. Saturday was "chores day," and each of us had our assignments. And my mother could be tough. She had little patience for self-indulgence. My sister and I rarely earned praise for behavior or achievements that were expected. "Why would

I applaud you for something you were supposed to do?" she would admonish if I tried to fish for compliments. And if I came home to report the latest drama in search of a sympathetic ear, my mother would have none of it. Her first reaction would be "Well, what did you do?" In retrospect, I see that she was trying to teach me that I had power and agency. Fair enough, but it still drove me crazy.

But that toughness was always accompanied by unwavering love and loyalty and support. If Maya or I was having a bad day, or if the weather had been gray and depressing for too long, she would throw what she liked to call an "unbirthday party," with unbirthday cake and unbirthday presents. Other times, she'd make some of our favorite things—chocolate chip pancakes or her "Special K" cereal cookies ("K" for Kamala). And often, she would get out the sewing machine and make clothes for us or for our Barbies. She even let Maya and me pick out the color of the family car, a Dodge Dart that she drove everywhere. We chose yellow—our favorite color at the time—and if she regretted having empowered us with the decision, she never let on. (On the plus side, it was always easy to find our car in a parking lot.)

Three times a week, I would go up the street to Mrs. Jones's house. She was a classically trained pianist, but there weren't many options in the field for a black woman, so she became a piano teacher. And she was strict and serious. Every time I looked over at the clock to see how much time was left in the lesson, she would rap my knuckles with a ruler. Other nights, I would go over to Aunt Mary's house, and Uncle Sherman and I would play chess. He was a great player, and he loved to talk to me about the bigger implications of the game: the idea of being strategic, of having a plan, of thinking things through multiple steps ahead, of predicting your opponent's actions and adjusting yours to outmaneuver them. Every once in a while, he would let me win.

On Sundays, our mother would send us off to the 23rd Avenue Church of God, piled with the other kids in the back of Mrs. Shelton's station wagon. My earliest memories of the teachings of the Bible were of a loving God, a God who asked us to "speak up for those who cannot speak for themselves" and to "defend the rights of the poor and needy." This is where I learned that "faith" is a verb; I believe we must live our faith and show faith in action.

Maya and I sang in the children's choir, where my favorite hymn was "Fill My Cup, Lord." I remember one Mother's Day, we recited an ode to moms. Each of us posed as one of the letters in the word "mother." I was cast as the letter T, and I stood there proudly, arms stretched out to both sides. "T is for the time she cares for me and loves me in every way."

My favorite night of the week was Thursday. On Thursdays, you could always find us in an unassuming beige building at the corner of what was then Grove Street and Derby. Once a mortuary, the building I knew was bursting with life, home to a pioneering black cultural center: Rainbow Sign.

Rainbow Sign was a performance space, cinema, art gallery, dance studio, and more. It had a restaurant with a big kitchen, and somebody was always cooking up something delicious—smothered chicken, meatballs in gravy, candied yams, corn bread, peach cobbler. By day, you could take classes in dance and foreign languages, or workshops in theater and art. At night, there were screenings, lectures, and performances from some of the most prominent black thinkers and leaders of the day—musicians, painters, poets, writers, filmmakers, scholars, dancers, and politicians—men and women at the vanguard of American culture and critical thought.

Rainbow Sign was the brainchild of visionary concert promoter Mary Ann Pollar, who started the center with ten other black women in September 1971. Its name was inspired by a verse from the black spiritual "Mary Don't You Weep"; the lyric "God gave Noah the rainbow sign; no more water, the fire next time . . ." was printed on the membership brochure. James Baldwin, of course, had memorably used this same verse for his book *The Fire Next Time*. Baldwin was a close friend of Pollar's and a regular guest at the club.

My mother, Maya, and I went to Rainbow Sign often. Everyone in the neighborhood knew us as "Shyamala and the girls." We were a unit. A team. And when we'd show up, we were always greeted with big smiles and warm hugs. Rainbow Sign had a communal orientation and an inclusive vibe. It was a place designed to spread knowledge, awareness, and power. Its informal motto was "For the love of people." Families with children were especially welcome at Rainbow Sign—an approach that reflected both the values and the vision of the women at its helm.

Pollar once told a journalist, "Hidden under everything we do, the best entertainment we put on, there is always a message: Look about you. Think about this." The center hosted a program specifically for kids through high school age, which included not only arts education but also a parallel version of the adult programming, in which young people could meet and interact directly with the center's guest speakers and performers.

The Bay Area was home to so many extraordinary black leaders and was bursting with black pride in some places. People had migrated there from all over the country. This meant that kids like me who spent time at Rainbow Sign were exposed to dozens of extra-ordinary men and women who showed us what we could become. In 1971, Congresswoman Shirley Chisholm paid a visit while she was exploring a run for president. Talk about strength! "Unbought and Unbossed," just as her campaign slogan promised. Alice Walker, who went on to win the Pulitzer Prize for *The Color Purple,* did a reading at Rainbow Sign. So did Maya Angelou, the first black female best-selling author, thanks to her autobiography, *I Know Why the Caged Bird Sings.* Nina Simone performed at Rainbow Sign when I was seven years old. I would later learn that Warren Widener, Berkeley's first black mayor, proclaimed March 31, 1972, Nina Simone Day to commemorate her two-day appearance.

I loved the electric atmosphere at Rainbow Sign—the laughter, the food, the energy. I loved the powerful orations from the stage and the witty, sometimes unruly audience banter. It was where I learned that artistic expression, ambition, and intelligence were cool. It was where I came to understand that there is no better way to feed some-one's brain than by bringing together food, poetry, politics, music, dance, and art.

It was also where I saw the logical extension of my mother's daily lessons, where I could begin to imagine what my future might hold for me. My mother was raising us to believe that "It's too hard!" was never an acceptable excuse; that being a good person meant standing for something larger than yourself; that success is measured in part by what you help others achieve and accomplish. She would tell us, "Fight systems in a way that causes them to be fairer, and don't be limited by what has always been." At Rainbow Sign, I'd see those values in action, those principles personified. It was a citizen's upbringing, the only kind I knew, and one I assumed everyone else was experiencing, too.

I was happy just where I was. But when I was in middle school, we had to leave. My mother was offered a unique opportunity in Montreal, teaching at McGill University and conducting research at the Jewish General Hospital. It was an exciting step in advancing her career.

It was not, however, an exciting opportunity for me. I was twelve years old, and the thought of moving away from sunny California in February, in the middle of the school year, to a French-speaking foreign city covered in twelve feet of snow was distressing, to say the least. My mother tried to make it sound like an adventure, taking us to buy our first down jackets and mittens, as though we were going to be explorers of the great northern winter. But it was hard for me to see it that way. It was made worse when my mother told us that she wanted us to learn the language, so she was enrolling us in a neighborhood school for native French speakers, Notre-Dame-des-Neiges— Our Lady of the Snows.

It was a difficult transition, since the only French I knew was from my ballet classes, where Madame Bovie, my ballet teacher, would shout, *"Demi-plié,* and up!" I used to joke that I felt like a duck, because all day long at our new school I'd be saying, *"Quoi? Quoi? Quoi?"* ("What? What? What?")

I was sure to take my upbringing with me to Montreal. One day, Maya and I held a demonstration in front of our building, protesting the fact that kids weren't allowed to play soccer on the lawn. I'm happy to report that our demands were met.

Eventually I convinced my mother to let me switch to a fine

arts school, where I tried out violin, French horn, and kettle drum alongside my studies in history and math. One year, we performed "Free to Be . . . You and Me" from start to finish.

By the time I got to high school, I had adjusted to our new surroundings. I still missed home, my friends and family, and was always so happy to return during the summer and holidays, when we'd stay with my father or Mrs. Shelton. But I'd gotten used to most of it. What I hadn't gotten used to was the feeling of being homesick for my country. I felt this constant sense of yearning to be back home. There was no question in my mind I'd return home for college.

I invited both of my parents to come to my graduation, even though I knew they wouldn't speak to each other. I still wanted them both to be there for me. I'll never forget sitting in the first couple of rows of the auditorium, looking out at the audience. My mother was nowhere to be found. "Where is she?" I thought. "Is she not here because my father is?" We were about to get started. And then, all of a sudden, the back door of the auditorium opened and my mother— who, most days, wore jeans and tennis shoes to her lab—walked in wearing a very bright red dress and heels. She was never one to let the situation get the better of her.

During high school, I started thinking more concretely about my future—college and beyond. I'd always assumed I would have a career; I'd seen the satisfaction my parents derived from their work. I'd also seen a series of extraordinary women—Aunt Mary, Mrs. Wilson, Mrs. Shelton, and my mother most of all—leading in their respective fields of influence, and the difference they were making in others' lives.

Though the seed was planted very early on, I'm not sure when, exactly, I decided I wanted to be a lawyer. Some of my greatest heroes were lawyers: Thurgood Marshall, Charles Hamilton Houston, Constance Baker Motley—giants of the civil rights movement. I cared a lot about fairness, and I saw the law as a tool that can help make things fair. But I think what most drew me to the profession was the way people around me trusted and relied on lawyers. Uncle Sherman and our close friend Henry were lawyers, and any time someone had a problem, within the family or the neighborhood, the first thing you'd hear was "Call Henry. Call Sherman. They'll know what to do. They'll know how to make sense of this." I wanted to be able to do that. I wanted to be the one people called. I wanted to be the one who could help.

So when it came to college, I wanted to get off on the right foot. And what better place to do that, I thought, than at Thurgood Marshall's alma mater?

I had always heard stories about what a wonderful place Howard University was, especially from Aunt Chris, who had gone there. Howard is an institution with an extraordinary legacy, one that has endured and thrived since its founding, two years after the Civil War. It endured when the doors of higher education were largely closed to black students. It endured when segregation and discrimination were the law of the land. It endured when few recognized the potential and capacity of young black men and women to be leaders. Generations of students had been nurtured and edified at Howard, equipped with the confidence to aim high and the tools to make the climb. I wanted to be one of them—and in the fall of 1982, I moved into Eton Towers, my first college dorm.

I'll always remember walking into Cramton Auditorium for my freshman orientation. The room was packed. I stood in the back, looked around, and thought, "This is heaven!" There were hundreds of people, and everyone looked like me. Some were children of Howard alumni; others were the first in their families to go to college. Some had been in predominantly black schools their whole lives; others had long been one of only a few people of color in their classroom or their neighborhood. Some came from cities, some from rural communities, and some from African countries, the Caribbean, and throughout the African diaspora.

As was the case for most Howard students, my favorite place to hang out was an area we called the Yard, a grass-covered space the size of a city block, right smack in the heart of the campus. On any given day, you could stand in the middle of the Yard and see, on your right, young dancers practicing their steps or musicians playing instruments. Look to your left and there were briefcase-toting students strolling out of the business school, and medical students in their white coats, heading back to the lab. Groups of students might be in a circle of laughter, or locked in deep discussion. A columnist for *The Hilltop*, the school newspaper, with the star of the football team. A gospel choir singer with the president of the math club.

That was the beauty of Howard. Every signal told students that we could be anything—that we were young, gifted, and black, and we shouldn't let anything get in the way of our success. The campus was a place where you didn't have to be confined to the box of another person's choosing. At Howard, you could come as you were and leave as the person you aspired to be. There were no false choices.

We weren't just told we had the capacity to be great; we were challenged to live up to that potential. There was an expectation that we would cultivate and use our talents to take on roles of leadership and have an impact on other people, on our country, and maybe even on the world.

I dove in with gusto. Freshman year, I ran for my first elected office: freshman class representative of the Liberal Arts Student Council. It was my very first campaign. No opponent I've faced since was as tough as Jersey Girl Shelley Young, and that says a lot, coming from a person from Oakland.

I chaired the economics society and competed on the debate team. I pledged a sorority, my beloved Alpha Kappa Alpha, founded by nine women at Howard more than a century ago. On Fridays, my friends and I would dress up in our best clothes and peacock around the Yard. On weekends, we went down to the National Mall to protest apartheid in South Africa.

While at Howard, in addition to being a student, I had many jobs. I interned at the Federal Trade Commission, where I was responsible for "clips," which meant combing all the morning newspapers, cutting out any articles that mentioned the agency, and pasting them onto sheets of paper to copy and distribute to senior staff. I also did research in the National Archives and was a tour guide at the U.S. Bureau of Engraving and Printing. My fellow tour guides and I were all given walkie-talkies and ID numbers; I was "TG-10," a code name that made me feel like a Secret Service agent. Once, I emerged from my shift to find Ruby Dee and Ossie Davis in the main area, waiting for a VIP tour after hours. They projected an aura like the luminaries they were, yet they made a special point of engaging me in conversation and telling me that it made them proud to see me as a young black woman working in public service. I've never forgotten how it made me feel as a young person to have these two icons, both larger than life, take the time to show an interest in me.

In the summer of my sophomore year, I got an internship with Senator Alan Cranston of California. Who could have known that some thirty years later, I would be elected to the same Senate seat? (I still have, framed, the thank-you letter from his office manager, which hangs in my Senate office near where my own interns sit. When I find myself riding the Senate subway with interns, I often tell them, "You're looking at your future!") I loved going to the Capitol Building every day that summer for work. It felt like the epicenter of change—and even as an intern sorting mail, I was thrilled to be a part of it. But I was even more mesmerized by the Supreme Court Building, across the street. I would walk across the street in the hot, humid summer, when you could cut the air with a butter knife, just so I could stand in awe of its magnificence and read the words engraved in marble above its entrance: EQUAL JUSTICE UNDER LAW. I imagined a world where that might be.

After Howard, I returned home to Oakland and enrolled at UC Hastings College of the Law. I was elected president of the Black Law Students Association (BLSA) during my second year in law school. At the time, black students were having a harder time finding employment than white students, and I wanted to change that. As BLSA president, I called the managing partners of all the major law firms and asked them to send representatives to a job fair we were hosting at a hotel.

When I realized that I wanted to work in the district attorney's office—that I had found my calling—I was excited to share the decision with my friends and family. And I wasn't surprised to find them incredulous. I had to defend my choice as one would a thesis.

America has a deep and dark history of people using the power of the prosecutor as an instrument of injustice. I knew this history well—of innocent men framed, of charges brought against people of color without sufficient evidence, of prosecutors hiding information that would exonerate defendants, of the disproportionate application of the law. I grew up with these stories—so I understood my community's wariness. But history told another story, too.

I knew the history of brave prosecutors who went after the Ku Klux Klan in the South. I knew the stories of prosecutors who went after corrupt politicians and corporate polluters. I knew the legacy of Robert Kennedy, who, as U.S. attorney general, sent Department of Justice officials to protect the Freedom Riders in 1961, and sent the U.S. Marshals to protect James Meredith when he enrolled at Ole Miss the next year.

I knew quite well that equal justice was an aspiration. I knew that the force of the law was applied unevenly, sometimes by design. But I also knew that what was wrong with the system didn't need to be an immutable fact. And I wanted to be part of changing that.

One of my mother's favorite sayings was "Don't let anybody tell you who you are. You tell *them* who you are." And so I did. I knew part of making change was what I'd seen all my life, surrounded by adults shouting and marching and demanding justice from the outside. But I also knew there was an important role on the inside, sitting at the table where the decisions were being made. When activists came marching and banging on the doors, I wanted to be on the other side to let them in.

I was going to be a prosecutor in my own image. I was going to do the job through the lens of my own experiences and perspectives, from wisdom gained at my mother's knee, in Rainbow Sign's hall, and on the Howard Yard.

An important part of what that wisdom told me was that when it came to criminal justice, we were being asked to accept false choices. For too long, we'd been told there were only two options: to be either tough on crime or soft on crime—an oversimplification that ignored the realities of public safety. You can want the police to stop crime in your neighborhood and also want them to stop using excessive force. You can want them to hunt down a killer on your streets and also want them to stop using racial profiling. You can believe in the need for consequence and accountability, especially for serious criminals, and also oppose unjust incarceration. I believed it was essential to weave all these varied strands together.

At the end of my summer internship, I was thrilled to accept a position as deputy district attorney. All I had to do was finish my final year of law school and take the bar exam, and then I'd be able to start my career in the courtroom.

I finished law school in the spring of 1989 and took the bar exam in July. In the waning weeks of summer, my future seemed so bright and so clear. The countdown to the life I imagined had begun.

And then, with a jolt, I was stopped in my tracks. In November, the state bar sent letters out to those who had taken the exam, and, to my utter devastation, I had failed. I couldn't get my head around it. It was almost too much to bear. My mother had always told me, "Don't do anything half-assed," and I had always taken that to heart. I was a hard worker. A perfectionist. Someone who didn't take things for granted. But there I was, letter in hand, realizing that in studying for the bar, I had put forward the most half-assed performance of my life.

Fortunately, I still had a job in the district attorney's office. They were going to keep me on, with clerk duties, and give me space to study to retake the exam in February. I was grateful for that, but it was hard to go into the office, feeling inadequate and incompetent. Just about everyone else who had been hired along with me had passed, and they were going to move on with their training without me. I remember walking by someone's office and hearing them say to someone else, "But she's so smart. How could she have not passed?" I felt miserable and embarrassed. I wondered if people thought I was a fraud. But I held my head up and kept going to work every day—and I passed on my second attempt. I was so proud and so honored the day I was sworn in as an officer of the court, and I showed up at the courthouse ready to start the work. But as it turns out, neither law school nor the bar exam really teach you what to do in court, and in those early days, it can feel like you've landed on another planet, where everyone speaks the language but you. As a clerk, you can represent the people in court under supervision. But this was the first time I'd be in trial on my own.

I had prepared, going over the facts of the case a dozen times. I'd practiced the questions I wanted to ask; internalized the precise wording of my legal motions. I'd researched and rehearsed every practice and custom—down to the skirt suit that was de rigueur for female attorneys, back before women were permitted to wear pants in the courtroom. I'd done everything I could. Still, the stakes were so high, it never felt like enough.

I walked into the courtroom, down the gallery aisle, and past the pews to the bar that separates defendants, families, witnesses, and other spectators from officials of the court. Chairs were arrayed in front of the bar for lawyers waiting for their cases to be called, and I took my seat among them. Nerves, excitement, and adrenaline jockeyed for position in my mind. But most of all, I was honored by and conscious of the immense responsibility I held—the duty to protect those who were among the most vulnerable and voiceless members of our society. When my turn came, I rose from my chair at the prosecutor's desk and stepped up to the podium, saying the words every prosecutor speaks:

"Kamala Harris, for the people."

The reason we have public offices of prosecution in America is that, in our country, a crime against any of us is considered a crime against all of us. Almost by definition, our criminal justice system involves matters in which the powerful have harmed the less powerful, and we do not expect the weaker party to secure justice alone; we make it a collective endeavor. That's why prosecutors don't represent the victim; they represent "the people"—society at large.

I kept that principle front and center as I worked with victims, whose dignity and safety were always paramount for me. It takes an enormous amount of courage for someone to share their story and endure cross-examination, knowing their credibility and most personal details may be on the line. But when they take the stand, they are doing so for the benefit of all of us—so that there will be consequences and accountability for those who violate the law.

"For the people" was my compass—and there was nothing I took more seriously than the power I now possessed. As an individual prosecutor, I had the discretion to decide whether to bring charges against someone and, if so, what and how many charges to bring. I could negotiate plea agreements, and provide sentencing and bail recommendations to the court. I was just starting out as a prosecutor, and yet I had the power to deprive a person of their liberty with the swipe of my pen.

When it came time for closing arguments, I approached the jury box. I decided to do it without notes so I wouldn't be looking down at a piece of paper, reading off my best arguments for why they should convict the defendant. I wanted to look the jurors in the eye. I felt that I should know my case well enough that I could close my eyes and see the entire incident in 360 degrees.

As I finished my closing and headed back to the prosecutor's table, I caught a glimpse of the audience. Amy Resner, my friend from the first day of orientation, was sitting there with a big smile on her face, cheering me on. Now we were both on our way.

The daily work was intense. At any given time, an individual prosecutor might be juggling more than one hundred cases. We started with lower-level work: arguing preliminary hearings, doing misdemeanor trials that covered things like DUIs and petty thefts. As the years passed, I got more and more trials under my belt and moved my way up the hierarchy of the office. In time, I would start prosecuting violent felonies, which took the work to a whole new level.

I would pore over police reports and interview witnesses. I would sit with the coroner and go through autopsy photographs, always cognizant that I was looking at somebody's child or parent. When police arrested a suspect, I would go down to the police station and stand on the other side of a two-way mirror and pass notes back and forth with investigators conducting the interview.

Once I started prosecuting felonies, I was assigned to homicide duty. I'd be given a briefcase on a Friday afternoon containing a pager (high-tech for the early nineties), a pen and pad, a copy of the penal code, and a list of critical numbers to call. For the next week, whenever the pager went off, it meant there had been a homicide and I was needed at the scene. Usually, that meant leaping out of bed between midnight and 6 a.m. My role was to make sure evidence was collected in the proper way, with all appropriate constitutional protections intact, so that it would be admissible in court. I often had to explain to victims and their families that there was a difference between what we knew happened and what we could prove happened. There is a giant chasm between arrest and conviction, and if you want to get from one to the other, you need legally obtained evidence.

I was at home in the courtroom. I understood its rhythm. I was comfortable with its idiosyncrasies. Eventually, I moved into a unit that focused on prosecuting sex crimes—putting rapists and child molesters behind bars. It was difficult, distressing, and deeply important work. I met so many girls, and sometimes boys, who had been abused, assaulted, neglected, all too often by people in relationships of trust.

What made these cases especially difficult was what was often needed to get a conviction: having the assault survivor testify. I spent a lot of those days meeting with survivors at Oakland's Highland General Hospital, walking them through what it would mean to take the stand, what that experience would be like. For some survivors, it was simply unimaginable to get on the witness stand and speak publicly about something they didn't even want to speak about privately.

There is so much pain and anguish associated with having experienced sexual violence. Containing that kind of emotional trauma to take the stand requires an extraordinary amount of courage and fortitude, especially when your abuser is also in the courtroom, when that abuser may be a family member or friend, and knowing you will be cross-examined by defense counsel whose job it is to convince the jury that you aren't telling the truth. I never faulted those who couldn't bring themselves to go through with it.

Often, as in the cases of the youngest children, the challenge of getting a conviction came down to the ability to testify, as much as the willingness. Those were the cases that haunted me most. I'll never forget a tiny, quiet six-year-old girl who was being molested by her sixteen-year-old brother. It was my job to sit with that sweet little child and see if I could get her to tell me her story—and whether she would be able to tell it again in front of a jury. I spent a lot of time with her, playing with toys, playing games, trying to build a relationship of trust. But as much as I tried, I knew—I just knew—that there was no way she could articulate to a jury what she had suffered. I remember walking out of the room and into a bathroom, where I broke down and cried. I wasn't going to have enough evidence to charge her brother. Without her testimony, I'd never be able to prove the allegations beyond a reasonable doubt. Despite all that prosecutorial power, I'm not sure I've ever felt quite so powerless.

These were just some of the challenges of defending children from sexual predators. There was also the jury itself, which sometimes seemed more inclined to believe adults than children. This was especially the case when it came to sexually exploited youth. I often think of a case I had involving a fourteen-year-old who had run away from her foster home with a group of young men from her neighborhood.

Instead of being her allies and protectors, they'd taken her to an empty apartment and gang-raped her. I could tell that she had learned at a young age that she couldn't trust adults; she wore an attitude of skepticism and hostility like a suit of armor. I felt for that poor girl, and the horrific childhood that had led her to this moment. But I was also acutely aware of how the jury might perceive her as she entered the courtroom, chewing gum, potentially coming off as almost contemptuous of the process.

I worried: Would they see her as the child she was, as an innocent victim of serial abuse? Or would they simply write her off as someone dressed "inappropriately," who had it coming?

Jurors are human beings, with human responses and reactions. I knew I had to meet them where they were if I was to have any chance of moving them to a more just interpretation of the facts.

I could see they weren't responding to her well. They didn't seem to like her. "The penal code was not created to protect some of us," I reminded the jury. "It is for all of us. This girl is a child. She needs to be protected from predators who are going to pounce. And one of the reasons the defendants picked her as their victim is that they thought you wouldn't care about her enough to believe her." In the end, we got a conviction, but I'm not sure the verdict meant much to the girl. She vanished after the trial. I asked some investigators to help me try to find her, but, though we had gotten a sketchy report that she was being trafficked on the streets of San Francisco, we could never confirm it. I never saw her again.

It was hard not to feel the weight of the systemic problems we were up against. Putting this young girl's abusers in prison meant they wouldn't be able to hurt other children. But what about the one they had already gotten their hands on? How had our system helped her?

A conviction was never going to make her whole, nor was it enough to get her out of the cycle of violence in which she was trapped. That reality, and what to do about it, bounced back and forth in my head—sometimes in the back of my mind, sometimes at the front of my skull. But it would be a few years before I could tackle it head-on.

In 1998, after nine years in the Alameda County District Attorney's office, I was recruited across the bay to the San Francisco District Attorney's Office. I was hired to run the career criminal unit, which focused on violent and serial offenders. I was hesitant to go at first, and not just because I loved working in the Alameda County courthouse. At the time, the San Francisco DA's office had a dubious reputation.

I was concerned by stories of dysfunction in the office. At the same time, it was a promotion: I would be running a unit, overseeing a team of prosecutors. This was a chance to grow. Plus, my friend and mentor Dick Iglehart, who was then the chief assistant district attorney, was actively encouraging me to come. With some trepidation, I accepted the offer—and soon found that my concerns had been warranted.

The office was a mess. Just one computer for every two lawyers, no filing system, and no database to track cases. It was rumored that when attorneys were finished with a case, some would toss the files in the trash. This was the late 1990s, and yet the office still didn't have email.

There was also a huge backlog of cases that were languishing, un-investigated, unprosecuted. Lawyers were frustrated with the police for not investigating cases. Police were frustrated with the district attorney because his office was failing to get convictions. The decisions being made at the top appeared to be arbitrary and random, and staff morale was close to rock bottom. That toxic environment was made even worse by a series of firings. One Friday, fourteen lawyers came back from lunch to find pink slips on their chairs. It was devastating. People cried and yelled, and soon their fear turned into paranoia. Lawyers were afraid of one another—afraid of backstabbing by colleagues trying to protect their own jobs. Some people started skipping out on the goodbye parties of their fired compatriots, worried that their attendance would mark them as targets for firing, too.

It was incredibly frustrating, and not just in terms of the day-to-day work. I believed the district attorney was undercutting the whole idea of what a progressive prosecutor could be. My vision of a progressive prosecutor was someone who used the power of the office with a sense of fairness, perspective, and experience, someone who was clear about the need to hold serious criminals accountable and who understood that the best way to create safe communities was to prevent crime in the first place. To do those things effectively, you also need to run a professional operation.

After eighteen months, I got a lifeline. The San Francisco city attorney, Louise Renne, called me with a job offer. Louise was the first woman to hold that office. She was a groundbreaker, and she was fearless, taking on entrenched interests ranging from gun manufacturers and tobacco companies to male-only clubs. There was an opening to lead the division in her office that handled child and family services; she wanted to know if I'd be interested. I told her I would take the job but that I didn't just want to be a lawyer dealing with individual cases; I wanted to work on policy that could improve the system as a whole. Too often, young people in foster care migrated to juvenile detention and then into the adult criminal system. I wanted to work on policies that would stem that devastating flow.

Louise was all for it.

I spent two years at the city attorney's office. I started by co-founding a task force to study the issues of sexually exploited youth. We put together a group of experts, survivors, and community members to help guide the work—a series of recommendations we would present to the San Francisco Board of Supervisors.

Norma Hotaling was my partner in that effort. She had firsthand experience with the challenges we were tackling. She had been abused as a girl, and ended up homeless and addicted to heroin. She was arrested for prostitution more than thirty times. But hers was one of the few such stories that have a happy ending. Norma got clean. She went to college. She got a degree in health education. And as soon as she graduated, she put that degree to use, creating a program designed to rescue women from prostitution that is widely replicated today. I couldn't think of a better person to have teamed up with, and I admire her for having the courage to tell her story and put it to use for the benefit of so many others.

One of our priorities was creating a safe place for prostituted youth to get love and support and treatment. I knew from years of experience that the survivors we were trying to help usually had nowhere to go. In most cases, their parents weren't in the picture. Many of them had run away from foster care. People often wondered why it was that exploited kids picked up by the police would go right back to the pimps or older prostitutes who "took care of them." It didn't seem so strange to me—where else were these kids able to turn?

Our task force proposed establishing a safe house for sexually exploited youth—a sanctuary that would offer substance abuse and mental health treatment; the resources needed to get back to school; and a network of support to keep vulnerable young people safe, healthy, and on track. We advocated for funding to create the safe house, as well as to run a public education campaign. We put posters up in public bathrooms and on buses, where at-risk youth would be able to get the information they needed without their pimp hovering over them.

We also believed it was important to disrupt the network of brothels masquerading as massage parlors, where so many people were being sexually exploited, so we asked the board of supervisors to direct law enforcement to investigate them as one of their top priorities.

To our delight, the board of supervisors adopted and funded our recommendations. We were able to rescue scores of runaways within the first couple of years. Law enforcement, meanwhile, shut down nearly three dozen brothels in the city.

The work was meaningful, empowering, and proof that I could do serious policy work without being a legislator. It also boosted my confidence that when I saw problems, I could be the one to help devise the solutions. All those times my mother had pressed me—"Well, what did *you* do?"—suddenly made a lot more sense. I realized I didn't have to wait for someone else to take the lead; I could start making things happen on my own.

I think it was that realization that turned my sights to elected office. Of all the problems I saw in front of me, few were in more urgent need of fixing than the district attorney's office. While we were making important gains at the city attorney's office, the district attorney's office was self-destructing. Talented career prosecutors were seeing their efforts undervalued and feeling stymied in the vital work to which they'd devoted their lives. Meanwhile, violent felons were walking free. I knew this. We all knew this. But suddenly it wasn't just an important problem to be solved. It was an important problem *I* could solve.

I wanted to honor, support, and empower the DA's office as a whole. But in order to run the office, I would have to run *for* office. A political campaign would be a huge undertaking, and one I clearly couldn't embark upon lightly. I turned to my friends, my family, my colleagues, my mentors. We had long, animated debates (another thesis to defend). We weighed the pros and cons, and then we weighed them all again.

People were generally supportive of the idea, but they were worried, too. My would-be opponent and former boss was already a household name. He also had a reputation as a fighter; in fact, his nickname was Kayo (as in K.O.)—a tribute to the many knockouts he scored in his boxing youth. A campaign would be not only bruising but also expensive, and I had no experience as a fund-raiser.

Was this really the time for me to run? I had no way of knowing. But more and more, I was coming to feel that "wait and see" wasn't an option. I thought of James Baldwin, whose words had defined so much of the civil rights struggle. "There is never a time in the future in which we will work out our salvation," he'd written. "The challenge is in the moment; the time is always now."

Two

A VOICE FOR JUSTICE

"Kamala, let's go. Come on, we're going to be late." My mother was losing patience. "Just a second, Mommy," I called back. (Yes, my mother was and always will be "Mommy" to me.) We were on our way to campaign headquarters, where volunteers were gathering. My mother often took charge of the volunteer operation, and she didn't dillydally. Everyone knew that when Shyamala spoke, you listened.

We drove from my apartment, near Market Street, past the wealth and attractions of San Francisco's downtown to a predominantly black neighborhood in the southeast part of town known as Bayview–Hunters Point. The Bayview had been home to the Hunters Point Naval Shipyard, which helped to build America's fighting fleet in the mid-twentieth century. In the 1940s, the prospect of good jobs and affordable housing around the shipyard lured thousands of black

Americans who were seeking opportunity and relief from the pain and injustice of segregation. These workers bent the steel and welded the plates that helped our nation win the Second World War.

But like too many similar neighborhoods in America, the Bayview had been left behind in the postwar era. When the shipyard closed, nothing came to take its place. Beautiful old houses were boarded up; toxic waste polluted the soil, water, and air; drugs and violence poisoned the streets; and poverty of the worst kind settled in for the long haul. It was a community disproportionately represented in the criminal justice system and also plagued by unsolved crimes. Families in the Bayview, many of which had generational roots in San Francisco, were cut off—literally and figuratively—from the promise of the thriving city they called home. The Bayview was the kind of place that no one in the city ever saw unless they made it their business to go there. You didn't pass it on the freeway. You didn't cross it to get from one part of the city to another. It was, in deeply tragic ways, invisible to the world beyond it. I wanted to be a part of changing that. So I headquartered my campaign at 3rd Avenue and Galvez, right in the heart of the Bayview.

The political consultants thought I was nuts. They said no campaign volunteers would ever come to the Bayview from other parts of the city. But it was places like the Bayview that had inspired me to run in the first place. I wasn't running so I could have a fancy office downtown. I was running for the chance to represent people whose voices weren't being heard, and to bring the promise of public safety to every neighborhood, not just some. Besides, I didn't believe that people wouldn't come to the Bayview. And I was right: They did come. By the dozens.

San Francisco, like our country as a whole, is diverse yet deeply segregated—more mosaic than melting pot. Yet our campaign attracted people representing the full vibrancy of the whole community. Volunteers and supporters poured in from Chinatown, the Castro, Pacific Heights, the Mission District: white, black, Asian, and Latinx; wealthy and working-class; male and female; old and young; gay and straight. A group of teenage graffiti artists decorated the back wall of campaign headquarters, spray-painting JUSTICE in giant letters. HQ buzzed with volunteers, some calling voters, some sitting together around a table stuffing envelopes, others picking up clipboards so they could go door-to-door talking to people in the community about what we were trying to do.

We pulled up to headquarters just in time. I let my mother out.

"You have the ironing board?" she asked.

"Yeah, of course, it's in the back seat."

"Okay. I love you," she said as she shut the car door.

As I drove away, I could hear her call, "Kamala, what about the duct tape?"

I had the duct tape.

I got back on the road and drove toward the nearest supermarket. It was a Saturday morning, the equivalent of rush hour in the grocery aisles. I pulled into the parking lot, snuck my car into one of the few open spots, and grabbed the ironing board, the tape, and a campaign sign that looked slightly worn from being tossed in and out of the car.

If you think running for office sounds glamorous, I wish you could have seen me striding through the parking lot with an ironing board under my arm. I remember the kids who would look curiously at the ironing board and point, and the moms who would hustle them past. I couldn't blame them. I must have looked out of place—if not totally out of my mind.

But an ironing board makes for the perfect standing desk. I set it up in front of the supermarket entrance, just off to the side, near the carts, and taped up a sign that read KAMALA HARRIS, A VOICE FOR JUSTICE. When the campaign was just getting started, my friend Andrea Dew Steele and I had put together my first piece of campaign literature: a basic, one-page, black-and-white bio and summary of my positions. Andrea would later found Emerge America, an organization that recruits and trains Democratic women to run for elected office nationwide. I put several stacks of my flyer on the ironing board and, next to it, a clipboard with a sign-up sheet. Then I got to work.

Shoppers rolled their carts out the automatic doors, squinting at the sunlight, trying to remember where they parked the car. And then, out of left field:

"Hi! I'm Kamala Harris. I'm running for district attorney, and I hope to have your support."

In truth, I would have settled for them just remembering my name. Early on in the campaign, we did a poll to see how many people in the county of San Francisco had heard of me. The answer was a whopping 6 percent. As in six of every one hundred people had heard of me before. I couldn't help but wonder: Was my mother one of the people they'd randomly called?

But I hadn't gotten into this thinking it would be easy. I knew I'd have to work hard to introduce myself and what I stood for to a whole lot of people who had no idea who I was.

For some first-time candidates, interacting with strangers can feel awkward, and understandably so. It isn't easy to initiate a conversation with someone who passes you on the street, or to try to connect with them at the bus stop on their way home after work, or to walk into a merchant's business and try to strike up a conversation with the owner. I got my share of polite—and occasionally not so polite—rebuffs, like a telemarketer calling during dinner. But more often than not, I encountered people who were welcoming, open, and eager to talk about the issues affecting their daily lives and their hopes for their family and their community—whether that meant cracking down on domestic violence or creating better options for at-risk kids. Years later, I still run into people who remember our interactions at those bus stops.

It may sound strange, but the thing it reminded me of most was jury selection. When I worked as a prosecutor, I spent a lot of time in the courtroom, talking to people who'd been called for jury duty from every part of the community. My job was to ask them questions over the course of a few minutes and, based on that, try to figure out their priorities and perspectives. Campaigning was kind of like that, but without opposing counsel trying to cut me off. I loved being able to engage. Sometimes a mom would come out of the grocery store with a toddler in the shopping cart seat, and we'd find ourselves spending a good twenty minutes talking about her life, and her struggles, and her daughter's Halloween costume. Before we parted, I'd look her in the eye and say, "I hope I can have your support." It's amazing how often people would tell me that no one had ever asked them that directly before.

Still, this process didn't come naturally to me. I was always more than happy to talk about the work to be done. But voters wanted to hear about more than just policy. They wanted to know about me personally—who I was, what my life had been like, the experiences that had shaped me. They wanted to understand who I was on a fundamental level. But I'd been raised not to talk about myself. I'd been raised with the belief that there was something narcissistic about doing so. Something vain. And so, even though I understood what was motivating their questions, it took some time before I got used to it.

There were multiple candidates in my first DA's race, and a runoff was inevitable. But our polling (which had markedly improved over time) suggested that if we just made the runoff, we could win five weeks later.

I spent Election Day on the streets shaking hands, from the pre-dawn commute until the polls closed. Chrisette, one of my closest friends, flew in to help with the last-minute campaigning. It felt like the final quarter-mile sprint at the end of a marathon—thrilling in its own way. My family, friends, senior campaign staff members, and I went out to dinner as the results started rolling in. My campaign manager, Jim Stearns, was at the elections office watching the count and calling in the numbers. Over the course of the meal, my dear friend Mark Leno, who was then a member of the California State Assembly, kept track of the counts along with Maya, my campaign consultant Jim Rivaldo, and my friend Matthew Rothschild. With each precinct that reported, and between bites of pasta, they would update the tally on the paper tablecloth.

Modern campaigns rely on big data, analytics, and sophisticated voter turnout models. But in my experience, I've found that a friend, a pen, and a bowl of spaghetti are just as effective.

We were getting ready to leave when Maya grabbed my arm. A new update had come in.

"Oh, my God, you did it!" she exclaimed. "You made the runoff!" I did the math myself to make sure she was right. I remember looking at Maya and Maya looking at me and both of us saying, "Can you believe it—we're really in this!"

The runoff was held five weeks later. It rained that day, and I spent it getting soaked as I shook hands with voters at bus stops. That night, as I'd hoped, we won a decisive victory.

We held a party at campaign headquarters, and I walked out to speak as "We Are the Champions" blasted through the room. Looking out at the crowd—friends, family, mentors, volunteers from the campaign—I saw one community. There were people from the poorest neighborhoods and the richest. Police officers alongside advocates fighting for police reform. Young people cheering with senior citizens. It was a reflection of what I've always believed to be true: when it comes to the things that matter most, we have so much more in common than what separates us.

At the time of this writing, it's been almost fifteen years since my inauguration as district attorney. I have spent almost every day since working, in some way or another, on reforming the criminal justice system. I spent two terms in its pursuit as district attorney and nearly two terms as attorney general, and I introduced criminal justice reform legislation within my first six weeks as a United States senator. Though I understood, fully, that inauguration morning in 2004, how important the issues were to me, I never could have imagined that they would lead me from San Francisco to Sacramento to Washington, DC.

My inauguration ceremony for district attorney took place in the

Herbst Theatre, in the San Francisco War Memorial and Performing Arts Center—the same stage where the United Nations Charter had been signed in 1945. Now we were making a different kind of history, but unity was still the message of the day. My mother stood between me and Ronald George, the Republican chief justice of the California Supreme Court, who I chose to swear me in. My strongest memory is of looking at her and seeing the pure pride on her face.

The room was packed to overflowing, hundreds of people from all corners of the city. Drummers drummed. A youth choir sang. One of my pastors gave a beautiful invocation. Chinese dragon dancers roamed the aisles. The San Francisco Gay Men's Chorus serenaded us all. It was multicultural, multiracial, a little frenzied in all the best and most beautiful ways.

Jerry Brown, then mayor of Oakland, was sitting in the front row; he told me that his father had taken the same oath of office sixty years ago to the day. And with Gavin Newsom's swearing-in as mayor the same day as mine, there was a palpable sense in the city that a new chapter was opening for San Francisco politics—and what might be possible for us all.

I made my way through the crowd, shaking hands and getting hugs and taking in the joy of it all. As the festivities were winding down, a man came up to me with his two young daughters.

"I brought them here today," he said, "so they could see what someone who looked like them could grow up to do."

After the inauguration, I snuck away to see my new office. I wanted to know what it felt like to sit in the chair. My communications director, Debbie Mesloh, and I drove to the Hall of Justice. Standing right next to the freeway, "850" as it was known (for 850

Bryant Street), was a gray, solemn, and imposing building; I used to joke that it was a "horribly wonderful" place to work. In addition to the district attorney's office, the building housed the police department, the criminal courts, the city tow office, the county jail, and the city coroner's office. There was no doubt this was a place where people's lives were changed, sometimes forever.

"Oh, wow." I surveyed my office. Or, more accurately, I looked around the empty room. It had been stripped of almost everything as part of the transition. A metal cabinet sat against one wall with a 1980s Wang computer on top of it. (Mind you, it was 2004.) No wonder the office hadn't gotten email yet. A plastic-lined wastebasket stood in the corner; a few loose wires stuck out of the floor. Out the window of my new office I could see a row of bail bonds businesses—a daily reminder of the ways in which the criminal justice system is more punishing to the poor. There was no desk in the office, just a chair where the desk had been. But that was okay. It was the chair I had come for. I took my seat.

Now it was quiet. And for the first time since the day began, I was alone with my thoughts, taking it all in, contemplating the surreal.

I had run because I knew I could do the job—and I believed I could do it better than it had been done. Still, I knew I represented something much bigger than my own experience. At the time, there weren't many district attorneys who looked like me or had my background. There still aren't. A report in 2015 found that 95 percent of our country's elected prosecutors were white, and 79 percent were white men.

No part of me would more fully inform my perspective than the decade I had spent on the front lines of the criminal justice system as a line prosecutor. I knew it backward and forward. For what it was, for what it wasn't, and for what it could be. The courthouse was supposed to be the epicenter of justice; but it was often a great epicenter of injustice. I knew both to be true.

I had been around the courtroom long enough to see victims of violence show up years later as perpetrators of violence. I worked with children who had grown up in neighborhoods so crime ridden that they had rates of PTSD as high as those growing up in war zones. I had worked with kids in foster care who changed homes six times before turning eighteen. I had seen them run away, from one bad circumstance into another, only to get caught in the gears of the system, with no prospect for breaking free. I had seen children marked for a bleak future solely because of the circumstances of their birth and the zip codes in which they lived. As deputy DA, my job had been to hold violators of the law accountable. But didn't the system owe them and their communities some accountability, too?

What the system doled out instead was an era of mass incarceration that has further devastated already disadvantaged communities. The United States puts more people in prison than any country in the world. All told, we had more than 2.1 million people locked up in state and federal prisons in 2018. To put that in perspective: there are fifteen American states that have smaller populations than that. The war on drugs pulled a lot of people into the system; it turned the criminal justice system into an assembly line. I saw it up close.

Early in my career, I was assigned to a part of the Alameda County DA's office known as the bridge, where lawyers in small offices would handle drug cases by the hundreds. There were bad actors in the piles, to be sure, plenty of dealers selling to kids or forcing kids to sell for them. But too many case files told a different story: a man arrested for simple possession of a few rocks of crack, a woman arrested for being under the influence while sitting on her stoop.

The cases were as easy to prove as they were tragic to charge. In the rush to clean up the streets, we were criminalizing a public health crisis. And without a focus on treatment and prevention, the crack epidemic spread like a deadly virus, burning through city after city until it had stolen a generation of people.

As I sat alone in my new office, I recalled a time, as a young prosecutor, when I overheard some of my colleagues in the hallway.

"Should we add the gang enhancement?" one of them asked.

"Can we show he was in a gang?" the other said.

"Come on, you saw what he was wearing, you saw which corner they picked him up on. Guy's got the tape of that rapper, what's his name?"

I stepped out into the hallway. "Hey, guys, just so you know: I have family that live in that neighborhood. I've got friends who dress in that style. And I've got a tape of that rapper in my car right now."

I reflected on it all—about why I ran for office, whom I had come there to help, and the difference between getting convictions and having conviction. In the end, I knew I was there for the victims. Both the victims of crimes committed and the victims of a broken criminal justice system.

For me, to be a progressive prosecutor is to understand—and act on—this dichotomy. It is to understand that when a person takes another's life, or a child is molested, or a woman raped, the perpetrators deserve severe consequences. That is one imperative of justice. But it is also to understand that fairness is in short supply in a justice system that is supposed to guarantee it. The job of a progressive prosecutor is to look out for the overlooked, to speak up for those whose voices aren't being heard, to see and address the causes of crime, not just their consequences, and to shine a light on the inequality and unfairness that lead to injustice. It is to recognize that not everyone needs punishment, that what many need, quite plainly, is help.

There was a knock at the door. It was Debbie. "You ready?" she asked, smiling.

"I'll be there in a second," I told her. I breathed in the silence for another moment. Then I pulled a pen and a yellow notepad from my briefcase and started to make a list.

I had just sat down at my desk when my administrative assistant came in. "Boss, there's another mom out here."

"Thanks, I'll be right out."

I walked down the hallway to the lobby to greet her. I'd been on the job only a few weeks, but it was not the first time I'd taken this walk. This was not the first time a woman had shown up and said, "I want to speak to Kamala. I will only speak to Kamala." I knew exactly why she was there. She was the mother of a murdered child.

The woman nearly collapsed in my arms. Her devastation was visceral. She was grieving and exhausted. And yet her being there at all was a testament to her strength. She was there for her baby, the baby she'd lost, a young man killed by gunfire in the streets. It had been months since her son's death, and yet the killer still walked free. The case was one of the more than seventy unsolved homicides languishing in the San Francisco Police Department when I took office.

I had known some of these mothers, and others I had met while I was campaigning. They were almost all black or Latina from high-crime neighborhoods, and all of them loved their children deeply. They had come together to form a group, Mothers of Homicide Victims. It was part support group, part advocacy organization. They leaned on one another to work through their grief. And they organized to get justice for their sons.

They weren't sure if I could help them, but they knew that I would at least see them. And I mean literally see them. See their pain, see their anguish, see their souls—which were bleeding. First and foremost, they knew I would see them as loving, grieving mothers.

This is part of the tragedy. When people hear that a mother has lost a child to cancer or a car accident or war, the natural response is collective sympathy and concern. But when a woman loses her son to violence in the streets, the response from the public is often different, almost a collective shrug, as though it's an expected eventuality. Not the horrific tragedy of losing a child, but rather just another statistic. As though the circumstances of her son's death define the value of his life. As though the loss she has suffered is less valid, less painful, less worthy of compassion.

I walked her back to my office so we could have some privacy to talk. She told me her son had been shot and killed, that no one had been arrested, that no one seemed to care. She described the day she had to go to the coroner's office to identify his body—how she couldn't get that image out of her head, of him lifeless in a place so cold. She had left messages for the homicide inspector, she said, suggesting possible leads, but she never heard back. Nothing had happened, nothing seemed to be happening, and she couldn't understand why. She grasped my hand and looked me straight in the eye. "He mattered," she said. "He still matters to me."

"He matters to me, too," I reassured her. His life should have

mattered to everyone. I told my team to get the entire squad of homicide inspectors to convene in my conference room as soon as possible.
I wanted to know what was going on with all of these cases.

The homicide inspectors showed up not knowing what to expect.
At the time I didn't know it was uncommon for the district attorney
to summon them for a meeting. One by one, I asked them to tell me
the status of the unresolved homicide cases and pressed them for details about what they were going to do to help us get justice for these
families. I had very pointed questions, and I pushed the inspectors
hard—harder, I later learned, than they were expecting. This ruffled
some feathers. But it was the right thing to do, and it needed to be
done—regardless of whether it had ever been done before.

They took my call to action seriously. Within a month of the
meeting, the police department launched a new campaign to try to
encourage witnesses to step forward. And in time, we were able to
reduce the backlog of unsolved homicides by 25 percent. Not every
case could be solved, but we made sure we worked hard to ensure that
every one that could be was.

Some people were surprised I was so relentless. And I know some
others questioned how I, as a black woman, could countenance being
part of "the machine" putting more young men of color behind bars.
There is no doubt that the criminal justice system has deep flaws,
that it is broken in fundamental ways. And we need to deal with that.
But we cannot overlook or ignore that mother's pain, that child's
death, that murderer who still walks the streets. I believe there must
be serious consequences for people who commit serious crimes.

I've handled cases for just about every crime imaginable—
including a man who had literally scalped his girlfriend during an
argument. I've prosecuted sadistic criminals who have committed

the most heinous, unspeakable acts against other people. I've been at homicide scenes where people had been killed, and I've won guilty verdicts against those who did the killing. I've faced cold-blooded murderers in the courtroom as a judge laid down a sentence of life in prison. And I haven't shied away from calling for harsher sentences in certain cases. In 2004, for example, I got a bill passed in California to lengthen the sentences for so-called johns who paid to have sex with underage girls. I believed that should be treated as child sexual assault.

But let's be clear: the situation is not the same—nor should it be—when it comes to less serious crimes. I remember the first time I visited the county jail. So many young men, and they were mostly black or brown or poor. Too many were there because of addiction and desperation and poverty. They were fathers who missed their kids. They were young adults, many of whom had been pulled into gangs with no real choice in the matter. The majority weren't there for violent offenses, and yet they had become drops in the sea of those swept up in a wave of mass incarceration. People whose lives had been destroyed, along with their families and their communities. They represented a living monument to lost potential, and I wanted to tear it down.

In 1977, in the heart of the San Francisco neighborhood known as Western Addition, my friend Lateefah Simon was born. She grew up in what was once a middle-class neighborhood as the crack epidemic was starting to take hold. She saw, firsthand, what it was doing to her community—the self-destructive addiction it fueled, the burden it placed on families that were already struggling to get by with little semblance of a safety net, the way it disappeared fathers and corroded even a mother's most deep-seated instinct to care for her child. When Lateefah was a young girl, her desire was to help people, but as she got older, she became one of the many who needed help. She ended up on probation for shoplifting. She dropped out of high school.

But then someone intervened. Lateefah was a teenager, working eight hours a day at Taco Bell, when an outreach worker told her about an opportunity. There was an organization in San Francisco, the Center for Young Women's Development, that provided social services, including job training, to girls and young women who were on the streets or in trouble. The center was recruiting for new staff to work there. Lateefah saw a lifeline and grabbed hold.

She started working for the center when she was a teenager and raising a daughter of her own; soon she was unstoppable. She was everywhere: at local government meetings, calling for changes to help girls who'd been trafficked; on the streets of poor neighborhoods handing out condoms and candy bars, along with information about how to get help; and at the center itself, working with vulnerable girls from her neighborhood. "I saw resilience in these young women," she recalled. "There were people who had absolutely nothing but were somehow able to make it through the day. And the next day. And the next."

The center's board members were so impressed by Lateefah's tenacity, skills, and leadership that they asked her to become executive director when she was just nineteen years old. She said yes—and that was when I came to know her.

At the city attorney's office, I had been working with the same community of women that Lateefah had. I had been holding "know your rights" sessions for vulnerable women all across the city, and I asked Lateefah to join our efforts. I could see that Lateefah was a genius, and it turned out I wasn't the only one who thought so. In 2003, she became the youngest woman to ever win the prestigious MacArthur "Genius" award (with only a GED).

When I became district attorney, I often thought to myself, "What if Lateefah had been picked up for a bag of weed instead of shoplifting? What if she'd been sentenced to prison instead of probation?" I knew what a felony conviction meant. It wasn't just about the time in prison; it was about what happens afterwards. As a country, we specialize in releasing inmates into desperate, hopeless situations. We give them a little bit of money and a bus ticket and we send them on their way with a felony conviction on their record—not the kind of experience most employers are looking for. In so many cases, finding themselves rejected in the hiring process, they have no way of making money. From the moment they leave, they are in danger of returning. They end up in the same neighborhood, with the same people, on the same corner; the only difference is that they've now served time. Prison has its own gravitational pull, often inescapable; of the hundreds of thousands of prisoners we release as a country every year, nearly 70 percent commit a crime within three years. The status quo isn't working.

I brought a small group of trusted advisers together, including my bold and brilliant chief of policy, Tim Silard, and posed a question: What would it take to put together a reentry program that actually worked? Put another way, if the best way of providing public safety is preventing crime in the first place, what can we do to prevent people from reoffending?

What if we could really get them back on track?

That question would become the name of the program Tim and I developed together: Back on Track. At the heart of the program was my belief in the power of redemption. Redemption is an age-old concept rooted in many religions. It is a concept that presupposes that we will all make mistakes, and for some, that mistake will rise to the level of being a crime. Yes, there must be consequences and accountability. But after that debt to society has been paid, is it not the sign of a civil society that we allow people to earn their way back?

There was tremendous pushback at first. At the time, criminal justice policy was still trending toward things like harsher sentences or militarizing the police. The guiding belief among many was that the criminal justice system wasn't punitive enough. More than a decade later, that attitude has, thankfully, evolved, opening up space for a more balanced approach. Reentry programs like Back on Track are now part of the mainstream conversation. But in those days, I faced intensive backlash, including from people I worked with on a regular basis. They saw a prosecutor's job as putting people in prison, not focusing on what happens to them when they get out. That was someone else's problem. I was accused of wasting precious time and resources. People would say to me, "You should be locking them up instead of letting them out."

But we persevered. It was one of the things I valued about running the office. In the end, it was up to me whether we were going to pursue the initiative. I would hear out my critics, but I wouldn't be constrained by them. I wanted to make a difference. I wanted to prove it could be done.

So Tim and I got to work. We wanted to create opportunities by running participants through a rigorous program that I often compared to boot camp. It would include job training, GED courses, community service, parenting and financial literacy classes, as well as drug testing and therapy. The DA's office led the charge, but we recruited a range of critical partners—from Goodwill Industries, which oversaw community service and employment training, to the San Francisco Chamber of Commerce and its member companies, which helped find jobs for program participants, to local trade unions, which provided valuable apprenticeship opportunities.

Though compassionate in its approach, Back on Track was intense by design. This was not a social welfare program; it was a law enforcement program. All of the first participants were nonviolent first-time offenders who had started their journey to the Hall of Justice in the back of a squad car. Participants had to first plead guilty and accept responsibility for the actions that had brought them there. We promised that if participants completed the program successfully, we would have their charges expunged, which gave them even more reason to put in the effort. We hadn't designed a program that was about incremental improvement around the edges. It was about transformation. We knew what these young people were capable of achieving—and we wanted them to see it in themselves. We wanted every participant to reach for the highest bar.

When it came time to identify someone to run the program, one name immediately came to mind. I called Lateefah.

At first, she was reluctant. She had never imagined herself as the kind of person who would work for the DA. "I never wanted to work for the Man," she told me.

"Well, don't worry," I laughed. "You won't be working for the Man. You'll be working for me."

Lateefah worked incredibly hard. And so did the Back on Track students. And on a night I'll never forget, we got to share in the fruits of that effort together.

Tim, Lateefah, and many others from my office joined me after the court had closed for the evening. We headed down the hall toward the jury assembly room. When we entered, the room was filled with people carrying flowers and balloons. The bustling, joyous mood was not typical in a jury room, to say the least. But this was not a typical night. I walked to the front of the room and opened the ceremonies for the first Back on Track graduation ceremony.

Through the main door, a group of eighteen men and women walked down the aisle to take their seats. With few exceptions, this was the first time in their lives they had ever worn graduation robes. Only a handful of them had ever had an occasion to which they could invite their family, an occasion that would make their loved ones cry happy tears. This celebration was hard-won, and they deserved every minute of it.

In the year since they started the program, each of them had, at a minimum, earned a GED and landed a steady job. They had all done community service—more than two hundred hours of it. The fathers among them had paid all of their outstanding child support payments. And they were all drug free. They proved they could do it— and that it could be done.

In exchange for that effort and that success, we were there to keep our promise. In addition to a diploma, the graduates would have their records cleared by a judge who was standing by.

A number of superior court judges volunteered to preside over Back on Track graduations, including my friend John Dearman, a former social worker who became the longest-serving judge in San Francisco's history. Another among them was Judge Thelton Henderson, an icon in the civil rights movement, who in 1963 lent his car to

Martin Luther King Jr. so Dr. King could make his way to Selma after his own car broke down.

Back on Track quickly proved its merit. After two years, only 10 percent of Back on Track graduates had reoffended, as compared with 50 percent for others convicted of similar crimes. It represented smart, effective stewardship of taxpayer dollars, too: Our program cost about $5,000 per participant. For comparison, it costs $10,000 to prosecute a felony case and another $40,000 or more to house someone for a year in the county jail.

Local officials don't have the ability to make national policy. They have no authority beyond their jurisdiction. But when they land on good ideas, even on a small scale, they can create examples that others can replicate. That was a key goal of ours in creating Back on Track. We wanted to show leaders at every level of government in every state in the union that a reentry initiative could work and was worth trying. So we were especially gratified when the Obama Justice Department adopted Back on Track as a model program.

When I later ran for attorney general, I did so, in no small part, to take the program statewide. And that's exactly what we did, working in partnership with the LA County Sheriff's Department to create Back on Track–Los Angeles (BOT-LA), in the largest county jail system in California.

I remember one day, I went out to visit a group of program participants with two of my special assistant attorneys general, Jeff Tsai and Daniel Suvor. When we arrived, we were told that the men had created a musical group and they wanted to perform a song they'd written for me. "That's great! What do they call themselves?" I asked. The answer made me smile: ContraBand. They were a wonderful sight. There was an older man in a yarmulke; a skinny guy doing his best Michael Jackson imitation; a guitarist who was definitely influenced by Santana; and a keyboardist who was channeling the Eagles. It turned out the song was called "Back on Track." The chorus was "I'm back on track and I'm not going back." They were really getting into it, having so much fun, all of them looking so proud.

We all clapped and cheered. I was laughing, but I found myself tearing up, too. I was so touched by their sincerity, which I hoped others could see in them. There was such beauty in the supposed impossibility of it all.

Whenever we held a Back on Track graduation during my time as DA, we'd make sure that current program participants were there to see what their future could hold. And whenever I spoke at those ceremonies, I'd tell the graduates what I knew to be true: that the program depended a lot more on them than on us. This accomplishment was theirs, and I wanted to make sure they knew it. But I wanted them to know that it was also bigger than themselves.

"People are watching you," I'd tell them. "They are watching you. And when they see your success, they'll think, 'Maybe we can duplicate that. Maybe we should try it back home.' You should feel inspired by that, by knowing that your individual success here will someday create an opportunity for someone you've never met before in some other part of the country."

When I first started as DA and I took out that notepad and made a to-do list, there was a lot I wanted to get done, a lot that needed to get done. I wanted to make sure I accounted for all of it. I even included "Paint the walls." I was serious, too. I've always believed there is no problem too small to fix. I know it may sound trivial, but people were working in offices that hadn't been painted in years. Not only was it a metaphor for the atrophy that had spread across the department—it was just plain depressing. The staff was demoralized. They felt undervalued, disempowered, and beaten down. Painting the walls was a tangible way to signal that I noticed—and that things were going to change.

I sent the staff a survey asking what they needed most to make the job better. One of the most common requests was for new photocopiers. It turned out that lawyers were spending hours pleading with an ancient machine and trying in vain to clear troublesome paper jams. So I ordered new copiers right away, and we celebrated more than you might expect when they arrived.

These were simple things. But the larger goal was restoring professionalism as the highest value. I knew that there was a direct link between professionalizing the operation and making sure it delivered justice. People needed to be at the top of their game. I was leading a DA's office with a former culture that pitted people against one another. I wanted to turn that on its head and make sure we worked as a team. Every Monday afternoon, I'd have all the felony trial lawyers come into the library and present their cases and the verdicts from the previous week to a roomful of their colleagues. When it was your turn, you'd stand up and talk about the legal issues of your case, how the defense was presented, how the judge had responded, any issues you'd had with witnesses, and so on. At the end, I always led the applause, no matter the outcome of the case. It wasn't so much about winning or losing. It was about applauding the professionalism of the performance.

Professionalism, as I see it, is in part about what happens inside an office. But it's also about how people carry themselves outside the office. When I trained younger lawyers, I'd say, "Let's be clear. You represent the people. So I expect you to get to know exactly who the people are." I'd tell my team to learn about the communities where they didn't live, to follow neighborhood news, to go to local festivals and community forums. "For the people" means for *them*. All of them.

The San Francisco District Attorney's Office was certainly not the only government agency that was operating poorly. And I certainly wasn't the first person to take over a mismanaged organization and focus on managing it better. But the stakes of repairing the DA's office were greater than making the trains (or, in San Francisco's case, cable cars) run on time; greater than improving morale and efficiency; greater than budgets and backlogs and conviction rates. At stake was justice itself. In a DA's office, dysfunction necessarily leads to injustice. Prosecutors are human beings; when they are not at their best, they do not perform their best—and that could mean people who should go to prison walk free and people who shouldn't go to prison end up behind bars. Such is the individual power of prosecutorial discretion.

I had divided my to-do list into three categories: short-, medium-, and long-term. Short-term meant "a couple of weeks," medium-term meant "a couple of years," and long-term meant "as long as it takes." It was that far side of the ledger where I wrote down the most intractable problems we were facing—the ones you can't expect to solve on your own, over a term, perhaps even over a career. That's where the most important work is. That's where you take the bigger view—not of the political moment but of the historical one. The core problems of the criminal justice system are not new. There are thinkers and activists and leaders who have been fighting to change the system for generations. I got to meet many of them when I was a child. You don't add the intractable problems to the list because they are new, but because they are big, because people have been fighting against them for dozens—maybe even hundreds—of years, and that duty is now yours. What matters is how well you run the portion of the race that is yours.

It was my mother who had instilled that in me. I grew up surrounded by people who were battling for civil rights and equal justice. But I had also seen it in her work. My mother was a breast cancer researcher. Like her colleagues, she dreamed of the day we'd find a cure. But she wasn't fixated on that distant dream; she focused on the work right in front of her. The work that would move us closer, day by day, year by year, until we crossed the finish line. "Focus on what's in front of you and the rest will follow," she would say.

That is the spirit we need to bring to building a more perfect union: recognition that we are part of a longer story, and we are responsible for how our chapter gets written. In the battle to build a smarter, fairer, more effective criminal justice system, there is an enormous amount of work to do. We know what the problems are. So let's roll up our sleeves and start fixing them.

One of the key issues I focused on during my first year in the Senate was the country's bail system—the process by which you can be released from jail while you await trial. It's an issue that has only begun to get the attention it deserves, given the scope and scale of the injustice it exacts on people's lives.

In this country, you are innocent until proven guilty and—unless you are a danger to others or highly likely to flee the jurisdiction—you shouldn't have to sit in jail waiting for your court date. This is the basic premise of due process: you get to hold on to your liberty unless and until a jury convicts you and a judge sentences you. It's why the Bill of Rights explicitly prohibits excessive bail. That's what justice is supposed to look like.

What it should not look like is the system we have in America today. The median bail in the United States is $10,000. But in American households with an income of $45,000, the median savings account balance is $2,530. The disparity is so high that at any given time, roughly nine out of ten people who are detained can't afford to pay to get out.

By its very design, the cash bail system favors the wealthy and penalizes the poor. If you can pay cash up front, you can leave, and when your trial is over, you'll get all of your money back. If you can't afford it, you either languish in jail or have to pay a bail bondsman, which costs a steep fee you will never get back.

When I was district attorney, I knew that every day, families were leaving the Hall of Justice, crossing the street, walking into those bail bonds offices, having done whatever it took to get the cash to pay the bondsmen—pawning their possessions, securing predatory payday loans, asking for help from their friends or at church. I also knew that people with defensible cases were taking guilty pleas just so they could get out of jail and back to their job or home to their kids.

The New York Times Magazine told the story of a struggling single mother who spent two weeks on Rikers Island, arrested and charged with endangering the welfare of a child, because she'd left her baby with a friend at a shelter while she bought diapers at Target. This young woman could not afford her $1,500 bail, and by the time she was released, her child was in foster care. In another case, sixteen-year-old Kalief Browder was arrested in New York on charges that he had stolen a backpack. When his family couldn't scrape together the $3,000 bail, Kalief went to jail while he awaited his trial. He would end up spending the next three years waiting, endlessly waiting, much of it in solitary confinement, not having ever been tried or convicted of anything. It was a tragic story from beginning to end: in 2015, soon after he was finally released from Rikers, Kalief committed suicide.

The criminal justice system punishes people for their poverty. Where is the justice in that? And where is the sense? How does that advance public safety? Between 2000 and 2014, 95 percent of the growth in the jail population came from people awaiting trial. This is a group of largely nonviolent defendants who haven't been proven guilty, and we're spending $38 million a day to imprison them while they await their day in court. Whether or not someone can get bailed out of jail shouldn't be based on how much money he has in the bank. Or the color of his skin: black men pay 35 percent higher bail than white men for the same charge. Latino men pay nearly 20 percent more. This isn't the stuff of coincidences. It is systemic. And we have to change it.

In 2017, I introduced a bill in the Senate to encourage states to replace their bail systems, moving away from arbitrarily assigning cash bail and toward systems where a person's actual risk of danger or flight is evaluated. If someone poses a threat to the public, we should detain them. If someone is likely to flee, we should detain them. But if not, we shouldn't be in the business of charging money in exchange for liberty. My lead co-sponsor in this effort is Rand Paul, a Republican senator from Kentucky with whom I vehemently disagree on most things. But this is one of those issues that he and I agree on— that all of us should agree on. It's an issue that can—and does— transcend politics, and, one way or another, we're going to get it done.

Something else it's past time we get done is dismantling the failed war on drugs—starting with legalizing marijuana. According to the FBI, more people were arrested for marijuana possession than for all violent crimes in 2016. Between 2001 and 2010, more than seven million people were arrested for simple possession of marijuana. They are disproportionately black and brown. One stark example: during the first three months of 2018, 93 percent of the people the NYPD arrested for marijuana possession were people of color. These racial disparities are staggering and unconscionable. We need to legalize marijuana and regulate it. And we need to expunge nonviolent marijuana-related offenses from the records of the millions of people who have been arrested and incarcerated so they can get on with their lives.

But let's do it with eyes wide open, understanding that there is unfinished business when it comes to legalization. There is no widely used equivalent to a breathalyzer that law enforcement officials agree is consistently reliable. We need to invest in a solution. We also need to acknowledge what we don't know about the effects of marijuana. Because marijuana has been deemed a Schedule 1 drug, doctors and scientists have been able to do only limited research on its effects. We need to understand any risks. And that means committing ourselves to doing the research, listening to what the science tells us, and acting on that information in our approach.

We also need to stop treating drug addiction like a public safety crisis instead of what it is: a public health crisis. When people suffering from drug addiction end up involved in the criminal justice system, our ambition has to be to get them help. It's time that we all accept that addiction is a disease, that it wreaks havoc on people's lives in ways they don't want and never intended. It's time we recognize that addiction does not discriminate, and that our laws shouldn't either. When someone is suffering from addiction, their situation is made worse, not better, by involvement in the criminal justice system. What they need is treatment, and we should fight for a system that provides it.

And even when people have committed offenses that require jail time, we should reject the notion that they are irredeemable or that they don't deserve a second chance. We still have mandatory minimums on the books, many of which have a disproportionate impact across racial lines. And we have to unravel the decadeslong effort to make sentencing guidelines excessively harsh to the point of being inhumane.

Thankfully, we have started to see progress: In the decade after we introduced Back on Track, some thirty-three states have adopted new sentencing and corrections policies aimed at promoting alternatives to incarceration and reducing recidivism. And since 2010, twenty-three states have reduced their prison populations. But there is still much more work to do to ensure that punishments are proportionate to the offense.

We also need to address what happens behind the prison gates. Women now represent the fastest-growing segment of our incarcerated population. Most of them are mothers, and the vast majority are survivors of violent trauma that usually goes undiagnosed and untreated. Many are imprisoned in facilities that don't support basic hygiene or reproductive health. As you read this, there are women being shackled while they're pregnant. In some states, they are shackled while giving birth. I have visited women in prison, heard stories of the ways they face the risk of sexual violence when supervised by male guards in the bathroom or shower. In 2017, I was proud to co-sponsor a bill to deal with some of these issues. This is a conversation we rarely have in this country—and we need to.

In the near term, one of the most urgent challenges is the fight against those who are ripping apart the critical progress we've made in recent years. The current administration has reescalated the war on drugs, reemphasized incarceration over rehabilitation, and rolled back investigations into civil rights violations at police departments that began during the Obama administration. They are even trying to tear up agreements made between the Obama Justice Department and certain police departments that are meant to end policies and practices that violate people's constitutional rights. We can't go backward on these issues when we have only begun to scratch the surface of progress. We have to act with fierce urgency. Justice demands it.

One thing we must do is take on, head-on, the racial bias that operates throughout our criminal justice system. And that effort starts with our stating clearly and unequivocally that black lives matter—and speaking truth about what that means. The facts are clear: Nearly four years after Ferguson, Missouri, became the flashpoint for the Black Lives Matter movement, the state attorney general reported that black drivers there are 85 percent more likely to be pulled over than their white neighbors. Across the nation, when a police officer stops a black driver, he is three times more likely to search the car than when the driver is white. Black men use drugs at the same rate as white men, but they are arrested twice as often for it. And then they pay more than a third more than their counterparts, on average, in bail. Black men are six times as likely as white men to be incarcerated. And when they are convicted, black men get sen-

tences nearly 20 percent longer than those given to their white counterparts. Latino men don't fare much better. It is truly appalling.

It's one thing to say that black lives matter. But awareness and
solidarity aren't enough. We need to accept hard truths about the
systemic racism that has allowed this to happen. And we need to turn
that understanding into policies and practices that can actually
change it.

When I was attorney general, I brought the senior leadership of
our investigative bureau together, led by Larry Wallace, the director
of my office's Bureau of Law Enforcement, and told them that I
wanted to institute an implicit bias and procedural justice training
program for our agents. Implicit bias lives in split seconds. It is the
unconscious shorthand that our brains use to help us make a quick
judgment about a stranger. Frontline officers, more than most, have
to make split-second judgments all the time, where implicit bias can
have a deadly outcome.

The presentation of the subject matter made for a difficult
conversation—and understandably so. These senior leaders had dedicated their lives and taken an oath to law enforcement. It wasn't easy
to have to reckon with the idea that the men and women of their
bureau carry bias with them, that it affects the community, and that
they need to be trained to deal with it. But it was an honest conversation, and in the end, the leadership not only agreed it was important,
but they also agreed to help create, shape, and lead the training while
advocating for its necessity up and down the chain.

Larry and my special assistant attorney general, Suzy Loftus, then
worked to develop a curriculum that could be adopted by police
academies and offered to law enforcement agencies statewide. We part-
nered with the Oakland and Stockton police departments and the

California Partnership for Safe Communities to create the training program, and brought in Professor Jennifer Eberhardt from Stanford University to evaluate its effectiveness. It became the first statewide implicit bias and procedural justice course offered anywhere in the country.

None of us were naive about what our training course could accomplish. We knew that such an effort, alone, would not rid the system of bias. And we surely knew that explicit bias, not just implicit bias, permeated the system. Racism is real in America, and police departments are not immune. At the same time, we knew that better training would make a real difference, that for most members of law enforcement, a better understanding of their own implicit biases could be revelatory. We knew that the hard conversations involved in the training course were the kind that stayed with a person, the kind of thing they'd take with them to the streets.

We need to speak another truth: police brutality occurs in America and we have to root it out wherever we find it. With the advent of the smartphone, what was well known only to certain communities is now being seen by the world. People can no longer pretend it isn't happening. It cannot be ignored or denied when we see video of Walter Scott, unarmed, shot in the back as he ran from an officer. We cannot ignore the horrified cries of Philando Castile's girlfriend after he was shot seven times by a police officer while reaching for his driver's license—all with her four-year-old daughter in the back seat. "It's okay, Mommy . . . it's okay. I'm right here with you," the little girl said, in a heartbreaking attempt to comfort. We cannot forget Eric Garner's desperate words—"I can't breathe"—as a police officer strangled him to death during an arrest for selling cigarettes.

And we must remember that tragedies like these occur over and over again, most of them unfilmed and unseen. If people fear murder and beatings and harassment from the police who patrol their streets, can we really say that we live in a free society?

And what does it say about our standards of justice when police officers are so rarely held accountable for these incidents? The Minnesota officer who shot Philando Castile was tried for second-degree manslaughter. But he was acquitted. In Ohio, a police officer climbed onto the hood of a car after a car chase and fired forty-nine times at its occupants, Timothy Russell and Malissa Williams, both of whom were unarmed. The officer was charged—and acquitted. In Pennsylvania, a police officer shot an unarmed driver in the back while he lay facedown in the snow. But he, too, was acquitted of murder.

If there aren't serious consequences for police brutality in our justice system, what kind of message does that send to police officers? And what kind of message does it send to the community? Public safety depends on public trust. It depends on people believing they will be treated fairly and transparently. It depends on a justice system that is steeped in the notions of objectivity and impartiality. It depends on the basic decency our Constitution demands.

But when black and brown people are more likely to be stopped, arrested, and convicted than their white counterparts; when police departments are outfitted like military regiments; when egregious use of deadly force is not met with consequence, is it any wonder that the very credibility of these public institutions is on the line?

I say this as someone who has spent most of my career working with law enforcement. I say this as someone who has a great deal of respect for police officers. I know that most police officers deserve to be proud of their public service and commended for the way they do their jobs. I know how difficult and dangerous the job is, day in and day out, and I know how hard it is for the officers' families, who have to wonder if the person they love will be coming home at the end of each shift. I've been to too many funerals of officers killed in the line of duty. But I also know this: it is a false choice to suggest that you must either be for the police or for police accountability. I am for both. Most people I know are for both. Let's speak some truth about that, too.

Make no mistake: we need to take on this and every aspect of our broken criminal justice system. We need to change our laws and our standards. And we need to elect people who will make it their mission to do so.

So let's recruit more progressives into prosecutors' offices, where many of the biggest problems and best solutions start. Prosecutors are among the most powerful actors in our system of justice. They have the power to prioritize what they work on. They can choose to focus their time and attention on anything from corporate and consumer fraudsters to sexual predators. They have the power to put criminals behind bars, but they also have the discretion to dismiss cases where police used excessive force, or conducted a search and seizure without probable cause. We need people who come from all walks of life and different backgrounds and experiences to sit at the table and wield that kind of power.

We also need to keep the pressure on from the outside, where organizations and individuals can create meaningful change. When I was attorney general, I made sure ours was the first state law enforcement agency to require body cameras for its agents. I did it because it was the right thing to do. But I was able to do it because the Black Lives Matter movement had created intense pressure. By forcing these issues onto the national agenda, the movement created an environment on the outside that helped give me the space to get it done on the inside. That's often how change happens. And I credit the movement for those reforms just as much as anyone in my office, including me.

Engaging in the fight for civil rights and social justice is not for the faint of heart. It is as difficult as it is important, and the wins may never taste as sweet as the losses taste sour. But count yourself as part of the lineage of those who refused to relent. And when we're feeling frustrated and discouraged by the obstacles in front of us, let's channel the words of Constance Baker Motley, one of my inspirations as the first black American woman appointed to the federal judiciary. "Lack of encouragement never deterred me," she wrote. "In fact, I think the effect was just the opposite. I was the kind of person who would not be put down."

Three

UNDERWATER

We were renters for most of my childhood, and my mother took incredible pride in our home. It was always ready for company, with fresh-cut flowers. The walls were decorated with big posters of artwork by LeRoy Clarke and other artists from the Studio Museum in Harlem, where Uncle Freddy worked. There were statues from her travels in India, Africa, and elsewhere. She cared a great deal about making our apartment a home, and it always felt warm and complete. But I knew my mother always wanted something more. She wanted to be a homeowner.

She would be the first to point out the practical considerations—that it was a smart investment. But it was so much more than that. It was about her earning a full slice of the American Dream.

My mother had wanted to buy her first home while Maya and I were still young—a place to grow up with a sense of permanence. But it would take many years before she could save up enough money for a down payment.

I was in high school when it happened. Maya and I had just gotten home from school when she pulled out the pictures to show us—a one-level dark-gray house on a cul-de-sac, with a shingled roof, a beautiful lawn in front, an outdoor space on the side for a barbecue. She was so excited to show us, and we were so excited to see it—not only because it meant we got to move back to Oakland, but because of the intense joy we saw in her face. She had earned it, quite literally. "This is our house!" I would tell my friends, proudly showing off the pictures. It was going to be our piece of the world.

That memory was on my mind when I traveled to Fresno, California, in 2010, in the midst of a devastating foreclosure crisis in which so many people had their own piece of the world destroyed.

Fresno is the largest city in California's San Joaquin Valley, an area that has been described as the "Garden of the Sun." The San Joaquin Valley is one of the world's most abundant agricultural regions, providing a significant share of the fruits and vegetables consumed in the United States. Amid the acres of almond trees and vineyards full of grapes live about four million people, a population roughly the size of Connecticut's.

Many middle-class families saw a life in Fresno as their best shot at the American Dream. It was a place with promise, a place where they could afford a real single-family home on a suburban street, a place that represented America's vitality, mobility, and hope. In the early 2000s, the population of the San Joaquin Valley was young and growing, and nearly 40 percent Latinx. For so many people who moved there, the six-hour round-trip commute to their jobs in San

Francisco or Sacramento was exhausting, but a worthy price to pay for what they got in exchange: the sense of dignity, pride, and security that came with becoming an American homeowner.

New suburban developments seemed to sprout up every month, taking root in the fertile soil as if they were another cash crop. That wasn't far off. Fresno's real estate boom was fueled by broader economic trends, trends that ultimately sparked an economic inferno.

In the wake of 9/11, central banks around the world slashed their interest rates. This capital-rich environment prompted lenders to become increasingly aggressive, luring more and more borrowers with enticing loan offers like "interest only," "zero down," and even "NINJA" (no income, no job, no assets). High-risk subprime mortgages flooded the housing market, with teaser rates seemed too good to be true. Lenders reassured home buyers (and themselves) that homeowners would just refinance their mortgages before their payments spiked. The reward was worth the risk, because, as they saw it, housing prices were only and always destined to go up.

Meanwhile, global investors were on the hunt for greater returns, which led them toward ever riskier opportunities to place their bets. Wall Street financiers were only too happy to meet this voracious demand, creating newfangled securities backed by the same deeply questionable mortgages. Investors who bought those mortgaged-backed securities believed that the banks had done their due diligence, only bundling together home loans that could and would be paid on time. Few realized they were actually purchasing ticking time bombs.

Remarkably, about half of all of these mortgage-backed securities ended up on the balance sheets of big banks after they realized that holding the securities, rather than the mortgages themselves, would help them avoid traditional regulation. The cycle fed on itself, spinning faster and faster, until it spun right off the rails. In 2006, the housing market peaked. A major housing crisis loomed.

Banks and investors tried to dump their bad securities, which only made things worse. Wall Street started to implode. Bear Stearns failed. Lehman Brothers filed for bankruptcy. Credit started drying up. The economy went into freefall. By 2009, homes in the Fresno area had lost more than half their value, the largest decline in the nation. At the same time, people living in Fresno were losing their jobs in droves; by November 2010, the unemployment rate had soared to 17 percent.

Meanwhile, the teaser rates on loans had expired, and borrowers' mortgages were doubling. Scam artists and fraudsters descended like vultures, promising frantic homeowners relief from foreclosure, only to take their money and run.

This happened all over the country. Consider the story of Karina and Juan Santillan, who bought a home twenty miles east of Los Angeles in 1999. Juan had worked for twenty years at an ink-manufacturing plant, while Karina sold insurance. "A few years after they bought their home, the Santillans say, people started knocking on their door selling financial products," *The Atlantic* reported. "It was easy money, the Santillans were told. Borrow against your house, it's sure to gain value." Like millions of Americans, the Santillans were persuaded to take out an adjustable-rate mortgage on their home. At the time, their monthly payment was $1,200. By 2009 it had risen to $3,000—and Karina had lost her job. Suddenly at risk of losing their house, they contacted a company that promised to protect them. After paying $6,800 for services that were supposed to help, they realized they had been scammed. Ten years after purchasing their home, they were forced to tell their four children they were going to have to leave.

This pattern played out with particular force in Fresno and Stockton. Local leaders pleaded with the federal government to declare the region a disaster area and send help. "Disaster area" was an apt description: entire neighborhoods were abandoned, and the area was suffering one of the highest foreclosure rates in the nation. Sometimes families were struggling so hard to pay their mortgages that they would abruptly pick up and leave. I heard stories of pets being abandoned because their owners could no longer afford to keep them—a phenomenon the Humane Society was reporting all across the country, from Little Rock to Cleveland to Albuquerque. When I visited Fresno, I was told that abandoned dogs had been seen roaming in packs. I felt like I was walking through the aftermath of a natural disaster. But this disaster was man-made.

When the crash finally bottomed out, 8.4 million Americans nationwide had lost their jobs. Roughly 5 million homeowners were at least two months behind on their mortgages. And 2.5 million foreclosures had been initiated.

Two and a half million foreclosures initiated. There is something clinical about saying it that way. Something that makes the human tragedy and trauma seem abstract.

Foreclosure is not a statistic.

Foreclosure is a husband suffering in silence, knowing he's in trouble but too ashamed to tell his partner that he has failed. Foreclosure is a mother on the phone with her bank, pleading for more time— just until the school year is over. Foreclosure is the sheriff knocking at your door and ordering you out of your home. It is a grandmother on the sidewalk in tears, watching her life's possessions being removed from her house by strangers and left exposed in the yard. It is learning from a neighbor that your house was just auctioned off on the steps of City Hall. It is the changing of locks, the immolation of dreams. It is a child learning for the first time that parents can be terrified, too.

Homeowners told me countless stories of personal catastrophe. And as the months dragged on, the news media continued to surface strange reports about irregularities in the foreclosure process. We learned about people whose banks couldn't find their mortgage documents. There were stories of people discovering that they actually owed tens of thousands of dollars less than the banks said they did. A man in Florida had his house foreclosed on and put up for sale—even though he'd bought the house with cash and never *had* a mortgage.

Tales emerged of a process that became known as dual tracking. Through a program with the federal government, banks were working with borrowers on one track to modify loan terms, which was supposed to make it easier for people to stay in their homes. But often borrowers were working on a second track, too, foreclosing on homes anyway, even after making such modifications, even after the homeowner had spent several months paying the new reduced amount. The banks left homeowners with no explanation, no point of contact, and no recourse.

Clearly, something had gone awry. But it wasn't until the end of September 2010 that a major part of the scandal would break wide open. That was when we learned that the country's largest banks—including Bank of America, JPMorgan Chase, and Wells Fargo—had been illegally foreclosing on people's homes since 2007, using a practice that became known as "robo-signing."

We learned that to speed up the foreclosure process, financial institutions and their mortgage servicers hired people with no formal financial training—from Walmart floor workers to hair stylists—and placed them in "foreclosure expert" positions with one responsibility: sign off on foreclosures by the thousands.

In depositions, robo-signers acknowledged that they had little or no familiarity with the documents they were paid to approve. The job wasn't to understand and evaluate; it was simply to sign their name, or to forge someone else's. They got paid $10 an hour. And they got bonuses for volume. There was no accountability. No transparency. None of the due diligence required by law. From the banks' point of view, it seemed the faster they got bad loans off their balance sheet, the faster their stock price would rebound. And if that meant breaking the law, so be it. They could afford the fine. It was painful to me when I realized that the banks apparently viewed a fine as just the cost of doing business. It became clear to me that they had built it into their bottom line. It was a damning portrait of an aspect of Wall Street culture that persists, the part that seems to care little—if at all—about the collateral damage caused by recklessness and greed.

I had seen it up close in the district attorney's office, where we'd prosecuted mortgage scammers for defrauding the elderly and veterans. In 2009, as DA, I created a mortgage fraud unit to fill in the areas of chronic under-enforcement by the federal government. But as the foreclosure crisis ballooned, I was eager to take on bigger culprits, to go after the bad-acting banks themselves. And it seemed I might have a chance.

On October 13, 2010, the attorneys general of all fifty states agreed to join together in what's known as a multistate investigation.

It was billed as a comprehensive, nationwide law enforcement effort to uncover the banks' actions in the foreclosure crisis.

I was eager to join the fight, but there was just one small problem: I wasn't yet California's attorney general.

I was in the middle of my campaign when the multistate was announced, and there were still three weeks left until Election Day. The polls were predicting a very close race.

On Election Night 2010, I lost the race for attorney general. Three weeks later, I won.

I'd started the evening with what had become a ritual: a friends-and-family dinner. Then we headed to the Election Night party, which we held on the San Francisco waterfront, in the headquarters of my dear friend Mimi Silbert's Delancey Street Foundation—a leading residential self-help and job training organization for addicts, substance abusers, the formerly incarcerated, and others trying to turn their lives around. We arrived as results started to trickle in from precincts around the state. In the main room, supporters were gathered, waiting in anticipation for the results. Behind them stood risers for TV cameras and press pointed at the stage. We went in through the back and into a side room where my staff was gathered. They had arranged four tables into a square, and most of them were sitting there, staring at their laptops, hitting *refresh* on the websites keeping track of the tally. I greeted everyone, my spirits high, and thanked them for all their hard work.

Then Ace Smith, my chief strategist, pulled me aside.

"How's it looking?" I asked.

"It's going to be a very long night," Ace said. My opponent was in the lead.

I'd always known that I could take nothing for granted. Even plenty of fellow Democrats had considered me a long shot, and some hadn't held back in saying so. One longtime political strategist announced to an audience at UC Irvine that there was no way I could win, because I was "a woman running for attorney general, a woman who is a minority, a woman who is a minority who is anti–death penalty, a woman who is a minority who is anti–death penalty who is DA of wacky San Francisco." Old stereotypes die hard. I was convinced that my perspective and experience made me the strongest candidate in the race, but I didn't know if the voters would agree. The past few weeks, I'd done so much knocking on wood that my knuckles were bruised.

By 10 p.m., we were not much closer to knowing the outcome of the race. I was trailing, but we knew that a lot of precincts had yet to report. Ace suggested that I go out and address the crowd. "The cameras aren't going to stay much longer," he said, "so if you have a message for your supporters tonight, I think you should do that now." It sounded like a smart idea to me.

I left the staff room, spent a few quiet minutes thinking about what I would say, then straightened my suit jacket and walked into the main room and onto the stage. I told the audience that it was going to be a long night, but that it was going to be a good night, too. My opponent was losing ground by the minute, I assured them. I reminded them what our campaign was about and what we stood for. "This campaign is so much bigger than me. It is so much bigger than any one person."

At some point during my speech, I noticed a shift in the room.

People seemed to be getting emotional. Back in the staff room, I later learned, two of my best friends, Chrisette and Vanessa, were sitting on the couch, sipping wine, listening to my speech. Chrisette turned to Vanessa:

"I don't think she knows."

"I don't think she knows, either."

"You gonna tell her?"

"Nope. You?"

"Nope."

I was just finishing my remarks when I saw Debbie Mesloh, my longtime communications adviser, approaching. She mouthed to me, "Get off the stage and go to the back room, now." That wasn't reassuring. I finished my remarks and was making my way to Debbie when I was intercepted by a reporter and her cameraman.

"So what do you think happened?" she asked, putting the microphone in my face.

"I think we ran a really great race and it's going to be a long night," I said.

The reporter seemed confused, and so was I. The more questions she asked, the more it was clear we weren't connecting at all. Clearly something had happened, and I was out of the loop. When I finally got back to the staff room, I learned what. While I'd been onstage, talking about what lay ahead, the *San Francisco Chronicle* had called the race for my opponent. No wonder people were crying! I'd been the only one out there who thought we were still in the game.

Realizing that our hometown paper had called the race against us felt like a punch in the gut. The mood was grim as my team and I huddled together in the greenroom. After so many months of working so hard, excitement was giving way to exhaustion. I looked around at the slumping shoulders and sad expressions. I couldn't bear the thought of sending our volunteers home feeling this way.

Ace called me over. "Listen, I'm looking at the numbers, and a lot of our strongest areas haven't come in. They called the race too early. We're still in this."

I knew he couldn't see the future—but Ace wasn't the kind of person who blew smoke. He knew California down to the precinct level, better than perhaps anyone in the state. If he thought we were still in it, I believed him. I told my supporters we weren't giving up.

My opponent had a different view of things. Around 11 p.m., he stood up in front of the cameras and delivered a speech in Los Angeles declaring victory. But we waited. And waited—getting regular updates from the field and trying to keep one another's spirits high.

Around 1 a.m., I leaned over to my childhood friend Derreck, who was like a cousin and who owned a chicken and waffle restaurant in Oakland. "Is your kitchen still open?"

"Don't worry," he promised. "I'll take care of it."

Sure enough, the next thing I knew, Delancey Street was filled with the mouthwatering aroma of fried chicken and corn bread and greens and candied yams. We all gathered around the aluminum pans and ate. About an hour later, with 89 percent of the precincts in, we were tied.

Finally, I turned to Maya. "I'm exhausted. Do you think anybody's going to have a problem if I leave?"

"Everybody will be fine," she assured me. "People are waiting for you to leave so they can, too."

I went home and got maybe an hour or two of sleep, only to be jolted back awake by the sound of news helicopters circling in the sky.

The Giants were celebrating their first World Series win in more than fifty years with a parade down Market Street. Most of the city was dressed in orange and black.

But the Giants' victory wasn't the only good news. More votes had come in, and I was now ahead in the race, albeit only by a few thousand votes. From the lowest of lows, now it felt like our campaign had vaulted to the peak of the mountain—on a day when music was rising from the streets and confetti raining down from the skies.

With two million votes still waiting to be tallied, there was a good chance we weren't going to know the results for weeks. The counties had about a month to finish counting and certify their tallies.

My phone rang. It was John Keker, a storied lawyer in the Bay Area and a dear friend. He told me that he was assembling a team of top lawyers. "Kamala, we're ready to convene to defend you if there's a recount." If there was going to be a recount, it wasn't going to happen any time soon. The earliest that either of us could request one would be November 30.

In the meantime, members of my campaign staff, led by my campaign manager, Brian Brokaw, activated dozens of volunteers, who put off their vacation plans and got back to work. They fanned out across the state, in county after county, to monitor the vote counting in real time and report any irregularities. Days extended into weeks. Thanksgiving was fast approaching. And all the while, there was a roller coaster of results, making the whole thing pretty excruciating. It reminded me of my days trying cases, when a jury would go off to deliberate and there was nothing left to do but wait. We reconciled ourselves to the fact that nothing was likely to happen with the count over Thanksgiving weekend, so we sent everyone home to be with their families.

Early Wednesday morning, I headed for the airport to catch a flight to New York. I was going to spend the holiday with Maya, my brother-in-law, Tony, and my niece, Meena.

As we were pulling off the highway, I got a text from a district attorney who had supported my opponent. "I look forward to working with you," it read.

I called my campaign team. "What's going on? Have you heard anything?" I asked.

"We're hearing he's going to have a press conference. That's all we know right now." I was just pulling into the airport terminal. "We'll check into it and get back to you." I made it through security and onto the plane without hearing another word. I was in an aisle seat, and fellow passengers, in their Giants caps and jerseys, were walking past me asking, "Kamala, have you won yet? Do you know what's going on?" All I could do was smile and say, "I don't know. I don't know."

I took out my phone and realized that, going through the airport, I'd missed an incoming call. There was a voicemail from my opponent asking me to call him back. I dialed his number as the cabin doors were closing and the flight attendants were directing passengers to put their cell phones away.

"I want you to know I'll be conceding," he said.

"You ran a great race," I said.

"I hope you know how big a job this is going to be," he added.

"Have a nice Thanksgiving with your family," I replied.

And that was it. Of the nearly nine million ballots cast statewide, I had won by the equivalent of three votes per precinct. I was so relieved, so excited, so ready to start. I wanted to call everyone, but the next thing I knew, we were barreling down the runway, and then we were in the air—with no Wi-Fi. My twenty-one-day election night was over, and all I could do was sit there. Alone with my thoughts. For five hours.

Because the count had taken so long, there was only a month to process the victory before my swearing-in. And beyond the election, I was also still processing the grief of my mother's death. She'd passed away the year before, in February 2009, as the long, hard-fought campaign was just getting under way. I will say more about this in a chapter to come, but, needless to say, it was crushing to lose her. I knew what my election would have meant to her. How I wished she could be there to see it.

When January 3, 2011, arrived, I walked down the stairs of the California Museum for Women, History, and the Arts, in Sacramento, to greet the standing-room-only crowd. We had arranged for a wonderful inaugural ceremony, with Bishop T. Larry Kirkland Sr. giving the opening invocation and a gospel singer at the close. Flags were waving, dignitaries were there, observers peered down from the balcony. Maya held Mrs. Shelton's Bible as I took the oath of office. But what I remember most vividly about the day was the worry I felt about saying my mother's name in my address while keeping my composure. I'd practiced over and over again, and choked up every time. But it was important to me that her name be spoken in that room, because none of what I had achieved would have been possible without her.

"Today, with this oath," I told the crowd, "we affirm the principle that every Californian matters."

It was a principle that would be put to the test in the heady weeks that followed. Later that month, 37,000 homeowners lined up in Los Angeles to plead with banks to modify their mortgages so they could stay in their homes. In Florida, there were lines that quite literally stretched for days. "In the 1930s, we had bread lines," said Scott Pelley on *60 Minutes*, during a segment on the foreclosure crisis. "Venture out before dawn in America today and you'll find mortgage lines."

On my first day in office, I gathered my senior team and told them that we needed to get involved right away in the multistate investigation into the banks. I had appointed Michael Troncoso, a longtime member of my team, as chief counsel in the attorney general's office, and Brian Nelson as special assistant attorney general. I asked them to dig in and get us up to speed.

Inside the office we were preparing for battle. Outside the office, we were constantly reminded of who we were fighting for. At every event we held, there was always a group of people—sometimes five or ten or twenty—who had come in the hope of seeing me and asking for my help, face-to-face. Most brought their paperwork with them— accordion folders and manila envelopes overflowing with mortgage documents and foreclosure notices and handwritten notes. Some had driven hundreds of miles to find me.

I'll never forget the woman who interrupted a small health care event I was doing at Stanford. She stood up in the audience, tears streaming down her face, desperation in her voice. "I need help. You need to help me. I need you to help call the bank and tell them to let me stay in my home. Please, I'm begging you." It was heartbreaking.

I also knew there were tens of thousands of people just like her, fighting for their lives, who didn't have the ability to track down the attorney general in person. So we went directly to them, holding roundtable meetings in community centers across the state. I wanted them to see us. I also wanted my team to see them, so that when we were sitting across from the bank executives in a conference room, we'd remember who we were representing. At one of these convenings, I was speaking to a man about the problems he was having with the banks. His young son was playing quietly nearby. And then the little boy came over and looked up at his father.

"Daddy, what does 'underwater' mean?"

I could see the awful fear in his eyes. He thought his father was literally drowning.

It was a terrible thing to contemplate. But the metaphor was apt: a lot of people had gone under. Still more were clinging by their fingernails to the edge. And every day that went by, more and more of those desperate people were losing their grip.

Over the course of our battle with the banks, we'd heard so many stories that underscored that these issues weren't intellectual or academic; they were about people's lives. At one homeowners' roundtable, a woman described with pride the home she had saved up to buy in 1997—the first home she'd ever purchased as an adult. After falling one month behind on a loan payment in early 2009, she'd called her lender asking for advice. Representatives for the lender said they could help, but after months of their insisting she produce and fax them endless paperwork, of sending her documents without explanation and demanding that she sign, of keeping her in the dark as she sought answers to her questions, her home was foreclosed upon from under her feet.

Fighting back tears as she shared her story with me, she said, "I'm sorry. I know it's just a house . . ." But she knew, as we all do, that it's never "just a house."

My first opportunity to get personally involved in the multistate talks arrived in early March. The National Association of Attorneys General—whose acronym, NAAG, is appropriate—was holding its annual multiday meeting at the Fairmont hotel, in Washington, DC. I flew in with my team. All fifty attorneys general were there, seated in alphabetical order by state. I took my spot between Arkansas and Colorado.

As the conversation turned from general business to the multistate investigation, it suddenly became clear to me that the investigation wasn't complete; there were still many unanswered questions. Yet they were talking settlement. They had a number on the table, and I got the impression that it was basically a done deal. All that seemed left to do was divide the money among the states—and that was exactly what was happening.

I was dumbfounded. What was the number based on? How did they come up with it? How could we negotiate a settlement when we hadn't completed an investigation?

But what shocked me most wasn't the choosing of an arbitrary dollar figure. It was that in exchange for settling, the banks were going to be given a wholesale release against any potential future claims—a blank check of immunity for whatever crimes they might have committed. That meant that by settling with them on the issue of robo-signing, we could be prohibited from bringing a future case against them that related to the mortgage-backed securities that had caused the crash.

During a break in the session, I gathered my team. The settlement was going to be on the agenda again in the afternoon.

"I'm not going to that meeting," I told them. "This thing is baked." I knew that if I joined the meeting, the conversation would just pick up where it had left off. They weren't going to turn back just because a new AG expressed concerns. But if they knew I would pull out of the negotiations if I had to, that might move some minds. California had more foreclosures than any other state, making it the biggest exposure of liability for the banks. If the banks couldn't get a settlement with me, they weren't going to settle with anyone. It was one thing to know I had this leverage; it was another to convince the others I was willing to use it. If I skipped the afternoon session, my empty chair would express that message better than I ever could.

My staff and I left the Fairmont and took a cab to the Justice Department. We called Tom Perrelli on the way, to let him know we were coming. Perrelli was the U.S. associate attorney general. It was his job, among other things, to oversee the multistate investigation on behalf of the federal government. I told him that of the ten cities hit hardest by the foreclosure crisis at the time, seven were in California; that it was my job to get to the bottom of it; and that I couldn't sign on to anything that was going to preclude me from doing my own investigation.

Perrelli made the case that my investigation wouldn't yield what I hoped it would, that going after the big banks was not something any one state could do, even the biggest in the nation. And, he added, that kind of litigation was going to take many years. By the time I got what California deserved, the people who needed help would have already lost their homes. This was the reason there hadn't been a thorough investigation; there simply wasn't time.

Later that afternoon, I met with Elizabeth Warren, who at that time was working at the Treasury Department, building what would become the Consumer Financial Protection Bureau. I raised the same concerns with her, and she was sympathetic and supportive. As an administration official, she couldn't outright tell us to go our own way, but I got the strong sense that she would understand if I persisted.

We flew home that night and got right to work. I had been told that, as things stood, California was going to get somewhere between $2 billion and $4 billion in the settlement. Some of the lawyers in the office thought it was a big number, big enough to take. My point to them was: Compared with what? If the banks' illegal scheme had caused a lot more than $2 billion to $4 billion in damage, then those really big numbers would start to look really small.

The immediate challenge was that our office wasn't equipped to answer that riddle. It was a problem that required economists and data scientists, not lawyers. Recognizing the hole in our game, I decided to hire some experts and put them to work crunching the numbers. I wanted to know how many underwater homeowners there were county by county so that we could target relief to the highest pain points. I also wanted to understand what we were dealing with in very human terms: How many people was the money going to help? How many would be left to fend for themselves? How many children were affected by the foreclosure crisis?

The results were as unacceptable as I had feared. Compared with the devastation, the banks were offering crumbs on the table, nowhere near enough to compensate for the damage they had caused.

"We need to be prepared to walk away from the settlement," I told my team. "There's no way I'm taking this offer." I told them that it was time to open up our own independent investigation. "Look, we're a guest at someone else's party and we don't have our own car," I said. "We need our own ride so that when we're ready to leave, we can leave."

Even before taking office, I'd planned with my team to launch a statewide effort to investigate the fraud. Now was the time. That May, we announced the California Attorney General's Mortgage Fraud Strike Force, a unit of the best and brightest lawyers from our consumer fraud, corporate fraud, and criminal divisions, as well as sworn investigators.

The robo-signing settlement was a critical part of the investigation, but our scope was even wider. I wanted to go after Fannie Mae and Freddie Mac, which owned 62 percent of new mortgages nationwide. I wanted to investigate the mortgage-backed securities that JPMorgan Chase had sold to the California public employee pension fund. And I wanted to go after the predators who had exploited these vulnerable communities, promising to save homeowners from foreclosure for a price—only to steal what little they had left.

The fact that we were doing our own investigation aggravated the multistate negotiators. The banks were furious that I was causing trouble. The settlement was now in doubt. But this had been my goal. Now, instead of merely noting my concerns, the state attorneys general and the banks would have to answer them, too.

Over the course of the summer, we focused on two tracks: the investigation on one, the settlement talks on the other. For my team, that meant working all hours of the day and night—traveling up and down the state and back and forth to Washington. Still, the negotiations were getting nowhere. The banks balked at our demands. At the same time, the rate of foreclosures picked up significantly in California.

In August, the New York attorney general pulled out of the multistate negotiations. In the aftermath, it seemed that everyone's eyes had turned to me. Would I leave the negotiations, too?

I wasn't yet ready to do that. I wanted to exhaust every reasonable possibility that the banks would meet our demands. There were important reforms that were part of the negotiation, and I wanted to see them implemented. We were being presented with a false choice: the reforms or the money. I wanted both.

And I knew that time was of the essence. In a homicide case, the body is cold; you're talking about punishment and restitution after the fact. In this situation, the harm was still unfolding. While negotiations went on, hundreds of thousands of more homeowners had gotten foreclosure notices. It was happening every day and in real time. There were huge areas, entire zip codes, where people were hundreds of thousands of dollars underwater. My team and I pored over the numbers weekly—a dashboard of despair, describing how many people were thirty, sixty, ninety days from losing their homes.

Before I walked away from the table, I wanted to take one last shot at getting a fair deal and some real relief for my state.

To that point, the day-to-day negotiations had been led by Michael and a team of veterans of the California Department of Justice. The next meeting was being held in September, and the general counsels of the major banks had asked me to attend. I was sure they wanted me there so they could size me up from across the table—this new attorney general from out of nowhere. Good. I wanted to size them up, too.

We arrived at the offices of Debevoise & Plimpton, the Washington law firm that was hosting the meeting. We were led into a large conference room where more than a dozen people were gathered.

After a few polite hellos, we took our seats around a long, imposing conference table. I sat at one head of the table. The chief counsels of the big banks were there, along with a team of Wall Street's best lawyers, including a man known as the "trauma surgeon of Wall Street."

The meeting was tense from the moment it began. Bank of America's counsel opened by turning to my negotiating team and complaining about the terrible pain we were putting the banks through. I'm not kidding. She said that the process was frustrating, that the bank had been through enormous trauma, that employees there were working to respond to all the investigations and regulatory changes since the crash. Everyone was exhausted, she told us. And she wanted answers from California. What was the holdup?

I ripped right in. "You want to talk about pain? Do you have any understanding of the pain that you've caused?" I felt it viscerally. It made me so angry to see homeowners' suffering downplayed or dismissed. "There are a million children in California who aren't going to be able to go to their school anymore because their parents lost their home. If you want to talk about pain, I'll tell you about some pain."

The bank representatives were calm but defensive. They essentially said the homeowners were to blame for getting into mortgages they couldn't afford. I wasn't having any of that. I kept thinking about what the home-buying process looks like in real life.

For the vast majority of families, buying a home is the biggest financial transaction they will ever be involved in. It's one of the most affirming moments in a person's adult life, a testament to all your hard work. You trust the people involved in the process. When the banker tells you that you qualify for a loan, you trust that she's reviewed the numbers and won't let you take on more than you can handle. When the offer is accepted, the broker is so happy for you, you'd think he's going to move into the house with you. And when it comes time to finish the paperwork, it's basically a signing ceremony. You might as well be popping champagne. Your broker is there, your banker is there, and you believe they have your best interests at heart. When they put a stack of paper in front of you, you trust them, and you sign. And sign. And sign. And sign.

I surveyed the roomful of lawyers, and I was certain that not one of them had read every word of their own mortgage documents before buying their first house. When I bought my apartment, I didn't.

The bankers spoke about mortgages seemingly without any sense of what they represented to the people involved, or who those people were. To me, it sounded as though they had made terrible assumptions about the character and values of struggling homeowners. I'd met many of those people. And for them, buying a home was not just about an investment. It was about attainment, self-fulfillment. I thought about Mr. Shelton, who was always in the front yard, pruning his roses in the morning, always mowing or watering or fertilizing. At one point, I asked one of the lawyers, "Haven't you ever known somebody who was proud of their lawn?"

The back and forth continued. They seemed to be under the misimpression that I could be bullied into submission. I wasn't budging. Toward the end of the meeting, the general counsel of JPMorgan chimed in with what he apparently thought was a smart tactic. He told me that his parents were from California and that they had voted for me and liked me. And he knew there were a lot of voters back home who would be really happy with me if I just settled. It was great politics—he was sure of it.

I looked him straight in the eye: "Do I need to remind you this is a law enforcement action?" The room went quiet. After forty-five minutes, the conversation had gone on long enough.

"Look, your offer doesn't come near acknowledging the damage you have caused," I told them. "And you should know that I mean what I say. I'm going to investigate everything. Everything."

The general counsel of Wells Fargo turned to me.

"Well, if you're going to keep investigating, why should we settle with you?"

"You have to make that decision for yourself," I told him.

As I left the meeting, I made the decision to pull out of the negotiations altogether.

I wrote a letter announcing my decision—but I waited to release it until Friday evening, after the markets had closed. I knew that my words could move markets, and that wasn't my intention. This wasn't about grandstanding or making a scene or tanking share prices. This was about trying to get justice for millions of people who needed and deserved help.

"Last week, I went to Washington, DC, in hopes of moving our discussions forward," I wrote. "But it became clear to me that California was being asked for a broader release of claims than we can accept and to excuse conduct that has not been adequately investigated. After much consideration, I have concluded that this is not the deal California homeowners have been waiting for."

I started getting phone calls. From friends who were afraid that I had made too powerful an enemy. From political consultants who warned me to brace myself because the banks were going to spend tens of millions of dollars to throw me out of office. From the governor of California: "I hope you know what you're doing." From White House officials and cabinet secretaries, trying to bring me back to the talks. The pressure was intense—and constant—and it was coming from all sides: from longtime allies and longtime adversaries and everyone in between.

But there was another kind of pressure, too. Millions of homeowners had raised their voices, along with activists and advocacy organizations that were mobilizing based on our strategy. We knew we weren't alone.

Still, this period was hard. Before bed, I would say a small prayer: "God, please help me do the right thing." I'd pray that I was choosing the right path, and for the courage to stay the course. Most of all, I'd pray that the families counting on me remained safe and secure. I knew how much was at stake.

I often found myself thinking about my mother and what she would have done. I know she would have told me to hold fast to conviction; to listen to my gut. Tough decisions are tough precisely because the outcome isn't clear. But your gut will tell you if you're on the right track. And you'll know what decision to make.

During those days, Beau Biden, Delaware's attorney general, became an incredible friend and colleague. The banks were in Beau's backyard, and the foreclosure crisis hadn't hit Delaware as hard as it had other states. By some measures, he had every reason to keep his head down and toe the line. But that wasn't who Beau was. Beau was a man of principle and courage.

From the very beginning, he had consistently objected to the deal. He hammered on the points that I was making, too: not enough money; no investigation into the scope of the fraud. Like me, he wanted testimony and documents. He wanted proof that the banks even owned the mortgages they were foreclosing on. And he never budged from that position. He had also opened up his own investigation, and we were actively sharing the information we uncovered. There were periods, when I was taking heat, when Beau and I talked every day, sometimes multiple times a day. We had each other's backs.

I had other great allies in the fight, too. Martha Coakley, then the attorney general of Massachusetts, was tough and smart and meticulous in her work. My now–Senate colleague Catherine Cortez-Masto was Nevada's attorney general at the time, and she became a formidable ally as well. Nevada, like California, had been pummeled by the crisis, and Catherine, who'd been in office since 2007, had formed her own Mortgage Fraud Strike Force in 2008. She, like me, was determined to fight the banks, and in December 2011 she and I joined forces to probe foreclosure fraud and misconduct. I could not have asked for better or more resolute teammates.

At the height of this period, I was constantly traveling the country with my team. I'll never forget the time we flew out to Washington, DC, dressed for the winter, only to find out that we would need to go to Florida the following day. Brian and I ended up racing into a clothing store in Georgetown to find more weather-appropriate attire. It was an awkward moment of levity as we critiqued each other's choices off the rack.

By January, the banks were exasperated. Michael came into my office.

"I just got off the phone with the general counsel of JPMorgan," he said. "I told him what the deal was—that we weren't budging off our position."

"What did he say?" I asked.

"He wouldn't stop screaming at me. He says it's over. That we pushed too far. It was really intense. And then he hung up."

I pulled my team into my office and we tried to figure out a next step—if there was one to be taken. Had we killed the possibility of any deal? Was there still a chance? I needed to be sure. We sat in silence for a while, thinking it through, until an idea popped into my head. I shouted for my assistant next door (which was the same intercom system we had used growing up). "Get me Jamie Dimon on the phone." Dimon was and—as of this writing—remains the chairman and CEO of JPMorgan Chase.

My team freaked out. "You can't call him. He's represented by an attorney!"

"I don't care. Get him on the phone."

I was tired of feeling caged, of talking through lawyers and other intermediaries in endless obfuscation. I wanted to go right to the source, and I believed the situation demanded it.

About ten seconds later, my assistant popped her head into my office. "Mr. Dimon is on the line." I took off my earrings (the Oakland in me) and picked up the receiver.

"You're trying to steal from my shareholders!" he yelled, almost as soon as he heard my voice. I gave it right back. "*Your* shareholders? *Your* shareholders? *My* shareholders are the homeowners of California! You come and see them. Talk to them about who got robbed." It stayed at that level for a while. We were like dogs in a fight. A member of my senior team later recalled thinking, "This was either a really good or a colossally bad idea."

I shared with Dimon the way his lawyers were presenting his position, and why it was unacceptable to me. As temperatures cooled, I got into the details of my demands so that he would understand exactly what I needed—not through the filter of his general counsel, but directly from me. At the end of the conversation, he said he would talk to his board and see what they could do.

I'll never know what happened on Dimon's side. But I do know that two weeks later, the banks gave in. When all was said and done, instead of the $2 billion to $4 billion that was originally on the table, we secured an $18 billion deal, which ultimately grew to $20 billion in relief to homeowners. It was a tremendous victory for the people of California.

As part of the settlement, the federal government was going to assign a monitor to make sure the banks complied. But given how much exposure California had, that didn't satisfy me. I was going to hire our own monitor and authorize her to oversee the agreement's implementation in our state.

I had been asked to fly to Washington to be part of the larger announcement, a major press conference and celebration that would take place at the Department of Justice and the White House. But I wanted to be at home with my team. It was our victory to share together. And we needed to gear up for the next battle ahead.

The settlement was just the beginning. In addition to money, the agreement required banks to provide homeowners with a number of reforms to make the process of fighting a foreclosure easier. But the settlement required those measures to be in place for only three years. If we wanted to protect homeowners in California from abuses in the future, we were going to need legislation to make the terms of the settlement permanent. I wanted the banks to be permanently prohibited from engaging in their notoriously predatory practices. And I wanted individual homeowners to have the right to sue when banks broke the rules. In coordination with our allies in the legislature, we put these ideas together into what we named the California Homeowner Bill of Rights.

But getting a new law that related to the banks passed through the legislature was going to be a problem. The banks had enormous influence in Sacramento. California legislators had tried to pass similar legislation on at least two prior occasions, only to be defeated by bank resistance. This was going to have to be a full-court press.

The reception to the bill was cold at first. People told me it was dead on arrival. They said the banking lobby was too strong to overcome. The rightness of the legislation seemed to have little to do with the calculation.

I met with John Pérez, who was speaker of the state assembly at the time, to come up with a strategy to turn the bill into law. John is an exceptional man, savvy in both policy and politics. He and I were in complete agreement about the importance of a Homeowner Bill of Rights, and he was ready to work to leverage his power to take on the banks.

I remember at one point during this effort, Speaker Pérez invited me to the Democratic policy retreat of the state assembly at the Leland Stanford Mansion, in Sacramento. Pérez, who had made sure to be in charge of seating assignments, strategically placed me at a table with a couple of strong allies, as well as a few legislators who needed some persuading. We spent much of the dinner talking about the bill. By that point, I knew more than I ever imagined I would about how the banks had acted, all the ways in which they had victimized homeowners. Being able to talk through those experiences with the group seemed to help. When the dinner was over, I had the sense that I had changed one or two of their minds.

None of the legislators ever explicitly said they were siding with the banks. But in conversation after conversation, they would try to find any technical excuse they could for why they couldn't support the bill. *If only you'd done this. If only you'd done that. If only that semicolon wasn't there.*

I'll never forget one Democratic legislator saying to me, "Well, Kamala, I don't know what's so bad about these foreclosures. They're good for our local economy. Because when a house is foreclosed upon and abandoned, that means they have to hire painters and gardeners to clean it up." Really? Really? Did this guy also support arson because it keeps fire extinguisher companies in business? It was stunning to me how people would justify being in the pocket of the banks.

While Speaker Pérez spent time focusing on the inside game, I went on the road, using the bully pulpit to evangelize for a fairer, more just system for homeowners. I was joined in the effort by a number of groups that had been championing homeowner rights and were mounting a pressure campaign to get the bill passed. Organized labor was critically important to this effort. Their ability to mobilize supporters was stunning. So many people called their legislators that they crashed the phone lines.

But it wasn't just labor's organizing efforts that mattered. It was their very presence. There was a cynical way of thinking in Sacramento: When a home is foreclosed on, the family living there is likely to move out of your district. They will no longer be your constituents. So their anger is only a temporary problem for you. The banks, on the other hand, are a permanent presence in the state capital, and their anger could result in retribution. What organized labor made clear was that there was also a permanent presence in the capital that was going to fight intensely for workers, not just so they could have better wages, but so they could be treated with dignity in every aspect of their lives, including buying a home. It sent a powerful message: Side with the banks, answer to labor.

As the vote drew near, I started walking the halls of the capitol building, knocking unannounced on legislators' doors. A lot of people refused to see me. I dispatched key members of my team as well. Brian Nelson, my special assistant attorney general, recalls that I would sometimes call him at his desk, and if he answered, he was in trouble. "Why are you sitting at your desk?" I'd ask. "Why aren't you walking the halls of the capitol? I know you have important work, but nothing is more important than this. You gotta be walking the halls! No one should be able to avoid having a face-to-face conversation with one of us."

When the bill came to the floor for a vote, we still didn't have a majority. Many legislators were planning not to vote so they wouldn't have to take a position one way or the other. But we needed forty-one people to vote yes. Abstentions were tantamount to voting no.

Speaker Pérez had a plan. He was going to hold the vote open while we continued to pressure people to come to our side. If they didn't want to vote, he implied, the vote was just going to stay open forever. At the beginning of the proceeding, he had an ally make a point of parliamentary inquiry.

"What's the longest the roll has ever been open?" the legislator asked.

"To my understanding," Pérez said, "the longest the roll has ever been open was an hour and forty-five minutes, and you know how competitive I am. I'm willing to go a lot longer than that!" At that point, everyone understood he was serious, and green lights started flashing as votes were cast.

I was in the office of Darrell Steinberg, the senate president pro tem, who had also played an instrumental role, watching the floor action on a closed-circuit television. I watched for legislators who weren't yet on the floor or who were milling around in the back. "I saw you didn't vote," I would text. "Go vote. It's time." We moved person to person, one by one, as John repeated the same phrase over and over again. "Have all members voted who decided to vote? Have all members voted who decided to vote?" He sounded like an auctioneer.

It felt like it lasted forever. But in reality it took only about five minutes of this before we got our forty-first vote cast. John closed the vote, and we declared victory. The bill passed the state senate as well and was signed into law by the governor. We had done what we had been told was impossible. It was as gratifying a moment as I can remember, and a reminder that even in the sausage making of politics, inspiring things can happen and good work can be done.

Meanwhile, the Mortgage Fraud Strike Force was pushing hard. The unit would go on to investigate and prosecute a number of major mortgage scams. The head of one of the larger scams was sentenced to twenty-four years in state prison. Because of the efforts of a truly extraordinary team, we were able to secure—on top of the $18 billion—$300 million from JPMorgan to reimburse the state pension system for losses on investments in mortgage-backed securities. We also secured $550 million from SunTrust Mortgage, $200 million from Citigroup, and another $500 million from Bank of America—all in connection with the mortgage crisis.

These were important wins, to be sure. But they weren't the kinds of victories we wanted to celebrate, because, for all the people these actions helped, millions of Americans across the country were still hurting. And despite the billions we recovered, a lot of people still lost their homes. The structural damage to the economy was so profound that, even with some relief, many people couldn't pay their mortgages and still make ends meet. The jobs weren't there. And neither were the wages.

Countless Americans saw their credit destroyed. Parents' dreams of financing their children's education evaporated like mist. Families faced multiple stresses simultaneously—from joblessness to homelessness to abruptly having to switch school districts. One analysis published in *The Lancet* suggested that "the rise in US unemployment during the recession [was] associated with a 3.8% increase in the suicide rate, corresponding to about 1330 suicides."

In many ways, the impact of the crash is still with us in 2018. In Fresno, the overwhelming majority of homes are still valued below their prerecession levels. Nationally, middle-class wealth was nearly wiped out and much of it hasn't returned.

Studies suggest that the burden hit black families disproportionately. An independent report of the Social Science Research Council, commissioned by the American Civil Liberties Union, found that, whereas white and black families alike were hit hard by the 2007–2009 crisis, by 2011 "the typical white family's losses slowed to zero, while the typical black family lost an additional 13 percent of its wealth." The consequence: "For a typical Black family, median wealth in 2031 will be almost $98,000 lower than it would have been without the Great Recession."

In other words, tomorrow's generations will suffer as a result of yesterday's folly and greed. We cannot change what has already happened. But we can make sure it never happens again.

The culture on Wall Street hasn't changed. Only some of the rules have. And the banks are waging a full-scale battle to repeal the Obama-era Wall Street reforms that have helped hold them in check. Where they have failed to repeal them, they have done everything they can to get around them. According to an analysis from *The Wall Street Journal*, between 2010 and 2017, major banks invested $345 billion in subprime loans—funneling the money to nonbank financial institutions, or so-called shadow banks.

"Banks say their new approach of lending to nonbank lenders is safer than dealing directly with consumers with bad credit and companies with shaky balance sheets," noted the *Journal*. "Yet these relationships mean that banks are still deeply intertwined with the riskier loans they say they swore off after the financial crisis."

Meanwhile, in 2017, the president appointed a man to run the Consumer Financial Protection Bureau who has referred to that very bureau as "a joke," and who set about actively dismantling it from the inside. In 2018, instead of tightening the rules on Wall Street, Congress rolled back essential protections, releasing midsize banks from the regulations meant to keep them in check. This is more than unacceptable. It's outrageous.

There is still much to be done. If we agree that we are tired of banks getting away with such reckless behavior, if we agree that we can't let the banks drag us into another recession, if we agree that homeowners deserve to be treated with dignity and respect, not as lines on a balance sheet to be packaged and sold, then there's only one way to achieve the change we seek: with our voices and our votes.

Four

WEDDING BELLS

Whenever I travel to a country for the first time, I try to visit the highest court in the land. They are monuments of a certain kind, built not just to house a courtroom but to convey a message. In New Delhi, for example, the Supreme Court of India is designed to symbolize the balancing scales of justice. In Jerusalem, Israel's iconic Supreme Court building combines straight lines—which represent the immutable nature of the law—with curved walls and glass that represent the fluid nature of justice. These are buildings that speak.

The same can be said of the United States Supreme Court Building, which, to my mind, is the most beautiful of them all. Its architecture harks back to the earliest days of democracy, as though you are standing in front of a modern-day Parthenon. It is grand and commanding while also dignified and restrained. As you walk up the steps toward an extraordinary portico of Corinthian columns, you can see a nation's founding aspirations in its architecture. It is there that the words EQUAL JUSTICE UNDER LAW are engraved in stone. And it was that promise that brought me to the Supreme Court Building on March 26, 2013.

When I arrived, the building was admittedly not looking its finest. It was encased in scaffolding, part of an overdue repair effort after a large chunk of marble broke off and fell to the ground. To minimize the unsightly view, a life-size, high-resolution photograph of the facade had been printed on a scrim and draped across the entrance. It was about as realistic as one of those oversize beach T-shirts with a bikini body printed on the front. Even so, the majesty of the building was unmistakable.

I was escorted to my seat in the courtroom. Because the Supreme Court justices don't allow photography or video inside, this is a place that most of the country never sees. I certainly hadn't before that day. I gazed around in awe: the stunning pink marble; the vivid red draping and intricate ceiling; the imposing bench with its nine empty chairs. I kept thinking about all the history that had been made inside these walls. But unlike a museum or a place like Gettysburg, where history is preserved for posterity, the Supreme Court is a place where history is active and alive, where it continues to unfold with every decision.

A little after 10 a.m., we rose as the nine justices entered the courtroom and took their seats.

"We'll hear argument this morning in Case 12-144, *Hollingsworth v. Perry*," said Chief Justice John Roberts.

This was the case against Proposition 8, a California ballot initiative that passed in 2008, prohibiting marriages for same-sex couples in the state. It had been a long time coming.

California may have a reputation as a bastion of liberalism, but in the year 2000, California voters approved a ballot initiative—Prop 22 (also known as the Knight Initiative, after its author, state senator William "Pete" Knight)—that required the state to define marriage as a union between people of the opposite sex. For years we fought it—in the streets, at the ballot box, and in the courts. Even my then school-aged niece, Meena, got in on the action; I remember one time going to pick her up at her high school and being told she was in a student meeting. When I got to the classroom, young Meena was in front, rallying her peers: "This isn't a Knight Initiative—it's a nightmare!"

During Valentine's Day week in 2004, then–San Francisco mayor Gavin Newsom decided to allow marriages for same-sex couples to proceed anyway.

I was on my way to the airport to catch a flight to Los Angeles, but I decided to pass by San Francisco City Hall before I left. There were throngs of people lined up around the block, waiting to get in. They were counting down the minutes before a government would finally recognize their right to marry whomever they loved. The joy and anticipation were palpable. Some of them had been waiting decades.

I got out of my car and walked up the steps of City Hall, where I bumped into a city official. "Kamala, come and help us," she said, a glowing smile on her face. "We need more people to perform the marriages." I was delighted to be a part of it.

I was quickly sworn in, along with numerous city officials. We stood together performing marriages in the hallway, crowded into every nook and cranny of City Hall. There was all this wonderful excitement building as we welcomed the throngs of loving couples, one by one, to be married then and there. It was unlike anything I had ever been a part of before. And it was beautiful.

But not long after, the marriages were invalidated. The couples who had been so happy and hopeful received letters telling them that their marriage licenses would not be recognized under the law. It was, for each and every one of them, a devastating setback.

In May 2008, the California Supreme Court came to the rescue. The court held that the same-sex marriage ban was unconstitutional, which paved the way for LGBTQ couples to realize the equal dignity they had always deserved. Ronald George, who had sworn me in as district attorney of San Francisco, wrote the majority opinion. And over the next six months, eighteen thousand same-sex couples exchanged wedding vows in California.

But in November 2008, on the same night that Barack Obama was elected president, the people of California narrowly voted to pass Prop 8, an amendment to the California Constitution that stripped same-sex couples of their right to marry. Because this was a constitutional amendment, it couldn't be overturned by the legislature or the state court system. No new marriages could be performed. Couples who had already been married were placed in a cruel limbo.

There was one clear route left to justice: the federal courts. The American Foundation for Equal Rights, then led by Chad Griffin, decided that the best way to respond was to bring suit against the state of California, arguing that Prop 8 violated the protections granted to every citizen in the Fourteenth Amendment: equal protection and due process under the law. This was a matter of civil rights and civil justice, and Griffin and his team planned to take the case all the way to the Supreme Court. The organization hired the lawyers who had argued against each other in *Bush v. Gore,* then filed a lawsuit on behalf of two same-sex couples—Kris Perry and Sandy Stier; Paul Katami and Jeff Zarrillo—whose job was to represent in court

My parents met at Berkeley during the civil rights movement. They were married soon after.

My mother and her dear friend Auntie Lenore were part of the protests against Birmingham atrocities.

At twenty-five years old, Mommy had a college degree, a PhD, and me.

Proud daddy on his way to a doctorate in economics at Berkeley. (April 1965)

When I was ten months old, I visited Spanish Town, Jamaica. This is me with my mother and my paternal grandfather, Oscar Joseph.

With my great grandmother Iris Finegan in Jamaica.

Visiting my uncle Freddy in Harlem. Harlem was always
a magical place for me. (September 1966)

Couldn't have been more excited
to welcome my baby sister, Maya.
(March 1967)

Grandpa and me when we visited him and my grandmother in Lusaka, Zambia. He was sent on a diplomatic mission by India to assist the African nation when it gained independence. Grandpa was one of my favorite people in the world and one of the earliest and most lasting influences in my life.

Christmas 1968. Sisters waiting for Santa Claus.

Mommy, Maya, and me outside of our apartment on Milvia Street
after my parents separated. From then on, we were known
as Shyamala and the girls. (January 1970)

Sporting my 'fro. (Summer of 1970)

My class at Thousand Oaks Elementary School was only the second
in Berkeley to be integrated. This is Mrs. Wilson's first grade.
That's me in the middle, in the white sweater.

This is my sixth birthday party. Included in this photo is Stacey Johnson, my best friend in kindergarten and still one of my closest friends today.

Maya and me at Madam Bovie's Ballet Studio. I loved dancing as a child. I still do.

My favorite pleather jacket at age seven. (December 1971)

Hanging out with my family in Jamaica. Maya is off to the right.

My maternal grandparents came to visit in 1972. You can see my mom's yellow Dodge Dart to the left. We lived just up those stairs, above the nursery school.

Long before "take your kid to work day," my mother often
took us to her lab in Berkeley. She had two goals in life:
to raise her two daughters and to end breast cancer.

This is Maya and me in the front
yard of our building. You can see the
Bancroft Nursery sign just behind us.
We lived upstairs.

My mother always said to me, "Kamala,
you may be the first to do many things.
Make sure you're not the last."

In front of Mrs. Shelton's house, holding her granddaughter Saniyyah. The house was always full of children, good cooking, and lots of love. (Summer 1978)

During my freshman year at Howard University, almost every weekend was spent at the Mall protesting apartheid and calling for divestment. Here I am with Gwen Whitfield. (November 1982)

Visiting my paternal grandmother, Beryl, in Jamaica.

Graduating from University of California Hastings College of the
Law in May 1989. My first grade teacher, Mrs. Wilson (left),
came to cheer me on. My mom was pretty proud, too.

Even after I started working in the Alameda County District Attorney's Office, I would return to Mrs. Shelton's kitchen, where I always knew I would receive a warm hug and delicious food.

We held the campaign kickoff for my DA's race at the Women's Building in San Francisco. My mother is addressing the crowd. She could also regularly be found organizing volunteers, licking envelopes, and generally doing anything that was needed. Also pictured: San Francisco Supervisors Sophie Maxwell and Fiona Ma, and State Assembly Member Mark Leno.

I'm blessed with an amazing family. I'll never be able to thank Auntie Chris, Uncle Freddy, and Aunt Mary enough for their constant encouragement and support. They always showed up for me, as they did here at a campaign event for my DA's race that we held at a San Francisco jazz club.

On Election Night in November 2003, we went to dinner as the vote tallies started to come in. My brother-in-law, Tony West, along with my dear friends Matthew Rothschild and Mark Leno, and my campaign consultant Jim Rivaldo, are writing down early returns on the paper tablecloth. We tore off the tally and I still have it framed in my office.

I won the runoff five weeks later, becoming the first female district attorney of San Francisco. Here I am at campaign headquarters, standing before the word "justice," which volunteers had spray painted on the walls. Behind my left shoulder is my mother. Behind her are Chris Cunnie and City Attorney Dennis Herrera. Chris would later become chief of my bureau of investigations.

After my inauguration, I went over to my new office to see what it would be like. It was totally empty except for a chair in the middle. I was happy to take my seat.

I loved having my mother with me at community events.
Here we are at the Chinese New Year parade. (2007)

the millions of people just like them, people who simply wanted to be accorded the human dignity of marrying the person they loved.

It would take eight months for the lawsuit to make its way to the first stage of the fight: the U.S. federal district court. Inside that courtroom, a judge would hear from witnesses, review evidence, and, based on the facts before him, decide whether Prop 8 had violated the civil rights of Kris, Sandy, Jeff, and Paul. On August 4, 2010, Chief Judge Vaughn Walker ruled in their favor, concluding that Prop 8 was indeed unconstitutional and affirming the right of same-sex couples to marry. It was fantastic and important news. But, as is common practice, the judge decided he was going to wait to enforce the ruling until it was appealed to a higher court—a legal concept known as a stay.

I was in the middle of my race for attorney general when the ruling came down, and it quickly became a central issue in the campaign. The California attorney general had the right to appeal the decision. Jerry Brown, whom I was running to succeed, had refused to defend the measure in court. I, too, made clear that I had no intention of spending a penny of the attorney general's office's resources defending Prop 8. My opponent took the other view—a sharp distinction between us. I understood that it wasn't just about principle; it was about practical outcomes. If California refused to appeal the ruling, the lower court judge could lift the stay and the state could start issuing marriage licenses again right away. If California did appeal the ruling, on the other hand, it would take years before marriages could begin.

When I won the election, my refusal to appeal the decision should have been the end of it. But proponents of Prop 8 were unwilling to give up the fight. In an unusual move, they joined together to appeal the ruling themselves. In my view, they had no basis for doing so. Your right to free speech doesn't give you the right to intervene in a court proceeding. You don't get to be a party in a lawsuit simply because you have strong feelings about something. In order to bring a case in court, you are required to have standing, which means, among other things, that you have suffered or might suffer an actual injury. (In more colloquial terms, I think of it as my New Jersey–raised husband might explain it: you have to be able to provide a concrete answer to the question "Whatsittoya?")

Kris Perry had standing to sue the state when Prop 8 passed because it injured her; it stripped her of a civil right. We had a law on the books that treated one group of Americans differently from all other Americans, and fundamentally that was unfair. But when Prop 8 was invalidated in federal court, that decision gave protections to one group without taking away anything from anyone. The constitutional principle was clear. Those people who wanted to deny same-sex couples the benefits of equal protection and due process under the U.S. Constitution could not do so simply because they didn't like the notion. They would always have their freedom of expression. But they did not have the power to deny other Americans their fundamental rights.

And yet the appeal proceeded. The ruling stayed on hold. It would take more than a year before the Ninth Circuit Court of Appeals issued its decision. Each day of delay represented justice denied—and much, much more. Each day of delay was a day a devoted couple couldn't consecrate their commitment. Each day of delay was a day a grandmother passed away before the wedding she would have loved to see. Each day of delay was a day a child was left wondering "Why can't my parents get married, too?"

There was much to applaud in the Ninth Circuit's ruling. A three-judge panel affirmed the lower court's decision that Prop 8 had deprived same-sex couples of their civil rights in California. But the court didn't take issue with the Prop 8 proponents' right to appeal. Instead, the court issued a stay in its ruling and allowed them to appeal once again—this time to the Supreme Court.

As I sat listening to the oral arguments, the Supreme Court justices homed in on the issue of standing. Justice Stephen Breyer questioned whether the Prop 8 proponents were "no more than a group of five people who feel really strongly." Justice Sonia Sotomayor wanted to know how the lower court's ruling had caused the proponents an injury "separate from that of every other taxpayer to have laws enforced." But when the arguments were over, there was really no way to tell what the decision would be.

As I left the Supreme Court, there were hundreds of people gathered, waving rainbow flags, holding signs, waiting anxiously for justice. It made me smile. They were why I had become a lawyer in the first place. It was in the courtroom, I believed, that you could translate that passion into action and precedent and law.

I looked out at their faces and imagined all the people who had stood in the same place for similar reasons: black parents with their children, fighting against segregation in schools; young women marching and shouting, holding signs that said KEEP ABORTION LEGAL; civil rights activists demonstrating against poll taxes and literacy tests and laws prohibiting interracial marriage.

In everyday life, they might have seemed like they had nothing in common. But on these steps, they shared something profound: in one form or another, they had faced treatment "directly subversive of the principle of equality," as Chief Justice Earl Warren had once put it.

And in one way or another, they believed the Constitution could set them free. They revered that document, in the words of Franklin Roosevelt, "not because it is old but because it is ever new, not in the worship of its past alone but in the faith of the living who keep it young, now and in the years to come." So they marched. And they fought. And they waited.

I knew that nothing was certain. The Supreme Court had made some terrible decisions in its past. In 1889, it upheld a law—still not overturned—that specifically excluded Chinese people from immigrating to America. In 1896, it held that racial segregation did not violate the Constitution. In 1944, it held that there was nothing unconstitutional about the forced internment of Japanese Americans. In 1986, it held that gay relationships could be criminalized. In 2010, it ushered in an era of dark money in politics with its ruling in *Citizens United*. And on the day before we would hear the ruling in our case, the Court's conservative justices invalidated—and gutted—a critical part of the Voting Rights Act. Nothing was certain.

But on the morning of June 26, 2013, we received wonderful news. The Supreme Court agreed that Prop 8 proponents had no standing to appeal, and dismissed the case in a 5–4 decision. That meant the lower court ruling would stand. And that meant marriage equality was the law again in California—finally.

I was in my Los Angeles office when the word came through. A spontaneous celebration broke out, with whoops and applause ricocheting through the hallways. After so many years of struggle and setback, love had finally conquered all.

I gathered my team to discuss a plan of action. I wanted the marriages to begin right away. But that couldn't happen until the Ninth

Circuit Court of Appeals lifted its stay, and the appellate court said it would take weeks to do so. This was unacceptable to me.

As I headed to a press conference to discuss the victory, my staff cautioned against challenging the court to act. There was decorum around these things, and my publicly weighing in might offend. But this was no time for decorum. Our fellow Americans had been waiting far too long. And so I leaned into the microphone and called on the Ninth Circuit to lift the stay as quickly as possible.

Two days later, I was in my San Francisco office with my team for a Friday afternoon strategy meeting, where we were discussing transnational criminal organizations ranging from drug smugglers to human and weapons traffickers. We were deep in conversation about a recently opened investigation when my assistant Cortney Bright came in and passed me a note. "The Ninth Circuit made a decision." I read the note to the team, and we lost all ability to focus on the work at hand. We needed to know the answer.

A short while later, Cortney was back. The Ninth Circuit had lifted the stay. The state could begin issuing marriage licenses right away. We erupted in cheers.

My phone rang, and it was Chad Griffin. He was with Kris Perry and Sandy Stier.

"Kamala, we're coming to San Francisco. Sandy and Kris are going to be the first marriage, and we want you to perform the ceremony."

"Of course! I would love to!" I told Chad. "Nothing would make me more proud."

Normally, I had to travel by official car, but this time I insisted that we walk. As my team and I made our way to City Hall, I recalled the famous image of Thurgood Marshall striding purposefully with

Autherine Lucy, who had been denied admission to the University of Alabama, one of the first tests of integration. Though we were the only ones in the street this time, it felt like we were leading our part of a parade—one that stretched through generations. We were following in the footsteps of giants, and widening the trail for our time.

When we reached City Hall, we made our way to the clerk's office, where a crowd was already gathering in the hallway. Kris and Sandy arrived soon after, beaming and ready to go.

"Congratulations!" I exclaimed as I hugged them both. They had been through so much, for so long. We were laughing and chatting when a reporter and a cameraman came over to ask me a question. He'd heard there might be an appeal and wanted to know what I thought about it.

I just looked at him and smiled. "Wedding bells are about to ring!"

Meanwhile, news started to spread, and people started coming to City Hall by the hundreds. Some to celebrate. Some to get married. Some just to bear witness. We could hear the Gay Men's Chorus singing, their voices soaring in the rotunda. As we filed into that confined space together, everyone experiencing pure joy, the feeling was magical.

We were preparing for the ceremony when somebody pulled me aside to say that the clerk in Los Angeles was refusing to issue marriage licenses until he heard from the state. He clearly needed direction. It was as simple as passing me the phone.

"This is Kamala Harris," I said. "You must start the marriages immediately."

"All right!" he responded, sounding relieved. "I will take that as our notice and we will issue the licenses now."

I thanked him. "And enjoy it!" I added. "It's going to be fun."

A short time later, I took my spot on the balcony and watched Kris and Sandy, followed by their loved ones and friends, walk up the stairs of City Hall. They made an elegant pair, in matching beige and white. Sandy was holding a bouquet of white roses. Two days earlier, they had become living symbols of justice. Now, as they took their final steps toward me—through the same building in which Harvey Milk had lived and died defending the dignity of all people—I could feel history being made.

"Today we witness not only the joining of Kris and Sandy, but the realization of their dream—marriage. . . . By joining the case against Proposition 8, they represented thousands of couples like themselves in the fight for marriage equality. Through the ups and downs, the struggles and the triumphs, they came out victorious."

Kris and Sandy exchanged their vows, and their son, Elliott, handed over the rings. I had the honor and privilege to say, "By virtue of the power and authority vested in me by the state of California, I now declare you spouses for life."

There were hundreds of weddings that day, all across the state, each one of them an expression of love and justice and hope. San Francisco City Hall was lit in the colors of the rainbow—a beautiful tribute to the beautiful words "I do!"

When I got home that evening, I had a chance to reflect on the day. My thoughts turned to a man I wished could have been there to see it. Jim Rivaldo was a San Francisco political strategist, one of the co-founders of *The National Lampoon,* and a leading member of the gay community who had been a key player in getting Harvey Milk elected to the San Francisco Board of Supervisors in 1977. He was truly brilliant, and when I first ran for district attorney, he was one of my most important advisers. My family and I loved him, especially my mother. In the years after my first election, we would see him often. He spent Thanksgiving with us the year before he died, in 2007. My mother cared for him at his bedside, trying to keep him comfortable in his final days.

I wanted to talk to him. I wanted to share the moment with him. But even in his absence, I knew exactly what he would have said: *We're not done yet.*

It would take another two years before the Supreme Court recognized marriage equality in all fifty states. And today, it is still the case under federal law that an employer can fire an employee if they identify as LGBTQ. It is still the case, in statehouses across the country, that transgender rights are getting trampled. This is still very much an active civil rights battle.

What happened with Prop 8 was an important part of a longer journey, one that began before America was its own nation and one that will continue for decades to come. It is the story of people fighting for their humanity—for the simple idea that we should all be equal and free. It is the story of people fighting for the promise made to all future generations at the signing of the Declaration of Independence: that no government has the right to rob us of our life or our liberty or our humble pursuit of happiness.

In the years to come, what matters most is that we see ourselves in one another's struggles. Whether we are fighting for transgender rights or for an end to racial bias, whether we are fighting against housing discrimination or insidious immigration laws, no matter who we are or how we look or how little it may seem we have in common, the truth is, in the battle for civil rights and economic justice, we are all the same. In the words of the great Bayard Rustin, organizer of the 1963 March on Washington, "We are all one, and if we don't know it, we will learn it the hard way."

A few months after Kris and Sandy got married, I was on my way to an event at a nonprofit organization called the California Endowment, run by my friend Robert K. Ross, a health philanthropist. The endowment is headquartered in a beautiful, modern space, and during my time as attorney general, we often used it to hold big events. On this particular day, the topic for discussion was one few might have expected to be on an attorney general's agenda. I was there to talk about elementary school truancy, and to initiate a discussion about solutions.

When I first started as attorney general, I told my executive team that I wanted to make elementary school truancy a top priority for my office. Those who didn't know me must have thought I was joking. Why would the state's top law enforcement official want to focus on whether seven-year-olds are going to school or not? But those who had been with me for a while knew I wasn't messing around. Indeed, instituting a statewide plan on truancy was part of the reason I'd run for the office in the first place.

When I was district attorney, much of the work I had done in crime prevention focused on interventions later in life. Back on Track, for example, was all about helping young adults avoid prison time and the consequences that flow from a felony conviction. But I was equally concerned about early interventions, about the kinds of steps we could take as a community—and a country—to keep children safe and on track to begin with. I wanted to identify key moments in a child's life when my office could make a difference.

It was during that process that I started connecting a series of research-related dots. The first dot concerned the importance of third-grade reading proficiency. Studies show that the end of third grade is a critical milestone for students. Up until that point, the curriculum focuses on teaching students to learn to read. In fourth grade, there's a shift, and students transition to reading in order to learn. If students can't read, they can't learn, and they fall further behind, month after month and year after year—which forces them onto a nearly inescapable path to poverty. The door of opportunity closes on them when they're barely four feet tall. I believe it is tantamount to a crime when a child goes without an education.

At the same time, I was focused on a rash of homicides in the city and county of San Francisco. It was an issue for leaders across the area, in and out of government, so there was a lot of activity and concern about what we should do to address it. When we studied the data, we learned that more than 80 percent of prisoners were high school dropouts.

I went to see the school district superintendent, a wonderful woman named Arlene Ackerman, to ask her about the high school dropout rate. She told me that a significant percentage of their habitually truant high school students had missed their elementary school classes, too—for weeks, even months at a time. That, to me, was a call to action. The connections were so clear. You could map the path for children who started drifting away from the classroom when they were young. The truant child became the wanderer . . . who became the target for gang recruiters . . . who became the young drug courier . . .

who became the perpetrator—or the victim—of violence. If we didn't see that child in elementary school, where they belonged, chances were we'd see them later in prison, in the hospital, or dead.

Some of my political advisers worried that tackling truancy would not be a popular issue. Even today, others don't appreciate the intention behind my approach; they assume that my motivation was to lock up parents, when of course that was never the goal. Our effort was designed to connect parents to resources that could help them get their kids back into school, where they belonged. We were trying to support parents, not punish them—and in the vast majority of cases, we succeeded.

Still, I was willing to be the bad guy if it meant highlighting an issue that otherwise would have received too little attention. Political capital doesn't gain interest. You have to spend it to make a difference.

My office joined with the city and the school district, and we developed a truancy initiative. I'm proud to say that by 2009, we had reduced truancy among San Francisco's elementary school children by 23 percent.

As we dug into the issue, what we found was quite different from what a number of my colleagues expected. Stereotypes held that a child becomes a chronically truant student because his or her parents don't care about the child's future. But the truth is different. The truth is that the vast majority of parents have a natural desire to parent their children well. They want to be good fathers and mothers. They just may not have the skills or the resources they need.

Imagine a single parent, working two minimum-wage shift jobs, six days a week, and still trapped below the poverty line. She gets paid hourly, with no vacation or sick leave. If her three-year-old daughter runs a fever, she can't bring her to the day care she took a second job to pay for. There's no money for a babysitter, but if she stays home, she's not going to be able to afford diapers for the rest of the month. It's already been hard enough saving money to buy new shoes for her eleven-year-old son, whose feet seem to grow a whole size every few months.

What amounts to a headache for those with means takes the form of desperation for those without. If a parent in that situation asks her son to stay home from school for a day in order to take care of his little sister, we can't accuse her of loving her children any less. This is a matter of circumstance and condition, not of character. She wants to be the best parent she can.

The goal of our truancy prevention initiative was to step in and provide support. We wanted the schools to reach out to parents with information: not only about the links between high truancy, illiteracy, and high crime, but, importantly, about resources they might not have been aware of—support the city and school district offered to make it easier to get their kids to school.

When we were first putting the initiative together, the draft guidance to the school districts told them to notify the parent with whom the child lived in case there was a truancy issue. This was usually the mother.

"Wait a minute," I asked. "What about the father?"

"Well, in a lot of these cases," one of my staffers explained, "the kids don't live with the father and the father isn't paying child support."

"So what?" I replied. "He may not be paying child support. It doesn't mean he doesn't want his child to go to school every day." And sure enough, in one of these cases, a young man found out that his daughter wasn't going to school every day and ended up changing his schedule to take her there each morning. He even started volunteering in her classroom.

When I became attorney general, I wanted to use the power of my office to expose the truancy crisis across the state. I knew the cameras would show up for a lot of what I did, and I wanted to shine a spotlight on this issue and appeal to people's self-interest. Like it or not, most people prioritize their own safety over the education of someone else's child. I wanted to make them see that if we didn't prioritize education now, it would be a public safety matter later.

Our first report, the results of which I was announcing that day at the California Endowment, estimated that we had approximately a million truant elementary school kids across the state. And in too many schools, nearly everyone was truant: one school had a truancy rate higher than 92 percent.

And so as I took the stage, what might have seemed like a tangential topic for the state's attorney general became the heart of impassioned remarks, in which I called on educators and policy makers, inside the room and beyond it, to step up and acknowledge the severity of the crisis.

While I was speaking, I noticed that two of my staffers were whispering to each other while pointing to a man in the audience. I couldn't hear them, but I knew exactly what they were saying: "Who's that guy? Is that him?" And I knew they were saying it because that guy was Doug.

Six months earlier, I hadn't known who that guy Doug was, either. I just knew that my best friend, Chrisette, was blowing up my phone. I was in the middle of a meeting, and my phone wouldn't stop buzzing. I ignored her call the first several times, but then I started to get worried. Her children are my godchildren. Had something happened?

I stepped out and called her.

"What's going on? Is everything okay?"

"Yes, everything is great. You're going on a date," she said.

"I am?"

"You are," she replied with total certainty. "I just met this guy. He's cute and he's the managing partner of his law firm and I think you're going to really like him. He's based in Los Angeles, but you're always here for work anyway."

Chrisette is like a sister to me, and I knew there was no use in arguing with her.

"What's his name?" I asked.

"His name is Doug Emhoff, but promise me you won't Google him. Don't overthink it. Just meet him. I already gave him your number. He's going to reach out."

Part of me groaned, but at the same time, I appreciated Chrisette's take-charge approach. She was one of the only people to whom I could talk candidly about my personal life. As a single, professional woman in my forties, and very much in the public eye, dating wasn't easy. I knew that if I brought a man with me to an event, people would immediately start to speculate about our relationship. I also knew that single women in politics are viewed differently than single men. We don't get the same latitude when it comes to our social lives. I had no interest in inviting that kind of scrutiny unless I was close to sure I'd found "the One"—which meant that for years, I kept my personal life compartmentalized from my career.

A few nights later, I was on my way to an event when I received a text from a number I didn't recognize. Doug was watching a basketball game with a friend, and he'd worked up the courage to send me an awkward text. "Hey! It's Doug. Just saying hi! I'm at the Lakers game." I wrote back to say hi, and we made plans to talk the following day. Then I punctuated it with my own bit of awkwardness—"Go Lakers!"—even though I'm really a Warriors fan.

The next morning, I was leaving the gym before work when I noticed that I had missed a call from Doug. Even though I had suggested we connect the following day, I hadn't expected him to reach out that early. But I found it pretty endearing, I'll admit. In fact, while I was writing this chapter, I sat down with Doug and asked him to explain what was going through his head when he made that call. This is what he said:

> I got up early that morning. I had an early meeting. And as I was driving to work, I couldn't get you off my mind. And I kept saying to myself, "It's eight thirty a.m., it's way too early to call her. That would be ridiculous. Don't be that guy. Just don't. Don't call her. Don't do it." And then, "Oh no, I just rang her number," and, "Oh no, it's ringing.

The voicemail, which I still have saved to this day, was long and a little rambling. He sounded like a nice guy, though, and I was intrigued to learn more. Doug, on the other hand, was pretty sure that he had ruined his chances. The way he tells it, he thought his voicemail had been disastrous and that he'd likely never hear from me again. He had to restrain himself from calling again and leaving another long-winded message trying to explain away the first one.

But fate was smiling on us. As it happens, I own an apartment in San Francisco, and, after saving up for years to redo my kitchen, the work was finally about to start. That day, I was supposed to meet the contractor and his team to show them in and give them keys, but when I got to the apartment, I learned the contractor was running late, and I would have to wait.

In other words, I found myself with a free hour for lunch— something that almost never happened. So I decided I'd give Doug a call. Maybe he was on a lunch break, too.

He answered, and we ended up on the phone for the entire hour. It sounds corny, I know, but the conversation just flowed; and even though I'm sure that both of us were trying extra hard to seem witty and interesting, most of all I remember us cracking each other up, joking and laughing at ourselves and with each other, just the way we do now. By the time the contractor arrived, I was genuinely excited to meet this Doug guy in person. We made dinner plans for Saturday night in Los Angeles. I could hardly wait to fly down.

Doug suggested that we meet first at his place. I suggested that he pick me up instead. "Okay, but I just need you to know I'm not a really good driver," he said. "Thanks for letting me know," I replied with a chuckle. There was no pretense or posing with Doug, no arrogance or boasting. He seemed so genuinely comfortable with himself. It's part of why I liked him immediately.

The morning after our first date, Doug emailed me with all of his available dates for the next couple of months. "I'm too old to play games or hide the ball," the email read. "I really like you, and I want to see if we can make this work." In fact, he was eager to see me that Saturday, but I had a long-scheduled girls' weekend on the calendar.

"That's no problem," he said. "I could come up and you and I could just sneak off on the margins." I appreciated his enthusiasm, but I had to explain to him that, no, that's not how a girls' weekend works. We planned a second date for later that week instead.

For our third date, Doug decided that a grand gesture was in order. He flew to Sacramento to meet me for dinner. After that, we knew we had something special. We agreed to commit to each other for six months, and to reevaluate our relationship at the end of it. Attending a speech about the ills of truancy isn't exactly what most people think of as a romantic date, but the event was Doug's coming out—the first time I'd invited him to join me at a professional gathering. Hence the whispering and pointing among my team, who had heard rumors of his existence but hadn't seen him with their own eyes. They would later refer to that era as A.D.—"After Doug." They loved how much he made me laugh. I did, too.

Doug had been married once before, and he had two kids, Cole and Ella—named after John Coltrane and Ella Fitzgerald. When Doug and I first started dating, Ella was in middle school and Cole was in high school; Doug shared custody with his first wife, Kerstin. I had—and have—tremendous admiration and respect for Kerstin. I could tell from the way Doug talked about his kids that she was a terrific mother—and in later months, as Kerstin and I got to know each other, we really hit it off ourselves and became friends. (We sometimes joke that our modern family is almost a little too functional.)

After our second date, Doug was ready to introduce me to Cole and Ella, and I was eager to meet them, too. But as a child of divorce, I knew how hard it can be when your parents start to date other people. So I slowed things down. Other than occasionally talking to the kids when Doug had me on speakerphone in the car, I wanted to make sure that Doug and I had something real and lasting before I waded into Cole's and Ella's lives.

Doug and I put a lot of thought into when and how that first meeting should transpire. We waited until about two months after we'd met, although in my memory it feels like we'd been together for a long time—maybe because the buildup was so great, or because, by the time the big day finally arrived, I felt like I'd loved Doug for years.

I woke up that morning feeling incredibly excited, but also with some butterflies in my stomach. Until that moment, I'd known Cole and Ella as gorgeous faces in Doug's photographs, charming characters in his stories, the central figures in his heart. Now I was finally going to meet these two amazing young people. It was a momentous occasion.

On my way home from my LA office, I picked up a tin of cookies and tied a festive ribbon in a bow around it. I got rid of my suit, changed into jeans and my Chuck Taylors, took a few deep breaths, and got a ride to Doug's house. On the way over, I tried to imagine how the first few minutes would go. I ran scenarios in my head and tried to land on the perfect things to say. The tin of cookies was sitting beside me on the seat, a silent witness to my rehearsing. Would the kids think the cookies were really nice or really weird? Maybe the ribbon was too much.

The ribbon was probably too much. But Cole and Ella could not have been more welcoming. They'd been wanting to meet me, too. We talked for a few minutes, then piled into Doug's car for dinner together. Doug and I had decided the kids should choose where we ate, to make everything as comfortable as possible. They'd picked a place that had been a favorite since they were younger—a seafood hut off the Pacific Coast Highway called the Reel Inn. It was about an hour away in traffic, which gave us some quality car time to get to know one another. Cole, it turned out, was a music aficionado, and he was excited to share some of his latest discoveries with me.

"I just started listening to Roy Ayers," he said. "Do you know him?"

I sang back: "Everybody loves the sunshine, sunshine, folks get down in the sunshine . . ."

"You know it!"

"Of course I know it!"

We put on the song, and then another and another. The four of us sang together with the windows rolled down as we drove up the coast to dinner.

The Reel Inn was casual and unpretentious. It was hard not to feel at ease. We waited in line with trays at a counter, the menu of fresh fish written on a blackboard on the wall. The cashier gave us numbers, much like at a deli, and when our order was called, we took our trays to some picnic tables with a view of the ocean, just as the sun was beginning to set. When we were done eating, Cole and Ella told us that they were going to head over to Cole's school to see an art show where some of their friends' work would be displayed. They wanted to know if we wanted to join them.

"Of course!" I said, as if this was a totally normal thing. It sounded great to me. Then Doug whispered to me, "They must like you. They never invite me to anything." We went to the school together, and Ella—a gifted artist—expertly guided us through the exhibit. Lots of their friends were there, too, and we had fun mingling and making conversation with the students and their parents. Doug later joked that I got completely inundated with their lives that night, but I think it's more accurate to say that I was hooked, and Cole and Ella reeled me in.

At the end of March 2014, I had two trips planned. One was to Mexico, where I was coordinating with senior officials in the fight against transnational criminal organizations and human traffickers. The other was to Italy, where Doug and I were looking forward to a romantic getaway. The respective itineraries were, in a word, different. At home, Doug and I stayed up late looking at pictures and guidebooks and planning our itinerary for Florence. At the office, I was working to put together and lead a bipartisan delegation of state attorneys general to join me in Mexico City.

Mexico-based transnational crime was—and is—a major threat, and California was a primary target. That March, my office had released a report that found, for example, that 70 percent of the U.S. supply of methamphetamine was coming through the San Diego port of entry on California's southern border. The report also drew attention to ways in which Mexican-based drug trafficking was being amplified in the United States as cartels formed alliances with gangs on California streets and in California prisons.

The challenges posed to California law enforcement—and thereby the rest of the country—were significant, and I wanted to meet with Mexican officials to work through a joint plan to take on the cartels.

We spent three days in Mexico—four other state attorneys general and I—and were able to come away with a plan for concrete action. We signed a letter of intent with the National Banking and Securities Commission of Mexico to establish an anti-money-laundering enforcement effort. Money laundering fuels transnational criminal organizations, and by creating a communication and cooperation agreement with

Mexico, we hoped to improve our ability to investigate and disrupt this financing.

On March 26, 2014, I arrived back at my apartment in San Francisco, feeling like the trip had been a real success. But it was late in the evening when I got home, and now I had a small problem: my trip with Doug was starting early the next morning, and I'd had no time to pack.

Shortly after I arrived at my apartment, Doug texted to say he was on his way from the airport. When he got to the apartment, I was in the middle of a frantic search. I couldn't find my black pants, and I was intensely frustrated about it.

It was ridiculous, of course, but it was one of those moments when the balancing act caught up with me—a balancing act that many working women, and some men, know all too well. Just like my mother, I've internalized the idea that everything I do deserves 100 percent, but sometimes it feels like the numbers won't work. There just isn't enough of me to go around. This was one of those times. I had a hundred things racing through my mind in the aftermath of the Mexico trip, and a hundred more as I contemplated the work I'd missed while I was away. Meanwhile, I was trying to shift mental gears for a getaway with my sweetheart—but my packing list and my to-do list were competing hard for real estate in my brain. I was beating myself up for trying to do too much, even as I worried that I wasn't doing quite enough, and all of this stress coalesced in the form of a search for my black pants.

Which I couldn't find. My closet was a mess.

As a result, I was frazzled, and when Doug arrived he seemed out of sorts as well. He was acting strange—a little stiff, a little quiet.

"Do you mind if we get takeout instead of going out to eat?" I asked him. "I didn't plan for this very well and I need time to pack."

"Of course," he said. "How about the Thai place we like?"

"Sounds great," I replied. I rifled through a kitchen drawer and produced a tattered paper menu. "How about pad thai?"

Doug turned to me. "I want to spend my life with you."

That was sweet, but he was always sweet like that. Truth be told, I didn't register the significance of what he'd said at all. I didn't even look up. My mind was still on the black pants.

"That's nice, honey," I said, rubbing his arm as I looked over the menu. "Should we have chicken or shrimp on the pad thai?"

"No, I want to spend my life with you," he said again. When I looked up, he was getting down on one knee. He'd concocted an elaborate plan to propose to me in front of the Ponte Vecchio, in Florence. But once he had the ring, it was burning a hole in his pocket. He couldn't keep it secret.

I looked at him there, on one knee, and burst into tears. Mind you, these were not graceful Hollywood tears streaming down a glistening cheek. No, I'm talking about snorting and grunting, with mascara smudging my face. Doug reached for my hand and I held my breath and smiled back. Then he asked me to marry him, and I bellowed a tear-soaked "Yes!"

Doug and I were married on Friday, August 22, 2014, in an intimate ceremony with the people we loved. Maya officiated; Meena read from Maya Angelou. In keeping with our respective Indian and Jewish heritage, I put a flower garland around Doug's neck, and he stomped on a glass. And then it was done.

Cole, Ella, and I agreed that we didn't like the term "stepmom." Instead they call me their "Momala."

One of my favorite routines is Sunday family dinner. This is a routine I instituted once Doug and I got engaged. When he and I first started dating, he was a single dad sharing custody with Kerstin. Family dinner had been Chinese takeout and plastic forks, which the kids spirited off to their bedrooms. I changed that. Now everyone knows that Sunday family dinner is nonnegotiable, that we come together, all of us around the table, relatives and friends always welcome, and I cook a meal for us to share. It's really important to me.

Everyone quickly got into the routine and found their role to play. Cole sets the table, picks the music, and pitches in as sous chef in the kitchen. Ella makes restaurant-quality guacamole and exquisite desserts, including a gorgeous fresh fruit tart, where she folds the dough in magnificent ways, topped off with homemade whipped cream. Doug bought himself a pair of onion goggles, which he dons with great fanfare when it's time to chop—and let me tell you, there is nothing more attractive than a man in onion goggles.

I make the main dish—maybe a rich pork stew or spaghetti Bolognese or an Indian biryani or chicken with feta cheese, lemon rind, and fresh oregano from the garden. Usually I'll start cooking on Saturday, and sometimes even Friday, though if I've been on the road I'll pull it all together quickly—something simpler, like fish tacos. It doesn't always go as planned: sometimes the pizza dough doesn't rise or the sauce won't thicken or we're missing a key ingredient and I have to improvise. That's all okay. Sunday family dinner is about something more than the meal.

When dinner is finished, the kids do the dishes. I once told them the story of Uncle Freddy. Because he lived in a small basement apartment in Harlem with a tiny kitchen, Uncle Freddy would clean every single dish or utensil he used as soon as he was done using it.

And in time, the kids turned "Uncle Freddy" into a verb. When it's time to clean, they promise to "Uncle Freddy" the place. And they do a pretty good job!

I know that not everyone likes to cook, but it's centering for me. And as long as I'm making Sunday family dinner, I know I'm in control of my life—doing something that matters for the people I love, so we can share that quality time together.

Early one morning in that busy summer of 2014, my phone rang at the side of my bed. I picked it up to find Eric Holder, then the U.S. attorney general, on the other end of the line. He told me he had a question.

"I'm going to be stepping down soon. Are you interested?"

It was, needless to say, a lot to take in. Did I want to be United States attorney general? Did I want to hold the office that Bobby Kennedy once held? Of course I did. This was the kind of job I used to daydream about during lectures in law school. And this wasn't just any moment or any president. This was Barack Obama, my friend and my president, whose leadership I so admired and whom I had been so proud to support. To join his cabinet would have been the honor of my life.

And yet I wasn't sure if I truly wanted the job. By the time Holder stepped down, there would be fewer than two years left in the administration. What kind of opportunity would I have to create a real agenda?

The next time Holder and I spoke, I brought up Back on Track. I said that if there was a budget at the Department of Justice to fund and create incentives for local reentry initiatives, then I would be interested in the job. I wanted to be able to create real reform at a national level, with an approach that prioritized prevention. Alas, as Holder explained, there wasn't any existing budget for such an effort, and any new funding would have to be approved by Congress— which we both knew was not going to happen.

That was disheartening. But I still knew the job wasn't something to be turned down lightly. Like every lawyer I know, I listed the pros and cons on a yellow pad. I batted the options back and forth with Doug and other members of the family. I did my best to argue both sides.

One day, one of my best friends suggested we take a hike in the Windy Hill Open Space Preserve, near Palo Alto. She thought the outdoor air and beautiful rolling hilltops might refresh my state of mind—and she was right. Away from the office, the contours of my choice came into sharper relief. With every step, I saw more clearly what I wanted to do, and why.

Inevitably, there would be limitations that came with the job. I took that as a given. But as I talked with my friend, and she raised all the right questions, I realized the real reason behind my resistance to the offer: I already had a job I loved, and work I still wanted to do.

I thought about my first days as California attorney general, when I'd learned that we had a big backlog of rape kits. I thought about all the work we were putting in to reduce the backlog, about the innovations we deployed to triple the number of cases that could be handled. Earlier in 2014, my Rapid DNA Service team received an award from the Department of Justice for our achievements. I thought about our work on human trafficking, too, which had been an unseen problem for so long, and our efforts to combat the brutal criminal organizations and street gangs that traded in human lives.

I thought about the fight I'd been able to lead, first as district attorney and then as attorney general, to stop defendants in hate crimes from using what's known as the "gay and trans panic defense." In 2002, a seventeen-year-old woman, Gwen Araujo, had been brutally beaten and murdered in Newark, California. Her killers, two of whom had been involved with her sexually, had tried to justify their actions in court by claiming that they had panicked upon learning that Araujo was transgender, to the point of temporary insanity. It was ludicrous. As district attorney, I had organized a conference of prosecutors and law enforcement officials from across the country to push back against the idea that criminal conduct could be mitigated by prejudice. And as attorney general, in that summer of 2014, I was working with the governor and state legislature on what would be a successful effort to ban such a defense statewide. I thought about how much that meant to me.

I thought about the Bureau of Children's Justice, a new initiative I was still developing with one of my special assistant attorneys general, Jill Habig, which would be entirely devoted to making sure the rights of all of California's children were protected. There was a lot on that agenda, and I was eager to see it all through.

I thought about the work we were doing to prepare to open up state crime data to the public, a first-of-its-kind transparency initiative led by special assistant attorneys general Daniel Suvor and Justin Erlich, which we would call OpenJustice.

Likewise, we were taking Back on Track and my truancy initiative statewide.

And then there were the corporate predators who took advantage of students and veterans and homeowners and the poor. I loved being the voice and advocate for the people they mistreated. The lawyers on my team knew how serious I was about holding corporate predators accountable. They would joke that "Kamala" meant "Get more commas in that settlement price."

And of course, the banks. The fight with them was still ongoing. We were still bringing lawsuits, and I had no plans of backing down.

By the time our hike was over, my friend and I both knew I'd made my decision. It wouldn't be about the title or the perception of prestige. What mattered to me was the work. And when it came to the work that mattered most, I wasn't finished yet.

Later that evening, I called Holder to let him know. Then Doug and I curled up on the couch with the kids and a big bowl of popcorn and, for the second time, watched *Iron Man 2*.

Five

I SAY WE FIGHT

I 'll always remember how I felt in November 1992, as a twenty-eight-year-old prosecutor, driving across the bridge from my home in Oakland into San Francisco to celebrate the victory of newly elected U.S. senators Barbara Boxer and Dianne Feinstein. They were the first female senators from California, and the first two women to represent any state at the same time. Their election was a highlight of the so-called Year of the Woman, and an inspiration to girls and women everywhere, including me.

I recalled that celebration twenty-two years later when, in early January 2015, Senator Boxer posted a video of herself in conversation with her oldest grandchild, Zach. She talked about the issues she cared about, the issues for which she'd fought over three decades in Congress—a strong middle class, a woman's right to choose, the environment, civil rights, human rights—and underscored that she wasn't going to give them up. But, as she told Zach, she wanted to come home to California. And so she wouldn't be running for re-election.

November 2016 was almost two years away, but I had a decision to make. Should I run to replace Senator Boxer? It would be an opportunity to take the issues we were driving forward in the California attorney general's office and bring them to the national stage. Becoming a U.S. senator would be a natural extension of the work I was already doing—fighting for families feeling the burden of stagnant wages, soaring housing costs, and diminishing opportunity; for people imprisoned in a broken criminal justice system; for students exploited by predatory lenders and burdened by skyrocketing tuition; for victims of fraud and white-collar crime; for immigrant communities, for women, for older people. I knew it mattered whose voice was represented at the table where national priorities and policies are set.

I announced my candidacy on January 13, 2015. Eventually, so did thirty-three others. Doug, for whom it was his first major campaign, had to get used to a new kind of scrutiny. We still laugh about the time a reporter asked me who would play me in a movie about my life. I deflected—said I didn't know. Doug was not as prudent. He answered the question and the resulting article said he was "delighted" at the prospect of being played by Bradley Cooper.

I tackled the race as I had every other, meeting as many people as I could, listening carefully to their concerns, mapping a plan of action to address them. As the campaign rolled on, my team and I crisscrossed the state in what we called the Kamoji bus, because of the giant emoji caricature of me painted on the back door.

Because of California's unique "jungle primary," I ultimately found myself in a runoff against fellow Democrat Loretta Sanchez, a long-time member of Congress. She was a tough, determined opponent who kept fighting until the end. I was fortunate enough to have on my team some of the best people in the business—my brilliant campaign manager, Juan Rodriguez, and my longtime strategic advisers Sean Clegg and Ace Smith, along with Ellie Caple, and an extraordinarily dedicated group of staff and volunteers. My goddaughter, Helena, was among them. She started a newsletter, interviewing the staff and chronicling our efforts. Our team was in it together every step of the way, and I couldn't have done it without them.

The two-year campaign passed both fast and slow. But even as I focused on my state, my campaign, and the work before me, something ugly and alarming was infecting the presidential election. The Republican primary was turning into a race to the bottom—a race to anger, a race to blame, a race to fan the flames of xenophobic nativism. And the man who prevailed crossed every boundary of decency and integrity—bragging about sexually assaulting women; mocking people with disabilities; race baiting; demonizing immigrants; attacking war heroes and Gold Star families; and fomenting hostility, even hatred, toward the press.

As a result, Election Night 2016 was not a night for cheering. It was no longer about the race that had just ended. It was about the fight that was clearly now beginning. Drawing on the words of Coretta Scott King, I reminded the audience that freedom must be fought for and won by every generation.

"It is the very nature of this fight for civil rights and justice and equality that whatever gains we make, they will not be permanent. So we must be vigilant," I said. "Understanding that, do not despair. Do not be overwhelmed. Do not throw up our hands when it is time to roll up our sleeves and fight for who we are."

I didn't know, when I spoke to my supporters that night, exactly what was to come. But I did know this: we would need to stand strong and stand together.

On Thursday, November 10, less than forty-eight hours after my election, I visited the headquarters of the Coalition for Humane Immigrant Rights of Los Angeles (CHIRLA).

CHIRLA is one of Los Angeles's oldest immigrant rights advocacy organizations. It was founded in 1986, after President Reagan, a former California governor, signed the Immigration Reform and Control Act, which, among other things, gave legal status to undocumented immigrants who had entered the United States before 1982. CHIRLA's original mission was to inform immigrants about the process by which they could apply for legal status and about their rights to work. It trained community organizers, challenged anti-immigrant laws like California's Proposition 187, which prohibited undocumented immigrants from getting nonemergency public services, and it eventually took on a national portfolio by building coalitions all across the country. It was the first place I wanted to speak officially as senator-elect.

Angelica Salas, CHIRLA's indefatigable executive director, was there to greet me when I arrived. The room was full. It was full of strong, brave women—young women to mothers to grandmothers to great-grandmothers—working women who did everything from domestic work to home health care work, some of whom spoke fluent English and some of whom spoke only Spanish, all of them ready to fight.

In their courage, their dignity, and their determination, they reminded me of my mother. Standing among them, I thought about the duality of the immigrant experience in America.

On the one hand, it is an experience characterized by an extraordinary sense of hopefulness and purpose, a deep belief in the power of the American Dream—an experience of possibility. At the same time, it is an experience too often scarred by stereotyping and scapegoating, in which discrimination, both explicit and implicit, is part of everyday life.

My mother was the strongest person I have ever known, but I always felt protective of her, too. In part, I suppose, that instinct to protect comes from being the older child. But I also knew my mother was a target. I saw it, and it made me mad. I have too many memories of my brilliant mother being treated as though she were dumb because of her accent. Memories of her being followed around a department store with suspicion, because surely a brown-skinned woman like her couldn't afford the dress or blouse that she had chosen.

I also remember how seriously she took any encounter with government officials. Whenever we would come back from traveling abroad, my mother made sure Maya and I were on our best behavior as we went through customs. "Stand up straight. Don't laugh. Don't fidget. Have all your stuff. Be prepared." She knew that every word she spoke would be judged, and she wanted us to be ready. The first time Doug and I went through customs together, my muscle memory kicked in. I was preparing myself in the usual way, making sure we had everything just right and in order. Meanwhile, Doug was as relaxed as ever. It frustrated me that he was so casual. He was genuinely perplexed, innocently wondering, "What's the problem?" We had been raised in different realities. It was eye-opening for us both.

For as long as ours has been a nation of immigrants, we have been a nation that fears immigrants. Fear of the other is woven into the fabric of our American culture, and unscrupulous people in power have exploited that fear in pursuit of political advantage. In the mid-1850s, the first significant third-party movement in the United States, the so-called Know-Nothing Party, rose to popularity on an anti-immigrant platform. In 1882, an act of Congress banned Chinese immigrants to the country. In 1917, Congress overrode President Woodrow Wilson's veto in order to establish a host of new restrictions on immigrants, including a literacy requirement. Concerns about growing numbers of newcomers from Southern and Eastern Europe resulted in the imposition of immigration quotas in 1924. In 1939, nearly 1,000 German Jews fleeing the Nazis in a ship called the *St. Louis* were turned away from the United States. A plan to allow 20,000 Jewish children into the country was outright rejected. And shortly after, the U.S. government interned some 117,000 people of Japanese ancestry.

More recently, as globalization has robbed the country of millions of jobs and displaced huge swaths of the middle class, immigrants have become convenient targets for blame. When the Great Recession ravaged rural America, a number of Republican politicians pointed to immigration as the problem, even as they filibustered a bill that would have created new jobs. Despite the profound role they have played in building and shaping America, immigrants who come here to seek a better life have always made for an easy scapegoat.

Our country was built by many hands, by people from every part of the world. And over the centuries, immigrants have helped to lift and fuel the economy—providing labor to industrialize it and brainpower to create society-altering innovations. Immigrants and their children were the creative minds behind many of our best-known brands—from Levi Strauss to Estée Lauder. Sergey Brin, the cofounder of Google, was a Russian immigrant. Jerry Yang, co-founder of Yahoo!, came here from Taiwan. Mike Krieger, the co-founder of

Instagram, is an immigrant from Brazil. Arianna Huffington, co-founder of *The Huffington Post,* was born in Greece. In fact, in 2016, researchers at the National Foundation for American Policy found that more than half of Silicon Valley's billion-dollar startups were founded by one or more immigrants.

I stood by the podium at CHIRLA, with an American flag and stars-and-stripes balloons in the backdrop, as a mother—a house cleaner from the San Fernando Valley—spoke in Spanish about her fears of deportation. I could barely translate her words, but I understood their meaning and I could feel her anguish. It was visible in her eyes, in her posture. She wanted to be able to tell her children that everything would be okay, but she knew she couldn't.

I thought of the nearly six million American children who live in a home with at least one undocumented family member and the trauma and stress that the election had wrought. I had heard many stories of safety plans that were being put in place—mothers telling their children, "If Mommy doesn't come home right after work, call your aunt or uncle to come and get you." It reminded me of the safety plans I'd seen when I was working with victims of domestic abuse. In both cases, there needed to be a contingency plan to mitigate against an impending harm.

Advocates working with families told us how children were afraid to go to school, not knowing if their parents would still be there when they got home. Parents canceled their children's pediatrician appointments out of fear that ICE would be waiting for them. Likewise, I knew that parents, at that moment, were facing harrowing decisions about what to do with their American children if they were deported. Should the children stay with a relative in the United States? Should they go with their parents to a country that they had never known?

Either option was heartbreaking to imagine. And I knew it wasn't just undocumented people who were terrified. According to research published in *American Behavioral Scientist,* all Latinx immigrants—whether citizens, legal residents, or undocumented—experience the fear of deportation at the same rates. I wanted them to know I had their back.

"This is a time in our country for coalition building," I said, reminded of the work I had seen and done through the years. "We are going to fight for the ideals of this country," I told them, "and we are not going to let up until we have won."

I left CHIRLA two days after the election feeling both encouraged and worried. I knew we were preparing for battle together. But I knew, too, that we were underdogs in the fight. We were going to have to steel ourselves for all that was to come.

Things moved very quickly. The following week, Doug and I flew across the country to Washington for new senators' orientation. A bipartisan group of senators and their spouses hosted us for three jam-packed days of sessions, during which we were informed about Senate rules and procedures, ethics, and how to set up a Senate office. Doug studied the spouses' binder like a Talmudic scholar.

Nathan Barankin, my number two in the California Department of Justice, agreed to move his family to Washington, and he began the intensive process of selecting and vetting my new team as my chief of staff. We had only the period between Election Day and New Year's to build the office virtually from scratch—poring over some five thousand résumés to fill a host of positions from policy and constituent relations to communications, correspondence, and more. Hiring a diverse staff was important to me—veterans, women, people of color. I wanted my staff in Washington and our state offices to reflect the people we represent.

Ella was now in her senior year of high school, which meant that Doug would be spending at least every other week in Los Angeles. This was the hardest part of it all, being away from Ella. Before becoming a senator, I had gone to every one of her swim meets, every one of her basketball games. Kerstin and I usually embarrassed Ella as we sat together and loudly cheered her name. I hated that I would have to miss some of those games now. And I hated that we would have so much less quality time in person, especially because she was about to go off to college, as Cole had done several years earlier. I was committed to flying home as many weekends as I could, which was important to me for so many reasons—to see my constituents, feel the pulse on the ground, and, crucially, cook Sunday family dinner.

The worst was several months later when I realized I wasn't going to be able to go to Ella's graduation. Fired FBI director James Comey had been invited to testify before the Senate Intelligence Committee that same day about the Russia investigation and his firing, and, given the significance to our national security, there was no way I could miss it. When I called to tell her, she was so understanding, but I felt awful about it. I had conversations with some of my female colleagues afterwards. Maggie Hassan bucked me up. "Our kids love us for who we are and the sacrifices we make," she said. "They get it." In the case of Ella and Cole, I'm so lucky to know that's true. When the hearing was over, I dashed to the airport and flew back to California. I missed the graduation ceremony but made it home in time for family dinner that night.

Doug and I rented a temporary apartment not far from the Capitol, along with minimal furniture—a pair of stools, a bed, a foldout couch for when the kids came to visit, and, for Doug, a big-screen TV. With things happening so quickly, there wasn't much time on the margins for grocery shopping or cooking, though I did make turkey chili one night and froze enough to last us for weeks.

I was sworn in on January 3, 2017, by Vice President Joe Biden during his final month in office, and moved into a basement office alongside other newly elected senators. While not every Senate committee had available seats, I was appointed to four based on my expertise and background: Intelligence, Homeland Security, Budget, and Environment and Public Works.

One week later, the Homeland Security Committee held a confirmation hearing for General John Kelly, who had been nominated for secretary of Homeland Security. I chose to focus my questions to him on the Deferred Action for Childhood Arrivals program (DACA), which was created in 2012 by the Obama administration to protect eligible undocumented youth from deportation and allow them to obtain work permits.

"Hundreds of thousands of DACA recipients around the country are afraid right now for what this incoming administration might do to them and also what it might do to their unauthorized family members," I said.

I went on to explain that in order to qualify for the program, recipients had submitted extensive paperwork to the federal government, including detailed information about themselves and their loved ones. Each person's case was reviewed and vetted according to specific criteria. The young person must not have been convicted of a felony, a significant misdemeanor, or three or more misdemeanors.

They must not have been deemed a threat to public safety or national security. They had to be in school or have already earned a high school diploma or certificate, or been honorably discharged from the armed forces. They had to provide proof of identity, proof of time and admission in the United States, proof of school completion or military status, and biometric information. Only if they cleared this extensive vetting would they get DACA status.

In addition, when they applied, the Department of Homeland Security (DHS) assured them it would follow its long-standing practice not to use their information for law enforcement purposes except in very limited circumstances. "These young people," I said to General Kelly, "are now worried that the information they provided in good faith to our government may now be used to track them down and lead to their removal." Hundreds of thousands of them have relied on our representations.

"Do you agree that we would not use this information against them?" I asked. Kelly wouldn't directly answer the question. I next read to him from a government document—frequently asked questions about the DACA program. There was a question that asked "If my case is referred to ICE [U.S. Immigration and Customs Enforcement] for immigration enforcement purposes or if I receive an NTA [Notice to Appear], will information related to my family members and guardians also be referred to ICE for immigration enforcement purposes?" The answer to the question on the government document was no.

"Are you willing to maintain that policy?" I asked. Again, Kelly deflected. I pressed harder. "Do you intend to use the limited law enforcement resources of DHS to remove [DACA recipients] from the country?" Once again, he refused to answer the question directly.

"Would you agree that state and local law enforcement agencies are uniquely situated to protect the public safety of their own communities?"

"I would agree," he said.

"Are you aware that state and local law enforcement leaders across the country have publicly stated that they depend on the cooperation of immigrant communities" to prosecute criminal activity and come forward as witnesses to crime?

"I've read that."

"And are you aware that when the government has applied indiscriminate immigration sweeps, many local law enforcement agencies have been concerned and have complained that there has been a decrease in immigrants reporting crimes against themselves and others?"

"I was not aware of that."

"Will you make it your priority to become aware of the impact on immigrant communities, in terms of their reluctance to report crimes against themselves, their family members, or others, when they are concerned that DHS may direct sweeps against entire immigrant communities?"

"You have my commitment. I'll get briefed on this. Again I fall back on, really—the law will guide me, if confirmed, in everything that I do."

That wasn't enough.

As a former district attorney and attorney general, I had a lot of experience with this issue. I knew that victims of crime—be it rape, be it child sexual assault, be it fraud—simply will not come forward if they believe they are the ones who will be treated as criminals. I also knew that predators use this knowledge to their advantage, exploiting the vulnerability of certain groups who they know will keep quiet. I don't ever want a victim of a crime to be afraid to wave down a passing patrol car to get help. Such a system serves the predators, not the public. It renders all of us less safe. As attorney general, I had crafted legislation to help ensure that undocumented immigrants who stepped forward to testify about crimes, or to report them, were shielded from deportation for doing so. I knew this would help prosecutors obtain convictions while strengthening the relationship of trust between law enforcement and immigrant communities.

In the end, I voted against John Kelly's confirmation and pressed my colleagues to do the same. He wasn't prepared to keep the nation's promises, and I wasn't prepared to put him in charge of them.

Whether he ever got briefed on the consequences of indiscriminate immigration enforcement, I will never know. What I do know is that in the first hundred days of the administration, immigration arrests increased by more than 37 percent. The administration chose to make all unauthorized immigrants a priority for deportation, regardless of whether they were otherwise law-abiding members of the community. Arrests of undocumented immigrants with no criminal record nearly doubled.

The policies have had far-reaching consequences for children. As the Center for American Progress documented, ICE officials raided a meatpacking plant in Tennessee where they arrested ninety-seven workers. It was one of the largest workplace raids in ten years. All told, 160 children had a parent arrested in the raid. The next day, 20 percent of the Latinx students in a nearby county were absent from school as parents feared that they—or their children—would be arrested as well. In 2016, a quarter of all kids in the United States under the age of five lived in immigrant families. These children have had to live in the grip of the fear that, at any moment, their parents could be abruptly taken away from them.

Children of immigrants also faced a new kind of torment. Teachers around the country have reported spikes in bullying that echoes the administration's rhetoric. Kids are being taunted by other kids, told they will be deported, told their parents will be deported, told they should go back where they came from. The words of one prominent, powerful bully have been mimicked and adopted as the rallying cry of bullies everywhere.

Of course, it's not just the children of immigrants who are affected. According to the Migration Policy Institute, for example, at least 20 percent of early childhood educators are immigrants. Immigrants also represent a large percentage of people working in the early child care industry—and those numbers have tripled over the past two decades. These caregivers—primarily women—nurture millions of children each and every day. The risks to their safety and security in this country due to overbroad immigration enforcement are a risk to us all. This cannot be overlooked.

On January 20, 2017, I attended the presidential inauguration, along with fellow members of the United States Congress. My Senate colleagues and I gathered in the Senate chamber and walked, two by two, through the Capitol Building, exiting the West Front onto the inaugural platform, where risers and chairs were arrayed for the ceremony. As we walked to our seats, we were handed plastic ponchos in case of rain. Doug was sitting with his new pals in the spouses' section, closer to the stage than I was. He turned around and gave me a wave.

By some twist of fate, the skies opened up just as the transition of power was complete. Some supporters of the president took the rain as a sign of blessing, but for me and so many others, dark clouds were settling in.

Renewal, it turned out, decided to reveal itself the next day. In the runup to Inauguration Day, activists had planned a Women's March in cities all across the country. But given the organic, decentralized way the march had come together—sparked by a Facebook post from a grandmother in Hawaii the day after the election and organized in a matter of weeks by a diverse group of activists, many of whom had never met before—no one knew exactly how it would unfold.

Reality exceeded all expectations: more than four million people showed up in the streets nationwide, with sister marches in countries around the world.

In Washington, the crowd was so massive that it packed the entire route, end to end—a vibrant sea of pink-hatted people of all ages, races, genders, and orientations. Marchers carried handmade signs that expressed the full range of emotions we all felt, from disbelief to determination, horror, purpose, and hope: IT'S 2017. WTF? . . . STILL I RISE . . . GIRLS JUST WANT TO HAVE FUNDAMENTAL RIGHTS . . . MEN OF QUALITY DON'T FEAR EQUALITY . . . WE THE PEOPLE.

I saw white-haired grandmothers and blue-haired college students; flannel-clad hipsters and down-jacketed soccer moms; toddlers in strollers and teenagers in the trees; men and women in solidarity, side by side. Amazingly, amid the throng, I ran into Aunt Lenore, who engulfed me in a giant bear hug. She told me that her daughter Lilah, who was at the time a leader in the Service Employees International Union (SEIU), was in the crowd as well. They had come out to march together, carrying forward the banner of social justice that Lenore and my mother had held high as students at Berkeley half a century before.

I had been asked to speak, and as I climbed up to the stage, I was overwhelmed by the size and spirit of the crowd stretching out before me as far as I could see. There were so many people that cellular networks had gone down, yet the energy was electric. No one could move, but everyone seemed to understand that the march was a glimpse of a new kind of coalition whose true strength had yet to be tested. "Even if you're not sitting in the White House, even if you are not a member of the United States Congress, even if you don't run a big corporate super PAC, you have the power. And we the people have the power!" I told the marchers. "And there is nothing more powerful than a group of determined sistahs, marching alongside with their partners and their determined sons and brothers and fathers, standing up for what we know is right!"

I talked about women's issues, at least what I see as women's issues: the economy, national security, health care, education, criminal justice reform, climate change. I said that if you are a woman who is an immigrant and you don't want your family torn apart, you know that immigration reform is a women's issue. I said that if you are a woman who is working off student loans, you know that the crushing burden of student debt is a women's issue. I said that if you are a black mother trying to raise a son, you know that Black Lives Matter is a women's issue. "And if you are a woman, period, you know we deserve a country with equal pay and access to health care, including a safe and legal abortion, protected as a fundamental and constitutional right." I affirmed that together we are powerful, and cannot be written off.

A few days later, Doug and I were in our new apartment in DC, eating dinner on stools at our kitchen counter, when breaking news cut across the television. The president had signed an executive order banning travel to the United States from seven Muslim-majority countries—Iraq, Iran, Libya, Somalia, Sudan, Syria, and Yemen—for a period of 90 days. He barred refugees from coming to the United States for 120 days and barred refugees from Syria indefinitely.

Travelers started getting detained at airports, unable to speak with lawyers. Families were panicking as their loved ones failed to emerge from airport security. I received calls from activists and lawyers, including Meena, who had rushed to airports to try to help people who were being detained. There was chaos.

So I called John Kelly. By then he had been confirmed as secretary of homeland security, and I needed to find out what was going on and to make sure that anyone being detained would get access to a lawyer. There were a lot of ways Secretary Kelly could have shown his responsiveness, a lot of information he could have provided. Indeed, the American people had a right to this information, and, given my oversight role on the Senate Homeland Security Committee, I intended to get it. Instead, he said gruffly, "Why are you calling me at home with this?" That was his chief concern.

By the time we got off the phone, it was clear that he didn't understand the depth of what was going on. He said he'd get back to me, but he never did. And by the next day, the nation had erupted in spontaneous protest, knowing full well that the travel ban was really a Muslim ban, and that there were few things more antithetical to our founding ideals. Enshrined in the First Amendment is the notion that not only would America establish no official religion of its own, but the government has no authority to prohibit anyone's activities based on their religion.

I was new to Washington and still learning how things worked. This episode taught me that calling this secretary of homeland security was a wasted effort. We needed a law. The first bill I introduced in the Senate was the Access to Counsel Act, which prohibits federal officials from denying access to a lawyer for anyone detained trying to reach the United States. But we were in an uphill fight, made harder by the political circumstances of the moment.

Four days after the travel ban was executed, Neil Gorsuch was nominated to the Supreme Court to fill a seat that had been open since Antonin Scalia's death almost a year earlier. President Obama had nominated a highly respected United States circuit judge, Merrick Garland, to serve. But in an unprecedented show of partisan obstruction, Republicans refused to hold even one hearing on Garland's nomination. They were rewarded for their recalcitrance. Gorsuch was confirmed by the Senate in April 2017, shifting the balance of power on the Court back toward the conservative justices. Fifteen months later, Justice Gorsuch cast the deciding vote in one of the most shameful decision's in the Court's recent history: the decision to uphold the president's travel ban.

Six

WE ARE BETTER
THAN THIS

On February 16, 2017, I gave my maiden speech on the floor of the United States Senate. It was a humbling experience. In recent years, the Senate has been known largely as a body of gridlock and partisanship. Once revered as the country's most deliberative body, it has often proved to be anything but. And yet as I stood there, it was the giants of the Senate who came to mind, and the extraordinary work that had been done on that very floor. It was here that the New Deal came to life and the economy was saved. It was here that Social Security earned passage and, later, Medicaid and Medicare. The Civil Rights Act, the Voting Rights Act, the War on Poverty—all fought for and won right here in this body. At my Senate desk once sat Eugene McCarthy, who sponsored the Immigration and Nationality Act of 1965, which ended quotas and established rules aimed at reunifying immigrant families.

I opened my speech exactly as those who know me would have expected. "Above all, I rise today with a sense of gratitude for all those upon whose shoulders we stand. For me, it starts with my mother, Shyamala Harris."

I told her immigration story, the story of her self-determination, the story that made Maya and me, and made us Americans. "And I know she's looking down on us today. And, knowing my mother, she's probably saying, 'Kamala, what on earth is going on down there? We have got to stand up for our values!'"

I didn't mince words. I talked about the unprecedented series of executive actions taken in the early weeks of the administration, actions that hit our immigrant and religious communities like a cold front, "striking a chilling fear in the hearts of millions of good, hard-working people."

I talked about the outsize impact on the state of California, because I believe California is a microcosm of who we are as Americans. I explained that we have farmers and environmentalists, welders and technologists, Republicans, Democrats, Independents, and more veterans, and more immigrants—documented and undocumented—than any state in the nation. When it came to DACA, I reiterated what I had said in Kelly's confirmation hearing: that we had promised recipients that we would not use their personal information against them, and that we could not go back on our promise to these kids and their families.

I spoke as a lifelong prosecutor and former attorney general of the largest state in this country when I said that the administration's Muslim ban and immigration actions presented a real and present threat to our public safety. Instead of making us more safe, the increased raids and executive orders instill fear. "For this reason," I said, "studies have shown Latinos are more than 40 percent less likely to call 911 when they have been a victim of a crime. This climate of fear drives people underground and into the shadows, making them less likely to report crimes against themselves or others. Fewer victims reporting crime and fewer witnesses coming forward."

I also talked about the economic consequences, noting that immigrants make up 10 percent of California's workforce and contribute $130 billion to our state's gross domestic product. "Immigrants own small businesses, they till the land, they care for children and the elderly, they work in our labs, attend our universities, and serve in our military. So these actions are not only cruel. They cause ripple effects that harm our public safety and our economy."

I closed my remarks with a call to action: that we have a responsibility to draw a line and say no—that as a coequal branch of government, it is our duty to uphold the ideals of this country.

The next month, I invited a young woman from Fresno who is a University of California at Merced alumna, a biomedical researcher, and a DACA recipient to be my guest at a joint session of Congress. Yuriana Aguilar's parents moved their family from Mexico to Fresno when Yuriana was just five years old. None of them had papers. Her parents were agricultural workers who supported the family by selling vegetables. Still, as Yuriana recalls, "somehow they knew in order to succeed, you have to have an education." Yuriana took her parents' message to heart—literally. Today she works at Rush Medical College, in Chicago, studying how the heart's electrical system functions. DACA made it possible for her to pursue her education and earn a PhD.

Yuriana has described how, when she first heard about the creation of DACA, she cried with relief. Then she went back to her research, doing her part to help others live healthier lives. As she says, "Science

doesn't have borders—there are no limitations on its advancement."
My mother would have loved her.

When we talk about DACA recipients, Yuriana's commitment to
giving back to our country is the rule, not the exception. The vast
majority of DACA recipients are employed—more than 75 percent of
them. They wear our nation's uniform, they study at our colleges and
universities, and they work in U.S. companies large and small. In fact,
if DACA recipients were deported, it is estimated that the U.S. economy as a whole could lose as much as $460 billion over a decade. These
young people are contributing to our country in meaningful ways.

I kept Yuriana top of mind over the course of the drama that
would unfold through the year. She was the first person I thought of
when, on September 5, 2017, Attorney General Jeff Sessions cruelly
and arbitrarily announced that the administration was ending the
DACA program, throwing the fates of hundreds of thousands of people into limbo.

Without DACA, eligible young people who had been brought to
the United States as children are faced with a terrible choice: they can
live here without papers and in fear of deportation or leave the only
country they've ever known. They have no path to citizenship. They
can't leave the country and get in line to immigrate here. There is no
line. And for this administration, that's the point.

Congress can fix this. There is bipartisan legislation in the House
and the Senate that I've co-sponsored—the DREAM Act—which
gives these young people a permanent path to citizenship. Every day
that the DREAM Act goes unpassed is another day they have to live
in fear—despite having done everything we asked them to.

I've met many Dreamers over the years, and on a nearly daily basis
throughout my first year in the U.S. Senate. They bravely came to

Washington to meet with members of Congress and tell their stories. There was one day when I was supposed to meet with five Dreamers from California who were in town as part of a group from all over the country. The others wanted to join, too, so I invited them into my conference room. It was packed, standing room only, with people lined up against the walls.

I was struck by one of the California kids, Sergio, who was a student at the University of California at Irvine. He talked about his mother working in Mexico, unable to make ends meet, and the decision she had made to come to the United States to give him a chance at a better life. He talked about how hard he had worked through school and how he had focused a lot of his energy on doing outreach to help people get health care. Like so many Dreamers, he was taking on a life of service. That's the thing about the Dreamers: they really do believe in the promise of this country. It is their country, too.

There was so much passion in Sergio's eyes. But I knew he was also frightened. The administration's decision to end DACA had been so dispiriting and demoralizing, so counter to the better history of our country, so counter to the promise of opportunity on which he had relied. And as he and most of them searched my eyes, looking for confidence that they would be okay, I fought the pain of knowing how wrong and unfair the situation was, and that I could not, on my own, control the outcome. It pains me still today.

Three days after Sessions announced his actions, the University of California filed suit against the administration "for wrongly and unconstitutionally violating the rights of the University and its students" by rescinding the DACA program on "nothing more than unreasoned executive whim." The president of the University of California system, Janet Napolitano, had served as President Obama's homeland security secretary and had been responsible for drafting and overseeing the DACA program as originally conceived. For her, and for all of us, this was personal.

On January 10, 2018, the federal court sided with the university, issuing a temporary nationwide injunction blocking the government's decision. This was a huge relief, as it restarted the DACA program and halted the administration action. But the operative word is "temporary." Congress must still act to provide these young people with permanent protection from deportation, which can come only through legislation. Until then, Dreamers will remain in constant fear that a new court decision could rip them away from their families and the only country they've called home. And with a solid conservative majority on the Supreme Court, there's every reason to believe that such a reversal could be forthcoming.

February 2018 was a pivotal month in the immigration fight. The administration continued its cruel and outrageous conduct, going so far as to remove a reference to the United States as "a nation of immigrants" from the mission statement of the agency responsible for citizenship and immigration services. Meanwhile, the administration and many congressional Republicans effectively held the Dreamers hostage.

As part of the budget bill debates to fund the government, the Senate had agreed to take a vote on the DREAM Act, which would create a path to citizenship for the Dreamers. But there was a catch. In exchange, the legislation included $25 billion in taxpayer money to build a wall on the border with Mexico.

There were a number of reasons why I opposed this. Purely from a dollars-and-cents perspective, it was a total waste of taxpayer money.

I am a strong believer in border security—but experts agree that a wall will not secure our border. Moreover, I worried that those billions of dollars would be used to implement the administration's anti-immigrant agenda—including raids that target California and its residents, and families across the country. For the same price tag, we could do anything from funding a full-scale effort to combat the opioid crisis to expanding rural broadband and upgrading critical infrastructure.

But there was a bigger reason to oppose the border wall. A useless wall on the southern border would be nothing more than a symbol, a monument standing in opposition to not just everything I value, but to the fundamental values upon which this country was built. The Statue of Liberty is the monument that defines to the world who we are. Emma Lazarus's words—"Give me your tired, your poor, your huddled masses yearning to breathe free"—speak to our true character: a generous country that respects and embraces those who have made the difficult journey to our shores, often fleeing harm; that sees our quintessentially optimistic, can-do spirit in those who aspire to make the American Dream their own. How could I vote to build what would be little more than a monument, designed to send the cold, hard message "KEEP OUT"?

The immigration debate is so often defined by false choices. I remember a town hall I held in Sacramento, where a group of the president's supporters showed up. One man said he thought I cared more about undocumented immigrants than I cared about the American people. It was a false choice. I care deeply about them both. Similarly, the budget debate was offering a false choice: fund the government or oppose the wall. I believed we could do both.

In the end, we were presented with two bills. I was proud to support the first, a bipartisan compromise drafted by Senators Chris Coons, a Democrat from Delaware, and the late John McCain, a Republican from Arizona, which included measures to protect Dreamers from deportation and provide them with a path to citizenship, and did not include funding for the wall. The other proposal—which included the DREAM Act in exchange for the wall—was something I simply couldn't get behind, regardless of the pressure. I voted against it. Ultimately, neither of the bills became law.

The fight on behalf of Dreamers continues. And here's what I believe: These young people were brought into our country, in many cases before they could walk or talk, through no choice of their own. This is the only country they've ever known. This is their home, and they're contributing. So I won't let up until they are recognized as the Americans they are.

There's a region in Central America known as the Northern Triangle, which includes three countries: El Salvador, Guatemala, and Honduras. Together these countries have the menacing distinction of being among the most violent in the world. Between 1979 and 1992, El Salvador was undone by civil war that left as many as 75,000 dead. Between 1960 and 1996, Guatemala's civil war resulted in the deaths of 200,000 civilians. Honduras didn't have a civil war of its own, but the violence in neighboring countries bled across its borders and made it, too, one of the world's most dangerous places to live.

Even after the wars ended, the violence didn't. A broken economy with deep poverty and few jobs, awash in weapons and generational destruction, led to the formation of organized criminal organizations that used murder, rape, and other sexual violence to control territory and take over large swaths of the region. In the years since, more people have been killed and kidnapped in the Northern Triangle than in some of the world's most brutal wars. Between 2011 and 2014, nearly fifty thousand people were murdered in the Northern Triangle, and just 5 percent of the deaths resulted in judicial convictions.

For residents of these countries, life is often defined by terror. Gang violence, drug trafficking, and corruption are rampant. The largest and most notorious of these transnational criminal organizations, MS-13 and the Mara 18, are reported to include as many as 85,000 members worldwide. They extort small business owners and residents in poor neighborhoods into paying hundreds of millions of dollars each and every year. Those who don't pay risk death, for them and their families. The gangs recruit young men to join their ranks through threats and intimidation, and they force teenage girls to endure sexual violence as so-called gang girlfriends.

Indeed, for women and girls in these countries, violence is systemic. In July 2014, the UN Special Rapporteur on Violence Against Women reported that violent deaths of women in Honduras had risen by 263.4 percent between 2005 and 2013. There are stories of children being robbed, raped, murdered—including an eleven-year-old girl in Honduras whose killers slashed her throat and stuffed her underwear in it. If there was a ground zero for brutality and bleakness, the Northern Triangle would be it.

The only option is escape. And so hundreds of thousands of people have fled the region into neighboring countries and up through Mexico to the United States. In the past, we have welcomed asylum seekers in accordance with international law, granting them special protected status because of the severity of the hardships they face. Sometimes they come as families. But all too often, the journey is impossible to afford, leaving parents with an excruciating choice: Do they keep their children close but in the midst of mortal peril, or do they send them to the United States, knowing that if they survive the perilous journey they will have a chance to be safe and free?

In the summer of 2014, an unprecedented surge of tens of thousands of children and adolescents fled the violence of the Northern Triangle through human smuggling networks that brought them to the United States.

I was attorney general at the time, sitting at home watching the evening news, when I saw an image that struck a chord. In Murrieta, California—a town roughly halfway between Los Angeles and San Diego—several buses carrying roughly 140 undocumented children and parents were on their way to a processing center. A crowd had gathered, blocking the street, waving flags and signs and yelling, "Nobody wants you!" "You're not welcome!" "Turn around and go back home!" There were children inside the buses, looking out of their windows at faces filled with hate and vitriol. Their only wrong was that they had fled horrific violence.

And it wasn't just the protesters in the streets. At the same time, a big push was coming out of DC to expedite the decision-making process so that they could quickly turn undocumented kids and families back. The aim was to assess and reach asylum decisions in about two weeks. Now, to be clear, the process requires someone to make a decision about whether the asylum seeker was fleeing real harm. That means that children have to share facts and tell their story in a comprehensive way.

I knew, having prosecuted child sexual assault, that in these types of cases, it takes a long time to earn a child's trust, and for a child to be able to tell his or her story in a court of law. What was worse, I learned that these asylum-seeking kids had no right to a lawyer to guide them through the process. And that mattered a great deal. If you don't have a lawyer, there's about a 90 percent chance that you will lose your asylum case. If you have legal advice, there's about a 50 percent chance you will prevail. Given that deportation would take these children back into the heart of danger, whether or not they had a lawyer was a matter of life and death.

I had to do something about this, and I knew there wasn't any time to waste. So I personally got on the phone with managing partners of some of the most prestigious law firms in California, as well as corporate lawyers from big entertainment companies like Walt Disney and Warner Bros. Entertainment, and asked them to come to my office to help me make sure these children, some as young as eight years old, had lawyers, and thus had access to due process. Representatives from dozens of law firms convened in the conference room of my downtown Los Angeles office, and I took on the role of auctioneer.

"Okay, can I get five hundred hours of pro bono from you? How about you? And you? What about your firm? What can you guys do for us?" Soon after, we held a similar meeting in Northern California, where I did the same. We rallied the private lawyers to work through one of the community agencies that was offering legal services to help unaccompanied kids. Then I sponsored legislation to provide $3 million to other nonprofits that were providing these children with legal representation.

This was my first experience with the crisis in the Northern

Triangle and the consequences it had wrought on children and families. But it wouldn't be the last.

In January 2017, one of the new administration's first orders of business was signing an executive order that revoked the temporary protected status of immigrants from the Northern Triangle. As a result, some 350,000 immigrants are in the process of losing their right to live and work in the United States. The administration also ordered a change in the way asylum cases are considered, making it more difficult for immigrants to establish a legal basis for staying in the United States. Between February and June 2017, the number of applicants found to be eligible for asylum dropped by 10 percent.

In March 2017, Secretary Kelly went on CNN, where he was asked about a report that, in order to deter more people from the Northern Triangle from coming to the United States, he was actively considering the possibility of forcibly separating parents from their children at the border. "I would do almost anything to deter the people from Central America from getting on this very, very dangerous network that brings them up through Mexico into the United States," he said, confirming that it was under consideration.

Shortly thereafter, Elaine Duke, the deputy secretary of homeland security, appeared before the Homeland Security Committee. "Do you know when this is supposed to take effect?" I asked her, trying to gauge the likelihood that something so atrocious could be under way.

"It is not a decision," she said. "The Secretary—I talked to him personally about it. He considers it still a possibility. They are looking at a wide range of deterrents, and it was raised as a possible method of deterrence but there is no decision made and there is no implementation plan currently."

It was an unacceptable answer. The next month, when Kelly appeared before the committee, I grilled him on the issue. He was evasive about whether this policy was under consideration, but he refused to rule it out.

"So are you unwilling, sir, to issue a written directive that it is the policy of this department to not separate children from their mothers unless the life of the child is in danger?"

"I don't need to do that."

I continued to press for answers through the end of 2017 and into 2018, but DHS was not forthcoming. Then, on April 6, 2018, Attorney General Sessions announced a zero-tolerance policy at the border, meaning that the administration would refer for criminal prosecution any adult crossing the border illegally, regardless of the reason, and that this could include separating children from their parents. We learned through a *New York Times* report several days later that, despite DHS's insistence that there was no separation policy, seven hundred children had been separated from their parents since the previous October, including one hundred who were under the age of four.

There are few things more cruel, more inhumane, more fundamentally evil than ripping a child from her parent's arms. We should all know this to be true on a gut level. But if we needed more proof, we could look at a statement released by Dr. Colleen Kraft, president of the American Academy of Pediatrics, on behalf of the organization, stating that she was appalled by the new policy. Dr. Kraft wrote about the extraordinary stress and trauma of family separation, which "can cause irreparable harm, disrupting a child's brain architecture and affecting his or her short- and long-term health." These findings are shared by the American Medical Association, which has called for an end to the policy, noting that the children the U.S. government is forcibly separating from their parents may be scarred for life.

The administration claimed that it wouldn't separate families seeking asylum if they arrived at an official port of entry, as opposed to other parts of the border. But that didn't hold true. There were reports of a six-year-old girl from the Democratic Republic of Congo who was taken from her mother when they arrived at the San Diego port of entry seeking asylum, even though the mother was able to establish a credible fear of persecution. This was just one of many documented cases of family separation at ports of entry. A blind six-year-old was taken from her mother. So was an eighteen-month-old. This wasn't just a tragedy; it was a violation of international law. It was a human rights abuse. And the toll it took was not just on the children. After a man from Honduras was separated from his wife, after his three-year-old son was ripped from his arms, after he was placed in an isolation cell, the trauma led him to take his own life.

On May 15, Kirstjen Nielsen, who had been confirmed as homeland security secretary after Kelly was named White House chief of staff, came before our committee. I told her that I was extremely concerned about the administration's repeated attacks on some of the most vulnerable communities, children and pregnant women in particular, as enforced by DHS. I pointed to the DACA program, to the separation of children at the border, and to an agency directive that allows for more detentions of pregnant women. I expressed concern about a new information-sharing system between the Office of Refugee Resettlement and ICE that is likely to have a chilling effect on sponsors who otherwise would be willing to come forward to provide care for unaccompanied minors, because of fear that doing so would lead to their own deportation.

I also noted that the previous week, *The Washington Post* had reported that Nielsen was considering undermining an agreement that ensures standards of care for immigrant children, such as the provision of meals and recreation, and calls for them to be placed in the least restrictive setting possible.

I told her that the administration had routinely provided misleading information to the committee and had even gone so far as to claim that policies many consider to be cruel, such as routinely separating families, are carried out in the best interest of the child.

"So my question to you is, last Thursday, *The New York Times* reported that the president has directed you to separate parents from children when they cross into the United States as a way to deter illegal immigrants, is that correct? Have you been directed to separate parents from children as a method of deterrence of undocumented immigration?"

"I have not been directed to do that for purposes of deterrence, no."

"What purpose have you been given for separating parents from their children?"

"So my decision has been that anyone who breaks the law will be prosecuted. If you're a parent or you're a single person or you happen to have a family, if you cross between the ports of entry we will refer you for prosecution. You have broken U.S. law."

Again I pressed. "So your agency will be separating children from their parents—"

"No, what we'll be doing is prosecuting parents who have broken the law, just as we do every day in the United States of America."

"But if that parent has a four-year-old child, what do you plan on doing with that child?"

"The child, under law, goes to HHS for care and custody."

"They will be separated from their parent. And so my question—"

"Just like we do in the United States every day."

"So they will be separated from their parent, and my question then is when you are separating children from their parents, do you have a protocol in place about how that should be done and are you training the people who will actually remove a child from their parent on how to do that in the least traumatic way? I would hope you do train on how to do that, and so the question is, and the request has been, to give us the information about how you are training and what the protocols are for separating a child from their parent."

"I'm happy to provide you with the training information," she said, though she never did. Once again, Nielsen made the false claim that she had stuck with through the entire process: "Again, we do not have a policy to separate children from their parents," she said. "Our policy is if you break the law, we will prosecute you. You have an option to go to a port of entry and not illegally cross into our country."

Let's call this what it is. The White House and DHS were using children—babies—as pawns in a profoundly misguided and inhumane policy to deter immigration. Attorney General Sessions admitted as much—proudly, it appeared, while quoting scripture to justify the abuse:

"Persons who violate the law of our nation are subject to prosecution. I would cite you to the Apostle Paul and his clear and wise command in Romans 13 to obey the laws of the government because God has ordained them for purpose and order," he said, seemingly forgetting or omitting all of the teachings of Christ in the process.

For an added dose of cruelty, Sessions got rid of the right of women and children to seek asylum because of domestic abuse.

I often describe the balance of our democracy as resting on four legs: three independent, coequal branches of government and a free,

independent press. As this horror unfolded, the press worked tire-
lessly to safeguard our true values. Crews of reporters went down to
our southern border, filming, filing, and reporting in real time, showing Americans what was really going on, bringing the crisis into our
living rooms. The vivid daily coverage informed and inspired a public
outcry that eventually forced the administration to backtrack, at least
temporarily.

On June 20, 2018, the president signed an executive order that
ended its family separation practice. But that did not put an end to
the story. Rather than separating families, the new administration
policy was to hold those families indefinitely behind bars. As of this
writing, jailing innocent children remains the policy of the United
States. Children remain separated from their parents. And in the aftermath of the executive order, we were still greeted with headlines
like this one, from *The Texas Tribune:* "Immigrant Toddlers Ordered
to Appear in Court Alone."

On a hot, dry day at the end of June, I visited the Otay Mesa
Detention Center, not far from the border between California and
Mexico. I've seen many prisons. Otay Mesa was identical in appearance. To get in the facility, which is surrounded by chain-link fences
and barbed wire, you have to pass through multiple checkpoints. One
gate opens, you stand in the middle area, and then it shuts behind
you before another opens ahead. For anyone detained there, it sends
a strong signal that you are locked away from the world.

Once inside the building, I met with mothers who'd been separated from their children. They were wearing blue jumpsuits with the
word DETAINEE in block letters on their backs. I asked the facility
staff to give us some privacy. They stood about twenty yards away

while I asked the mothers about their experiences and came to understand the deep trauma they had endured.

Olga told me that she hadn't seen her four children—ages seventeen, sixteen, twelve, and eight—in nearly two months and that she
wasn't even sure where they were. She had fled domestic violence in
Honduras, taking a flight to Mexico. She stopped at the Tapachula
shelter, in Mexico, where she learned that there was a caravan helping
asylum seekers get to the United States. It wasn't going to cost her any
money, and it was going to drop her off in Tijuana just south of the
border. They provided her and her family with food on the journey
and offered to help her with the process of seeking asylum. She said
she traveled by airline, train, and bus and at some points walked,
though she was often able to hitchhike. People along the way had
wanted to help.

When she arrived in Tijuana, she and her family were taken to
churches and shelters, and eventually presented themselves to the
U.S. Border Patrol. They were led to a holding cell and told to wait to
be processed. That was when her children were taken from her, with
no warning or explanation. She pleaded with the Border Patrol agents
to tell her where her children had been taken. She presented their
birth certificates. She needed answers. Desperately. But no answers
were given. All she knew was that her three girls were being held together while her son was all by himself. Eventually a social worker
was able to connect her by phone to her kids, who weren't sure exactly
where they were. She had come to believe that they were all in New
York City, and though they said they were okay, it was hard to imagine that could be true.

Another woman from Honduras had a similar story. She, too, had fled the country because she was being abused, and she had brought her eight-year-old son, Mauro, with her. Her son was also taken from her cell with no explanation. The deportation officers told her that he was in Los Angeles, but even they weren't sure. She had brought him with her because she thought he would be safe in the United States. But now that hope seemed lost.

The Department of Homeland Security had said that families seeking asylum at ports of entry would not be separated from one another. But when another woman at Otay Mesa, Morena, left El Salvador and presented herself with her two boys—ages twelve and five—at the San Ysidro Land Port of Entry processing center, her children were ripped away from her. She pleaded with the agents not to take her kids, but to no avail. She had to wait fifteen days to call her sons, because detainees were charged eighty-five cents per minute for calls and she didn't have any money. She had to earn some by working at the facility. Morena had worked for seven days straight and was paid only four dollars. Olga had worked for twelve days and was also paid just four dollars. They said that when they tried to report abuse, they were yelled at. They told me they'd received a lot of verbal abuse from the officers, and had been forced to work late at night after long days of waiting for their hearings.

Six weeks had passed and Morena was still unable to get in touch with her children. She called the facility where she was told they'd been taken, but the phone just kept ringing, with no answer. She told me that the only time they were allowed to make phone calls was when their kids were in class and unavailable. Morena said she was finding it hard to eat because she was so distraught over not seeing or speaking to her children in such a long time.

When I spoke with the guards at the detention center, I had a lot of questions, and the answers didn't add up. They told me, for example, that videoconferencing with kids was a service they offered that was available anytime and for free. They assured me that phone calls were free, too. But when I asked the mothers if they knew this, they immediately said no. They didn't even know that videoconferencing was available. And when I returned to Washington and took part in a Judiciary Committee hearing with Matthew Albence, executive associate director of enforcement and removal operations at ICE, our exchange on this topic was revealing.

I told Albence how, during my visit to Otay Mesa, I'd learned from the parents being detained that when they were performing labor, such as cleaning toilets or doing laundry, they were paid one dollar a day. "Are you familiar with that policy? Or practice?" I asked.

"Many of the individuals that are in ICE custody are eligible to apply and work in a voluntary work program," Albence replied. "It's not mandatory; it's voluntary if they choose to do so. Many do choose to do so, just to pass the time, while they're awaiting their hearing or their removal—"

"Do you think that people voluntarily choose to clean toilets to pass their time? Is that what you're saying?"

"I can say that we have a large number of individuals within our custody that volunteer to work in the work program."

"To clean toilets? Sir, is that what you're saying?"

"I don't know every task that these individuals are assigned, but again, it's voluntary."

Voluntary? I don't think so.

The most shocking answer I got during my time at Otay Mesa was when I asked the detention facility staff the question many people had asked me: "Who is responsible for leading the process to reunite these families?" They looked around at one another blankly for a few seconds, until one (who was apparently more senior than the others) answered, "That would be me." He then admitted that he had no idea what the plan was or the status of any reunification efforts.

We would later learn that federal records linking parents and children had disappeared. In some cases, for unfathomable reasons, records had actually been destroyed. When a federal court ruled that families had to be reunited within thirty days, government officials had to resort to DNA tests to try to figure out which children belonged with which family.

Before I left the detention facility, I reassured the mothers that they weren't alone—that there were so many people standing with them and fighting for them, and that I would do everything in my power to help them. As I walked down the long driveway toward the exit, I saw that solidarity personified. Hundreds of people had gathered outside the fence, holding vigil in support of the families. People of all ages and backgrounds—children, students, parents, and grandparents—had traveled to Otay Mesa because they shared the anguish and the heartbreak of the mothers inside.

I joined the throng of supporters, many of whom were carrying signs. ESTAMOS CON USTEDES . . . FAMILIES BELONG TOGETHER . . . WE WON'T BACK DOWN. Beneath the blazing summer sun, I told the press what I had seen.

"These mothers have given their testimony, if you will, have shared their stories, and they are personal stories of a human rights abuse being committed by the United States government. And we are so much better than this, and we have got to fight against this. This is contrary to all of the principles that we hold dear and that give us a sense of who we are when we are proud to be Americans. But we have no reason to be proud of this."

These mothers had made the dangerous journey to America with their children because they knew that the danger of staying in their home country was even worse. They have the legal right to seek asylum, but when they arrive, we call them criminals. We treat them like criminals. That is not the sign of a civil society, nor is it a sign of compassion. The United States government has brought great shame to the American people.

The values at stake here are so much bigger than an immigration debate.

Nothing makes a child feel more secure than being tucked in by a parent at the end of a day, getting a kiss and a hug, a good-night story, falling asleep to the sound of their voice. Nothing is more important to a parent than talking with their child at night before the child goes to sleep, answering their questions, comforting and reassuring them in the face of any fears, making sure they know that everything will be okay. Parents and children everywhere relate to these rituals. They are part of the human experience.

As family reunification began, we heard horrific stories that showed us just how shameful this administration's actions have been. The *Los Angeles Times* reported on a three-year-old boy who was separated from his father at the border. "At night, Andriy sometimes wakes up screaming in the bunk bed he shares with his mother and baby brother." We saw video of six-year-old Jefferson reunited with his father after nearly two months of separation. The child's body was covered in a rash; his face was bruised; his eyes were vacant. His father cried, enveloping the boy in a hug. Jefferson was stiff and expressionless. We also learned, through *PBS NewsHour,* of a fourteen-month-old who was returned to his parents, after eighty-five days, covered in lice, apparently having not been bathed. It is hard to imagine anything crueler than such blatant state-sponsored child abuse.

A mother who was separated from her children said that she had been kept in a cell with nearly fifty other mothers. She recounted that officers told them they weren't allowed to eat because they were asking about their children. A pregnant woman fainted out of hunger. She said of the separated children that they had no shoes or blankets in the detention center and that there were people in the cells who had to sleep on their feet. The children were demeaned, she said, called "animals" and "donkeys." These are surely just the examples we know, representative of horrors in the thousands that we may never hear of. These children, ripped away from their parents, will suffer lifelong trauma because of the actions of this administration. This behavior is not just immoral; it is inhuman. And I've introduced a bill in the Senate to put body cameras on immigration agents so we can deter such bad behavior and create transparency and accountability.

A society is judged by the way it treats its children—and history will judge us harshly for this. Most Americans know that already. Most Americans are appalled and ashamed. We are better than this. And we must make right the wrongs that this administration has committed in our name.

Seven

EVERY BODY

How are you adjusting?" I asked.

"So far so good," Maya replied. "But we haven't had a winter yet."

It was 2008, and Maya was visiting from New York, where she had recently taken a job as vice president of democracy, rights, and justice at the Ford Foundation. We had lived in different cities before, but for many years our homes were never more than a short car ride away from each other. Now she was almost three thousand miles away. I was adjusting, too.

We were in a restaurant, waiting for our mother, who had asked us to meet her for lunch. All three of us were excited to be back in the same city, even for a brief time. We'd come a long way from the Berkeley flatlands, but we were still Shyamala and the girls.

"The foundation is doing amazing things," she said. "And I'm going to be—"

Maya stopped talking midsentence. She was looking over my shoulder. I turned around. Our mother had just walked in. Mommy—the least vain person I knew—looked like she was ready for a photo shoot. She was dressed in bright silk, clearly wearing makeup (which she never did), her hair professionally blown out. My sister and I exchanged a glance.

"What's going on?" I mouthed to Maya as our mother approached our table. She raised an eyebrow and shrugged. She was just as confused as I was.

We hugged and greeted one another, and our mother sat down. A waiter brought us a basket of bread. We reviewed our menus and ordered our food, making lighthearted conversation.

And then my mother took a deep breath and reached out to us both across the table.

"I've been diagnosed with colon cancer," she said.

Cancer. My mother. Please, no.

I know that many of you can relate to the emotions I felt in that moment. Even just reflecting back on it now, it fills me with anxiety and dread. It was one of the worst days of my life.

And the hard truth of life is that every one of us will go through an experience like this sooner or later, whether it is coming to terms with a loved one's mortal illness or experiencing our own. As my mother herself understood so well from a lifetime of looking at cancer cells under the microscope, no matter who we are or where we are from, our bodies are essentially the same. They work the same way—and they break down the same way, too. No one gets a pass. At some point, nearly all of us will face a prognosis that requires profound interaction with the health care system.

So much comes with this realization: pain, worry, depression, fear.

And it is all made worse by the fact that America's health care system is broken. The United States spends more on health care than any other advanced economy, but we don't see better outcomes in exchange. Incredibly, in many parts of the country, life expectancy is actually shrinking, and when it comes to maternal mortality, the United States is one of only thirteen countries where rates have gotten worse over the past twenty-five years. Meanwhile, working families are overwhelmed by medical bills, which are one of America's leading causes of personal bankruptcy.

I want to be clear that I have tremendous respect for the women and men in the medical profession. For so many of them, the call to medicine stems from a deep desire to help others—from helping a baby come into the world to extending the time that person has on earth. But in our nation's approach to health care, we've created a bizarre dichotomy: we are simultaneously home to the most sophisticated medical institutions in the world and to structural dysfunction that deprives millions of Americans of equal access to health care, a basic human right.

Unlike many other wealthy nations, the United States does not provide universal health care for our citizens. Instead, Americans need some form of private health insurance to cover the costs of their care, unless they are senior citizens, severely disabled, or lower income, making them eligible for Medicare or Medicaid. Generally speaking, private insurance is employer based, and the breadth and depth of coverage varies, as does the portion of the insurance premium that the employee is expected to pay. For years, those premiums have been going up—and doing so much faster than wages. A system where access to health care depends on how much you make has created enormous disparities. A 2016 study found a ten-year gap in life expectancy in America between the most affluent women and the poorest. That means that being poor reduces your life expectancy more than a lifetime of smoking cigarettes.

The Affordable Care Act (ACA), aka Obamacare, went a long way toward making health insurance more accessible and affordable, offering tax credits to those who can't cover their premiums and expanding Medicaid to cover millions of people. But after it passed, Republican leaders made it an intense partisan issue and worked to sabotage, strip, and subvert it; indeed, the Senate leader openly declared that it should be repealed "root and branch." Their arguments ranged from comparing the Affordable Care Act to colonial taxation by King George III to suggesting that the president might somehow, someday decree that the government would pay for only one baby to be born in a hospital per family. But for all their posturing and falsehoods, the GOP hadn't bothered to devise a serious alternative. They were playing politics with people's lives—and they still are.

There have been more than a hundred lawsuits challenging the ACA since its passage. Republican governors blocked seventeen states from expanding Medicaid, leaving millions in places like Florida, Texas, Missouri, and Maine without affordable coverage. In numerous states, Republican lawmakers have passed laws restricting the ability of health care officials to help people enroll in insurance plans, despite a law that provides funding for that explicit purpose.

In 2017, the first executive order from the new administration ordered federal agencies to "exercise all authority and discretion available to them to waive, defer, grant exemptions from, or delay the implementation of any provision or requirement of the [Affordable Care] Act that would impose a fiscal burden." The administration halted ACA cost-sharing payments that would have provided more affordable health insurance for middle-class families and individuals and even canceled an advertising campaign to alert people about the 2017 open enrollment period, going so far as to pull ads that were already fully paid for. The result of these efforts has been deep uncertainty and instability in the insurance markets, which has resulted in soaring premiums, forcing people all over the country to give up their health insurance altogether.

And this was on top of the efforts of congressional Republicans to fully repeal the ACA—more than fifty times. In July 2017, their push to end Obamacare was thwarted by just three votes—but they will surely try again. Repealing the ACA would result in tens of millions of people losing their health insurance. It would allow insurance companies to reinstate lifetime limits, driving countless Americans into bankruptcy, and permit insurance companies to once again deny coverage based on preexisting conditions, from asthma to high blood pressure, diabetes to cancer. We all remember what that was like. We know we can't go back.

In early 2011, just after I was elected attorney general of California, I went in to see my dentist for a checkup. The dental hygienist, Chrystal, and I knew each other from past visits, and it had been awhile since I'd seen her. Chrystal asked me how I'd been. I told her I'd been elected. I asked her how she'd been. She told me she was pregnant. It was great news.

As a dental hygienist, she was working for a few different dentists but wasn't considered a full-time employee of any of them. This was before the ACA was in place, so Chrystal was on private insurance with only basic coverage—just enough to cover her annual exams. When Chrystal found out she was pregnant, she went to her insurance company to apply for prenatal coverage.

But she was denied. They told her she had a preexisting condition.

I was alarmed. "You okay? What's wrong?" I asked. "What's the preexisting condition?" And she told me it was that she was pregnant. That was why the insurer had turned her down. When she applied to another health care company for insurance, again she was denied. Why? Preexisting condition. What was it? She was pregnant. I couldn't believe what I was hearing.

This young woman was forced to go into her sixth month of pregnancy before she received a sonogram. Thankfully, there was a free clinic in San Francisco where she could get her prenatal care. Thank God Chrystal had a strong and beautiful baby named Jaxxen and they're both doing well today.

But think about that for a minute. This is the world we could return to if they abolish the ACA: women denied health care coverage for perpetuating the species. Let's remember the words of Mark Twain: "What, sir, would the people of the earth be without women? They would be scarce, sir, almighty scarce."

The Affordable Care Act provided a lot of relief. But there are still structural realities that make health care too costly for working families. As anyone who's been to the doctor knows, in addition to premiums, there are also deductibles and co-payments for prescription drugs and health care services to worry about, which could end up costing thousands of dollars out of pocket.

Compared with people in other wealthy countries, Americans face extraordinarily high prescription drug prices. In 2016, for example, the same dose of Crestor, a medication that treats high cholesterol, cost 62 percent more in the United States than just across the border in Canada. This disparity exists with drug after drug. Fifty-eight percent of Americans take prescription drugs; one in four take four or more; and among those currently taking prescription drugs, one in four find their medications difficult to afford.

Why are Americans paying so much more for the medicines we need? Because, unlike many other advanced countries, the U.S. government doesn't negotiate prices on prescription drugs. When a government is purchasing medicines in bulk, it can negotiate a better price and pass those cost savings to consumers—much like the cost savings you enjoy at a wholesale grocery like Costco. But the current U.S. health care system doesn't allow for such deal making.

Medicare, which covers about fifty-five million people, could have incredible bargaining power to drive significantly lower prescription prices through negotiation. But lawmakers from both parties, at the behest of the pharmaceutical lobby, have prohibited Medicare from doing so. Individual health insurance plans are allowed to negotiate, but with their relatively small numbers of enrollees, they have little leverage to make a dent in prices.

The alternative to negotiating lower prices ourselves is to import cheaper drugs from countries that do. Imagine, for example, that you need Crestor. What if you could buy it from Canada at a significant discount? One of my very first votes in Congress would have enabled just that by allowing Americans to purchase drugs from our northern neighbor. The amendment I voted for earned significant bipartisan support, but the powerful pharmaceutical lobby helped kill it in its tracks.

Pharmaceutical companies have wielded influence over Congress for years, and their power is intensifying. A report by Citizens for Responsibility and Ethics in Washington (CREW) found 153 companies and organizations lobbying in the area of drug pricing in 2017, a number that had quadrupled over the previous five years. In 2016, fearing that Congress might actually do something to get drug prices under control, PhRMA, the trade association that represents the largest drugmakers, increased its membership dues by 50 percent so it could raise $100 million more with which to fight. It should come as no surprise that over the past decade, pharmaceutical companies have spent about $2.5 billion on lobbying. Imagine the new drug trials they could have funded instead.

These efforts have also helped prop up a system by which pharmaceutical companies can quash competition from generic brands, preventing more affordable versions of a medication from reaching the market for years. And in the meantime, they continue to raise prices without any compunction.

Take pharmaceutical manufacturer Mylan. Mylan raised the price of the EpiPen—a lifesaving treatment for anaphylactic shock—by nearly 500 percent over seven years. Between October 2013 and April 2014, the company increased the price of Pravastatin, a statin that helps reduce cholesterol and prevent heart disease, by 573 percent. During that same period, Mylan jacked the price of Albuterol, a common treatment for asthma, from $11 to $434. You don't need to be a prosecutor to see something wrong with a 4,000 percent price hike.

Prescription medicines are not luxury goods. Quite the opposite. We don't want to need them! No one aspires to be allergic to peanuts, or to suffer from heart disease or asthma. I'll always remember the terror I felt when Meena had a childhood asthma attack so bad that Maya had to call 911. It's heartless and wrong for companies to make a fortune by exploiting the fact that their customers literally cannot live without their products.

At the same time that pharmaceutical companies are dramatically raising their prices, they are also cutting down on the amount they spend on research and development of new drug treatments. In January 2018, for example, Pfizer announced that it would no longer participate in neuroscience research, meaning an end to its work on Alzheimer's disease and Parkinson's disease, which together affect tens of millions of people around the world.

Too many of our fellow Americans are getting crushed under the weight of high drug prices—having to choose between taking the medications they need and buying other essentials like food. And that's not to mention the financial peril they face if they go to the emergency room.

Over the course of six months, *Vox* investigated more than 1,400 emergency room bills and found a series of troubling anecdotes about patients blindsided by outrageous fees. In one example, parents brought their baby to the ER after he fell and hit his head. There wasn't any blood, but the parents were worried, so they had an ambulance take him to the hospital. The doctors determined that the baby was fine. He was given a bottle of formula and discharged less than four hours after he'd arrived. When the bill came, the parents found out they owed the hospital nearly $19,000. In another case, a woman broke her ankle and had emergency surgery. Despite the fact that she had medical coverage, her insurance company decided that the hospital had charged too much money. Instead of paying in full, they passed $31,250 in fees on to her. In still another case, a patient in a motorcycle accident actually confirmed on the phone, before going into surgery, that the hospital he'd been taken to was in his insurance company's network. But the surgeon who operated on him wasn't. As a result, he was expected to pay $7,294.

And what if you are one of the more than forty-three million Americans who require mental health care at some point during the year? Even if you have insurance, it is extremely difficult to find mental health care providers who will take it. Almost half of psychiatrists don't take insurance. On the whole, mental health care providers have no incentive to sign a contract to join an insurance company's network because they are reimbursed at such low rates. As a result, if you need mental health treatment, you are likely to have to go out of network. And because continuous care is incredibly expensive, people tend to forgo it altogether. Depression is increasing in the United States, especially among young people. But more and more, it's only people who can pay out of pocket who can access the care they need.

The problem with mental health care isn't just cost. It's also a general lack of qualified providers. According to the Department of Health and Human Services, the United States will need to add 10,000 mental health care providers by 2025 just to meet the expected demand. And when you focus on the problem on a regional level, the challenge is even greater. Alabama has only 1 mental health professional for every 1,260 people; Texas, just 1 per every 1,070 people; West Virginia, 1 per every 950 people. A report from New American Economy found that roughly 60 percent of America's counties lack a single psychiatrist. In rural counties, home to 27 million people, there are only 590 psychiatrists—that's 1 for every 45,762 people.

Even in Maine, the state with the best access to mental health care, 41.4 percent of adults with mental illness do not receive treatment. Think about that for a minute. Imagine if, in your hometown, four out of every ten broken legs went unaddressed, four out of every ten infections went untreated, four out of every ten heart attacks were ignored. We would say, "That's unacceptable!"—and rightly so. It's

Even though my opponent in the 2010 attorney general race declared victory on election night, we knew that it was too close to call. We huddled around computers and checked tallies through the night. It took twenty-one days for all the ballots to be counted and for me to be declared the winner. Every vote counts! From left to right: Justin Erlich, Dereck Johnson, Tony West, me, Meena, Maya, Ace Smith, and Brian Brokaw.

California Supreme Court Justice Tani Cantil-Sakauye swears me in at the Women's Museum in Sacramento. Maya is holding Mrs. Shelton's Bible.

Governor Jerry Brown signs our California Homeowner Bill of Rights. Speaker John Pérez, Senate President Darrell Steinberg, and Assembly Member Nancy Skinner all helped enormously in getting the bill passed.

My team traveled with me to Mexico City to work on our collaboration with Mexican attorneys general to combat transnational criminal organizations. From left to right: Mateo Munoz, Travis LeBlanc, me, Michael Trancoso, Brian Nelson, and Larry Wallace, who was the director of the law enforcement division for the California Department of Justice.

Performing the wedding of Sandy Stier (left) and Kris Perry (right) on the balcony of San Francisco City Hall on June 28, 2013.

On September 30, 2013, I stood on the stage of the California Endowment for the statewide launch of our elementary school truancy initiative, where I explained that 82 percent of prisoners are high school dropouts. It was also the day that my team first met Doug.

On October 10, 2013, I announced a lawsuit against for-profit Corinthian Colleges, Inc., which defrauded students and investors across the state. We successfully advocated that the students' loans be forgiven.

One of the most joyful days of my life was marrying my sweetheart, Doug. We were married at the courthouse in Santa Barbara, CA, on August 22, 2014.

At the courthouse on the day of our marriage, with my family. Left to right: Tony, Aunt Chinni, Maya, me, Aunt Sarala, Uncle Subash (Chinni's husband), and Meena.

Doug congratulates me for winning reelection as California's attorney general in November 2014. We're at the Delancey Street Foundation, which is run by my dear friend Mimi Silbert.

Visiting the Pitchess Detention Center in Castaic on March 11, 2015, where we were starting Back on Track–Los Angeles. In partnership with the sheriff's department and the Ford Foundation, we were there to provide services to the inmates to help them with their reentry back into society. Left to right: Me, LA sheriff Jim McDonnell, Dan Suvor, Doug Wood, and Jeff Tsai.

A morning walk along the bay with my dear Ella. (March 2015)

Venus Johnson, my associate attorney general and de facto chief of staff, and me, working on issues related to law enforcement. I can't thank Venus enough for her leadership. (April 2016)

Campaigning up and down the state on the Fearless for the People bus, with a Kamoji always waving to passersby. My campaign team, from left to right: Juan Rodriguez, Ellie Caple, Sean Clegg, Jill Habig, and Daniel Lopez.

Chrisette Hudlin, my best friend, got her kids (and my godchildren) Helena and Alexander into the spirit of the campaign. Helena was an active volunteer in the campaign office, where she started her own newsletter, interviewing campaign staff. She was one of the toughest interviews I've ever done.

Doug and me jumping off the Kamoji bus on the last full day of campaigning.
Ready for action! (November 7, 2016)

Nathan Barankin and I have come a long way together. He was
my number two in the attorney general's office in Sacramento
and joined me in Washington, DC, as my chief of staff.

Election Night celebration at Exchange LA. (November 8, 2016)

Vice President Biden swearing me in as a United States Senator in the Old Senate Chamber at the U.S. Capitol. (January 3, 2017)

Members of Congress joined the Women's March on Washington on January 21, 2017. Left to right: Rep. Brenda Lawrence (D-MI), Rep. Yvette Clarke (D-NY), Rep. Barbara Lee (D-CA), Rep. Sheila Jackson Lee (D-TX), Rep. Grace Meng (D-NY), me, Emily's List President Stephanie Schriock, Rep. Jackie Speier (D-CA), and Rep. Doris Matsui (D-CA).

I am a proud graduate of Howard University, an institution that has inspired, nurtured, and challenged its students to take on roles of leadership. I was honored to deliver the commencement speech at my alma mater. (May 13, 2017)

Cole graduated from Colorado College on May 22, 2017. Doug, Kerstin, and I were there to celebrate with him.

The devastation and loss for the victims of the Santa Rosa fire was beyond description.

Visiting with first responders during the Santa Rosa fire in Northern California. This firefighter lost his home in the same blaze he was battling. His bravery and his sacrifice were deeply moving. I'll never forget him. (October 2017)

Traveling with a delegation to Puerto Rico to survey the vast destruction from Hurricane Maria. It was critical to witness the devastation felt by our fellow citizens. (November 2017)

With John Laird, Secretary of the California Natural Resources Agency, touring Lake Oroville, where damage to the reservoir's spillways caused flooding and forced the temporary evacuation of 100,000 people.

On March 20, 2018, the Senate Intelligence Committee held a news conference where we presented our findings and recommendations on threats to election infrastructure. Left to right: Sen. Richard Burr (R-NC), Sen. Susan Collins (R-ME), me, Sen. Mark Warner (D-VA), Sen. James Lankford (R-OK), Sen. Martin Heinrich (D-NM), Sen. Joe Manchin (D-WV), and Sen. Angus King (I-ME).

On March 24, 2018, I joined the millions of people around the county in the March for Our Lives to advocate for reasonable gun safety laws. I attended the Los Angeles march, where I met with young community leaders from The Brotherhood Crusade, who are highlighting the impact of gun violence in the community.

Calling for an end to the barbaric practice of family separation, I visited the Otay Mesa Detention Center in Southern California, where mothers who had been separated from their children were being held, on June 22, 2018. I met with them in the prison and then gave a news conference outside. To my left is a great leader: Angelica Salas of CHIRLA.

With Doug and Meena celebrating the San Francisco Pride Parade. (June 2018)

Marching at the Martin Luther King Day Parade in Los Angeles. Left to right: Heather Hutt, Areva Martin, me, Rabbi Jonathan Klein, Doug, Cole, Ella, and Angelica Salas. (January 15, 2018)

In this crowd are survivors of sexual assault who fearlessly spoke truth to powerful forces and refused to be silenced. I am inspired by their courage.

Hanging with a few Dreamers. Let's find time between the marching and the shouting to dance, sing, and laugh—to be joyful warriors.

just as unacceptable that mental illness goes unaddressed, untreated, and ignored.

My mother's cancer treatment acquired a grim kind of routine. During the day, I would take her to the hospital for chemotherapy. We'd see many of the same people every time—men and women of all different ages, hooked up to a machine that was infusing their bodies with the toxic drugs they hoped would save their lives. It took on a strange familiarity, an abnormal sense of normalcy. If I had to, I'd drop her off and pick her up when chemo was done, but I preferred to wait and keep her company, and she preferred it, too.

Sometimes the chemo would steal her appetite. Other times she was hungry, and I would get her buttery croissants that she loved from a bakery nearby. More than once, she had to be admitted to the hospital with complications, and I remember a lot of hard days and nights under those fluorescent lights. When my mother was asleep, I would walk down the long corridors, glancing into the rooms as I passed. Sometimes people would look up. Sometimes they wouldn't. And all too often, they were lying there alone. I left that experience convinced that no one should have to face a hospital stay without support—and that many do.

My mother's circumstance could feel overwhelming. Chemotherapy is depleting; oftentimes my mother was too wiped out to do anything but sleep. Meanwhile, there were so many medications, possible side effects, counterindications, and things to keep track of. What if she had a bad reaction to a new medicine, as happened more than once? I had to coordinate her care, make sure her doctors were talking to one another, and ensure that she was getting the proper treatment. I often wondered how my mother would have fared if we hadn't been there to speak up on her behalf.

I came away believing that we should mandate patient advocates with medical expertise so that anyone dealing with an acute illness has a trustworthy, capable champion by their side. After all, we have decided that when their liberty is at stake, people are entitled to an attorney. We do this because we understand that most people don't speak the language of the courtroom, and even if they do, in high-pressure situations it's difficult to make objective judgments. The same is true in a hospital. Emotions are running high. People are placed into a new environment where a specialized language is being spoken, with complex, unfamiliar terms and phrases. And they may have to make decisions while they are frightened or in pain or heavily medicated—or all three. They're expected to be strong enough to monitor themselves at a moment when they feel deeply vulnerable. We should have expert advocates to shoulder that burden so that patients and their families can focus on healing.

We should also speak truth about the racial disparities in our health care system. In 1985, then–Secretary of Health and Human Services Margaret Heckler released a pathbreaking Report of the Secretary's Task Force on Black and Minority Health. As she wrote at the time, despite significant progress in the American health picture overall, "there was a continuing disparity in the burden of death and illness experienced by blacks and other minority Americans as compared with our nation's population as a whole." In her words, this disparity was "an affront both to our ideals and to the ongoing genius of American medicine."

I was in college when she commissioned this study. What have we seen in the three decades since then? The gaps have narrowed, but they are pervasive—and communities of color pay the price. According to the 2015 Kelly Report on Health Disparities in America, black Americans have higher mortality rates than any other group in eight of the top ten causes of death.

In segregated cities like Baltimore, there are twenty-year gaps in the life expectancy of those living in poor black American neighborhoods and those living in wealthier and whiter areas. "A baby born in Cheswolde, in Baltimore's far northwest corner, can expect to live until age eighty-seven," writes Olga Khazan in *The Atlantic*. "Nine miles away in Clifton-Berea, near where *The Wire* was filmed, the life expectancy is sixty-seven, roughly the same as that of Rwanda, and twelve years shorter than the American average."

These disparities begin in the delivery room. Black babies are twice as likely as white babies to die in infancy, a stunning disparity that is wider than in 1850, when slavery was still legal. In fact, infant mortality rates for black babies today are higher than they were for white infants at the time of the Heckler Report. In other words, today, black infants are less likely to survive their first year than white babies were in the early 1980s.

Black women are also at least three times as likely to die due to complications relating to pregnancy than white women—a shocking gulf that transcends socioeconomic status. A major five-year study in New York City found that college-educated black women are more likely to face severe complications in pregnancy or childbirth than white women who never made it through high school.

There are a number of factors that put black men, women, and children at a disadvantage. Hundreds of years of institutionalized discrimination in housing, employment, and educational opportunity have left black Americans more likely to lack access to health care, to live in poor neighborhoods with limited healthy food options, and to have fewer community health care resources.

And because black Americans are more likely than their white counterparts to be born and raised in low-income, high-crime neighborhoods, they are more likely to experience a phenomenon known as toxic stress, the result of trauma caused by things ranging from witnessing violence to experiencing it. This causes not just psychological anguish, but also physical changes. To borrow the words of toxic stress expert Dr. Nadine Burke Harris, founder of the Center for Youth Wellness, in Bayview–Hunters Point, "child adversity literally gets under our skin and has the potential to change our health."

One study found that children who go through at least six adverse childhood experiences could see their life expectancy reduced by more than twenty years. Physiological stress leads to hypertension, which results in higher rates of infant and maternal mortality, among other conditions. Research has even found that certain levels of stress shorten our telomeres, which are structures that hold our chromosomes together. As we age, our telomeres naturally get shorter until cells start dying, which leads to disease. A study at the University of Michigan measured the telomere length in hundreds of women and found that black women were biologically more than seven years older than white women their age.

But environmental circumstances alone cannot explain health care disparities.

It's also the case that black Americans experience poorer care when they go to the doctor. White patients are 10 percent more likely to get screened for high cholesterol than black Americans, even though rates of heart disease and stroke are higher among black Americans.

Black patients are also less likely to be treated using procedures to repair blocked arteries. White women are more likely to get breast cancer screenings than black women and Latinas. And women of color are more likely to have their symptoms dismissed by their doctor, regardless of their economic status.

When tennis star Serena Williams, one of the greatest athletes of all time, delivered her baby, she had serious complications. The day after an emergency C-section, Williams started having trouble breathing. She had a history of pulmonary embolisms, or blood clots, and, having experienced them before, she suspected she was having another. She told *Vogue* magazine that she walked out of her hospital room so that her mom wouldn't worry and told her nurse that she needed a CT scan and an IV blood thinner right away. But the nurse was skeptical. She thought Williams must have been confused because of her pain medication. Williams persisted. Rather than give her the CT scan and IV drip, the doctor arrived with an ultrasound machine.

"I was like, a Doppler?" Williams recalled. "I told you, I need a CT scan and a heparin drip," she stressed to the medical team. When they finally sent her for a CT, they discovered that she was right after all. "I was like, listen to Dr. Williams!" she told *Vogue.* There were further complications that required surgery and left her bedridden for six weeks. If someone like Serena Williams can go through such an ordeal, imagine what happens to other patients who articulate symptoms and are ignored.

What accounts for these inequities in the care of our fellow citizens? A growing body of research suggests that part of the problem is unconscious, implicit bias—similar to what we see in police departments. All of us absorb social stereotypes and assumptions, often without ever realizing it. But left unexamined, they risk leading us to behave in discriminatory ways, which can have profound consequences in fields like law enforcement, criminal justice, education, and health.

Some enlightened members of the medical profession are working to address this problem. At UC San Francisco, all first-year medical students take a class on the discriminatory effect of these biases. Before they begin, they are given an implicit bias association test that measures their unconscious attitudes, not just about race but about gender, weight, and age. Research has found that 75 percent of those who take the test—no matter their race—show an unconscious preference for white people.

How do we close the divide? It starts by speaking the uncomfortable truth that it exists, and then we can break the problem into parts we can tackle one by one. First and foremost, we need every medical school in the country to require implicit bias training for their students. When people are given the knowledge that implicit bias is real, and that we all have it, it gives them room to think about it in their daily actions and make better decisions.

We also need medical schools to focus proactively on bringing more diversity into the field. As of 2013, only about 9 percent of our country's physicians are nonwhite, and only 4 percent are black. This is the first gap we need to close if we intend to close the others. It won't be easy. It'll be a generational challenge. But it's time we get started.

Most critically, however, improving health outcomes across the board demands that we transform the health care system itself. I believe that health care should be a right, but in a system where the quality of your care does indeed depend on your station in life, the reality is that health care is still a privilege in this country. And we need that to change. It's why we need Medicare for All.

Imagine if U.S. health care coverage was based not on how much you can pay but instead on your health needs. The purpose of the system would be to maximize good health care outcomes rather than maximizing profits. That, in itself, would be revolutionary. Getting sick would no longer mean risking bankruptcy. Employers would no longer have to spend so much to provide health insurance to their employees. And the system itself would run far more efficiently, as we see when we compare the high administrative costs of private health insurance companies with the lower costs of Medicare.

But even if we could snap our fingers and make Medicare for All a reality, this alone would not alleviate all of the problems in the system.

For starters, we need to dramatically increase funding to the National Institutes of Health to step in and fill the innovation gap that pharmaceutical companies have left. I remember how proud my mother was to work with the NIH as a peer reviewer and collaborator with other experts in her field. She would speak of her time there with such reverence that when I was a girl, I imagined Bethesda, Maryland, where the agency is located, to be a place filled with castles and spires. I might have been wrong about the architecture, but not about the beauty of scientific collaboration—and certainly not about the fact that the NIH is a national treasure. If we want our children to have cures for humanity's most terrible diseases, we should invest in our national medical researchers, instead of relying on companies that would rather funnel money to their shareholders.

We also need to protect patients and taxpayers from fraud. And that means putting bad actors under a microscope. Consider for-profit dialysis companies, which offer one of the worst examples of bad practices.

Dialysis is a process by which a machine cleans the blood of patients who are in kidney failure. Kidney disease remains the ninth leading cause of death in America, but for a person in kidney failure, dialysis is a lifesaving treatment and an important bridge between loss of kidney function and getting a kidney transplant (which is a cheaper alternative with a much better prognosis). Across the country, nearly 500,000 patients are on dialysis, going three times a week to have their blood circulated out of their body through a multi-hour process that mimics a healthy kidney's function.

Who are these patients? Disproportionately, they come from low-income communities. People living in certain zip codes are far more likely to end up with kidney failure, which is most commonly the result of diabetes and high blood pressure. Black Americans develop kidney failure at 3.5 times the rate of white Americans, and they constitute nearly one-third of all U.S. patients who receive dialysis.

The two largest dialysis companies, DaVita Inc. and Fresenius Medical Care, have both found themselves in legal hot water. In 2016, Fresenius agreed to pay $250 million to settle thousands of lawsuits. According to *The New York Times,* "Fresenius's own medical office sent an internal memo to doctors in the company's dialysis centers saying that failure to properly use one of the company's products appeared to be causing a sharp increase in sudden deaths from cardiac arrest." Yet the company chose not to warn doctors in non-Fresenius clinics who were using the product until after the memo had been leaked to the Food and Drug Administration.

In 2014, DaVita agreed to pay $350 million to resolve claims of illegal kickbacks, in a scheme where it allegedly sold an interest in its clinics to physicians and physician groups in exchange for their driving patients to those clinics. In 2015, the company agreed to pay $495 million to settle a whistle-blower case in which it was accused of fraudulently overcharging Medicare. DaVita was sued in 2017 for keeping its clinics so understaffed and requiring such high-speed care and turnover that patients' lives were endangered. It's time to crack down on this kind of behavior.

Finally, we will need to overhaul public health policy so that it does a better job of providing mental health care to all Americans. That effort will have to begin by ensuring that more mental health professionals contract with Medicare in the first place. There's only one way to solve this problem: We need to raise Medicare reimbursement rates. As the largest single payer of health care services, the federal government must lead the way to ensure we pay all mental health professionals what they deserve.

We also need to encourage a new generation of Americans to go into the mental health care field. Let's create a model similar to Teach for America or the Peace Corps—an apprenticeship system that has as its core mission the goal of getting people to serve their country through mental health training.

Let's also do away with laws that strip funding from mental health care services. There's an old law known as the IMD exclusion, for example, that prohibits Medicaid from paying for treatment in mental health facilities with more than sixteen beds. This rule has hollowed out mental health care hospitals and left most people with severe mental health conditions to fend for themselves.

Ultimately, I believe we should provide mental health care on demand. And when I say "on demand," I mean that whoever you are and wherever you are, mental health treatment is available if you need it. In addition to requiring far more practitioners, meeting this goal will require investment in and expansion of telemedicine so patients can access mental health care no matter where they live. This is especially important for people in rural areas, where nearly 100 hospitals have closed over the past several years. So far, studies have shown that telemedicine is generally as effective as in-person treatment. But further research and development can surely improve its value.

I n the days before being sworn in as senator, I read a newspaper profile of Chillicothe, Ohio, a small city in southeastern Ohio's Ross County. It's located in the foothills of the Appalachian Mountains, with sprawling fields of soybeans and corn and a skyline marked by the smokestacks of a paper mill that has operated continually for more than a hundred years. Kenworth has its largest truck-manufacturing plant in Chillicothe and pays middle-class wages. The local hospital is one of the county's largest employers. But the grand history and pride that once defined this classically American town have been replaced by a sense of despair.

Seventy-seven thousand people call Ross County home. In 2015 alone, doctors in the county prescribed 1.6 million opioid pills. That same year, thirty-eight people died from accidental overdose. The following year, another forty lost their lives. "Now you can get heroin quicker in these communities than you can get pizza," Teri Minney, head of Ross County's Heroin Partnership Project, told *The Washington Post*. "They're delivering." According to the *Post*, addicts in Ross

County often shoot up in public places, hoping that if they overdose, paramedics or police officers will revive them. "One day in September, police and paramedics responded to thirteen separate overdose calls, including one fatality: a man who died in an apartment right on Main Street. Meanwhile, a woman overdosed in her car as it idled at a Valero gas station with her two-year-old daughter in the back seat."

As has happened in other areas with heavy opioid use, the violent crime rate has gone up, as have incidents of theft. So have the numbers of opioid-addicted babies born, and of children requiring foster care. According to local officials, two hundred children were placed into state care in 2016, 75 percent of whom had parents with opioid addictions. The surge has required that the county nearly double its child services budget, which now makes up more than 10 percent of the total county budget. What was once one of the happiest places in Ohio is now clouded by a fog of hopelessness.

Similar stories are repeating themselves in every state in America. The human toll has rocked the nation to its core. Entire communities have been destroyed. And the opioid epidemic does not discriminate. It has hit people across every demographic, and infected rural, suburban, and urban areas alike. For so many people, what began as a legitimate desire to reduce pain became an overpowering addiction. Now the pain they feel isn't from the original back injury or post-surgery healing; it is the pain that comes from quitting. "It's like having the flu and laying in the street while people run over you while you're puking," one Chillicothe addict described to *The Washington Post.*

The opioid epidemic has killed more than 350,000 Americans in the past two decades. But the national health crisis we face today is itself the result of a failure of public health intervention, from the moment OxyContin was approved to be sold. It is a different story than the one we witnessed during the crack cocaine epidemic—now, instead of people dealing drugs on the corner, people in suits and ties and white coats are dealing a drug while drugmakers cover up the dangers.

It started in 1995, when the FDA approved OxyContin and allowed its manufacturer, Purdue Pharma, to make the claim that, unlike previous opioids (Percocet and Vicodin), OxyContin was "believed to reduce" appeal to drug abusers because it was longer acting. Purdue Pharma seized on this claim and, in 1996, began the largest marketing campaign in pharmaceutical history based on the idea that OxyContin wasn't addictive. The company's executives testified in Congress to this effect and ran a whole program to convince doctors and patients that pain should be treated more aggressively than in the past, and that it could be done with little fear of addiction, as long as that pain pill was OxyContin. This despite the fact that company officials had received information that pills were being crushed and snorted, and that doctors were being criminally charged with selling prescriptions to patients.

According to a time line developed by *Mother Jones*, by 2002, doctors in the United States were prescribing twenty-three times more OxyContin than they had in 1996. By 2004, the Federation of State Medical Boards actually recommended sanctions against doctors who undertreated pain.

Pill mills started to pop up all over the country, where doctors would sell prescriptions and pills for cash. Between 2007 and 2012, three major drug distributors—McKesson, Cardinal Health, and AmerisourceBergen—made $17 billion by saturating West Virginia with opioids. By 2009, the United States was consuming more than

90 percent of the world's hydrocodone and more than 80 percent of its oxycodone. By 2012, sixteen years after OxyContin reached the market, health care providers had written 259 million prescriptions for opioids. For perspective, there are about 126 million households in America.

By the late 1990s, heroin use in the United States had declined quite dramatically from its 1960s and '70s peak. But as opioid addictions skyrocketed in the early 2000s, heroin traffickers found a highly motivated consumer base for their product, which was significantly cheaper and easier to obtain than prescription medication. According to the National Institutes of Health, roughly 80 percent of Americans who become addicted to heroin start with a prescription for opioids.

The danger worsened in 2013 as fentanyl, an exceptionally deadly synthetic opioid with fifty times the strength of heroin, made its way from China into the American heroin supply. The CDC estimates that there were 72,000 drug overdose deaths in America in 2017 alone. That's nearly twice what it was ten years earlier. And in 2018, the CDC released a report finding that opioid deaths are still rising in nearly every segment of the country.

When I was attorney general, I made the fight against opioids one of my highest priorities. We took down a large-scale transnational drug-trafficking organization in 2011 while sponsoring legislation to make it more difficult to print fraudulent prescription pads. We went after pill mills and shut down so-called recovery centers that were overprescribing, leading to patient deaths. When funding to my department's drug-monitoring program was cut, we fought tooth and nail until I got the budget restored. The system allowed prescribers and pharmacists to quickly access a patient's prescription history and make sure the patient wasn't seeking the same painkillers from different doctors simultaneously. We went after criminals who were selling opioids on Craigslist and filed a lawsuit against a pharmaceutical company for inflating prices for opioid addiction treatment.

How has the federal government responded? Not in the way one would hope. According to a joint investigation by *60 Minutes* and *The Washington Post* in 2017, Congress "effectively stripped the DEA of its most potent weapon against large drug companies suspected of spilling prescription narcotics onto the nation's streets. . . . The law was the crowning achievement of a multifaceted campaign by the drug industry to weaken aggressive DEA enforcement efforts against drug distribution companies that were supplying corrupt doctors and pharmacists who peddled narcotics on the black market."

In 2017, the administration declared the opioid crisis a public health emergency, but the fund they used to deal with it had only—I kid you not—$57,000 in it. That represents less than one dollar for each person who died of a drug overdose that year. It's unconscionable. And if Republicans had succeeded in repealing the Affordable Care Act, they would have taken addiction treatment coverage away from three million Americans.

This is a crisis that deserves a major federal mobilization. We need to declare a national state of emergency, which would provide more funding, right away, to help combat this disease—giving places like Chillicothe, Ohio, more resources to pay for addiction treatment, hospital services, skills training, and more.

We need to address the challenge at every point along the spectrum, beginning with providing supportive treatment programs for those whom experts call "pre-contemplators"—that is, people who are not yet ready to commit to treatment.

We need to make sure that people who are addicted have access to medication-assisted treatment (MAT)—drugs like buprenorphine, which prevents withdrawal symptoms and cravings without producing the kind of high that heroin or OxyContin does. Many insurance companies will cover the cost of opioids while charging more than $200 a month for buprenorphine. That has to change. We have to change it.

At the same time, we need to create a federal standard for substance use disorder treatment. Right now, in many states across the country, it's possible to open an addiction treatment center without being qualified to do so. There are no requirements for proper training or evidence-based treatment. As a result, too many Americans who have worked up the courage and strength to go to rehab arrive only to find that, for all the expense, they are not getting proper care and the treatment doesn't work.

We also need to reinstate the DEA's authority to go after the major pharmaceutical manufacturers and distributors for their role in creating and sustaining the crisis. And we need to invest resources in law enforcement efforts to cut off the supply of fentanyl from China.

Finally, we need to understand that, at its core, this is a public health issue, not a criminal justice issue. We can't keep repeating the mistakes of the failed war on drugs that put so many people addicted to crack in prison. It is normal human behavior to want to stop feeling pain, whether physical or emotional, and people will find ways to do so. Sometimes that will mean getting help, and sometimes it will mean getting hooked on heroin. Our job is not to punish our friends and family members and neighbors by throwing them in prison. It is to put them on a sustainable path to better manage their pain.

. . .

As my mother's condition worsened, she needed more care than we could provide her. We wanted to hire a home health care aide to help her—and me. But my mother didn't want help.

"I'm fine. I don't need anybody," she would say, even though she could barely get out of bed. There was a fight to be had about it, but I didn't want to have it. Cancer—the disease she'd devoted her life to defeating—was now wreaking its havoc on her. Her body was giving out. The medication was making it difficult for her to function—to be herself. I didn't want to be the one who took her dignity away.

So we muddled through. I cooked elaborate meals for her, filling the house with the smells of childhood, which reminded us both of happier times. When I wasn't at the office, I was most often with her, telling stories, holding hands, helping her through the misery of chemotherapy. I bought her hats after she lost her hair, and soft clothes to make her as comfortable as I could.

There isn't a smooth, steady decline, I would learn. The process isn't gradual. My mother would reach a plateau and stay there for weeks or months, then, seemingly overnight, fall to the plateau beneath it. During one especially hard spell, I convinced her to spend two weeks at the Jewish Home for the Aged—a place known for some of the kindest and best care—where she could get the round-the-clock care she needed. We packed her up and drove over to the home. The staff was incredibly kind to our family. They gave my mother a tour of the facility, showed her to her room, introduced her to the doctors and nurses, and explained the routine of her care.

At one point, one of the doctors pulled me aside. "How's my DA?"

she asked. The question caught me off guard. I had been so focused on my mother's well-being I hadn't made room for anything else, but the question cracked through the strength I had mustered and hadn't wanted to betray. I started to choke up. I was scared. I was sad. Most of all, I wasn't ready.

She asked me if I had heard of "anticipatory grief." I hadn't, but the term made perfect sense. So much of me was in denial. I couldn't bring myself to believe that I was going to have to say goodbye. But underneath it, I was aware. And I had started grieving my mother's loss already. There was something validating about that, about understanding what was happening to me. Putting a label on things can help you cope with them, I've learned. It doesn't make you stop feeling your emotion, but you can put it somewhere if you can name it. And now I could.

When the tour was over, I unzipped my mother's suitcase so that I could help her move in. But she had other plans. She was sitting cross-legged on the bed, all five feet of her, when she said firmly, "Okay, this was nice. Let's leave."

"Mommy, you're going to stay here for two weeks, remember?"

"No, I'm not. Nn-nnn. I'm not staying for two weeks." She turned to the medical team, who were still in the room. "This has been great. Thank you. We're leaving."

And so we did.

She ended up in the hospital not long after that. That was when I started to see another change. For as long as I could remember, my mother loved to watch the news and read the newspaper. When Maya and I were kids, she'd insist we sit down in front of Walter Cronkite each night before dinner. She loved to digest everything that was happening in the world. But suddenly, she had no interest. Her mighty brain had decided it had had enough. Though she still had room for us.

I remember that I had just gotten into the attorney general's race and she asked me how it was going.

"Mommy, these guys are saying they're gonna kick my ass."

My mother had been lying on her side. She rolled over, looked at me, and just unveiled the biggest smile. She knew who she had raised. She knew her fighting spirit was alive and well inside me.

When it was time for hospice care, we took her home and, finally, she let a hospice nurse come with us. Maya and I still didn't believe that she could die, to the point that when she said she wanted to go to India, we booked plane tickets and started planning. We worked out how we could get her on a plane, and made arrangements for a nurse to come with us. We were all in a great state of delusion—especially me. I couldn't bear to tell my mother no—not because she couldn't take it, but because I couldn't. Whether it was a question of bringing a nurse home or staying in the nursing home or going to India, I didn't want to accept what saying no to her meant. I didn't want to accept that she was running out of time.

One night, Maya, Tony, Meena, and I were all at my mother's house when Aunt Mary and Aunt Lenore, who had flown into town, came for a visit. I decided to cook again. I'll never forget that night—I was making Alice Waters's recipe for beef stew. I had browned the cubes of beef and they were cooking down in red wine, and all of a sudden my brain figured out what was happening around me. I started to hyperventilate—short breaths in and out. I felt like I might faint. All of a sudden, the delusion was gone. I had to face reality. I was going to lose my mother and there was nothing I could do.

We had called our uncle in India to let him know that she was too sick to make it. He got on a plane from Delhi to see her. I now realize that she waited for his arrival, waited to say goodbye. She passed away the very next morning.

One of the last questions she asked the hospice nurse, the last concern on her mind, was "Are my daughters going to be okay?" She was focused on being our mother until the very end.

And though I miss her every day, I carry her with me wherever I go. I think of her all the time. Sometimes I look up and talk to her. I love her so much. And there is no title or honor on earth I'll treasure more than to say I am Shyamala Gopalan Harris's daughter. That is the truth I hold dearest of all.

Eight

THE COST OF LIVING

When I was getting ready to write this book, I spent a good deal of time going through photo albums, reminiscing with Maya, and unpacking old boxes, including things my mother had saved. It's been a blessing. I've had the chance to sit with good memories that don't always make it to the front of my mind.

When we were growing up, our mother always made chiles rellenos around Christmas. After she died, I wanted so badly to find the recipe. I searched everywhere I could, including online, but nothing matched my mother's version. I felt so defeated, as though I'd lost more than just the flavor of her cooking. And then, while I was digging through my cookbooks, I found a notebook, and as soon as I opened it, the recipe fell right out of the pages and onto the floor. I was transported just by reading my mother's handwriting. It was like she was there with me, still responding to my needs.

I also found a couple of pot holders that Maya and I had woven on plastic looms. Any reader who grew up in the 1970s probably knows just what I mean. Our mother made sure our hands were never idle, especially in front of the television. That's where I perfected my crochet shell stitch.

Our mother loved to talk with her hands, and she was always using her hands—to cook, to clean, to comfort. She was always busy. Work itself was something to value—hard work especially; and she made sure that we, her daughters, internalized that message and the importance of working with purpose.

She also showed us, in so many ways, how much she valued all work, not just her own. When something good would happen at the lab, my mother would come home with flowers for our babysitter.

"I wouldn't have been able to do what I did if you didn't do what you do," she would say. "Thank you for everything."

She saw the dignity in the work that society requires to function. She believed that everyone deserves respect for the work they do, and that hard effort should be rewarded and honored.

I'd hear the same thing at Rainbow Sign, where speakers would talk about Dr. King's Poor People's Campaign, about his belief that "all labor has dignity," and his effort to make it so.

As part of that effort, Dr. King had gone to Memphis in 1968 to join black sanitation workers in their fight for basic decency. Day in and day out, these workers rode the trucks that hauled away the city's garbage. The city didn't provide uniforms; instead, workers were forced to befoul their own clothes on the job. They worked long hours without water to drink or a place to wash their hands. "Most of the tubs had holes in them," one sanitation worker recounted. "Garbage leaking all over you." He described how, when the workers got home in the evening, they'd remove their shoes and clothes at the door and maggots would fall out.

For this hard, indispensable work, they received little more than minimum wage. They didn't get overtime pay. They had no sick leave. If they were injured at work and needed time to mend—as happened often—they were likely to be fired. And if bad weather made trash collection impossible, they were sent home without pay. Many needed government assistance to feed their families.

When the city refused to compensate the families of two sanitation workers who were crushed to death by their trash compactor, it became too much for the others to bear. With great courage, 1,300 Memphis sanitation workers went on strike, demanding safer conditions, better pay and benefits, and recognition of their union. They were on strike for their families, for their children, and for themselves. It was, above all else, a battle for dignity. The signs they held at marches said simply I AM A MAN.

When King arrived at Bishop Charles Mason Temple, in Memphis, on March 18, 1968, a crowd of 25,000 people had gathered to hear him speak.

"So often we overlook the work and the significance of those who are not in professional jobs, of those who are not in the so-called big jobs," he said. "But let me say to you tonight, that whenever you are engaged in work that serves humanity and is for the building of humanity, it has dignity and it has worth."

"We are tired," King said to the audience in Memphis. "We are tired of our children having to attend overcrowded, inferior, quality-less schools. We are tired of having to live in dilapidated substandard housing conditions. . . . We are tired of walking the streets in search of jobs that do not exist . . . of working our hands off and laboring every day and not even making a wage adequate to get the basic necessities of life."

Sixteen days later, King returned to Memphis to march on behalf of the strikers—speaking again at Bishop Charles Mason Temple, where he declared, "I've been to the mountaintop." The next evening, April 4, 1968, he was killed by an assassin. Two months after that, on June 5, Robert F. Kennedy was murdered as well. The nation's clearest voices and strongest leaders in the fight for economic justice had been suddenly, irrevocably silenced.

That was half a century ago. In some ways, we have come so far since then. And in others, we have barely budged. I remind people that when you adjust for inflation, the federal minimum wage is actually lower now than when Dr. King spoke of "starvation wages" in 1968. What does that say about how our country values the sanctity and dignity of work?

Americans are a hardworking bunch. We pride ourselves on our work ethic. And for generations, most of us have been raised to believe that there are few things more honorable than putting in an honest day's work to take care of our family. We grew up trusting that when we worked hard and did well, we would be rewarded for our effort. But the truth is, for most Americans, it hasn't been that way for an awfully long time.

Whenever there is a major push to pressure Congress into doing the right thing, activists and elected leaders implore the American people to call and write their representatives. These days, the phone lines are overwhelmed by Americans engaged in an extraordinary thing: exercising democracy. And in a number of cases, it has really mattered. I believe that repeal of the Affordable Care Act failed in 2017 because congressional Republicans had taken a nonpartisan issue—access to affordable health care—and made it a partisan one, and the people just weren't having it. It activated and energized folks to fight back, and because of the pressure they put on key senators, the people prevailed. That means that millions of people still have health coverage because individual Americans picked up the phone and wrote letters.

For me, reading these letters isn't just about understanding where people stand on major policy issues. It's about understanding what their lives are like, both the joys and the fears. When people write to me, it is often as a last resort. They are struggling, and in real trouble, but nothing else they've tried has worked. And so they turn to me and share with me the things that have upended their lives.

Dear Senator Harris,

My husband and I work full time jobs yet we still struggle every week to make ends meet. I get full [health care] coverage for my two-year-old son [for] which I thank God every day, but can't figure out why my husband and I can't get full coverage either?

. . . We can't get help with daycare because we "make too much money" but yet we can't even afford to pay $50 a month for daycare, so we depend on family, [but] they have their own problems, so there have been too many occasions [when] we lose money because we can't get a babysitter for us to go to work.

. . . I am begging with my life that this needs to change!! Please for the love of God HELP!! This is just not ok! I am confused,

angry, frustrated, and I feel so betrayed by our government! I don't EVER ask for help unless I need it and I seriously need it!!

Every letter stands on its own. But together, they tell the same story. It is the story of Americans trapped in a cost-of-living crisis, where everything from housing and health care to child care and education is way more expensive than it used to be while wages remain as low as they've been for decades. The letters I receive consistently tell the story of the hollowing out of the middle class, and of an economic life defined by intense struggle.

When I wake up in the middle of the night with a thought on my mind, I remind myself that in countless households around the country, someone else is wide awake, too. Millions of someone elses. And I imagine that the majority of them are asking themselves questions about their greatest fears: Am I going to be able to provide a good life for my children? What if I can never make ends meet? How will I get through the month?

The American people have not given up on the American Dream. I know this to be true. But when you can't sleep at night, how can you dream?

How can you dream when, on average, a year of child care for a baby or toddler is more expensive than a year of in-state public college tuition? How can you dream when the cost of higher education has gone up more than three times faster than wages since I was in school in the eighties? How can you dream when you are drowning in student loan debt?

How can you dream if you make minimum wage and work forty hours a week, knowing that, in 99 percent of U.S. counties, you can't afford the market-rate rent on the average one-bedroom apartment?

How can you dream when your pay barely budges no matter how hard you work, while everything else keeps getting so much more expensive? How can you dream when your son is sick but you can't afford your copay or deductible?

A middle-class life isn't what it used to be. And right now it isn't what it's supposed to be. Being middle-class ought to mean having financial security and stability. But how is that possible when the cost of living is so high that you live one setback away from catastrophe? An injury. An illness. Nobody expects life to be easy, but it's not supposed to be a life-altering crisis when your car's transmission fails.

And yet for so many, it is. One setback and the savings account gets emptied. Another and the retirement account goes, too. Soon you're carrying a bigger balance on your credit card than you know is safe, but what choice do you have? You have to get the car fixed if you're going to keep your job. There is rent or a mortgage to pay.

According to one survey, 57 percent of Americans don't have enough cash to cover a $500 unexpected expense. That's one of the reasons I've introduced the LIFT the Middle Class Tax Act in the U.S. Senate, a bill that creates a major new middle-class tax credit that would provide eligible families up to $6,000 a year—the equivalent of $500 a month. Families would be able to receive the credit as a monthly stipend, rather than wait for a refund the following year. It's a different kind of safety net, one that prevents hardworking people from falling out of the middle class, or gives them a fair shot at attaining it for their families. This is the kind of tax relief we can provide when we stop giving endless tax cuts to corporations and the wealthy.

I think of Mr. and Mrs. Shelton. She was a nursery school teacher and he was a construction worker, and on those incomes they were able to purchase a two-bedroom home that was everything they dreamed of, and everything they had worked for. But at the time of this writing, that house is listed on Zillow at $886,000, which would be impossible to purchase on the salaries of a teacher and a construction worker. I recognize that California has become extraordinarily expensive, but this is a problem in major metropolitan areas all across the country. According to a 2018 analysis by Redfin, in cities like Denver and Phoenix, less than 1 percent of the homes on the market were affordable on the average teacher's salary.

In rural areas, housing affordability issues aren't as severe, but communities have been devastated by a lack of jobs. According to a recent report, only 3 percent of job growth in the twenty-first century has come from rural areas. That has forced people to find work far away from home, which leaves them with an awful choice: endure an hours-long commute every day, or move away from the place where their family has lived for a generation, the place where their friends live, where their kids play little league baseball, where they have always gone to church.

I also think of the workers I've met along the way who are severely undervalued in this economy. Several years ago, I met a woman named Wendy through SEIU and got to spend the day with her, watching her work up close. She had changed jobs when her elderly mother got sick, becoming a home health care worker so she could be the one to take care of her day and night. That meant everything from lifting her mother out of her bed to dressing her, feeding her, assisting her in the bathroom, measuring and tracking her vitals, helping her into her wheelchair and taking her out for a walk, and keeping her cognitively engaged throughout. It was detailed and demanding work, physically, mentally, and emotionally.

And yet, in 2017, the average home health aide in the United States was earning too little to keep a four-person household above the poverty line. And because they are often contractors, they aren't always eligible for employee benefits. That strikes me as outrageous. As the baby boomer generation continues to retire, we're going to need more home health aides—1.2 million by 2026. And this is how we intend to treat them? What does this say about the value we place on caring for older Americans? What does this say about how we honor our elders?

The cost-of-living crisis is especially hard on women. Women are still paid, on average, eighty cents on the dollar compared with men—a gap that is even more punishing for black American women, who are paid only sixty-three cents for every dollar earned by white men. As the National Women's Law Center points out, that means a black woman who works full time, year-round, comes up more than $21,000 behind her white male counterpart. That affects everyone in her home. It's even worse for Latinas, who make just fifty-four cents on the dollar.

Politicians talk a big game about the value of hard work. But it's time we speak some truth. The truth is that the economy stopped rewarding and valuing most hard work a long time ago. And we've got to acknowledge that if we're going to change it.

Let's start by reflecting on how we got here.

For several decades after the Second World War, workers got pay raises when companies did well. And the government gave people a hand up, offering free education through the GI Bill. The productivity gains necessary to grow the economy were remarkable. In the three decades after the war, productivity improved a staggering 97 percent. The difference then was that everyone shared in the bounty.

During that same period, worker wages grew 90 percent. That's how the United States was able to build the world's largest middle class.

But in the 1970s and '80s, corporate America decided to go its own way. Instead of spending their earnings on workers, the corporations decided that their only real obligation was to their shareholders. From big business's perspective, it was those who owned a piece of the company who deserved the lion's share of the riches, not the people who made the company run. So while productivity improved 74 percent between 1973 and 2013, worker compensation rose just 9 percent.

In the 1980s, President Reagan made that idea core to the Republican Party's view of economics. Cut taxes for corporations. Cut taxes for shareholders. Oppose minimum wage increases. Oppose the very idea of a minimum wage. Dismantle organized labor, the most powerful force fighting for workers in Washington. Roll back government oversight. Ignore the collateral damage.

This was the ushering-in of a new era of selfishness and greed. And it was frighteningly effective. Corporate profits have soared, but American workers haven't gotten a meaningful raise in forty years. And yet there is no shame, it seems, in CEOs making more than three hundred times the wage of their average worker.

The goal of economic growth has to be to grow the pie. But if all that's left for workers are the crumbs, what kind of economy are we really building?

This was the context in which we entered the twenty-first century. The American people got sandwiched between forces beyond their control—on one side, outsourcing and offshoring that eviscerated the manufacturing sector, and on the other, the worst recession since the Great Depression. Suddenly, the jobs were gone. Communities turned into ghost towns.

I read so many letters that underscore the significance of the passage of time. A man, sixty-two, who lost everything in the Great Recession, who has nothing left for retirement and is running out of working years. A couple dealing with a family health crisis, who can't afford to pay their medical bills and still cover the monthly rent. They need help right now; they can't wait. Anyone stuck in a cycle of financial desperation will tell you it's an emergency. That there is no time for delay. Dinner has to go on the table tonight. Gas has to go in the tank in the morning. The bills have to be paid tomorrow. The rent is due at the end of the week. There is truly no time to spare.

During this period there have also been a rash of corporate predators who have taken advantage of—and often ruined—vulnerable people. Among the worst examples of these predators are the for-profit colleges that became the darlings of Wall Street during this time. Generations of Americans have been told that their best shot at opportunity is to get a degree. And a lot of folks took that advice to heart and went for it, sometimes at great cost to themselves and their families.

Dear Senator Harris,

At one point, I considered getting two jobs to provide for my son and me. I concluded the best solution for me was to go back to school and continue to work my minimum wage job, so my son wouldn't miss out on quality time with me. I decided I would struggle through poverty long enough to complete school. This is a reality for a lot of Americans.

The problem is that a lot of people signed up at for-profit colleges that promised them a great education and a great future, when, in truth, the degrees they were offering weren't worth much of anything.

When I was attorney general of California, we took on Corinthian Colleges Inc., one of the largest for-profit college scams in the country. In order to get students and investors to sign up, Corinthian representatives lied incessantly. They told investors that more than 60 percent of their students were successfully placed in sustainable jobs. They charged the students enormous amounts for their degrees and told them that some programs had 100 percent job placement rates, even when there was no evidence that a single graduate had received a job. They advertised programs they didn't offer and penalized their telemarketers if they revealed the truth to prospective students.

Even more venal was the way Corinthian went after vulnerable people. They targeted people living at the poverty line; people who had decided to go back to school and earn a degree so they could better take care of themselves and the people they loved; people who had lost jobs during the Great Recession and who believed their best chance in the job market was to acquire a new set of skills. Corinthian's internal documents betrayed the company's attitude toward its own students: they called their target demographic "isolated," "impatient" men and women with "low self-esteem," who have "few people in their lives who care about them" and who are "stuck" and "unable to see and plan well" for their own future. As far as I was concerned, this conduct was no different from the criminal predators I've known—purposely targeting those most in need.

Of course, most public companies don't act in such a predatory way. But a central tenant of corporate governance—to create value for shareholders even if it's to the detriment of workers—has created a great deal of harm of its own.

For example, to raise stock prices, executives engage in a concept called "buybacks," in which a company buys its own stock off the market, often causing the stock price to jump. Putting aside whether or not buybacks are ever an appropriate tool, let's acknowledge how extreme its use has become.

Between 2003 and 2012, S&P 500 companies spent 91 percent of their earnings on buybacks and dividends for shareholders. That leaves 9 percent to invest across the entire company, in everything from research and development to worker wages.

What's the result of all this? It's been great for the richest 1 percent of American households, who now own 40 percent of the nation's wealth, which adds up to roughly $40 trillion. But it's been a financial nightmare for the middle class. According to research done by United Way, 43 percent of households can't afford basic expenses: a roof over their head, food on the table, child care, health care, transportation, and a cell phone.

What are people supposed to think about a government that has left them behind? How are you supposed to feel when you're drowning and no one is coming to your aid, and then you turn on the television and hear that the economy is doing great? Great for whom?

It's not great for people who have had to move hours away from their job just to find an affordable place to live. It's not great for people who are dropping out of the workforce because they can't afford child care. It's not great for the people who are giving up on their dream of going to college because they know they can't afford it.

And yet with millions of Americans hanging by a thread, the White House reached for scissors. In 2017, the administration cut taxes for people who didn't need it and raised taxes on people who can't afford it. They sabotaged the Affordable Care Act, driving up premiums. They ignited a trade war that could lead to higher prices on things we all buy, from groceries to cars. They nominated judges intent on destroying organized labor. They canceled a pay raise for federal civil servants—everyone from transportation security officers to food inspectors, park rangers, medical personnel, and more. They even halted the debt relief policy that we put in place to help Corinthian Colleges' victims. And for good measure, they did away with net neutrality, which will allow internet companies to charge a premium for popular websites for the first time, adding an unacceptable new bill to the stack.

Dear Senator Harris,

I'm a high school student and most of my school work depends on the internet and the tools it gives us. My school is small and doesn't have much money, plus I come from a poor background and my parents struggle to make ends meet. If you take away Net Neutrality, you're basically taking away all the tools the internet provides students like me to succeed in school and adding more problems to poor families all over the nation.

We are running out of time. That's the hard truth. And not just in terms of dealing with what is so urgent right now. We are running out of time to deal with major changes to come. With the rise of artificial intelligence, we are likely to face an automation crisis in this country, with millions of jobs on the line.

Industries are changing. Self-driving trucks could cost 3.5 million truck drivers their jobs. The entire tax preparation business could disappear, too. The McKinsey Global Institute found that as many as 375 million people worldwide will need to switch jobs because of automation and predicts that 23 percent of current working hours could become automated by 2030. Another analysis suggests that automation could displace 2.5 million jobs a year in the near term. We have seen, already, the cost of displacement. But nothing has yet prepared us for what is to come.

We will also have to cope with the realities of climate change, which is as much an economic crisis as it is an environmental one. In 2017, extreme weather events in America—things like hurricanes, tornadoes, droughts, and floods—killed more than 362 people, displaced more than one million, and caused more than $300 billion in damage. Experts predict that over time, things will get much worse. The economic toll will follow—hitting states in the South and the lower Midwest the hardest. After Hurricane Harvey hit the Gulf Coast in 2017, a study found that in Houston, three of every ten affected residents fell behind on their rent or mortgage; 25 percent had trouble paying for meals.

Climate change imperils industries, too. Temperature and current changes in the oceans are already hurting the fishing industry. The agriculture industry faces dangers on multiple fronts: a rise in invasive species, pests, fungus, and disease; changing weather patterns that will lower yields; and the constant fear of drought.

Put bluntly, we have work to do. Hard work. Indispensable work. We have everything we need—all of the raw ingredients—to build an economy for the twenty-first century that is fair and sturdy, an economy that rewards the work of those who sustain it. But we have to hurry. And we have to be willing to speak truth.

We need to acknowledge that the jobs of the future are going to require people to earn an education after high school, whether it's a certification or a university degree. This isn't optional anymore. If we want to be true to the principle that all Americans deserve access to public education, then we can't stop funding it after high school. We need to invest in our workforce, now and in the future, and that means we're going to have to invest in more post–high school education, too. It means, among other things, that we have to make debt-free college a reality.

Let's speak truth about housing affordability. We can't have a functioning society if people can't afford to live in it. The housing crisis is not something we can just shrug off as if it is a fact of nature. We've got to make a major effort, from changing zoning laws to encourage new and affordable housing to giving relief to people who are struggling—right now—to pay their rent. For starters, I introduced a Senate bill that would give overburdened renters some relief. If someone is paying more than 30 percent of their income in rent and utilities, they would receive a new refundable tax credit to help defray their housing costs. But there's much more to do.

Let's speak truth about child care. If we don't find a way to make it affordable, we're not only subjugating people in financial crisis; we are also making it harder for women to stay in the workforce when they want to. This is one of the systemic barriers to women's growth and success in the workplace. We need to tear it down.

And let's speak truth about what we have to build up. To put people to work in well-paid jobs, and to prevent our economy from lagging, we should be investing in rebuilding our nation's infrastructure. We have roads and bridges that need building and upgrading. We have broadband internet infrastructure to build in rural areas that still lack it. We have new wind farms and transmission lines that need installing. We have airports that need modernizing and subways in dire need of repair. If not for ourselves, shouldn't we at least do this work for our children and grandchildren?

Let's also speak truth about organized labor, which has been systematically dismantled by the Republican Party. Less than 7 percent of the private workforce is represented by unions today, and a 2018 Supreme Court ruling is likely to decimate public sector union membership as well. Many people have already written the obituary for the labor movement. But we can't accept that. Unions are the ones lobbying in Washington exclusively on behalf of workers. They are the only ones who have given the power to the people in the workplace. In the midst of a Republican effort to hollow out the middle class, it is the unions that have successfully compelled management to pay better wages and provide better benefits. We need a rebirth of organized labor in America.

And let's speak one final truth: big corporations and the richest people in the richest country in the world can afford to pay their fair share of taxes so that we can fix the economy. It's necessary, it's moral, and it's wise.

Nine

SMART ON SECURITY

When I arrived in the Senate, I was surprised to learn that there was a seat open on the Senate Select Committee on Intelligence. I asked outgoing senator Barbara Boxer why this was. She told me that the committee's work was fascinating, meaningful, and critical to the country, but that most of it took place behind closed doors. Members of the committee couldn't talk publicly about their activities, because reviewing the country's most sensitive intelligence involved the highest levels of security clearance. Consequently, she explained, there usually wasn't much of a spotlight on the committee.

That didn't matter to me. I knew that, by the very nature of the job, if I had something important to say, I could find a bouquet of microphones to speak into. But when it came to the daily work, I wanted to be informed in real time about the threats facing my constituents and our country.

So I joined the Senate Intelligence Committee, fully expecting the work to be done in the shadows, away from the press and outside the day-to-day focus of the national conversation. But days after I was sworn in as a United States senator, those expectations were upended. On January 6, 2017, the intelligence community released a public assessment that determined that Russia had conducted multiple cyber operations against the United States, with the intent of influencing the outcome of the 2016 presidential election. Suddenly our work—an investigation into what had gone so terribly wrong—would become one of the most consequential undertakings in the history of the Senate.

Most of what I do on the committee involves classified information, so there's a real limit to what I can write about here. But there are times when the intelligence community releases its assessments to the public, stripped of the information sources and methods by which the information was obtained, and meticulously written to avoid revealing anything that could compromise national security or endanger people's lives. And there are times when our committee works in close coordination with the intelligence community to release our own assessments publicly so that we can balance the critical need for the American people to know what is happening from our oversight perspective against the equally critical need to keep our intelligence-gathering efforts covert. I can—and will—reference that work.

Twice a week, for two hours at a time, members of the Intelligence Committee get together behind closed doors to speak with the men and women who lead our seventeen intelligence agencies and receive briefings on the latest information. I can't tell you the details of what we talk about, but I can tell you what it's like. For starters, the room we gather in is known as a SCIF, which stands for Sensitive Compartmented Information Facility. It has been designed to prevent eavesdropping of any kind. Before we enter, we have to put our cell phones in a cupboard outside the door. Inside, we take classified notes by hand, and even those must be kept locked away in the SCIF.

When the committee holds public hearings, Democrats sit on one side of the dais and Republicans on the other as we face witnesses and cameras. But inside the SCIF and away from the cameras, it is a very different environment. Often senators take off their jackets. We get down to business. It is not just the absence of cameras and the seating arrangement that changes the dynamic; it is the work itself. The rigid partisanship that has paralyzed much of Washington somehow fades as we enter the room. We are, all of us, keenly focused on the weight of the work we are undertaking and its consequences. There is simply no room for anything other than a focus on America's national security and the protection of Americans' privacy and civil liberties. The public can't be there, nor the media, nor other senators who aren't on the committee. It's just us, to do oversight with global reach. It is invigorating, even inspiring. It is a scene I wish the American people could see, if just for a moment. It is a reminder that even in Washington, some things can be bigger than politics.

My work on the Intelligence Committee and the Homeland Security Committee covers a broad range of issues, from building and maintaining counterterrorism capability at home and abroad to the work of disrupting and destroying ISIS; to protecting and securing our borders; to the challenge of nuclear proliferation; and to the ever delicate balance between gathering intelligence and protecting civil liberties. But rather than run through the laundry list of issues we deal with in all their complexity, I want to focus on a few of the threats that keep me up at night.

First and foremost, I think of cybersecurity—a new front in a new kind of battle. If we had a daily visual of attacks under way—of explosions in our cities, of Russian, Chinese, North Korean, and Iranian warplanes overhead—the American people would insist that we respond, clear in the knowledge that the future of the American experiment was very much at risk. But cyber warfare is silent warfare, and its consequences are often difficult to grasp before the damage is done. I sometimes refer to it as a war without blood: there are no soldiers in the field, no bullets and bombs. But the reality is cyber warfare aims to weaponize infrastructure and, at its worst, could result in casualties. Imagine, for example, a cyberattack on railroad switching signals or hospital generators or a nuclear power plant.

The intelligence community and private companies alike are waging a defensive battle against cyberattacks on a minute-by-minute basis. But the reality is that we still remain unprepared for this new kind of terrain. Our systems and infrastructure need to be seriously upgraded.

We are currently under attack. Our elections are top of mind, especially given the nefarious—and effective—attacks by the Russian government. The January 2017 assessment found that "Russian President Vladimir Putin ordered an influence campaign in 2016 aimed at the U.S. presidential election. Russia's goals were to undermine public faith in the U.S. democratic process, denigrate Secretary Clinton, and harm her electability and potential presidency." Though many have become numb to it through the news cycle, the significance of this finding is hard to overstate. The intelligence community assessed, with a high degree of confidence, that Russia's intelligence services conducted cyber operations to hack into a U.S. presidential campaign and to release data they gathered with the intent of influencing the outcome of the election.

Russian agents and propagandists exploited U.S. social media platforms such as Facebook, Twitter, and YouTube to spread false and inflammatory information about Secretary Clinton and to stoke divisions in the United States. And what I think is very telling is exactly how they went about it.

They focused on hot-button issues, from race to LGBTQ and immigrant rights. This means that they knew that racism and other forms of hate have always been our nation's Achilles' heel. They knew precisely where to strike us, deliberately targeting—and tearing away at—some of the most painful, divisive parts of our nation's history.

I first made this point during an Intelligence Committee meeting. A few days later, I was sitting at my desk on the Senate floor, the last one in the far back. I had chosen the desk for two reasons: it wasn't visible on the C-SPAN cameras, which made it easier for me to concentrate on the work at hand. But, more important, it was the desk closest to the candy drawer.

I looked up and noticed that Senator James Lankford, a Republican from Oklahoma, was walking toward me, literally crossing the aisle so we could have a conversation.

"Kamala, I've been listening to what you've been saying about race as our Achilles' heel, and I think you're on to something important," he said. "Personally, I think it starts with the question 'Have you had a family over to your house that doesn't look like you? Have you ever really had that kind of interaction? I think that's a good place to start."

"I'm glad to hear you say that," I told him. "We have to start somewhere."

Lankford and I sat across from each other in closed sessions of the Intelligence Committee, and though there are very few things we agree about when it comes to policy, I found him to be genuinely kind and thoughtful. It didn't take long for us to build a friendship.

Together with our colleagues on the committee, we spent more than a year working with the intelligence community to understand the information that led to the January 2017 assessment about Russian attacks. Of particular interest to me was the threat of Russian penetration of our election equipment itself. In May 2018, we released our preliminary findings on the issue of election security. We let the public know that in 2016, the Russian government had conducted a coordinated cyber campaign against the election infrastructures of at least eighteen individual states, and possibly as many as twenty-one. Other states also saw malicious activity, which the intelligence community has been unable to attribute to Russia. What we do know is that Russian operatives scanned election databases looking for vulnerabilities. They attempted to break in. And in some cases, they were actually successful in penetrating voter registration databases. Thankfully, as of May 2018, our committee had not seen any evidence that actual vote tallies or voter registration rolls were changed. But given our limited information on state audits and forensic examinations of states' own election infrastructures, we cannot rule out that activities were successfully carried out that we just don't know about yet.

In our report, we raised concerns about a number of potential vulnerabilities that remain in our election infrastructure. Voting systems are outdated, and many of them do not have a paper record of votes. Without a paper record, there is no way to reliably audit a vote tally and confirm that numbers haven't been changed. We found that thirty states use paperless voting machines in some jurisdictions, and that five states use them exclusively, leaving them vulnerable to manipulation that cannot be reconciled and reversed. We also found that many of our election systems are connected to the internet, leaving them open to hacking. Even systems not regularly connected to the internet are nevertheless updated by software that must be downloaded from the internet.

It's misleading to suggest that impenetrable cybersecurity is possible; our focus must be on defending against, detecting, deterring, managing, and mitigating any effort to do us harm. There's a grim joke: What's the difference between being hacked and not being hacked? Knowing you've been hacked. The truth hurts—but we simply can't afford to be naive.

To help members of Congress and their staffs understand the nature of the risk, I invited a computer science and engineering professor from the University of Michigan to visit the Capitol and demonstrate the ease with which a hacker could change an election's outcome. We gathered in a room in the Capitol Visitor Center, where the professor had set up a paperless voting machine used in numerous states, including swing states like Florida, Pennsylvania, and Virginia. Four senators participated—Senators Lankford, Richard Burr, Claire McCaskill, and me—and the room was filled with staffers who had come to better understand the process.

The professor simulated a vote for president, where we were given a choice between George Washington and the infamous Revolutionary War traitor Benedict Arnold. As you might imagine, all four of us voted for George Washington. But when the result came back,

Benedict Arnold had prevailed. The professor had used malicious code to hack the software of the voting machine in a way that assured Arnold's victory, no matter how the four of us had voted.

He told us that the machine was very easily hacked, enough so that, in a demonstration elsewhere, he turned one into a video game console and played *Pac-Man* on it. Can you imagine?

America's electoral infrastructure consists of outdated machines and local officials who often have little or no cyber-threat training. When you consider how many major corporations have experienced data breaches, despite having invested in the best cybersecurity money can buy, our vulnerability becomes all the more stark. Some might think it is alarmist to be talking this way, but I think we should be preparing to defend against the worst-case scenario: that foreign actors will target these outmoded machines and manipulate vote tallies. Given Russia's unprecedented effort to undermine confidence in our election system while attempting to interfere with the outcome of a presidential election, there's no question that the Kremlin is emboldened—along with other state and nonstate actors—to try again.

At the time, James Lankford and I were the only members of the Senate who served on both the Homeland Security and Intelligence Committees. As such, we were uniquely suited to come together in a nonpartisan way to develop legislation to combat these attacks. At the end of December 2017, together with other senators, we introduced a bill—the Secure Elections Act—that would protect the United States from future foreign interference in our elections.

The legislation—which grew out of hearings and testimony in front of both the Homeland Security and Intelligence Committees, would improve cybersecurity information sharing between federal and state agencies. It would create a process by which election officials could receive top-secret security clearance, allowing them to have timely access to classified material (as in a case where we learned that Russia had attacked their machines). It would establish clear expert guidelines for securing election systems—including, for example, the need for paper ballots. Russia might be able to hack a machine from afar, but it can't hack a piece of paper. And it would provide $386 million in grants for cybersecurity improvements.

It would also establish what's known as a bug bounty program for election infrastructure. Commonly used in tech firms, a bug bounty is a system by which altruistic hackers are paid for identifying software vulnerabilities. It's an economically efficient way to quickly patch bugs that could be exploited by malicious actors. We owe it to ourselves to continually test our system's security, just as we'd test the smoke alarm in our home. No one wants to wait for the house to catch on fire in order to realize the battery's dead.

Remarkably, despite the bill's bipartisan support, as of this writing, it has yet to receive a vote in the United States Senate. Though it was introduced nearly a year before the 2018 midterm elections, the White House opposed the bill, and the Senate majority leader refused to bring it to the floor. And so I am, indeed, kept up at night, knowing the scale of our vulnerabilities and knowing that actions we should be taking immediately have stalled out without any justification.

It's also important to remember that election systems aren't the only area in which we are vulnerable to foreign interference.

In March 2018, for example, the Department of Homeland Security and the FBI issued a joint alert that showed that Russian hackers had gained access to the computer systems of organizations and U.S.

government entities in sectors ranging from energy and water to aviation and manufacturing. DHS and the FBI described the actions as a "multi-stage intrusion campaign by Russian government cyber actors who targeted commercial facilities' networks and staged malware, conducted spear phishing, and gained remote access into energy sector networks." After they got access, the Russians did extensive reconnaissance. They were able to gain access to at least one power plant's control system. And they placed tools in the systems that would allow them, in certain cases, to shut down power plants at will.

This is, needless to say, an extraordinary vulnerability. Millions of Americans recall the blackout of August 2003, when an electricity surge overloaded the grid covering parts of eight northeastern states. Major cities were plunged into darkness. Fire departments rushed to free people from elevators as building temperatures rose. Hundreds of trains were stopped in their tracks, and thousands of passengers had to be rescued from darkened subway tunnels. Waste treatment plants lost power; 490 million gallons of raw sewage were spilled in New York City alone. Cell phone service was disrupted. ATMs went down. Hospitals had to rely on generators to care for vulnerable patients. Analysts later concluded that mortality rates in New York City rose 28 percent during the two-day blackout.

In the intelligence community's Worldwide Threat Assessment in 2018, the director of national intelligence detailed increased risks to critical infrastructure over the coming year. "The use of cyberattacks as a foreign policy tool outside of military conflict has been mostly limited to sporadic lower-level attacks," the report explained. "Russia, Iran, and North Korea, however, are testing more aggressive cyberattacks that pose growing threats to the United States and U.S. partners."

Iran, which in the past has attacked a large U.S. corporation and stolen personal data, is expected to continue its work penetrating the United States' cyber infrastructure. North Korea, which conducted a destructive attack on Sony in November 2014, and which the U.S. government identified as responsible for a massive cyberattack in the United Kingdom that paralyzed that country's health care system, is expected to use its cyber operations to steal money in the wake of sanctions, as it did in 2016, when it took $81 million from the Bangladesh Bank. China, meanwhile, has been advancing its own cyberattack capabilities since 2015 and has directed attacks at U.S. private industry, particularly defense contractors and IT and communications firms whose products and services support worldwide networks. An investigation by the Office of the United States Trade Representative found that Chinese theft of American intellectual property costs us more than $200 billion annually.

And then there are nonstate actors. As the DNI threat assessment indicates, "Transnational criminals will continue to conduct for-profit cyber-enabled crimes, such as theft and extortion against US networks." This is costly business: in February 2018, cybersecurity software provider McAfee and the nonpartisan Center for Strategic and International Studies released a report that put such cybercrime's toll in North America at $140 billion to $175 billion. And we can also expect state actors to fund such criminal activity, which represents both an inexpensive and deniable way for them to pursue their malicious aims.

Cybersecurity has to become one of our highest priorities in this new age. It's not enough to make sure that our troops have the very best weapons when they go into battle. We also have to make sure our military, intelligence community, and private sector have the very best cyber defenses to protect against these new and ever-changing threats. As General Keith Alexander, former NSA director and inaugural head of U.S. Cyber Command, said in 2016, Department of Defense systems are probed by hackers about 250,000 times an hour. That's six million times each day.

In a world where tech can be weaponized, we need to deploy the very best technology in order to respond. And that means constantly upgrading our efforts so that we are always a step ahead.

I remember that when I first became attorney general, in 2011, I was shocked by what we lacked in terms of technology. So I put together a team, led by Special Assistant Attorney General Travis LeBlanc, to upgrade and overhaul our system so that we could better fight crime in the digital era. In my first year in office, we organized an "eCrime Unit," which we staffed with attorneys and investigators who focused on technology-related crimes like identity theft and cyber exploitation. I spent much of the remainder of my tenure working to institutionalize California's technological advantages. Those efforts culminated in the creation of our Cyber Crime Center, which gave all of our tech crime fighters access to state-of-the-art digital forensics capabilities, making California one of the first states to do so.

But in addition to deploying our best technology now, we need to invest in the innovations and breakthroughs that we'll need in order to stay protected down the line. That's one of the reasons I've put forward a bill to invest in quantum computing, a frontier technology that would put the United States at the forefront of the race for technological superiority. Our pursuit of innovation cannot be viewed from an economic lens alone. It matters to national security, too. It's also one of the reasons I believe we must be a country that welcomes highly skilled students and professionals from around the world to study at our universities and work at our companies.

Ultimately, I believe we are going to need to develop a cyber doctrine. As a matter of principle, we will have to decide when and whether a cyberattack is an act of war, and what kind of response it warrants.

On January 12, 2017, Mike Pompeo came before the Senate Intelligence Committee for his confirmation hearing as CIA director. By tradition, questions at public hearings are asked in order of seniority, so, as the newest member of the committee, I questioned Pompeo last. Throughout the hearings, I listened as my colleagues asked Pompeo a wide range of questions, touching on traditional issues ranging from intelligence sharing and collection to preventing terrorist attacks in the United States and abroad. When it was finally my turn, I focused on a subject area that seemed to surprise Pompeo and others on the committee. I wanted to know how his public position rejecting the science of climate change was going to impact his role at the top of America's intelligence apparatus.

Right-wing pundits from Fox to the Heritage Foundation took great pleasure in calling my questions "dumb," "ridiculous," and "off-base." Evidently, they felt my concerns were divorced from issues of national security. But they were wrong. This was about analytic objectivity and not politicizing intelligence. The CIA had already made an unclassified assessment regarding the threat of climate change. Pompeo's previous statements disregarded the CIA assessment. How would he brief the president? Would he let his personal views override the findings of CIA professionals when it came to climate change—and, if so, what would that mean for other dire threats against our nation?

Climate change can be seen from many angles. Some see it purely as an environmental issue. They point to the destruction of habitats, the melting of ice sheets, and a coming mass extinction of species. Others see it as a public health issue that demands a world where clean air and clean water are readily available. There is also the economic dimension of climate change: ask farmers about the complexity of their work, about their precise and measured focus on weather patterns, about the incredibly narrow margins that exist between a successful harvest and a ruinous one, and you will come to understand that extreme weather events and unpredictable shifts in the climate are nothing to dismiss.

But when you speak to generals, when you speak to senior members of the intelligence community and experts on international conflicts, you will find that they look at climate change as a national security threat—a "threat multiplier" that will exacerbate poverty and political instability, creating conditions that enable violence, despair, even terrorism. An unstable, erratic climate will beget an unstable, erratic world.

For example, climate change will lead to droughts. Droughts will lead to famine. Famine will drive desperate people to leave their homes in search of sustenance. Massive flows of displaced people will lead to refugee crises. Refugee crises will lead to tension and instability across borders.

Climate change also increases the risk of deadly global pandemics making their way to the United States. The Centers for Disease Control and Prevention reported that between 2006 and 2016, the number of Americans infected by diseases like West Nile, Zika, and Lyme more than tripled. As temperatures continue to warm, diseases are flourishing in parts of America where they wouldn't have been able to survive in the past. In fact, the CDC has already identified nine types of infections that had never been seen before in the United States.

The hard truth is that climate change is going to cause terrible instability and desperation, and that will put American national security at risk. That's why former CIA director John Brennan has said that when CIA analysts look for deeper causes of rising instability in the world, one of the causes they point to is climate change. That's why, as part of President Obama's national security strategy, climate change was identified as a national security threat of the highest priority. That's why the Pentagon has been ahead of the curve in developing resilience to the effects of climate change, including strategies to protect the dozens of military bases that will be affected by rising seas and extreme weather events. And it's why I didn't hesitate in asking the person who would become the nation's CIA director how and whether climate change would be a factor in his strategy to protect the American people.

This isn't the stuff of science fiction or of a dystopian novel set far in the future. Climate-driven crisis is already on the rise. In late 2017, for example, water reserves fell so low in Cape Town, South Africa, that the city of more than three million people, South Africa's second largest, was at risk of having its taps run dry. Residents started showering over buckets so that they could reuse the water in their washing machines. Farmers had to abandon about a quarter of their crops.

This is an issue we will face at home, too, and it's a matter of national security that we prepare for it. We need a diversified water security strategy to ensure a reliable, sustainable supply. Growing up in California, I understood from an early age that the water supply is precious and precarious. In elementary school, my classmates and I studied ecology; I remember my mother smiling when she had to explain to me the difference between a *conservative* and a *conservationist*. I saw the drought of 1976–77 through a child's eyes— unflushed toilets, shower timers, and dried-out brown lawns. I think a lot about water security, and I never take it for granted.

A diversified approach would work on multiple fronts simultaneously. Conservation is the cheapest, most effective way to increase our water resources. But we also need to update our aging water infrastructure, improve our storm water capture and storage capacity, and make smart investments in water recycling, purification, and desalination.

There's a lot we can learn from friends and partners who have already made such investments—especially Israel, a global leader on water security issues. In February 2018, I traveled to Israel and toured its Sorek desalination plant, which uses reverse osmosis to produce clean drinking water from the sea. I had a glass. It tasted as good as any water I've ever had.

And that's not all. As many have said, the Israelis have made the desert bloom. They've done so in part by successfully reclaiming 86 percent of their wastewater and purifying it for agricultural reuse. By contrast, the United States, which produces 32 billion gallons of municipal wastewater each day, reclaims only 7 to 8 percent. Surely we can do better than that.

Conserving water and safeguarding against scarcity must be a top priority. The same can be said, in this era of climate change, for the need to protect against floods. In India, Bangladesh, and Nepal, flooding in the summer of 2017 killed 1,200 people and affected more than 40 million. Nearly 1 million homes were destroyed. In 2010, flooding in Pakistan rocked 20 percent of the country, killing more than 1,700 people and affecting at least 12 million. Here at home, the destructive force of Hurricane Maria left the island of Puerto Rico in ruins. I visited Puerto Rico in November 2017 and saw some of that devastation firsthand—homes obliterated, roads collapsed and destroyed, and a community in crisis. It was disheartening. The official death toll has been revised from 64 to more than 2,900, but a report from scientists at Harvard's T. H. Chan School of Public Health estimates that the storm and its aftermath were responsible for the deaths of at least 4,600 American citizens in Puerto Rico.

And if it isn't floods, it's fires. Fires aren't caused by climate change, but they are exacerbated by it. Higher temperatures and longer dry spells turn our forests into kindling. California has always had wildfires, but because of climate change, they are becoming more frequent and getting bigger and bigger. When I was attorney general, I had toured a fire overhead by helicopter. From that height, the scale of the devastation came into view—entire streets, entire neighborhoods burned to the ground. It looked like a graveyard, with chimneys as headstones.

In August 2018, I flew home to California to meet with firefighters and evacuees from the Mendocino Complex Fire, which burned more than 450,000 acres, making it the largest fire in the state's history.

When I arrived in Lake County, I went to a convention center where evacuated families were being sheltered temporarily. Some of them knew they had lost their homes and all of their possessions. Others were left to wonder. I met a mom who was pregnant with her third child. She was trying to keep her family's spirits up. I remember how proud her daughter was to show me how neatly she had tidied the sheets on top of the Red Cross cots where they now slept.

A year earlier, I met a firefighter who lost his own home in a fire he was fighting. He said he had always thought he understood the pain of losing everything, given how often he had seen it happen to others—but that it was so much worse than he imagined. Still, he reminded himself and me, it wasn't as bad as the families that got the call that their husband or son had been one of the many firefighters who lost their lives that year.

There is a theme that runs through all of these issues, be it cybersecurity or climate change or keeping aggressors like Russia and North Korea in check. Though the United States is a superpower, there are real limits to what we can do alone. In order to keep the American people safe, in order to ensure that our national interests and homeland are secure, we must work in partnership with our allies—economically, diplomatically, and militarily. We must protect NATO, the most important defensive treaty the world has ever known, especially in the face of Russia's increasingly flagrant aggression. We must rejoin the Paris Agreement, because only together can we reverse the trends of climate change and prevent some of its more terrifying outcomes. And we must remind ourselves that the work we do to protect the American people must also be in service of American values. That the actions we take project a message to the world about who we are.

It was that final truism that I held in mind when Gina Haspel came before our committee in a confirmation hearing to replace Mike Pompeo as CIA director. Haspel, a thirty-three-year veteran of the CIA, had been at the agency during a time when prisoners were tortured. She had been asked many questions about this work by other senators—about whether her actions had been legal; about whether she would ever authorize such actions again.

When it was my turn to speak, I underscored that this hearing wasn't about the incredible and unquestionable importance of the service and sacrifice of the men and women of the CIA, nor was it about the agency's mission, both of which I wholeheartedly support. The hearing, I explained, was about her suitability to be the director of the CIA, and it was our job, as senators, to understand that who we chose for that position would send a signal to the men and women of the agency, the American people, and our neighbors around the world about our values and our moral authority. With that in mind, I initiated what became a revealing exchange:

"So one question I have not heard you answer is: Do you believe that the previous interrogation techniques were immoral?"

Haspel paused as she considered the answer. "Senator, I believe that CIA officers to whom you refer—"

"It's a yes-or-no answer. Do you believe the previous interrogation techniques were immoral? I'm not asking do you believe they were legal; I'm asking do you believe they were immoral?"

She paused again. "Senator, I believe that CIA did extraordinary work to prevent another attack on this country, given the legal tools that we were authorized to use."

"Please answer yes or no. Do you believe in hindsight that those techniques were immoral?"

"Senator, what I believe sitting here today is that I support the higher moral standard we have decided to hold ourselves to."

"Can you please answer the question?"

"Senator, I think I've answered the question."

"No, you have not. Do you believe the previous techniques—now armed with hindsight—do you believe they were immoral? Yes or no?"

"Senator, I believe that we should hold ourselves to the moral standard outlined in the Army Field Manual."

Shortly after Haspel refused to answer the question, the late Senator John McCain, who had been subjected to five years of brutal torture as a prisoner of war in North Vietnam, released a statement saying that he would not support her confirmation as CIA director.

"Like many Americans, I understand the urgency that drove the decision to resort to so-called enhanced interrogation methods after our country was attacked," McCain wrote. "I know that those who used enhanced interrogation methods and those who approved them wanted to protect Americans from harm. I appreciate their dilemma and the strain of their duty. But as I have argued many times, the methods we employ to keep our nation safe must be as right and just as the values we aspire to live up to and promote in the world.

"I believe Gina Haspel is a patriot who loves our country and has devoted her professional life to its service and defense," he continued. "However, Ms. Haspel's role in overseeing the use of torture by Americans is disturbing. Her refusal to acknowledge torture's immorality is disqualifying. I believe the Senate should exercise its duty of advice and consent and reject this nomination."

We live in an uncertain world, one filled with complexity and danger. The challenges we face in the future will be new and nuanced, and they will require us to mobilize based on being smart, not on being afraid. There will be hard decisions to make, to be sure, of the kind that no previous generation has had to consider. And yet it will serve us well to remember what it was that helped us protect the American people and secure the peace in the generations leading up to this moment. We must remember that we are a nation of laws, that we stand for the rule of law. We must remember what we have worked and in some cases bled for: an international order that promotes peace and cooperation; a commitment to democracy, here and around the world; a rejection of despots and tyrants and dictators who rule their countries based on their self-interest alone, not the interests of the people they are meant to serve. Imperfect though we have been, ours is a history in pursuit of a better, safer, freer world. In the years to come, with all the challenges to come, we cannot lose sight of who we are and who we can be.

Ten

WHAT I'VE LEARNED

Early in my career, one of the first cases I tried was a hit-and-run case in Judge Jeffrey Horner's Oakland courtroom. To illustrate my argument, I had printed out a map on a large sheet of paper, which I pinned to an easel with butterfly clips. I needed the map so that I could show the jury the driver's path.

I don't remember all the details of the case, but I do remember this map, because I kept stumbling over north, south, east, and west. To acknowledge my own gaffes, at some point in the proceedings I cracked a self-deprecating joke before the jury. Not long after, during a break, Judge Horner called me into his chamber. "Don't you ever do that again," he said. "You figure it out. Figure it out."

His words stuck with me, along with so many lessons I've absorbed along the way—foundational wisdom from my mother; encouragement and guidance from family members, friends, and trusted mentors; and the powerful examples I've witnessed, both good and bad, that have shaped my understanding of what it takes to lead effectively, what it takes to achieve one's objectives, and what we owe to one another in the process.

These lessons have been informed by my own life experience and leavened by their application over the course of my career. Today they find expression in a series of brief phrases, ones my team members hear so often they'll probably laugh when they read this chapter. One year, my team even had blue stress balls made, with NO FALSE CHOICES emblazoned in white letters.

Of course, it isn't possible to reduce the complexity of leadership to simple slogans. But my team and I rely on these mantras as touchstones and guideposts—as starting points for policy conversations and as ways to determine whether we're on the right track. I'm sharing them here because they say a lot about my personal philosophy and style. And maybe they will help to shape your thinking in some way, as the wisdom earned by other people has helped shape mine.

TEST THE HYPOTHESIS

When I was a kid, I used to accompany my mother to the lab, where she'd give me jobs to do. Cleaning test tubes, mainly. I think she probably knew early on that I wasn't going to follow her into the sciences. It was the humanities and the arts that spoke to me, even as I was in awe of my mother and her colleagues and their work.

But when you're the daughter of a scientist, science has a way of shaping how you think. Our mother used to talk to Maya and me about the scientific method as if it were a way of life. When I'd ask her why something was the way it was, she wasn't content to just give me the answer. She wanted me to formulate my own hypothesis, to use that as a starting point for further investigation, and to challenge my assumptions. This was how she did her work in the lab. The experiments she ran each day were aimed at figuring out whether her ideas would stand after being tested. It was about kicking the tires. She would collect and analyze the data, and draw conclusions from that evidence. If the results didn't support the hypothesis, she would reevaluate.

Innovation is the pursuit of what can be, unburdened by what has been. And we pursue innovation not because we're bored but because we want to make things faster, more efficient, more effective, more accurate. In science, in medicine, in technology, we embrace the culture of innovation—hypotheses, experiments, and all. We expect mistakes; we just don't want to make the same mistake twice. We expect imperfections; it's basic for us. We've gotten used to the idea that software will need to be tweaked and updated. We don't have any problem with the concept of "bug fixes" and upgrades. We know that the more we test something, the clearer we'll understand what works and what doesn't, and the better the final product or process will be.

But in the realm of public policy, we seem to have trouble embracing innovation. That's in part because when you're running for public office and you stand before the voters, you aren't expected to have a hypothesis; you're expected to have "the Plan." The problem is, when you roll out any innovation, new policy, or plan for the first time, there are likely to be glitches, and because you're in the public eye, those glitches are likely to end up on the front page in bold lettering. When the HealthCare.gov website crashed two hours after it launched in 2013, the problem, though temporary, became a stand-in for describing the entire pursuit of affordable health care coverage as folly.

The point is, when you are in public office, there really is a lot of risk associated with pursuing bold actions. Even so, I believe it is our obligation to do so. It is inherent in the oaths we take.

The point of being a public official is to find solutions to problems, especially the most intractable, and to have a vision for the future. I've always said that political capital doesn't gain interest. You have to spend it, and be willing to take the hit. You have to be willing to test your hypothesis and find out if your solution works, based on metrics and data. Blind adherence to tradition should not be the measure of success.

Michael Tubbs, the mayor of Stockton, California, understands this idea better than just about anyone I know. He became mayor, at twenty-six, of a city that had been hammered by the foreclosure crisis and forced into bankruptcy. His city still contends with high poverty and crime and, now, rising rents. Tubbs asked a team of researchers to identify novel ways he could fight poverty, and one of the ideas they came back with was a guaranteed income program. The concept is that giving people direct cash payments can help them make ends meet while giving the economy a boost. And that was a hypothesis he was willing to test. The city is putting together a pilot program, beginning in February 2019, in which it will give a random group of a hundred residents $500 a month for eighteen months to spend however they want. Researchers will check in with the participants regularly during the program. At the end of that time, the city will have a trove of data that will help the mayor—and countless political leaders—determine the effectiveness of such a model.

Another much discussed idea for helping the American workforce is to create a jobs guarantee program. Rather than guarantee a base cash payment, a federal jobs guarantee could ensure that anyone who wants to work will have a good-paying job with dignity. It's an idea straight out of President Franklin Roosevelt's Economic Bill of Rights. Is it possible? Would it work? If it's part of "the Plan" you're running on, you're compelled to say yes. But the better answer is "Let's find out." I signed on to legislation in the Senate to create a model program that will help us do just that. One way or the other, I am confident that the data that comes from such a program will inform our approach.

GO TO THE SCENE

There's a small community in Southern California called Mira Loma that sits just north of the Santa Ana River, at the western edge of Riverside County. It was, for a long time, a rural community, a place of grape vineyards and dairy farms, a place where people loved to ride horses and to raise their children away from the smog of industrial Los Angeles. But in the late 1980s, things started to change.

The rise of globalization meant that the United States would start importing a lot more goods from around the world, and many of those shipping containers from Asia were ending up at Southern California harbors. So nearby Riverside County started approving huge warehouse projects and distribution centers into which trucks would drop off the cargo they picked up at the docks. By the time I was attorney general, there were approximately ninety such mega-complexes in Mira Loma.

Life was transformed for the 4,500 families living in Mira Loma. Farms were dug up and paved over. Traffic became unbearable. The quiet rural community was swallowed up by an industrial warehousing district. And the air turned toxic. Every day, trucks made more than 15,000 trips on Mira Loma's main roads, bringing with them soot and other particulate matter. Soon Mira Loma had one of the highest rates of diesel pollution in the state—well beyond state and federal air quality standards.

Researchers at the University of Southern California conducted a study that found that pollution was linked to poor lung development and other serious illnesses in Mira Loma children. The federal Environmental Protection Agency had already expressed its own concerns about health dangers associated with such filthy air. But things were only getting worse.

The circumstances of Mira Loma were brought to my attention when I learned that the county had approved another complex of warehouses, which would facilitate another 1,500 truck trips through Mira Loma every day. Residents sued to stop it, arguing that the county had failed to take the health concerns seriously and hadn't done the work to mitigate the harm this would cause to a population already experiencing dangerous health impacts. They argued that the county had failed to follow state standards meant to protect communities like theirs. After reviewing the documents, I agreed.

"I want to join the lawsuit," I told my team. "Let's show those families the state has their back."

That could have been the end of it. I was confident that, with state resources behind them, the community would have what it needed to prevail. But taking action wasn't enough. Understanding the circumstances strictly through the lens of briefing documents and discussions with lawyers wasn't enough. I wanted to go to the scene.

As we approached Mira Loma, I could see a towering mass of haze and smog enveloping the community and the surrounding areas. The sun shone through, but with a gray, refracted tint as the toxic cloud settled in. When I got out of the car, the pollution stung my eyes. I could taste it in the air. I could wipe the dust and soot off surfaces with my fingers.

I went into a small meeting room where members of the community had gathered to tell me their stories. One person told me that every day, when the wind changes, he started breathing the fumes. Another told me that it's not safe for children to play outside. More than half the households had children under eighteen, and they were stuck indoors. A soft-spoken woman told me that she was glad I was there, because they had been fighting for a long time and no one ever seemed to listen.

One man told me that they have to wash the soot off their driveways, and clean their clotheslines before they hang any clothes. He worried about the trees in his backyard, which had stopped bearing fruit and were dying. And he expressed his concern for people in the community who were suffering from higher rates of cancer, asthma, and heart disease.

At first, that was all he said. But when the microphone came back to him, the group encouraged him to tell the more personal story that had brought him to the meeting.

"It's hard for me to talk about it. . . . But, I mean, I'll do it to help this community."

Through tears, he began. "I had a daughter . . . and she died before she was fifteen years old. And instead of planning for her fifteenth birthday . . . I was planning for her funeral. . . . She died of lung cancer. Sometimes it's hard for me to talk about it. But if this can help, I'm just telling my story."

It did help. The fight against the county would take place in courtrooms and conference rooms, and we would be not just the voice but the vessel through which the community's story would be told. To really understand the pain that a community is coping with, it's not enough to imagine what it must be like. Smart policies cannot be created in an ivory tower, and arguments aren't won by facts alone. What matters just as much is being there whenever possible, in person, ears and eyes wide open, talking to the folks living closest to the challenge. It mattered that we were there to hear this anguished father's story and the stories of other families in Mira Loma.

It mattered when I visited soldiers in Iraq who were waiting for their next mission, and sailors in San Diego, preparing to deploy for months on a nuclear submarine. It is one thing to talk about the needs of the military and intelligence communities in a Senate hearing room. It is another to go to the scene and make real, in-person connections with the men and women who are serving. I spent a good deal of time with the troops, talked about their specialties and their training, about the challenges of their work and how a combination of bravery and duty had led them to this life. But we talked about other things, too: what they missed, what they feared, what they had left behind, the sacrifice their families had to make while they were gone. It was personal, and that mattered.

It mattered when I visited a Syrian refugee camp in Jordan so that I could get an up-close view of what life was like for the people trapped there—70 percent of them women and children. We drove around the encampment, which seemed to stretch endlessly in all directions, each makeshift dwelling representing a family that had fled war and slaughter. I insisted that we get out of the cars. We walked down a street they had nicknamed the Champs-Élysées, after the famous shopping street in Paris, and we admired the stalls of clothes and food.

At one point, three kids ran up and started talking to me. One of them, a ten-year-old in a blue soccer shirt, took a real liking to me. We took a selfie together and then he asked, through interpreters, if I would come meet his family. I said of course, and I followed him through the camp to where they were living.

When I got there, a large extended family was there to greet me. They had two small dwellings between them and had created a little courtyard between the two, with a board as an overhang. His grandparents were there—the matriarch and patriarch of the family—and they were incredibly welcoming when I arrived.

"Will you stay for tea?" the grandfather asked me. "I'd be honored," I replied.

The grandmother went behind the hut, where there was a water spigot and a small gas camp stove. The next thing I knew she was back, bearing a tray with beautiful glasses, a plate of sweets, and a teapot.

We were all sitting there cross-legged, drinking our tea. I was ready to ask all about them—the story of how they got there, the experience of living in the refugee camp—when the grandfather started to speak.

"Okay, I've invited you into my home. I've given you tea. I've fed you. Now tell me, who are you?"

EMBRACE THE MUNDANE

Bill Gates is obsessed with fertilizer. "I go to meetings where it's a serious topic of conversation," he writes. "I read books about its benefits and the problems with overusing it. It's the kind of topic I have to remind myself not to talk about too much at cocktail parties, since most people don't find it as interesting as I do." Why the fascination? He explains that 40 percent of people on earth owe their lives to higher crop outputs that were made possible only because of fertilizer. It was the literal fuel for the Green Revolution, which helped lift hundreds of millions of people out of poverty. What Gates understands is that there is a big difference between announcing a plan to end world hunger and actually ending it. And closing the gap depends on seemingly mundane details like fertilizer and weather patterns and the height of wheat.

Politics is a realm where the grand pronouncement often takes the place of the painstaking and detail-oriented work of getting meaningful things done. This isn't to say that there's anything inherently wrong with grand pronouncements. Good leadership requires vision and aspiration. It requires the articulation of bold ideas that move people to action. But it is often the mastery of the seemingly unimportant details, the careful execution of the tedious tasks, and the dedicated work done outside of the public eye that make the changes we seek possible.

Embracing the mundane also means making sure that our solutions actually work for the people who need them. When I was attorney general of California, for example, and I went after the for-profit Corinthian Colleges, I was concerned about what would happen to students who'd been defrauded. The students had the right to transfer to another school, get their loan discharged, or get their money back, but the paperwork involved was quite complicated. Most students had no idea how to begin, or even that they had these options in the first place.

We had prevailed in the case, but the students wouldn't actually receive the benefit of the financial relief unless they could navigate the bureaucracy. So my office created a website that walked students, step by step, through this complex process. I wanted to make it as simple as possible for someone to exercise their rights and get actual relief. As we were developing the website, I'd often have our team show it to me, and I'd literally click through the process myself. More than once, I hit a snag. I'd tell them, "If I don't understand it, how will the students?" That meant the team had to rework the interface and the text. But as frustrating as the exercise might have been, it resulted in a better product. Taking the time to perfect the details made the tool more relevant for the students who needed it.

My point is: you have to sweat the small stuff—because sometimes it turns out that the small stuff is actually the big stuff. I read a story once about a principal at a St. Louis elementary school who wanted to take on rampant truancy in her school. When she talked to parents, she realized that many of the kids didn't have clean clothes. Either they didn't have access to washing machines or their families couldn't afford detergent or the power had been shut off. Students were embarrassed to show up at school in dirty clothes. "I think people don't talk about not having clean clothes because it makes you want to cry or go home or run away or something," a student explained. "It doesn't feel good."

So the principal had a washer and dryer installed at her school, and she invited students who had missed more than ten days of class to do their laundry on campus. According to *CityLab*, in the first year of the initiative, more than 90 percent of the students they tracked boosted their attendance.

WORDS MATTER

Words have the ability to empower and to deceive, the power to soothe and to hurt. They can spread important ideas and wrongheaded ones.

They can spur people to action, for good or ill. Words are incredibly powerful, and people in power, whose words can carry furthest and fastest, have an obligation—a duty—to speak them with precision and wisdom. Scripture tells us, "The one who has knowledge uses words with restraint, and whoever has understanding is even-tempered."

I am keenly aware of the potential power that lives in my words—as someone who represents nearly forty million people, who seeks to give voice to the voiceless. And so when I speak, I do so with the knowledge that the words I choose matter.

First, what we call things, and how we define them, shapes how people think about them. Too often, words are used to degrade our impressions of issues, or of one another. It's why I insisted on better terminology in my work with sexually exploited youth. It was not right to refer to these individuals as "teen prostitutes." They were young people who were being exploited and preyed upon by adults.

When I was attorney general, I prosecuted a case against a man who had started a website called UGotPosted.com, which invited people to upload sexually explicit content featuring their former sexual partners. The man who ran the website would then demand payment from those who had been exploited in exchange for removing the images. In the press, and in common parlance, the act of posting the images was described as "revenge porn." In my office, people shorthanded the case as the "revenge porn" case.

I wasn't having any of that. Revenge is something you inflict on someone who has wronged you. These people hadn't wronged their perpetrators. It wasn't revenge. Nor was it pornography. The victims had never intended for the images to be publicly displayed. It was internet-based extortion, plain and simple, so we referred to it as cyber exploitation. I directed my team that we were not to use the term "revenge porn." I encouraged the media not to use the term, either. And I did so for one fundamental reason: words matter.

Second, I choose to speak truth. Even when it's uncomfortable. Even when it leaves people feeling uneasy. When you speak truth, people won't always walk away feeling good—and sometimes you won't feel so great about the reaction you receive. But at least all parties will walk away knowing it was an honest conversation.

That is not to say that all truth is uncomfortable, or that the intention is to cause discomfort. Many truths are incredibly hopeful. I am simply saying that the job of an elected official is not to sing a lullaby and soothe the country into a sense of complacency. The job is to speak truth, even in a moment that does not welcome or invite its utterance.

SHOW THE MATH

Many of us remember taking math tests in grade school, where it wasn't enough to simply answer a question. You had to show your work. That way, your teacher could see how your logic unfolded, step by step. If you got the solution right, the teacher would know that you hadn't just made a lucky guess. And if you got it wrong, she could see exactly where and why—and help you correct your mistake.

"Showing the math" is an approach that I've embraced throughout my career. In part, it's a methodology that helps me and my team test the logic of our own proposals and solutions. When we force ourselves to lay out our assumptions, we often find that there are certain parts of our arguments that assume things they shouldn't. So we go back and revisit them, we revise them, we dive deeper so that when we are ready to put forth a proposal, we can be confident in its soundness.

At the same time, I think leaders who are asking for the public's trust have a responsibility to show the math, too. We can't make other people's decisions for them, but we have to be able to show how we reached ours.

That's why, when I taught young lawyers how to put together a closing argument, I would remind them that it wasn't enough to get up in front of the jury and just tell them, "You must find eight." Their job was to get up there and show the jury that two plus two plus two plus two leads, categorically, to eight. I'd tell them to break down every element. Explain the logic of their argument. Show the jury how they reached their conclusion.

When you show people the math, you give them the tools to decide whether they agree with the solution. And even if they don't agree with everything, they may find that they agree with you most of the way—a kind of policy-making "partial credit" that can form the basis for constructive collaboration.

NO ONE SHOULD HAVE TO FIGHT ALONE

In the spring of 1966, Cesar Chavez led a 340-mile march of Latinx and Filipino farmworkers from California's Central Valley to its state capital in an effort to spur action and direct the country's eyes at the unconscionable ways that farmworkers were being treated. That summer, the United Farm Workers was formed, and under Chavez's leadership, it would become one of the most important civil rights and labor rights organizations in the country.

At the same time, two thousand miles away, Martin Luther King

Jr. was leading the Chicago Freedom Movement. Through speeches and rallies and marches and meetings, he demanded everything from the end of housing discrimination to the need for high-quality education for all.

In September 1966, King sent Chavez a telegram. He wrote about the many fronts on which the battle for equality must be fought—"in the urban slums, in the sweat shops of the factories and fields. Our separate struggles are really one—a struggle for freedom, for dignity, and for humanity."

That is the sentiment I believe we all must embrace. There are so many ongoing struggles in this country—against racism and sexism, against discrimination based on religion, national origin, and sexual orientation. Each of these struggles is unique. Each deserves its own attention and effort. And it would be wrong to suggest that the differences don't matter, or that one solution or one fight will alone solve them all. But at the same time, we should embrace the point that King made to Chavez—that what these struggles have in common is the pursuit of freedom, of basic human dignity. Black Lives Matter can't just be a rallying call for black people, but a banner under which all decent people will stand. The #MeToo movement cannot make lasting structural changes for women in the workplace unless the effort is joined by men. Victories by one group can lead to victories for others, in the courts and in society as a whole. None of us—none of us—should have to fight alone.

And if we are lucky enough to be in a position of power, if our voice and our actions can mobilize change, don't we have a special obligation? Being an ally can't just be about nodding when someone says something we agree with—important as that is. It must also be about action. It's our job to stand up for those who are not at the table where life-altering decisions are made. Not just those people who look like us. Not just those who need what we need. Not just those who have gained an audience with us. Our duty is to improve the human condition—in every way we can, for everyone who needs it.

IF IT'S WORTH FIGHTING FOR, IT'S A FIGHT WORTH HAVING

"On Monday, I stood in front of your office," a protester named Ana Maria Archila exclaimed to Republican senator Jeff Flake, of Arizona, as he got into an elevator. "I told the story of my sexual assault. I told it because I recognized in Dr. Ford's story that she is telling the truth. What you are doing is allowing someone who actually violated a woman to sit on the Supreme Court! This is not tolerable!"

As she spoke, Senator Flake nodded his head but didn't make eye contact. Then another survivor, Maria Gallagher, spoke up: "I was sexually assaulted and nobody believed me. I didn't tell anyone, and you're telling all women that they don't matter, that they should just stay quiet because if they tell you what happened to them you are going to ignore them. That's what happened to me, and that's what you are telling all women in America, that they don't matter."

Senator Flake continued to avoid the woman's gaze. "Look at me when I'm talking to you!" she said, her voice breaking. "You are telling me that my assault doesn't matter, that what happened to me doesn't matter, and that you're going to let people who do these things into power. That's what you're telling me when you vote for him. Don't look away from me!" The elevators closed, and Senator Flake made his way to the room where the Judiciary Committee was holding a vote on the confirmation of Brett Kavanaugh.

I had been appointed to the Judiciary Committee ten months earlier and had expected, at some point, to be part of a Supreme Court confirmation process. But when Anthony Kennedy announced his retirement on June 27, 2018, I counted myself among the millions of people who were stunned and dismayed, especially when we learned that Judge Kavanaugh had been chosen to replace him.

Before we ever knew the name Christine Blasey Ford, we knew from Judge Kavanaugh's public statements, his writings, and his judicial record that he was hostile to civil rights and voting rights and reproductive rights. We knew he would be a reliable vote against unions, against the environment, against corporate regulation.

We knew before his first set of confirmation hearings that there was something in his past that Judge Kavanaugh and the White House were trying to hide. We knew it because 90 percent of Judge Kavanaugh's record was withheld from members of the Judiciary Committee.

We were convinced after those first hearings that Brett Kavanaugh had misled the Senate under oath: about his involvement with stolen documents, about his work with controversial judicial nominees, about his role in Bush-era warrantless wiretapping.

We knew all of this first. And then we learned her name. And then we learned her story.

We learned that when she was in high school, Christine Blasey Ford had gone to a gathering at a house with several people, where Brett Kavanaugh had forced himself on top of her, had grinded against her, and had groped her while trying to take off her clothes. We learned that when she tried to scream, he had put his hand over her mouth, that she believed he was going to rape her, that she feared he might inadvertently kill her.

"I was able to get up and run out of the room," Dr. Ford explained as she testified under oath in front of the Judiciary Committee about the attack. "Directly across from the bedroom was a small bathroom. I ran inside the bathroom and locked the door. I heard Brett and Mark leave the bedroom laughing and loudly walk down the narrow stairs, pinballing off the walls on the way down.

"I waited, and when I did not hear them come back up the stairs, I left the bathroom, ran down the stairs, through the living room, and left the house," she continued. "I remember being on the street and feeling an enormous sense of relief that I had escaped from the house and that Brett and Mark were not coming after me."

I watched her in such awe as she told her story. In front of Dr. Ford sat all twenty-one members of the Senate Judiciary Committee, looking down from a raised dais. Behind her sat an audience of many strangers. To her left was Rachel Mitchell, an Arizona prosecutor who would question Dr. Ford instead of the Republican committee members—all men—who apparently doubted their own ability to question her. There were bodyguards in the room, too, whose protection Dr. Ford now needed. And, of course, there were the cameras, broadcasting every moment, every movement, every word spoken and tear shed in front of a national audience. This was no place for a person to have to talk about the worst day of her life.

And yet there she was in front of us and the world—even after death threats, even after having to leave her home, even after countless vile attacks hurled at her online. Christine Blasey Ford came to Washington out of a sense of what she called her civic duty and testified in one of the most extraordinary displays of courage I have seen in my lifetime.

Then Judge Kavanaugh responded.

"This whole two-week effort has been a calculated and orchestrated political hit," Kavanaugh railed at the committee, "fueled with apparent pent-up anger about President Trump and the 2016 election, fear that has been unfairly stoked about my judicial record, revenge on behalf of the Clintons, and millions of dollars in money from outside left-wing opposition groups!" Fuming, he declared that "the behavior of several of the Democratic members of this committee at the hearing a few weeks ago was an embarrassment." He went on for forty-five minutes. And that was just his opening statement.

"I like beer. I like beer," Kavanaugh said in response to a question from Senator Sheldon Whitehouse, a Democrat from Rhode Island. "I don't know if you do. Do you like beer, Senator, or not? What do you like to drink? Senator, what do you like to drink?"

Minnesota senator Amy Klobuchar, also a Democrat, asked, "So you're saying there's never been a case where you drank so much that you didn't remember what happened the night before, or part of what happened?"

"It's—you're asking about, you know, blackout," he said, with visible frustration. "I don't know. Have you?"

"Could you answer the question, Judge? I just—so you—that's not happened. Is that your answer?"

"Yeah," he said smugly. "And I'm curious if you have."

"I have no drinking problem, Judge," she said, not moments after having described how alcoholism had deeply affected her father.

"Yeah, nor do I," he retorted. It was, if anything, a revealing moment from a man who had sworn up and down that he always treats women with respect.

Near the end of the hearing, it was my turn to question the witness. As everyone was aware, Dr. Ford had taken and passed a polygraph examination. She had called for outside witnesses and expert witnesses to testify. And, most important, she had called for an FBI investigation. I asked Kavanaugh if he would do the same. He repeatedly evaded answering—just as he had done on many questions from my colleagues up to that point. The contrast between Dr. Ford's sincerity and Judge Kavanaugh's caginess was striking.

As was his willingness to mislead the committee. He gave patently false statements about the meanings of certain terms he'd written in his high school yearbook. He downplayed key aspects of his drinking. He was dishonest about the kinds of gatherings he attended in high school.

And that temper. Judge Kavanaugh's flagrant behavior was so outside the norms of judicial standards that in the days after the hearing, the American Bar Association reopened its evaluation of him, and more than 2,400 academics signed an open letter to the Senate saying they were "united, as professors of law and scholars of judicial institutions, in believing that he did not display the impartiality and judicial temperament requisite to sit on the highest court of our land."

And yet from the moment the hearing was over, it seemed the Republican caucus was ready and eager to move on, and that, despite Kavanaugh's performance and despite Dr. Ford's testimony, the committee would push forward with a vote. Shortly after Judge Kavanaugh finished testifying on Thursday night, Republican leaders scheduled a committee vote on his nomination for Friday morning.

There are many reasons why survivors of sexual assault don't report, and one is the fear—or assumption—that they will not be believed. "I was calculating daily the risk/benefit for me of coming forward, and wondering if I would just be jumping in front of a train that was going where it was going anyway," Dr. Ford had testified that morning, "and that I would just be personally annihilated."

As Republican senators pressed ahead, that fear seemed all too justified. Those senators were choosing not to believe Christine Blasey Ford, even though she had risked everything to warn them about what she knew, even though she had reached out before Judge Kavanaugh had even been nominated, even though she had no reason to lie.

They chose not to believe Dr. Ford even as they refused to do a real investigation, even though she had corroborating information that backed up her claims, even though Judge Kavanaugh had more than one accuser. For Judge Kavanaugh's defenders, the cost of believing her—the cost of the truth itself—was simply too high.

"This has been about raw power," I said the next morning after leading a walkout of the committee hearing. "You're seeing that on display in the hearing this morning; you're seeing that in the process from the beginning. . . . This is a failure of this body to do what it has always said it is about, which is to be deliberative."

When I returned to the chamber, there were rumblings. It appeared that Senator Flake had been affected by the survivors who'd stopped him in the elevator on the way to the hearing that morning. After consultation with Senator Chris Coons, a Democrat from Delaware, and others, Senator Flake called for a delay to the final vote so the FBI could be given a week to investigate further. It gave us an unexpected reprieve.

We know now that the victory felt in that moment was fleeting—but that does not diminish its significance. Two survivors of sexual assault standing in front of an elevator seemed to change the mind of a senator whom most saw as immovable, securing an FBI investigation and forcing a delay in an out-of-control process. In that moment, those two brave women were more powerful than all the Democratic senators on the Judiciary Committee. Together they paused history—and gave us one last chance to prevail.

But the White House had one more card to play. The administration limited the scope of the investigation, dictating whom the FBI could speak to, even preventing agents from following up with Dr. Ford and Judge Kavanaugh themselves. And yet for key swing senators, the fact that there had been an investigation of any kind was enough. On October 6, 2018, I stood on the Senate floor and watched as Judge Kavanaugh got confirmed.

I have been writing these words in the days since, even as I finish this manuscript. Like many Americans, I am still processing what our country has just been through. But for now, I will say this: It would be a mistake to downplay the consequences of having Justice Kavanaugh on the Supreme Court. With this lifetime appointment, he will be in a position, along with the conservative majority on the court, to end a woman's right to choose as we know it; to invalidate the Affordable Care Act; to undo the legal basis by which corporations are regulated; to unravel fundamental rights to vote, to marry, and to privacy.

I worry about the ways his partisanship and temperament will infect the court, how it will color his decision making, how it will disadvantage so many who seek relief in the courts. I worry about what it will do to the court itself to have a man credibly accused of sexual assault among its justices. I worry about the message that has been sent yet again to Americans and the world: that in our country, today, someone can rage, lash out, resist accountability, and still ascend to a position of extraordinary power over other people's lives.

But here's what I am not worried about: I am not worried about our commitment to the fight for a better country. I am not worried that this experience has diminished our will. We chose this fight not because we were sure we could win but because we were sure it was right. Because that should be all that matters. And I know it is no bromide of consolation to say what is certainly true: that even though we didn't prevail, this fight mattered.

Dr. Ford did not come forward in vain. As Senator Patrick Leahy said of her decision to speak, "Bravery is contagious." The cameras and microphones that Dr. Ford never sought carried her story and her message far beyond our committee room, inspiring women and men to tell the stories of their sexual assaults, many for the first time. On the day that Dr. Ford testified, the National Sexual Assault Hotline saw a 200 percent increase in calls. Women were calling in to C-SPAN to share their stories. Writing op-eds. Telling their husbands and fathers. They were speaking their truth—and, in so doing, making plainer than ever the pervasiveness of sexual violence.

These survivors took no pleasure in reliving their own pain. Many who came forward had no intention of seeking justice, much less an expectation of receiving it. But they spoke out, like the survivors of Harvey Weinstein, Larry Nassar, and Bill Cosby, like survivors of abuse in the Catholic Church, to help ensure that this conversation will never again be limited to whispers. Sexual violence is real. It is wrong. It affects men as well as women. And no one should suffer in silence. The faces, the voices, the crowds who filled the hearing room and the Hart Building and the streets outside the Supreme Court, the people who flooded social media with messages of solidarity and shared anguish, all command us to listen, to respect, to believe, and to act. Their voices, like Dr. Ford's, will have lasting reach.

Indeed, though this battle is over, the scope of its impact is yet to be seen. History has shown that one person's willingness to stand up for what is right can be the spark that ignites far-reaching change. Anita Hill's testimony wasn't enough to keep Clarence Thomas off the Supreme Court in 1991, but it brought the term "sexual harassment" into the mainstream and started a national conversation. Less than two months after Hill's testimony, Congress passed the Civil Rights Act of 1991, which expanded the remedies available to victims of sexual harassment. The following year, Democratic women took the 1992 elections by storm, doubling the number of women in the House and tripling the number of women in the Senate.

I am not naive. I walk the same halls where one Republican senator told survivors of sexual assault to "grow up," and where another described protesting survivors as a "mob," even as the president he serves was inciting a crowd to humiliate Dr. Ford. I know—we all know—that there are miles still to go before women are accorded the full respect and dignity we deserve. But I am heartened by the unprecedented numbers of women running for office, and the many more who have been politically energized. I am heartened by the new bonds being forged across boundaries of race, age, background, experience, and gender as women and men stand shoulder to shoulder for justice, equality, and basic rights.

This progress is the product of a movement. A movement that started before Anita Hill ever testified and will continue long after Dr. Ford becomes a hero in our children's history books. We will grow stronger through every effort, even when we face setbacks. We will draw wisdom from every chapter, even when those lessons are hard. We will face what is to come with conviction that change is possible—knowing that truth is like the sun. It always rises.

YOU MAY BE THE FIRST.
DON'T BE THE LAST.

I was in the middle of my first campaign for district attorney when I got a call from an old law school friend, Lisa, who was working as a career counselor at a nearby law school. She had met a young black woman named Venus Johnson, a second-year law student who had grown up in Oakland, the child of an immigrant, with dreams of becoming a prosecutor. Not surprisingly, when my friend heard Venus's story, she thought of me.

We arranged to spend a day together in the fall of 2003, and from the moment I shook Venus's hand, I could feel this incredible sense of commonality. I could see myself in her. She was kind enough to spend the day following me around while I campaigned and ran errands. At one point, we ended up shopping for a wedding present for one of my dear friends. (I settled on bedding.) At another, we drove past a storefront that had a sign for my opponent in the window.

"Come on, let's go," I told Venus as I grabbed one of my own signs out of the trunk. We went in and I shook hands with the store owner and asked him for his support.

"But . . . um . . . I have another candidate's sign in my window," he said, not sure what to make of me. "That's okay," I told him. "You can put mine in the window, too!" He agreed, and we were on our way.

Over lunch, Venus and I talked about the reasons she wanted to be a prosecutor, and the kind of work she had hoped to do. I learned that her father had a long career in law enforcement, and that she always imagined herself fighting on behalf of victims. I told her that I had taken a similar path and recommended she follow her instincts and join the Alameda County District Attorney's Office. I'd be happy, I told her, to make some calls on her behalf.

She seemed to wonder why I was doing this for her. I told her that there was something my mother used to say that I always held close. "You may be the first. Don't be the last." My mother had gotten to where she was because of the help of mentors. I had gotten to where I was because of mentors, too. And I intended to be a mentor to as many people as I could during the course of my career.

A few years after my first conversation with Venus, she got the job she'd been dreaming of in the Alameda County DA's Office. She worked there for eight years, and, like me, she specialized in helping victims of sexual violence. We spoke regularly over those years. In 2014, she joined me in the attorney general's office, and about one year into her working for me on legislative matters, I had a specific request for her.

I called her into my office. "I want you to be my associate attorney general and my de facto chief of staff." There was a pregnant pause. "Me?" she asked. "Yes, you!" I've had a lot of good fortune in my life, but I'm not sure I've ever felt as lucky as the moment she said yes. She was as wonderful at the job as I thought she would be. In addition to keeping things moving, staffing me, and being the last person in line to ensure that I was prepared for meetings and press conferences, she helped to manage a complex bureaucracy and lead major initiatives on my behalf as a legal and policy adviser. I couldn't have asked for a better member of the team.

During those years, we spent a lot of time together. We've continued to speak since our time in the attorney general's office. Sometimes about her cases. Sometimes about career moves she was considering. Once about a recipe for a really amazing chicken broth.

Venus was part of the inspiration for a speech I often give, especially in front of groups of young women. I like to induct them into what I call the Role Models Club.

I tell them that, whatever profession they choose, they've got to keep raising their hands, to share—and take credit for—their good ideas, and to know that they deserve to rise as high as they dare to climb. I also tell them that when they see others in need, they've got to go out of their way to lift them up.

I tell them that sometimes members of the Role Models Club can feel alone. Sometimes they may think, "Do I have to carry this burden by myself?" The fact is, they will find themselves in rooms where no one else looks like them. And breaking barriers can be scary. When you break through a glass ceiling, you're going to get cut, and it's going to hurt. It is not without pain. But I ask them to look around at one another and hold that image in their brains and their hearts and their souls. I tell them to remember that they are never in those rooms alone—that we are all in there with them, cheering them on. And so when they stand up, when they speak out, when they express their thoughts and feelings, they should know that we're right there in that room with them and we've got their back. I know Venus always has mine.

I 've seen a lot in my years of public service. And what I've learned can't all be boiled down. But I've come away with the firm belief that people are fundamentally good. And that, given the chance, they will usually reach out a hand to help their neighbor.

I've learned, through history and experience, that not all progress is gradual or linear. Sometimes it simply goes from one plateau to another. Sometimes we fall back tragically. Sometimes we leap forward and achieve things beyond the realm of what we thought possible. I believe that our job is to provide the force propulsion that will get us to a higher plane.

We have yet to achieve that perfect union. Alongside the great achievements of the American experiment lies a dark history that we have to deal with in the present. In the face of powerful headwinds, it's easy to become tired. To become overwhelmed. But we cannot give up. The beginning of our downfall comes when we stop aspiring.

Let me speak one final truth: For all of our differences, for all the battles, for all the fights, we are still one American family, and we should act like it. We have so much more in common than what separates us. We need to paint a picture of the future in which everyone can see themselves, and everyone is seen. A vibrant portrait of a vibrant United States, where everyone is treated with equal dignity and each of us has the opportunities to make the most of our own lives. That is the vision worth fighting for, born out of love of country.

It is an age-old fight. And what we know about it is this: Victories won can be lost in complacency. Battles lost can be won with new effort. Every generation has to recommit to the work, to the effort, and to the true meaning of the word "patriot." A patriot is not someone who condones the conduct of our country, whatever it does; it is someone who fights every day for the ideals of the country, whatever it takes.

What I have seen, especially since becoming a United States senator, is that this is a fight born out of optimism, too. I see hundreds of Dreamers walking the halls of the Capitol who believe that if they are heard, they can make a difference. And they will. I see it in the parents who traveled from all over the country to Washington with their disabled children, to show Congress the faces of those who would lose coverage if the Affordable Care Act was repealed. I see it in the women who fight every day for the right to make their own decisions about their bodies. I see it in the Parkland survivors, who march and fight and organize for gun safety laws, and who have achieved significant victories that tell them a better future is possible.

When I travel our country, I see that optimism in the eyes of five- and seven- and ten-year-olds who feel a sense of purpose in being part of the fight. I see it, and feel it, in the energy of the people I meet. Yes, people are marching. Yes, people are shouting. But they are doing it from a place of optimism. That's why they've got their babies with them. That's why my parents took me in a stroller to civil rights marches. Because as overwhelming as the circumstances may be, they believe, as I do, that a better future is possible for us all.

My daily challenge to myself is to be part of the solution, to be a joyful warrior in the battle to come. My challenge to you is to join that effort. To stand up for our ideals and our values. Let's not throw up our hands when it's time to roll up our sleeves. Not now. Not tomorrow. Not ever.

Years from now, our children and our grandchildren will look up and lock eyes with us. They will ask us where we were when the stakes were so high. They will ask us what it was like. I don't want us to just tell them how we felt. I want us to tell them what we did.

ACKNOWLEDGMENTS

When I sat down to write about my life, I didn't expect the process to become a life experience of its own. During one of the most tumultuous years in recent memory, my weeks started early and ended late, and I spent most weekends working on this book: recalling the professional experiences that had led up to it; revisiting the childhood that formed my way of thinking; and reflecting on what this inflection point represents. Writing this book has reinforced for me what drew me to public service and what will always be worth fighting for, and I am so grateful to everyone in my life who helped me along the way. There are a lot of you to thank.

First, I want to thank the people of California, whom I've been so honored to represent. Thank you for believing in a brighter future for our state and our nation, and for working so hard to make it so. Thank you for believing in me, for putting your trust in me all these years. I want you to know that I try hard to earn it every day. And I want to especially thank the people who wrote letters to me and let me share excerpts in this book. Your stories matter.

I also want to thank my extraordinary Senate staff, in Washington and California, for the critical work you do each day on behalf of the American people. I am so grateful for your sense of purpose and your dedication. I know this work is personal to each of you. In particular, I want to thank Tyrone Gale, who started with me as my press secretary on day one in the Senate, and whom we recently lost to cancer. Tyrone is irreplaceable. He was an exceptional talent and an exceptional person—kind, warm, generous, and deeply committed to public service. Those of us who knew him will carry his memory forward, and try each day to live up to the example he set.

Like everything in my life, this book would not have been possible without the love, support, and help of family. Doug, thank you for your advice, encouragement, and feedback on this project. Cole and Ella, you are an endless source of love and pure joy for me. As I watch you enter the world, choosing your own unique paths, it makes me so proud, every day, to be your Momala.

Maya, writing this book was like reliving our childhood. The list of things I have to thank you for is too long for these pages. So let me use this simply to thank you for the input and insights you offered throughout this process. Thank you, also, for bringing me a brother in Tony, and for Meena. Meena, I remember you at two years old, walking around the house, literally in my shoes. Now you're a leader in your own right who has forged an important path and whose advice I cherish. Thank you for everything, especially for my baby nieces, Amara and Leela, and their amazing dad, Nik.

Thank you to my father, who, when I was a young girl, encouraged me to be fearless. Thank you to my Chittis, Sarala and Chinni, and to my uncle Balu, for the love you've shared with me across great distances. Thank you to Auntie Lenore for being such an important part of my life, and to Uncle Aubrey, for sharing memories of those early days during the writing process. And thank you to Mimi and Denise for always encouraging me.

To Chrisette and Reggie, thank you for encouraging me to write this book at the earliest stage. I've mentioned many of my dearest personal friends in this book and could have written volumes more about the experiences we've shared. Suffice it to say, I am so grateful to Amy, Chrisette, Lo, Stacey, Vanessa, and everyone (too many to mention here) with whom I've been blessed to travel this journey of life. When people ask me the secret to life, I tell them it's having good friends who become your family. That's what you've all been for me, and what I've tried to be for you. And thank you for all the godchildren you've brought into my life.

This book would not have been possible without the support of my broader family, too—staff and former staff who have been at my side throughout the years.

Thank you to my longtime advisers, Ace Smith, Sean Clegg, and Juan Rodriguez, for always being there for me, and for your insights and perspectives through the years.

I am deeply grateful to my former staff from my days as attorney general and district attorney. You've all gone off to do such wonderful things but have remained part of the family. There are so many to whom I am grateful. Special thanks to Venus Johnson, Debbie Mesloh, Brian Nelson, Lateefah Simon, Dan Suvor, Michael Troncoso, and others for all your help with this project. And thank you to Josie Duffy Rice, who is like a niece to me, for your comments and suggestions on the manuscript. I have so much respect for your perspective and your perceptions. I also want to thank John Pérez, whom I still refer to as Mr. Speaker, as well as Marc Elias for your wise counsel.

Of course, none of this would be possible without the extraordinary team at Penguin, led by Scott Moyers. Scott, you were the best editor a person could have asked for, and I will always be grateful to you for understanding the vision of the book I wanted to write. Thank you to Creative Artists Agency, in particular to Mollie Glick, David Larabell, Craig Gering, Michelle Kydd Lee, and Ryder White, for all of your work to make this happen.

I want to thank my collaborators, Vinca LaFleur and Dylan Loewe, for your commitment, compassion, and yes, your patience. You made this process a joy.

And a big thank-you to their research and fact-checking team: Brian Agler, Zach Hindin, Steven Kelly, Machmud Makhmudov, Maggie Mallon, and Raul Quintana. And thank you to Dorothy Hearst for our important early work together on this project

Finally, I want to thank all the people I love that are no longer with us. I don't know what kind of book distribution Penguin has in heaven, but, Aunt Mary, Uncle Freddy, Uncle Sherman, Mr. and Mrs. Shelton, Aunt Chris, Auntie Bea, Henry Ramsey, Jim Rivaldo, Mrs. Wilson, and my grandparents: this book is a tribute to how much you meant to me, how much of my life was shaped by you, how much you mattered.

Mommy, you are the star of this book because you were the reason for everything. It's been almost ten years since we lost you, and I miss you so much. Life without you is still hard to accept. But I believe you are staring down at us. When I am stuck with a hard decision, I ask, "What would Mommy think?" And in that way, you are here. It is my sincerest hope that this book will help those who never met you understand the kind of person you were. What it meant to be Shyamala Harris. And what it means to be her daughter.

NOTES

PREFACE

xiii **Shortly after, the Associated Press:** Phil Willon, "Kamala Harris Breaks a Color Barrier with Her U.S. Senate Win," *Los Angeles Times,* November 8, 2016, http://www.latimes.com/politics/la-pol-ca-senate-race-kamala-harris -wins-20161108-story.html.

xv **"We cannot play ostrich," he said:** Thurgood Marshall, "The Meaning of Liberty," acceptance speech after receiving the Liberty Award on July 4, 1992, http://www.naacpldf.org/press-release/thurgood-marshalls-stirring -acceptance-speech-after-receiving-prestigious-liberty-award-on-july-4-1992.

CHAPTER 1: FOR THE PEOPLE

8 **They met on Sundays:** Donna Murch, "The Campus and the Street: Race, Migration, and the Origins of the Black Panther Party in Oakland, CA," *Souls* 9, no. 4 (2007): 333–45, https://doi.org/10.1080/10999940701703794.

9 **SFSU had a student-run:** Martha Biondi, *The Black Revolution on Campus* (Berkeley: University of California Press, 2012), 47.

17   **Pollar once told a journalist:** Richard Ramella, "The Rainbow Sign Can Use Some Help," *Berkeley Gazette*, April 18, 1975, 14.

32   **"The penal code was not created":** Scott Duke Harris, "In Search of Elusive Justice," *Los Angeles Times Magazine,* October 24, 2004, http://articles .latimes.com/2004/oct/24/magazine/tm-kamala43.

34   **She was a groundbreaker:** Harris, "In Search of Elusive Justice."

CHAPTER 2: A VOICE FOR JUSTICE

40   **toxic waste polluted the soil:** *Pollution, Health, Environmental Racism and Injustice: A Toxic Inventory of Bayview Hunters Point, San Francisco* (San Francisco: Hunters Point Mothers Environmental Health and Justice Committee, Huntersview Tenants Association, and Greenaction for Health & Environmental Justice, 2012), http://greenaction.org/wp-content /uploads/2012/08/TheStateoftheEnvironment090204Final.pdf.

45   **I introduced criminal justice reform legislation:** A Bill to Clarify the Rights of All Persons Who Are Held or Detained at a Port of Entry or at Any Detention Facility Overseen by U.S. Customs and Border Protection or U.S. Immigration and Customs Enforcement, S. 349, 115th Cong. (2017–2018), https://www.congress.gov/bill/115th-congress/senate-bill/349.

47   **95 percent of our country's:** Nicolas Fandos, "A Study Documents the Paucity of Black Elected Prosecutors: Zero in Most States," *New York Times,* July 7, 2015, https://www.nytimes.com/2015/07/07/us/a-study-documents -the-paucity-of-black-elected-prosecutors-zero-in-most-states.html.

48   **All told, we had more:** The University of London, Institute of Criminal Policy Research, *World Prison Brief,* accessed October 25, 2018, http://www .prisonstudies.org/highest-to-lowest/prison-population-total?field_region _taxonomy_tid=All.

53   **In 2004, for example:** Lee Romney, "Bill Would Fight Child Prostitution," *Los Angeles Times,* September 5, 2004, http://articles.latimes.com/2004 /sep/05/local/me-child5.

54   **Lateefah was a teenager:** Kevin Cartwright, "Activist Awarded for Work with Troubled Youth," *The Crisis* 111, no. 1 (January/February 2004): 9, https://books.google.com/books?id=Ice84BEC2yoC&pg.

54   **"I saw resilience in these young women":** Carolyn Jones, "Lateefah Simon: Youth Advocate Nominated as Visionary of the Year," *SFGate*, January 5,

2015, https://www.sfgate.com/visionsf/article/Lateefah-Simon-Youth-advocate
-nominated-as-5993578.php.

55 **nearly 70 percent commit a crime:** "NRRC Facts and Trends," National
Reentry Resource Center, Council of State Governments Justice Center,
https://csgjusticecenter.org/nrrc/facts-and-trends.

58 **Another among them was:** Bob Egelko, "Judge Thelton Henderson Ending
Long Career Rallying for Oppressed," *San Francisco Chronicle,* January 15,
2017, https://www.sfchronicle.com/bayarea/article/Judge-Thelton
-Henderson-ending-long-career-10859424.php; Associated Press, "Judge
Thelton Henderson, Lawyer Fired for Loaning MLK a Car, Retiring,"
Al.com, January 20, 2017, https://www.al.com/news/birmingham/index.ssf
/2017/01/judge_thelton_henderson_lawyer.html; and Jenifer Warren, "Judge
Is No Stranger to Controversy," *Los Angeles Times,* December 16, 1996,
http://articles.latimes.com/1996-12-16/news/mn-9670_1_federal-judges.

59 **It represented smart, effective stewardship:** U.S. Department of Justice,
Office of Justice Programs, *Back on Track: A Problem-Solving Reentry Court,*
by Jacquelyn L. Rivers and Lenore Anderson, FS 00316 (Washington, DC,
September 2009), https://www.bja.gov/Publications/backontrackfs.pdf.

64 **the median savings account:** Board of Governors of the Federal Reserve
System, Survey of Consumer Finances, 2016 (Washington, DC, 2016),
https://www.federalreserve.gov/econres/scfindex.htm.

64 *The New York Times Magazine* **told:** Nick Pinto, "The Bail Trap," *New York
Times Magazine,* August 13, 2015, https://www.nytimes.com/2015
/08/16/magazine/the-bail-trap.html.

65 **Latino men pay nearly:** Kamala Harris and Rand Paul, "To Shrink Jails,
Let's Reform Bail," op-ed, *New York Times,* July 20, 2017, https://www
.nytimes.com/2017/07/20/opinion/kamala-harris-and-rand-paul-lets-reform
-bail.html.

66 **According to the FBI, more people:** Christopher Ingraham, "More People
Were Arrested Last Year over Pot Than for Murder, Rape, Aggravated
Assault and Robbery—Combined," *Wonkblog, Washington Post,* September
26, 2017, https://www.washingtonpost.com/news/wonk/wp/2017/09/26/more
-people-were-arrested-last-year-over-pot-than-for-murder-rape-aggravated
-assault-and-robbery-combined.

66 **Between 2001 and 2010:** "Marijuana Arrests by the Numbers," ACLU,
https://www.aclu.org/gallery/marijuana-arrests-numbers.

66 **93 percent of the people:** John Annese, "NYPD Ripped for 'Racially Biased Practices' After Stats Show Cops Still Targeting Minorities for Pot Arrests," *New York Daily News,* April 27, 2018, http://www.nydailynews.com /new-york/nyc-crime/nypd-targeting-minorities-marijuana-arrests-2018 -article-1.3957719.

67 **In the decade after we:** *33 States Reform Criminal Justice Policies Through Justice Reinvestment* (Philadelphia: Pew Charitable Trusts, November 2016), http://www.pewtrusts.org/-/media/assets/2017/08/33_states_reform _criminal_justice_policies_through_justice_reinvestment.pdf.

67 **And since 2010, twenty-three states:** Chris Mai and Ram Subramanian, *The Price of Prisons: Examining State Spending Trends, 2010–2015* (New York: Vera Institute of Justice, May 2017), https://www.vera.org/publications /price-of-prisons-2015-state-spending-trends.

68 **Nearly four years after Ferguson:** Jim Salter, "Missouri Report: Blacks 85 Percent More Likely to Be Stopped," AP News, June 1, 2018, https://apnews .com/58d9ad846ef14b93915ee26d3cf4663e.

68 **three times more likely to:** C.K., "Black Boys Are the Least Likely of Any Group to Escape Poverty," *The Economist,* April 2, 2018, https: //www.economist.com/blogs/democracyinamerica/2018/04/broken-ladder.

68 **they are arrested twice as often:** C.K., "Black Boys."

68 **six times as likely as white men:** Janelle Jones, John Schmitt, and Valerie Wilson, *50 Years After the Kerner Commission* (Washington, DC: Economic Policy Institute, February 26, 2018), https://www.epi.org/publication /50-years-after-the-kerner-commission.

68–69 **sentences nearly 20 percent longer:** American Civil Liberties Union, "Written Submission of the American Civil Liberties Union on Racial Disparities in Sentencing Hearing on Reports of Racism in the Justice System of the United States," submitted to the Inter-American Commission on Human Rights, 153rd Session, October 27, 2014, https://www.aclu.org /sites/default/files/assets/141027_iachr_racial_disparities_aclu_submission _0.pdf.

CHAPTER 3: UNDERWATER

76 **"Garden of the Sun":** Wallace Smith, *Garden of the Sun: A History of the San Joaquin Valley, 1772–1939,* ed. William B. Secrest Jr., 2nd ed. (Fresno, CA: Craven Street Books, 2004).

76 **nearly 40 percent Latinx:** Michael B. Teitz, Charles Dietzel, and William

Fulton, *Urban Development Futures in the San Joaquin Valley* (San Francisco: Public Policy Institute of California, 2005), 18, http://www.solimar.org /pdf/urbandevsanjoaquin.pdf.

78 **lost more than half their value:** Bonhia Lee, "Emerging from the Bust, Fresno Housing Market Is Healthiest Nationwide," *Fresno Bee,* January 5, 2016, https://www.fresnobee.com/news/business/article53168660.html.

78 **the unemployment rate had soared:** U.S. Bureau of Labor Statistics, *Unemployment Rate in Fresno, CA (MSA),* retrieved from FRED, Federal Reserve Bank of St. Louis, https://fred.stlouisfed.org/series/FRES406UR.

78–79 **Ten years after purchasing their home:** Alana Semuels, "The Never-Ending Foreclosure," *The Atlantic,* December 1, 2017, https://www.theatlantic.com /business/archive/2017/12/the-neverending-foreclosure/547181.

79 **the Humane Society was reporting:** "Hidden Victims of Mortgage Crisis: Pets," NBC News, January 29, 2008, http://www.nbcnews.com/id/22900994 /ns/business-real_estate/t/hidden-victims-mortgage-crisis-pets/#. W2dfby2ZOEI; and Linton Weeks, "The Recession and Pets: Hard Times for Snoopy," *All Things Considered,* NPR, April 6, 2009, https://www.npr .org/templates/story/story.php?storyId=102238430.

79 **Roughly 5 million homeowners:** "2010's Record-Breaking Foreclosure Crisis: By the Numbers," *The Week,* January 14, 2011, http://theweek.com /articles/488017/2010s-recordbreaking-foreclosure-crisis-by-numbers.

79 **And 2.5 million foreclosures:** "2010's Record-Breaking Foreclosure Crisis."

80 **That was when we learned:** U.S. Department of Housing and Urban Development settlement see https://www.hud.gov/sites/documents/ NATLSETEXECSUM(2).PDF and https://archives.hud.gov/news/2012/ SettlementFeb92012.cfm.

81 **to speed up the foreclosure process:** " 'Robo-Signers' Add to Foreclosure Fraud Mess," NBC News, October 13, 2010, http://www.nbcnews.com/id /39641329/ns/business-real_estate/t/robo-signers-add-foreclosure-fraud-mess.

83 **"a woman running for attorney general":** ProsperitasMember, "Pundits Explain Why Kamala Will Never Win (Oops)," YouTube video, 3:00, posted December 7, 2010, https://www.youtube.com/watch?v=1HemG2iLkTY.

86 **I was now ahead in the race:** Jon Brooks, "Video: Steve Cooley Prematurely Declares Victory Last Night," KQED News, November 3, 2010, https: //www.kqed.org/news/4195/video-steve-cooley-prematurely-declares-victory -last-night.

87 **Of the nearly nine million ballots cast:** Jack Leonard, "Kamala Harris Wins Attorney General's Race as Steve Cooley Concedes [Updated]," *Los Angeles*

Times, November 24, 2010, http://latimesblogs.latimes.com/lanow/2010/11
/steve-cooley-kamala-harris-attorney-general.html.

89 **37,000 homeowners lined up:** CBS News, "The Next Housing Shock," *60
Minutes* report, YouTube video, 14:06, posted April 3, 2011, https://www
.youtube.com/watch?v=QwrO6jhtC5E.

89 **"In the 1930s, we had bread lines":** Ryan Chittum, *"60 Minutes* with a
Good Look at the Foreclosure Scandal," *Columbia Journalism Review,* April
5, 2011, https://archives.cjr.org/the_audit/60_minutes_with_a_good_look
_at.php; and CBS News, "The Next Housing Shock."

90 **the lender said they could help:** California Department of Justice, "Attorney
General Kamala D. Harris Convenes Roundtable with Foreclosure
Victims," YouTube video, 15:59, posted November 22, 2011, https://www
.youtube.com/watch?v=QbycqFzva5Q.

94 **which owned 62 percent of new mortgages:** Douglas J. Elliott, "The Federal
Role in Housing Finance: Principal Issues and Policy Proposals," in *The
Future of Housing Finance: Restructuring the U.S. Residential Mortgage
Market,* ed. Martin Neil Baily (Washington, DC: Brookings Institution
Press, 2011), https://www.brookings.edu/wp-content/uploads/2016/07
/thefutureofhousingfinance_chapter.pdf.

100 **in December 2011 she and I:** State of California Department of Justice,
Office of the Attorney General, "Attorneys General of California and
Nevada Announce Mortgage Investigation Alliance," press release,
December 6, 2011, https://www.oag.ca.gov/news/press-releases/attorneys
-general-california-and-nevada-announce-mortgage-investigation-alliance.

107 **Parents' dreams of financing:** Janis Bowdler, Roberto Quercia, and David
Andrew Smith, *The Foreclosure Generation: The Long-Term Impact of the
Housing Crisis on Latino Children and Families* (Washington, DC:
National Council of La Raza, 2010), https://communitycapital.unc.edu
/files/2010/02/Foreclosure-Generation.pdf.

107 **"the rise in US unemployment":** Aaron Reeves et al., "Increase in State
Suicide Rates in the USA During Economic Recession," *The Lancet* 380,
no. 9856 (November 24, 2012): 1813–14, https://www.thelancet.com/journals
/lancet/article/PIIS0140-6736%2812%2961910-2/fulltext.

107 **In Fresno, the overwhelming majority:** Patrick Clark, "Most U.S. Homes
Are Worth Less Than Before the Crash," Bloomberg, May 3, 2017, https:
//www.bloomberg.com/news/articles/2017-05-03/most-u-s-homes-are-worth
-less-than-before-the-crash.

107 **the burden hit black families disproportionately:** Sarah Burd-Sharps and

Rebecca Rasch, *Impact of the US Housing Crisis on the Racial Wealth Gap Across Generations* (New York: Social Research Council, June 2015), https://www.aclu.org/files/field_document/discrimlend_final.pdf.

108 $345 billion in subprime loans: Peter Rudegeair, Rachel Louise Ensign, and Coulter Jones, "Big Banks Find a Back Door to Finance Subprime Loans," *Wall Street Journal,* April 10, 2018, https://www.wsj.com/articles/big-banks -find-a-back-door-to-finance-subprime-loans-1523352601.

CHAPTER 4: WEDDING BELLS

112 eighteen thousand same-sex couples: "Fed Court OKs Immediate Gay Marriages in California; SF Conducts 1st," KPIX CBS San Francisco, June 28, 2013, http://sanfrancisco.cbslocal.com/2013/06/28/federal-court-oks-gay -marriage-to-resume-in-california-immediately.

115 Justice Stephen Breyer questioned: *Hollingsworth v. Perry,* 558 U.S. 183 (2010), oral arguments, March 26, 2013, https://www.supremecourt.gov /oral_arguments/argument_transcripts/2012/12-144_5if6.pdf.

116 "not because it is old": Franklin D. Roosevelt, "Address on Constitution Day, Washington, D.C.," speech delivered September 17, 1937, American Presidency Project, http://www.presidency.ucsb.edu/ws/?pid=15459.

119 hundreds of weddings that day: Malia Wollan, "California Couples Line Up to Marry After Stay on Same-Sex Marriage Is Lifted," *New York Times,* June 29, 2013, https://www.nytimes.com/2013/06/30/us/california-couples-line -up-to-marry-after-stay-on-same-sex-marriage-is-lifted.html.

123 by 2009, we had reduced truancy: Jill Tucker, "Pressuring Parents Helps S.F. Slash Truancy 23%," SFGate, June 9, 2009, https://www.sfgate .com/news/article/Pressuring-parents-helps-S-F-slash-truancy-23-3228481 .php.

125 Our first report, the results: State of California Department of Justice, Office of the Attorney General, "Report on California Elementary School Truancy Crisis: One Million Truant Students, Billions in Economic Harm," press release, September 30, 2013, https://oag.ca.gov/news/press-releases/report -california-elementary-school-truancy-crisis-one-million-truant-students.

CHAPTER 5: I SAY WE FIGHT

147 more than half of Silicon Valley's: Farhad Manjoo, "Why Silicon Valley Wouldn't Work Without Immigrants," *New York Times,* February 8, 2017, https://www.nytimes.com/2017/02/08/technology/personaltech/why-silicon-valley-wouldnt-work-without-immigrants.html.

147 **She wanted to be able to tell:** Phil Willon, "Newly Elected Kamala Harris Vows to Defy Trump on Immigration," *Los Angeles Times,* November 20, 2016, http://www.latimes.com/politics/la-pol-ca-senate-kamala-harris-trump-20161110-story.html.

147 **nearly six million American children:** Leila Schochet, "Trump's Immigration Policies Are Harming American Children," Center for American Progress, July 31, 2017, https://www.americanprogress.org/issues/early-childhood/reports/2017/07/31/436377/trumps-immigration-policies-harming-american-children.

148 **the fear of deportation:** Randy Capps et al., *Implications of Immigration Enforcement Activities for the Well-Being of Children in Immigrant Families: A Review of the Literature* (Washington, DC: Urban Institute and Migration Policy Institute, September 2015), https://www.urban.org/sites/default/files/alfresco/publication-exhibits/2000405/2000405-Implications-of-Immigration-Enforcement-Activities-for-the-Well-Being-of-Children-in-Immigrant-Families.pdf; and Seline Szkupinski Quiroga, Dulce M. Medina, and Jennifer Glick, "In the Belly of the Beast: Effects of Anti-Immigration Policy on Latino Community Members," *American Behavioral Scientist* 58, no. 13 (2014): 1723–42, https://doi.org/10.1177/0002764214537270.

153 **in the first hundred days:** Schochet, "Trump's Immigration Policies."

153 **arrested ninety-seven workers:** Caroline Scown, "Countering the Effects of Trump's Immigration Policies in Schools," Center for American Progress, May 3, 2018, https://www.americanprogress.org/issues/education-k-12/news/2018/05/03/450274/countering-effects-trumps-immigration-policies-schools.

153 **20 percent of the Latinx students:** Scown, "Countering the Effects."

153 **In 2016, a quarter of all kids:** Leila Schochet, "Trump's Attack on Immigrants Is Breaking the Backbone of America's Child Care System," Center for American Progress, February 5, 2018, https://www.americanprogress.org/issues/early-childhood/news/2018/02/05/445676/trumps-attack-immigrants-breaking-backbone-americas-child-care-system.

154 **20 percent of early childhood educators:** Schochet, "Trump's Attack on Immigrants."

154 **those numbers have tripled:** Schochet, "Trump's Attack on Immigrants."

CHAPTER 6: WE ARE BETTER THAN THIS

161 **"somehow they knew"**: Sankar Raman, "A Cardiac Scientist with Heart,"
The Immigrant Story, July 10, 2017, http://theimmigrantstory.org/scientist.

162 **as much as $460 billion**: Zoe Henry, "800,000 Workers, $460 Billion in
Economic Output, Dozens of Entrepreneurs: What the U.S. Loses if DACA
Goes Away," *Inc.*, March 5, 2018, https://www.inc.com/zoe-henry/dreamer
-entrepreneurs-respond-to-daca-uncertainty.html.

166 **There's a region in Central America**: Rocio Cara Labrador and Danielle
Renwick, "Central America's Violent Northern Triangle," Council on
Foreign Relations, June 26, 2018, https://www.cfr.org/backgrounder/central
-americas-violent-northern-triangle.

167 **nearly fifty thousand people were murdered**: Labrador and Renwick,
"Violent Northern Triangle."

167 **MS-13 and the Mara 18**: Labrador and Renwick, "Violent Northern
Triangle."

167 **violent deaths of women in Honduras**: "Special Rapporteur on Violence
Against Women Finalizes Country Mission to Honduras and Calls for
Urgent Action to Address the Culture of Impunity for Crimes Against
Women and Girls," Office of the United Nations High Commissioner for
Human Rights, https://www.ohchr.org/EN/NewsEvents/Pages/DisplayNews
.aspx?NewsID=14833.

167 **an eleven-year-old girl in Honduras**: Sonia Nazario, "The Children of
the Drug Wars," *New York Times*, July 11, 2014, https://www.nytimes
.com/2014/07/13/opinion/sunday/a-refugee-crisis-not-an-immigration-crisis
.html.

167 **If there was a ground zero**: Labrador and Renwick, "Violent Northern
Triangle."

169 **about a 50 percent chance**: *Continued Rise in Asylum Denial Rates:
Impact of Representation and Nationality,* Transactional Records Access
Clearinghouse (TRAC) at Syracuse University, December 13, 2016, http:
//trac.syr.edu/immigration/reports/448.

170 **some 350,000 immigrants**: Labrador and Renwick, "Violent Northern
Triangle."

170 **dropped by 10 percent**: Anneliese Hermann, *Asylum in the Trump Era*
(Washington, DC: Center for American Progress, June 13, 2018), https:
//www.americanprogress.org/issues/immigration/reports/2018/06/13/452025
/asylum-trump-era.

171 **seven hundred children had been separated:** Caitlin Dickerson, "Hundreds of Immigrant Children Have Been Taken from Parents at U.S. Border," *New York Times,* April 20, 2018, https://www.nytimes.com/2018/04/20/us/immigrant-children-separation-ice.html.

171 **the extraordinary stress and trauma:** Colleen Kraft, "AAP Statement Opposing Separation of Children and Parents at the Border," American Academy of Pediatrics, May 8, 2018, https://www.aap.org/en-us/about-the-aap/aap-press-room/Pages/StatementOpposingSeparationofChildrenandParents.aspx.

174 **"Persons who violate the law":** Julie Zauzmer and Keith McMillan, "Sessions Cites Bible Passage Used to Defend Slavery in Defense of Separating Immigrant Families," *Washington Post,* June 15, 2018, https://www.washingtonpost.com/news/acts-of-faith/wp/2018/06/14/jeff-sessions-points-to-the-bible-in-defense-of-separating-immigrant-families.

174 **Sessions got rid of the right:** Katie Benner and Caitlin Dickerson, "Sessions Says Domestic and Gang Violence Are Not Grounds for Asylum," *New York Times,* June 11, 2018, https://www.nytimes.com/2018/06/11/us/politics/sessions-domestic-violence-asylum.html.

178 **"I don't know every task":** Kamala D. Harris, U.S. Senator for California, "At Hearing on Family Separations, Harris Blasts Immoral Separations and Inhumane Detention of Pregnant Women," press release, July 31, 2018, https://www.harris.senate.gov/news/press-releases/at-hearing-on-family-separations-harris-blasts-immoral-separations-and-inhumane-detention-of-pregnant-women.

179 **resort to DNA tests:** Caitlin Dickerson, "Trump Administration in Chaotic Scramble to Reunify Migrant Families," *New York Times,* July 5, 2018, https://www.nytimes.com/2018/07/05/us/migrant-children-chaos-family-separation.html.

179 **"These mothers have given":** "Sen. Kamala Harris Visits Otay Mesa Detention Center," NBC 7 San Diego, June 22, 2018, https://www.nbcsandiego.com/on-air/as-seen-on/Sen_-Kamala-Harris-Visits-Otay-Mesa-Detention-Center_San-Diego-486286761.html.

180 **"At night, Andriy sometimes":** Brittny Mejia, "A 3-Year-Old Was Separated from His Father at the Border. Now His Parents Are Dealing with His Trauma," *Los Angeles Times,* July 3, 2018, http://www.latimes.com/local/lanow/la-me-ln-separation-trauma-20180627-story.html.

180 **Jefferson was stiff:** Esmeralda Bermudez, " 'I'm Here. I'm Here.' Father Reunited with Son amid Tears, Relief and Fear of What's Next," *Los Angeles Times,* July 15, 2018, http://www.latimes.com/local/california/la-me-family -reunion-20180715-htmlstory.html.

181 **a fourteen-month-old who was returned:** Lisa Desjardins, Joshua Barajas, and Daniel Bush, " 'My Son Is Not the Same': New Testimony Paints Bleak Picture of Family Separation," *PBS NewsHour,* July 5, 2018 (updated July 6, 2018), https://www.pbs.org/newshour/politics/my-son-is-not-the-same-new -testimony-paints-bleak-picture-of-family-separation.

181 **A pregnant woman fainted:** Desjardins, Barajas, and Bush, "My Son."

181 **The children were demeaned:** Desjardins, Barajas, and Bush, "My Son."

181 **Most Americans are appalled:** Eleanor O'Neil, "Immigration Issues: Public Opinion on Family Separation, DACA, and a Border Wall," *AEIdeas* (blog), American Enterprise Institute, June 21, 2018, https://www.aei.org /publication/immigration-issues-public-opinion-on-family-separation-daca -and-a-border-wall.

CHAPTER 7: EVERY BODY

185 **the United States is one of only:** Linda Villarosa, "Why America's Black Mothers and Babies Are in Life-or-Death Crisis," *New York Times Magazine,* April 11, 2018.

185 **a ten-year gap in life expectancy:** Dave A. Chokshi, "Income, Poverty, and Health Inequality," *Journal of the American Medical Association* 319, no. 13 (2018): 1312–13, https://jamanetwork.com/journals/jama/fullarticle /2677433.

186 **the Senate leader openly declared:** Jillian Rayfield, "McConnell at CPAC: Repeal Obamacare 'Root and Branch,' " *Salon,* March 15, 2013, https://www .salon.com/2013/03/15/mcconnell_at_cpac_repeal_obamacare_root _and_branch.

186 **comparing the Affordable Care Act:** Jack Gurdon, "Rand Paul: The Republican Frontrunner in Seven Quotes," *Telegraph,* October 2, 2014, https://www.telegraph.co.uk/news/worldnews/us-politics/11134793/Rand -Paul-the-Republican-frontrunner-in-seven-quotes.html.

186 **suggesting that the president might:** "25 Unforgettable Obamacare Quotes," *Politico,* July 16, 2013, https://www.politico.com/gallery /2013/07/25-unforgettable-obamacare-quotes-001595?slide=11.

187 **Repealing the ACA would result:** "H.R. 1628, Obamacare Repeal Reconciliation Act of 2017," cost estimate and analysis, Congressional Budget Office, July 19, 2017, https://www.cbo.gov/publication/52939.

187 **It would allow insurance companies:** U.S. Department of Health and Human Services, Office of Health Policy, *Health Insurance Coverage for Americans with Pre-Existing Conditions: The Impact of the Affordable Care Act* (Washington, DC, January 5, 2017), https://aspe.hhs.gov/system/files /pdf/255396/Pre-ExistingConditions.pdf.

188 **Compared with people in other:** "How Prescription Drug Prices Compare Internationally," *Wall Street Journal,* December 1, 2015, https://graphics.wsj .com/table/GlobalDrug_1201.

188 **the same dose of Crestor:** Rachel Bluth, "Should the U.S. Make It Easier to Import Prescription Drugs?" *PBS NewsHour,* March 22, 2017, https://www .pbs.org/newshour/health/u-s-make-easier-import-prescription-drugs.

188–89 **Fifty-eight percent of Americans take:** "Public Opinion on Prescription Drugs and Their Prices," Henry J. Kaiser Family Foundation, https://www .kff.org/slideshow/public-opinion-on-prescription-drugs-and-their-prices.

189 **One of my very first votes:** Zack Struver, "Klobuchar Drug Importation Amendment Sees Votes Crossing the Aisle," Knowledge Ecology International, January 13, 2017, https://www.keionline.org/23248.

189 **found 153 companies:** John Morgan, *A Bitter Pill: How Big Pharma Lobbies to Keep Prescription Drug Prices High* (Washington, DC: Citizens for Responsibility and Ethics in Washington, 2018), https://www .citizensforethics.org/a-bitter-pill-how-big-pharma-lobbies-to-keep-prescription -drug-prices-high.

190 **increased its membership dues:** Morgan, *A Bitter Pill.*

190 **about $2.5 billion on lobbying:** Morgan, *A Bitter Pill.*

190 **increased the price of Pravastatin:** Morgan, *A Bitter Pill.*

190 **jacked the price of Albuterol:** Morgan, *A Bitter Pill.*

191 **owed the hospital nearly $19,000:** Jenny Gold and Sarah Kliff, "A Baby Was Treated with a Nap and a Bottle of Formula. His Parents Received an $18,000 Bill," *Vox,* July 20, 2018, https://www.vox.com/2018/6/28 /17506232/emergency-room-bill-fees-health-insurance-baby.

191 **passed $31,250 in fees:** Gold and Kliff, "Nap and a Bottle."

191 **he was expected to pay $7,294:** Sarah Kliff, "He Went to an In-Network Emergency Room. He Still Ended Up with a $7,924 Bill," *Vox,* May 23,

2018, https://www.vox.com/2018/5/23/17353284/emergency-room-doctor -out-of-network.

192 **Depression is increasing:** "Depression Is on the Rise in the US, Especially Among Young Teens," *Science Daily,* October 30, 2017, https://www .sciencedaily.com/releases/2017/10/171030134631.htm.

192 **Alabama has only 1:** "Mental Health in America, Access to Care Data," Mental Health America, http://www.mentalhealthamerica.net/issues /mental-health-america-access-care-data.

192 **roughly 60 percent of America's counties:** New American Economy, "New Study Shows 60 Percent of U.S. Counties Without a Single Psychiatrist," press release, October 23, 2017, https://www.newamericaneconomy.org/press-release /new-study-shows-60-percent-of-u-s-counties-without-a-single-psychiatrist.

192 **only 590 psychiatrists:** New American Economy, "New Study Shows."

192 **41.4 percent of adults with mental illness:** "The State of Mental Health in America," Mental Health America, October 7, 2018, http://www .mentalhealthamerica.net/issues/state-mental-health-america.

194 **"there was a continuing disparity":** U.S. Department of Health and Human Services, *Report of the Secretary's Task Force on Black and Minority Health,* vol. 1, by Margaret M. Heckler (Washington, DC, 1985), https://ia800501 .us.archive.org/32/items/reportofsecretar00usde/reportofsecretar00usde.pdf.

195 **black Americans have higher mortality rates:** Robin L. Kelly, *2015 Kelly Report: Health Disparities in America* (Washington, DC: Office of Congresswoman Robin L. Kelly, IL-02, 2015), 11, https://robinkelly.house .gov/sites/robinkelly.house.gov/files/2015%20Kelly%20Report_0.pdf.

195 **"A baby born in Cheswolde":** Olga Khazan, "Being Black in America Can Be Hazardous to Your Health," *The Atlantic,* July/August 2018, https: //www.theatlantic.com/magazine/archive/2018/07/being-black-in-america -can-be-hazardous-to-your-health/561740.

195 **Black babies are twice as likely:** Villarosa, "Why America's Black Mothers and Babies."

195 **black infants are less likely:** From the Heckler Report: "Moreover, in 1981, Blacks suffered 20 infant deaths per 1,000 live births, still twice the White level of 10.5, but similar to the White rate of 1960." U.S. Department of Health and Human Services, *Black and Minority Health,* 2; "Infant Mortality," Centers for Disease Control and Prevention, https://www.cdc .gov/reproductivehealth/maternalinfanthealth/infantmortality.htm.

195 **at least three times as likely:** Villarosa, "America's Black Mothers and Babies."

195 **A major five-year study:** New York City Department of Health and Mental Hygiene, *Severe Maternal Morbidity in New York City, 2008–2012* (New York, 2017), https://www1.nyc.gov/assets/doh/downloads/pdf/data/maternal -morbidity-report-08-12.pdf; and Nina Martin and Renee Montagne, "Black Mothers Keep Dying After Giving Birth. Shalon Irving's Story Explains Why," *All Things Considered*, NPR, December 7, 2017, https://www.npr .org/2017/12/07/568948782/Black-mothers-keep-dying-after-giving-birth -shalon-irvings-story-explains-why.

196 **"child adversity literally":** David Bornstein, "Treating the Lifelong Harm of Childhood Trauma," *New York Times*, January 30, 2018, https://www .nytimes.com/2018/01/30/opinion/treating-the-lifelong-harm-of-childhood -trauma.html.

196 **could see their life expectancy reduced:** Khazan, "Being Black in America."

196 **telomere length in hundreds of women:** Khazan, "Being Black in America."

196 **White patients are 10 percent more likely:** Robert Pearl, "Why Health Care Is Different if You're Black, Latino or Poor," *Forbes*, March 5, 2015, https: //www.forbes.com/sites/robertpearl/2015/03/05/healthcare-black-latino -poor/#650c70d37869.

197 **Black patients are also less likely:** Quinn Capers IV, "To Reduce Health-Care Disparities We Must Address Biases in Medical School Admissions," *The Hill*, April 14, 2018, https://thehill.com/opinion/healthcare/383154-to -reduce-health-care-disparities-we-must-address-biases-in-medical-school.

197 **more likely to get breast cancer screenings:** Pearl, "Why Health Care Is Different."

197 **regardless of their economic status:** Villarosa, "America's Black Mothers and Babies."

197 **Rather than give her the CT scan:** Rob Haskell, "Serena Williams on Motherhood, Marriage, and Making Her Comeback," *Vogue*, January 10, 2018, https://www.vogue.com/article/serena-williams-vogue-cover-interview -february-2018.

197 **If someone like Serena Williams:** Haskell, "Serena Williams," *Vogue*.

198 **Research has found that 75 percent:** April Dembosky, "Training Doctors to Spot Their Own Racial Biases," CNN, September 7, 2015, https://www.cnn .com/2015/09/07/health/healthcare-racial-bias/index.html.

198 **As of 2013, only about 9 percent:** "Diversity in the Physician Workforce: Facts & Figures 2014," Association of American Medical Colleges, 2014, http://www.aamcdiversityfactsandfigures.org.

200 **the ninth leading cause of death:** "End Stage Renal Disease in the United States," National Kidney Foundation, updated January 2016, https://www.kidney.org/news/newsroom/factsheets/End-Stage-Renal-Disease-in-the-US.

200 **develop kidney failure at 3.5 times:** "Low Income Linked to Higher Levels of Kidney Disease Among African Americans," National Kidney Foundation, November 5, 2012, https://www.kidney.org/news/newsroom/nr/Low-Income-Linked-to-Higher-Levels-of-Kidney-Disease.

200 **"Fresenius's own medical office":** Andrew Pollack, "Dialysis Equipment Maker Settles Lawsuit for $250 Million," *New York Times,* February 18, 2016, https://www.nytimes.com/2016/02/19/business/dialysis-equipment-maker-settles-lawsuit-for-250-million.html.

201 **DaVita agreed to pay $350 million:** U.S. Department of Justice, "DaVita to Pay $350 Million to Resolve Allegations of Illegal Kickbacks," press release, October 22, 2014, https://www.justice.gov/opa/pr/davita-pay-350-million-resolve-allegations-illegal-kickbacks.

201 **DaVita was sued in 2017:** DaVita have not admitted any liability to these claims.

202 **doctors in the county prescribed 1.6 million:** Melanie Saltzman, "Ohio Sues Big Pharma over Increase in Opioid-Related Deaths," *PBS NewsHour,* October 7, 2017, https://www.pbs.org/newshour/show/ohio-sues-big-pharma-increase-opioid-related-deaths.

202 **thirty-eight people died from accidental overdose:** Joel Achenbach, "No Longer 'Mayberry': A Small Ohio City Fights an Epidemic of Self-Destruction," *Washington Post,* December 29, 2016, https://www.washingtonpost.com/national/health-science/no-longer-mayberry-a-small-ohio-city-fights-an-epidemic-of-self-destruction/2016/12/29/a95076f2-9a01-11e6-b3c9-f662adaa0048_story.html.

202 **another forty lost their lives:** "Fentanyl and Related Drugs like Carfentanil as Well as Cocaine Drove Increase in Overdose Deaths," in Ohio Department of Health, *2016 Ohio Drug Overdose Data: General Findings* (Columbus, 2016), https://www.odh.ohio.gov/-/media/ODH/ASSETS/Files/health/injury-prevention/2016-Ohio-Drug-Overdose-Report-FINAL.pdf.

202 **"Now you can get heroin quicker":** Achenbach, "No Longer 'Mayberry.'"

203 **"One day in September":** Achenbach, "No Longer 'Mayberry.'"

203 **the violent crime rate has gone up:** Achenbach, "No Longer 'Mayberry.'"

203 **two hundred children were placed:** Paula Seligson and Tim Reid, "Unbudgeted: How the Opioid Crisis Is Blowing a Hole in Small-Town America's Finances," Reuters, September 27, 2017, https://www.reuters.com

/article/us-usa-opioids-budgets/unbudgeted-how-the-opioid-crisis-is
-blowing-a-hole-in-small-town-americas-finances-idUSKCN1BU2LP.

203 **The surge has required:** Seligson and Reid, "Unbudgeted."

203 **"It's like having the flu":** Achenbach, "No Longer 'Mayberry.'"

204 **This despite the fact that company:** Justice Department findings in Barry
Meier, "Origins of an Epidemic: Purdue Pharma Knew Its Opioids Were
Widely Abused," *New York Times*, May 29, 2018, https://www.nytimes.
com/2018/05/29/health/purdue-opioids-oxycontin.html.

204 **Between 2007 and 2012:** Julia Lurie, "A Brief, Blood-Boiling History of the
Opioid Epidemic," *Mother Jones*, January/February 2017, https://www
.motherjones.com/crime-justice/2017/12/a-brief-blood-boiling
-history-of-the-opioid-epidemic.

204 **the United States was consuming:** Lurie, "History of the Opioid Epidemic."

205 **259 million prescriptions for opioids:** Lurie, "History of the Opioid Epidemic."

205 **roughly 80 percent of Americans:** Keith Humphries, "How Legal Drug
Companies Helped Revive the Heroin Trade," *Wonkblog, Washington Post,*
June 15, 2018, https://www.washingtonpost.com/news/wonk/wp/2018/06
/15/how-legal-drug-companies-helped-revive-the-heroin-trade.

205 **opioid deaths are still rising:** Karen Kaplan, "Opioid Overdose Deaths Are
Still Rising in Nearly Every Segment of the Country, CDC Says," *Los Angeles
Times,* March 29, 2018, http://www.latimes.com/science
/sciencenow/la-sci-sn-opioid-overdose-deaths-20180329-htmlstory.html.

206 **"effectively stripped the DEA":** Scott Higham and Lenny Bernstein, "The
Drug Industry's Triumph Over the DEA," *Washington Post,* October 15,
2017, https://www.washingtonpost.com/graphics/2017/investigations
/dea-drug-industry-congress.

207 **Many insurance companies will cover:** German Lopez, "She Paid Nothing
for Opioid Painkillers. Her Addiction Treatment Costs More Than $200 a
Month," *Vox,* June 4, 2018, https://www.vox.com/science-and-health
/2018/6/4/17388756/opioid-epidemic-health-insurance-buprenorphine.

CHAPTER 8: THE COST OF LIVING

214 **"Most of the tubs":** Steven Ross, Allison Graham, and David Appleby, *At the
River I Stand* (San Francisco: California Newsreel, 1993), documentary film,
56 min., https://search.alexanderstreet.com/preview/work
/bibliographic_entity%7Cvideo_work%7C1858429.

215 **"So often we overlook"**: Martin Luther King Jr., "All Labor Has Dignity," King Series, ed. Michael K. Honey (Boston: Beacon Press, 2011).

215 **"We are tired," King said:** King, "All Labor Has Dignity."

218 **a year of child care for a baby:** Tanza Loudenback, "In 33 US States It Costs More to Send Your Kid to Childcare Than College," *Business Insider,* October 12, 2016, http://www.businessinsider.com/costs-of-childcare-in-33-us-states-is-higher-than-college-tuition-2016-10.

218 **more than three times faster:** Michelle Jamrisko and Ilan Kolet, "College Costs Surge 500% in U.S. Since 1985: Chart of the Day," Bloomberg, August 26, 2013, https://www.bloomberg.com/news/articles/2013-08-26/college-costs-surge-500-in-u-s-since-1985-chart-of-the-day.

220 **less than 1 percent of the homes:** Jenny Luna, "Buying a Home Is Nearly Impossible for Teachers in These Cities," *Mother Jones,* February 4, 2017, https://www.motherjones.com/politics/2017/02/buying-house-nearly-impossible-teachers-these-cities-2.

221 **1.2 million by 2026:** U.S. Department of Labor, Bureau of Labor Statistics, "Fastest Growing Occupations," *Occupational Outlook Handbook*, April 13, 2018, www.bls.gov/ooh/fastest-growing.htm.

221 **more than $21,000 behind:** Brandie Temple and Jasmine Tucker, *Equal Pay for Black Women* (Washington, DC: National Women's Law Center, July 2017), https://nwlc.org/resources/equal-pay-for-black-women.

222 **worker wages grew 90 percent:** Lawrence Mishel, Elise Gould, and Josh Bivens, *Wage Stagnation in Nine Charts* (Washington, DC: Economic Policy Institute, 2015), http://www.epi.org/publication/charting-wage-stagnation.

222 **worker compensation rose just 9 percent:** Mishel, Gould, and Bivens, *Wage Stagnation.*

222 **CEOs making more than three hundred:** Diana Hembree, "CEO Pay Skyrockets to 361 Times That of the Average Worker," *Forbes,* May 22, 2018, https://www.forbes.com/sites/dianahembree/2018/05/22/ceo-pay-skyrockets-to-361-times-that-of-the-average-worker.

225 **40 percent of the nation's wealth:** Christopher Ingraham, "The Richest 1 Percent Now Owns More of the Country's Wealth Than at Any Time in the Past 50 Years," *Wonkblog, Washington Post,* December 6, 2017.

225 **adds up to roughly $40 trillion:** Harriet Torrey, "Americans' Wealth Surpasses $100 Trillion," *Wall Street Journal,* June 7, 2018, https://www.wsj.com/articles/u-s-net-worth-surpasses-100-trillion-1528387386.

225 **43 percent of households can't afford:** Quentin Fottrell, "50 Million American Households Can't Even Afford Basic Living Expenses," *MarketWatch,* June 9, 2018, https://www.marketwatch.com/story/50-million -american-households-cant-afford-basic-living-expenses-2018-05-18.

227 **375 million people worldwide:** Daniela Hernandez, "Seven Jobs Robots Will Create—or Expand," *Wall Street Journal,* https://www.wsj.com/articles /seven-jobs-robots-will-createor-expand-1525054021.

227 **23 percent of current working hours:** James Manyika et al., *Jobs Lost, Jobs Gained: Workforce Transitions in a Time of Automation* (Washington, DC: McKinsey Global Institute, 2017), https://www.mckinsey.com/~/media /McKinsey/Featured%20Insights/Future%20of%20Organizations/ What%20the%20future%20of%20work%20will%20mean%20for %20jobs%20skills%20and%20wages/MGI-Jobs-Lost-Jobs-Gained-Report -December-6-2017.ashx.

227 **2.5 million jobs a year:** Karen Harris, Austin Kimson, and Andrew Schwedel, "Quick and Painful: Brace for Job Automation's Next Wave," Bain and Company, March 7, 2018, http://www.bain.com/publications/articles /quick-and-painful-brace-for-job-automations-next-wave-labor-2030-snap -chart.aspx.

227 **In 2017, extreme weather events:** Jeff Goodell, "Welcome to the Age of Climate Migration," *Rolling Stone,* February 25, 2018, https://www .rollingstone.com/politics/politics-news/welcome-to-the-age-of-climate -migration-202221.

227 **The economic toll will follow:** Eileen Drage O'Reilly and Alison Snyder, "Where Climate Change Will Hit the U.S. Hardest," *Axios,* June 29, 2017, https://www.axios.com/where-climate-change-will-hit-the-us-hardest -1513303282-6566eea4-6369-4588-88cc-c2886db20b70.html.

227 **After Hurricane Harvey hit:** Goodell, "Age of Climate Migration."

CHAPTER 9: SMART ON SECURITY

240 **490 million gallons:** Andrea Elliott, "Sewage Spill During the Blackout Exposed a Lingering City Problem," *New York Times,* August 28, 2003, https://www.nytimes.com/2003/08/28/nyregion/sewage-spill-during-the -blackout-exposed-a-lingering-city-problem.html.

240 **mortality rates in New York City:** G. Brooke Anderson and Michelle L. Bell, "Lights Out: Impact of the August 2003 Power Outage on Mortality in

New York, NY," *Epidemiology* 23, no. 2 (March 2012): 189–93, https: //www.ncbi.nlm.nih.gov/pmc/articles/PMC3276729.

241 **Chinese theft of American intellectual property:** Sherisse Pham, "How Much Has the US Lost from China's IP Theft?" *CNN Business,* March 23, 2018, https://money.cnn.com/2018/03/23/technology/china-us-trump-tariffs -ip-theft/index.html.

241 **cybercrime's toll in North America:** James Lewis, *Economic Impact of Cybercrime—No Slowing Down* (Washington, DC: Center for Strategic and International Studies and McAfee, February 2018), https://www.mcafee.com /enterprise/en-us/assets/reports/restricted/economic-impact-cybercrime.pdf.

242 **six million times each day:** Keith Alexander, "U.S. Cybersecurity Policy and the Role of USCYBERCOM," transcript of remarks at Center for Strategic and International Studies Cybersecurity Policy Debate Series, Washington, DC, June 3, 2010, https://www.nsa.gov/news-features/speeches-testimonies /speeches/100603-alenander-transcript.shtml.

242 **Cyber Crime Center:** State of California Department of Justice, Office of the Attorney General, "Attorney General Kamala D. Harris Announces Creation of eCrime Unit Targeting Technology Crimes," press release, December 13, 2011, https://oag.ca.gov/news/press-releases/attorney-general -kamala-d-harris-announces-creation-ecrime-unit-targeting; and State of California Department of Justice, Office of the Attorney General, "Attorney General Kamala D. Harris Announces California Cyber Crime Center Initiative in Fresno," press release, October 10, 2016, https://oag.ca.gov /news/press-releases/attorney-general-kamala-d-harris-announces -california-cyber-crime-center.

243 **Right-wing pundits from Fox:** Hans A. von Spakovsky, "Nominated for a Cabinet Position? Liberal Senators Just Want to Know Your Position on 'Climate Change,'" Heritage Foundation, February 24, 2017, https://www .heritage.org/environment/commentary/nominated-cabinet-position-liberal -senators-just-want-know-your-position.

243 **"dumb," "ridiculous," and "off-base":** See Andrew Seifter, "Yes, CIA Director Nominee Mike Pompeo Needs to Answer Questions About Climate Change," *Media Matters for America* blog, January 13, 2017, https://www.mediamatters.org/blog/2017/01/13/yes-cia-director-nominee -mike-pompeo-needs-answer-questions-about-climate-change/215013.

244 **diseases are flourishing:** Centers for Disease Control and Prevention, "Illnesses from Mosquito, Tick, and Flea Bites Increasing in the US," press

release, May 1, 2018, https://www.cdc.gov/media/releases/2018/p0501-vs
-vector-borne.html.

245 **the CDC has already identified:** Centers for Disease Control and
Prevention, "Mosquito, Tick, and Flea Bites."

245 **Farmers had to abandon:** Krista Mahr, "How Cape Town Was Saved from
Running Out of Water," *Guardian,* May 4, 2018, https://www.theguardian
.com/world/2018/may/04/back-from-the-brink-how-cape-town-
cracked-its-water-crisis.

246 **reclaims only 7 to 8 percent:** U.S. Environmental Protection Agency and
CDM Smith, *2017 Potable Reuse Compendium (Washington, DC, 2017),
30,* https://www.epa.gov/sites/production/files/2018-01/documents
/potablereusecompendium_3.pdf.

246 **Nearly 1 million homes:** Ben Westcott and Steve George, "Asia Under
Water: How 137 Million People's Lives Are Being Put at Risk," CNN,
August 30, 2017, https://www.cnn.com/2017/07/24/asia/climate-change
-floods-asia/index.html.

247 **The official death toll:** Leyla Santiago, Catherine E. Shoichet, and Jason
Kravarik, "Puerto Rico's New Hurricane Maria Death Toll Is 46 Times Higher
Than the Government's Previous Count," CNN, August 28, 2018, https
://www.cnn.com/2018/08/28/health/puerto-rico-gw-report-excess-deaths.

247 **at least 4,600 American citizens:** See Nishant Kishore et al., "Mortality in
Puerto Rico After Hurricane Maria," *New England Journal of Medicine*
379, no. 2 (July 12, 2018): 162–70, https://www.nejm.org/doi/full/10.1056
/NEJMsa1803972#article_citing_articles.

CHAPTER 10: WHAT I'VE LEARNED

262 **helped lift hundreds of millions:** Bill Gates, "Here's My Plan to Improve
Our World—and How You Can Help," *Wired,* November 12, 2013, https
://www.wired.com/2013/11/bill-gates-wired-essay.

263 **"I think people don't talk":** Mimi Kirk, "One Answer to School Attendance:
Washing Machines," *CityLab,* August 22, 2016, https://www.citylab.com
/solutions/2016/08/school-attendance-washing-machines/496649.

268 **"This is not tolerable!":** Niraj Chokshi and Astead W. Herndon, "Jeff Flake
Is Confronted on Video by Sexual Assault Survivors," *New York Times,*
September 28, 2018, https://www.nytimes.com/2018/09/28/us/politics
/jeff-flake-protesters-kavanaugh.html.

268 **"that they don't matter"**: Jesus Rodriguez, "Woman Who Confronted Flake 'Relieved' He Called for Delaying Kavanaugh Vote," *Politico,* September 28, 2018, https://www.politico.com/story/2018/09/28/jeff-flake-protester -kavanaugh-852971.

269 **Kavanaugh had misled the Senate:** Paul Blumenthal and Jennifer Bendery, "All the Lies Brett Kavanaugh Told," *Huffington Post,* October 1, 2018, https://www.huffingtonpost.com/entry/brett-kavanaugh-lies_us _5bb26190e4b027da00d61fcd.

269 **We learned that when she was in high school:** "Kavanaugh Hearing: Transcript," *Washington Post* (transcript courtesy of Bloomberg Government), https://www.washingtonpost.com/news/national/wp/2018/09/27/kavanaugh -hearing-transcript. Subsequent references to information presented during the Kavanaugh hearing may also be found here.

272 **American Bar Association reopened:** Associated Press, "American Bar Association Reopens Kavanaugh Evaluation," *PBS News Hour,* October 5, 2018, https://www.pbs.org/newshour/politics/american-bar-association -reopens-kavanaugh-evaluation.

272 **"united, as professors of law"**: Susan Svrluga, " 'Unfathomable': More Than 2,400 Law Professors Sign Letter Opposing Kavanaugh's Confirmation," *Grade Point* (blog), *Washington Post,* October 4, 2018, https://www .washingtonpost.com/education/2018/10/04/unprecedented-unfathomable -more-than-law-professors-sign-letter-after-kavanaugh-hearing.

272 **"I was calculating daily the risk/benefit"**: "Kavanaugh Hearing: Transcript."

275 **a 200 percent increase in calls:** Holly Yan, "The National Sexual Assault Hotline Got a 201% Increase in Calls During the Kavanaugh Hearing," CNN, September 28, 2018, https://www.cnn.com/2018/09/24/health/ national-sexual-assault-hotline-spike/index.html.

INDEX